The New World

Book Four
Of
The Eleusis Cycle

D. Brumbley

Content Warning

This book contains content that some readers might find triggering, such as:

Combat violence
Mass casualty events
Sexual content (explicit)
Dom/Sub dynamic
CnC
Arranged marriages
Cheating
Sexual assault / rape (implied, off-page)
Genetic experimentation
Medical trauma
Mentions of pregnancy complications
Torture
Apocalyptic scenarios
Pandemic / disease
Institutional gaslighting / emotional manipulation
Forced pregnancy
PTSD / trauma responses

Read with Care

To all of you
who look for a better world
but haven't found it.
Yet.

CONTENTS

PROLOGUE

Four months had passed since the attack. Four months since their last contact with Eleusis. A new year was upon them already, and yet nothing felt renewed or optimistic.

Susan had, her entire life, been a quiet girl, a quiet teenager, and a quiet woman. Ever since the attack in the mountains, the world seemed *too* quiet, even for her. She tried her best, just like everyone else, to find ways to be happy, but it was difficult in times like these. Especially because her entire world was in a state of unrest and unease. Ben was her world. Her children were her world. Her children were safe, but caged like the rest of them.

Ben had his two youngest sisters around, and Danny, at least. After losing his father and then Anna and Cory so quickly after, Ben was even quieter than Susan. The world was too quiet around them, filled with dangers that mostly they couldn't even see.

Susan worked hard to make a small cake to celebrate, though, even though the ingredients weren't easy to come by. She grabbed the cake in one hand and scooped Maddie out of her playpen before she called out for their son. "Matthew!" She had checked on him ten minutes ago and he was working on building a huge house out of legos. "If you want some cake, you get your little tush in here. We're going to take it out to Daddy!"

If there was one summons guaranteed to get a three-year-old's legs pumping, it was a promise of cake, and the little boy tripped and fell over himself as he sprinted down the hallway. Unfazed, he got up, brushed himself off, and continued running as if nothing had happened. If there was one virtue to the Bickford Estate, it was extensive hallways in which children had ample opportunity to stretch their legs. "Caaaaaaaaaaaake!!" He screamed excitedly, still wired from the fact that he was being permitted to stay up past his usual bedtime and continue playing with his toys.

Susan laughed at Matthew's enthusiasm but she stopped him short of being able to dive into the cake pan in her hands. "Can you carry the forks out and Daddy's drink?" She nodded toward the table where there were three forks and a large water bottle for Ben. "I'm sure he's thirsty out there."

"Carry, carry, carry, carry . . ." Matthew tended to make a song out of things as he complied, especially when he was in a good mood. Ben thought the boy had made it his own personal task in life to make up for the quiet disposition of his parents and bring balance with his own noise. "We see fireworks?" He asked as they walked, looking up at the ceiling as if he could see fireworks through the ceiling of the house.

"I don't think so, buddy." Susan said gently, since she knew he was looking forward to fireworks. Larissa had a new baby to take care of, and Liam and Logan were together, but gone from the area. No one really wanted to bring any attention to the estate, though Susan never knew what to think of one of Liam's wives, Brianne. Maybe she would want to put on a show. "I think it will just be cake this year. Is that okay?"

"New year! Want see fireworks!" He had gone gaga over them the year before, and they had apparently left a lasting impression. Probably because he had barely been learning to talk at the time and had been excessively proud of himself for being able to say the word 'fireworks' at all. "Want see fireworks! Want see fireworks!" Chanting was a good way to get what he wanted, right?

Susan endured the chanting until they got out of the house and she paused to bend down to get a little closer to Matthew; with Maddie still on her hip and cake still in her hand. "I hope we will see them, okay bud? I don't know. But we have chocolate cake. That's your favorite, right?"

The promise of cake as an immediate treat outweighed his hypothetical fireworks, and the whole rest of the way out of the house, he wove a haphazard path back and forth behind his mother, scooping in the air with his tiny fork as if he was already eating the cake. The singing to himself continued, in varying tones of "Cake" with every step, including a few impromptu dance moves. The boy never stopped moving for an instant. Thank goodness their daughter was, at least so far, a great deal more mellow.

They had to take the lift inside the watchtower that overlooked the Bickford estate fields in order to get up to where Ben was standing sentry duty. It was harder to spot a person under a canopy from satellite photographs, even if that canopy had been damaged and now only covered half the former watch station.

Ben saw them coming, and had his gun laid aside, high out of Matthew's reach, when they finally reached him. "I'm amazed he's still awake." He glanced around again, then pulled Susan into a quick but warm kiss. "Her, I'm less surprised about. She never sleeps."

"That's because she wants to eat all the time." Matthew was already telling his father that he made the cake with mommy and that chocolate was his favorite and that they should eat it *now*. Susan told Matthew to give his father a fork before they all moved to sit down on the floor. "No one said anything about fireworks, but he's desperate to see them."

"I don't think we'll have any of those tonight, buddy." Ben gave Matthew a smile, but the boy was inconsolable about the fireworks until the first bite of cake hit his lips. Then nothing else in the world mattered. "Don't get me wrong, if I know Bree, she's probably trying to organize some kind of light-show inside and there's a very real possibility that she'll blow something up, but it's not going to be one of their usual shows, that's for damn sure."

"I thought maybe she would. But I don't know, she's different without Liam around. At least between her and Rachel, though, they're holding each other up pretty well." Susan bounced Maddie in her lap gently as she watched Matthew messily devour his cake, but she could only smile at him, messy or not. Cake was rare for them. She didn't blame Matthew for being excited about it. "Quiet New Year. But at least we're here together."

"I'll take that over the alternative." He said with a grateful bite of the cake. He'd had better cake in his life, but he knew what Susan had produced from the ingredients they had was more or less a miracle, and he was grateful.

"I keep going back and forth, up here at night." He glanced away from them through the mesh that wove through the railings beneath the control panels, but caught no sign of any kind of movement. Not that he expected any at that point. "I keep hearing about things happening in different parts of the world, the attack in Florida, the siege in Johannesburg that lasted three days a few weeks ago, all the crazy . . . stuff . . . that happened in the Parisian ruins. Part of me wishes I was involved just so we could be *doing* something. Even if I know that's not the answer. I hate just watching."

"You stayed here for us. I know that." Susan looked down at

Maddie and Matthew, Matthew who was working on a second, smaller piece of cake. "Hopefully you won't end up resenting us, or resenting me for it."

"I said I wish I could help, not that I've got a death wish." He gave her a faint smile, but it wasn't hard for her to know what really had him on edge about not being more involved. They'd had no news whatsoever of Anna and very little about Cory since the attack in the mountains, and from everything they had heard, they had no reason to think or trust that either of them were alive. There were contacts at first about Cory. Then communications became strained. The best they could hope for was that Anna had somehow been taken prisoner, and that wasn't something Ben wanted to contemplate. If he knew his sister, he imagined she would prefer death to captivity.

"I'm gonna go the rest of my life wishing there was more I could do. It's the way Dad was, and I don't see any other decent way of living." He glanced out again at the rest of the world with a shrug. "Someday soon, this is gonna be over, one way or another. Either the world's gonna get better or it's gonna get worse. I'll just have more work to do if it gets worse, that's all."

Susan pulled Ben into a kiss that started on his cheek and moved to his lips. "When you're off duty, we're going to celebrate the new year in a way that will make you stop worrying for a little bit. You've been up here too long."

Matthew was too young to care what his parents were doing to each other when he didn't require them to do something for him, and Maddie thought it was fun to be squished between them for a while in what seemed to her a hug more than anything else. "My relief is supposed to be up here at two. You think you can get these two into a mild comatose state by then?" Matthew was learning words a little too quickly and Ben had to invent new ways to say things that wouldn't set him off.

"I can definitely do that." Susan assured with another kiss, since she felt like she and Ben were always busy, but they knew their family was the most important thing. "I'm all about making as many babies with you as I can." She teased with a smile, since she wanted to make him smile as well. "What do you think?"

"When I married you, I signed up for everything I could give you." Ben reminded her with a reserved grin. In private, and especially toward the beginning of their relationship, he'd been quite the hopeless romantic, though he never made a particularly big show of that. The difficulties of their lives had left that aspect of him a great deal more subdued than before, but he certainly never backed down from a challenge when she was in the mood to issue him one. "Though that one had me rethinking high numbers for a while." He nodded at Matthew, who was trying in vain to reach the controls. "Don't touch that, buddy, you're not supposed to stand on that."

"I want to be tall! I want fireworks!"

Ben groaned. Apparently cake hadn't been able to distract the boy forever. He ignored Matthew and looked back down at Madeline instead. "Especially if you can promise me the rest of our kids will be like this one, I'm in for as many as you're up for." He tickled Maddie's shoulder to make her squirm, and chuckled quietly through another kiss and another bite of cake.

"Keep giving me girls and we'll see." Susan replied with a smile before she looked over at Matthew again. Susan handed Maddie to Ben so he could eat his cake in relative peace while she picked up Matthew to walk him around the tower a bit and let him touch the things he was actually allowed to touch. It seemed like there really weren't going to be any fireworks that year, at least not until Ben came to bed later that night and they could create their own.

"I move this, and go BOOM!" Matthew moved some of the inert controls as if it would accomplish anything, but his mother kept him from getting too destructive. He stomped along the panel above the controls for a while pretending that he was a monster, but then suddenly turned and looked up at the sky, pointing excitedly. "Fireworks, Mommy! Fireworks!"

Susan looked up immediately and her stomach sank as she saw what Matthew called fireworks. There was a brilliant cascade of tiny flashes of light far above the darkness of the world.

Someone was blowing up a space station.

Her stomach twisted as she thought about the last station that had been blown out of the sky. "That can't reach us here, can it?" She wasn't able to look away but she trusted Ben's opinion.

Ben was up on his feet quickly with Madeline clutched in one arm, looking up through the half of the watchtower that was open to the sky. The so-called "fireworks" were happening around a station in low orbit, clearly a smaller station that was much longer than it was broad. "No, it's moving too fast." He watched anyway, and though it was too far away for them to see individual blasts or explosions, the lights erupting all along the length of the station were unmistakably catastrophic.

"I wish I knew if that was something to celebrate or not. It's hard to know anymore. If that's the rebels taking down a military station, great. Let's watch fireworks. If it's the Consortium taking down a rebel station . . ." he wished he was surprised, and hated the fact that he wasn't. That was the world they lived in. Thousands of people visibly dying in the sky was, if not commonplace, at least no longer surprising.

"They're not our enemy, the people up there, but it kind of feels like we are on opposite sides." Susan kept Matthew close, even though he was entertained instead of scared. "Well, buddy, looks like you got a show after all." Susan felt sick saying so, but there was nothing they could do but watch.

"I guarantee it's mostly good people doing the dying up there, not the ones who deserve it." He watched the fight go on a little longer as Matthew squealed in delight. The lights weren't huge or dramatic, but they were certainly brighter and more violent than the starlight behind them. "It's moving on. It won't fall anywhere around here if it does fall."

"That's good news, if nothing else." Susan watched a little longer, then ripped her gaze away to look at Matthew. "I think it's time to go get washed up and go to bed, Mister. Daddy has to get back to watching over us."

As Matthew protested and whined in obligatory three-year-old fashion, Ben held Maddie against his chest as he watched the station fly across the sky. It hadn't been in sight for very long, and he imagined the fight must have been going on since the far side of the world. He had no idea if it would go around again or not. All the world could do was watch as humanity tore itself apart.

When it was finally out of sight, Matthew stopped protesting, and Ben leaned down to kiss Maddie's cheek before he handed her back to her mother. "I'll be inside as soon as my relief gets here." He promised with a kiss. They could always retreat to the world they had between themselves. At least until the rest of the world inevitably threatened even that refuge. "I love you. Get some rest before I get inside."

"I love you too, Ben." Susan replied with another kiss, even with Maddie between them. She reached one hand up and caressed along his cheek gently. "Happy New Year. Maybe this one will finally bring something good, for all of us."

1

Full consciousness all at once. As if he hadn't slept.

He knew he had, since the fatigue was at just a little more distance than it had been a few hours before. That was all sleep accomplished. It pushed the exhaustion away, but it kept falling back in on him all the same, pulled in close by the gravity of the world he lived in.

Logan took in a deep breath and stretched his neck to make sure it hadn't gotten too bent out of shape during his nap. A few hours, that was all he could ever spare anymore, and often even that was too much. Far too much. His neck was fine, so he looked down at the rather strange contraption he called a bed. Liam had made it for him a month before, just a frame for him to back his wheelchair into and lean back until his head and shoulders were resting on a pillow. His body didn't care what was happening to his legs anymore, so why worry if they were comfortable? Lie back on half a bed and that was plenty for him.

He unlocked his wheelchair from the frame and leaned forward until the front wheels hit the floor. At the impact, some of the screens in the room came on, displaying updates and messages he'd received since he went to sleep. His eyes flew over a few of them in mild alarm, and when he reached the last of them, he heaved a deep sigh and rolled out of the room.

Back to work trying to fix a world that was intent on tearing itself apart.

"Renata." He didn't even look around for her, since he knew one of his two secretaries would be nearby at all times, and if it wasn't Renata, her assistant would quickly let him know where she was. It was Renata herself who appeared, though, in the dark corridors. "Tell Tatyana I want her in the war room and get me the personnel and inventory files from Thirteen. If you run into any walls, get them from Jason. I'm sure he's already pulled them by now."

"Of course." Renata replied automatically, ever the dedicated and consistent secretary, wherever Logan was. Where he went, she went. It seemed like she didn't even have a life outside of doing what Logan commanded, but he knew that wasn't true. She was social whenever she had the chance to be. "Is there anything that you need first, Mr. Bickford?"

Logan started the roll down the hall toward the war room, but let himself drift a little so he could rub some more of the sleep from his face. "Coffee." He said in the gravelly voice that sleep and life in general left him with. "Please." He added a little too late for it to have been actually associated with the initial request. But he figured better late than never.

"I haven't asked you how you're doing for a while, Renata." He asked in the same tired voice. He felt bad about it, but he knew she knew better than to expect anything else from him. "We're what, twenty kilometers from the rest of your family? But I haven't so much as seen you leave the bunker since we got here."

"You know me better than most, Mr. Bickford." Renata said with split attention, as usual, since she was always doing something at the same time as having a conversation. If someone had her full attention, it was rare. She was a busy woman, after all, working for the president. She glanced up from her tablet once and gave him a reassuring but small smile. "If I wasn't doing well, I believe you'd notice. Anyway, we have important things to attend to. Maybe I'll be social again once we're not being hunted."

"Maybe we all will." Nothing he said lately sounded terribly hopeful, but no one expected that from Logan. His children were taken, the love of his childhood and his first wife was dead, and his second wife might be dead as well, for all anyone knew. The Consortium learned that silence was one of the most effective weapons of all time against a man like Logan. "If there is something you need or I become more of an asshole than you're accustomed to dealing with, I expect you to be the one to tell me. Just know that I'm grateful for your social sacrifices."

"You're not being any more difficult than usual." Renata assured him as she turned her attention back to her tablet. "Hopefully Jason will have good news today." She said it every day, at least once. She was hopeful that Mercury was alive, along with the children, and until someone confirmed if they were dead, she would never let that hope die. Initial health scans gave them information about Mercury and the babies, but those had been locked down. Logan needed hope, even if he seemed to thrive on his anger more than anything else. Renata wouldn't let him forget there was still hope. "I'll get your coffee, Sir. Tatyana has already confirmed she is on her way. The personnel files are loading into your tablet now."

"Thank you, Renata." He said in his usual grumble, then continued down the hall. It always seemed like a long, long way to go, but considering he very rarely ever went farther than the trip between his room and the war room, he knew he shouldn't complain. He never did complain outwardly, it was just one more thing that he tossed into the fire at the back of his mind to keep himself on edge. He had to stay on edge. There was too much to do and too little being accomplished.

The war room and the rest of the quarters they had moved into were in one of the last places he knew the Consortium was ever likely to look. Bogota, like so many cities mostly still populated because of the memory of the Pre-Crisis world, was nothing but a shell of its former self. Logan had looked through what seemed like endless memories and films set in its streets and found nothing resembling the overgrown corpse of a town that remained.

When they were offered asylum by the Amazonian Prime Minister, Logan imagined that their situation would improve over the Labyrinth they had left back in the Rockies, but he wasn't sure that was the case. During the Crisis, the city had died along with most of the world. The Santamaria Bullring had been cemented over as if it was some kind of nuclear reactor gone bad, and had been abandoned ever since. They had found decomposed corpses, four centuries old, still unburied when Xander had the idea to relocate inside it, and they spent weeks cleaning out the place to make a halfway livable home. Nonetheless, the arena was space enough for them to dock several of the strike ships they stole from the Consortium, and the corridors beneath were as hospitable as war required them to be.

The War Room itself was the open space that had once been the great arena. All the stands had been retrofitted for use as docks for the ships, and there were partitions set up everywhere for different subsets of rebel operations. There were targeting exercises going on in the parts of the stands that weren't occupied by ships, and troops moving back and forth from the tunnels that ran under the rest of the city. They were spread out in abandoned sectors all through old Bogota, moving unseen, living entirely away from the sunlight and any sensors that could find them, but with room to breathe. That was all Logan required. For the moment.

"Status of the Madagascar flight." He rolled out onto the concrete floor that remained when all the sand had been swept away.

"On target, sir." One of the aides nearby reported, knowing better than to need Logan to address him directly or give details on what kind of status he required. "Estimated contact 428, all involved locked in. No recognition detected, no intercepted warnings. Monitoring at the Madagascar base shows no break from routine."

Good. One thing going right. "Any report from the Jakarta chapter?"

"Yes, Sir. Notes in your tablet, Sir." Yet another Aide responded, stepping closer to Logan away from his station. "Two teams lost in reconnaissance. Fariz intends to double down."

"Of course he does. Tell him I want to meet with him in two hours and he does not have authorization to move until I've reviewed the report. Send the message to Beth as well and make sure he knows it." Logan had a thousand strings of the web they were stringing all over the world running through his mind at the same time, all the time, and they all had an effect on all the others. His coffee could not arrive fast enough.

Renata arrived at the same time as Tatyana with a fresh mug of coffee, and she didn't spare a moment to look at Tatyana except dismissively. Tatyana still didn't have a great reputation, but Renata knew the woman didn't care about that. "Here is your coffee, Sir."

Tatyana looked Renata up and down and then shook her head as she turned her attention to Logan. "I'm beginning to wonder exactly how much your secretary *loves* you, Bickford."

"Insult my secretary, Tatyana, and I will see to it that you are assigned to monitor a weather station in Antarctica until the war is over." There wasn't even any fire in his threat as he lifted the mug to his lips, but she didn't have any reason to doubt that he would do as he said. A month after the attack in the Rockies, he had simply been nearby when someone had suggested in passing that Mercury had been the one to lead the Consortium directly to the Bickford estate, since her father was a station Captain, after all. The offending gossipmonger had been immediately and dispassionately stripped of all rank and ordered to scrub toilets the rest of his natural life. He still worked in the arena, and all it usually took was a cold glare from Logan to send him scurrying to find the nearest bathroom to clean. "Tell me what happened on Thirteen."

"They were trying to tighten down on the stations, and Thirteen wouldn't have it. So the Board infiltrated their people and turned them against each other. We were getting some of the conversations here and there between the leadership . . . they're trying to crack down on things up there. Remind people who's in charge and that the enemy is down here, not up there."

"Well that seems to be working out well for them." He couldn't allow himself to be happy about that kind of news, but his mind had already moved past emotional responses to the practicality of the entire situation. How it could be used. What it would mean for their own efforts. "Have they started trying to spin what happened in their media yet, or are they continuing their policy of keeping their foot firmly in their mouth?" He sipped gratefully at his coffee.

"They're calling it a 'rebel action', but by calling it such, it looks like we infiltrated them. Not that they had to go in and squash a rebellion within their own station." Tatyana shrugged as she tapped on her tablet and popped up a hologram of some news headlines so Logan could see them. "They're pushing too hard. People are getting angry. Especially the stations that are used to more relaxed governance. Three, for example. They don't call it the Edge for no reason. Artists, musicians, drugs, whores. People don't like their lifestyle disrupted by the government."

"Except Three is also big enough to push back if Prime tries to push them." Logan said thoughtfully. His eyes scanned the headlines, but he didn't move any more than he had to. Any movement involved effort and pain, and he avoided both unless they were necessary. "And Two is nearly the size of Prime. So they pick on the little kids getting uppity to try and keep the bigger kids on the playground afraid of them. Typical."

He sounded almost disappointed, and began looking through the files Renata had loaded for him about Thirteen. Jason had already grabbed the files he knew Logan would want. He would have to either compliment the man on his efficiency or start getting more unpredictable. "It looks like they didn't completely destroy the place. See what you can find out about those who are left. Any inroads we can make with those who are left in the sky will come in handy soon."

"Those that are left are any ranking officials with the Consortium. They want their own to clean up the mess and reinstate order." Tatyana brought up a list of confirmed survivors. "Only most of them lost someone or several people in the attack. I think the Board assumed that if they lost someone, then they would be more apt to know things are serious. I think it just made them angry."

"Good. I can work with angry." The sighed response came out more like a growl. "Get a team on research and have them make the contacts. If they're successful, start putting through our Sleeper procedures. They're primarily a supply and distribution station, and I want that foothold."

He finally looked up at her once he was done giving the order. He knew Tatyana was an exceptionally capable woman, and he had tried to use her as much as possible since the assault on the mountains. He knew better than to think that she was happy about someone who, in her eyes, was brand new to the life of a rebel being thrust into the spotlight as he had been, but he also trusted her. There were very few people in the world about whom he could say any such thing. "Do you foresee any difficulty with that?"

"There is always difficulty these days." Tatyana stared at Logan, but then she gave him a brief nod. "I'll see what I can do." She looked around at the floating information and back at Logan. "Is that all?" She typically refused to address him as Sir, even though most did. He didn't scare her. He could try to take away whatever he wanted from her, and it didn't scare her. Tatyana had followers and power in her own right, but she wasn't fighting for power. She was fighting for the cause. For retribution. For revenge. And it wasn't from Logan Bickford.

"For now. I'd like daily updates on your team's progress with the contacts, and make sure Philip is looped in as well. He's doing some work with Five that could tie into this." All the intricacies of maintaining orbital life made his head swim, but he pushed those thoughts aside for the moment. He could review what he knew about all the strings later in one of his staff briefings.

He was already working on his tablet to reach out and send a few of his more pressing questions to those from whom he knew he could get decent answers, but he decided to actually call his next communicant. She wasn't far away, but it was more effort for him to move than it was to call.

"I apologize if I woke you, Mrs. Tanaka." He said as soon as she answered, with audio only. He couldn't blame her for that. It wasn't a time of the morning he or anyone else had ever termed 'decent' for human activity. "Are you up to speed on the developments coming out of Station Thirteen?"

"I am, Mr. Bickford." Hitomi replied before she launched into her report. "Ships have been coming and going quickly to remove bodies and those seriously injured. If you want to get in there, now is the time."

"I have some people already working on it. We don't have anything in position for a physical presence, but given the playground-bully the Consortium brass is turning into these days, it won't be hard to reach people." He wanted to reach out himself to manage some of that work, but he had to pull himself back from even considering it. *You are limited. Now more than ever. Do what you can. Delegate the rest.*

"I wanted your opinion on the spin I've been told they're trying to put on this, and see if your team can work on twisting the message to give us some anchors there. If they're blaming this attack on us somehow to cover up their own housekeeping, I'd like a way to make that work to our advantage instead of theirs. What are your people seeing?" Aiko's parents had been incredibly worn down since the Twist had been destroyed, understandably, but Logan had done his best to make sure they were both active in the efforts to prosecute their rebellion. Mr. Tanaka was hit or miss even on good days, but his wife had definitely shown she had her own daughter's constant resilience.

"They can spin it however they like, but it's not what we're seeing. We're seeing devastation and Consortium soldiers with weapons pushing around the victims. Is there any way that we can relay this video feed to you so you can have it? We've been having some trouble recording the feed, since seeing it is one thing, keeping it is another. If you can release some of this footage to the others . . ."

"Patch it through to Jason. He's running all the storage and distribution processes. I think Jessie is working on the actual social media side, so make sure they get a handle on it and they'll incorporate it with what they've already got." More delegating. He had to push it. He had to remember to push it at all times. Speed. Off balance. That was important. "Do you have anything else for me? I'm sure you've got your hands full with the attack, but if there's anything else your people are seeing that I need to know about, now is a good time."

"There is something else." As a side project, the Tanakas had been going through reports like crazy, mis-labeled reports specifically, for information that the Consortium might hide under other information. Mostly the things they found hadn't been valuable, until recently. "We found some genetics reports, and what caught our attention was that a few of them had our son's name on them." She said carefully before she continued. "They were recent reports, and since we know Kazuo is . . . gone, we believe they're from reports connected to our granddaughter. So we have reason to believe that she is alive." If their granddaughter was alive, then there was definite reason to believe there were other children alive too. Maybe Logan's.

That revelation, even more than the coffee that Logan had already downed, made him sit forward in his chair and lean attentively on the desk as he listened. "That's . . . that's amazing news, Hitomi. Have you started cross-checking with some of the other taken children and rebels yet?" Hope was a thing in short supply, even if it was also the fuel that kept them all moving on a day-to-day basis. He would take any and as much of it as he could get.

"We've found two others. No more than that, yet, since it seems they are keeping this information buried and certainly not together." He could hear a heavy sigh on the other end, but all it indicated was that Hitomi was struggling to tell him the extent of what she was thinking. "Kazuo is gone. Aiko is . . ." She shook her head, even though he couldn't see her. "If this is Kassie, then Will could be there too. We are desperate to find our grandchildren."

"I'd say that finding a study like that is an excellent indication they're still alive." Logan mustered his most comforting tone, though it wasn't something that came easily to him. "This is great work, Hitomi. Thank you for bringing it to my attention. When you send the data to Jason, tell him I've asked him to make assisting you with this branch of your search a priority. There are a lot of people down here on the ground who are waiting for news the same as I know you and Nobu are. I, for one, am going to sleep just a little better tonight knowing there's a chance." A chance was enough. A chance had to be enough, otherwise there was no point to anything they were doing.

"I've been watching for any indicators of yours in particular. I hope I find something soon. I'll speak with Jason about this and we'll keep working at it." She paused and took a deep breath. "Anything else, Sir?"

"That's more than enough for one morning. Keep it up. And whoever made that connection or made that discovery, get me their name so I can be sure to send them a message to thank them. Keep me updated." He signed off the call and sighed, allowing himself a single moment to lean on the table in front of him and let that news work its way through his mind.

There were negative sides to the story, certainly, since the fact of medical records about kidnapped children almost certainly meant that they were all being held prisoner and hostage, but he wasn't going to approach it that way yet. If the Consortium wanted to control them with the threat of their children, they'd have done so already.

Or would they have just allowed them to think their children were dead as a means of destroying all hope in those they were fighting, and held back the possibility of threat with a hostage situation for when they perceived things to be going worse for them?

Plots within plots. Threats within threats. That was his life. That was all their lives. That was the kind of life that needed to end.

"Renata." He spoke into his communicator once he'd made the connection. "I'm going across the ring. I'll be back once I've finished with the Al-Jabbars. Hold my appointments until then. I know I have a meeting with the Scandinavians. I'll get to them when I get back." He pushed himself away from the desk and began the long push across the ring. He knew he could've gotten someone to take the bars of his wheelchair and push him the rest of the way to his destination, but that was not something he was going to allow. If they were looking to him to lead, he didn't need to be seen being pushed. Plus, Doc Weber was continually getting on him to get more exercise instead of sitting at a desk all day. They were going to have to disagree on his priorities for the time being.

"Of course, Sir." Renata said immediately, as she usually did, but she kept the connection open for a little bit longer. "That's good news, the Tanakas' discovery." She hadn't been listening to the conversation, but she could see the information transferred to Logan directly. She could see everything that crossed over to him, unless it was specifically labeled personal. But it was part of her job to make sure only the important things actually made it to Logan. "If they've got Kazuo and Kameron's baby, then certainly . . . I just mean, they don't have any reason to harm innocent children."

Logan knew Renata was Orbital by birth, but he always tried not to hold that against her, since she had also been a rebel most of her adolescent and adult life. But her defenses of the Consortium, however small they were, always served to remind him of the very different perspective under which she grew up.

"I agree that they don't have any reason to do it. I don't for a moment imagine that a lack of reason is going to stop them. Harm is a relative term, and they'll justify whatever they want to do any way they want. All I care about is that we find some kind of proof that the children and the others who were taken are still alive. If we can find that, there's a lot of people down here who are going to be a lot more interested in getting a move on."

He was already wheeling himself into the wall of the far side of the small stadium, heading for some of the areas that had been converted hastily to living quarters. It was still an incredibly cramped situation for everyone concerned, but if he had his way about it, they wouldn't be holed up in a bullfighting stadium for too much longer.

"You're right, Sir." She said quickly afterward. "I'll hold your appointments until you're done with your meeting."

"Thank you, Renata." He closed the connection with a sigh, since he knew he was heading into a particular conversation that was incredibly unlikely to have the same kind of civility he had come to expect from people he'd worked with before. But he couldn't expect the whole world to be respectful and understanding. A lot of people were very much on edge, and it wasn't their fault they hadn't been living there on that edge every second of the past two years.

When he got to the portion of the residential area he'd headed for, he was a little surprised to see Liam already there, but he knew he shouldn't have been. Liam hadn't been very involved in running things outside of the people from the midwest, at least while they were still in the mountains. Since unifying the army and bringing in crews from all over the world, though, and especially since the attack, Liam had been . . . much more of a presence. He seemed to have anticipated Logan's visit, though from the look on Khadijah's face, it didn't seem to be going well.

"Good morning, Mr. Bickford." Liam was incapable of being completely serious unless absolutely necessary. That much hadn't changed. "You're right on time. Ms. Al-Jabbar here was just telling me how pointless it is to try and make contact with anyone on Three who could help us make inroads after the Thirteen incident a few hours ago. Which is funny to me, since I thought you all on Three were supposed to be the biggest badasses in the solar system."

Khadi gave Liam a death glare before she looked over at Logan. "Three is far more complicated than just making contact." She replied sharply. "You have to contact someone who is willing to talk to the right people without reporting anything. Three is .. . they are not interested in engaging the Consortium any more than necessary. Especially not for a small station."

"We wouldn't be asking for any action immediately." Logan said quietly, trying to keep his frustration with Orbitals in general from showing too much in his voice or his expression. "The countries of Earth are finally beginning to realize that the Consortium meant it when they declared war. They're also beginning to realize that none of them can fight it on their own. As much as everyone would love to be the ringleader of the resistance, at the moment we control the largest piece of the offensive. A few of the Stations have been able to start their own cells on their own terms, but whatever it is, it won't be enough. Not now and not twenty years from now. Your station is the key to bringing all the others in line. So we recognize fully it's much more complicated than making a contact. But that's what we're asking for as a beginning."

Khadi sighed, but it was a dramatic sigh. She was a dramatic person, but she was also a literal model. It came with the territory. "Look, I know people, but . . . if you really want to convince them this is worth their while, you're going to have to send someone to Three to have the conversation. They will see value in risking it to talk to them. They'll take it to heart more. If you just send a written or verbal message, it's essentially worthless."

Logan considered that in silence for a while, but it was Liam who spoke first. "And if we do send someone, would you be willing to go along to make sure that person gets in touch with the right people on the station?"

"Anyone I put you in contact with would want me to be there." Khadi was vague about why, but she was pretty famous in her own right, even more famous once her brother's face was splashed everywhere as one of the leading rebels against the Consortium. "So if anyone is going to Three, I would be going too."

"Yeah, I assumed that." Liam snapped back, since he wasn't going to take the woman's diva attitude without giving some of his own back. Instead of watching her, though, he looked over at Logan. "So when can we leave?"

"You've got one of the most recognizable faces in the world." Logan said in a bored tone, since he figured Liam was using the moment as a possible opportunity to get into space. "You'd get three steps inside the dock and be scanned and detained."

"Because my face is your face?" Liam gave Logan his own glare. "There's something to be said for keeping a low profile. We're all targets now. Doesn't mean we should hold back from getting shit done."

Khadi looked between the men and she looked at Logan with a shrug. "A lot of people's faces are recognizable now. If he wants to go, let him. I know the ins and outs, I should be able to get us in without getting him caught. He's on a mission, clearly. Probably because he's in the longest dry spell of his life."

"One of his wives is up there." Logan defended, without contradicting her, then looked over at Liam. "Can I speak to you for a minute?"

Liam didn't agree out loud, but he did step away anyway, heading down the corridor to put some distance between them and the rest of the occupants of the makeshift home. He waited patiently for Logan to catch up on two wheels instead of two legs, but he was glaring down at his brother once they were more or less alone. "There's no reason not to send me, Logan. I've got people who would go with me, who wouldn't be suspected, and we've got plenty of intercepts around the planet that I can get to and piggyback up. Khadi and I both."

"You're not gonna talk me into this by telling me it's the same as a trip to the Waste to pick up booze, Liam. You're talking about crossing battle lines to try and get into orbit to begin with, and then going somewhere we have no reason to expect Gwen and the others to be." Logan countered with his own serious expression.

"If anyone leaves this rock headed directly for Prime, they're gonna get shot to hell. I'm not a fucking idiot." Liam kept his voice down, but his tone was unmistakable. He was in no mood to take Logan's shit, especially after dealing with him and being his right hand for the past four months. "If we're going to get people into space now, and we fucking have to, I'll remind you, then we're gonna have to come at Prime sideways, through channels that aren't going to be suspected. This is as good a place to start with that as any. And if I go up there, looking like you, then whoever I meet with is going to know we mean fucking business."

Logan stared up at his brother for a while arguing with himself. "You really want to lead this? Yourself? A few months ago, you wanted to keep your eyes on supplies and practical governance and . . ."

"A few months ago, I thought this was about exposing the Consortium and then riding the wave when the world blew itself up. But exposed as it is, the world doesn't seem to give a shit, and I'm tired of waiting. This needs to get done, and I can do it." Liam glanced over at the space where the Al-Jabbars were still waiting on an answer, and gave Logan a sigh. "I'm also not exactly asking your permission. I want to work within the larger scope here, and I think that's what I'm doing. It's something that needs to get done. You said it yourself. We get Three, we get an ally and a foothold, and we can work from there."

"You're not ready for something like this, Liam." Logan thought his brother understood that. Understood the stakes and the consequences of what was going on. "You're not . . ."

"I'm about ten minutes fucking younger than you, Logan." Liam's tone surprisingly didn't get more angry. It stayed flat and cold. Logan was distracted enough by it to wonder if that was what he sounded like to other people. "And I may not be the leader of the hoping-to-be-free world like you are, but I know what the fuck is happening here. That's my wife up there. It's your children. It's our family, one way or the other. You've got no good reason not to send me up there, and I've got every reason to go. So let me handle it."

Logan didn't respond for a long time, but eventually gave in. "Handle it then, Liam. When you have your team picked out and you've got a plan for how to get to Three, bring it to me so I can make sure it's coordinated with all the other moving parts."

"Thanks." Liam knew he had crossed a line with the conversation, but he wasn't going to stand around just because his brother was permanently bathed in his own hatred. "I'll handle it. And I'll keep you updated." He let the moment of tension last just a little longer, then put a hand on Logan's shoulder and headed back toward Khadi to continue the conversation.

Khadi's eyebrow raised slightly to signify she was curious about the conversation, but she didn't ask outright. "So are we doing this?" She crossed her arms, leaning back habitually in a pose that looked like it belonged on a magazine cover. She could still hear the echoes of photographers' voices in her mind throwing out tag phrases of confidence and power postures. Usually it was easy to be confident, but she in no way was a fighter or even a good rebel, even though she was trying for Orion's sake. She had been raised with everything she ever wanted or needed and had been beautiful and tall even as a little girl. Her appearance demanded attention, and she always got it, but she was never a fighter like her brothers. "It's going to take me a little time to set something up, if we are."

"We are. It's gonna be you, me, and a dozen or so of my closest friends." He confirmed in a tone that was too lighthearted to be completely genuine. "Are your parents and your sister-in-law gonna come too? I can't say I recommend it, but your turf, your call."

"No, they're not. My sister needs to be where she's safest with her son, and my parents need to be here in case . . . in case someone hears from Orion." Khadi chewed on her bottom lip carefully. "They already lost one son. They haven't given up hope for Orion because they can't handle losing another. So you may be after a fiancee or a wife or . . . I don't know. I've heard mixed stories. But they're after a son. My brother. We all have skin in this."

"Fiancee." He verified for her, though it was only a technicality. He still thought of Gwen as one of his wives. "Your brother had a hell of a lot of people with him on Eleusis when we lost touch. And if we or they had managed to make contact again since, our tech people would've known about it. That means it's whoever was up there when shit went down against all our people. I like your brother's odds."

"I hope you're right." Khadi looked him over again. "I'm sorry about giving you a hard time. This place . . . brings out the worst in people."

"You mean Earth, or the equator?" It was blisteringly hot almost all the time in the bullfighting arena, though it was almost always worse outside than it was inside, thanks to all the concrete around them and the fact that most of their inhabited spaces were underground.

"Both, I think." She admitted honestly as she looked around briefly. "I was happy up there in Orbit. And I don't think it makes me terrible for being happy there. I lived a good and reputable life."

"I'll take your word for it on the reputable part." As much as she gave him grief for his incredibly long dry spell (which she wasn't wrong about) he hadn't so much as even looked at Khadijah any more than necessary since they started working together. He had no interest in Orbitals, but he was going to keep himself from saying so out loud. "What do you need from me to start getting your plans together?"

"A little bit of patience." She said with a renewed glare, since they both glared at each other more than anything else. "I can do this, but I don't need you breathing down my neck to get it done."

The mention of him breathing down her neck forced his imagination into a meditation on the kinds of positions he would have to have her in for him to be literally breathing down the back of her neck, but he cut off that train of thought as quickly as possible. God, it had been a long time. "I'll let you update me when you've made progress, then. I'm gonna get to work finding us a window to get back into orbit. Are we talking weeks or days on your end?"

"A couple of days, that's it." She looked over at him again. It was too bad he was a complete ass ninety-nine percent of the time. She could use a friend at a time like this. Especially because coming down to Earth had been hard enough. She only had her parents to talk to, and they were depressing to be around. Not that she blamed them for it, but Orion would have found the humor in any situation. "You're not talking to a nobody here." She reminded him quickly. "I'm pretty fucking famous, you know."

"Right." Liam said with the kind of half-smile that he would've given to a four-year-old who claimed the same thing. "And at some point, maybe that's gonna actually matter again. Right now, not so much."

"Why do you have to be such an ass?" Khadi replied flatly, since his ridiculous complacent smile really got under her skin and made her want to smack him across the face. "It matters to me. What if I said something like that to you about your farm with your cornfields or whatever else? Do you think that you matter any more than I do?"

"They're wheat fields, mostly." He answered with a slight shrug. "I'm not gonna get into some kind of cosmic debate with you about who matters and who doesn't. I know who matters to me and you know who matters to you. That's why we're both here. So if being famous matters to you, great. Go on being famous. Being a farmer and a husband matters to me. So I'm gonna go on doing that. Me being a farmer has helped feed people who are fighting this war. So I think that's important. If you being famous gets us some contacts up on Three that moves this war forward, then you being famous might start mattering to me. But until your skills at looking good in heels and flashing a disinterested smile down a runway becomes tangibly useful to what we're doing here, no, that doesn't matter to me."

Khadi shook her head again and let out another sigh. "I'm not even going to call you by your name anymore. You're just The Ass from now on. And not because you have a nice one." She added with another glare. If only her glare could actually shoot daggers. "I'll send you a message as soon as I get it set up."

"That's *Mister* Ass to you. Maybe we should both call each other that. Yours has to have helped you get some of that fame you care about, right?" He leaned to the side to get a look at her as he started to walk away. "I'll wait for your call, Miss Ass." He needed to put as much distance between himself and the intolerably narcissistic woman as possible. She was gorgeous, he was in no way immune to that aspect of her, but every conversation he'd had with the woman had left him incurably annoyed. Some people saw the world in ways he had no desire to understand.

"You're damn right this ass got me some of it." She threw a runway-ready look over her shoulder when she got to the door. What made things even worse was that Liam was always eye-level with her, and his eyes were unrelenting. Both Bickford men were that way. But at least Logan didn't purposefully irritate her. "You'll be thinking about it when you're alone with your hand later." She shot at him before she opened the door. "Be ready whenever I get things arranged. We're both eager to get shit moving."

"Eager. Bet that had something to do with your fame too." He clearly wasn't one to back down, but he didn't expect her to be either, and slid out past her into the busy corridor with another look over her as he walked away. He was already taking out his communicator, since there were a lot of moving pieces if they were going to succeed. He couldn't believe he was basing something so important on a bimbo like Khadi, but they all had to work with what they had.

*****

Hours later, Logan leaned forward on his desk and tried to keep his composure, though the woman on the other end of the communication seemed hell bent on trying to make him lose it.

"With all due respect, Prime Minister, the Consortium has never declared war before. So when you try to tell me that this kind of posturing is the same kind of gambit we've seen from them before, I am forced to violently disagree. They have moved past any kind of power play or fear mongering about rebel activity and will continue along their present course until the nations of the world submit themselves to its authority. The reasons for that submission are less important than the submission itself, and they have already shown they will employ whatever means necessary to accomplish their ends. This is not a time for neutrality or standoffish policy."

"You're trying to unite people that don't want to be united, Mr. Bickford." She sighed loudly, since she was just as frustrated as he was. "You're assuming people want a war, that they'll put their short lives on hold to endure something that could further devastate Earth. For what? Because the Consortium is bad-mouthing Earth and attacking their own? The people of Orbit are beyond our jurisdiction. They wanted it that way. We don't owe them anything, just as they have often shown that we are the last concern on their minds."

"You're right to be concerned for your people." He agreed, since he could see the woman's perspective and he knew she was far from stupid or short-sighted. That was part of what was so frustrating about the conversation. "I'm concerned for mine. The Northern Federation is a comparatively small political block on the global scale, and as you said, you're certainly not first on the

Consortium's list of concerns. Their primary concern right now is the Mediterranean coalition, the Polynesian block, and the North American territories, all of whom have made themselves a massive pain in the Consortium's Orbital ass. They're more populous than you are, they have more resources, more reason to be a part of the fight. I know you're familiar with each of those heads of state. Misipati has always spoken very highly of you, and I know how much Francesca's friendship and support meant to you during your recent successful campaign."

Logan kept his voice as even as possible, but he knew enough about the woman to know that some aspects of what he said weren't common knowledge. He didn't want to threaten her, but he did want her to know that his alliances with the powers of the world were becoming deeper and more thorough every day, rather than just a thing of rumor and suspicion. "What you and your people need to examine is the possibility that the greater powers of the world are not enough. You need to think about what happens if the Mediterranean or Polynesians fall or are somehow corrupted, again, by the Consortium, and if your people will still be the last thing on their minds when that happens."

The line was silent after he said that, but the woman's voice was colder when she responded. "I don't take well to veiled threats, Mr. Bickford. I understand what you are saying and what you're attempting to do. I believe what you are doing is a valiant effort, but I'm simply not going to put suffering people on the line against the Consortium. I will ensure that all trading and resource transfers cease. Communications also. But I refuse to send our military resources, small as they are, up into orbit to fight the Consortium. It's a suicide mission, and my people are not ready to die for a cause like this. You would be better off pleading your case to Orbitals."

Cold as the woman's tone was, a smile actually worked its way across his face, though he could see the concern on Renata's face across the table from him at the expression. *Is she always wondering when I'm going to just crack? I wish I could tell her she was wrong to worry.*

"The thought had crossed my mind, Gretchen. If I may call you Gretchen." He didn't give her time to answer. "I understand your reluctance to commit your military, but I'm glad you see the wisdom in cementing your territory's neutrality with an embargo on trading and communication. In the future, as the situation between Earth and the Consortium continues to develop, I hope you'll keep what I've said in mind. When things change, they will change quickly, and the decisions made during that change will have far-reaching effects."

When things change, he said. Logan Bickford was certainly confident about his plan. "I will keep everything you've said in mind, Mr. Bickford. As for now, I believe we've reached an impasse when it comes to military needs. I will, however, organize an effort to reach out to my people as a result of this conversation. If it turns out that they *are* willing to die for your cause, perhaps we can revisit this issue at a later date. You clearly know how to get in touch with me if you wish to do so."

"The point of war isn't to die for a cause, Prime Minister." Apparently she wasn't going to give him permission to call her Gretchen. "The point of war is to make sure your enemy dies for theirs. I look forward to hearing from you again. Be well."

The Prime Minister gave Logan a clipped farewell before ending the communication and Renata looked over at Logan again with concern. "Sir?" She thought she would start by asking a question, since she was so confused. "She said no, but you don't look upset by it."

"She didn't say no. She said not right now. I realize that kind of thinking may make me sound like an asshole, but in this context, I believe it applies." He took a sip of the water nearby and managed to keep from wincing at the harsh bottled taste. He never could get used to it, no matter how long they were away from his home.

"If I could call every single head of state on Earth and get that same response from all of them, I would consider it a good day. She's cutting off trade and communication with orbit, and that's as good a 'fuck you' as anyone who's watching needs when it comes to political relations. She'll cut that off, the Consortium will in some way level sanctions against them and declare them to be formally in league with us, and create their own self-fulfilling prophecy."

"So what you're happy about, just to clarify," Xander said with his own disapproving stare from across the table, "is that you successfully prodded the Northern Territories into possibly provoking an attack from the Consortium on their people."

"Yes." Logan answered without hesitation or apology. "Because anything that moves resources or people or power away from the Consortium is a step toward a world without a

Consortium. You have some objection to that?"

"I make my own sacrifices." Xander's face was inscrutable. "I'm glad to make any sacrifices that need to be made and take as many people as are willing along with me, but I'm not gonna move innocent or unwilling people around on a chessboard because it's to my advantage."

"That's why you've been fighting this war for forty years and barely made a dent." Logan shot back, his stare even across the table. "I'll make some calls to the Mediterraneans to see what kind of outreach I can have them arrange to support the North in case of an attack by the Consortium, if it'll ease your conscience. But I'm not gonna apologize to you or anybody else for moving people away from the Consortium and pushing this war forward. That's my job."

Renata looked between the men and sat back in her chair as she went through her tablet. She didn't always agree with the choices Logan made, but she had lived through the same hell in the Initiative he had, except without a magnifying glass over her like Logan had endured over him. Probably because Renata never ended up getting pregnant. "Are you ready for your next meeting, then, Sir?" Renata trusted that Logan was acting in the best interest of the greater good. That was all anyone could ask of anyone anymore.

Rather than prolonging the fight, Xander was the one to get up from the table and walk away, leaving Logan and Tatyana on opposing corners of it with Renata sitting near Logan to facilitate and monitor for other priorities. "Let's give Mr. Montgomery a moment." He knew Tatyana had something to say, since she usually did, and he was impressed that she was restraining herself as well as she was. "Who's next for this afternoon, Renata?"

Instead of staying to hear Renata rattle off Logan's schedule, Tatyana got up and walked out after Xander, since she was far more concerned about him than anyone else in the universe. "Xander." She spoke softer than usual, but her tone was still firm. "Are you alright?"

"Yeah." He answered reluctantly, glaring off at the stadium seating where people were working on the fighters or being taught how to fly them. Logan had everyone on a rotating system of education while they waited for another strike, so that everyone would eventually know at least a little about everything. Everything in the place moved and flowed as Logan dictated, every moment of the day, and Xander couldn't bring himself to be exactly angry about it. "Part of me is still wondering when everything changed, I guess." He shook his head as he turned to face her. "I don't mind, but I feel like I should. I can't even disagree with the guy, but that doesn't mean I have to like it."

Tatyana approached him slowly and reached out for his hand. She knew in some ways she'd become more distant and cold, and in others . . . well, she was holding his fucking hand. That showed vulnerability she never allowed before. "Everything changed when the rebellion turned into a war. I've learned recently that I can fight and kill until doomsday and not flinch even once, but when I see an entire war in front of me, possibly spanning two planets and more, I can't . . . I can't really manage that. He doesn't really have anything else to live for."

She didn't even look back, because she didn't care if Logan heard anything she said or what he would attempt to do about it. Tatyana didn't give two shits about Logan. She had always cared about the cause, and Logan happened to be on her side. That was what she cared about. The right side. "Shit changes. Who cares? We go with it. It's what has to be done."

"I'm sure they started off thinking the same way." Xander sighed, but squeezed her hand anyway. "I guess I didn't really think before now about the difference between a rebellion and a war. I'm a rebel, not a soldier. I'll be happy when we have a target and a plan. That's the life I'm good at."

Tatyana nodded in complete agreement, since she felt exactly the same way. "I didn't think about it much until recently." She yanked him closer so she could kiss him roughly. "I want to shoot those motherfuckers with you by my side. That's what I want."

She could feel him relax by degrees under the kiss, until he had a handful of her shirt by the end of it and they were both sweating just a little more in the heat of the arena. "Simple tastes. Good portion of the reason I love you, woman."

She nodded and pulled him into another kiss before she said anything else. "I love you too, Xander." Tatyana didn't say it very often, but when she did, she always meant it wholeheartedly. "Don't let Logan get to you. He's just trying to survive by being an even bigger dick than the rest of us."

"Yeah . . . I guarantee he's not." He glanced down and kissed her one more time before heading back toward the table with her. "Only a matter of time before we've got another target to go after.

Then the world will start making sense again." As they got close to the table again, though, Renata was speaking with a small team out of their communications personnel, who were usually tasked with listening in on as many Orbital conversations as possible.

For Logan's part, he was apparently just ending a phone call. "You don't have to like it or even agree, Jason. Your brain might move a hell of a lot faster than mine, but I understand the risks just as well as you do. Coordinate with Olivia's people and get it done." He closed the call without waiting for a response, rubbing at his temples.

"Coordinate with Olivia's people?" Tatyana asked as she walked back in with Xander. "What are you coordinating now?"

Logan looked up at her, making eye contact in a rare show of actual interpersonal connection. Those moments had become more and more rare for Logan since the attack in the mountains, and the degree to which they were unsettling had increased along with their rarity. "I'll tell you, but you should know beforehand, you're not going to like it."

Tatyana felt as though she should roll her eyes at Logan. Instead she just glared. "I rarely like any news you have to give me, Logan Bickford."

"Oh, but you're gonna like this a whole lot less. Even less than my usual." He actually smiled up at her, and that was the most rare, and most unsettling, of all possible expressions. "Make sure your schedule's clear later tonight. We've got a conference call you're not going to want to miss, with some people you really, really don't like."

2

Mercury sat on the edge of an exam table in a skimpy exam gown, with light music being played in the room, feeling more uncomfortable than she had ever been in her life.

She was in her element. She should have felt calm, she should have felt comforted by the sight of tools all around her she knew better than most. It looked exactly like many of the rooms she herself had used to examine pregnant women as a practicing doctor. And yet, none of it felt the same.

It was a part of a distant past, a past that she looked back on and thought about how naive she had been, how stupid she had been for blindly trusting the Consortium. The girl that Mercury had been didn't exist anymore. She had been shattered by everything the Consortium threw at her and more, and the version of Mercury that was left was a patchwork quilt of the woman she was trying to be.

She wasn't nervous because she was afraid something bad was going to happen to her. So far, very little 'bad' had happened to her or anyone else, but she knew that they were just 'in a holding pattern,' as Orion had liked to call it. Mercury was valuable because she was developed for a purpose, that much she had figured out, but she didn't really know more than that. She knew she was valuable because her sons were the product of her and an earthling. She was valuable because of the baby girls still growing inside her, but she didn't have nearly the answers she wanted.

She was a rat. A rat trapped in a cage with other rats who all wanted to get out but didn't want to lose what was important to them. Who knew what would happen to her boys if she put up a fight? Who knew what they would do to her daughters if she refused to do as they said? She was powerless. As she sat there on the exam table staring at the screen where they would project her ultrasound, all she could think about was exactly how pathetically powerless she was. They all were.

"You have a lot to be glad about." Her doctor was saying. Even in her own practice, it had been fairly rare for men to be practicing obstetricians, but her doctor had all the manners of one. Comforting words, more than a little grey in his beard, and an air of confidence that could only have been achieved by years of experience with thousands of pregnancies.

"Your girls both seem to be progressing nicely, though one seems to be outpacing the other just slightly, as is common with twins, as you're obviously aware. There is a potential, given the smaller girl's bloodwork, that she will carry and present the clotting and vascular disorder your record shows that you were warned about upon your admission to the Eleusis Initiative, but we won't have any way to know for sure until she's born and is living entirely on her own blood supply. In any event, it's treatable, just something to bear in mind."

"I was doing research about the disorder." Mercury replied without even looking at the man as she settled back against the pillow the nurse put on the table for her. They were supposed to do an anatomy scan, just to make sure her twins had all of the parts they should have and that they all looked to be working correctly. She was, if nothing else, happy to be able to hear their heartbeats. That would help her day significantly. "I was doing research on a lot of things before they stuck me in here like a lab rat." She said sharply, but she expected the man wouldn't really react. He was trained to be polite on all occasions and so far, his bedside manner had been exactly in line with the Consortium's teachings.

"Rats are afforded considerably fewer courtesies than you and the others have been, Doctor." He had taken care to address her with respect, at the very least, even if the end result of respectful imprisonment was still imprisonment. "I've reviewed some of your previous research. I was a little puzzled at the direction you chose to move with it. It seemed you were looking for incidents of coexistence with CV-immunity. It was a marker I haven't seen anyone look for previously. I can't say I agree it's fruitful for further study, given the natural limitations of CV research, but still, it was a unique approach."

"You don't think so?" She asked curiously as the nurse prepared her for the sonogram by moving about and maintaining her privacy by draping blankets over her but leaving her stomach exposed. Mercury was bigger now with the girls than she had been with the boys at this stage, but she attributed it to her second pregnancy and the fact that Orion was no small man. "What happens if somehow the CV mutates and it can travel? You can imagine the devastation humankind could suffer again if there isn't a cure? It's dangerous. It needs to be controlled *and* eradicated. For all of our sakes."

"You're talking like a first-year medical student, Doctor." The man was condescending without being malicious, and he shook his head as he prepped the gel, which was pre-heated for her comfort, just like everything else about the procedure. "Lucky for you, I've taught more than a few of those classes. I know the cycle as well as anybody else, I expect. The history. Every effort to vaccinate against the virus only weakened the immune systems of those who were vaccinated until they normally died of common non-lethal illnesses. Attempts at quarantine, even on community levels, never made it past the first generation. Eventually, someone needs contact with the outside world, and that always leads to infection. Usually worse than typical levels because of a complete lack of prepared immune response. Treatments administered away from other sources of contagion are effective at removing the virus and placing it in a state of complete remission, but attempts at mass treatment, even enforced treatment, were met with mass resistance in the twenty-second century. Come on, Doctor. You know all this."

"I know the literature." She said with a bored and flat tone as she looked up at the ceiling, since she read *so* much literature about CV. "But I've studied it closer than most. I've read so much literature I used to dream about it. All you're doing is reciting someone else's work, which is all you can do. You've never known someone dying from CV. Probably never will."

"And does your personal data tell you something more than thousands of scientists for four generations immediately after the Crisis?" He wasn't letting the device linger on a complete picture of her children for the time being, going through and grabbing measurements mechanically from both the twins in a sequence as intrinsic as signing his own name. "You're breaking yourself against a problem that already has a solution. One that your rebels have done nothing but help to destroy."

"And that doesn't sound strange to you?" Mercury finally lowered her gaze from the ceiling, but she looked at her girls first before she turned her attention to the condescending doctor. She hoped she hadn't once sounded like this man. She hoped she was kinder than that, though she didn't know what she had really been like before. A curious, young doctor. Mercury felt as though she had aged so much in such a short time.

"It doesn't sound strange that the best minds of thousands of scientists, generations of genius . . . they just couldn't figure it out?" She turned her attention away from the doctor and back to her squirming babies with loud and perfectly thumping hearts. "It sounds to me like you believe in a system that wants you to stay inside the lines, Doctor. And it also sounds like you like the lines. I don't blame you. I do too, usually."

"I think living outside the lines always sounds like the best way to get where you want to go." He said in a somewhat kinder tone. His condescension was genuine, even if there was nothing else redeeming about it. "It always feels like what we want is something we could have if we could just bend this one tiny little rule or bypass this one safeguard. No one would have to know. But that never works. History teaches us how often that works. Sometimes people change the world by seeing farther than the rest. Most people make mistakes that end up costing them their lives. Or worse, costing other people their lives."

He gave her a look that told her he was very distinctly thinking of her and 'her rebels' when he said so. "And yes, I do believe in it. I believe that working in accordance with science and practical understanding is the best way to move anything forward. Best way to have children, best way to run a society. Not blind idealism that gets carried away with itself every single time it gets a little power."

Mercury stared at her little girls without saying anything for a moment that felt like it was going to stretch on forever. "I dedicated my entire life to being a good doctor, the best doctor, and to being the best intellectual that I could be. I did everything the way the Consortium wanted me to live my life. I followed the rules, I exercised regularly, I ate right, I studied hard, I worked hard. I was nothing but grateful for everything that they gave me, every opportunity. I lost sleep over my application into the Initiative. I wanted to get in so much I couldn't do anything else but count the days. I wanted to make a difference because the Consortium had given me so much." Mercury felt her eyes filling with tears, but she didn't care. Tears were more a part of her life than anything else anymore. "I followed protocol and put my name into the Matching system. I met the perfect Match."

She stared at her daughters as her voice broke over the thought of Orion, since he was gone, and she was sure the universe wasn't going to give him back to her. "I did everything the way I thought I was supposed to do it. The way I was raised to do it. The way the Consortium told me to do it. And then they tried to kill me and every other person who they inducted into the Initiative." She finally looked away from the screen to the doctor. "They were going to kill me. As though I meant not a single thing to any one of them. After every moment I had spent working for them, dedicated toward their causes. These babies you're going to deliver? They wouldn't exist if I hadn't done something. I would be dead. I don't want to be dead. I want to live. And if that makes me a rebel, then so be it."

"You were married to one of the most notorious terrorists in history, Dr. Finnegan." They had seen, by her own protestations, that her last name had been changed to Al-Jabbar, but no one had ever called her that the entire time she'd been on the station. "A man who's bound to go down in history as a mass-murderer and a known degenerate. You've taken enough psychology to be able to diagnose the kinds of symptoms he exhibits. You don't need me to tell you. You can say what you want about all the work you did for the Consortium and the excellent doctor that I fully admit you became, but when you try to somehow reconcile the doctor you were with the rebel you've become, you're going to have to forgive me when I can't stop myself from laughing. The two are worlds apart." He froze a number of images for her and left them up on the screen, pulling the equipment away to start cleaning up, since he'd gotten all he needed. "The fact that you can't perceive that just goes to show the kind of corrupting influence the kind of rebel ideology you've adopted can have, even on a great mind like yours."

Mercury sat up enough to wipe the gel off of herself and she actually smiled at the doctor a little. She honestly couldn't tell who was more 'corrupt', herself or him. "Maybe what you perceive and what I perceive is different. I, for example, believe that a person in a leadership position within the Consortium should not be able to drug and rape a woman just for his perverse pleasure. To me, that is corrupt." She tossed aside the gel-covered towel and covered herself up as much as she could, though her backside was still hanging out of the ridiculous robe. "I wasn't only married to him. I was in love with him. Deeply, deeply in love with him. Make sure you put that on your notes before you submit them to the psychiatrist."

He seemed mildly surprised at the acid in her reply, but he nodded, his professional bedside manner resuming smoothly. "Do you have any other questions about your girls, or anything else you'd like me to include in your chart, Dr. Finnegan?"

"No, there's nothing else that you can tell me that I particularly care about. My daughters are healthy." She started to get off the exam table to get back to her standard-issue clothing. "Unless you have more you feel you need to tell me."

"Nothing that I expect you to take to heart." He said sadly, finishing up some last notes on a terminal nearby. "Oh, there was one more thing. We received some instructions this morning that there have been some changes in your access permissions. You're still restricted from communications, of course, but we were told to let you know that you have full research database privileges now. Even more than you had when you still had your license, as a matter of fact. Your access was granted by the Directors themselves."

"I see." Mercury continued to get dressed even though the nurse and the doctor hadn't left the room. She was their lab rat. They could handle a little nudity. "Am I being asked to research a particular topic, or . . . they wanted to give me access for some strange reason just to watch what I do with it?"

"I wasn't informed of any particular reason for the access change, only that it was altered and you were to be told about it." The man shrugged, not even looking at her as she finished dressing. "If I had to wager a guess, though I'm not much for gambling or guesswork, I'd say it's because there's no harm in letting a researcher do what she does best. Knowledge is knowledge, even if it's uncovered by a rebel mind."

Mercury couldn't help but laugh. "Spoken like a true Consortium doctor." She finished getting dressed and turned her attention back to the older man. "Thank you for your time, nonetheless."

"Of course. I'm at your service." He stepped out of the room and when the door opened, one of the ever-present guards stood just outside waiting for her, hands meekly clasped in front of him, firearm strapped along one of his thighs as a silent means of encouraging obedience.

Mercury wasn't sure why they felt the guns were necessary

with a group of distinct non-combatants, but she didn't make a comment about it when she looked over at the guard. "Where to now? Back to the maze?"

"Only place ye belong." The man said in a thick accent for which he made no apologies. "And just fer yer smart mouth, no cheese for ye. Seein' as yer more of a mouse than a rat."

"A mouse? Why do you say that?" She asked curiously, though she wasn't at all apologizing for her mouth. The universe had been cruel to her too many times, and yet somehow she was always polite even if a little sarcastic.

"Every now and then, a rat at least bites. Could do ye some 'arm, even if it's just a nip." It wasn't a long walk between the clinic and the door to the corridor in which she and the rest of the prisoners lived. He and the other guards were mostly there to make sure they didn't attempt any kind of escape while out of their isolated world. Once inside it, it was almost possible to forget, temporarily, that they were prisoners at all. Temporarily. "A mouse, though, 'at's just a pest, nothin' more."

"A pest. I see." Mercury looked over at the man and then really stared at him before she said anything else. "You know, I honestly cannot remember if all the people I knew before were as rude as most of you are around here and I just didn't recognize it, or if they just handpicked the lot of you because you're so unhappy that they didn't have anywhere else to put you except with women and children who are mostly innocent."

"I used te work security on Seven." He answered without missing a beat, giving her a sideways glare. "I knew ye back then, before ye lost yer mind. O' course, ye never spared anyone but yer own reflection a second look back then and I dinnae expect ye te start doin' so now. Four months 'ere in these 'alls and ye've never once acted like ye even recognized me." He wasn't a very striking man by appearance, dark brown hair and pale green eyes mostly washed of color over a scruffy beard, middling height and not-unpleasing features. "And yeah, ye'd be fair in sayin' people 'ave always been rude as most of us. Ye were always too busy with yer own mind te even notice. That makes ye just as bad as the rest."

"You're probably right about that. I'm just as bad as the rest." She looked him over again and turned her attention to the door he was reaching out to open with his badge. "I'm sorry that I didn't recognize you. I should have." Mercury wasn't a fighter and she certainly had no reason to fight now, with her boys inside and waiting for her. Even if she got out with her children, she wouldn't get far. There was nowhere to go, and no one to save her. This was her life.

"You are what you are, mouse. Same as the rest of us." He pressed a button and closed the glass doors on the corridor, leaving her in the hallway with the rest of the prison cell rooms behind her. They could always see the guards watching over them day or night, since the corridor was always lit to deny them any natural sense of time.

"Is everything alright, Señora?" Diego's voice came from nearby, where he was sitting outside his unit with two of his children and one of his wives. His boys were old enough to understand vaguely what was happening, but too young still to even be considered young men, as much as they tried to act otherwise. Captivity had dulled the man's usual ready smile and forced away most of his sense of humor, but he was still always the first to jump in and help whenever someone among the captives needed it, including Mercury with her boys.

Mercury looked back at the guard and walked in and nodded, giving Diego as much of a smile as she could muster. He was a kind man, especially to try and help her as much as he did when he had a very large family of his own. She saw the benefit of multiple wives and a big family now, after being alone with twin boys, Anna's children, and pregnant with two more. "They were just checking on the girls. And lecturing me about how I was married to two of the most infamous terrorists of our time. Nevermind that at least one of them is dead now. Why does it matter?"

"I didn't know your giant very well." Diego said with a shrug. "But from what I do know, I'm gonna need to see a body before I believe he's dead." They all had their own kind of hope that they needed to hold onto, since they had been kept away from everything in the world that they couldn't observe from their own windows for months.

"Anyway, there's somebody waitin' for you at your unit. Gwen wouldn't let 'em inside, don't worry, but they said they'd wait. Real polite-like. Got manners, no' like the rest o' these . . ." Diego had a habit of lapsing into long strings of Spanish that he seemed to assume everyone else could always understand, but his meaning was usually more or less clear from the expression on his face. The fact that one of his wives snapped at him for saying whatever he'd said in front of their children immediately afterward was indication enough of however rude whatever he'd said had been.

"Thank you for keeping an eye on them, and Gwen too." She said with a genuine smile, since it was easier to be around friends than around anyone else. However, she didn't like the sound of whatever was waiting for her at her unit. "I better go check what it is all about." She went up to Diego and gave him a kiss on the cheek before she moved on past and headed toward her unit. She was even more grateful for Gwen than she ever had been, since she appreciated anyone who would stand up and protect her children.

When she got to her unit, she could see what Diego was talking about. The man who was waiting for her was so clean and smooth-looking he was more than a little feminine, his suit in the newest Orbital styles, even down to a stylized pin going along the left side of his collar to pin a part of his tie. The small stud earring in one ear didn't help him look in any way more masculine. Nearby, Melissa and Kameron were standing outside the open door of their own unit, William and Kassie apparently asleep inside. Neither of them were armed, of course, but Kameron didn't have to be armed to look dangerous. It was something that came naturally to her.

"Dr. Finnegan." The man said respectfully as she got closer. His accent was vaguely French, and he almost bowed, his manner was so formal. "My name is Martin. I hope everything went well with your appointment?"

Mercury raised a rust-colored eyebrow to inspect the man critically before she said anything. She was always trying to figure things out before she was told anything. It was just how her mind worked. "Martin. What can I do for you?" She asked without making any mention of her appointment. He didn't need details from her about her appointment, mostly because she assumed by the way he looked that he could have access to them and she wouldn't have a say in it anyway. But at least she could make him work for information.

There was a brief moment of hesitation, in which she could almost see him trying to work through the fact that she had completely ignored his question. There was no way to continue polite conversation along the same lines under those terms, so he carried on with a rough break instead of any other available smooth ones.

"I am here to invite you to dinner this evening. Mr. and Mrs. Alpert extend their invitation for you to join them in their personal unit at 19:00. It is their hope that you will be their guest, as they've expressed an interest in meeting you and making your further acquaintance. What may I tell them?"

Mercury's face remained a sheet of stone in confusion for a moment before she burst out laughing. There was no way the Alperts wanted to meet with her. Her father had told her about them in the past, and nothing she knew about them gave her the impression they were interested in hosting a terrorist lab rat for a dinner party. "The Alperts? Want to see me? I don't believe that."

"That's your prerogative, Doctor." The man looked neither surprised nor offended at her refusal, still patiently waiting for her answer. "It is now 17:06, and I'm given to understand that the chef has already begun work on your meal for the evening. If you accept, I will return to escort you at 18:45." There was no trace of dissembling or game-playing on his face, so if the man wasn't toying with her, he was either honest or a complete psychopath. It was anyone's guess which was more likely.

Mercury laughed a little bit more. "Sure. Of course, I'll meet with them. They have absolutely no reason to want to meet with me, but sure. As long as I can get a sitter." She smiled after that, since of course there would be someone who could watch her children, but she wanted to ask Gwen anyway.

"You have roughly one hour and forty-five minutes to work out your own childcare arrangements. I'm sure you'll find something satisfactory." He gave her another one of his nods that was just a little too low to be normal, then headed past her back to the one and only door in or out of their detention wing.

Mercury sighed as she turned back to her unit, but she looked over at Kameron and Melissa afterward. "Do you think the two of you could make a party out of it with the kids and help Gwen while I'm gone? Three versus six seems a little more reasonable."

"We'll take them over to Diego's and have the party there." Melissa watched the man leave with the same suspicion on her face as had been in Mercury's laugh. The Swedish blonde bombshell still managed to look gorgeous even in the jumpsuits, mostly because she constantly refused to wear hers completely zipped up like most of the other captives. Sitting just outside their own unit she had her jumpsuit rolled down and tied around her waist, sitting in just her bra and the covering of her extensively colorful tattoos. "You're not worried? About the Alperts?"

"Of course I am." Mercury replied softly before she looked over at Kameron, but Kam just shrugged. "What in the world would they want to see me for?" She looked up toward one of the cameras, then sighed as she looked at Melissa and Kam again. "Unless they think I have information that I don't have. It's not like Logan and I discussed his work. And even when we did, that was a long time ago. I wasn't with Logan when we were taken."

"Well, they want *something*." Melissa sounded much more worried than Kam did, and was looking back and forth between them as if she was trying to figure out why the blood pressure in the hallway wasn't higher. "And whatever it is, you . . . probably shouldn't give it to them. Because if they're asking, it means it's something they can't get by force, or they would have already."

Mercury looked over Melissa with all of her tattoos, chewing on her bottom lip. "I'm not interested in giving them anything they want." She looked between the women and then she looked down at her ever-growing belly. "I meant to talk to you about something else, Melissa. I was able to get some tools . . ."

That was more than enough to get Melissa's attention, and she reversed the way she had her legs crossed to face Mercury directly. "Tools? What kind of tools? I've got a thing for hammers and screwdrivers."

"I asked for something that you are intimately familiar with, and they didn't see the harm in giving it to me. But I have a favor to ask." Mercury left the vague response hanging before she disappeared into her unit and then came back out with a tattoo gun. "I was hoping you could help me with this."

Melissa gasped dramatically and actually fell off her chair to crawl across the hallways floor to Mercury's knees. She was a little over the top. Just a little. "Is that . . .?" Her hands actually shook as she reached out for it, holding it like some kind of sacred object. She let out a gasping sigh the likes of which Mercury had only heard out of the woman when Mercury had been babysitting their children and they had mistakenly left a door cracked. "Oh my . . . you . . ."

"I think it's because they don't care what we do to the outside of our bodies in here, but I've been thinking a lot about Orion and Logan and . . . I want something to remember them by. Also I think it's adorable to see how Kameron smiles when she sees how happy you are. We could use some happiness around here."

Kameron *was* smiling as she watched Melissa's reaction but she tried to look less obvious after Mercury made her point. "So I like to see my wife happy. It's not a crime."

Melissa flicked her hair over her shoulder as she gave Kam a glowing smile. She actually shivered as she turned back around and looked at the tattoo gun, checking over each of its components and running her fingers along the parts with another satisfied purr. "I . . . mmmmm. Okay, I need a minute. But yes, I'd love to do something for you. Of course I would."

Mercury relaxed a little, since she did have a little concern that Melissa might say no, but she didn't know why she thought that way. "I don't need anything complicated, though I don't doubt your skills. I just want their names here," she held out and exposed one wrist. "And here." She showed her other wrist. "Orion and Logan. On two pulse points." She stared at her wrists before she looked up at Melissa again. "I was wondering if you could make the lettering look like the lines on a heartbeat monitor. Both of them are the reasons why I have anything to live for here. The boys and the girls they gave me. Otherwise my life was my career. And I don't think I'll ever be allowed to practice medicine ever again."

Melissa's elation quickly turned subdued, but she hadn't gotten up from where she knelt on the floor at Mercury's feet, looking down over her wrists. "I'll draw something up, Mercury. It'll be good. I promise."

Mercury took a deep breath to sigh and she gave Melissa a small smile before she nodded. "I know. You draw such beautiful things." She looked at Melissa's colorful body art again and then down at her wrists. "I miss them both. Being so angry felt wrong once they said he was dead."

Melissa sat back on the floor with the tattoo gun, still turning it over and over in her hands as she thought about the job ahead of her. "And . . . if they were lying? If they're still alive?" They never knew what was true and what was a trap when the Consortium was behind it, and Mercury was one of the few who believed most of what they had been told. Many of the others were still very much in denial about what happened to their loved ones.

Mercury shook her head again. "I don't think they have reason to lie to prisoners. I don't know that I even believe Logan loved me like he loved Anna. I'm tired of being angry over it, certainly. Everyone should have a life that makes them happy. You and

Kam have each other. He had always loved Anna. I knew that from the moment I met him."

"He loved you." Melissa said weakly, since she hadn't known Logan that well, but she had been around for some key moments in their short history. "I was there, in the docks. Hiding and just trying to stay out of the way, mostly, but I was there when he attacked the Kaplans. Now, I haven't had a chance to scratch any bitches' eyes out for looking at my honey wrong, but I know what it looks like when somebody's settling a score for someone they love." Melissa wasn't sure if she was speaking out of turn or not, but she always watched people, and she knew what she saw.

Mercury wanted to believe that, but she shook her head again anyway. "He owned me. There's a difference." She never admitted what kind of relationship had occurred between her and Logan, not because she was necessarily ashamed, mostly because she didn't want to be the reason for Logan's fall from power. "He didn't like anyone touching what was his. I was happy to be his, I gave him everything, every part of me. It still wasn't enough when Anna presented herself." She held up her hand. "It doesn't matter. He's dead. And if he's not, he's avenging Anna's death. I'm okay with it."

Melissa wasn't going to argue with her about something no one inside their detention center could definitively answer, so she just nodded and got up to go back toward her unit and prepare. "I'll have something drawn up by the time you get back from the Alperts later. We can work on it when all the little monsters are asleep."

"Thank you. You should be able to request the ink through the shopping portal." She replied with a subdued smile and when Kameron gave her a nod, she headed back to her unit to relieve Gwen. The girl hadn't been with the babies too long, but Mercury didn't like to abuse good childcare.

* * * * *

Martin returned promptly at 7:44, typical Consortium punctuality at work. Even more typical of the man's Consortium mentality was the disparaging look he gave the jumpsuit she wore to visit the Alperts, even though they were the only clothes the prisoners were given.

Their progress through Prime seemed to go on forever, and

there were no guards with her besides the tall man with a sashay to his walk. They passed down corridors filled with common citizens going about their lives, all of them staring as the obvious prisoner moved among them. She could tell when they entered the restricted area, as the suits around her became a great deal more stylish and the hallways went from merely efficient to broad and polished.

When she finally arrived, the rotation of the station had the feeling of roughly half Earth gravity. Her hair took just a little longer than normal to fall back into place with every step. Martin himself didn't accompany her into the unit, clearly feeling unworthy to do so, but he announced her at the stylized double doors, which opened a few moments later to admit her without making them wait.

"Come in, Doctor." She had heard Dominic Alpert's voice before in speeches, but never in person. It was a mid-range tenor and sounded every bit as kindly and professional as her doctor sounded only a few hours before. The man himself was nowhere to be seen, but the luxury of the suite that opened up to invite her in was beyond anything else she'd ever seen, in Orbit or on Earth. The place crackled and gleamed with crystalline light, colors refracting everywhere against white walls and perfect white carpets. Some of the crystal was in sculptures, others were simply in fixtures around the room meant for nothing but ornamentation.

Mercury stood still just inside the door as she took in the ridiculous ornamentation. She thought about how much a waste it all was, but the art was still beautiful. It was as though the chairs of the Board had decided to live in an art gallery, some kind of museum dedicated to the beauty of the world they chose to oppress.

Mercury could already feel her eyes glazing over as they moved from piece to exquisite piece, until she saw something that looked familiar.

That wasn't right.

As she moved closer, Mercury's stomach sank, and the gravity in the room felt suddenly inadequate. She reached up and touched the corner of the canvas, where her initials rested, painted by her own hand.

They had one of her paintings from the unit she left behind on Seven.

Why did they have one of her paintings?

"A beautiful piece." Dominic's voice came again, this time from behind her in the ostentatious reception area. He walked up with a wine glass in either hand, though the liquid in the glasses was actually a shade of light purple rather than the reds or whites she was used to. Dominic himself looked like the kind of man who belonged in the middle of such an effluence of wealth. His clothing was cut in simple styles, but he had small touches of elegance about every aspect of his appearance, small accents of gold along the seams of his coat and bits of crystal woven into the tie pinned along his collar.

"I particularly like your use of the light. So many artists get that wrong, especially with spacescapes. But you have all the right lights and shadows in beautiful contrast. I loved it the first moment I saw it."

Mercury felt a particular chill run down her spine, but she tried not to appear as disturbed as she felt. They were doing this on purpose, she just didn't know why yet. "I didn't know you were an admirer of my work. I didn't show it to many people. This was in my unit on Seven."

"Yes, it was. My wife and I procured it after you and your comrades destroyed Station Nine and declared yourselves rebels against the Consortium." He said it all calmly, as if he was still describing how much he admired the painting he examined past her shoulder. "We have the rest of your collection as well, set aside in storage. This one was our favorite, though, so we decided you, and it, deserved an honored place here in the gallery."

"I think it's interesting you define the incident on Nine as an act of rebellion when I see it as an act of survival." Mercury didn't have any reason to respect the man in front of him, nor did she have any reason to hold her tongue. She was his prisoner. "Why did you ask me here?"

"Dinner." He said matter-of-factly, nodding toward a hall leading away from the gallery and all of its neutral upholstery. "And curiosity. But dinner first. Curiosities, like wine, are best left out to breathe for a while." He looked down at the wine glass in her hands, left completely untouched, then gave her a smile that looked as practiced as a doctor's bedside manner as he took it back.

"How silly of me. I quite forgot your rather unfortunate history with drinks poured by strangers. My apologies. There's another bottle chilling in the dining room unopened. Hopefully you'll accept some of that one." He took a brief sip from the glass he handed her as he turned to move in the direction he had indicated without looking back.

It made it worse that he knew that much detail, since she knew she had only ever told Logan and Orion. "Unfortunate." She repeated carefully as she followed behind the man. "Yes, how *unfortunate* your leadership decided it was perfectly acceptable to drug and rape a woman repeatedly for their own twisted pleasure."

"Well, that was their primary motivation, certainly. Stephen and Maria have always been driven by their own desires, unconventional as they are." He didn't seem bothered by her accusation at all, and didn't even look back to acknowledge it. "However, they have also always been excellent scientists with equal dedication to their craft as their own desires. Their violation of you yielded a number of very interesting results given the bloodwork they took from you throughout the experience."

They reached the dining room and he stepped to one side, indicating a seat at a small, round table off to one side of the room. There was a long and impossibly-ornate dining table that ran the entire length of the room, set with beautifully-engraved cutlery and flatware, but apparently that evening's dinner was to be more intimate. The small, round table was set only for three. "That data helped to expedite a number of chains of research concerning the agent they slipped you at the outset, and inspired Maria to create an anti-anxiety medication from a variant of the drug that is now seeing promising early use in Northern Africa."

Mercury hated that hearing about medical advancement actually gave her a little bit of comfort, especially because she had been tortured and tormented for the advancement to occur in the first place. "I don't care about their research. I don't care about anything you could possibly tell me, *Dominic*. I have no information you could possibly want." She wasn't expecting to lose her temper, but it was happening despite her best efforts to stop it. She was so tired of being an experiment. All she wanted was to live her life in peace.

He looked over at her and actually laughed, then stepped up to pull her chair out for her, bits of crystal and colored glass glinting in the soft lights of the room as he did so. "I'm very sorry, you've quite mistaken the purpose of tonight's dinner, Dr. Finnegan. This is not an interrogation. And, as beautiful as you are, my sexual tastes and my wife's have never tended to the abusive. If anything, Doctor, you are here so that we can give *you* some information that, in my estimation, is long overdue."

She looked at him with only suspicion as she sat down in the chair that was pulled out for her, but she still felt completely out of place in her prisoner jumpsuit in his fancy dining area. It was as though she was a small fish dining with a shark, and the shark kept telling her she wasn't his taste.

Mercury looked up when a perfectly-put-together blonde woman entered in a fancy dress, heels, and glittering jewels. Who dressed up like that for dinner with a prisoner?

"I'm so sorry I'm late, my dear." Mrs. Alpert said as she went to give her husband a kiss and he moved to pull out his chair for her as well. She smiled as she sat down and looked over at Mercury. "It is good to see you, Doctor. Thank you for joining us."

"Expressing gratitude for something about which a person had no choice seems nonsensical. You are not welcome." She was still trying to figure out what information they could have that she would want, unless they were going to tell her that Orion or Logan was alive. Even then, Mercury knew better than to believe them.

"Well, we did ask, and you did agree." Dominic offered another of his brief shrugs. He took a bottle of wine and pulled the cork with a pointed look at Mercury, then poured all three glasses for the three of them to taste. He let Mercury decide which one she wanted and sipped from his own before looking back at the door to the kitchens as their first course came out.

Mercury had been to her share of staff receptions and yearly banquets with the hospital, even though she had normally found an excuse to work instead. The servants who came out with their aperitif were a stark reminder of the world she had left behind, in perfect uniforms with perfectly neutral faces and efficient gestures. It was a different world, but it was the world she had come from. The world she had once belonged in.

Mercury only took a sip from her glass and put it aside, even though it clearly tasted expensive. "Most research shows that small amounts of alcohol doesn't harm unborn children. Nevertheless, I won't need more." She looked at one of the servants as she attempted to ignore the people in front of her. "Water, please."

They responded to her just as politely and quickly as if she was one of the Alperts themselves, and her wine glass was quickly replaced with one of ice water.

"If you'll allow us a curiosity, Doctor," Dominic said once he'd thanked the servants and they were alone again for the moment, "I'd like to ask what you have in mind for your first priority of research given your newly-restored access to our databases. Have you given it any thought yet?"

"I promised Orion I would figure out a way to make sure that his son will grow up without any problems caused by his variety of gigantism." She was grateful for the water as soon as it arrived, and she drank half of it quickly. "So I'm aiming to keep my promise."

"His gigantism? Really?" Dominic smiled in a manner that was so bright and affable it threatened to wreak havoc on her brain. Everything about him spoke of a person she could, and possibly should, have genuinely liked. He and his wife were polite, pleasant, and appeared genuinely interested in her life and interests. Sitting with them on their own terms, in finery that threatened any memory that there was anything wrong, made it difficult to think of them as the enemy.

"Some of the traces in the samples we've taken of Leo's blood so far showed some interesting inhibition factors you've been testing so far. We also have some of Captain Al-Jabbar's blood samples left in storage, and his fully sequenced code should be available as well, I'm almost sure of it. We can make them available to you if they'll be helpful with your research."

"That would be." She replied in a small voice, since it made her want to cry at the knowledge that she would still have access to Orion's blood but not to him. She missed him so much it was a physical pain in her chest. "My daughters are not showing as many problems."

"Well, my understanding is that the majority of cases show genetic traces through the Y chromosome, so with twin daughters, it makes sense that it's less likely to be transmitted." Dominic didn't talk like a doctor most of the time, but he seemed confident of what he was saying nonetheless. "I'm glad to hear your daughters are developing without any foreseeable difficulties. And I'm sure with the right resources, you'll find an effective method of helping Leo. With others like Orion, there has been a high rate of difficulties. One woman I recall reading about a few years ago grew to 3.23 meters before her heart was no longer capable of keeping up with the strain. That was, of course, on Earth."

"Fortunately, Leo is only measuring slightly larger than he

should at his age. And his mother is not a tall woman. I'm hoping that will help him until I can find a solution. And I will." She took a few of the small food items she didn't entirely recognize.

"I have every confidence." Dominic's smile was as pleasant as always, and he actually turned to Sara for a while so that they could discuss a few details of their day, as if Mercury was some intimate friend of theirs rather than a prisoner they had brought to have a meal with them. The specifics of what they talked about were completely innocent, and dealt more with confirming schedules with each other than anything else. When he finally looked back over at her, they were on their second round of palate-cleansing between courses. "How's your salad, Doctor?"

Mercury paused mid-bite and she looked down at her plate as though she should be worried about it. "It . . . is fine." Her stomach twisted in nervousness. "Is something wrong with it?"

"No, I just wanted to know if you were enjoying your meal." He smiled and poked his fork toward her plate, taking a last bite of his own salad. "We have no interest in harming you, Doctor. You have one of the most brilliant minds of your generation. If you put it to use in your present situation, I'm sure you'll come to that conclusion. We have no interest in bringing any harm to you or to the others with you. You are imprisoned because you are self-confessed rebels against the authority and practices of the Consortium, so it follows that we cannot permit you to move freely, but that does not immediately mean we wish you harm. On the contrary, we have a great deal of respect for you and your accomplishments, even given the circumstances."

"I've been hunted for the better part of two years. Hunted within the confines of the Initiative by the Kaplans, hunted by your people on Earth. That feeling doesn't just go away." Mercury put her fork down and turned her attention back to the water. "I don't really know why you're keeping us alive, unless you want my research, but I'm hoping you'll clarify. Eventually. Between your wine and your scheduling with your wife."

Dominic nodded understandingly, and set down his own fork with a sip of his wine, settling back in his chair. "Some clarification to accompany the main course, then. That is a perfectly reasonable expectation."

He reached out and tapped a few places on the small table between them, which was seamlessly integrated with the room around them. The lights dimmed somewhat and images of Earth came up on the plain walls, the small bits and flecks of ornamentation making different parts of the world sparkle out more than others as the images flowed over the space. "If you'd be so kind, Doctor, I'd like you to tell us a story, as you know it. It will make our own clarifications much simpler if you give us a place to begin."

He tapped something else, and numbers began to fly up on the walls surrounding the view of Earth. Population totals, density charts, life expectancy statistics and more. "The year is 2057, two years before what is usually marked as the formal beginning of the Crisis." The population numbers in front of her showed 11.3 billion people on the planet. According to most research she had read, the human race hadn't even produced that many people in four centuries' worth of generations since. "To your knowledge, what comes next?"

"Some animals and plants begin showing strange mutations and some were dying off before any human was sick enough to be diagnosed with the unknown virus. Some crops grew too fast and went bad before they could be harvested. Some animals became sick and died quickly, but everyone was blaming the overuse of modified pesticides. Economies started to feel the pinch first, since resources were jumping up in value."

"Very good. So few people ever manage to associate those things with what followed. Even in most history texts." He seemed genuinely pleased to hear her answer, and nodded for her to continue after taking a sip of his wine. "Most texts begin with the Threat of the Three a year and a half later, after the treaty between China, India and Indonesia. Would you agree with that assessment as the beginning of the end?"

Mercury nodded as she quickly combed through all the information she had in her head about it. "People started getting sick and no one had an explanation, so the three countries with the largest populations decided to work together to try and come up with a solution. Between pesticides and the theory that it was a strangely mutated flu, they couldn't figure it out. But not enough people were getting sick and dying yet, they were just getting sick but not getting better." She wasn't even looking at the Alperts as she thought about all of her research. She divided her attention between the numbers on the walls and her food.

"The animals started getting better five years after they were recorded to be showing strange mutations and unprecedented death. By that time, though, lots of people were dying and no one cared about the animals. I never could figure out how the animals started defeating it naturally and humankind never did. They still have trace amounts of CV, most animals and plants, but it seems to enhance their quality, actually. They mature faster, but they don't rot faster. A cow lives as long as a cow should on Earth. I cannot tell you how many cow samples I looked at for a connection. Somehow they became mostly immune to CV and people never did."

"You were so close." Dominic was truly smiling, like some kind of father figure watching his little girl try to ice skate for the first time. "*So* close. As you say, many people ignored the animal side of the Crisis, even in the early days of research. So close."

He shook his head and tapped a few buttons on the table to advance the timeline, centering one map of the world on a location in northern India that was both very familiar and at the same time looked very strange on the map. In the 21st century it had been land. In the 24th century, only a vast crater lake remained. "The fusion reactor at Banang Co. The Big Bang that most people blame for humanity's demise."

Mercury looked at the pictures he brought up and she shook her head. "But CV isn't actually affected by radioactivity. It was actually used as a last-ditch method to try and cure it. It was called the double-fire method, since people claimed it was fighting fire with fire." She stared at the reactor and then she looked over at Dominic. "They were attempting to use known methods against an unknown virus. The only thing that has worked is to remove humankind from Earth and to administer immunotherapy over at least a month, preferably longer."

Mercury couldn't help but think about Logan briefly, since their romance really blossomed in her exam room on Nine. During his treatments. "The treatments are multi-step. They replace white blood cells with artificially created, non-exposed cells. After that, treatments suppress the immune system's response, since those with CV have an overactive immune system, which makes them vulnerable, but overall hasn't had too negative a response . . ."

When she met Dominic's eyes again, she stopped her explanation of the treatments, since she knew he would know plenty. She just shook her head. "When administered on Earth, the effects simply stall CV's destruction on the human body. It can give a projected decade more to human life if they faithfully take treatment every day for their entire lives. But the treatments are expensive on Earth, and hard to acquire. Even then, no recorded subject has been able to use it faithfully enough to extend life more than around two years."

"That's the best data we've seen as well." He nodded down to her plate. "Try the fish. It's a specialty of my chef's, and quite good for fetal development." He finally placed his wine glass back on the table as he settled in to speak. "First of all, thank you for indulging us in that recitation, and for all your conjectures. I want you to know how truly impressed we've always been with you. Especially as you've pushed forward in your CV research over the years without funding or any form of encouragement. You are an inspiration, and we admire that." There was no 'but' to his statement, and when he continued, he had reset the Earth on the wall to 2058.

"The first trials were naturally carried out on animals and plant life, as the researchers attempted to find combinations that could be tolerated by the world itself without adverse effects. This had actually been going on since 2051, but trials increased in size, quantity, and variance of environment so that a broad baseline of sustainability could be achieved. The earliest batches decades before had been relatively stable but nearly wiped out the world's honeybee population. The variant in 51 proved more stable, and eventually a level of acceptable loss was reached for the rest of the world's flora and fauna, to be compensated by the increased productivity and sustainability you yourself mentioned."

Mercury didn't like to be told what to eat and when to eat, but she couldn't deny that he was right about the fish and fetal development. She cut up the fish and started to eat it slowly, but she didn't have much to say about his explanation. "The bees never really recovered. Most animals did. The bees were slow, and still, it's hard to find honey on Earth."

"They're interesting creatures. Not to fret, though, there are a number of environments on Eleusis where we expect them to thrive." He was looking at her like he was waiting for her to grasp the punchline of a joke, but when her face showed no greater grasp of what he'd said, he moved on. "One other facet of the Crisis that most overlook, including yourself, is the political climate of the time and other surviving records of scientific inquiry. The three great treaties were understood in their own time to be a silent declaration of war, and each alliance was hell bent on surviving what they had started. The watchdogs of the time placed the hands of the doomsday clock within seconds of midnight, and it remained that way for more than a decade of posturing and international tensions."

He took a sip of wine to wet his tongue before he continued. "Only scientific communities and a few religious sects were capable of rising above the noise. Communities began placing themselves in orbit rather than live on the ground, making a better world up here than the one they left. If the political course had been left unchecked, the success of the fusion reactor at Banang Co would have meant the ultimate success of the Threat of the Three. The other nations of the world would not tolerate that kind of failure. Eleven billion people caught in the crossfire. You can imagine what the world would have looked like when they were finished with it."

"The world already looks pretty desolate." She chewed on a small piece of fish. "I didn't do much research on the political climate. It seemed separate from the virus, except that perhaps heavily populated areas obviously made it spread faster."

"That is true, though not for the reasons you were perfectly justified in believing." He gave a brief laugh. "There is no such thing as a true separation between politics and science. We would like to believe there is. We are told that there must be a separation in order to practice true science, and that is not an incorrect teaching. Science itself, the act of research and the testing of truth, must be conducted aside from political biases, or indeed from any biases whatsoever. But science always functions within and is applied based on political prejudice. That is the reality. It was also a reality the first Board of Directors was attempting to ignore or avoid by establishing themselves here in space. They wanted to be impartial, objective, free from the controlling influences of their own home countries to whom they supposedly still owed allegiance. They were ripped apart over and over again by the conflicts escalating on the ground, until the Board at the time decided that such a situation could not be tolerated."

He pressed a button, and different contingencies began playing out on the screens around her, images of missiles being fired all over the world, armies moving in rapid-fire maneuvers, people starving, people surrendering, people fighting back, more people dying, the images moved too fast to follow, and yet it was an old story. One that had played out millions of times in the history of the world.

"97.4 percent of all contingency simulations showed the complete annihilation of humanity within twenty years. There was a 0.04% chance of peaceful political reconciliation, and only a 0.8% chance of the survival of the species over fifty years."

He took a sip of his wine, watching Mercury's reactions to the news as he laid out the situation for her. "Now, even being generous in stating that those procedural contingency analyses were flawed, which they so often are, and giving humanity a slightly larger margin for error, those are not numbers that they at the time were prepared to accept. They aren't numbers that I would be prepared to accept now, were I presented with them."

Mercury stared at the numbers and slowly put her fork down before she turned her attention back to the man . . . if she could even call him that . . . and his wife in front of her. "Crisis Virus was made." She found herself wringing her hands in her lap as soon as she realized it wasn't some devastating odd phenomenon, but a tool. She had spent the better part of her life trying to cure an entire planet of a virus she was now sure they already had the cure for. "You murdered billions of people based on conjecture?"

"I was born forty-eight years ago, Doctor Finnegan. Our *predecessors* murdered billions of people based on available data." He described the act with the same tone in which he had described her painting, as if the use of Crisis was the same kind of artistry with light and darkness that had been contained in her own brush strokes.

"Their skills in conjecture and extrapolation seemed quite finely honed, though. The mortality counts were almost exactly what they had anticipated based on preceding trials. The cases you mentioned, of people coming down with the symptoms prior to the Banang Co explosion. Those at incredibly high latitudes avoided exposure more than had been anticipated, and continue to do so because of natural weather patterns, but to our knowledge, no one's ever investigated that phenomenon." He glanced down at her wringing hands and picked up his wine again. "There is more, but if you need a moment, I understand."

She thought about what she could do in that moment, she thought about throwing her plate, her silverware, her glass, everything, at the people in front of her. She looked over at Sara, a notoriously quiet woman in any setting, but she seemed as little perturbed about the history in her husband's recitation as Dominic himself. Mercury wanted to scream. She had watched people die on Earth. She had watched them die in slow and painful ways because of CV. She had read story after story, child after child . . .

"There were children. Children born that were CV-immune. Most of them died in accidents." So said the reports, but now she didn't know what to think. She thought it was strange before. Now she felt it was entirely on purpose. While she didn't actually move or even flinch, her blood was beginning to boil.

"It might shock you, given your current state of mind, to know just how many of those were legitimately accidental. Not all of them, certainly, but most of them." He seemed similarly impressed that she wasn't screaming, but continued when it was clear she was listening.

"In order to understand *why* most CV-immune children die in childhood or in accidents, I am afraid I must alter your understanding of history one step further, Doctor. And it is this one further fundamental alteration which I hoped to clarify for you this evening." He reached under the table and opened a small drawer, out of which he took a vial the length of his hand in a small stand. It was filled with a clear fluid that appeared as pristine as water at first glance, but against the brilliance of the table, she could see that it tinted its background a dark grey, like steel made clarified liquid.

"In the year 2020, a pharmaceutical company was researching methods of treating auto-immune diseases, using different compounds that were known to augment immune system response to treat patients in early stages of various disorders, strengthening them against secondary infections. The developer of this particular company went bankrupt when its human trials ended in catastrophe for over a hundred test subjects.

"These subjects, though the majority, were not the only participants of the study. The observing physicians saw, in those who survived, the expected increase in immune system response. Their auto-immune disorders were completely erased, and for years after the study, the patients reported never once getting so much as a cold.

"Then when they reached middle age, they found themselves developing rapid-onset cancer symptoms, moving more quickly and aggressively than anyone had ever seen before. The drug was found to be the only common thread between the patients, but the original developers were no longer in business. Some of them were dead. The patients all died of their exposure, and all that remained was the investigating research company that they had hired to find the cause of their deaths." He flicked the vial lightly to stir the liquid inside by way of demonstration.

"Those researchers were, naturally, some of the first to move their operations into orbit, and one of them sat on the first Board of Directors. Mass production of the compound was relatively simple and universally disregarded as simply another pharmaceutical production operation. Initial exposures moved too slowly to avoid risk of mass hysteria and possible blame from conspiracy theorists. But when a research article showed the likelihood of Banang Co losing its stability, the Board at the time acted to saturate the ground for a kilometer surrounding the reactor. In the course of the eruption, debris, fallout, and wind patterns ensured worldwide distribution within a matter of weeks."

Mercury closed her eyes for a moment as she tried to process all of the information.

Her life's work had failed because of a misdirection. CV, the so-called Crisis Virus, wasn't even a virus. It was a toxin. One that no one even knew to look for.

Eventually she opened her eyes and leveled a stare at the Alperts. Some of the information didn't make sense. "Fallout doesn't last this long. The particles would have been absorbed and metabolized by now. Broken down." Even as she spoke the words, she knew what they meant. It meant as much as the contaminant would persist in the ecology of Earth at every level, there had to be some amount of it continually being introduced around the world. Some amount produced and distributed by the Consortium itself.

Dominic smiled, first at Mercury and then over at his wife. "I told you she was smarter than the Kaplans."

"Good thing we have her here with us, then." Mrs. Alpert looked over at Mercury with a smile, but her gaze flicked toward Mercury's belly and back up to her eyes. "Those babies of yours are something quite special, Mercury. Just like you are."

"All three of you share a trait that some have developed naturally, but which you obviously already know you were engineered to carry, that being a true immunity to CV." He wiggled the vial on the table again, and picked it up to place it closer to her plate, a vial filled with the source and sustenance of humanity's worst nightmares. "This is yours for the purposes of your research as well, since I'm sure you have any number of questions it should be able to help you answer."

Mercury reached out to touch the vial and when she took it in her hand, she wanted to hurl it back at the Alperts and hope that it broke and poisoned them both. "I assume you've made certain you're also immune, then?"

"We were both born with immunity. All children of sitting Board members and many of their associates have the coding ensured. It's been that way for several generations now." He sounded very matter-of-fact about it, and waved in the servants to take their plates, since it didn't seem Mercury was in the mood to finish. "We'll wait a few minutes for dessert, thank you. We'll let you know when we're ready." He dismissed the servants with one of his usual smiles, but there was none of the sick pleasure in it that had once haunted her nightmares from Stephen and Maria's faces. He was merely being polite, but he seemed happy to be doing so. "The knife at your right hand would make a better offensive weapon if you have violence in mind, Doctor. Stainless steel, surgical grade. Should feel quite familiar to you."

Mercury made no move closer to the knife, even though a part of her mind begged her body to move. It would do no good. "I'm not a fighter. Or a murderer, though lives have been lost at my hands. I usually do my best to *prevent* it." Mercury cleared her throat. "It would do me no good to kill you. I would be sacrificing myself and my daughters to do it, and that's not a sacrifice I'm willing to make." She put a hand on her belly and took a deep breath. "Why are you telling me this? Why do you want me to continue my research when you already have answers?"

"We know a great deal, but we know better than most just how much we still don't know. You have shown yourself to be one of the finest researchers in the system. We believe in promoting that as much as possible." The display on the wall advanced through the following years after the crisis to show the cliff that humanity had fallen from, and their slow, incremental rise afterward to be even the smallest fraction of its former self.

"We have you here tonight partly because we felt it would be a courtesy, given your research, to discuss the facts of history with you as candidly as possible and afford you the opportunity to ask questions. I'm sure you still have a great many. But you are also here because the information you've been given, regarding the true origin of CV, its true nature, will soon be revealed to the rest of the world." The tiniest hint of malice entered the man's eyes, but it was so fleeting that it might have been so simple as a trick of the light. "Some of the research we recovered from your data banks in the mountains after the attack was incredibly promising, and pointed you directly along the path to this realization. We're confident you would have uncovered the truth on your own given more time to do your work. Your research and its inevitable conclusions will be released to the world as a recent discovery that will forever alter mankind's perspective on the Crisis."

Mercury still wasn't sure why, after all this time, they were going to release the information. Unless they were going to benefit from it. "So, what, so you'll convince the people of Earth that you can save them? If they don't rebel? You have the answers to save the planet as long as they remain meek and submissive?"

"Human behavior is far from an exact science, even now, but a general rule is that people do not, in a popular vein, support war. Prolonged violence. Rebellion. Individuals seek power, change, dominance. People on the whole wish to live in peace, even as you said yourself. People don't want to join a rebellion. People want to go home, and well they should. If they are given terms for how that might be accomplished, no matter what those terms are, they will usually accept. Especially if choosing to rebel would mean siding with those who uncovered the truth about the Crisis and elected to say nothing to the world for decades. Who chose not to tell even you, their friend and ally." The look on his face was so empathetically offended it looked genuine. Was it genuine? What was honest about the man and what wasn't? There was no way to tell. "I'm speaking, of course, about your friends the Montgomeries."

"I think you underestimate the people of Earth, and I think you overestimate your own people." Mercury said without missing a beat. "You can do whatever you like, play your political game, but it's not going to work this time. You've mistreated earth for too long. You've mistreated *everyone* for too long."

The disappointment in Dominic's eyes was every bit as genuine as every other emotion he showed her, and he sighed before he shook his head. "We are here for science, Doctor. Not politics, not countries, not religion, not to be kind or cruel or warm or cold. Only science. You are free to judge us however you like for our perceived moral infringements, but we are here, as we have always been, to facilitate the growth and expansion of the human race. That could not have been achieved in the twenty-first century, not by humanity as it was then.

"Humanity as it is now has become capable of so much more. Capable of walking from star to star and studying out the answers to a billion billion questions we don't even yet know to ask. The Consortium is responsible for that elevation over the past three centuries, and is the only organization in human history to offer it the chance to truly move forward. That is the future you and your rebels have been intent on destroying these past two years." The sadness was in full force in the man's eyes, truly lamenting Mercury's choice to rebel and grieving for the disloyalty of such a mind.

"Did you bring me here to convince me to *not* rebel? If you wanted to do that, you wouldn't have put me into an Initiative with the intention of killing me. You wouldn't bring me here and trap me prisoner with the intention of killing me. Don't deny it." She had no doubt in her mind that they intended on killing her, but only when their need for her was complete. "I would have been glad, and I *was* glad to serve the Consortium and to build up knowledge for the good of humankind. I worked tirelessly for that very cause. You and yours were the ones to change that. You did it by breaking up my marriage. You did it again by hunting my family and the people I love. You have no one to blame but yourselves for the *waste* of a mind like mine. You made me. You needed me. And then you corrupted me."

"The only corruption possible or meaningful in this world is a corruption of reason. Of intellect." He still didn't sound angry or even defensive, merely stating a counterargument to her own claims. "There are two choices in front of you, Doctor, at the most basic and reductive level of analysis. You may continue in your present loyalties, continue to work to subvert the cause of the Consortium whenever possible and foster dissent among the people of Earth, or you can choose to support the Consortium in its efforts to move humanity forward among the stars, to heal what is broken in Earth itself.

"Either choice has consequences, as all choices do. Choose to rebel and all those about whom you care deeply will be destroyed, including your children. Choose to remove yourself from them, either to re-enlist with the Consortium or simply to cease your support for their activities in favor of resuming your former career, and you will find yourself and all those who choose the same path both forgiven for your rebellion and well-placed within your old accustomed society." He looked away at the image of Earth on the walls nearby, and sighed as he looked back at her, hope still alive in his eyes. "There will be worlds without end to see once the rebels have been corrected. Yours are the right eyes to see them, if you will allow yourself the chance."

Mercury looked down at her belly and then placed both hands on either side. "Why would you destroy them for the choices I make?" She looked up at the Alperts with a gaze that was pleading for her own reasons. "The children are innocent in all of this. You've already taken their fathers."

"Their fathers were aggressors against the Consortium, and they were each directly responsible for the deaths of people who had done them no harm." There was something in Dominic's eyes that Mercury couldn't quite place, but she recognized the look of analysis that she had seen in the mirror whenever she was examining a patient. "You have been kept in captivity only because neither you nor many of those with you have been shown to be directly responsible for such crimes, although there are charges pending against several of them which will have to wait until the rebellion outside our walls has been entirely subdued. I also admit that I misspoke when I stated that your children would be destroyed. We of course would never wish harm to a child. But your relationship with your children, on the other hand, will be severed should you choose to persist in your current flawed ideology."

Mercury closed her eyes and took a deep breath. Orion was dead. Logan was dead. Anna was dead. Her parents . . . she had no idea what had happened to her parents. They had been with her for a little while, but then they had been removed and she had never seen them again. Everyone that mattered to Mercury was gone except for those under the age of two. She had to do everything in her power to keep them safe, and the Alperts clearly knew it.

"Alright." She opened her eyes. "Alright, I'll re-enlist and work for the Consortium again. I'll renounce all rebel ties." She met Dominic's eyes for a moment before she continued. "But not yet." She took another deep breath. "If you keep me in there, then perhaps I can change the minds of others too. People that you think are valuable, people that would be helpful to the Consortium. All I have left are the children, and I won't lose them too." And she hoped, deep down, if she dragged her feet then maybe the rebels would break them out. But right now, she needed to look as desperate as she felt and she needed to keep her children safe.

The way Dominic looked at her, it seemed as though he could see straight through her thoughts and desires as clearly as the crystal surrounding them in the lavish apartment. He let her sweat out her counteroffer for a long, tense silence, in which the only sound was of ice settling in the bucket holding the bottle of wine nearby.

"The potential of every life is a valuable commodity, of course." He seemed to agree with her terms, and his smile was as if they were old friends merely teasing each other about something rather than the givers and receivers of death threats one against the other. "Full disclosures on the nature of CV will be broadcast tomorrow evening through all appropriate news channels. Following that, we don't anticipate taking long to clean up what remains of the rebels once the governments of Earth are finished taking their own bite out of them. Following that, we plan to have transportation to Eleusis restored within a few weeks, and the Initiative itself back in progress. How long, in your view, would it be fruitful for you to remain with the other rebels?"

"A month. Any longer than that, and I doubt anyone could be convinced." She said gently, but a month was more time than she had now, and she needed more time. Somehow she had to get it.

"A month, then." Dominic agreed, a little too quickly. Did that mean he was planning to kill her before then, and it didn't really matter what she had asked? Did that mean he wasn't planning to kill her at all and she could have had whatever she asked for? There was no way to know. There was no way to be sure of anything with the Alperts.

He pressed a button on the table in front of him, at which the doors to the servant quarters opened almost immediately to admit some of the most delicious scents she had experienced in months. The desserts placed on the table were ornate and delicate creations of spun sugar and fruit and cream. The centerpiece of her plate was a single red strawberry dipped in perfectly smooth chocolate.

They knew her. They knew too much about her.

"Enjoy, Doctor."

3

Orion took another glance over the most recent aerial scans of the Consortium compound, glancing nervously at the sky as he wondered about what the weather would be like in the hour it would take him to move between their campsite and the new location. Storms were a tricky thing, the electrical storms especially. They tended to wake and excite the Behemoths, who would go to the highest point in their vicinity when the lightning got bad enough, as if inviting the storm to come and visit them.

Even Carl and Aiko hadn't been able to fully predict the electrical storms during the months and months they had spent on the planet, and none of those who came through the Twist in the main assault had exactly been meteorologists. All they knew was that they were approaching the end of the Eleusis summer, from the way the ambient temperature slowly dropped from one day to the next.

No one knew precisely what to expect. Four months (Earth time) had taught them to plan for the worst at all times.

"Carmina." He said loudly enough to be heard, which didn't take much in the mostly-silent camp. People knew better than to waste energy anymore. They either worked in their assigned functions, kept up camp life, or they rested, waiting for the next engagement. Carl, Orion, and Carmina worked together to make sure people didn't sit idle too long but didn't have too much work on their hands. It was a delicate balance. War was a delicate thing. But it was a thing they had been training for all their lives.

It didn't take long for Carmina to get up, even though her body was always aching and she was eager to sleep. Or rest, at least. "I hear ya, Al Jabbar. What do you want?"

"I need your sharpshooters." He said without looking up from the map under his fingers. "They've gotten wise the last few times we've tried a direct assault on the northeast corner and waited us out, just out of range of our energy weapons. If we goad them into supporting the corner the same way, just out of range, we'll have time for at least a few good volleys at them with your snipers. Help bring the ratio down a little farther."

"We can't over-utilize. We're limited on bullets, remember." Carmina got up from her lover's side so she could walk to where Orion was always planning one thing or another. The rest of them were a bit worn down, but not Orion. "I'm beginning to wonder if we should try waiting again. Draw them out there. There can't be that many of them left."

"There aren't." Orion still didn't look up, checking and rechecking his guesses every moment. "Kim's last estimate puts their personnel at somewhere around two hundred seventy. Which means they've only got about forty more than we do, and we know not all theirs are military. We've been weeding them down since we got here, and they know it. They're not coming out here."

He looked over at her when she didn't agree, and he knew he had to change tactics somehow if he wanted her agreement. He meant what he said about her sharpshooters. "How's this: we get up within the range of our siege-line, then all of us take our time getting into the best positions we can find. Lie in for a couple hours to make sure they're not looking for us, let them know we can hit them out of nowhere. Your people can get a nap. We'll wake them up before the shooting starts."

"Fine." Carmina said as she glanced back to where she was napping. "Do you want to leave now? We could use the rest. All the surveying just to find some decent shit to eat is wearing." Surviving and camping were certainly two different things. They were surviving. Surviving with little to no clothing, since there wasn't enough fur to go around. Surviving on dried meat and some fruits and vegetables, but the offerings of the landscape were starting to die off as it got colder. Survival was getting more difficult. Somehow they would have to claim the compound to survive. What Carl and Aiko had survived before was not sustainable for their numbers, at least not from their current location and vantage.

"As soon as you and Francis can get your people together, yes. No point in waiting." No one questioned Carl's status as the ultimate commander in the camp, since there had been more than one occasion on which he had pulled rank on Orion or Carmina, but more and more as the days went on, Carl had turned to being in charge of the camp and keeping people alive. Orion and Carmina typically handled the offensive side of their operations. "I'll get Zoe and a few others to bring supplies and we'll wait for you by watchpoint six."

"We'll meet you there." Carmina replied simply before she headed off without another word. Maybe they could finally get something done this time.

Orion leaned over the map just a little longer before starting away toward one of the many hiding-holes dug for their small army. They did their best to stay hidden over the months they had been stranded, and most of their preferred fortifications were just below ground level, strung out in a broad half-circle to form a perimeter around the Consortium compound. It was hard to find anyone in particular at any given time, but Orion did his best to keep track.

On his way to get Zoe, Orion decided to stop by the single tent they had with them when they arrived on Eleusis. It had been given over to Carl and Aiko to serve partly as a command tent, partly as an infirmary, and partly as a home for the two of them. Or at least, it had been just the two of them when they first arrived.

The newest member of Carl and Aiko's family was crying as Orion walked up, but that was nothing new. The baby had been cranky for most of his life, and everyone in the camp knew that Aiko and Carl were doing their best for the child. Sometimes there was only so much that could be done, especially with limited resources.

Orion stepped into the portion of the tent that was permitted for public access, and continued inside when he saw that there was no one else within but Carl and Aiko. Carl was working on calming the baby while Aiko worked to create one of her many mixtures. There were piles of herbs and other supplies in makeshift baskets against one side of the tent, all for Aiko's personal use and ingenuity. "Another one of Dave's bright and shiny mornings?"

"His name is David." Carl said with a fatigued glare, since it wasn't the first time he'd made the correction, and he knew it wouldn't be the last. "He had a pretty decent night and was having a decent morning until just a few minutes ago. Must have smelled you coming from a hundred meters away."

"Well, when the eels stop swarming along the shore, I'll go back to taking a bath at least once a week." Orion promised without malice in his voice, looking back and forth between the two of them. "Just wanted to let you know I'm taking Carmina, Francis, Zoe, and about a dozen others up to the northeast corner of the compound for some target practice."

Aiko was finishing up a mixture she drank half of in a hurry before she walked over to give Carl the other half. She found that as long as she stayed hydrated, there was an Eleusis herb that boosted her milk supply, which was what she needed for her gigantic, hungry baby. Carl's sons couldn't be anything less than large. "Are you sure that's a good idea? What if another storm comes in soon?"

"We'll be situated in the V-cut. It's been safe from the electrical storms during previous fights, but if it gets bad, there's always the caves at the base on the lee side. We'll be sheltered from natural problems." Orion had thought through the position of their attack, but he couldn't keep the small quiver from his voice as he said it.

"You won't be sheltered from the plasma guns they've got set up on that corner." Carl reminded him, since that was the whole reason they had mostly left that corner alone in the first place.

"They can't shoot what they can't see. I'm taking Carmina's sharpshooters. We're gonna take our time getting settled in, get some rest, and only hit once we've got their attention."

Aiko glanced over at Carl before she grabbed David so she could feed him again. "You've been pushing really hard recently." She said as kindly as she could to Orion. "Did you think about what we discussed before? As it gets colder, we can't keep going at it like this. We have to start preparing to survive an Eleusis winter."

"Our best chance of doing that is by clearing out that compound." Orion responded just as gently, but he had never budged since they arrived and he showed no signs of doing so that morning. "This fight has gone on too long already. We may have confirmed that they can't reach Earth right now, but every day that goes by, the chances go up that eventually Earth will reach them. That they will reach *us*. If that happens before we take the compound, we are fucked."

"Even if we have taken the compound, if it's the Consortium coming through the Twist, we're still fucked." Carl said, fatigue clear in his voice in spite of what he'd said about sleeping decently the night before.

"I'd rather fight them from inside that compound than out here in the wilderness." Orion kept his voice down for David's sake, even if it was one of the rare times he was quiet. "The answer is not to step away and let them fortify that compound through the winter while we keep withering in exhaustion and borderline starvation. We need to press harder and smarter."

"I'm worried about how much longer everyone can last pushing this hard." Aiko replied softly as she looked down at David who was content to have his breakfast and snuggle close. She missed Will every day, but having a baby to hold helped a little. She refused to believe that William was dead, even though some people believed everyone they left behind was dead or dying. She refused to believe it. Aiko, Carl, and William had survived a year on Eleusis without anyone else. Will was a strong little boy. "But you're the commander. Not me."

Carl considered the proposition for a while quietly, but he knew Orion had already given orders to prepare and he wasn't going to countermand him now in front of everyone else. They didn't need to be seen to be fighting internally as well as against the Consortium. "It's cleared for today. My concern with an operation like this isn't the goons inside the walls, it's Henri. It's the kind of mission he loves to see us try."

"He was last sighted inside the walls two days ago. No one's seen him leave since." Orion protested, though he knew what Carl was going to say before he even opened his mouth.

"When it comes to Henri, that's almost meaningless." Carl shook his head. "If we could find whatever tunnels or cave systems he's using to get in and out of the compound, that would be huge, but it's also the longest of long-shots. Just be careful today. I can authorize now, but we do need to think about buckling down for the winter, Orion. I've already got our people working day and night gathering, and before long, we're going to need to bring down and portion out another Behemoth. The last one cost us two men so the rest of us could eat. Those are not odds I want to accept any more than you do, but they're what's in front of us."

Orion just nodded, since he knew the situation as well as Carl did, they just saw it differently. "I'll do what I can to make the math work in our favor today, then."

"Be careful." Aiko said as she looked up at Orion with a weary smile. "We don't want to lose you too."

"I thought you said I was too stubborn to die?" He asked with the faintest trace of his old humor, giving both of them a quick smile as he saluted and left the tent.

Zoe Hearn was as unlikely a sidekick as any military officer had ever picked up in history, but within a week of being stranded on Eleusis, Orion had found her more than capable when it came to helping run the camp and seeing to the conservation of their supplies. She was also no pushover in a fight, and he'd seen her take down more than her own fair share of the Consortium's people in their many engagements over the preceding months.

Every day in the camp, he was glad that she was around.

Every day fighting their enemies, he was glad she was on *his* side.

"Time for some target practice." He said when he found her, near the supply tents coordinating efforts with the gatherers as usual. "You got two or three others with an itch to do something productive, bring 'em along. Plan is to be up there most of the day."

"Most of the day, huh?" Zoe looked around at the gatherers and nodded toward the exit so they could get going and get to work. They had their assignments already. "What are we doing now, Boss?"

"Same thing as every other day. Try to kill people." He shrugged off the comment, since it truly had turned into a stalemated war between the two sides, and taking aim at another human being had become something of a daily activity. "We're gonna sneak up near six, lie in wait for a while, coax some of them out of hiding and let Carmina's people do some sniper work. Need a couple of psychopaths to come and hang around for a while and then draw out some fire."

"A psychopath, you say? Flattery will get you everywhere. Sign me up." Zoe grabbed her personal survival kit and a couple personal items, and she always had a gun at her hip. "You know just what to say to get me excited, Boss." She teased before she threw her bag over her back.

"High possibility of killing somebody and even higher possibility of getting blown-up. Your list of turn-ons gets weirder the longer I know you, Lieutenant." It was strange to have risen in the ranks to the point where he could comfortably give orders to others, but necessity had made him comfortable with command. "Grab two or three you think best for the loud and obvious strike team and a couple more for support. Since you're so perky this morning, I'm gonna have you and one of your fellow whack jobs investigating the caves while the rest of us get ourselves into position."

"Oooh, the caves!" Zoe said with a little too much enthusiasm, but she really was excited. If they ever did get back to Earth, she was going to be rich from all the surveying they had to do. "So I get to go rock-shopping while we wait?" They had found all sorts of raw gemstone deposits in the nearby caves, most of which they didn't have the gear to extract.

"Absolutely. If you find one big enough to throw at the Consortium and give somebody a concussion, I'll be excited. Otherwise, let's keep the prospecting to a minimum. I want a way in and under, and I swear to fucking god if you make that dirty the way you did last time, I will put you on latrine duty for a month."

"You're supposed to laugh, not be all stuck up about it. You know we all want a way in and under." She replied as she waggled her eyebrows and laughed. "Don't put me on latrine duty, Boss. I can't help myself."

He sighed, but he appreciated her humor. It was a reminder of how far he'd come in four months, but he kept her around because he needed to be reminded. "I'll tell you what, you or one of your psychopaths finds a way up the skirt of that compound so we can come up and fuck those bastards in the ass, the finder gets to keep mining rights for the hill where you find it once we remake contact with Earth."

He had no idea if he was going to be able to keep that promise or not, but they'd been given military authority by Logan and the other rebel leaders. So if they managed to come out winners against the Consortium, he imagined they'd have at least some ability to make good. They had no idea if the gemstones in the caves around the Consortium compound were a rarity on the planet or if the entire place was somehow much more gemstone-rich than Earth had been, but Orion knew Zoe, for one, planned on finding out. "Does that sound like a deal you can live with, Lieutenant?"

"Hell yes." She replied with a grin. "Maybe when I'm rich, I'll get a man who doesn't care how fucking weird I am. And you know, likes nerdy girls who like guns. They have to exist somewhere, right?" Zoe was fairly average in appearance, average height, average weight, dark brown hair that she kept tied back.

The only extremity of her appearance was the abundance of crazy in her eyes and the feral smile to match.

"Yeah, in whatever psych ward we dragged you out of when we recruited you, I'm sure." He had to smile just a little more genuinely at her exuberance, but he checked his own weapons and started off across the field to where he had said he would meet Carmina. With the death of the summer, Orion had taken to not wearing a shirt and only wearing a jumpsuit that had been cut up to make a pair of loose-fitted shorts above his boots.

They were only going to go get themselves covered with underbrush for the sniper lying-in anyway, so there was no point getting any more dressed than he already was. The Eleusis sun didn't lend itself to sunburn in the first place, on account of Eleusis' well-padded atmosphere, a fact which all of them were deeply grateful for. What little beard his face was predisposed to grow had grown in over four months, giving him a more wild appearance, but it was just barely enough to give the depth of his eyes a particular edge of unpredictability. "Be quick about it. We'll get moving as soon as Carmina has her people together."

Zoe gave him a nod so she could go find some friends, but she wasn't usually one to drag her feet anyway.

Orion had always been an excellent marksman, since his first days with the military when he found out that his vision was better than 20/20 and didn't show any signs of degeneration. But it was one thing to shoot a target half a kilometer away under ideal conditions and quite another to shoot at one two hundred meters away while crushed against the ground, looking out a hole in the turf only a few centimeters wide. It was one thing to be amazing under perfect conditions. Under conditions like the ones they had lived through on Eleusis, all he wanted was to survive.

For the better part of two hours, he and the rest of Carmina's squad put together roughage covers and slowly made their way through the V-cut in the hills above the Consortium compound, moving just a few meters at a time. They had never attempted to fire at the compound from that angle before, simply because the V-cut typically left them exposed to the Consortium's fire, and the entire slope was more or less a killing field.

He couldn't spare the visibility to look out and check on the others as they moved along the slope, but he'd been taught well by Carmina's people, and he had confidence in their ability not to be seen. He only knew Carmina was close by because the two of them had chosen the same high track to follow to a promontory overlooking the compound. It was the most exposed patch of ground, but also the most advantageous. Francis came up behind them, making Orion nervous that someone in the compound would notice so much variance on a single promontory, but the little he'd seen of the compound below said that people were mostly inside.

"Alright." He whispered into his comm, once the last of Carmina's snipers had reported reaching their position. "Everybody get comfortable, we're gonna be up here a while."

"Sentry position four, be advised, they've set up some new cameras since the last time we were out here. East wall, ten meters down from the red bell tree." One of the others radioed in warning.

"Saw it before I started my run. My position has a clear shot of it. I'll take it out before anything else starts. You fuckers call dibs on your own pieces of property out here and stay out of my house."

"Play nice, babies. It's all one house out here. Our house." Orion hushed the banter quickly, since he wanted them to conserve energy as much as possible. They would need it, if they had any luck.

Zoe was sprawled out on Eleusis grass that ate her up but she knew Orion was close by, so she laid there and looked up at the Eleusis sky. "I'm surprised Carl let us come out." She whispered to Orion. "I heard him talking to Aiko the other day. They think you're losing yourself in this."

Orion took a long time to respond, his eyes scanning the compound for any sign of life, or more importantly, any sign that they were seen. He knew she was asking because she cared, and he knew there was a right answer. Or at least, that there was an answer that would forestall most following conversation. It just wasn't an answer he could give honestly.

"What else is there?" He asked pointedly. "If we ran, the Consortium would eventually just carpet-bomb whatever part of the world we chose to settle into. When flight is suicide, fight is the only option left."

"Everyone has a *reason*, though." Zoe asked gently, since she was always prying. "What is your reason for pushing so hard? What are you fighting for? I mean, you've pushed for some seriously crazy shit. Not that it hasn't been fun. But still."

He knew she was right, and he knew he should have felt guilty about some of the things he'd asked of his comrades than he did. He'd led more than a few crazy adventures that had gotten some of their people killed, though they had always taken more of the Consortium's fighters than they had lost. Orion tried to tell himself that made it okay, even if he knew the honesty of the math just helped to hide the lie.

"There are people in that compound that we know they're keeping as slaves. I don't know how they justify that to themselves, but there's no way anybody's gonna justify that to me. There's people in that compound we've known about for a long, long time, and they're people who need to do the universe a favor and stop breathing its oxygen. I do what I do and I push how I push because it needs to get done. I don't need a better reason than that."

Even though he had one. Anyone who had known him at all before they were stranded on Eleusis knew what his reasons were, even if he never talked about them. He had someone to avenge. He didn't labor any longer under the delusion that Anna had survived, as he had for the first few weeks of the stalemate. But even if he no longer believed she had survived, he would still destroy everyone who'd had a hand in her death.

"I hope you get what you're waiting for." Zoe replied after letting a moment of silence linger between them. "You've lost a lot. More than many." She knew he had basically lost everyone that meant anything to him, since his immediate family had been in the mountains when they were under attack, and his kids and wife . . . well, the Consortium had pretty much cleaned house in central North America.

"I'm waiting to see every one of those fuckers in a shallow grave." He continued to glare ahead at the compound, watching a small group of their researchers move warily from one building to another. "As soon as that happens, I'll have someplace to dance again." He had never understood the poetry behind someone dancing on someone else's grave, but for the people who had killed his family, who had killed Anna . . . he would fucking tango. "So yeah, there's a reason why everybody puts me in with your Psychopath Patrol. I'm one of you now. So when we lay out a mass grave for these assholes, I'll bring the music, you bring the booze."

"You know I've been saving some." She patted the bag at her

side cheerfully. "There's a small flask in there waiting for a special occasion. Especially because Aiko won't tell me the best fruit around here to ferment and make into Eleusis booze. She's very controlling for being so tiny."

Orion let out a brief laugh, since he couldn't disagree. As much as he liked Aiko, she wasn't wrong about the woman being controlling. "Well, she's one of the brains of this outfit, you can't be too pissed off at her for trying to keep the rest of us sober."

His light mood was immediately ruined by the sight of a pair of figures crossing the compound in the distance, out of range of their sniper fire but not out of range of their scopes. They found out only a few days after being stranded that Maria and Stephen Kaplan were both present in the compound, and Orion couldn't help the murderous rage that came over him every time they were seen. "Speaking of brains, there's the brains of this shithole right there. What I wouldn't give for a good, solid thermonuclear weapon right now. Strap the two of them to it and drop it in the ocean."

Zoe didn't have to get up to see who he was talking about. "She's a doctor, right? A shrink?" She thought about everything else she knew about the Kaplans. "Why the fuck do they need one of those on Eleusis? Are their own people that fucked up they need someone to talk to on a daily basis?"

"She's not just a shrink. She runs the medical programs for the Initiative. Which I'm guessing includes whatever fucked-up shit they've been doing to the Numbers." It had been an easy way of referring to the people who occasionally were released from the compound, rather than having to remind themselves every moment that they were either slaves or somehow mindless drones. "Wouldn't fucking surprise me if they were completely her idea." He examined the range of the shot it would take to reach Maria again, and growled a little when it clearly came up short.

"Do you think the Numbers can even be saved?" She asked with actual curiosity, since she was really doubtful. "The ones we've found alive . . . they don't even seem like people anymore."

"We're not gonna know until we get in there and get a picture of what's going on with them. The ones they send outside the walls seem like they've been . . . used up, maybe. That's not the right word. I don't know, they just seem tired. The rest of them still inside might not be as far along, or as far gone. If they're not, maybe they can be turned around and they can help explain what the fuck has been going on in there."

"Maybe." Zoe replied with obvious doubt. When she sat up she saw more figures, though, and Zoe tensed up immediately. "They're not alone."

Orion saw movement as well, and reached a hand up slowly to his communicator, tucked by his face for easy access. "All eyes on the corner. There's movement. Might be a welcome for us, might be just people moving. If there are more than a dozen Consortium guns in sight, start calling targets." They had to make an impression and make a difference that day. So if the Consortium was going to send out the troops and make it easy, he wasn't going to complain.

Carmina's voice chimed in not long after. "We have some in our sights. It looks like either they know we're here, or they're expecting something."

"Well, they're not shooting at us yet." Orion said in an attempt at optimism. If the Consortium knew they were there before Zoe and her crazies had even gotten started, they were all more deeply fucked than he had thought. "They're definitely looking for us, though."

It was a group of non-military personnel who were coming out of a nearby building, looking along the slopes just outside of the compound for any trace of movement. Orion was confident that they were all as invisible as it was possible to get, but if the Consortium had some kind of heat-mapping tech on their central watchtower, it was possible that they had been seen by thermal scans. "If anybody gets a clear shot at either of the Kaplans or the Montgomery traitor, take it at will. Otherwise, hold fire. We need to see what these fuckers are up to."

Zoe started moving very slowly through the grass away from Orion, almost like a cat who was going after her prey. She slithered through the tall grasses so she could attempt to make a distraction if they needed to do things quicker than they planned. "I think we are going to have to speed up our timeline, Al-Jabbar."

Orion hated it when things got away from him, when it turned out that, yet again, the Consortium managed to get one more step ahead of him. No matter how good he thought his position was, how carefully he planned something, it always got taken away. They couldn't let that continue. They couldn't let it just keep slipping. Everything would fall. Everything that was left.

"Well, we didn't come all this way and get all dressed up not to party. If they're gonna give us some scientists to shoot at, I'll take it. Zoe, take your people down into the rubble at your two o'clock, then start blasting the research building with the panels along the upper floor. Flashers only, don't waste bullets. Should be enough to take out the glass and incapacitate whoever's inside, at least. I want to try and empty this security post to give us something to shoot at."

"Sure thing, Boss." And then just like that, Zoe had slithered too far away to converse with Orion without being loud about it. She was whispering plans to the rest of her group, and they disappeared to do exactly what Orion had asked. Make a distraction. Destroy the glass. Incapacitate.

He watched her group move, and knew that if he could see them moving, so could anyone who knew what to look for on the other side of the wall. He had hoped to lie low for a while, but if he wasn't going to get that chance, he wasn't going to get it. That was life. They had to take the chances that were given to them.

"They're watching Zoe's people." Francis' voice came from nearby, unexpectedly close on the far side of Carmina. The man should have left more room, but Orion supposed the two of them were accustomed to being cozy. "So either they can't see us, or they're more interested in them. I don't blame them, I'd be more interested in them too."

Orion watched the building he told them to target, adjusting the sight on his rifle with a deep breath. "I count five Numbers on the second floor, look like they're just . . . standing there, with the frosted glass. Few more in white coats, headed downstairs. Zoe, hit them first if you can manage it. That should bring everybody else running."

"I'm going to get closer, Orion." Carmina announced, since she wanted the chance to hit as many fuckers as she could. She was tired, and she knew it compromised her accuracy a bit, but if they could make some headway, maybe that meant some more fucking sleep. She looked over at Francis and nodded, asking him silently to follow.

Zoe, who was still moving away from the rest, finally got to the spot where she felt that it was the best to cause a mess, and she targeted her flashers at the glass. It started shattering even before she could say anything, and shit started going crazy. What the hell? Had the Consortium been watching the entire time? How did they know . . .

Before anyone could even follow what was happening, Zoe could feel waves of concussive force hit the ground in front of her as if a bomb had gone off, even though there had been no audible explosion. They'd felt the defensive weapons of the Consortium before, but they thought the force weapons were on the far side of the compound, far away from that day's operation. Their own buildings were being compromised as collateral damage to try and rip into Zoe and her team, but the way the first wave hit, it threw her and half a dozen of her friends backward twenty paces. The force of it was still smashing into them in waves, but it diminished significantly the farther they got from the source.

Orion started swearing and immediately started shooting at everything he could see. There were a few fighters who came out at the sound of the destruction, all three of them fell within seconds. Others came out of the security station to meet the same end, but those who followed were more wise, taking cover as they tried to return fire. His team was efficient, not firing unless they knew they had a kill shot, but he still heard at least one of his comrades cry out in muffled agony as a shot found its way through someone's face. They were going to get their asses handed to them. Again.

Not again. Not again.

Carmina and her sharpshooters, though, were doing some damage as the focus turned on Orion and everyone around him. Carmina took out two Consortium dumbasses easily, and the more that fell, the more confident she felt to move closer. "Al-Jabbar, they're going down like flies over here!" She nailed a couple more before something else happened. Uniforms started disappearing and . . . then there were prisoners. "Fuck, they're sending out Numbers?"

"Don't shoot the Numbers!" Orion ordered several times over the comms, but it meant that shots from their side were getting infrequent, while the Consortium continued to fire straight past the line of their human shields. The Numbers moved out in front of the research building and navigated the rubble nimbly, standing in front of the soldiers with their arms out to provide as much cover as possible, even as they looked terrified of the hail of bullets.

Orion had one last clear shot at a soldier before the Numbers caught up with him, and he saw the man go down in a satisfying lump on the other end of his scope. The Number that had been sent to guard him, however, screamed in pain as if he had been the one who had been shot. What in the world was going on? Were they prisoners or were they followers?

Zoe piped in over her radio, but she did not sound good. "The Numbers are everywhere, Orion! We're getting rained on over here! We're pulling back!"

"No!" Carmina called out and pressed closer. Her snipers could kill around the Numbers. Even if they were screaming in pain, they weren't really in pain, were they? "I'm going closer! I'm going to try to nab one of the Numbers! We need answers!"

"Answers don't mean shit if we don't live long enough to hear them!" Orion was frantic, but furious. How had they known? There was no way they could have been prepared with a counterassault like this at every point along their perimeter at all times. Could they? He refused to believe that. Believing that would mean believing there was no chance of victory. Orion would never accept that. Something had gone wrong, somewhere. He just didn't know where. "Pull back, Carmina, there's another wave coming out at your ten o'clock! Zoe, pull back and try to give the snipers some cover!"

Carmina wasn't answering Orion any longer, mostly out of defiance, but Zoe and her group tried to cover where he wanted them until Zoe let out a small gasp over her radio. "Holy fuck, Orion. Look. Look! It's . . . It's . . ."

Time might as well have stopped for Orion once he saw what Zoe was talking about, and even the gunshots all around them lost his interest. There were dozens of bodies moving out of the research building in white jumpsuits to place themselves between the walls and the researchers.

There, in the line of fire, was Anna.

He could see fear on her face, since she was getting shot at, after all, but she certainly wasn't looking behind her as if there was anyone she actually wanted to protect. What the hell could they have threatened her with to make her protect them like that? There was no way. Not the woman he'd known.

"Carmina, pull back!" He ordered again, and a few of her people actually listened, unlike Carmina herself. The Consortium managed to turn the percussion cannons in their direction, and Orion's next scream for a retreat was drowned out completely by the intangible force of the subharmonics that blasted apart the world in front of him. The shock of it blew him and those around him back up the hillside and cracked one of his shoulders against the ground.

He scrambled to join Zoe, since he knew they had no other option but retreat. He could see that a few of Carmina's people made it to the line of Numbers along the ruins of the compound wall, and one pair of her snipers was dragging one of the Numbers, literally kicking and screaming, up the hill to join the retreat. He couldn't see where Anna had gone in the chaos, but he knew he hadn't imagined her. He knew he hadn't.

Zoe and most of the others were in full retreat without looking back since none of them were interested in shooting at innocent prisoners and the risk was too great that they would hit a Number. She made sure all of the men she had dragged with her on the mission were still alive and retreating, and fortunately, they were. Carmina and her snipers was a different story, but they could worry about their own asses.

"Did you . . . did you see her?" She replied between breaths as they ran. "She's knocked up! They sent out a knocked up prisoner into gunfire?! They are some seriously twisted fuckers!"

"I saw her." Orion growled on their way up the hill. He saw another one of Carmina's fighters go down beside him, and as another wave of percussion canonfire hit the hillside, he felt one of the rocks torn up from the blast rip through part of his leg. The blast also threw every one of them that was upright a dozen feet farther up the slope, which sent many of them sailing over the V-cut in the hills they had crept through earlier. It put them out of range of the compound, but for Orion, it only made the situation worse. It was just more distance between him and Anna.

When no more of their people seemed to come through the gap, Orion turned to one of Zoe's people, all of them still panting for breath. "What was the count, Taras?" The man had an excellent memory, but it was always best to get information when it was fresh. The man was a little unhinged in more than just a joking way.

"Six . . . six of ours, Boss." He said as his head twitched uncontrollably, his eyes fixed on the same patch of ground as he focused, breathing irregularly. "Six dead or left dying, likely to die, almost certainly dead, have to leave them. Three cap . . . ca-captured, Carmina, Francis and Brett. Brett and Francis had injuries, not sure if captured or dead. Maybe dead. Maybe. Saw . . . . saw sixty-two . . . one, two three, four . . . sixty-six. Sixty-six of the Consortium people dead. Probably dead. Very shot. Sixty . . . maybe sixty-five. One, two, three . . ." the man fell off to muttering to himself over the numbers, obviously reliving every moment of the short-lived battle in his mind.

Zoe only glanced back once she heard Carmina and Francis were taken, which actually was a big blow to their operation, even if they had lost far fewer people than the Consortium. "Your leg, Al-Jabbar." She panted her words when they felt far enough to slow down a little. "Let me wrap it."

Orion was reluctant to stop for any reason, but he did, looking around at the rest of those around him to make sure everyone was more or less alright. "Hodge, Kurtz, take the rest of your squad and get back to camp, get the report to Carl. Take the Number with you." Carmina's people still had the woman strung between them, though she was still screaming to be taken back. What the hell was wrong with these people? "Blindfold her before you take her too far." He said with concern in his voice besides the pain from his leg. He didn't want the woman spying on their camp and taking information back to the Consortium if she did manage to escape as she was so eager to do.

As soon as the others were moving, even with a blindfolded, thrashing, screaming woman who they had freed, Zoe knelt down to work on whatever she could do for Orion's leg until they could get back to Aiko. He was bleeding steadily, so she opened up her bag and went digging for antiseptic and binding cloth. Aiko had them well prepared, or as prepared as they could get. Zoe also had a couple salves to help with numbing and infection. "Talk about whatever is going on in your brain. You keep it all in too much."

"She's alive." He said quietly, as the rest of her personal squad of psychopaths set up a quick perimeter and set a couple of them up in the cut to watch for any kind of pursuit. If they actually sent any out, it would be a first, but they had to watch for it anyway. "She's alive and she's visibly pregnant. That means she's at least five or six months along. Which means she's carrying a dead man's baby." Orion tried to be hopeful about what happened in the mountains during their attack, but that optimism hadn't lasted long for him. Their way home was by gaining control of the compound and waiting for the next strike from the Consortium once they got their own Twist working again. They couldn't hope for any help from rebels still living on Earth, with their own Twist destroyed.

"She's alive." Zoe tried to emphasize to comfort him, though she didn't know what state of "alive" Anna was really in. "We'll figure out a way to save her. I know you basically hate her, but I know you don't want her dead. Clearly."

He grunted in pain as she worked on his leg, but it was at least a clean injury. Something he could live through, unlike a few of the cracked ribs and internal injuries he had suffered in the first attack that Aiko and the other nurses still thought were just ticking time bombs waiting to kill him at the wrong moment. He was going to die, on the ground, on the losing side of a war that needed to be won.

"I don't hate her." He wasn't sure when Zoe of all people had become his confidante, but he knew it was partly because Carl normally filled the position and had better things to do. Zoe was easily the least-judgmental friend he'd ever had, mostly on account of her self-confessed insanity. "I tried to for a long time. But you can never hate somebody you've loved that much. You can just do a better and better job of lying to yourself about it." He groaned as she began tying off the bandage, and glared down at her after the look she gave him. "And yes, before you ask, I've considered a career writing greeting cards."

Zoe snickered and finished tying things off before she stood up to inspect it. "Should last until we get to Aiko. Hopefully her concoctions keep the infection away." She looked up into Orion's eyes and tried to give him a weak smile, even though they literally just fought for their lives. Again. "It's good you don't hate her. Cuz she's gonna need a fucking friend if we get her out of that place. Who knows what they've done to her in there. Hell, who even knows if that baby isn't one of theirs? How much would that suck if that was Kaplan's baby or some messed up shit like that?"

"You know, when most people have an idea that fucked up, they keep it to themselves." He got up on his leg and started testing it out. He wanted to limp, but he knew they needed to move faster than that. "It's not Kaplan's. She wouldn't be that far along already. We've only been here four months. And it's not mine, because she'd be about to pop by now if it was. Which means it belongs to a dead man." He winced in pain, but forced himself to walk at a more or less normal pace.

"Then it belongs to a dead man. A dead man can't do jack shit for her. You can." Zoe helped support him anyway so they could get moving. "Like I said, she's gonna need you if you're willing to help her."

"What do you think I've been trying to do the last four fucking months?" He was still panicked from the fight and the fact that they had lost Carmina, but he was also even more frantic than before because they had seen Anna.

Months of hoping she was alive, convincing himself that she was alive, convincing himself that she *had* to be alive, was all rushing through his head at once. "You wanted to know why, now you do. And now I know I wasn't a complete psychopath for believing it this whole time." He looked over at her with as much of a smile as he could manage. "No offense. I'm fond of psychopaths, I'm just not very good at being one myself."

"I had high hopes. And you let me down." She shook her head as she continued to help him along. "But I'm glad you were right, for your sake in the very least. You needed some real, tangible evidence for your hope-fire."

"My hope-fire. That's a good way of describing it." He walked in silence the rest of the way back to the camp, since his thoughts were still swirling. All he had been able to think about for months were strategies of how to get into the compound, how to even the score, bring the numbers more into their favor. Now all he could think about was getting Anna out. She was a Number. They made her into . . . something else. He was going to find out what it was and he was going to do something about it.

4

Every day felt a little like her consciousness was trapped in the body of a robot. Except that robots couldn't feel sensations, they couldn't feel emotions, they couldn't feel physical pain or pleasure . . . she wished she was a consciousness trapped in a robot body. It would be easier.

Anna had daily instructions that she was supposed to follow without fail, and recently, she rebelled rarely against it because the daily tasks weren't the things really worth her effort to resist. So she saved her effort, her stamina, her fighting instinct . . . for the worst of it.

She saved it for whenever she had to see one of the Kaplans.

She saved it for whenever Henri came around to taunt her.

She saved it for the worst of times, so they would always know that even if she was bent over backwards, she still wasn't completely broken. She was a mouse to them, but she was a mouse trapped in a corner, and even a tiny little mouse had teeth.

Sunrise. She was in a small room, pristine, enough space for a bed, a toilet and sink, a tiny shower that was getting less easy to maneuver in while her belly grew. Anna opened her eyes and turned her head slowly toward the small, barred window where the sunlight was streaming through. Why were there bars, anyway? She wanted to leave, she wanted to run free more than anything, but she wasn't going to. She couldn't. She knew that. They knew it. What a waste.

Anna sat up slowly and let out a sigh as she moved to dangle her feet off of her bed. She was instructed to wake up at sunrise, shower, get dressed in her clothing, pull her hair back and report for a meal with the others. Anna did all of the things she was supposed to do, but she pushed off doing them until her body responded to the resistance. She watched the window until the sun had been up long enough that she started to feel physical pain, and once she got up to take a shower, it went away. She stayed in the shower long enough to feel the same pain, resist, and *then* she went on with her tasks. The only logical way to endure the pain, she figured, was to push it, embrace it, and then get used to it. It was working for her so far.

Most of the time.

Once Anna actually made her way to the cafeteria, she ordered her meal, perfectly adjusted for her health and for her baby's, and sat down next to the others. She sat next to the number ahead and behind her own number, and none of them looked up from their meals at each other. None of them touched each other. They barely touched their own forks and spoons, and when they got up from the table, they were careful not to even bump one another. It always ended badly.

Anna watched as several of the others finished before her because they hadn't dragged their feet like she did, but she remained at the table without pain. She was supposed to eat all of her food. Drink all of her beverage. No one told her to hurry, so she was pain-free as she took her time. She saved the drink for last every single day because she knew what was in it. She knew it was the reason why she was trapped, trapped in her very own body, but there was simply nothing she could do.

Silent resistance was all she had.

When she was alone and there was only a little food left, Stephen Kaplan approached the table. She hated that her body was instantly hyper-aware of his presence, and that her body ached for him to even just reach out and graze her cheek or her arm. Whatever the serum was, it made her want praise from her abusers, and she hated every second. What she wouldn't give for a metallic, empty, robot body. The ones made out of flesh were sick fuckers. Always wanting pleasure. Relief. Endorphins.

Stupid body.

"It's good to see you, Sir." She muttered softly as she stared at her food. It wasn't good to see him. It never was.

"It's good to see you too, Echo-23." Stephen's tone was every bit as fake as her own, but his falsification was condescension and contempt, glazed over and bound together with a sadism she had only previously thought she understood. "It's a beautiful day outside, don't you think? The weather is getting colder."

"Eleusis always has beautiful weather. Even in the storms." She replied still without looking up at him again. Anna gripped her utensils tighter so that she could ignore her body's achy feeling that she hated so much. She also felt a little stronger at resisting since she'd not had her daily dose yet. Her drink sat untouched above her tray.

"You know, Maria and I just finished a very interesting study. I think you would have enjoyed it." He slid down onto the bench next to her, facing outward. He didn't touch her, though he was easily within reach of her, and he didn't order her to get closer to him. Something else much more basic than words was doing that. He leaned backward on the table with a relaxed arm around her tray as he looked over at her.

"We took Delta-17 after breakfast a few days ago. She was like you, always saved the best of the day for last." He lifted his hand to run a fingertip around the rim of her glass, setting the cup just slightly off balance for a moment so as to upset the liquid within. "You remember Delta-17. She was the one who swore at me the entire time I was fucking her your third day here." It was a long way back in the haze that life had become, but the girl was as beautiful as most of their test subjects; blonde ringlets and violet eyes. "We put her into a hamster box. Took her almost three full days to die. I was impressed."

Anna didn't want to give him the satisfaction of commentary, her gaze fixed on the glass and the way his finger traced the rim. God, she hated that hand and yet she wanted it to touch her all the same. It made her sick. She was being bent, broken, and molded by their serum every single day. "Why did you put her in a hamster box? Was she disobedient?"

"No, not at all. D-17 was very obedient, right from the start. She didn't take as much encouragement as some." He continued his caress of the glass once he saw her watching, watching her the entire time. "It was just a question of practicality. If you're not learning something in life, then you're not really living. She didn't have anything else to teach us, so it made sense to let her teach us something about dying." He shrugged and reached up idly to push a stray strand of her hair back over her shoulder, his fingers not actually touching her skin directly at any point. "Even dying, she was no more than mildly above average. The longest lasters make it a full week past their missed dose. The weakest are dead within a single day."

Anna was visibly fighting the need to lean into his hand, since her body wanted to do one thing and her mind refused to let it. She took deep, careful breaths before she pulled her gaze from the glass and looked into Stephen's eyes directly. He wasn't going to win. He had destroyed so much of what mattered to her already, he wasn't going to destroy the rest. She needed to destroy him first.

"You . . ." She was struggling, clearly, but she was maintaining some control. For the moment. "I'm not ready to die." It was all she could get out, but there was so much more she wanted to say following that particular statement.

"I know." His Australian accent drawled out the word in satisfaction as he smiled. "But you will be soon. As soon as your daughter is born and we stamp a number on her palm, you'll be ready."

Anna's eyebrows turned in but she took another deep breath. She could feel her baby kicking in response to her intense physical response, but trial after trial, the Kaplans' drug hadn't passed through the placenta. Her baby was drug-free, not that they weren't trying their damndest to change that. "You . . . can't have her."

Her defiance made him grin, and it wasn't the first time it had provoked that kind of response from him. Every time she struggled, every time she resisted even in the slightest, he just got more excited. "Never say that to me again, Echo-23." He moved a single finger down along her neck to her collarbone, his physical touch reinforcing his command. It wasn't the first time he had forbidden her from saying anything, but she kept defying his order anyway. It was very promising.

Anna couldn't stifle the groan of pleasure she felt when he touched her, but she still didn't reach out for him. The utensils in her hands dug into her skin as she gripped them for dear life. "You . . . can't . . ."

"Can't?" He said with a laugh deep in his chest. "You of all people know that's not a word that applies to me, Echo-23. Especially when it comes to you. There's nothing you won't do for me." His touch moved lower, just a casual touch that could do so many un-casual things. "In fact, when your daughter is born, Maria and I are going to have you give her to us yourself."

She shook her head, but she was also distracted by his touch. Anna wanted to bite his hand or punch his motherfucking face, but instead she somehow found the strength to let go of her utensil and push his hand away. It was literally painful to do so, since she wanted his touch and she was denying him, but she didn't want his touch at all. Fucking human body. Robot. She wanted to be a robot.

He laughed all over again at that resistance, but as soon as she pushed his hand away, it was back faster than she could even see him move. The drug kept her vision just a little blurry and sometimes played tricks on her hearing too, though touch . . . touch was deeply heightened. She could feel every detail of the way his hand gripped her neck, reminding her and reminding her entire body of all the other times he'd begun to choke the life from her. She could feel the memory of everything else he'd done to her in those moments, the threat of everything he still intended to do. "I think I've found something you'll enjoy today, Echo-23. It's going to be a special day for you. There are some parts of you we've decided it's time you explored."

Anna tried to keep her breathing even as he gripped his hand around her neck, but she simultaneously wanted to kiss him and castrate him slowly. Even if castrating him caused her excruciating pain, it would be worth it. God, it would be worth it. She was only alive for her baby girl now anyway, and if they were really going to take her baby . . . dying for the chance of destroying Kaplan was a worthy cause. "Special . . ." She attempted to choke out, but she didn't struggle otherwise.

"Very special." He confirmed, his fingers caressing along her neck even as he squeezed a little tighter, listening for her to truly struggle to breathe before he let her go. "Drink it all. Then come with me." He got up after another casual caress along her chest, heading for the stairs that led up to Anna's least favorite place in the world.

Her nostrils flared as she took in a deep breath after a cough. Rather than pick it up, she just stared at the cup. She was hoping he would forget, but he never did. Anna's throat throbbed as she sat there, but eventually the drink won out. Her shoulders slumped as she reached out through the pain for the glass and downed it all in one drink. She hated the instant effect that it had of making her want to bolt after him, but she did get up and follow. She was already tired from fighting him so hard in just one conversation and her head was beginning to throb.

Stephen didn't so much as turn around to make sure she followed him. He could hear her footsteps in the hallway behind him, but he just walked past doors and branches of the hall, passing other slaves and a very few military personnel, all of whom gave him a wide berth as he passed.

"What did you dream about last night, Echo-23?" He had always asked her the question, and had never given her a satisfying answer as to why, but he had always smirked at her when he could tell she was lying.

"Earth." She answered honestly, since she had no reason to lie at the moment. "Earth, and rain, and my father. Who you can't torture because he's already fucking dead."

"Well, there's always grave-robbing." He laughed as if her father's death was a joke. Maybe it was, to him. Had he ever once cared about another human being? Genuinely cared? "Lucky for you, I've never been interested. I do miss rainstorms sometimes, though. Here, they're always more lightning than rain, it seems like. Not exactly good for going out and fucking in. I can understand why you'd dream about them. They're a decent thing to miss."

"Yes. They are." She looked out the windows at Eleusis as they walked and while she thought it was beautiful, she really did miss Earth. "Orion and Logan too." She admitted, not out of necessity, but because she wanted to. Talking about them eased emotional pain, even though she was talking to Kaplan. "Not about fucking them. Just seeing them again." Logan had left Kaplan on the brink of death once. She wished he was still around to do it again.

He looked over at her as they walked, as if they were friends taking a stroll instead of a monster and one of his favorite toys. "You should think about them the next time I'm inside you." The suggestion was always more than a suggestion, given how much of the drug they gave her every day and how long she had been taking it. Every order, every mere hint of desire from Stephen or Maria worked its way into her body at a chemical level, an instinctual level that went beyond rationality or even emotion.

A flicker of anger was visible in her expression, but then it went away. Sure. She could think about them. She could think about Logan beating Stephen into a fucking pathetic bloody pulp. She could think about Orion taking a gun and filling Stephen full of lead. Sure she could think about them. It might actually give her a little peace. "Okay."

He thought he knew what was going through her mind, that his suggestion was strong enough to force her into obedience on its own. His smile told her just how pleased he was at that kind of obedience. He liked to be challenged, but he really, really liked to win after every challenge he found.

He took her into a small room with just one other door and a huge window that obviously should have opened into another room past the door. There was a table and two chairs, one on either side. If she had been under arrest, the room would have made more sense. As it was, Stephen closed the door they came through and moved over to the glass, which at the moment was only reflecting their own faces back at them. "Have you ever wondered how we found you? All of you? In the mountains back on Earth and your attack here? How we knew you were coming and knew where to hunt you down?"

"I've pretty much believed that you sold your soul to the devil and you have fucked-up, greedy, rich bastards funding you every which way. It was a matter of time." She admitted, though she hated it. "But I really wish it had been later. When I could have been ready to put a fucking bullet in your brain."

Stephen seemed to take her comment much more seriously than she had intended it. The man had a bent for sarcasm himself, so it wasn't a matter of him not understanding hers, he just found literal interpretations much more interesting. "You know, I wasn't raised in a particularly religious fashion, so I never had the opportunity to gain the respect for the devil which I imagine he deserves. Maybe if I'd had a better upbringing, I'd have tried to make that kind of deal. But I've seen a little too much of the universe to try a deal with the devil now." He shrugged, and went to a control knob along one side of the window.

"No, our methods were actually much simpler with the lot of you. They just took more time than we thought they would." He pressed the knob and the window faded from opaque to mostly-translucent, still shaded in oddly grey tones with the difference in light level between the room in which they were standing and the room on the other side.

In the other room, on a hospital bed, with Maria standing beside him, was Oliver. She hadn't been permitted to see him since she first woke up inside the compound, but she had been given conflicting information about him ever since. Some days she was told he was dead, sometimes escaped, sometimes that he was sick and suffering. No answers were consistent.

Anna ran to the window and knocked on it before Kaplan could tell her not to, since she was all about acting first and fuck the consequences. She would be punished regardless. "Oliver!"

She cried out immediately. Anna had fallen in love with Oliver too, he had been a good friend to her. Support for her father in his last days. "Oliver!!"

"He can't hear you." Stephen said quietly, still laughing at her. "You can keep trying, but all he'll know is that somebody's knocking for him." Oliver looked up, his eyes dancing along the glass to try and see anything at all through it, but he clearly couldn't focus on her. His eyes were wide and wild, stretched as if they had been perpetually widened under the treatment of the Kaplans. "He's only been permitted to leave that room once since he woke from his injuries, and that was to see you, with his own eyes, one day when we had you and the rest of Echo rank doing exercises in the courtyard."

"Can I see him now?" She knew that he probably wouldn't let her, that they were torturing her with his nearness, but she asked anyway. They had their reasons for doing this. She just had to be on her toes so she didn't give them the satisfaction they were hoping for.

Stephen shook his head casually. "No. Not yet." He stepped up and knocked three perfect times on the glass near where Maria was standing on the other side, apparently some kind of pre-arranged signal for them. "Have I ever told you that you have a wonderful screaming voice? Oliver does too, but I like yours better."

Anna didn't like showing the anger that she felt, but it was obvious before she could hide it. "You're such a sick motherfucker. Every day. When someone finally kills you, even the flies will have a fucking kegger to celebrate."

Maria left Oliver's side to tap back and move to open the door. "You're just on time, my dear."

"I do pride myself on my timing." He kissed her deeply as she held the door open. When he let the kiss break, he was holding a handful of her shirt, as usual, and he turned to glare back at Anna without releasing it. "You are to come and stand in that corner. You are not to touch him, and you are not to speak. Confirm that you understand."

Anna's fingers twitched at her sides but she started walking to the corner where she was instructed to go, even before acknowledging what he said. "I understand." She growled, even though she had no intention of following what he said if she could fight it off. This was the first time she had seen Oliver since they had been attacked. He was *alive*. There was no way she would keep her mouth shut if she could fight it.

Oliver's reaction on the bed was similarly violent, but even though he opened his mouth to speak, all he could do was move his jaw like a fish out of water. There was something wrong with his legs, since he wasn't moving, but his hands twitched along the sides of the hospital bed as if they were instinctively looking for wheels to push himself closer to her. Finding nothing, he looked over at the Kaplans in terror and then laid himself back on the bed.

His eyes were a tangled box of emotions as he looked at Anna. She could see the love he'd once professed to her, the caring, but it was buried beneath trauma she saw in so many eyes of the other Numbers. Their life was one of fear and empty spaces in which the fear could be remembered, nothing more. But she could see guilt in the way he looked at her as well, in a way that she had never seen before. Whatever they had done with him, he was a very different man than the one she had known.

"Has he been talkative this morning?" Stephen had settled in against the glass with his hands on Maria's hips. He touched her every time they were in each other's presence, or he was ordering someone else to do the touching. Either way, there was rarely any interaction in which the two of them weren't getting fondled by someone, either each other or some of their playthings. Attending them at meals and sleeping in the corners of their room had been some of Anna's primary tasks for weeks after her arrival, just in case they were in the mood for her.

"More than most days. I told him right after I arrived he would get to see Echo-23 today. He had a lot to say about that." Maria said with a chuckle as she leaned into Stephen and his touches. "You left early, I was still asleep."

Anna wanted to throw up listening to the Kaplans, but she kept her attention firmly on Oliver. She gave him a small wave, since she couldn't touch him or speak to him, but she tried to give him a reassuring smile anyway. He was alive. It made her happy to see him, even if he was probably paralyzed. *I missed you.* She mouthed, hoping that he would understand what she said, even if she wasn't talking. Clearly she was still pregnant, though, and she touched her belly so that he would look at it. *The baby is okay.* She mouthed again, still trying to smile.

Her mouthed words didn't provoke any change in his

expression at first, but after a few moments of just staring at her, she saw a tear run down his cheek. When the Kaplans were kissing again (Stephen was apologizing for leaving, but had gotten called away on supplier business before the sun was up), his lips finally moved. *Boy or girl?*

Girl. Anna replied quickly with as warm a smile she could manage. Her own eyes filled with tears and a few trickled down her cheeks. *I love you.* She mouthed afterward, since seeing him brought her actual happiness in a place that she believed was literal hell on Eleusis.

That declaration got more tears from him, and she could see something in Oliver's eyes that she had never seen in Logan's or Orion's. Whatever they had done to Oliver over the four months they had been prisoners, it had broken him. Not just bodily, with the paralysis she could see by his lack of any movement whatsoever below the waist, but with the jumpy, paranoid flash of animal fear behind his eyes. She had seen it in other slaves every day, those who couldn't fight anymore, who couldn't resist anymore, who didn't have a reason, who could no longer keep themselves from becoming whatever the Kaplans wanted from one moment to the next. *I love you too.* He mouthed, but he was shaking with the force of the conflict in his body to make the effort. That kind of resistance could put a person into a seizure or worse, but the trembling in him didn't stop, it only grew more violent.

"Well. He looks pretty talkative to me." Stephen looked at the man over Maria's shoulder. "Have you told him yet this morning what we have planned for him today?"

Maria looked back at Oliver who was shaking and she l smiled as she nodded. "He knows what we have planned. He also knows he serves no purpose to us any longer." She glanced over at Anna who looked at them sharply as soon as Maria said the words.

"He has a purpose for me!" She shouted at the Kaplans, since she couldn't talk to Oliver directly. "You can't . . . don't kill him!"

"We have no intentions of killing him." Stephen said in a mild voice, then reached up into the coat he wore and pulled out a small handgun. He placed it on a small table just out of arm's reach for Anna, and flicked the safety off as it lay there between them. He didn't so much as look at Anna the whole time, since he knew she would stay where she was told. "Echo-30." Stephen began, looking over at Oliver. "Tell Echo-23 how you really came to be employed by her family."

Oliver grew more frantic, resistance welling up in him even as his mouth started to open of its own accord. He was staring at Stephen and Maria as if pleading for help, but neither of them would ever give any such thing. "I ca . . ." his voice was broken from screaming, and had acquired a raspy, heavy-whisper quality that didn't go away. "I . . ." just that much resistance was all he could muster, and Anna saw him slump under the relief of obedience once he started speaking, his eyes on the floor between them.

"When Nine fell, a group of rebels in the city where we were living at the time thought it was a good opportunity to make a name for themselves. They rioted through the town, and they killed my wife and our unborn daughter. I tried to fight back, and got swept up in the Consortium personnel dealing with those who had been injured. The Mistress had escaped to Earth after the explosion on Nine. She knew how much I hated the rebels. She put me to work taking care of them. I was sent to one hospice case after another, always of people who were suspected to have ties to the rebels. Any intelligence I received about them, I communicated back to her."

Anna stared at Oliver for a long time, but her tears didn't stop, they just continued as she stared in silence. She wasn't allowed to speak to him, but even if she was, she didn't know what she would say. He was sent to take care of her father because of her, even though her father and the rest of her family thought she was dead the entire time until she had pushed Logan enough to go home. Ultimately, it was still her fault, even if Oliver had been a plant. He never would have had information to give if she and Logan had stayed 'dead'. So much never would have happened if they had stayed 'dead'. Anna lost both Logan and Orion, and she had destroyed a wonderful marriage even before that. All because she was forever too selfish to stop herself from being stupid and reckless.

"You may talk to him now." Maria released Stephen's command on Anna, since they were both interchangeably in charge of all their toys.

"Why? Why would you work for them?" Anna asked incredulously, even though he had just admitted that he hated the rebels. "If you hated us . . . why did you . . . was it a lie? All of it?" She wanted to know if he actually loved her, or if he was just lying about that so he could stay alive.

"I didn't hate *you*." He said quickly, still a broken mess of tears. "I stopped hating . . . I couldn't hate the people I helped. I hated the rebels, I hated the rebellion for killing my wife, but the people . . . your father was a good man. The others I helped care for as they died were good people. But the chaos that the world turned into . . ." he shook his head, still broken about it, still torn. She had always known he had misgivings about some things, about the violence of it all, but it had seemed like the aversion of a healer to the work of death. It went deeper than that. Too deep to be rid of. "I hate the rebellion, I hate the Consortium, I hate all of it. But not you. Not your family. Not you."

"But you still told us where to find them." Stephen pushed, wanting to dig the wound in deeper. "You still sent us that message."

"No! I didn't! I only meant to . . ."

"Quiet." Stephen said quietly, but an order didn't have to be loud to have force. Oliver's lips kept working and his sobbing resumed, but he didn't say anything else. "You sent the message and alerted us of their location. That was all that was required of you. You did your work well."

Anna turned her attention to Stephen when he started talking, and though Oliver was sobbing, she didn't feel the anger that she knew they wanted her to feel. They were trying to play her like a stringed instrument, plucking at different chords to see what struck the loudest. If Oliver alerted their location, then he was the 'obvious' reason why her family was dead. Her children. Her siblings. Logan. But none of them would have been at risk if it weren't for her in the first place.

"You exploited a grieving man, a man who felt like he had nothing left in the world but his motherfucking vengeance." Anna didn't move from her spot, but she felt like throwing herself at the Kaplans. "You want me to hate him. You want me to want him dead. That's the only reason why I'm here, or why you're forcing him to tell me the fucking truth. But you know what? They're dead. They're dead and no confession is going to bring them back. He didn't kill them, you did. I did! I killed them by going there in the first place! So stop your motherfucking games . . ."

"You did." Stephen agreed, immediately and quietly silencing her tirade. "I'm glad you're taking responsibility, Echo-23. Some of the others have trouble with that. Echo-30 certainly did at first."

He turned back to Oliver, who was panting on the bed as if he'd just run a marathon. He was still trying to resist, but he was too weak to do so meaningfully. "For weeks, he denied that he had anything to do with what happened. Maintained that he had done what he thought was right in turning against us."

He shook his head in condescension, then looked back at Anna. "Eventually, you'll come to the same understanding. It won't even take you quite as long, not from here. Everything you've done since aiding in the destruction of Nine has led to suffering, Echo-23. Everything. It's destroyed your own family and countless others, and you are to blame for it, at least in part. You worked to make the world a worse place."

Anna looked back and forth between Stephen and Maria and she just busted up and started laughing. "That's what you think is going to break me? Fucking *guilt*?" She kept laughing in her spot until she was wiping at the tears that had never stopped. "Do you know how effective guilt is on someone like me? A whore? A fucking selfish piece of shit like me? I thought I was making a difference, going to the Initiative. But I already know that I did it for me. I got what I deserved. Your fucking guilt can go blow itself in a corner."

"We haven't even gotten started on your guilt yet." Stephen and Maria watched her laughing fit with mild disinterest, as they had watched everything else about her over the course of her time with them. They observed the world as if they weren't even a part of it, walking on some kind of oil slick coating the surface of an entire ocean of reality they themselves were too greasy to ever join. "Speaking of the whore label, though, you should be aware that the girl you're carrying does belong to Echo-30. Testing showed that very clearly early on. Now seemed the prudent time to tell you."

"I already knew that." She spat back at the Kaplans, even though she hadn't known for a hundred percent certainty. She looked back at Oliver and just stared at him for a moment. "I don't blame you. I still love you. Don't carry that with you. Don't let them . . ."

"I warned you not to speak." Stephen's voice was cold, but more disappointed than angry. "Remember the needle room." He said quietly, but his voice was a command to her brain, reaching into the pain centers of her mind by way of his voice. "Remember being trapped there, and be there again. Now."

Anna shook her head as she tried to fight the memories, she tried to stay in the moment and look at Oliver, but eventually the pain of it brought her to her knees. She didn't cry out or scream, but she was gasping and shaking on the floor.

"Stay there." Stephen crouched on the sterile tile floor, watching her writhe in pain that was entirely in her mind. Pain they had put there. Pain that could be evoked in a word.

There had been so much advancement in such a short time. Such a simple thing Maria had done, in retrospect, though the effects were profound in ways they hadn't yet fully explored. To find a chemical path into the mind of another person, to give them a very simple order: obedience. Then to lace that obedience and imprint it to a specific individual. Or a set of individuals, that didn't matter. Maria's serum worked on the mind of a subject, waiting to bond them to a specific receptor, a specific master. It didn't matter who that subject or who that master was. All that mattered was that in that moment, he and Maria were Anna's gods. "Stay there as if you'd been left in there for hours. Feel every moment."

"Stephen." Maria scolded gently. "How are we going to complete this interaction if she's no good to us for the rest of the day? I'm not getting rid of Echo-30, she is."

Stephen sighed, but he knew she was right. He stood up, but didn't rescind his order to Anna yet. "I know. I do get carried away playing with them sometimes. It will be better to put her in there and actually leave her for hours. Reality always hurts more than the mind. Most of the time, anyway." He sighed one more time and turned back to Anna. "Come out of it, Echo-23. Get on your feet."

Anna stopped shaking, but she couldn't get up immediately, and there was actually a small trickle of blood from her nose as she attempted to stand. It wasn't clear if mentally she had been in so much pain the bleeding happened as a response, or if she had bumped her nose on the floor, but regardless, her gaze looked far away from the pain she had endured.

"You will finish your punishment for your outburst later tonight. And you will beg for it to be granted to you." It wasn't an unusual command coming from Stephen. His tools were always the same. Pain, humiliation, abuse, always the same. But once he was finished with his reminder, he looked back over at Oliver. "Speak, Echo-30."

Oliver gulped, looking into Anna's eyes, since he'd been given no injunction against speaking to her, but clearly he had been given orders on what he did need to confess beforehand. "I've killed people fighting for the rebellion. I've caused hundreds of innocent people to die, including your own children. I was responsible. Even while we were sleeping together, I was responsible."

Anna nodded, though it was only because her whole body was still ringing in pain and she couldn't even think to respond in any other way. "Okay."

Stephen seemed satisfied by that, and picked up the gun he placed on the table, handing it to Anna grip-first. "Kill him." He hadn't given her permission to move from the spot where she was standing, and he purposefully didn't tell her to shoot him. He wanted her to remember choosing to use the gun and killing the man. He wanted that image in her mind forever for him to use against her.

Anna looked at the gun in her hand and she looked truly horrified as she looked between Stephen and Oliver. Anna had killed a lot of people. She remembered being with Orion, jumping from place to place, killing and moving on. But this was different. This was Oliver. "No." She replied in a shaky voice as tears ran down her cheeks. "I love him." Her hand wouldn't let go of the gun, though. She wanted to let go.

"Everyone you love dies." Stephen said slowly, the words working their way into her mind as fixed points of truth, as if she had known them all her life. "Your father, your brothers and sisters, your husbands, your children. They all die because of you. Now your lover will join them. They all die because of you. He's no different."

Anna looked at Oliver and cried harder. "I love you, Oliver." She stared at him, but she was pointing the gun at him against her will. She knew it would only take one shot, she was a skilled shooter, after all. "I'm going to name her Olivia. So she will always know you. She will."

Oliver nodded, tears chasing each other down his cheeks as he looked her in the eye. "I deserve this, Anna. You don't, but I do." He sniffed, grief and hopelessness contorting his face into a mask of pain that was a far cry from the man she had known. "Give her my love, and make sure she knows I loved her mother."

"Her mother loves you too." She said between sobs. "You'll

be free from them now. No more pain. With your wife and your baby . . ." Anna had to convince herself that something good would come out of it, though her hand was shaking because she was resisting. She closed her eyes at one point, but between her labored breathing she opened them again and stared at Oliver. "I'm so sorry."

The gunshot was ear-splitting. Her ears rang as the smoke trailed out of the end of the gun, but Oliver's body laid still. Her shot had been true, right through the center of his skull, killing him instantly. At least it had been humane. For him.

Anna went to her knees in sobs, and she could hear Stephen walking closer to her. He was probably going to taunt her and tell her that she deserved this feeling, this feeling of murdering someone she loved, but he didn't get the chance before she whipped herself around and shot him twice in the ribs.

His momentum of walking toward her carried him through the shock of being shot, and he fell over directly on top of the gun in her hand, pinning her wrist between his body and the floor as he writhed and gasped for breath, more in shock at being shot than anything else.

"Stephen!" Maria immediately rushed to her husband's aid and called for help. She ordered guards to take Anna back to her unit and restrain her, but she kept her attention on her husband, with her hands pressing on the wounds. "They were clean shots. No vital organs by the look of the bleeding. We'll get you fixed up, alright?"

Stephen nodded, clenching his teeth in pain, but there had been something very different about the way Stephen experienced pain ever since the beating he had taken at Logan's hands. He had been mostly dead for most of a year, and he had found when he was finally restored that he had a much easier time ignoring pain than he had before. Gunshots were a stretch, but he felt more anger than pain.

"I will break that woman." He snarled up from the floor, letting another pair of guards haul him up to help him get to an infirmary.

Anna didn't struggle as she was carried back to her unit, restrained, and then strapped down to her bed. The straps creaked as she tested them, but she didn't fight against them too hard. She was too busy trying to remember where she'd shot Kaplan and if there was even a possibility that he would die. He had forced her hand.

Oliver was dead. She could still see his dead eyes, but she didn't want to think about it.

"Please let him be dead." She whispered up toward the ceiling, unwilling to even turn her eyes away from her restraints to look at the rest of the world. No matter where she looked, there was nothing for her to see. "Anyone listening, please let him be dead."

"I'm sorry." The voice that came to her was from across the hall, more familiar than most other voices in the world, especially because she'd met four different men who bore it. "If you're looking for a deity with the ability to actually answer that prayer, you'll have to hang up and try your call again later. Who is it you're trying to pray into the next life, exactly?"

She wanted to tell the voice in the cell across from her to shut the fuck up, even though he'd never been particularly cruel to her. "I nailed that fucker Kaplan twice. He better fucking be dead."

"Ah. Stephen. Well done." The man's voice seemed genuinely pleased, and she could hear the canvas of his cot creaking from across the hall as he struggled to sit up. Moving never ceased to look painful for him, though he had never condescended to explain why. "If you can describe where the entry wounds for the gunshots were, I can probably give you a probability differential on his chances for survival."

"It happened really fast. He . . . he made me kill someone I loved." She replied in a voice that cracked too many times, but she took a deep breath. "I whipped around and shot him in the side, but I don't know if I nailed anything important."

"You're not overwhelming when it comes to detailed descriptions, but if you shot him in the side, your best hope is that you punctured his liver or one of his kidneys. If you didn't have a chance to focus on accuracy, though, there is maybe a fifteen percent chance of mortality. Probably less." He had never been particularly comforting or optimistic in the many estimates he had given her, but he was also normally right. "I didn't think either of those you previously loved were still alive, at last given information."

"Haven't you heard? I'm a whore. I love many men." She replied bitterly before she rested her head back against her pillow. "He also happened to be the father of this baby. And apparently a plant who gave our location to the Consortium. So it's complicated. I just found out about the last part."

"I see." The man assimilated the information like a computer, just like every other conversation she'd had with him. She had never once seen them let the man out of his cell, never seen them give him anything but food and water, but she'd seen him tortured more often than almost any other prisoner held there on Eleusis. Usually by Henri, one of his own clone-brothers.

As for Charles himself, he looked unlike any of the other Montgomeries she had met. He was taller, for one thing, which was strange considering the fact they were clones, but when she had asked why, he had declined to explain. He was also completely hairless, leaving him with a downright unsettling appearance.

With the Eleusis atmosphere and the complete lack of windows in his own cell, the man looked a great deal like an albino except for the multifaceted hazel of his eyes. The only sunlight he got every day was that which came in through Anna's window and struck his room. At first, she thought she was imagining Charles' routine of making sure he was sitting in the path of the sunlight each and every day, but the pattern had gone on too long for her to discount it as anything but intentional.

"My sympathies." He eventually said in his low, broken voice. "I have some experience with having your heart removed forcibly by those to whom it had previously been willingly given."

"You would think a heart like mine would learn." She shook her head, hating even the familiarity of the pillow rustling beneath it. "I can't even grieve over my family again, knowing he pointed us out. Because it doesn't matter who did it, me or Oliver. They're dead now." Anna closed her eyes. "Are we still going to try and get out of this place, Charles?"

"Getting out of here isn't altogether the problem." His accent was vaguely French, and was more similar to Henri than it was to Xander's Londoner or Jason's Midwest accent. There was a story behind that similarity the man had never told. "Getting out and surviving is the complicated part. Freedom means death for people like us."

He glanced down at his daily rations, still untouched just inside the bars of his cell. The tall glass of cloudy liquid they were required to drink each day was similarly untouched, but sat there like a silent threat they both understood too well. "It may not have quite the same effect on my brain it does on lesser minds, but withdrawal would still kill me. Probably faster than it would you, actually."

"Is there no one in this place that would help us? No one with any humanity?" She knew the answer to that already, but she wished it wasn't the truth. She wished she could believe there was *one* good person somewhere in the Consortium. Orion had been good. Mercury had been good, even if Anna had never liked her. But they weren't really members of the Consortium, they had just been citizens. "Can't we . . . I don't know, attach the serum fixation to each other to survive? That sounds ridiculous, but not as fucked up as the current situation."

"Well, everything I know about the compound they use is what I've derived from conjecture, so my medical opinion is going to be far from exact. Not to mention the fact that medicine was always a hobby for me to begin with, not a primary profession. That being said . . ." he shrugged, a slight movement of his shoulders she could see out of the corner of her eye while she stared up at her ceiling. "Theoretically, it's possible, but I would have to know more about the process the Kaplans are using to produce their formula in the first place, and their imprinting protocols. We don't currently have enough data to make a prediction."

"Well, what will it take, then?!? What will it take to get the data? Don't you want to get the fuck out of this place? I would rather fucking die as a starving person in the Eleusis forest with the fucking Behemoths after me than in here!"

"I've thought about a lot of ways I would rather die than here." His tone was immediately both angry and deadly, though the threat in it wasn't directed at Anna. "Like you, I would prefer almost any other alternative, but most of all, I would rather not die at all." He never could stand up for very long at a time, and he slowly lowered himself to the floor by the bars of his door so they could continue their conversation.

"There are four things I would require in order for us to proceed with any kind of escape plan. First, a better understanding of the obedience serum they've been giving us. Second, the necessary access to said serum in order to do something other than die after getting out of here. Third, my former associate Jeeta. I have been repeatedly threatened with the reality of her presence here, and have watched her tortured several times, so I have no reason to believe that she was returned to Earth. Fourth, an actual escape plan. With those four things, I would be more than happy to break you out of here, and anyone else who wanted to go along."

"Well, let's get fucking started. I'm done being their fucktoy. I'm so fucking done." She said even louder until she heard faint footsteps, and then she got louder. "I'm motherfucking *done* with this fucking shithole!"

"One more time, *ma petite.*" A voice that sounded very much like Charles', but wasn't, sounded just down the hallway from her. Henri eventually came and strolled into her cell, moving to sit on the side of her bed and smile down at her. "They did not hear you back on Earth, I don't think. Try it one more time, with a little more feeling."

"And fuck you too, you disgusting piece of shit." She growled from her bed, but it wasn't the threat she wanted it to be. "If only I could fucking shoot you too."

"I know you would enjoy that." Henri ran one hand up over her body casually, just because he could. He had stayed out of all the Kaplans' experiments on purpose, but that didn't mean he had abstained from enjoying the fruits of their research. All their research subjects were under compulsion not to resist advances from any staff members. In the first few weeks of Anna's captivity, there had been a parade of faces and other body parts to which she had been exposed. Henri's had frequently been among them. Him feeling her up while she was bound on her back didn't even break the top forty list of horrible things he had done to her.

"Unfortunately for you, I've been sent to punish you today, not the other way around. Stephen is in surgery and expected to live, so I've been given the task to make your life as miserable as possible until his surgery is finished and Maria can take over herself."

She squirmed a little as he ran his hand over her, since she hated his touch almost as much as she hated his cock. "I hope you don't mean that you're going to try and punish me with the tiny appendage you like to call a cock."

He grinned, and it reminded her just a little of the last place she'd called home. That was one thing that was the same across all four Montgomeries, that smile. It meant something different from all of them, but the smile itself was the same. "Big enough to make you scream more than once, and big enough for me to have whatever fun I want with it. No man can ask more than that. But keep talking." He encouraged her as he began undoing her straps to free her from the bed. He didn't need to be one of those with the authority to order her around. Anna knew from past experience that Henri always preferred a much more old-fashioned, hands-on approach to controlling prisoners.

Anna hated the fact that her brain was so fucked up on drugs that someone like Henri could get away with his atrocities. She hated that the body couldn't differentiate sensations sometimes, with the drugs fucking up everything. "Keep talking? You getting off on someone hating your guts again, you twisted motherfucker?"

"Well, when all you've gotten all your life is hatred, you learn to get off on what you're given. At this point, several shrinks have confirmed to me that clinically speaking, I'm incapable of knowing any different." He didn't seem bothered by that fact, he just shrugged and moved his hand down to start pulling up the loose clothing they always had the subjects wear. If he was assigned to torment her for the day, he might as well utilize the fact that she was already tied up for him. "I love it when people hate my guts, because everybody hates my guts. It's all the same to me."

"Seriously. What is it with you and women being tied up?" She growled again as she struggled against her restraints but she knew it wouldn't make any difference. She couldn't break free. She had tried a million times.

"If they're tied up, I'll have fewer cuts and bruises to heal from the next morning." He was every bit as bad as Stephen, but he was much more straightforward and aggressive about it. Stephen liked to toy with his victims, while Henri was just . . . vicious.

Anna closed her eyes as he continued to get himself ready to do whatever he wanted to her. "I'm not sure I'll even notice anything happening with that tiny dick of yours. You couldn't even get it up last time."

Henri laughed again, as he had every other time she had tried to humiliate him out of doing anything to her. Those tactics had occasionally worked on Stephen, leaving him to abuse her in other ways, but never on Henri. The man was dangerous in every way that a person could be. He was as stubborn as Xander, as intelligent as Charles, and as cunning as Jason, with none of the conscience or restraint with which the other three were burdened.

The communicator in Henri's pocket chimed, and he gave a huff of frustration before he took it out and propped the device up on her breasts to examine the message. His face darkened as he looked it over, and he groaned once he was finished, sliding it back into his pocket. "Looks like we have visitors, *cherie*. Let's go have a look and see what exactly they think they're going to accomplish."

"Visitors?" Anna asked curiously, but she was restrained and mostly naked at this point. What did he want her to do, exactly? "I don't know what you want me to do about visitors."

"I want you to get up and do as you're told. You're mine to deal with for the day, so wherever I go, you go too." He twisted her restraints deftly until they popped open, then got up off the bed and headed for the hallway, waiting for her to follow. Since her pregnancy was starting to show, it took her a little longer than it otherwise might have, and it clearly wore on his patience.

Anna rolled her eyes and followed after him, tugging her clothes back in place, but she couldn't help but smirk as she followed after him. "You're even more grumpy when you've been cock-blocked. It's hilarious."

"You remember what happened to you on your third day here, right? When you got Stephen good and pissed off at you?" He asked disinterestedly as they headed down the hallway.

Anna's smile faded, but her attitude didn't. "Yeah, well, I'm still here, aren't I?"

"Yes, you are. You're still *here*." He emphasized, with a smile of his own back at her. "Keep running your mouth every chance you get and I'll make what Stephen did to you just another part of your daily routine."

"You know, that's like telling someone that you're going to punch them in the face every day. Eventually the routine of it lessens how much it sucks. That's torture 101, Clone Henri."

"So you're telling me that after being here with us for four months, the place where you are sucks less than it did when you got here?" He smiled over at her as they turned a corner. "That the death of your daughter is going to hurt less because we've already killed your other children?"

"No, it's not going to hurt less. But I have no way to stop it from happening." She didn't have a way, *yet*, anyway. Anna felt like they were getting closer to the outside, but she didn't know why. "Are we leaving the building?"

"Not yet. I want to get a look first." They went around a corner and a wall of windows came in view, looking down on what was left of the compound barrier wall a dozen yards away. There were others present, mostly security personnel who had consistently ignored her existence the entire time she'd been a captive, but there were a few other researchers as well.

A pair of them, a man and an older woman, were talking to Henri as soon as he stepped out with Anna. "Heat-mapping has marked fifteen warm bodies on the slope just past the wall. We're waiting on our higher surveillance to give us a look at what's beyond, but the lightning storm is interfering with everything."

"You can say I was right." Henri said with a grin that clearly even his allies hated. "It won't kill you. But *they* might." He nodded out the window, trying to look over the heat-map to see where the snipers were positioned. "Have we got the cannons moved?"

It was the first time Anna had seen anything about people that were outside of the compound, and she immediately moved closer so she could see the map better. There were people out there. People that were trying to get into the Consortium compound and were trying to bring this fucking place down. She didn't know who the people were, but clearly they had to be her friends. Even if they were strangers, enemies of the Consortium were her friends. "I'm so fucking glad someone is still out there trying to kill you."

"So am I." Henri agreed amicably, as if they were longtime friends rather than recent and violent acquaintances. "What's life without somebody or something trying to kill you all the time? Sounds dull to me. Makes people lazy." The rest of those around him were moving and dispensing orders based on the single question he had asked. Henri just looked excited. "If they're here under sniper covers, then they think we don't know they're here. Still, it also means they could start their assault any time, which means we should start moving people to the tunnels."

"Why don't you go out and face them like a man? Only rats use tunnels, you asshole." Anna said with a look of disgust. "You must be afraid of them, if all you do is fight in secret."

"Well, if someone has a gun pointed at your head and you're not even a little bit afraid, you're either asleep or suicidal. I'm neither, at least not for today." He looked over the heat map again and handed it back to one of the others nearby. "But if you absolutely insist that we go and present ourselves to be shot, then that is what we'll do. Wagner, start sending out research teams from the front offices. Don't tell them how many we've got or where they are. I want to see if they're willing to start shooting or if they're still waiting on something else. And start prepping the cannons."

Anna watched as people scurried to follow orders, and she shook her head. "What makes these assholes so afraid of you? Did you swing around your tiny prick in front of them too?"

"Wow, you just pick one song and keep singing it, don't you?" Henri smiled over at her and went to stand beside her, laughing as he looked out through the windows. She knew from her few times outside in the sunlight that the windows were opaque from the outside, but the world was fairly clear from their point of view. Down below, a few parties were gathering up against the building in places they thought they would be safe before trying to make a run for the tunnels nearby. "Do we have an ID on any of the heat signatures?"

"Haven't been able to get a lock on any of them for long enough, Mr. Montgomery." Someone answered nearby, the voice trembling almost as much as the tablet in the man's hands. "The size of one of them, though, indicates either Espinoza or Al-Jabbar. They're the only two we have on record with the kind of height the signature is suggesting."

The impending assault hadn't stopped her cold in her tracks, but the sound of the last name she never should have been rid of certainly did. Orion was alive and on Eleusis? No. They were making it up. They had to be making it up. Anna moved closer as though she would see Orion out of the window. "You're lying." She said to no one in particular. "Orion Al-Jabbar is dead."

Henri looked over at her in surprise. "Is that your fantasy? The husband you left is dead and the husband you went back to is still alive on Earth somewhere fighting for you?" He chuckled and looked back at the hillside. "We're not in the habit of declaring someone dead around here until we get a positive ID and verify a lack of a pulse. Ripping their heart out or burying their head separately help as indicating factors too."

Anna actually winced at the idea of someone ripping Orion's heart out and then his head. "No, it's not my fantasy. All of them are dead. Orion. Logan. My children. Mercury."

"Interesting." Henri watched her with the eyes of a predator, and he had definitely seen the wince. "Let's say your giant *was* alive. And let's say we were to take him and dope him the same as the rest of you." He smiled slowly. "That could be fun, don't you think?"

"If he is alive, that means he's evaded you this long, and that means you're unlikely to catch him. He's a skilled and trained fighter, thanks to your Consortium. And if he was alive, he would kill you before you could inject him with any such shit." Anna's eyes were glued to the window.

God, was there actually a chance that Orion was alive? Even if he was, there was no way for her to get to him. Regardless, the world seemed a brighter place if he was.

She wished she could let him know how sorry she was.

She wished she could tell him she still loved him, even though he was happy with Mercury while she was still alive. Anna had too many months to think about everything. Ending things with Orion had been a mistake, and she only knew it because she and Logan weren't the people that they had once been when they first married.

Not that it mattered now.

Orion hated her, she knew that. But at least if she could tell him how sorry she was, maybe he wouldn't hate her so much. Logan and Oliver were gone. She had already missed two other chances to apologize for being a piece of shit.

Her defensiveness only made Henri laugh, and she could almost smell the anticipation on the man as he looked back out the window. "Once you confirm that it's Al-Jabbar, let me know. I'm going to enjoy this. How many personnel still need to be evacuated?"

"Most of the ward can be pulled back to the other wing, Mr. Montgomery, but there are still several. . ."

"Good, round them up and get some of your people out there. Start firing on the heat-map targets. I'm not going to let them just sit in cover and pick us off because they think they can surprise us. Once you've got a better lock on them, start in with the canons. Gamma group! Echo group! All your other orders pertaining to your schedule for today have been rescinded. You're with me. Come on."

Roughly seventy slaves in various shades of white and tan clothing turned at his order and hastened to catch up with him as he strode down the hallway. Clearly the man's twisted mind had come up with some kind of idea. As they walked, Anna could hear gunfire just outside the walls, but they quickly moved away from the glass and any indication of what was actually happening outside.

Anna kept watching the glass and as they got closer to the outdoors, Anna looked up at Henri. "It's not going to stop him or them, you know." She had figured out what he was going to do, and while she was momentarily horrified, she would rather die by Orion's gunshot than deal with the Kaplans and Henri for a single day more. "He hates me. And if they're here, they're going to kill everyone. Including us."

"That's the idea. Better they kill you than the rest of us who can actually do some good for the human race." Henri's casual attitude toward their lives knew no bounds, and when they got down to the entryway of the building, he proved it. "Alright, everybody whose brain has been chemically removed, form a line facing out, shoulder to shoulder, between here and the tunnel entry. You are to cover everyone moving from here to there. If any of them get shot, you'll wish you had been. That includes you." He said with a final slap to Anna's backside, shoving her forward hard enough that it was likely to leave a bruise on her ass for days.

Farther into the building, they felt the percussion cannons go off before they heard the sound of shattering glass, and Anna could see figures on the hillside being blown back and off balance by the force of the impact. Once started, the cannons kept firing every half a minute as they were all herded out to be human shields.

Anna kept her eyes open as long as she possibly could, but eventually when someone was shot next to her and fell to the ground, she closed her eyes briefly out of fear. She didn't really want to die, even though it would be sweet relief from the hell that had been her life. Anna didn't want to die because she didn't want Olivia to die. Olivia had an entire life to live, unless it was going to end right now. Anna couldn't defy the orders enough to run or even move that much, even though she wanted to fucking duck so she could let someone get a clear shot at Henri.

The situation on the hillside didn't go well for the rebels, and Anna had a front row seat for all of it. Several went down and were dragged by their comrades back up the hill to relative safety, and a few went down close enough to the ruins of the wall that some of the Consortium security officers ran out to take them prisoner. As the rebels were in retreat under the barrage of the cannon, though, Anna saw the tallest figure on the battlefield stand up, to his full height for once, and try to pull someone else up along with him. He towered over the woman next to him, and everyone else on the hillside. The 'someone else' had been pointing at her, and the figure looked her direction to follow.

She couldn't see any details of the man's appearance beneath the garb of the landscape he had piled on top of himself, but she could feel him look right at her, feel him pause, in the middle of a battlefield, to take her in.

Anna desperately wanted to run to him. She hoped he didn't hate her so much that he wouldn't at least help her get away, and she was already crying, even though he couldn't see that from his distance. She couldn't fight against the order enough to do anything except what she was supposed to do, even though she lifted her arm just enough to try and reach out for him. It wasn't much, but then she had to keep moving in order to use her body to protect the bastards behind her. He would get away. He would still be safe. She would still be stuck.

The moment she thought he would get away, she saw him go down as if he'd been shot. It was impossible to hear anything specific across the distance between them, but she could see pain in a person's body well enough, and he crumpled to the ground in a heap. The woman beside him helped drag him over the crest of the hill to get out of range and sight of the rest of those she was being forced to protect, and the last she saw of him, he was being thrown somewhere clear like a sack of ammunition.

Anna closed her eyes and tried to breathe through her tears as soon as she saw Orion go down, and she just couldn't move. She had killed Oliver that morning, and then she'd been given hope that Orion was still alive. Now was he really dead? They were right to tell her that she was the reason why everyone she loved was dead. If she hadn't been standing there at that moment, Orion never would have been distracted enough to get hurt. She probably killed him too. Again.

The assault didn't last long after that, and once the gunfire had died down, those who had retreated to the tunnels came back up cautiously. They moved back into their building to begin clearing away all the broken glass and relocate. Installing the percussion cannons inside a building rather than at some point along the perimeter fence had been a gamble with a great deal of cost behind it, but they had brought down several of the rebel fighters, and that was clearly something the Consortium security forces were comfortable with.

Henri was there to release the slaves from their orders, but he caught Anna before she could get away from him and back into her normal daily routine. He smiled at the tears covering her face and stepped in closer to her as she tried to catch her breath.

"I saw it too." He confirmed. "It was almost sweet, before you got him shot."

"He pointed at me." She looked into Henri's eyes, since she wasn't a woman who was fearful of anyone, even a man who had brutally raped her in a dozen ways. "He could have been instructing someone to fucking aim at me for all we know. So don't get smug about it."

He wasn't buying what she was trying to sell for a moment, and the smug look on his face didn't disappear. "I love it when people have hope. I truly, truly do." He nodded back toward the building. "Go find the cinder block room and get naked, then put your wrists in the restraints and stay there. I'll be there once this mess is cleaned up."

Anna stared at him for a moment and walked away. Of course he would want to fuck, since he felt victorious. He could do whatever he wanted to her body, it was just a body. But he wouldn't break her. They wouldn't get Olivia. He couldn't have her soul. If she still had one, anyway.

5

"Nope, nope, I think I'm okay now." Liam said with a final cough, his arm firmly in front of his mouth as he shook his head and groaned. He avoided throwing up by the barest of margins, and he was grateful that most of the people in the cargo section of the transport ship were either his friends or people whose opinions he didn't particularly care about.

"This . . . this is not the natural state of a person. Ugh . . . this . . . no, this is not for me. Very, very not for me." The ship had broken free of the atmosphere and cut its escape thrust just a few minutes before, and Liam felt as though all his internal organs were fighting over where they wanted to end up inside his body.

Khadi couldn't help the impulse to snicker, since he seemed like such a 'tough guy' but he wasn't looking so tough now.

"Here." She handed him a bottle with a spout. "Drink some of this. It's peppermint water with a bit of anti-nausea. Unless you want the risk of throwing something up and then possibly getting hit in the face with it."

Liam was a proud man most of the time, but he certainly wasn't proud enough to refuse something that might help. He took the spout and took a few awkward sips, some of the moisture spilling out onto his face and just . . . staying there. His attempts to wipe it off afterward were almost as hilarious as his near-vomiting, but eventually it soaked into his jumpsuit. "Thanks, that actually does help." He groaned again as he handed it back to her, since it still felt incredibly disorienting to have absolutely no handle on the world. "I'll bet all of you had a blast with this when you were kids. You got zero-g kid parks and shit like that?"

"Yes, they exist. But most kids don't get to just . . . play. At least not on Three." Khadi had seen how the kids played on Earth, how they had responsibilities, but they were also expected to run wild. "Most people are raised to be focused on something. Which is why the party life as adults is much larger than kid parks." She took a drink of the peppermint water herself and held it between them in case he wanted more. "Orion trained to be a pilot from childhood."

"Childhood like what, twelve? Thirteen?" He remembered other children that age starting to get the 'It's time to start getting serious about life' talk from their parents. Obviously his own situation had been a little different, since he'd had no parents by that time.

"Actually, I think Orion was six. Since our brother Ahmed was ahead of him in the programs too." She leaned her head back into the chair she was strapped into so her head wouldn't jostle so much. "My parents had me in fashion before I could even walk. It's just how things go."

The look of mildly-horrified confusion on Liam's face wasn't the first she'd seen when discussing her professional life with people from Earth. "Before you could even walk? That's . . . and you never felt, I don't know, trapped in it? Getting stuck without options like that would fucking kill me."

"Trapped? Oh, sometimes, I suppose. When I was a teenager. I didn't want to have to adhere to a strict diet or curfews, or work ridiculously long hours. But that's the business." Not that it mattered anymore. She wasn't in the business. She wasn't anything anymore. Except a rebel. "I didn't know any different, really."

"So what about now?" They still had several hours before they would reach their destination on Three, and Liam felt a little better while talking than he did when left alone with his thoughts and the incredibly unsettling feeling of being completely weightless. "Any plans for what you want to be if you grow up?"

Khadi laughed before she took a deep breath and sighed. "Alive?" She said softly as she closed her eyes. "Is that too morbid to say out loud? I'm no good for much on Earth, so I guess I would have to start over with something. If we manage to survive."

"Alive is good. Good prerequisite for most jobs that I know of. If there's such a thing as a corpse modeling industry, I'm sure you'd be great at it, but yeah, best to stay on this side of a gravestone." He took a few deep breaths and tentatively moved himself around the small area, just to see if he could get a feel for being weightless. "If you were working for that long, you'd have to know pretty much everything there is to know about the business, though, right? Making the clothes, getting them from one place to another, how to deal with fabric, how to network with people, how to manage schedules, photography, all the moving parts, right?"

"A basic knowledge, sure. And yes, I can make clothes, but I'm not a designer." She opened her eyes and watched him bounce around a little, but she stayed in her seat. It wasn't a new experience for her, after all. "Actually, I thought about bartending. Do you have much use for a bartender on Earth?"

"Yeah, of course." He laughed, since it seemed like such a ridiculous question. "Earth invented bartenders, not orbit." He gave her a teasing glare that normally pissed her off, but they were having a decently friendly conversation, for once. "You usually find them either in big cities or attached to really fucking rich households. There's actually a small suite set aside for one in the manor back home. Not that I think it ever got occupied by one, but it's there. You just have to have a place with enough people close enough together to need a place to get out and drink. Little hard to find that in the midwest."

"Huh. Well, I'm not going to go running off to the big city by myself. I can't do that to my parents or my sister-in-law. They deserve a quiet life after all of this." She thought briefly about her family and she hoped they were still okay. "Ahmed dying was hard enough. Now with Orion . . . it's just . . . hard."

Liam nodded, since he understood about things being hard. He hadn't lost his brother or sister yet, but with some of the batshit crazy ideas Logan had in mind, it felt like he was possibly about to do just that. "I didn't really know your brother that well, but everybody who did has nothing but good things to say about the guy, even before what happened in the mountains. Seems like every family is impacted these days. Doesn't make it any easier on anybody."

He hadn't imagined that years later, he would be capable of missing his parents, but he was. He wondered sometimes if he missed them even more than Logan ever had, just because he had never needed to become them the way Logan did. "If any of this works, and we manage to pull all this off, then you and the rest of your family will have your pick of where to relocate. Maybe even back to Three if you feel like it."

"I don't know. Too much has changed." Khadi took another sip of the water and took a deep breath and sighed it out. "My parents will want to harass me again about settling down and getting married. They said I need a family to settle my wild ways."

That got an outright laugh from Liam as he took the bottle from her and took another sip. "Yeah . . . that shtick sounds familiar. But what do you mean, 'again?' Were you married and settled down before and it just didn't stick?"

He had a nice laugh. She hated that she noticed his nice laugh. And his . . . no, she wasn't thinking about it. He had like ten wives already. "I was matched before. Never officially married. We had great sex, but I hated him otherwise. He was such an idiot, and so possessive, I felt like he was suffocating me a lot of the time. I spent a lot of time sleeping on Orion's couch."

"That sucks. Suffocating is never a good thing. Unless you're into it, and even then, it's usually only fun until you get off, and then the hand around the throat just isn't hot anymore." He shrugged and took another quick sip before he floated the beverage back over to her. "So what broke it off? Did it just end when he went to pull you off Three, or was it over before that?"

"Eventually he got tired of being blown off whenever he wanted to talk about marriage. He said he was looking at rings one day, and I told him I had no intention of getting married. He got mad, we yelled a lot, had some angry sex and then he moved out the next day." She shrugged and sighed again. "I do miss the sex. So . . . do you use the Match program on Earth too? I could use a new match."

He laughed once and watched her eyes, his expression slowly dropping. "No. That's . . . no. We don't. At least not in the midwest. Do you seriously not know anything about how relationships work on Earth? How . . . I don't know, *ninety percent* of the human race works?"

"Why should I know how things go on Earth? I never went to Earth until everything fell apart. I never intended to go to Earth. You can't be mad at me for not caring to know about something that didn't apply to my life at all." She glared at him and crossed her arms. "So then how do you know who you are compatible with? There are a lot of areas to cover. Attraction. Intelligence. Hobbies. Sexual preference, obviously. Education. Religious beliefs. Family, no family . . ."

"Wow. If I had that checklist running through my head, I'd need a computer to help me keep it straight too." He stopped trying to maneuver in the zero-g and strapped himself back down in his chair, since that gave at least a comforting illusion of pressure and a kind of gravity.

"I'll . . . let me put it to you this way. Logan and I knew a lot of our parents' friends growing up. We heard about them as grownups basically through their friends." He hadn't had to talk about his parents in a long time, but he was almost shocked at how little it bothered him. So much had been going on with his own life that he was just grateful to know as much about them as he did.

"My dad slept with somewhere between forty and fifty different women before he married my mom. My mom slept with almost that many guys. And even then, she only married my dad after Doc Weber had done a DNA test to confirm that he was the one who had knocked her up with our older brother. And they got married when they were about nineteen years old."

He could tell that none of what he'd said made sense to Khadijah, so he went on. "It meant my parents could have children together and they liked each other enough to try. James died when he could barely walk and talk, but Mom was already pregnant with me and Logan by then. Larissa wasn't that far behind the two of us. People only live until they're fifty, *maybe*. We don't waste a lot of time with the maybes. If you want a family, you get to work trying to make one until you find somebody you work with. And you go from there."

"But what if you don't want to think about children for a while? I mean, isn't birth control illegal? What if you just want to date and have great sex?" Khadi countered, since the m-word was not on her radar.

"Then you either make sure you get a girl who pays really close attention to when she can fuck you and when she shouldn't, or you prepare yourself to be around for her if the timing is more right than you wanted it to be." Liam had done his fair share of trying to get around that particular system, just like most people did on Earth, but his situation had ended . . . strangely, to say the least.

"If the whole world did as they wanted to, it would be a world full of people like me and Logan, who didn't know their parents past the age of ten because they were too busy dying in the most horrifying way imaginable. If you want to see your kids grow up and turn into people, you pop those kids out as fast as possible. Time is a luxury for us, and even rich sons of bitches like me and Logan can't afford to wait."

"Hopefully it won't always be that way." Khadi replied as she looked over at Liam. "I'm sorry about your parents. I kinda figured they were . . . gone, but losing them at the age of ten is pretty damn sad."

"There's a lot sadder in the world than mine. A lot better too, but a lot sadder." He nodded back over to her in confusion. "You're really gonna put your name back through a computer after it gave you a guy the first time who was no good except on his back?"

"Why not?" Khadi asked in confusion, since even though she'd had a bad experience once, she had a lot of faith in the system. It gave Orion trouble too, but the opposite kind. He had two women matched to him that he fell in love with. "How else am I going to meet someone if I'm going back to Earth? I see you more than most other people every day. And you're the only one that seems to crack a smile, even though you annoy the shit out of me most of the time."

"I thought you said I annoyed the shit out of you *all* the time. Is there some patch of time where I've been slacking on the job? Because if there is, it wasn't intentional." He teased with a quiet smile, but then he looked around at the rest of the passengers accompanying them to the station. "Earth people usually have a lot more fun. The whole rebel cause has kinda fucked with people's party-planning mentality.

"Do a lot of people have relationships like yours? I mean, with multiple spouses and everything? We don't really do that up in orbit." She looked truly intrigued instead of judgmental in any way. "It would be nice, I can see the benefits to it. It isn't two people together against the world, but more like a team. And hell, help with children, that's a definite perk. I suck with babies. I try so hard, and yet they always like to throw up, pee, or poop all over me. It's really rude."

"Babies shit on everyone. You're not special." The image of a baby doing some kind of mischief on the obsessively put-together woman in front of him was entertaining, and his grin showed it. "But yeah, there's a fair amount like ours around. Some go the other way, too, one woman with a few husbands. I haven't seen too many like that. The one I know best is Diego. Dated two women, then ended up marrying not just the two he dated but both their sisters too, when their own husbands died in the attacks after Nine. Son of a bitch stays busy."

"Clearly." She said with a shake of the head. "I wonder what convinces women to do it otherwise. I mean, are you just *that* good? I don't know if I believe that you are."

"You mean, you haven't heard the incredible story of the orgy at which all of my wives proclaimed their undying love for me mid-climax for all the town to hear?" He took the drink back from her with a sip. "I thought for sure that story would've gotten around to you by now."

"That did not happen." She argued as she grabbed the water back from him after he took a sip. Apparently the battle of egos had boiled down to a water bottle. "If that story is circulating, you most undoubtedly were the one to start it."

"Was I?" His grin was either incredible self-confidence or legitimate amusement that she hadn't heard it. Or both. "I was dating three women at the same time. Having fun, like you said. One was local, the other two were from out of town, and stayed because of me, for slightly different reasons. Pretty sure my dick was on the list of convincing factors, even if it wasn't the only thing on the list. Anyway, then Logan decided to go off to the Initiative and he decided I needed to get strapped down and serious about life, so he went and got all three of them to agree to marry me. What was I gonna say, no?"

"A *sane* man would have said no." She replied with a laugh as she drank another sip. Was she just drinking from it to keep it from him, or was she drinking from it because he had? She didn't need the calming effects like he did. "I know all too well how catty women can be. I spent my life around too many women, half of them hooking up with each other and causing drama because Stacy kissed Debra who slept with Megan . . ." Khadi just shook her head. "And then mix the men in that mess? God. You, in a house with three women, you're insane. Especially if they're all on the same cycle schedule. Then they all hate you at once."

"I call it Red Week." He smiled and leaned back in the chair and turned to prop his feet up, even though gravity wasn't exactly holding them in place. "When I'm by myself, I do, anyway. And there's more than one room between me and anybody else. And I do it in my head. Never out loud. I'm not a complete idiot." He shrugged, looking . . . oddly wistful.

She hadn't really seen him around his wives, hadn't met them herself during the chaos in the mountains. All she'd ever seen were pictures that he kept with him and pictures of Gwen, who he was trying to rescue.

"They get along fine, for the most part. Everything has its ups and downs. They've got their strengths, just like I do. Rachel has always been in charge of anything that's even remotely related to numbers. She keeps things running smoothly and doesn't actually mind being pregnant as much as the others did. Bree keeps things fun, not just for me but for all of us, and for the kids. Anybody starts taking themselves too seriously and she'll be there to knock the wind out of you and take you down a few pegs. And Gwen loves the babies. They all do, but she's the best with them. She takes care of people, especially little ones. Sees what they need, makes sure to get it to them. Me, I just grow crops and fight with farming machinery all day long. Out of all of us, I got the easy job."

"That, and fuck like a god, according to you." She replied with a smirk before she held out the water like a peace offering. "You sound like you have a good group of women. And I can tell that you love them. I guess that's all that really matters in the end."

"I figured I had already covered the fucking like a god part. Didn't want to brag." He shrugged in mock humility and finished what was left of the water. "This stuff actually really does help. Is there any more? Or is this just a prank on the Earth-born guy and I'm gonna start shitting out breath mints or something later on?"

"It's not a prank. I'm not that evil." She nodded toward a small refrigeration unit and unbuckled herself to push across to get another water. Khadi sailed across the shuttle with ease, landed exactly where she wanted to, and made it all look not just easy, but smooth. She grabbed another one for him and pushed off and grabbed onto his seat to stop herself, putting her squarely in front of him. "Here you go."

He took the drink but clearly he was watching her instead of what she was bringing with her. "Show-off." He looked up at her hair specifically, curling around her face in a way that he almost wished he had a camera to capture. He was sure she was trained for that. "I've seen some of your zero-g photo shoots. Kind of impressive how you get . . . you know . . ." he waved his free hand vaguely along where her body was, without actually touching her, "everything *exactly* where it should be going for the lens. That take a lot of practice? Gyrating with no Gs?"

"You've seen some of my photos?" She asked curiously as she stared him down. He looked uncomfortable. It was funny. Mostly.

"I thought you didn't know anything about my career?" She had the same dark eyes Orion had, and they demanded the same kind of attention Orion's did. "I'm flexible. I can make this," she waved a hand around her own body, "do whatever I need it to do."

He was definitely rendered uncomfortable by that, but it was far from the first time he'd been so close to a gorgeous woman. She was, however, easily the strangest woman he'd ever been around, or at least the most foreign. It only added to his . . . discomfort.

"I . . . believe that. I, um, I looked up your photos once we knew we were going to leave on this trip together. Just wanted to see a little about where you were coming from." He was a little wide-eyed as he thought back over them, and his eyes ran over her the way a man's eyes inevitably did whenever she got close. He might have been multiple-married, but he was still very, very human. "I think my favorite was the, um, the sunrise/sunset one? There was a lot of blue and black body paint involved and it looked like you were about halfway through a backflip. Your hair was doing . . . kind of the same thing it's doing now."

She was both confident in her body and mildly obsessive and self-conscious all the time. Khadi reached up to feel whatever her hair was doing, and her gaze went up, as if she could see her own hair. "It turned out really pretty." She replied without actually looking at him. "I had to get the same pose twice, which was hard. They took one picture at sunrise and another at sunset. They could have superimposed me, but they wanted authenticity."

"Pretty rare thing to find these days, even outside of the fashion business." He thought back to the pose she had held, and continued to be impressed, but also realized it was in his best interests to steer the topic in a direction that didn't have anything to do with what she could or could not do with the exceptional body in front of him. "So how did your parents get you into modeling before you could even walk? Is there a scientific test for babies who will one day be hot people?"

Khadi snickered and pulled back and away from being directly in front of him, since she didn't want to make him uncomfortable. However, he was the one who went looking for her pictures. "I was a cute baby. I have dimples that were more pronounced then, and between the hair, eyes, and my skin color . . . I was a fashion baby. A lot of the models now are genetically engineered."

"Kinda makes it unfair for anybody else trying to break into the industry." He looked her up and down as hundreds of men had before, but when Liam did it, it was slightly different than she was accustomed to. In orbit, men took one look at her, knew she was a model, and immediately started looking her up and down for any kind of imperfection. Anything to take her down off the pedestal she had been placed on by orbital society and their genetic expectations. When other Earth-born looked her over in the months she'd spent on the ground, it was as something outside their comfort zone and completely foreign. She was an Orbital, and that was enough to make them look at her as if they were wondering what kind of strangeness she might have been hiding under her skirt.

When Liam looked at her, though, all she saw was a man looking at a woman and enjoying what he saw. "Anybody competing against you for a modeling job would be like me going up against one of the Montgomeries in a quantum physics competition. That shit just ain't gonna happen."

She just laughed at that. "Oh, so you think I'm pretty now? Now that we're having an actual conversation and you're not biting my head off?" Khadi shook her head and glared at him, like usual, except her glare was more playful this time. "Also, obviously you know how to compliment a woman, you scored three of them. I know I'm pretty. Tell me something else. Like, I think you're extremely stubborn, but I think it's a virtue. Or . . . I've never seen anyone pull off facial hair like you do."

"Not seeing any facial hair from here. If you're rocking it, you're hiding it well. And I think stubbornness *can* be a virtue, but I'm not sure about whether that's the case with you or not. Get back to me after we've had a few more actual conversations." He considered her for a minute, since it was the first time a woman had told him point-blank not to compliment her appearance. In her case, it made sense. "I do appreciate a woman with balls, though. Your figurative stones are enormous, taking us back up here and working with us to make contact. I respect that. Gotta make it tough to walk sometimes, though."

"I can strut just fine, thank you very much." She said with a grin but it faded quickly as she thought about her reason why. "A lot of my confidence is just bravado. But I wanted to do *something*. Orion did so many things, and your cause seemed better than most. You want to find wife number three. True love. That's a good reason for anything. I hope someone would travel the universe for me someday."

"Well, it's possible we'll get to Three here in a little while and find out your match has had a change of heart and wants to try not to be an asshole." Liam shrugged. "People can change."

"I *might* believe that long enough to scratch an itch, but not any longer than that. I don't want him. I want someone better than that." She looked at Liam and smirked. "And he didn't have a beard, and you're kinda changing my mind about men and beards. It's a rugged look. Not many men in Orbit have facial hair."

"What, they genetically engineer that out too? Or do the men in orbit just prefer . . . not to look like men?"

"They look like men." She said with a smack to his arm. "They just look different than Earth men. It's called a *preference*." Khadi shook her head. "You're judgy. Do I not look like a woman because I look different from Earth women? Because I can prove that my tits are real."

"I am judgy, you're right." He didn't seem to mind that fact, and looked down at the jumpsuit she was wearing for flight. She had complained about it earlier, but it was what it was. "It's possible, and I'm not admitting guilt here, it's *possible* that the thought might have crossed my mind that they're not. You guys in space get all kinds of implants and enhancements. Tits would be far from the strangest thing to apply some artificiality to."

"Excuse you!" Khadi said loudly, clearly affronted. "The only thing that is enhanced about this body is the genetic code." She was already unzipping her suit, even though she knew it was wildly inappropriate to do so, but what did he think she had, metal cones for tits? "I'm not a goddamn alien, you know. I don't have robotic parts, I have real, working parts."

"Really? Not a single gear or motor in there anywhere? I'm a little disappointed. Just a little." All of those headed up to Three with them were scattered throughout the cargo wherever they could find a seat. There were a few others near him and Khadi at the beginning of the flight, but they had moved away in the event that Liam actually did throw up. They were tucked in between crates that were tied down four different ways to keep them from shifting mid-flight, with several other people near enough to hear, but nobody immediately visible from either of their seats. "Bionic arm? X-ray vision? Nothing?"

"Seriously? What the hell is a model going to do with a bionic arm or x-ray vision? What do you read down there for information? Comic books?" Khadi had her jumpsuit open to her navel and she pulled off her shirt underneath. Clearly she didn't care about taking off her clothes in front of everyone else.

She had a black bra underneath, though it wasn't nearly as fancy as he might have guessed. "They're real." She showed him, but then realized he might think she was surgically enhanced. "There are no scars from any magical surgeries." She lifted up the sides of her bra to show just about every part of her breasts except her nipple. "I'm just a normal woman. Ish."

"Heavy on the 'ish,' I think." He unbuckled himself and floated across the space between them to inspect them himself, since if the surgeon was good, he knew the scars wouldn't be visible from anything but up close. He put his hands on the arms of her chair and leaned in as she showcased herself. "Nothing on the side, nothing on the other . . ." he spun himself in mid-air so that he was upside down with his legs on the ceiling of the narrow cargo compartment, and so that he could get a better look at the underside of her chest as she proved her point. "Alright, no scars, but what's that tucked under Lefty? Is that a tattoo?"

"Lefty? Don't name my boobs. God, that is SUCH a man thing. It's the left breast. Lefty. Really." Khadi rolled her eyes and exposed her breast a little more. "Yes, it's a tiny little tattoo of a butterfly because technically under contract I wasn't allowed to mark up my body. Or pierce it. But I didn't think they would notice if it was black and tiny."

He twisted himself to get a better look, and gave her an appraising nod. "Nice. Though still weird you had some kind of lifelong contract that told you what you can and can't do with your body." He spun back to be right-side-up again, but didn't move back to his own seat immediately. He was going to get the hang of zero gravity if it killed him. He didn't want to be caught in it and be completely helpless. "Nobody's ever made me sign on a dotted line to say what I can and can't do with my own skin, but I've just never had the inclination. Now I want to get Melissa to do some work for me, but I just haven't figured out what yet."

"I didn't sign any lines, but that was how I was raised. I didn't really know any different." She shrugged and put her arms back into the sleeves of her jumpsuit, but she didn't zip it up and she didn't go after her shirt. It was a little more comfortable this way. "Do you want some help with how to float properly?"

"Oh what, now you're gonna tell me I'm floating wrong?" He

was still spinning a little in mid-air, but he corrected himself every time he came up against a surface, even if that surface was her knee.

Khadi grabbed him by the shoulders and straightened him out. "You're putting way too much force into it. Didn't anyone teach you about light touches and finesse?" She smirked and pointed at a spot by the refrigeration system and she pushed him toward it with just enough force to get him there without him slamming his face into a wall. "Don't wiggle or move so much. Just focus on the force and be aware of your surroundings."

He stayed mostly still on the way there, but he couldn't help trying to flip himself around to land on his feet along the way. It ended with him just hitting his shoulder on the wall and laughing, since clearly he was terrible at following instructions. "Focusing on the force. Not so great at the whole 'being aware of my surroundings' thing." He looked back at her, since his attention was clearly more on her than on his own movements. "It's like swimming, but with less chance of drowning and more of a chance of concussion."

"I guess you could say that." Khadi replied with a slow nod, since she hadn't really made the comparison before. "You'll get the hang of it. Maybe. Though I wouldn't try to have sex until you figure it out. Otherwise you're going to stick yourself in some really interesting places."

"Is that a specialty of yours? Zero gravity sex?" He took a hold of part of the unit next to him, bracing himself in a few different positions to see what might work best. "Man, that . . . I hadn't even thought about what that would be like. Lower-gravity would be nice, you get to really throw somebody around that way, but when you could send somebody across the room with just one smack to the ass, it'd be hard to really get the leverage you need."

"It's fun." Khadi said with a grin. "It's *messy*, but it's so fun. You can say that someone is bendy on Earth, but NO one is bendy like they are up here. Holy shit, it's fun." She looked him up and down before she let out a deep sigh. "We have got to stop talking about this, or else I'm going to have noisy, vivid dreams about a lumberjack Earth-man."

"Lumberjack? Nobody does that anymore. But I do have a couple flannel shirts if that helps you with your visuals." He pushed himself across the space, still a little too forcefully, but he was getting better every time he tried. "How do your dreams get noisy, exactly? Are you a screamer even in your sleep, or are things just noisy inside your subconscious?"

"I'm a talker. And everything else that goes with it." Khadi started to finally zip up the jumpsuit. "I have a vivid imagination. It's not a crime."

"I don't see anybody pressing charges." She saw him watch her zipper as it traveled back up over her chest, as he took a last look at the rest of her before she was out of sight again. He moved back to his own chair, but kept his eyes on her for the most part. "I'm more of a listener than a talker. Comes in handy."

"And here I thought you were a doer." She moved back to her seat and started to strap herself back in. "So, um, in your . . . relationships, do you spend time with only your wives or what?"

"That's, um . . . that's a little complicated." He wasn't sure if she was a tease with her questions and her stripping in front of him, or if she was just that comfortable with herself. He was thinking it was a little bit of both. "When we started this, the three of them and me, it was . . . well, one of my wives from back then is no longer part of the family. She decided this life wasn't for her. I met Gwen when Margo started feeling like she needed to leave, and that . . . yeah, that was complicated. The point is, with Rachel and Bree, and Gwen, it's always been understood that what's important is the family. I'm not gonna do anything to hurt my family or to hurt any of them, but families change. We decided to embrace that possibility instead of trying to fight any kind of change for any reason."

"Makes sense." Khadi replied vaguely before she glanced over at him again. "Sorry, I shouldn't be so nosy. I was just curious how it worked."

"You can be nosy. I'm a pretty open person." He got back into his seat and strapped in, since it was much easier than fighting a lack of gravity. "Don't have much choice about that, really. Three wives, soon to be four kids . . . Everything I've got is out in the open at all times and always will be. Nose away."

"Four kids, huh? How many are you trying to get?" She asked softly next to him.

"Started at the top of the alphabet. Just working my way down. Anders, Beckett, Chrissy, and in a few months, Dakota. Bree's just getting into her third trimester, I think." It had been too long since he saw his wives, and even being able to talk to them from the rebel headquarters in Bogota wasn't anywhere near enough.

"I wouldn't have started the alphabet if I didn't have the ambition to finish it. Bree said she had a breeze through Anders, and she's had a little more discomfort with Dax, but she says she's still planning on seven. Rachel's probably not gonna go quite that high. Haven't even had the chance to have that conversation with Gwen yet, but as much as she loves kids, I wouldn't be surprised if she was the one to want to go for double digits."

"Dear gods. You *are* ambitious aren't you? Twenty-six kids? You're insane. So insane. That's . . . what is wrong with you?" She asked with a laugh.

"Hey, I was raised to know we've got a world to repopulate. I mean to do my part." He meant that, but there was something more serious behind his answer as well. "I also love my kids. Having the first batch was just, you know, you want to make sure things get started and you've got a family to watch get older, but I like 'em. Probably because I'm not stuck with them twenty-four hours a day every single day, I'm told that helps with liking your own kids, but neither are any of their mothers."

"Like I said, a smart way to raise those little poop machines." Her gaze raked over him again. She hated that she was paying closer attention to him. It was easier to be annoyed. Maybe . . . Khadi leaned closer and dropped her voice to a whisper. "You know, both of us are suffering a dry spell. I won't tell if you won't. I'm not interested in fucking up anyone's life."

He clearly didn't say no right away, and leaned in closer to her in turn. "That depends. The rooms you got us to check into on Three . . . do they have gravity?"

Khadi was stunned into silence. "Are you saying yes, Lumberjack?"

"Well, I *thought* I was asking if they had gravity in the units you got for us, but I'm mostly asking that because when I fuck you, I'd rather not be flopping around like a first-timer." Everything about him sounded both casual and practical, but the way his grey eyes raked over her had much more to it than mere practicality. "But if there's no gravity and I have to let you be the one to show me how it's done, that's not a problem. Just curious."

When did this switch happen? When did she realize that she wanted a piece of him, and when did he realize it too? Khadi was blaming it squarely on her lack of interaction with the male sex in far too long. She opened her mouth to speak several times, but it was hard to think about what to say. "They have gravity, but it's not like Earth gravity. You still bounce more than you would down there."

"I don't really think extra bouncing is gonna be a downside, do you?" He wasn't making any move to touch her, but their seats were right next to each other, so if he wanted to, he wouldn't have to go far. "We've gotta get through the docks and decontamination, then make sure our passes get us into the residential sector, then we'll have some down time while we wait to make sure our cover story holds up. I like the sound of some down time, if you ask me." He looked down at her again, since he clearly had some ideas of how to spend the time.

"Seriously. You're just ON, aren't you?" Her cheeks burned with the idea of actually having sex. She desperately wanted sex. "I'm a little worried your bragging is just all talk."

"Fine. Be worried." He shrugged with a grin, moving as if to lean back in his seat, except the action was completely meaningless in zero gravity, so it ended up just looking awkward. "The more you think I'm just full of shit coming in, the better it's gonna be for me when you admit you were wrong." He glanced down at the zipper of her jumpsuit again. "Plus, you're the one who said your body can do whatever you want it to. I'm not the only braggy one here, thank you."

"Says the man who said he gave three women an orgasm at the same time. Which one is more believable, a bendy body or a triple-woman-orgasm?" She gave him another one of her glares, since it was the thing she did the most when Liam was around. "Just for further clarification, are you agreeing because it's me, or are you agreeing because your balls might shrivel up and fall off if you don't get laid?"

"First of all, you can't ask the question and then question the answer because it's the one you wanted. That doesn't make a whole lot of sense." The laugh he gave said he didn't mind, even if he was calling her on it. "Second, no, I'm not just interested because I'm seeing the world in shades of blue right now. I'm agreeing because you're not as insufferable and bitchy a human being as I thought you were.

"Also because every one of my wives talked about you back on Earth, at one point or another. Gwen told me about you after that one time you helped out in the nursery on a shift, because she said it was hilarious watching you try to change a little boy's diaper without getting pissed on. Apparently you're not much good at that. Rachel mentioned you after you jumped in on the middle of the textiles workshop and started giving orders about something, I forget what it was now. She said she appreciated a good bossy bitch when she saw one. And Bree . . . well, I'm pretty sure Bree was hot for you, but once you get to know Bree, that won't surprise you much."

"You kept all these details until *now*?" Khadi narrowed her eyes at him and shook her head. "You made it seem like you thought I was an idiot. Now you're telling me that your wives actually talked kindly about me at one point. And one is hot for me?" She jabbed at his arm with her long finger since he deserved it. "You. Are. An. Ass."

"I am. I really am." More facts about himself he didn't seem bothered by. "And I never thought you were an idiot, I just thought you were a bitch. I still do, it's just good to see the more useful sides of what you do with being as bitchy as you are. Women like you tend to be the ones who make the world go around and get shit done."

"Damn right I get shit done. Exhibit A." She motioned her arm to the rest of the shuttle where they were headed toward Three as he spoke. "But I'm not a bitch all of the time. I'm just motivated and bossy. That does not make a bitch." She kept her hand on his side and she slid a little closer to him in her seat. "Maybe we should have a trial of skill first. If you're a shitty kisser, then the whole thing is off." She almost wondered if he would hit a point where she had pushed too far, since they had quickly gone from enemies to flirting in one shuttle ride. Clearly she had the hots for him and had lied to herself about it.

"Really? A trial of skill?" He reached down to the harness buckle in front of her stomach and undid the latch to set her free of her seat. Once the straps were loose, he took a handful of the front of her jumpsuit and pulled her around the armrest between them and into his lap, though there wasn't much room in the seat to begin with. "You think I got four different women to agree to marry me at various times by being a shitty kisser? Really? That'd be a hell of a lot of luck or coincidence on my side."

"Well, you're attractive. And you said you were rich. How do I know if you're skilled or not?" She didn't want to insult him, but she did want him to prove her wrong. She *really* wanted him to be a good kisser.

He looked up into her eyes as he grinned under the challenge, but when he finally kissed her, he didn't just kiss her. Once she was settled into his lap and holding onto him, one of his huge hands moved up to brush a rough caress over her cheek and down to her neck. He held her as he drew her lips down to his, and his other arm tightened around her waist to press the rest of her against him as he captured her completely. His beard wasn't as rough or scratchy as it had looked like it would be, but it was definitely something that set the kiss apart from any other man she'd ever been with. The man she was pressing against was, however, rougher and harder than the rest of her sexual history, and a great deal stronger.

Khadi let him lead the kiss until she was completely drawn into it and she felt a *need* to kiss him back. He could hear little moans that caught in her throat as they kissed, and the knees of her endless legs pressed into his hips, since she couldn't wrap her legs around him. She was his height almost exactly, which lined everything up just a little too perfectly. One of her hands came up to tug on his beard as they kissed, since she really did like the sensation of kissing a bearded man.

He grinned under the touch, and his hands moved down over the rest of her torso as the jumpsuit would allow. It was made of thick fabric that was designed to protect them in the event of debris unexpectedly flying around a ship in transit, so they didn't permit much by way of sensation. "I'm glad you like the beard." His hands weren't shy, especially since he wasn't really touching her in the first place.

"Very much like the beard." She breathlessly responded with a groan as she held herself back from kissing him again. "I think I need to make sure it wasn't because I've been deprived. I need another trial kiss."

"How long have you been deprived, exactly?" He pulled her into another, slightly less fiery kiss, but the embrace kept deepening as they spoke. "I feel like I need to know exactly what kind of wound-up I'm getting into, here."

"Almost a year." She responded between kisses, since she was getting really worked up. "A really fucking long year."

"Holy shit." He looked her up and down as if seeing her as a new creature for the first time. "I'm amazed it took you this long to assault somebody. You don't strike me as the type who's built for celibacy." Certainly not from the way she was kissing him. He knew a girl in need when he felt her grinding herself against him relentlessly. Not that he was complaining.

"The world has been going to shit." She replied by way of explanation, but for some reason, she couldn't stop kissing him once she started. "Now I'm an enemy of the Consortium, and before they were paying my paychecks. I didn't need to worry about a boyfriend." She paused in her kisses to explain quickly. "Not that I'm looking for one now. Especially since you already have three wives. Or two and a fiancee. Whatever."

"Relax. You're not scaring me." He pulled her in for another kiss, and shifted beneath her to get the jumpsuit a little more comfortable. It was a hopeless cause, since the jumpsuit just wasn't built for a man to have a woman like Khadijah on top of him.

"There's a lot of people who've been putting a lot of things on hold because the world is going to shit. I decided while Logan was up on Nine not to let that be me. Somebody gives me the option of either watching paint dry and pissing myself while the world burns or fucking my way through the apocalypse, I'm gonna be the bastard whose wives are screaming and satisfied while it all falls down. Just my preferred way of doing things."

That made Khadi smile and she laughed a little against his lips. "That sounds like a hell of a way to go." She grabbed at the zipper of his jumpsuit and started pulling it down slowly. She just wanted to look. Just a little. "I'm not going to put on a show, even though I would say that we already have. I just want a peek." She chewed on her bottom lip but decided to taste along his skin as she kissed along his neck. "I might be bossy, but you sound like an asshole yourself."

He let her do and peek as she liked, and moved his hands down to her thighs so she could push back the jumpsuit to get a look at him. "That doesn't stop with me. You thought I was an asshole when you met me because most of the time, I am. The days of me shoving you around aren't gonna stop once I've shoved you down on a bed."

"What if I don't like it rough?" She challenged again as she pushed on his shoulder, though it was pushing on a solid mass of muscle. "You might break me. You're a lot stronger than any other man I've been with."

"Well that sounds like a risk you're looking forward to." He wasn't going to apologize for his physical condition, but she certainly didn't feel weak under his hands. "I'm not gonna make any promises about how controlled I'm gonna be in lower gravity, though. Just keep those legs around me tight, otherwise I might slam you into the ceiling without really trying."

"Do you have a hard time keeping it all straight? What one woman likes versus another?" She nipped at his skin with her teeth before she leaned back enough to look into his eyes. He really was incredibly attractive. Damn him for being so challenging *and* attractive. If Orion knew that she slept with Logan's twin, he would be so mad.

"Not really." He was as consummately casual as Logan was brooding and angry, and the contrast kept on getting stranger to witness, since she'd had more interaction with Logan than with Liam prior to their mission to Three. "I like something different with all of them too, so no, it's pretty easy to keep things straight. Some of them like getting woken up in the middle of the night, some would kill me for trying. Some of them like their hair pulled, some of them I very rarely sleep with any way but face to face. Some are more private, some would . . . probably let me fuck them on worldwide television and get off on the exposure. There's a range. I prefer it that way, honestly. If all of them liked it the same way, then I might have trouble getting them mixed up."

He unzipped her own suit a little just to have her slightly more exposed, though he wasn't going to put her on display again in the middle of the cargo bay. "Even a polygamist gets in trouble if he yells out the wrong name in bed."

That made her laugh again before she went back to kissing him, since it was too fun to stop. "So, you're a good kisser." She confessed when their lips parted again. "I still don't believe the 3-woman orgasm thing. That's a blatant lie. No man's dick is that magical."

"It's true, it just wasn't with my wives. Not with *all* of my wives." He corrected quickly. "Bree had a girlfriend when I met her, and they liked a challenge. I got in on things, and her girlfriend invited another girl, it was during a pretty hard party phase for me. Had one of them riding me, had the other two one in each hand. That was a fucking lot of work." He shook his head at the memory, since it was not something he was ever going to try again. "After that, Bree took more of an interest in me and her girlfriend ran off with the fourth wheel, so it all worked out pretty great, if you ask me."

She laughed again. "Okay, I'll believe it when she tells the story. So one of your wives is bisexual, then? Married a man . . . and has girlfriends on the side?"

"She's just . . . sexual. Two of them are, though I don't think Gwen would have stuck with a girlfriend by preference. Bree is just . . . if there had been any kind of sentient and fuckable life form on Eleusis when we got there, it would've been competition for Bree's affections. She likes it every way she can get it." He smiled at the resonant quality of her voice, and pulled her back up into a lingering kiss. "I like your laugh."

Since the compliment wasn't about her appearance, it surprised her, but she smiled afterward. "I'm glad you like my laugh. I like your smirk." She poked at his cheek playfully. "Though you don't have dimples like I do."

"Well, we can't all be genetically engineered supermodels." His hands found their way around to her ass in the next kiss, and he found himself appreciating the fact that she was tall enough to tower over him while she was in his lap. Bree was the tallest of his wives, but even she had never forced his head back while she had her way with him. "The last guy you were with, was it your clean-shaven, psycho-possessive idiot match?"

She nodded as she looked down at him with her hair falling around her face. Khadi appreciated that she made him lean his head back, she loved it when she actually saw an attractive man that was at least her height. "You make him sound crazy. But like I said, he was great in bed."

"Just wanted to make sure it wasn't some lousy lay I was competing against. When I set you on fire later I want you to be sure it's not just because your standards got lowered somewhere along the way." His confidence was every bit as constant as his casual tone, but she could see in the grey of his eyes that he fully intended to do as he said.

Khadi raised an eyebrow as she looked into his eyes. "We'll see." She refuted before she kissed him again and slid her hand inside the opening of his jumpsuit so she could slide her hand further. "I need to see what you're bragging about."

He adjusted himself in the seat to allow for her inspection, and leaned back with his arms out along the low, padded backs of the secured seats to either side of him. As she dug down into his jumpsuit and worked her way past his boxers, he let out a groan and looked up in her eyes. "Preview of coming attractions. You get me going any harder than this and the rest of this crew is gonna hear you singing my song."

"You have a song?" She snickered as she reached into his boxers to stroke him. She was being so brazen, and she loved it. It had been so long since she had touched a cock, and she missed it. "You don't need a song. It's fine without a song."

"My song is you screaming my name. You already said you were a talker." He leaned his head back and closed his eyes as they got jostled by the ship firing some thrusters to get them into position. His eyes flicked down to his crotch as she stroked him, giving another groan as his hips responded as much as the chair would permit. "So was I bragging, or am I up to your genetically-modified standards?"

"You have an impressive cock. But don't let it go to your head. Just because you have the right equipment doesn't mean you know what to do with it." She pulled her hand away as if she wasn't interested in stroking him anymore, but in truth, she didn't want to stop.

"Well I'm glad you're impressed." He gave a low growl when she took her hand away, but he didn't want to make a scene on the freighter any more than she did. "How much longer until we dock on Three again?"

"An hour or so." She reached out to tug on his beard before she leaned into him again so she could whisper into his ear. "Impatient?"

"Just as much as you are." He teased back, kissing her neck as she got close enough. "I heard that up in space, y'all are fixed until you decide it's time to start poppin' out kids. That true?"

"Doc Weber took it out." She said with a little bit of concern in her voice. "I had a tracker in my shoulder she had to take out, and she asked if I could think of anything else. I told her about the device they implanted. It was longer-lasting and more efficient than the sterilization shot. I told her I didn't know when I would see a doctor again that would know how to get it out, so she did it."

"That was fair thinking." He agreed, kissing her again to put aside the concern he'd heard from her. "I wish I could tell you I've got an on and off switch, but like you said, I'm pretty much just stuck at 'on' at all times."

"It wouldn't be the worst thing to happen in my life." She admitted, but she was hoping to wait to have a baby with someone who she was married to. "My parents would be happy, and they could help me if it happens."

"If all of us live that long." He wasn't going to pretend that a part of their immediate heat for each other was coming from the sheer danger of the situation they were about to walk into. They had every assurance from Jason they would be covered against all technological recognition while they were on Three, but things could and did go wrong with technology all the time. Still, riding the edge of danger was bound to give everyone involved a proverbial or literal hard-on, and he didn't mind being the object of Khadi's. "Look at it this way, if it does happen, then you can come at me and scream and you'll know the make-up sex afterward will be good enough to just about make it worth your while."

"I'm not going to blame you for something that would be a mutual fault. Especially because then your wives would know and I'm not going to screw up someone else's family." He was right about the possibility of dying, though, and it definitely upped the urgency for her. "Come with me." She pulled on his hand and floated away from his chair. She looked around and zipped off across the shuttle into what looked like a narrow passage that went down.

Everyone on the mission with them knew that Khadi and Liam were in charge of what was going to happen, so the two of them moving about the freighter was hardly cause for anyone to be concerned. Liam did his best to float casually as he followed her, waving at a few of their companions as he went. He didn't want anyone to get nervous. Tensions were high enough to begin with.

Khadi knew shuttle ships like the one they were on because of Orion, and she was particularly grateful for not ignoring her brother when she was looking for privacy. Khadi led him through the passage and into an open, dimly lit space that was obviously meant for cargo. They didn't have much. She grabbed his hand and kept moving past what little cargo there was and toward a door. When she opened it, a tiny trail of dim lights glowed and he could see a small bed inside. It was clearly a unit for one, but she yanked him in anyway.

"It's for long trips. Co-pilots take turns." She locked the door behind him and she moved to the bed. There were straps for arms and legs, clearly to keep someone down on the bed for resting. "How kinky are you, co-pilot?"

He looked over the straps with at least some of the same thoughts that had crossed her own twisted mind, and he shoved her down against the bed once he had braced himself with a hand on a strap, already pulling at the zipper for her jumpsuit. "I haven't found my kink line yet to know that I even have one to cross. Do your worst."

Khadi quickly got herself out of her clothes to reveal her black bra and a black thong to match. She held onto a strap as well as she helped him out of his suit. "Faster. Before you change your mind."

"You think me seeing you naked is gonna change my mind?" Maneuvering without gravity was still a very new thing for him, especially since the pilots were working to course-correct their ship to get them on par with Three, but he managed, with her help. He kissed her back against the bulkhead next to the door and down her neck, then unhooked her bra and threw it aside only for it to bounce off the wall and get tangled in one arm from his suit. He didn't care where their clothes ended up, though, since it left her bare enough that he and his beard could wreak havoc on her breasts. He'd been with women who had faked their chest before. He knew just from the way she felt that she hadn't been lying about being natural. Unfairly designed, maybe, but natural all the same.

Khadi groaned as soon as he put his lips on her breasts, since they desperately needed male attention and he was giving it to her. "Shit." She said between moans, since his tongue was threatening to damage her in the best way. "Gods, your tongue."

"Not even my best feature." He said against her chest, reaching down to pull her thong off and throw it aside. She seemed to enjoy the attention on her breasts, and he needed the practice of keeping himself more or less upright in the zero gravity, so he kept on going. God, it had been so long since he'd been with anyone. He hadn't been celibate so long since he hit puberty.

Khadi wrapped her arms around him so that she could keep his face buried in her breasts, but she couldn't help all the noises that escaped her mouth. "This is better . . . than glaring at you and arguing with you. But that's fun too."

"Good. Keep that up. I always need somebody to fight with." He managed to kick his jumpsuit off the rest of the way as the ship adjusted again, throwing them into one wall against Liam's shoulder hard enough to get a grunt from him. Not that he minded. His hands roamed over every part of her, spreading her thighs with a rough touch as his tongue continued to torture her breasts. "Pictures never do anybody justice." His lips continued moving down. "They never catch the way somebody moves. Certainly didn't capture half of you."

"I guess you never saw the naked pictures, then." She teased inside another moan as she dipped her hand down to yank his boxers off as well. She wondered if their clothes would come back to smack them in the face later, but she didn't think about that. Just the extremely attractive, rude, rough bulk of a man that was holding her close.

"Oh no, I definitely did." He groaned once he was bare against her, and kissed his way back up to her lips as their bodies spun in mid-air, grappling with each other without the benefit of clothes to hang onto. "Real you is still a fucking sight better than any pictures. I looked for porn, but apparently that was one line you decided not to cross."

Khadi wrapped her legs around his waist as quickly as she could, even though the force of it moved them together in the small space. "No porn. I was paid to wear clothes or take off clothes, but never paid to fuck. Never wanted to make that into business instead of pleasure." She kissed him harder and rougher, and even though she was thin, she still had an ass to grab onto and tits that were worth admiring. All thanks to genetic enhancements. "If you don't get your cock inside of me, I'm not going to be happy about this."

That made him laugh, but the two of them were too close for him to laugh for long. "Let's see how long you can stay bossy." He managed to get a hand on one of the straps of the bed in the room and pulled them against it, then pulled away enough to watch the look in her eyes as he reached down to guide himself into her.

His body forgot any kind of skill or pretense as he felt her body respond to his, and he lost himself in the kiss that followed.

"Finally." She groaned as she pressed her forehead to his after the kiss, her legs like a vise around him as she matched him. He didn't need to hold onto her, but she was glad that he was holding onto one of the straps at least. "No . . . toy . . can match a real man with an excellent dick."

His strength, especially in zero gravity, knocked her around a great deal more than any other experience she'd had while naked and weightless. He managed, at one point, to grab onto the side of the bed with both feet, leaving him free to grab her waist with both hands to drive himself into her. There was no top in space, no bottom, none of the usual control dynamics that functioned elsewhere. It felt like learning how to have sex all over again, but he loved it.

"You . . . mmmm . . . keep that up. Not the . . . yeah, that . . . fuckin' hell . . ." Her hair was flying every which way and he loved watching every ripple of it cascading around her ecstatic face. Pictures had truly not done the woman justice.

Khadi took every opportunity to run her hands over his sculpted body, especially because the lack of gravity was forcing both of them to use every muscle they had. His just kept flexing and making her even more wild for him. No wonder his wives were happy women. He was a hard-working lover.

The tension inside of her coiled and built, and she couldn't wait to feel it wash over her as he pulled her every which way. "You're . . . getting the hang . . . of no gravity."

"It's you I want to get the hang of." In one of the ship's many movements, they ended up lying sideways on the bed, and he latched onto the chance to grab the straps, both with his hands and feet, and press her between himself and the cushions. It was the closest to sex in gravity that they'd gotten so far, and the difference in his skills was immediately apparent to every single nerve ending in her body. He drove himself into her as her head laid back off the side of the bed in the momentary acceleration. Simultaneously, he was fucking her against the ceiling, the wall, the floor, anything. Nothing mattered except by perspective, and even perspective didn't matter under his mastery over both their bodies.

She could not talk once he got the hang of fucking her against every surface he could, and it was apparent by her moans that he was driving her wild. Khadi loved how he pushed off her orgasm as long as possible, but it still didn't take long before her head was tilted back in pleasure and she was moaning his name.

His relief at seeing and feeling her climax was almost comical, partly because in the next moment, she took him right along with her. He drove himself into her hard as her thighs clamped reflexively around his waist to relish the shared orgasm, and his hips moved with a mind of their own as he gasped her own name against her chest. In the delicious aftermath, he didn't remember to hold onto the straps of the bed or anything else, and the two of them started drifting, each still buried in the other as their bodies rang with heat.

Khadi wrapped her arms around him to keep him close since she didn't want to drift apart. "Being . . . down on Earth . . . my muscles are going to ache." She laughed softly against his hair. "This works all of your muscles."

"Damn right it does." He agreed as he caught them against a bulkhead before her back hit it, leaving them drifting mostly free in the air between the walls and the side of the bed. "You weren't kidding about being a talker. Not that I mind. And it turns out you've got a great name for yelling out during sex. Khadi . . . just kinda rolls off the climax."

She laughed again, which only made her more aware of him still buried inside of her, but she didn't care. Khadi kissed him hard and rough, though clearly still needy. "We still have a lot of time before we need to prepare for docking." Khadi kissed him again and again. "I mean, we might as well enjoy this . . . thing, while we're doing it, right?"

"Oh, so you're actually admitting that I wasn't just bragging, then?" While she had a firm grip on him, he took the chance to run his hands roughly over her breasts and down to her ass, making sure her body knew he wasn't done with her yet. "I already heard your body say it loud and clear, but I want to hear you admit that I made good on how good I think I am."

Khadi rolled her eyes. "I'm not going to say a damn thing to further inflate your ego." She liked his touch and him grabbing her ass, though. She wasn't going to admit that either. "You think what you want to think."

"I think I'm gonna make you say it, is what I think." He ground her against him with his hands on her ass, and leaned back just to get a good look at the rest of her, as if he was lying on his back and she was riding right on top of him, even if their positioning in the room was all wrong. It didn't matter where they were in the room, all he cared about was where he was in relation to Khadi. "You got me started now, and stopping isn't something I've ever been good at. I can be demanding, and I *will* eventually make you say uncle. That's who you decided to start fucking. Full disclosure."

She rolled her eyes again and shook her head. "You

underestimate . . ." When he thrust up into her again and she gasped, then she glared down at him instead of rolling her eyes. "You can't make . . ." Every time she started talking, he did something to make her gasp, like grabbing her ass that time. "Are you going to let me talk?!"

"Rather get back to making you scream." He said with another kiss, raking his hands over her chest until he could hold her by her shoulders to get the leverage against her that he wanted. It clearly hadn't taken him very long at all to recover from their last round.

"When you talk . . ." he said before another thrust, at which he himself was groaning, though grinning, "you start telling me what I can't do." He savored the sound of her hissing gasps as he turned her into fire all over again, the uncontrolled hunger in her hands as she ran them all over him. "You were warned."

"Eventually . . . I'll be able to . . . talk again." Mostly she was focused on kissing him again, though she clearly had things she wanted to say. Except he was distracting her. It was both infuriating and also fun. He was challenging her right back. "How are you even ready again?"

Once he got her back against a wall, he hung onto a set of bolts and pressed himself deep into her until she gasped and trembled a little under his kiss, then smiled through his own groan. "Your genes might be a work of art, but you're getting fucked by an all-natural freak of nature." His hands moved up over her back to press her completely against him, her ample chest straining against his own rock-hard muscles. "Two or three minutes, tops."

"Holy shit." She hissed as she felt him deep inside of her, which was impressive all in itself, since she wasn't a small woman. "You *are* a freak." Khadi replied with a moan, keeping her thoughts about how impressive he was to herself. She still wasn't going to inflate his ego. He had wives for that. "I've . . . never met anyone with . . . that kind of stamina." She wiggled and bucked herself against him, since she wasn't going to let him have all the fun. "Or such big a cock." Okay, maybe she would boost his ego just a *little*.

Clearly the inflation of his ego went a long way toward convincing him that he had her exactly where and how he wanted her, and when they bumped into the bed again, he reached for one of the straps and threaded her arms through to secure her. Once she was more or less tied down, his hands massaged up her body until his strong fingers interlaced with hers, leaving both of them stable but allowing both their bodies to do all the work. "I could do this all day." The breathless sound of it was half-boast, half-compliment, especially with the look he was giving her between kisses. "Especially with you. I love the way you move."

Khadi smiled, but she was a little hesitant, because she could feel in her own smile it was saying more than she had intended to say even without speaking a word. She kissed him again and sighed against his lips. "Don't look at me the way you're looking at me. We're two people on a crazy mission who desperately needed a good fuck. And this is better than good."

He returned the kiss before he answered, making sure to have her moaning again with his forehead against hers. "I'll look at you however I want." He challenged, then made sure the rest of her senses were too busy screaming in pleasure to let her say anything else.

* * * * *

Renata was quiet as usual as she walked into Logan's office with her infamous tablet in hand. She cleared her throat slightly, though she knew he knew she had arrived as soon as she had opened the door.

"The shuttle arrived safely at Station Three, Mr. Bickford. Your brother and Khadijah and the rest were allowed in without any problems. Miss Al-Jabbar's contact met them and escorted them into the station."

Logan let out a deep sigh that he felt like he'd been holding for hours, and nodded without looking up from the worktable in front of him. There were three envelopes sitting in front of him that he'd spent the last five hours writing by hand, since he didn't trust the words to any digital system and he simply didn't want to commit them to something that felt so impermanent as a collection of signals and light. Real ink on real paper was needed for some situations.

"Make sure the Al-Jabbars are informed as well, they'll want to know their daughter is safe so far." It had been a very quiet night other than those in the arena who were waiting nervously for news of a safe landing. Logan had to wonder how long it had been since he'd passed such a peaceful night. "What about my shuttle? Has it arrived yet?"

She hesitated to respond, but eventually she spoke after letting the silence linger, which was enough answer in itself. "Yes, Sir. Your shuttle is here." Renata didn't say anything else, but she did move closer to him in the dark. He rarely had more than a few lamps on at any given time.

"Sir, there has to be another way . . ." Renata had spent years of her life as Logan Bickford's personal secretary, his attendant. The Consortium had assigned her the job, but she had put her heart into it from the beginning. He was a worthy leader to support, and she had done everything she could to support him, including being his friend.

He laughed once, though the heart behind the laugh was too cauterized and stiffened to produce anything resembling humor in it. "I'm sure there's a better way out there somewhere, Renata. I really am. I just don't know what it is. Believe me, this is not something I'm looking forward to." He looked at the envelopes on the table and then pushed his wheelchair back away from it to allow himself to get moving.

Only when he had a little distance from the letters did he look up at his faithful assistant. "If the opportunity ever presents itself, and it becomes necessary to do so, I'd ask that you see those delivered, please." As she stepped up to the table, she saw that one of the letters was addressed to Anna, one to Mercury, and one simply to his children, with the parenthetical that a copy was to be delivered to all three of them on their sixteenth birthdays.

Renata looked at the letters before she looked at Logan and couldn't help the tears that blurred her vision as she met his eyes. As much as she tried not to be, she was an emotional person and the tears quietly started to slide down her cheeks. "I feel like I should be going with you."

He shook his head. "I wouldn't choose that. Not for anyone. You've been more than essential these past years. I quite literally couldn't tie my own shoes without you for quite a bit of it." He glanced down at his feet, but his heart wasn't in the joke, even if he knew it should have been. "I'll rest easier knowing that you're here helping the others on the council, and that you're safe when things go sideways. We've done a good job keeping most of the world out of the line of fire, you and me, but I'm afraid that's not how things are going to be here very soon."

She nodded and took a deep breath before she moved the rest of the way so that she could hug him. It was a rare occasion that she felt the need to hug Logan, but if he was going to die, she wanted him to know she cared about him and she felt as though he was a good man. "I would do it all again, Sir." She held the hug longer than she knew she should. "And I'll be here ready to resume work with you, should you return."

Logan returned the hug, glad for the comfort even though he would never admit it. He was even more glad she knew and cared enough about him as a friend to know he needed it. "Fair warning, if you ever do come back to work for me, it's going to be because this actually worked. Which means your job description and your pay grade are going to be drastically different, if I have anything to say about it."

She smiled at and nodded. "I'll want a Christmas bonus and everything." Renata backed away slowly, but her tears hadn't stopped. "I continue to hope that it will work. And that you'll find Mercury or your children up there somewhere. Best of luck to you, Sir."

"And to you, Renata." He squeezed her hand, then lowered his head again and rolled away through the arena.

Very few people had been told about his plan. That was part of the purpose of the plan in the first place. It was intended to be a surprise and intended to shock, and Logan was fairly sure he was going to achieve both effects.

Still, as he rolled over the cemented arena floor, past sleeping personnel and a few diligent watchmen monitoring international communications, he felt more alone than he had felt in a very long time. The chair left him feeling alone after the battle, but he hadn't been the only one who had survived. In a way, it had felt, for just a little while, as if the entire world had survived that battle along with him, that things on Earth still stood, for just a little longer, and for just a little while they stood together. In the months since, he had seen how untrue that was.

Some nations of the world were quietly on the side of the rebels. Some very few and very small nations of the world were loudly on the side of the rebels, and had been hammered relentlessly by the Consortium as a result. Some few other nations were loudly on the side of the Consortium, and were those doing the hammering. But the vast majority of the world's population, of its leaders, its supposed caretakers, were simply quiet, even after the Consortium's declaration of war and open hostility toward both its own people and the nations that had chosen to oppose them. Logan thought silence would be enough, but the months since the attack had taught him better.

Silence meant that the world was allowing itself to grow accustomed to the new normalcy of the Consortium's policies toward the human race. Silence meant either fear or consent, in the eyes of the Consortium. That was not something Logan was willing to permit.

The only people waiting for him just outside the arena beside the shuttle were Xander and Tatyana, together as always, watching him approach with the same doubts and disagreements in their eyes as had been there when he suggested the plan in the first place. For all their strategizing, though, they hadn't been able to come up with anything more likely to succeed. Logan couldn't blame them. They had explored every possible option, or at least it felt as though they had. They had to do something to tip the scales. To push the world over the brink into real change. The only person in a position to do so at the moment was him.

He took the earpiece from Tatyana and slid it into place, tapping it once to make sure she could hear him through it and nodding when she did the same for her own corresponding device. Beside them, the pilot disembarked under guard, looking confused as to why it seemed the shuttle was about to take off with no pilot and only a cripple for a passenger. "You two and Jason have everything set for the broadcast?"

"You know everything is prepared, Logan." Tatyana said flatly, since she still didn't support what he was planning but she was doing everything as he had asked. If the man wanted to die for his cause, there was only so much someone could say to stop him. "Are you?"

"Much as anybody can be." Logan said with another sigh and a shrug. "You two are better than anybody else I've ever met at beating somebody over the head with something until it sticks. Normally I wouldn't mean that as a compliment, but right now, I'm hoping it turns out to be of good use over the next few days. Don't take no for an answer, don't give up, don't let anybody off the hook, and don't surrender. Not like I have to tell either of you that. You two could write the book between you on not surrendering."

He knew he was stalling, and he couldn't really afford to, so he took both their hands, in a much more formal farewell than the one he'd gotten from Renata, as he'd known it would be. When he let go of Tatyana's hand, he looked back at the arena, then at the shuttle ahead of him, and nodded, as if he was saying farewell to himself as well. In several ways, he was.

"Who wants to live forever?" He asked no one in particular, expecting no one to answer.

He rolled himself up into the shuttle and moved himself into the pilot's seat, even if the craft was going to be piloted remotely. He secured his wheelchair behind him first, then secured himself in the seat before he leaned back and tapped the earpiece once. "Ready for liftoff when you are. Let's get this show on the road."

Liftoff and the initial push through the atmosphere brought back every bad memory of the Initiative that Logan had done his best to forget in the years since the last time he had left Earth's surface. The silence stretched on, since Tatyana wasn't exactly big on conversation or making small talk, especially given his intentions for the next few hours.

Only when he finally got out of the atmosphere and the stars began to look him in the eye did he feel like he could take a full breath. Tatyana had put a countdown on the control panel for him, to let him know when it would be time for the real show.

Prime wasn't a difficult station to align with, if the launch was timed correctly, since it was necessarily the slowest-orbiting station in the sky. Once he had reached the necessary height, the countdown set itself on forty-two minutes. More than enough time to accomplish what needed to be done.

When he finally worked up the courage to do so, he reached out and tapped a single button on the control panel, taking in a deep breath to steel himself against what was coming.

He could see an image of himself up on the panel in front of him, and he made eye contact with himself as well as he was able. "My name is Logan Bickford." He began simply, settling himself back into the chair. "Right now, nearly every device on or above the planet should be receiving some form of this message. Out of consideration for those who I'm waking up in the middle of the night, I'll keep this brief." He took a deep breath and pressed another button to start a whole host of information scrolling across the screen beside his face for the world to take in.

"I'm aboard the shuttle Immortality, bound for Station Prime. I'll be docking in roughly forty-five minutes. I am alone, and currently moving at the coordinates and along the vector on the screen with this message. I am unarmed." He said finally, his expression turning to one of challenge. When had his face turned to stone? He knew the answer, he just didn't want to think about the answer.

"Leaders of the Consortium, this message is addressed primarily to you. In your media and your propaganda, you have branded me a terrorist and an enemy of mankind. You have accused me of terrible crimes, and even offered a reward to any who capture me or provide evidence of my death. You have done this while prosecuting a war on humanity that is both unjustified and tyrannical, and you have made yourselves look every bit the fools you are in the process." He stopped long enough to let that sink in, which he knew it would. He had been living rent-free under the skin of the Consortium ever since the destruction of Nine.

"I am coming to Prime willingly and without resistance, to stand trial in front of the world for my supposed crimes. I do this not because I recognize your authority, but because I recognize that you have none. Over the centuries since the Crisis, you have usurped and bullied and dictated your way into every facet of life for millions of people across the world, and that influence, that oppression, isn't going to last much longer.

"You declared war on the nations of Earth because you've finally started to figure out that you need to be afraid. You've got reason to be. What you've got to be afraid of isn't me, it's everybody else in this world who is no longer going to live without the resources you hold back, the information you hoard for yourself, the path to Eleusis that you've had for five years and kept secret from the rest of the dying world. What you've got to be afraid of isn't anything that I can do myself, but everything the human race has finally started to realize it can do perfectly well without you.

"So I'm here to let you put me on trial for the crimes you say I've committed. Let the whole world watch, let the whole world judge between the Consortium, your pathetic lies, your genocidal policies, and the rest of the human race that wants to live full lives without you telling us how. You want me? I'm gonna make it easy for you." He ended with a sneer that he couldn't help.

"As for the rest of you back on Earth, I want everyone seeing this message to watch what comes next. Because what comes next is going to be the act of cowards and liars, who've got no ground to stand on. You watch what comes next, and you decide what you want to be a part of. If they shoot me out of the sky without a trial, you'll have your answer. If they throw me in a hole and you never see me again, you'll have your answer. If they give me this trial and they're forced to put together some kind of bullshit defense of themselves, you'll have your answer.

"This is our world, our lives, our fight." He finished with a last glare into the camera. "Eleusis waits for us, and the Consortium holds the keys to the doorway to get there. That opportunity belongs to the entire human race. A long life and open spaces for every child born to the human race." He said with a small catch in his throat, as he saw his own glare deepen. "A long life my own children will never see, since for all I know, the Consortium has already killed them, like they've murdered so many other innocents before their time."

He took a moment to compose himself, looking down and away from the control panel as notifications began popping up off the screen where the entire human race couldn't see them. His shuttle was already being shadowed by a few other crafts from the Consortium that launched as soon as he started to speak. They had targeted him, but hadn't fired. That was fine by him.

He finally looked back up at the camera with a sigh that turned into a low growl. "I wanted my children to live full lives on Eleusis. To have the time to live free. That's what I wanted for my children. All of you down on Earth and in these stations in orbit . . . of everyone left in the human race the Consortium hasn't yet managed to destroy, I want to know. Who wants to live forever?" He asked imploringly, looking into his own eyes and imagining the faces of every world leader he'd met with who had turned him down. Every fighter for the cause of the rebellion. Every station captain on the fence about their own loyalties.

"You know where I am. I'll be docking with Prime in thirty-six minutes. You have until then to decide if you're going to shoot me straight out of the sky or if you're willing to have this trial in front of the entire human race. It's your choice. I'll see you soon." He flicked a finger at the screen to cut off the transmission, and collapsed back in his chair to wait out the rest of the trip.

He had no idea if his gamble was going to pay off. He had no idea if the nations of the world would really pay attention to what was happening or if they would regard him as just another zealot fighting for what he considered freedom. He had no idea. But he knew he had to try.

The world needed a push to get it moving against the

Consortium. That was all it needed, just a push. He hoped it would be enough. It had to be enough.

The next half hour was the most nerve-wracking period of time he could remember, but the expected fire never came. He glided through the vacuum of space toward Prime, and received terse instructions regarding how and where to dock once he got there. The orders were followed by remote command, and Logan simply sat in the pilot's seat until the docking clamps had been fully engaged.

He was theirs now, to do with as they pleased. He took the earpiece out and cracked it in two between his hands, knowing that Tatyana was going to similarly destroy hers to keep it from being tracked. With it, his last lifeline back to the rebels disappeared, and he turned to glare at the back of the shuttle while he waited for the inevitable boarding party.

"Your move."

6

"What kind of security do we have on him?" Gehrig asked as she listened to her earpiece, though she was nearly running to meet with Hugo in interrogation. The Alperts were meeting them as well, though they might have gotten there already. When she was assured they had more than enough security, she hurried the rest of the way to meet with Hugo. "Are we sure we have the right one? It's not his twin?"

"They're finishing a full scan on him now, along with a full bloodwork panel." Clearly Hugo was worried about some of the same questions, since he didn't want to be the one who got duped by a stupid Earth-born child. Again. "Initial results show that he does have traces in his liver and lungs of some of the drugs we were pumping into them during his phase of the Initiative. And they've already confirmed the nerve injury he was rumored to have suffered during the attack on the mountains. So it looks like it really is Logan, not the other one." He was still nervous about the man's presence, but there was nothing they could do about it now. The Alperts had made their call and called the man's bluff.

"Have they promised him anything to get him to talk? They haven't updated me on anything. I hate it when they keep all the information to themselves. How are we supposed to do our jobs?"

"There's nothing to update." It wasn't often someone like Hugo Vance sounded nervous, but she had known him long enough to hear the faint tremor of both incredulity and anxiety in his voice as he said it. "He was taken into custody, bound, gagged, and carried to an interrogation cell. He's been stripped, searched, scanned, had blood drawn, and been given a jumpsuit. They haven't even removed the gag yet. There's nothing. I've got him on a closed feed right now and he's just . . . waiting."

"Waiting . . . for us? For death?" Gehrig let out a heavy sigh before she walked forward toward the interrogation room. "Let's get this over with. He came here for a reason. We might as well find out what it is. I don't believe all the junk he put out there. He's here as a distraction. He has to be."

"This isn't one of the Montgomeries we're dealing with, here." He reminded her as he moved toward the room as well. "This is Bickford. He was a pain in the ass back on Nine, he kicked both our asses in the fight in the mountains, and he's come here thinking he can do it again. I agree he's here for more than what he said, but with him, I can't imagine him being anything but the center of attention. It's just not the way the man is built."

"Well, with enough of Maria's serum, we can make anyone dance the way we want them to. Including Logan Bickford. With enough conditioning, we can make him sing our praises to the world. We just need time. He's offered himself up. Now we need to break him once and for all."

"That would be fine, if Maria or Stephen were on this side of the galaxy." Vance said in a low voice, since he didn't want to be heard by anyone in a stray corridor. "It'll help to break him down as it is, I admit, but without the two of them, there's no key to it. We're going to have to do this mostly the old-fashioned way."

"Or maybe we start using their drug without them." She clearly wasn't happy about Maria and Stephen not being there, since she blamed them for the situation on Eleusis, but there was nothing to be done about it.

She knocked on the door and waited to hear the click to would admit them into the room, since there was no reason to put anything off. She was surprised, though, that even though she had been informed the Alperts were there, Mrs. Alpert was actually missing. If she was gone, she was up to something.

"Victoria." Dominic said as soon as she came in, looking through the one-way glass into the interrogation cell where Logan was kept. Beyond the glass, there was a space for the interrogator to stand and move, with steel bars between the interrogator space and the actual cell of the prisoner, with a cot and a toilet, both bolted to the floor. In Logan's case, the bolts were rather redundant, since the man's paralysis appeared genuine. Still, they weren't going to take any chances with a man who had become such a thoroughgoing pain in their collective asses.

Dominic was sipping from a water bottle without taking his eyes off Logan, trying to figure out the man in front of them who had so dramatically turned himself over. "What are your thoughts on how we ought to proceed?"

Victoria looked at Logan in silence as she considered what to do with the man. She wanted to take a gun and shoot him in the skull, but clearly that wasn't an option. "We figure out how to break him. He thinks he's a man who has lost everything, and so he's willing to do whatever it takes to take us down. Do we go retrieve one of his children? Make him feel as though he has something at stake?"

"He already believes he's lost them once." Dominic said without looking away. "He's here to be a martyr. In order to convince him to be something else, especially to betray his own misguided cause, we will have to convince him that he has a better option, and a reason to believe he was wrong to fight against us as he has. If he's willing to die himself, then he may be willing to sacrifice his children as well. If he is, there will be no changing him. He wants to make this about extremes, and I'd rather not give him his way if we can avoid it."

"Finnegan has already agreed to leave their cause and come back to work for us." Victoria said as she kept her eyes on Logan. "If we can convince her, then maybe she can convince him in turn. I realize she was married to Al-Jabbar, but it might be an option." She moved closer to the glass to look at Logan like he was an animal for observation. "Are we going to repair his injuries?"

"I think that would be a good opening overture, yes. As a rule, I prefer carrots to sticks, and anything we can do to complicate his emotions toward the Consortium with gratitude, I believe will be a positive step." Even when offering healing, manipulation was the most important factor in any of Dominic's considerations. People were power, and influence over the actions of any given person was the definition of power.

"The positive spin will be that we saw no reason for anyone, even a criminal, to go through life as a cripple. The spin will be that Mr. Bickford actually came here as a part of a pre-arranged deal to get the use of his legs back, and all else has been a sham act. It will make for a good beginning in the perception of the public."

"Always ten steps ahead, right Dominic?" She tapped on the glass once, but before she could say anything else, she heard a door open and saw Mrs. Alpert walk in. With Mercury Finnegan right behind her. Victoria was surprised, but she obviously had the same idea. Just not so soon. "Doctor." She said politely, but she stepped away from the glass to watch.

Mercury still didn't know why she had been plucked from her area again by the Alperts, but she didn't have to walk too far into the room before she stopped dead in her tracks.

She turned slowly and stared at the person she saw through the glass. No. This wasn't real. They were playing tricks on her. It was Liam. No, it wasn't Liam, she could certainly tell them apart, couldn't she? He was paralyzed? What happened to him in the mountains? Why was he here? Was it a hologram to get a reaction out of her?

"You told me he was dead."

"We did not tell you he was alive." Dominic said from the glass, still sipping at his water. "I believe you'll find, if you remember accurately, all other mentions of Mr. Bickford's death could be interpreted as being hypothetical in nature. Is that the point you'd like to deliberate on at the present, or are there other questions you find more pressing?"

"What happened to him?" No one was stopping her from getting closer, so Mercury went up to the glass and put her hand on it, though she doubted she would actually be allowed to see him.

"Well, he hasn't exactly been forthcoming on details." Dominic said with a lifetime of sarcasm behind it. A few taps on the glass superimposed a full series of medical scans against the real image of Logan on the other side, showing the base of his spinal column and some of the bones and muscles in his legs. "We haven't had any other physicians look this over yet. He arrived a few hours ago. The auto-analysis diagnosed him with a pinched disc in his lower spine and severed nerves in both legs caused by some kind of trauma. From the look of his legs, my guess would be he was just inside their base in the mountains when most of it collapsed. Both femurs show signs of a clean break, no easy task, but he shows no nerve response in his legs whatsoever. If you want more of a story, you'll have to ask him. Eventually."

"Ask him? You're going to let me talk to him?" She continued to stare at Logan. He was so close, yet so far away. It was hard to be so close.

"Not today, I think." Dominic said with another glance up at the scans on the glass in front of them, then got rid of them with a few gestures and tapped out Mercury's name on one part of the screen. When they disappeared, she felt her own communicator chime in her pocket to let her know the files had been made available to her. "For now, you'll be his attending physician. It's our intention to correct the injuries he sustained, as a token of our good will."

Mercury slowly turned her head to look back at Dominic, since she knew that he was torturing her, she just didn't know why. She had agreed to abandon the rebel cause for the sake of her children. What more did they want from her? "I cannot be someone's physician without actually being able to examine them. Scans will never be complete without a physical examination."

"You'll have to work within the limitations you're given for now. You'll be permitted access to your patient at our discretion." He wasn't fazed by her insistence on seeing the patient, clearly. "We will permit you to observe his interrogations at your convenience, for diagnostic purposes, until such time as you are permitted to interact with him directly. Given the circumstances and Mr. Bickford's status as a wanted terrorist, this is not open for negotiation."

She wanted to argue or throw some kind of tantrum, but she knew it would be futile. Instead, Mercury just back at Logan again through the glass, forcing herself to take a deep breath. "You know, if you brought him here . . . if you brought *me* here to convince either of us to do something, you're not going to get what you want. He's a man devoted to his cause, and you killed the woman he was fighting for. Bringing me here isn't going to change the fact that you took Anna from him."

Dominic's lips moved upward in a slow smile at that accusation, but he didn't laugh. The man had one of the most wicked senses of humor she had ever encountered, but he was much more quiet about it than the others she had encountered. "He came to us, as a matter of fact." He turned his back on her and made a few more gestures on the glass, eventually pulling up the video that Logan had sent around the world just a few hours before, the manifesto he had dropped on the world and his call to arms.

Mercury watched the video clip without a single change in her expression or even her body language, even though she wanted to cry when his voice caught while he was talking about his children. She hated he was living with that guilt when all of his children were well and cared for by herself and Gwen and their other friends. "You're just further proving he's devoted to his cause. Involving me in this isn't going to change anything."

"Permitting you to help convince your friends in the resistance to surrender peacefully was one of the terms of your conditional release, Doctor." He said flatly, with another glance at Logan. "We'll see what you can accomplish when we deem it's time for you to make the attempt. For now, you can see Mr. Bickford surrendered himself willingly for trial, and you have access to his medical records. We will order and execute further diagnostic tests upon your recommendation, but for now, those are the limits of your capacity here." He turned to his wife, apparently forgetting Mercury even existed the moment his eyes weren't on her. "Sweetheart, you've always had more of a knack for this kind of thing than I have. Care to have a first crack at our guest?"

"Certainly, Dear." Sara Alpert said sweetly and headed into the room without even a second glance at Mercury. Mercury would have to watch in silence.

"Logan Bickford." She entered the room, smiling and pleasant as always, her heels clicking happily along the floor as she approached. She looked like a lawyer most of the time with her hair pinned in a low bun at the base of her neck, sporting a suit-jacket and pencil skirt. "We finally get a chance to meet. My name is Sara Alpert."

Logan's eyes widened slightly at her introduction, but then narrowed equally as he raised his head to look at her. "I'm glad to know I got your attention." He didn't look glad in any way, glaring up at her the same way he had been glaring down at the floor a moment before.

Logan had been many things over the time Mercury had known him; frustrated, aggressive, domineering, impetuous, controlling, forceful, stressed . . . but at the moment, all of those emotions were gone from the man on the other side of the glass and bars. All she could see in the eyes of the man looking back at Sara was rage. Barely controlled, frozen in ice, but rage that pushed through every word he said. "I'm not sure what I expected from the woman who could have brainchildren like the Initiative itself. I suppose actual fangs and a forked tail would have you standing out a little more than would be convenient."

"How creative of your mind to come up with something like that." She said sweetly, smiling all the while. "You've made things interesting for us by your little broadcast and your presence here. We were just discussing what we might ask of you, but your physical condition is rather concerning." She glanced back toward the glass since she knew who was on the other side, but clearly he did not. "Your physician is just on the other side of the glass evaluating your condition based on your scans. Would you like to provide more information so that we can assess your condition completely?"

"I'm here to stand trial, not so that your doctors can tell me to turn my head and cough." He said with the same glare. "So unless you plan on serving as my defense attorney, then no, I won't be answering questions about my condition."

"Alright. Well, we can handle that the hard way, if you like. If you're going to stand trial, then you're going to do it at your best. We intend to show the entire world that not only did we receive you without harm, but you will be given care and a trial. When you show the world how terrible we are, you'll be doing it while standing on your own two feet after we repair the damage you've done to your body."

She continued smiling at Logan as she moved a little bit closer to him. "Your doctors on Earth don't really have access to resources like we do. Very few of them would even dream about repairing a man with permanent paralysis. It's in our favor to remind the people of Earth what they do not have, and what we do." She looked him up and down. "Hopefully you won't fall in love with your new doctor, though. That sort of thing has a way of ending badly for you." She said offhandedly as she looked away from him and down at the palm-sized tablet she'd brought in with her.

The rage in Logan's face boiled a little more to the surface at the mention of falling in love with a doctor, and Mercury could see him grit his teeth, though he said nothing right away. He was at least still capable of measuring his words before he let them loose. That was something. "Everything you do is a reminder to Earth of what we've never had. More of that will be more evidence of everything you hold back that could benefit the rest of humanity."

"More of a reminder that we're needed." She looked up from her tablet. "Even your ex-wife, Dr. Finnegan, recognized that. After we captured her, along with many others, she agreed to continue her research with us and abandon all ties to the rebel cause. Clearly, if you had meant anything to her at all, she would not have abandoned your people and your cause so quickly. She even agreed to do research on her own children."

News of Mercury's survival, according to the woman in front of him, made Logan pause, watching Sara's face for any sign of deceit, after which he shook his head. "If you're telling even a quarter of the truth, and Mercury is still alive, she would never go back to work for you by her own choice. Not unless you threatened the others you took along with her. Including our children." He watched Sara's reaction, but she was as good a poker player as he had ever seen in his life. He didn't know what was true and what was lies when it came from anyone working for the Consortium, and he was tired of trying to sort out one from the other. "If she's alive, then whatever she's doing, however she's doing it, for whatever reasons, she's doing what needs to be done. Not for you, but for everyone. That's who she is."

"I didn't say she was alive, Mr. Bickford. I just wanted you to know that in the end, she abandoned you and your beliefs. If it makes you feel better to think she did it for the reasons you said, then by all means, I would not deny a crippled man the emotional relief of the lies he built up in his mind. It seemed as though she wanted to move on from the life she had on Earth. She never spoke of you fondly." Mercury rarely spoke of anything or anyone at all with much emotion, and so it certainly wasn't much of a stretch.

"She doesn't have much reason to speak of me fondly." He was still going to speak of Mercury in the present tense, for as long as he didn't have direct evidence of her death. He settled back on the narrow cot, leaning against the wall. "Whatever crime you choose to accuse me of, Mrs. Alpert, it will be secondary to the offenses I'm guilty of against Mercury. The happiest days of my life were spent with her, and the single decision I regret more than anything was the one that took her out of my life after our return to Earth. She has every reason not to speak fondly of me."

"There are crimes enough that we choose to accuse you of, but that will come out in time." Sara stared at him for a while longer and she shook her head. "You're so sure that you're going to defeat us. You cannot." Sara tapped on a tiny tablet in her hand and she looked up at Logan again. "Let's get you into surgery, Mr. Bickford. You'll have to forgive me, though. We didn't schedule an anesthesiologist to assist."

"Of course you didn't." The rage returned to his eyes, but incongruously, a smile accompanied the rage. "Keep something in mind, Mrs. Alpert. I came here and surrendered myself willingly into your custody, knowing everything you would likely do to me once I got here. Whatever happens, whatever you do, I may scream, I may suffer, but everything you do will prove to the world that you are everything I have accused you of being. Do as you like."

"We've broken far better minds, far stronger men, and people more stubborn than you. You will break, Mr. Bickford. And it will be a good day when you do." Sara leveled a stare at Logan until she heard a knock against the glass.

Mercury didn't know what broke inside of her, but the moment Mrs. Alpert said there would be no anesthesiologist, she was furious. "You cannot send a person into surgery like that without putting him under!" She was screaming at Dominic, but then she turned and knocked on the glass, as if she could somehow prove to Logan she was still there. That she was still alive. "Even if he's your enemy, you cannot do that to him! He surrendered!"

Dominic looked back at her calmly, and didn't even stop her from knocking on the glass, though she had clearly gotten Logan's attention in the process. "You've been tasked with developing a surgical plan for Mr. Bickford based on his current scans. If you are telling me you reject this task, there are other surgeons in the central hospital who can be relied upon to perform the operation."

"I refuse. I took an oath. I became a doctor to help people, not to torture them!" She couldn't stop screaming, and she knocked on the window again. "Logan!"

He had wondered if Sara was simply bluffing with her request about Mercury, but even though Logan couldn't hear Mercury screaming from the outer room, he could hear the banging on the glass. No one else was likely to be banging on the glass like that after he'd just admitted that his biggest mistake had been leaving Mercury. They wouldn't have any reason to bring anyone else to observe him, unless it was her, and they wanted to torture her just as much as they wanted to torture him. "Mercury!" He threw himself off the cot, and felt a distracted satisfaction that his sudden movement forced the Alpert bitch to take a half-step back away from him, bars or no bars.

He crawled quickly to the bars and pulled himself up until the weight of his body was at least partially resting on his locked legs. He was more than strong enough to hold himself against the bars, his eyes searching the one-way glass for wherever Mercury might have been. "Don't give up." He said in a grunt once he got more or less up to his feet, completely ignoring Sara's presence in the room. "Whatever's going on, don't give up. Not now."

Most of Mercury's life, she hadn't been an emotional person, but Orion and Logan had changed her in their own ways. Orion and Logan helped to teach her how to really feel, and seeing Logan again brought on sobs she hadn't felt in months. Living on Prime was the same almost every single day. But not this day. He couldn't see her, but she could see him. Mercury pressed her hands to the glass, even when guards finally came in to take her away. She never fought before, but this time, she was fighting. Mercury knocked on the glass as loudly as she could before she was grabbed by the arms and pulled forcibly away from the glass. "Logan!"

She had to be half-carried, half-dragged most of the way back to her unit, but when they finally reached the detention block, her guards merely stood and watched to make sure she went back in on her own.

In the broad corridor that was the main artery of the detention block, most of those who had been taken prisoner along with her and her children were gathered all together to watch the large screens along the walls. Logan's voice was playing from every one of them, his broadcasted call to arms and challenge to the Consortium. Why were they playing that video for the entire rebel contingent to see? It made no sense.

Mercury was still sobbing as she went back into the prison block, and people rushed to her, but they also thought it was because she was seeing Logan on the screen. Melissa rushed to her, and Mercury allowed herself to be led. "They have Logan. They're going to . . . surgery . . . non-medicated . . ."

"They're gonna what?!?" Melissa asked as she led Mercury back to her own unit, past dozens of staring faces and whispering voices, all of them sympathetic. They all knew she thought Logan was dead ever since they had been taken. Having that knowledge proven to be a lie so violently . . . that wasn't something anyone envied.

Back in Mercury's unit, Gwen was sitting next to the monitor they had been permitted to use to keep an eye on their sleeping children, watching the tiny screen where Leo, Lynnette, James, and Declan were all asleep, since it had been the middle of the night when Mercury had been taken from her bed to go see Logan. The children, at least, were still peaceful, but Gwen had been watching Logan's broadcast along with everyone else, and everyone had been affected by it in their own ways.

"That . . ." Melissa said when Mercury finally got the full details of her meeting with Logan out, "is . . . intensely fucked up. Even for . . . they can't just do that, right? I mean, every doctor takes that oath. No doctor would do that. Would they?"

"They do whatever they want to do." Mercury said between sniffles and hiccups. "They use experimental drugs. They rape people. They left Kameron to die when she was pregnant, you were with her. They aren't moral. They're more disgusting every single day that passes."

Melissa looked back and forth between Mercury and Gwen, hoping as always that someone, anyone but her, would have some kind of plan of action. "Well we can't just let them do . . . whatever the fuck they want to do! We need to *do* something! He just got done on that video telling us *not* to just sit back and do nothing! I know we've been round and round a thousand times about trying to do something from here, but there just . . ."

Melissa had felt, even before she entered the Initiative, as though her life had never once been her own. The Initiative had taken away what little choice she had even more than it had been restricted back on Earth. She had found the kind of freedom she wanted with Kameron, but the Consortium just kept coming back to put chains on her. More than almost anyone else in captivity, she continued to chafe against every restriction that was placed on them. "There has to be *something*."

"Like what, Mel?" Kameron finally responded, since she was always quiet when she was trying to figure something out. "We don't have any weapons or even very many people who would be any good with them. And we have all of the children here. I'm not willing to risk them, none of us are. They don't even give us metal utensils, for crying out loud. We've got nothing."

"I don't care if we've got . . ." Melissa began again, but paused when the lights in their unit flickered once as if the power was about to die. They had been tormented several times, early on, with complete darkness, making the children scream until they got accustomed to it and leaving the adults in a deep panic. The lights didn't go out, but the baby monitor on the table nearby flickered a few more times and went black.

When it came back, it was to a flickering image, unclear at first but quickly coming into focus, in bright and stark contrast to the night-vision by which they had been watching their children. *Patient is a 25-year-old male with fractures of both femurs and extensive muscle damage* . . . a voice was droning on, as all the women in the room watched nurses move around a surgical table. They were strapping Logan down in a hundred different ways, including a gag for his mouth that resembled some of the toys that he and Mercury had played with during their days on Station Nine. His eyes were empty and staring at the ceiling, but he blinked every once in a while, making it obvious that he was awake and aware of everything that was happening to him.

All three of the women stared at the monitor in horror for what felt like too long before Kameron moved quickly across the room toward the monitor. "Oh, fuck no." She picked up the monitor and threw it as hard as she could into the wall to shatter it. "Fucked up bastards."

The screen was gone, but the audio from the unwelcome broadcast remained, quiet enough that they had to strain to listen to it, but loud enough that they could hear the details of the doctors and nurses talking. Everything was sterilized, a brief outline of how they would proceed was given, and then . . . silence.

There was nothing but doctor instruction for a long time, but eventually they heard heavier breathing, then a sharp gasp, then a strangled whimper, then at last, full screaming. The doctors and nurses were still speaking in the background as if nothing whatsoever out of the ordinary was happening, though their tones were certainly subdued. When Logan's voice reached a fevered shriek, the audio faded as if pulling itself out of their reach, and it didn't return.

"Motherfucking twisted psychopaths." Kameron growled as Gwen and Melissa both moved to comfort Mercury who had put her hands up to her ears and resumed sobbing. Both Gwen and Melissa were crying as well, but Kam was just furious. Give her a fucking scalpel and she would love to take it along the spine of the fucking terrorists that called themselves doctors. "They'll pay for this. I promise."

Melissa had her hands over Mercury's to help cover her ears, but all three of them were sobbing by the time the sound mercifully faded. The horror of it lingered in the room in spite of the sound being gone, since they knew a surgery like the one Logan was in would take hours. Possibly multiple surgeries over multiple days. How many times would their unit be invaded by the sound of his screams while someone calmly asked for a scalpel?

In the agonizing silence, the first sound to break the torment of ignorance was Gwen's, as she started to sing. Part of the reason the children adored her was because of her singing, and in that moment, a happy little children's song was enough distraction to help them all try to regain some composure.

Melissa was the next to join in, but the four of them didn't let go of each other until the song had run its course through the room. They were captives who had nothing but each other and their children to hold onto, but it was enough to see them through one moment after another. That had to be enough.

"He wouldn't be here," Melissa began quietly, once all of them had more or less gotten past their sobbing and could speak in hushed tones within the small cluster they had formed on the floor, "unless there was a plan. He wants the trial, that's what he said, but he can't imagine they'll actually give him a fair one. Something else has to be happening. Something worth him coming here as a distraction."

"She's right." Gwen agreed, since she wanted to distract herself just as much as anyone else. It was Logan who they saw on the screen, but it was Liam who she saw in her mind. She was going to have nightmares. They all were. "There's a plan. There's always a plan."

They weren't interrupted with any more screaming, but there were no guarantees of what was going to happen, either to Logan or to anyone else. "I finished . . ." it had only been a few days since Mercury had given her the request, but they were captives, and Melissa was excited to have something to work on. "I finished your, um, your drawings. I can go grab them if it would help take your mind off things."

Mercury shook her head, even though she did eventually want to see what Melissa had created. She closed her eyes and slumped in the middle of the three women who were holding onto her as if they were guarding her. "Would you all . . . would you stay here with me?"

"Of course." Melissa answered for the rest of them, since there was no way they were going to leave Mercury or Gwen alone when Logan was somewhere being tortured. She squeezed Mercury's arm as she stayed seated on the floor near her. "He's gonna be alright." She promised. "He's too valuable for them to let him die.

He'll be alright."

Gwen and Kam both nodded in agreement, but then Gwen looked away, since she had no such assurance that Liam was even alive. Part of her hoped he was still back on the farm with Rachel and Bree. Bree would be due anytime, and his sister Larissa would have had her baby already. They needed Liam more than she did. Still, she missed him terribly. She missed them all. The life she wanted with the man she wanted had been right there and it was forever out of her reach.

There was a knock at the door some time after the screaming had finally been turned off, and Diego was on the other side when Kam went to answer it. From the look on his face, the broadcast of Logan screaming hadn't been isolated to just Mercury's unit.

"I won't bother you for long." He said in a low voice. They all kept themselves hushed most of the time, even if that wasn't likely to do any good for not getting overheard by the Consortium monitoring their rooms at all times. "But whatever needs to happen, just know that everybody's on board. You're the only military officer along with us, so when something has to go down, you say the word and everyone is ready to move. I don't even know what it would be, but everyone here is unanimously fed up with this shit."

Kam nodded as she looked up at the man, though she was still at a loss about what they could even do, especially with so many women and children that would not be able to defend themselves. "I'll try my best to come up with something. I never intended to die in here, so there has to be some way out."

"I don't know either." Diego said with a growl. The man was not built to be cooped up for very long. "But throwing ourselves at the problem has to be better than just sitting around here shitting ourselves."

"We'll figure it out. I promise. I have to come up with a plan." Kameron sighed and looked back into the darkness of the unit. "If we don't get out, they're going to break us all down until we're begging to be killed. Which is exactly what they want."

"I don't beg." Diego glanced back down the corridor where everyone was still gathered together for the reassurance of a large group. "And neither will anybody else in here." He knew there was no plan in place to deal with things yet, but as terrified as everyone was, the Consortium couldn't completely remove the renewed hope they felt at the fact that Logan was still alive, that the resistance itself was still alive outside their walls. Theories and conjecture had only been able to accomplish so much in keeping hope alive. Real evidence, even if that evidence was being brutally tortured, was something concrete for them to hold onto. "Just tell the doctor she's not alone. We'll get through this, all of us. Somehow."

7

As Aiko approached the space Orion had cleared for himself on the beach, he glared up at her, but kept working. He had been frantic when he got back to camp after the attack, partly because he'd been injured and partly because he had seen Anna alive inside the compound. He had been more than a little unhinged for hours afterward, but the next thing he knew, he woke up the next morning in his own cot. It hadn't taken much to deduce that Aiko had slipped him some kind of sedative in the strange-tasting water she had given him during his fit of obsessive planning.

He slipped out of his cot in the dark hours of the morning, and it had been several hours before anyone found him. Their camp tried to stay away from the beach, since there were creatures in the water that tended to hunt anyone who came too close to the water's edge. But the tide was out and would stay that way for the next few days, leaving almost fifty meters of dry, smooth sand between Orion's back and the surf.

In the sand in front of him, he had a collection of sticks he was using to draw and scheme and plot, and there were small twigs stuck into his map at various places. Orion himself was moving from one part of the map to another with narrowed eyes, deeply focused on his task, even if it was unintelligible to anyone else. Zoe's squad of psychopaths stood guard around him, one of them coming back from the water's edge with full canteens for everyone, since Eleusis oceans had just barely more salt content than Earth's freshwater streams, and were easily drinkable.

Orion hardly even noticed when he was handed his canteen, and took a sip without taking his eyes off the map, except to glare up at Aiko. "I slept great, thanks for asking."

"I *had* to sedate you." She defended immediately "You had a serious injury that needed to be seen to, and you wouldn't sit still for two seconds without going on and on about Anna. I'm very glad that she's not dead, but I still had to do what I needed to do."

"You and me both." He didn't even flinch as lightning struck the sea behind them in rapid succession, the way Eleusis storms almost always did. They were getting worse, and according to Aiko, they were only going to get much, much worse as they got closer to the equivalent of winter in that part of Eleusis. Something about a mountain range to the west and the electrical field of the planet . . . all things that Orion vaguely paid attention to once and no longer had the capacity to care about.

The strikes were so quick that the thunder bled into itself. Orion's eyes stayed fixed on his map, even as he leaned on what had apparently become his walking stick. "So does everyone else think I've officially earned some kind of psych-related demotion now?"

"No one is talking about you and your mental state to me, Orion." Aiko said as she tried to move closer to him. "If you get electrocuted out here, you're not going to do Anna any good. At least come back into the safety of the hideout."

"Lightning rod." He pointed absently down the beach a little ways to a large cluster of rocks, on which he had placed one of the lightning rods they had managed to fashion from stolen Consortium equipment. Some of their most successful raids had been conducted within the first few weeks of their imprisonment on Eleusis, during which they had managed to mostly clean out one of the Consortium's warehouses.

Unfortunately, most of what they had stolen had been hardware or tech, rather than artillery or food. The pallets of lightning rods came in handy for keeping their camp safe, though, and some of their engineers had done calculations to show the frequency at which they would have to be placed to ensure safety. They were stretching it by being exposed on the beach, but Orion wanted to get away from the rest of the camp for as long as possible.

"I might be the tallest person on the beach, but the water is still more appealing than I am, I'm pretty sure. I could be wrong. Wouldn't be the first time." He glanced up at Aiko briefly, then sighed as he looked back down at his map. "I'll come back up soon. I'm going to need one of the engineering teams, though. I have a lot of work for them."

Aiko was quiet as she sighed. She looked at his makeshift map before she said anything. "You have to eat when you come back up, do you hear me? This insanity has to slow down a little. We have to approach this as logically as we can, because anything half-assed is going to get us killed and possibly now Anna too."

"How far did you and Carl have to go for decent hunting?" Orion knew he was completely ignoring her questions and her instructions, but he needed to know. He hadn't been a part of many of the hunting parties that went out.

"There's a herd of green-backed Jumpers about three clicks inland." One of Zoe's Psychos answered excitedly. "Taste good with a little salt on the meat. Heart's nice and tender if you cook it a nice medium-rare. General said we weren't allowed to take out the whole herd because he thought it would show up on the compound's sensors, that big a change."

"I think we're a little past that at this point." Orion was still looking down at his map, but he looked up at the man for confirmation. "How big a herd?"

The man shrugged excitedly. "I dunno. Two, maybe three hundred head? Could be more? I'm not known for my counting."

Orion shifted his eyes over to Aiko, looking for her opinion. "What do you think? People here could use a good steak dinner, and I've got plans for what to do with the rest. Plans that aren't half-assed, crazy as they might be."

"If you think you can down a few without being trampled or getting anyone else killed, then I'm sure people would appreciate a good, warm meal. You should take Carl with you. He's starting to drive me a little crazy with how much he's hovering over me like I might break in half at any moment. Just don't you dare let him do anything crazy."

"I don't want to down one. I want to down them all." Orion looked back at the man who had spoken. "How would you do it?"

The man considered for a moment, leaning on a spear he had fashioned for himself. The man liked making sharp things. "We'd have to herd them into that one blind canyon up north. Set a palisade in the cut to pull up once they're inside, keep them from stampeding back out again, pick them off one by one as they try." He shrugged again, but he was grinning. "It'd be dangerous, but do-able."

"How long?" Orion didn't look frantic as he had the day before, just focused, even though it was easily the most dangerous Aiko had ever seen the man.

"Maybe two days? Scout the canyon, set the pikes, herd them

in on the morning of day three, leave the rest of the day to do the bloodwork." The man's face was placid as he talked about doing all the killing, just like the rest of Zoe's squad.

Aiko watched the guard scurry off after Orion nodded and she looked at Orion again with a confused expression. "What are you up to?" She crossed her arms, since she really did want to know his plans. "I'm your friend, you know. You can tell me things. I'm not Carl, but I'm still your friend."

"I know, Aiko." Orion said quietly, slumping slowly to crouch in the sand, still leaning heavily on his walking stick. "What we've tried so far, every tactic, every plan, has been well thought-out and well-executed. Orderly. And they've been ready for it every single time. Because they know how many of us there are, and they've been watching us as much as they can. Orderly conduct, however logical, isn't going to win here. We need chaos, which is something the Consortium isn't good at. So that's what I'm going to give them. And I'm going to *hope*," he emphasized with a deep sigh, "that the Consortium slugs are too busy pissing themselves to worry about ordering their slaves around. If we can do that, we can finish this thing. Finally."

She nodded slowly and watched him carefully to see if he was bleeding any more or if he needed any more pain medication. "I can give you something for your pain when you come back. You'll need it." She chewed on her bottom lip a little bit before she continued. "I heard Anna is pregnant."

Orion nodded slowly, since that had clearly been on his mind as well. "With the father either dead or on the other side of the galaxy." He tightened his grip on his walking stick and forced himself back up to his feet. "She's the only one of us who really understood. I think Logan did too, in his own way, but he kept trying to fight by . . . by rules. Politics. Anna's the only one who's ever understood the way this war needs to be fought. The only way this war can be won." He looked over at Zoe and nodded off after the man who left. "Take your squad and go help Sean. Ask Carl to send half a dozen engineers down here, if he'll let me borrow them for the next few days."

"Carl likes to give you what you want. He thinks he's making you happy." Zoe replied before she ran off as well, which left Orion with Aiko again.

"What do you mean?" She wasn't sure she understood what he was trying to say about Anna, or even if he wanted to talk about her. "I thought it was because she rushed into things that she got captured in the first place."

"That may be why she got captured. Doesn't mean she was wrong to do it." Orion agreed, finally looking back up the slope at Aiko on the other side of his map. "If all of us had been that committed, focused, straight into the compound and fuck the consequences, there's no telling what would've happened. It could've worked, it could've failed. But what doesn't work, what won't work, is what we've already done. Classic definition of insanity. So if you think about it," there was still the slightest hint of the old Orion beneath the gloom and intensity that had settled on him in the months they'd been left on Eleusis, and it showed every so faintly in his voice, "when acting in a sane fashion continues to fail, the only sane thing to do is something completely bat-shit crazy."

Aiko couldn't help but laugh just a little, and she gave Orion the smallest smile afterward. "There was a reason why the two of you were so great together. More than one reason, really."

All he could do in response to a comment like that was nod. "A lot of reasons." He looked over his map again, checking over the details without finding anything more. "I don't know what they're doing to her in there." He eventually said. "I don't know how they coerced her to do as they told her to do, I don't know how she's still alive, since they have to know who she is. But whatever else is going on in there, whatever else happened back on Earth, she's . . . she was my wife. I love her too much to let anything stop me from trying to get her the fuck out of there. And I do mean anything."

"I know. You'll get her out of there. I just hope you can find an answer about what's going on with her when you do. I'm extremely concerned that it's drug-related. The only things I've ever encountered that would change someone's behavior so drastically would have to be pharmacological in nature. You've seen what people are like when they're drunk. Or using a narcotic substance. Some kind of drug therapy has to be behind this. I wish I could test for it myself, but clearly I don't have those kinds of resources in the Eleusis wilderness. Just be aware of it, and if you get in there and she fights you, that could be why. That or severe conditioning. Just be aware."

"I hope you'll be able to figure it out once we get there, whatever it is. If my plan works, the Consortium people are going to clear out too fast to worry about destroying evidence on the way. You should have their notes or drugs or apparatus or whatever the fuck they're working with." He started walking away from the map, going around it so he wouldn't mess up any of his lines.

The lightning struck again in a fractured delta of spiked fissures above the sea, but Orion still didn't turn around. "I'll go get something to eat. Then, if Carl decides to indulge me on this, we're all gonna have plenty of work to do these next few days. If he does, I'm just hoping I don't get assassinated in my sleep by somebody who's tired of going along with my crazy ideas."

"You won't." She replied after flinching from the lightning and she started heading back, with or without Orion, even though he had agreed to get something to eat. "I'm going to run, since I'd like to not get zapped. It happened once. It wasn't funny at first, but if you ask Carl about it now, it makes him laugh. I'm still not convinced it was funny."

"I'll have to ask him about it. You're not exactly tall enough to make a good lightning rod, but run if you want to." He couldn't really run with his leg still healing, but he wasn't dallying either. Now that he had people in motion, he felt the need to be busy. That had been the way his entire life. Once he had orders, he needed to act. Life was that simple. Life should have been that simple.

"You go ahead. I'll get there." He hesitated before she could get moving again, though, looking around at the landscape past the beach. "Also, just making sure, East is that way, right?" He pointed his walking stick away from the direction of the Consortium compound, away from the beach at a shallow angle to the shoreline.

"Maybe I gave you too much sedative." Aiko said with a concerned look at Orion, but then she nodded. "East is that way."

"Thank you." He nodded to her, but didn't make any move to follow, quickly or otherwise, when she jogged away from the lightning. It left Orion as the tallest thing anywhere nearby, though the hills rolled up quickly into the inland canyons. There were flashes every few seconds over the sea behind him, but he wasn't worried. Or he tried not to be.

Soon he was alone on the scrub grass just a few dozen meters above the high end of the open sand. It was one of a thousand moments of solitude in which it had been easy to feel like he was the only human being who had ever set foot on the planet. So much of Eleusis was still unspoiled, but the small patch of the planet where humanity had first set foot had naturally been turned into a bloodbath. It saddened him without surprising him.

It had been . . . how long had it been? He couldn't easily remember the last time. Back when he was living on Three. Before anything. Before the Initiative. Before Mercury, before Anna, before Leo and Lynnette. Before the world had gone insane. Or before he had realized how little sanity the world had to spare in the first place.

He went slowly down onto his knees, sitting back on his heels, and carefully set aside his walking stick. It wasn't dawn, it wasn't noon, it wasn't afternoon or sunset or night, but he doubted he would have been able to remember enough for one of them anyway. And besides, he doubted anyone had yet established guidelines for the correct practice on another planet. Some things, though, he did remember. Some things he still believed in.

"*Alhamdul lillaahi rabbil 'aalameen; Ar-rahmaanir-raheem . . .*" He was surprised how easily the words flowed once he started. He was a child again, kneeling beside his parents. He had been gone from home before he was expected to begin daily prayers, but that hadn't stopped him from learning when he was young. *Praise is for God alone, Lord of the Universe, Most Compassionate, Most Merciful. Master of the Day of Judgment. We . . .* he shook his head, taking in a deep breath at the correction, *I . . . pray to you alone for help. Show me the straight path, the path of those you have blessed. Those who have not deserved your wrath, or gone astray.*

Had he gone astray? It had been a long time since he had believed, since he had felt the need to believe. Astray or not, they didn't deserve anybody's wrath. Nothing about what was happening with the Consortium was deserved. Nothing about the Consortium had anything to do with God.

His hands moved down to his ribs, where beneath his jumpsuit, there were two tattooed quotes in Arabic. Even though they were inked right into his skin, it had been a long time since he gave them any consideration. *To Allah belongeth the mystery of the heavens and the earth. Truly Allah is full of kindness, the most merciful toward mankind.* He recited the passages and sighed, bowing his head toward the scrub grass and folding himself in half to press his nose against the ground. *We could use some of that mercy toward mankind right about now. Some of that help and the straight path would be good too. And kindness. Kindness would be a switch.*

He knew it wasn't the most reverent prayer ever muttered by someone on their knees, but reverence wasn't something he was very good at.

I refuse to believe that letting these assholes control any world you created is a part of your will. Humans have had more than their fair share of fucked-up dictators and governments over the years, but this . . . I can't believe that this is your will, because it sure as hell isn't mine. If it isn't, then help me out, here. Please.

He stayed against the ground for a long time before he pushed himself back up to his feet, staring up into the cloud-covered sky and wondering, as always, if anyone or anything was listening. He always felt as though someone was, but faith didn't come easily to him beyond that vague impression. He would need more than just vague impressions to pull off the bat-shit crazy plans he had in mind.

* * * * *

It had been almost a week since the last rebel attack on the compound, and Stephen smiled as he checked the most recent round of reports. Heat-mapping from their high-placed sensors showed good news for them in the compound.

"It would appear," he said to the rest of the room around him, "that your friends have decided it's time to start stockpiling and lying in for the winter. Can't say I blame them." Stephen was naked, which was normal when he was inside his own suite. Anna had undressed him herself hours before, and done a great deal more to him besides. She was, as she had been instructed to be while in the Kaplans' chambers, kneeling on one side of the bed with her hands folded in her lap, her eyes on the floor like a good slave.

Next to her, Carmina and Francis were in the same posture, though the two of them were chafing against it a great deal more than Anna was. They had only been under the serum for a few days, but Anna knew from personal experience that even a single dose of the stuff was enough. "Our imaging shows they've called almost all their people into some hunting effort in the northern canyons. Makes sense, given how bad the storms are getting this season."

"Why do you . . . think we care?" Carmina spoke through

173

gritted teeth, but her posture didn't change.

"Well, people in your position usually like to think there's going to be an end to it." Stephen slid to the side of the bed Carmina was on, placing himself right in front of her in easy reach. She had been his new favorite toy ever since she'd been captured, mostly because of all the fight she still had left in her. "I thought I would let you know that doesn't appear to be likely. Certainly not before the spring."

"You think you're going to scare me? Or destroy me? It's going to take a worse fucker than you, Kaplan." Carmina growled and looked over briefly at Francis for support. "They'll kill you eventually. That's all that matters."

"That's part of what's wrong with you people." Stephen said in disappointment, glancing over at Anna. "Get me a drink. Tequila. From the Eleusis-brewed batch." He didn't even look at Anna any longer than to make sure she had heard the command and was moving to obey. "All you can think about is your little tasks. Who to kill, what you want for yourselves, what injustices you've suffered, you you you all the time. Tiny minds and tiny ambitions."

"You won't have any ambitions when you're dead. Big or small." Carmina replied with a growl as Anna poured the bastard a drink. She knew Anna couldn't control herself, but the sight still perturbed her. Though much worse things had happened over the last few days, and to Anna especially. It was as though the Kaplans and Henry were making Anna pay for the attack by the rebels.

Stephen shook his head and took his drink from Anna. "I would have thought you, of all people, would understand the ambitions of the Consortium, Carmina. More than most of them, you've been ruthless and direct in your methods, to accomplish your goals. You've never pretended to be moral, you've never apologized, and you've never backed down from a fight. Hell, you even did some of our work for us when you broke your people away from the rebels."

"Just stop engaging him." Anna said as she looked at Carmina. "He gets off on the threats, especially from you. Unless you enjoy getting your face fucked by his disgusting penis, I would shut up."

Stephen grinned at Anna's continued rebellion, but he kept looking at Carmina as he nodded in Anna's direction. "She's a little jealous. She wants to make sure as few other people get a taste of my cock as possible. More for her. You saw how she screamed."

Stephen loved very little more in the world than the look on Anna's face when he forced her to remember. Carmina had been much easier to break physically than Anna had, but Anna was much more rewarding as a result.

"You know how much I hate you. Which is why you love telling me that I don't."

"They're not going to give up." Carmina continued on, talking about the rebels. "You'll see."

"I know. That's what makes them so much fun." He looked over at Maria as she came back into the room from the bathroom. He never stopped being attracted to the woman, but when she had just gotten out of the shower, she was always particularly appealing. He took her hand as she got back onto the bed and laid back to put his head in her lap, still looking over at Carmina.

"Here's a hypothetical situation for you, and you can consider yourself under orders to answer. If your rebel friends continue their attacks, and eventually lose enough people that they will either retreat into the wilderness or open themselves up to be taken captive, like yourself, then their rebellion here on Eleusis will be over. If, hypothetically speaking, all of your rebels are either captive or dead, and the Consortium eventually re-establishes a Twist that can reach us here, will you still continue to insist that someone, someday, will come to rescue you?"

"I'm not looking to be rescued. I'm looking to have you destroyed." Carmina growled, and it made her angrier that Maria started laughing.

Maria ran her fingers through Stephen's hair in her lap and leaned back to get comfortable. She was relaxed and rather exhausted from the use of their slaves. "You've wasted most of your life trying to destroy the Consortium. To no result but failure. You should accept that."

"What's the point of acceptance?" Francis said beside Carmina, still every bit as defiant and wilful as the woman he loved. They had done their best to keep their captors from realizing their relationship with each other, and had succeeded so far. He gritted his teeth and pushed himself up off his knees to get to his feet, though every moment was clearly a struggle.

He was closest to where Maria was lounging against the pillows, and he forced himself forward against the edge of the bed. It was like he was weighed down with hundreds of pounds of weights and moving through a snowdrift to get to her, and he broke a sweat almost immediately at the resistance required. Even so, he pushed on and one of his hands started reaching out for Maria's throat.

Maria giggled as Francis tried so hard to get her, and she didn't even move away. "Husband, dear, I think he's trying to kill me."

Francis continued, and Stephen almost obligingly moved out of the way so Francis could get closer. "It looks that way." He ran his hands down Maria's legs as Francis leaned in. He managed to get one hand over Maria's collarbone, but he was struggling to get it closer to her throat. The rest of the man's body was getting up onto the couch as if strangling Maria wasn't his only intention. Stephen moved to the edge of the bed to watch. "He looks serious. Would you like me to do something about it?"

"Would you?" She said without moving, since she was glad to watch Francis try so hard. "I don't know if I can handle it."

"Don't sell yourself short." Stephen chuckled. The man had made a mistake in attempting to assault Maria with some kind of physical touch. The effects of the serum on their prisoners were both immediate and irresistible when it came to skin-to-skin contact. "I think you can handle it. Let him kill you just a little. Make the man happy."

"Oh, all right." She replied obligingly as she slid a little closer to Francis. Maria batted her eyelashes at him in an attempt to look quite vulnerable. "Are you really going to kill me, Francis?"

He did his best to close his hands around her neck, but all he managed to accomplish was a slight constriction of her airway. Even so, he was grunting and panting for breath, clearly struggling even more than Maria was. "I'm . . . going to . . ." She had just finished with him an hour before, but however brutal the man was, Maria had taken it and encouraged him into more. No matter what he tried, he hadn't been able to do any lasting harm, but he was clearly trying, even as his body betrayed him.

Stephen looked away as the battle continued, since he knew his wife. He knew she would get what she wanted, no matter what. He looked back at Carmina and leaned forward to raise her chin so she could look him in the eye. "Keep fantasizing about destroying me. You'll have as much success as he's having with my beautiful wife over there."

Anna watched as both of the Kaplans tortured their new toys, and she thought about how after months of drugs and conditioning, she still had the willpower to take a gun and shoot

Stephen. Francis couldn't convince himself to choke Maria, but she had managed to actually shoot Stephen. Maybe she wasn't immune to their shit, but she was stronger than it. Wasn't she?

By the time they were finished with their latest round of dissolute torture, Stephen left Carmina as a gasping, shuddering puddle of her former self just off the side of the bed, curled up in a ball as her body continued to betray her under Stephen's orders. Francis joined her, rolled into the fetal position as he stared at his hands that completely refused to do as they were told.

Stephen looked down at Carmina with a satisfied growl, running his hands over Maria as if the two of them had been the ones to satisfy each other instead of their victims. "I'll tell you what's going to happen once we've captured all of your friends. We're going to continue building the world we had in mind before you came here. One without all the petty infighting of Earth or Orbit, one where the human race finds answers instead of always asking all the same fucking questions and then fighting over them. You'll be working to build this place until you die. So will your children. So will their children. And they'll be making this world a worthwhile place."

Anna looked over the two newest victims, then up to the Kaplans. Too bad they didn't keep a gun nearby. She really wanted to try again.

"No comment for once?" Stephen grinned and turned to kiss the inside of Maria's thigh before looking up at his wife's face. "I think she's learning."

"Good." Maria said with a very satisfied sigh. "I'm sleepy. Let's get some sleep. They're no fun when they're exhausted anyway."

"Oh I don't think that's true. Besides, it's just barely morning. You used to have a lot more stamina." He accused her with a slap to her ass before he moved away from her again on the bed. "But fine, surrender if you insist. I'm going to . . ." He looked across the room as his communicator beeped, and he stepped directly over Carmina where she was still recovering against the floor.

"It's an alarm." He said with a look back at Maria. They'd gotten no warning the night before about anything they would need to have a warning issued for. He opened the message to a garbled image of a guard speaking into the device, but there was no clear audio.

"Report." Stephen said, but the only image that came through from the man was one of a panicked expression and people moving quickly behind him. "I said report, damn it! What's the alarm about? Are we under attack or not?"

"Sir . . . we are, Sir. It's just . . . we're not sure, Sir."

Stephen had no patience for incompetence or cowardice, and the voice on the other end of the connection was both shaken and confused. They could afford neither in their position. "Pull yourself the fuck together and tell me which it is. Are we being attacked or not?"

"Sir, the perimeter alarms tripped because we had a projectile incursion. But it was a . . . well it's . . . I've been informed that it's what the hunters call a Copperback, Sir. Like a mean-looking deer with fangs . . ."

"I know what a fucking Copperback is! What do you mean it was a projectile? It jumped a downed perimeter segment?"

"No, Sir, it . . . holy shit!" The voice and video on the other end of the line cut out abruptly, and Stephen could hear a number of dull thuds sound on the other end of the phone, one of which sounded like it hit the communicator the man had been holding.

"Soldier!" Stephen shouted, looking back at the captives and then moving to pick up his clothing. If they were under attack in some way, he needed to be clothed and he needed to be armed. "You three report to your cells and remain locked in unless Maria or Henry or myself gives you the order to leave. Confirm that you understand." He wasn't going to have a trio of slaves hanging around that had a history of pushing their boundaries every chance they got when he didn't even know what kind of attack they were under.

All of them agreed that they understood, but as Carmina and Francis started complying, Anna hesitated. "You can't use us as body armor if you lock us away, you know."

"Shut up and go back to your cell!" There were degrees of forcefulness that the Kaplans could use to impose their will on their slaves. That kind of shouting was the highest degree, and set every nerve in her body rushing to do as she had been told, while he pulled on a pair of pants and a shirt.

Maria was quick to get dressed as well, but her efforts were focused on getting in touch with Henry. He was the one who would know what was going on and why. "Montgomery. What is going on? Why are they hurling dead animals?"

"Believe me, I'm just as confused as you are." From the background noise, it sounded like he was in a hurry, but he didn't sound panicked. "Whatever it is, it's certainly something they've never tried before. I don't know if they're just out of other ammunition or what. I'm heading to the walls right now to do some scouting. I'll let you know what I find."

"If it's needed, meet at the emergency outlet." She said quickly, but once he agreed, she ended the contact. "He doesn't know what's going on. Let's find out."

Stephen watched to make sure Anna and Carmina and Francis were on their way through the halls to their cells, then headed out with Maria's hand in his. They had both had a very long and pleasantly exhausting night, but if the compound was in danger, they needed to go see what the hell was going on.

The compound had been built with further construction in mind. Each of the buildings was set apart from each of the others to allow for a broad plaza of cleared space between them, wide paths that served for moving people and equipment easily from place to place. In the center of the compound, in a clearing now surrounded mostly by rubble after the many attacks from the rebels, stood a small, temporary monument, a small tree only a dozen meters high with shining branches, which the early designers of the compound had intended one day to replace with a commemorative statue to celebrate the achievements of those pioneers who were responsible for surveying and taming the planet.

The small monument had been knocked on an angle, and there were several Copperbacks hanging from the various branches of it at grotesque angles.

As Stephen watched, a dozen more carcasses were flung into the compound over what remained of the outer walls, no longer falling in the middle of things, but splattering and shattering against every building and every pile of plaster and concrete that had once been fit for research or residence.

"What the fuck?" Stephen asked with his mouth hanging open. "What would . . ."

"Sir!" A guard was yelling nearby, running over to Stephen and Maria with a tablet in his hand and panic on his face. "Thermal imaging shows movement, Sir! We don't . . . the electrical storm is giving us a hell of a lot of interference, it could just be misreading, Sir, but it looks like there's . . . there's hundreds of them. I don't understand it, Sir. It goes against all intelligence."

Stephen held down his own horror at the possibility, since it simply wasn't a possibility. "Are you telling me that after almost five months, they've gotten reinforcements? That's bullshit, Private! We'd have picked up a working Twist on our sensors, no matter where it opened up on the planet! They can't have gotten reinforcements!"

"Sir, without visual verification, I can't . . . all I can tell you is what I'm looking at, Sir. And there's things . . . I don't know what this means, Sir. It doesn't make any sense."

"Where are they attacking from? You can see that much at least. Form fucking ranks! Call out the . . ."

"But it's from everywhere, Sir!" The man was about to piss his pants, if he hadn't done so already. "North side, through the gap, southeast, every side but the water, Sir! We're surrounded!"

Stephen reached out and punched the idiot square in the face, but managed to catch the tablet the man held on the backswing, looking through the data himself. He looked up every few seconds to make sure he wasn't in the path of the still-flying Copperbacks, but otherwise, he focused on his work.

"They made catapults." He showed Maria beside him. On some of the surveillance drones, they could see rudimentary catapults with huge piles of dead Copperbacks next to them, being flung regularly and with some precision by the rebels. They seemed to be falling farther and farther from the center of the compound, though. Were the catapults losing their efficiency already? Flimsy weapons, if they were.

"What the fuck are they doing? Besides providing us with steak dinners to last us until fucking Ragnarok, I mean?" He looked up at the sky as the ever-present lightning storm continued to intensify over them. The storms were always worst in the mornings when the temperature variations were most in flux.

Maria watched in both horror and fascination, because she knew there was a reason, but she didn't know what it was. Not knowing was always a fascinating challenge for someone like her. "They're not crazy. So that means they're doing it with a purpose. Since we don't know what that purpose is, my inkling is that we get ourselves to a safe place."

"If we don't know what kind of attack they're launching at us, how can we know where is safe?" Stephen was getting increasingly confused, but he looked around for a likely spot that would allow them to see what was going on while also being safe. "The south shore watchtower has tunnel access. We can see what's going on and if something goes wrong, we can get down to the tunnels."

"Perfect." Maria looked around again and started running after Stephen as they headed toward the watchtower. What the hell were the rebels doing? It didn't make any sense. At least not to her.

The compound wall joined up directly with the watchtower, and was one of the only parts of the wall that was still more or less intact. The scene they saw when they got up to the top of the wall segment was like something out of a nightmare. More than a kilometer away, Stephen could see where the rebels had set up some of their catapults, but their piles of Copperbacks were almost completely gone. There was an entire trail of animal carcasses from the walls of the compound leading outward, and as Stephen watched, the rebels suddenly abandoned their catapults. They didn't even run in the direction of the compound.

"What the fuck do they think they're going to accomplish?" Stephen was incredibly confused. Nothing about the attack was making any sense. The rebels were clearly amassed for some kind of attack, but there was no clear sign of what. If they were surrounded, especially by hundreds of fresh rebel reinforcements, then they would have to improvise.

Once he was sure Maria was keeping an eye on the exterior, he turned around to shout at the soldiers who were awaiting orders. "I said form up! Firing lines on all three fronts! Somebody get to the force cannons and get them hot. The rest of you form up to the northwest and southeast corridors. If the reinforcement reports are accurate, then we're matched! Move!"

He kept hearing a sound from out in the distance beyond the bared field of grass between the compound and the forest, but it was too far away for him to identify it, especially behind all the lightning strikes. The thunder from the electrical storms turned the morning clouds into grey noise that suppressed every other sound. "Motgomery, do you see anything?"

Henry was slow in responding, but eventually Stephen saw the man coming toward them along the rubble of a downed section of the compound wall, watching the exterior carefully as he moved. He was in his usual survival gear, his mask hanging off his belt beneath a wide and varied coat. "They're not . . ." He slowed as he got to the Kaplans near the watchtower, but there was real fear in his eyes as he watched the landscape, especially as the noises from the forest grew louder.

"They're insane." He finally said, all the blood draining from his face. "It's suicide. They're . . . we need to go. Now. All of us. Everyone you don't want dead, we need to go. Now."

"Full fucking sentences, you idiot! What the fuck are they doing?!" Anything that could legitimately scare a psychopath like Henry was not something Stephen wanted to see, but he wasn't going to abandon the compound they had been fighting for because one man was pissing himself.

"They're trying to lead . . ." Henry began to say, before the noises out in the forest suddenly got louder. Henry eventually was not going to stick around to see what was coming for them. "Run, you fucking pricks!" He was into the watchtower and rushing down the stairs before either of them could follow.

Stephen began to move to follow instinctively, but instead he stood near the doors and turned to watch. At first, he couldn't understand what he saw. They knew the rebels had a few dozen two-wheeled transport devices, though they were typically terrible on rough terrain and took a long time to charge under the Eleusis sun. Every one of those motorcycles seemed to be in use along the forest's edge, but it looked like there was lightning striking among them on the ground as well, between them and the forest behind them. One rebel drove the cycle, another sat behind with one of their weak energy weapons, shooting into the trees.

It made no sense. Until the forest started moving.

The roars of the Behemoths grew to a bellowing crescendo as the rebels led the house-sized beasts from the treeline. Every time they were shot with the electrical discharge from the rebel weapons, it seemed to just excite them, whipping them into a frenzy that drew them on rather than pushing them back or causing them pain. Each cycle pair seemed to have woken five or six of the beasts, and there were hundreds emerging from the forest in wave after wave.

As soon as the army of animals had reached the midpoint of the field where the animal carcasses began, the cyclists broke off and wove their way through the beasts, back toward the trees, but by then, the Behemoths had gotten the scent of fresh kills, and they only turned more frantic. The feeding frenzy started as soon as they got the scent of blood, and a few of the animals broke off from their assault, fighting with each other over some scrap of animal that had been left. The rest, however, followed the trail of bodies, each one crawling over the last to rush the compound's walls and the feast beyond.

Maria's face was a horrified mask as she saw the Behemoths headed straight for their compound. Nothing would survive. Nothing. "Stephen, let's go! Those things will destroy everything!!"

He knew they had to go, but it was still inexplicably difficult for him to pull himself away. That kind of senseless destruction . . . the sheer insanity of even trying it . . . he felt a twinge of respect for the rebels for the first time since Bickford had beaten him to a pulp.

"Alright. Let's go." He looked back at the compound, at everything they had accomplished. All the data they had gathered from their slaves had been backed up on orbital data servers, of course, so very little would actually be lost, but still. It had been an excellent beginning for their research from which he and Maria wanted to build. They would just have to survive until the Consortium could re-establish contact.

Even if the Behemoths spent the majority of their lives as a stationary part of the forest's ecosystem, the lightning and the artificial shocks of the rebels had driven them into fits, rushing the compound with long, spindly legs that looked like they belonged in the ocean rather than on land. They easily launched their huge bodies over the walls when their brethren had taken some of the easier carcasses outside. When the ranks inside the walls opened fire, the beasts roared in pain and turned the firing lines into well-disciplined bloodstains on the landscape. A few of the beasts fell to the defenders in the progress of the attack, but they moved too quickly and too aggressively for the defense to last more than a few minutes.

As pockets of resistance retreated into the research buildings and found safe spaces on rooftops from which to fire down on the creatures, the Behemoths threw themselves at the buildings themselves, until walls of glass and concrete came tumbling down, raining defenders along with them.

After an hour, the last sounds of gunfire had faded, and the compound had been turned into a massive feeding ground for the Behemoths. Bodies of every kind were everywhere, but one by one, the Behemoths made their way out of the compound and back to the forest. They were moving slower than they had during the feeding frenzy, like giant spiders dragging their overfilled bellies along the ground. A few of the creatures attempted to hole up in a corner of the compound wall, but they quickly seemed to settle into a kind of temporary hibernation, and seemed like nothing more than an overgrown portion of the manicured grounds.

Only when the beasts seemed settled did the rebels begin leading clean-up parties from the forest's edge. There were a few small pockets of resistance that had gotten wise enough not to challenge the beasts, but they were quickly dispatched. It took hours just to clear the grounds and some of the outbuildings, moving cautiously through every room and every twist and turn of the subterranean structures.

Those Consortium soldiers who surrendered were taken to the surface and held in a pack near one of the dormant Behemoths. Just in case.

Orion found that Zoe and her team had appointed themselves his own personal bodyguards, even though most of them had insisted on being given the opportunity to be among those riding the cycles and taunting the Behemoths as their part of the assault plan. As they moved through the compound, the seven Psychos around him couldn't stop grinning at the savagery of what they had accomplished, and a few of them kept giggling with glee as they stepped over Consortium soldiers who had been variously ripped asunder.

Orion told Carl in no uncertain terms that he was going to lead the team to clean out and inspect the building where they believed the slaves were housed, but he couldn't stop himself from hesitating as he stepped inside. The place looked like it was half-palace, half-prison, and he had to admit he was afraid of what they would find.

"Sean, Yolie, Kofi, take the top levels. Everybody else, room-by-room on the way down. Do not fire unless fired upon."

The group split up according to Orion's orders, but Zoe stayed close. She looked around and stopped at a medical kiosk where she threw open the doors. There were a few sedatives, and she tossed them to Orion. "You remember the last one that we took back. She died. If they're gonna fight us, we might as well make it easy on ourselves."

He nodded, then handed out the syringes to the others with them as they headed deeper into the building. "And easy on them. No way I'm gonna believe any of the Numbers volunteered for this program. I'm not interested in hurting or killing anybody who's here against their will." He kept the syringe handy, but also kept a hand on his gun so as to be ready in case there were more soldiers or guards lingering in the facility.

Boss. A click came from upstairs, Sean's voice crackling through their earpieces. *Upper floors are clear. Top floor looks like it's mostly just one big fuckpad, but there's some kind of refinery or chemical manufacturing on the floor just beneath. We've got a few staff members locked down, they surrendered willingly. Not Numbers.*

"Good. Tie them up in one of the corridors and finish your sweep. March them down here to the lobby when you're done." Orion couldn't suppress a smile at the fact that they'd hopefully found something that could be of use and some people who actually knew how to operate the contents. How useful such people would be was another question, but it wasn't one Orion was going to ask until they knew the place was clear.

* * * * *

Anna had no idea what the hell had just happened, but the silence was giving her more anxiety than the sound of battle. Or, more accurately, the sound of the Consortium getting their asses handed to them. She gripped the edge of her bed as she sat there on top of it, all the while wondering if everyone else was dead and she would be trapped in her cell until she died from dehydration or starvation.

"Charles?" She eventually called out, though she didn't know if he was okay or if he was even still there.

"I'm here." The lights in the slave quarters had been off even before Anna and those with her had returned, so all they were getting was the light through the angled windows, permitting no vision of anything outside in the compound itself. The angle of the sun kept things fairly dark for them for the time being, and Charles' cell was almost entirely in darkness.

"If our captors had won, they would have been down here an hour ago to gloat. From the sound of what happened outside and the occasional gunfire, I would say that the compound is being cleaned out systematically. But if you're asking what the initial attack was, I won't be of much help. I've never heard sounds like that before. To your knowledge, has the Consortium been stupid enough to actually try their hand in genetically engineering monsters? Because if they had, that's what I imagine they might have sounded like."

Monsters? Monsters. "No . . . it sounded like Behemoths. They're native Eleusis beasts." Anna looked up as though one could come crashing through the ceiling but then she turned her attention back to the conversation. "If Stephen and Maria are dead, what happens? Are we free of their control?"

Anna could hear the negative in the silence before Charles answered. "No. They've conducted that experiment already. Your dependence on the serum won't end just because they are unavailable to issue you commands. Whether they were dead or you were merely separated from them in some way, the obedience is still required at a chemical level. Without it, you'll enter withdrawal."

"Shit. Well, if dehydration or starvation don't kill us, that withdrawal definitely will." She looked down at her belly and then she sighed. "We'll figure a way out, Olivia."

When Orion and Zoe came through a set of reinforced double doors and a full block of cells with bars on the doors revealed itself, he lifted his gun and proceeded slowly. The first few cells were empty, sheets neatly folded on the simple cot, but the third rank was occupied. There was a dark-skinned, matronly woman sitting on her cot, with a middle-aged man sitting in the cell across from her, both of them staring at the wall rather than watching excitedly for whoever was coming.

"Who are you?" Orion asked quietly, glancing down the hall to make sure no one was guarding the prisoners. The block appeared to be abandoned, aside from whoever was actually inside the cells.

"I am Delta 12." The woman answered simply. She was expressionless, clearly waiting for further questioning or an order.

"You're wha . . . That's not a name. What's your name?" He could see the tattoo she'd been given of the number on her palm, but the woman's eyes were just . . . staring forward.

"Delta 12. My name is Delta 12." The woman's gaze eventually moved to Orion's, but it looked as though her eyes were just empty. "I have no other name."

"We're not with the Consortium." He explained, hoping that it would help. "We're not here trying to trick you or something. We're here to rescue you. The rest of us are clearing this place out as we speak. Whoever forced you to be Delta 12 is either gone or dead. You don't have to be anymore. It's over."

"I do not understand. How can I serve you?" She asked, since apparently this man was just a guard that was new. "I do not recognize you. You must be new. Welcome to Eleusis."

She didn't seem to understand what he was saying at all, but she could speak, and seemed reasonably alert. It was making less and less sense to him by the moment. "I'm Commander Orion Al-Jabbar, with the rebels against the Consortium. I don't want you to serve me. I'm here to free you. You don't have to serve anyone anymore."

Her expression darkened when he mentioned he was a rebel, and she backed away from him immediately. "Rebel? How did you get in? The Masters told us that the rebels were to be killed. Go! Get away! Security! Guard!"

Orion gave her a sarcastic look, and glanced down the hallway, as well as looking over Zoe and the others with him, before looking back at Delta-12. "Right. Keep screaming. Notice how *nobody* is answering? That's because they're all gone. Like I said. You don't serve them anymore. Because they're not here to be served. At all. Completely gone. No more Masters."

"No . . . no more Masters?" The woman's voice was breaking over the words. "No. No, it's not true. Are they hurt? Why did you hurt them? I love them!"

Orion was horrified as he watched, but eventually he shook his head and stepped away from the bars. "Hoo boy." He reached up and rubbed at the back of his neck, especially when the man in the cell across from Delta-12 appeared to be actually crying over the news.

"Start questioning the others one by one." He said to Zoe and the others. "If they give you the same song and dance as D12 over here, show even the least remorse that the Masters are dead, leave them in their cells. We can't risk the chaos if they're going to be a problem. Let me know if you run into anyone who seems like they're actually happy to be free."

Zoe looked more disgusted than horrified, but she was shaking her head at the reactions. "Probably the whole Delta sector. I can hear the tears already. This is fucking disturbing. And that's coming from me. So, you know, double it."

As they proceeded down the cell block, the entire Delta sector was in tears and panicked at the thought that the Masters were gone, and Orion couldn't get out of the sector fast enough. Near the end of it, there were a few holdovers who identified themselves as Gammas. They were even worse than the Deltas had been, clearly from the batch immediately prior. There were no Betas or Alphas except for a single, scrawny Alpha who actually closed his eyes and seemed to simply give up on life as soon as he was told that the Masters were gone. When Zoe checked him, there was no heartbeat.

When they continued along the block, they thankfully got to Echo-1, who appeared to be at least cautiously grateful to hear that the Masters were dead. There were still a few Orion didn't feel comfortable letting out of their cells, but there were a few he released, and who appeared to want to be helpful, even if they were overeager to be obedient.

"What's down there?" He asked one of those he released, looking at a staircase that led down off the block with its own set of barred doors.

"That's where they keep their favorites." The man said with obvious fear. "The ones they like to visit personally."

Orion's face fell as he looked back at the doors, then glanced at Zoe. They both knew who would be down there. Or who should be down there, if she was still alive. "Come on then." He held tightly to the railing to favor his injured leg on his way down.

When he got there, there were only half a dozen cells in a dead-end corridor. One of them held a busty redhead that nearly fit Mercury's description, but Orion could tell the difference. The woman's eyes were as vacant as the rest of the earlier slaves, and when he saw the Gamma on her hand, he didn't even bother speaking to her.

Across from her was a man who looked a great deal like Logan, and had even had his hair trimmed to match. Unlike the vacant expression in the eyes of the redhead, though, the man didn't even bother to get up or look around as they approached. He laid on his cot, completely naked, with bruises and burn scars and more than a few casts over his various joints. Orion felt like he was about to throw up, but he held the bile down as it tried to rise in his throat.

Someone was holding onto the bars of the cell at the back of the block, and as Orion approached, he felt his heart leap in his chest. He knew those hands. He knew the face that was sticking through the bars above them, though still a great deal closer to the ground than his own.

He took in the sight of Anna as he stepped in front of her cell, and didn't fight the tears that immediately welled up in his eyes.

"Hey." He said through a broken voice, his hands shaking as he moved to place them over her own. If she was as mentally far gone as the others or if they had done something else to her to make her think he was his enemy, it was a risk he was willing to take. "I, um, I was told my wife was down here someplace. You wouldn't know where I could find her, would you?"

Anna's own eyes welled up with tears and she did her best to ignore what the physical touch of his hands on hers did to her. She fought the impulse to pull away, since her body didn't recognize him as someone who was approved to touch her. It was his words that pierced her most, since he said she was his wife. Did he really still love her enough to call her that?

"Orion." She breathed through her bars. "You're alive. You're okay. I . . . it looked like you were shot."

"I was." He said with a casual shrug, as if it was the least serious thing that had ever happened to him. "I've been shot . . . What's it been, Zo, five? Six times since we got here? Including last week, I think it's six." He didn't care about getting shot. Not while Anna was alive in front of him. "Not a big deal. Nothing I'm not genetically designed to get over." He looked down at her bump, which was starting to make it difficult for her to approach the bars. "Did they do anything to fuck with your baby, or only you?"

She winced as he talked about her being fucked with, and then she looked down at her bump. "She's okay. Everything they tried couldn't get the drugs past the placenta. They were keeping me alive to get her in a few months." When Anna looked up from her bump, she had to pull her hands away. The instinct was too great.

"It's touch activated." She shook her head and wrung out her hands. "I never thought I would see you again but I thought over and over about what I would say if I could. It was all I could think about for so many days." She looked up into his dark eyes and savored the moment, since she truly didn't know how long it would last. "I know you're with Mercury. And you're happy together. I just want you to know how sorry I am. I fucked up, and I regret it more than anything else. I never should have betrayed you. I'm so sorry."

Touch-activated or not, he left his hands on the bars between them, since it was as close as he could get to her until he was sure she was alright in the head. "The mountains . . ." He realized there was no way she could know about what happened, and he sighed at the fact that he'd have to break it to her himself.

"We've been here, a few hundred of us, for the past five months, surviving out of range of the compound. When we retreated to the Twist the day of the attack, Henry followed us and threw a bomb through, same as we did to theirs. We've all been stranded here almost half a year. We don't know what's happened to anybody across the galaxy. We know they were under attack when we got cut off. From orbit, not from here." He looked down at the floor for a moment as he mourned for who had been lost, but met her eyes again. "I would've stayed anyway. There's no way I was gonna leave you here with them. I saw you go down, but I knew you were too stubborn to die."

Anna had been told over and over that everyone she loved was dead, but it definitely had more weight coming from Orion. She was still crying anyway, since she was glad that Orion had some kind of faith in her.

"This baby isn't Logan's. It was Oliver's. They . . . tortured him and . . . they made me . . . kill him. Bury him with my own hands." Anna took several deep breaths as she tried not to think about it. "Orion, I'm so fucked, I don't . . . I can't even leave this fucking cell without being ordered to. They ordered me to stay."

"You're not the only one we've heard that from. We ran into Carmina and Francis a few minutes ago. They couldn't leave either." Orion's face twisted into one of concern. "What the fuck did they do to you? All of you?"

"It was actually a rather ingenious breakthrough in neurochemical manipulation." A voice came from the cell opposite Anna's. Orion swung around quickly, cursing himself for not watching his own back, but Zoe hadn't been surprised by the man, so Orion relaxed a little.

The man was nothing but a voice in the darkness, but Orion could make out the shape of him sitting on his cot. "The simple version, for the sake of those of us in the room without a pharmaceutical or neuroscience background, is that the Kaplans discovered a means by which to implant the impulse for obedience within what is popularly referred to as an individual's subconscious. You can think of it as a kind of chemical hypnosis, with the receptors bound to certain designated individuals as activated at the moment of drug delivery. Namely the Kaplans and my brother. Henry."

Charles finally turned his face to look into the hallway, but still didn't get up from the cot. "You must be Orion. Anna's told me about you. Charles Montgomery. Strangely pleased to be liberated by you."

"Oh, for fuck's sake, not another one." Orion growled, but then looked back at Anna. "Is he right? It was a . . . some kind of drug?"

Anna nodded with tears streaming down her face. "Every day. It's a clear liquid in our morning meal. Some of the people in previous trials . . . they don't even know who they were before this. They worship the ground the Kaplans walk on." She knew her body wanted her to worship them too. It had betrayed her often enough.

"The Echo trial was for the 'especially resistant'. They want to modify it so no one would be able to resist eventually." Stephen told her a lot of things, mostly while forcing her to do a lot of unspeakable things. "They used it on Mercury too. In the beginning. One time. They talked about missing her sometimes."

"Yeah, I kinda gathered that from the redhead in the cell that looks just like her." He shook his head and turned around as one of his squad members stepped up with the key for the special cells. He opened Anna's door, even if she wouldn't be able to leave it. "So if it's something you take every day, then we'll just have to wait until the last dose wears off, right? Human body works through just about anything, given enough time and a liver that's not completely destroyed."

"Wait? No . . . we can't . . ." Anna shook her head almost violently, but she moved as close to the opening of her cell as she could. If Orion wanted to get closer to her, he would. If he didn't, he didn't. She wouldn't blame him. "I will die without it. I can't just go cold turkey. I imagine we could wean off of it slowly, but I don't know."

"Addictive hypnosis." Orion said with a grunt, since he hated the Kaplans even more the more he heard about them. He stepped through the door of the cell to be close to her, but he didn't touch her, since he wasn't sure what she meant by 'it' being touch-activated. He didn't want to hurt her, but he did want her to know he was there for her. "We'll find a way around it. We've already secured the lab upstairs where it looks like they were making the stuff. Maybe Aiko can figure out what they were doing and make some sense of it."

"If I may," Charles said from the other cell, pushing himself to his feet hobbling over to the bars, "I might be of help in that respect. The serum's never worked on me, due to some of my unfair advantages, but I have a basic understanding of its workings. I might be able to reverse-engineer a cure. Or at least something to help them wean off it, as she said."

Orion halfway turned around. "And I should trust you to do something like that why?"

"Because he hates a lot of the same people we do." Anna looked across her cell to Charles' cell. "Mostly Henry. But the Kaplans too." Anna looked over at Orion. "I trust him."

Orion watched her expression, then turned to look back across the corridor, clearly hesitating.

"Ah, yes, I see your conundrum." Charles said almost empathetically, as he struggled to hold himself upright against the bars.

"First of all, you're not inclined to trust me because you have a well-deserved distaste of at least one of my brothers, possibly more. We can be quite off-putting. Second, you've just been informed that your wife is under a form of chemical hypnosis and may, therefore, be unreliable in her own scruples. Since that information has come from me, you have an understandable double-blind when it comes to trusting me. I do not envy your position."

Charles' accent made the words sound even more condescending than they already were, which was saying something. "That being said, if you happen to have a firearm handy and you have my brother Henry in custody, I would happily volunteer to perform his execution as proof of my trustworthiness."

"We knew Xander and Jason. But I already told you that." Anna inched closer to Orion. She was having to fight the impulse to stay away to get closer to him. "Can I sit next to you?"

The question distracted Orion from the crisis of judgment he was having between trusting Charles or not trusting him. "Yeah, of course." He stepped into her cell and sat down gingerly on her bed, looking up at Zoe in the corridor. "Keep two of the squad on him at all times. Go find Carl. Tell him Anna vouches for him and I'm inclined to trust him. Just make sure he's watched."

Zoe opened up Charles' cell and stared at him for a second. "You're going to need to be carried, huh?"

Charles shook his head, hobbling out of the cell with a hand on the wall. The man's legs, once she could see them, appeared either deformed or diseased. The man himself was pale and hairless all over, and looked more frail than anyone else she'd seen on Eleusis so far. "It's possible. I haven't walked more than a hundred steps by myself in . . . seven or eight years now."

He stayed next to the wall as he hobbled along, but he clung to the bars of the cell beside his, his face falling as he looked in. "Her too." He pointed inside the cell at a woman who appeared to be asleep on her cot. "She's kept in an induced coma because we tried to break out too many times. The yellow syringe above the door put into her IV will bring her around."

"You have a girlfriend, then? Must suck in this place." Zoe opened up the other cell and helped Charles so he could administer the yellow syringe himself. "Coming from someone who is pretty fucked up, this place is jacked."

Charles spared her a quick glance as he waited for the stimulant to take effect, spending most of his attention on examining the woman to make sure she didn't have anything wrong with her he wasn't already aware of. It didn't take long for the woman to show signs of movement, and Charles put a hand on her arm to reassure her as she began to come around. "It's alright, Jeeta. I'm right here. It's me."

Jeeta immediately gasped when she could and she brought her hands to her neck out of instinct. Apparently she'd been sedated in a moment when she thought she was going to die. "Charles." She whispered when she realized it was someone she knew. "You got out again."

"I can't take credit for it this time. And take it slow, we're not in a hurry. For once." He took her hands and helped her sit up, then helped her disconnect the IV in her hand that had been there for much too long. "You've missed a few months this time. The rebels stayed put here after the attack where they put you under. They seem to have finally managed to break through and sweep this cesspool clear. How are you feeling?"

"Tired. Which seems so silly." She sat up but looked over at Charles, reaching out to put a hand on one of his cheeks. "I had so many nightmares. I kept seeing you die."

"Well, you've seen them kill me in any number of ways. I'm sure your imagination had more than enough raw material to work with." He still couldn't look at her whenever he accepted a touch from her. What existed between them was admittedly strange, and not something he'd ever had in his long life. But he turned his face aside and kissed her hand nonetheless, as his long fingers came up to clasp hers. "They turned the sound off on your monitors this time to make me think they had moved you. But your nurses kept coming every day at noon, so yet again, they weren't as clever as they thought. Can you walk?"

"I don't . . . I don't think so. Not yet." She felt so incredibly weak, but she hoped her strength would come back like every other time. "Where are we going?"

"Up to the manufacturing lab. The Kaplans are, according to our new friends, either dead or run off. There are, I'm estimating, at least a hundred slaves who are going to be in severe withdrawal by nightfall unless we can figure out how to give them a dose to keep them alive and taper them off." He laughed at the caustic look in her eyes.

"Yes, I know, I'm exhibiting some form of caring emotion regarding someone other than myself. Do try not to faint. That would be embarrassing having come right out of a coma. And no, before you ask, I don't know for certain that it's not like the other times. But if it is, then it's their most elaborate game yet, and I never credited the Alperts or the Kaplans, or especially my brother, with this degree of subtlety."

"I'll help in any way I can. You're the genius." She replied with a very weak smile. He didn't need to be reminded he was a genius, but she liked to remind him she appreciated his genius at least. His whole life he'd been scorned for it, but not by her.

"Of the two of us, you're the only one who's gone to medical school. I can process whatever needs to be processed as fast as anybody, but you're the one who actually knows what you're talking about." He reached out to caress her face, then helped her get to where she could put her feet on the floor and begin testing out her long-dormant muscles. They both had a lot of rehabilitation ahead of them, but they had to start somewhere.

Anna, though it took her a lot of effort, finally made it so she was sitting pressed up against Orion's side, even though she was still amazed he would let her get so close. "I'm sorry." She repeated after they were left alone, but she couldn't help herself. She never thought she'd have the chance to tell him how sorry she was about fucking things up so badly. "I'm so glad you're here, I'm so glad you're alive. I didn't know what you might be thinking when you saw me, if you hated me enough to not be happy I was still alive."

He looked over at her quietly for that, but then shook his head. "I was angry. For a long time. I was even still angry when I came here with you. Being with Mercury was something that I think healed us both, in our own ways. Things have always been simpler for us Orbitals than they are for you Earth-born." He gave her a small smile that was weak after five months without much practice.

"I stopped being angry eventually. After we'd gotten stuck here and I kept on not finding you when I went to look in the rubble where I saw you go down. I shouldn't have been angry in the first place. The only thing I stayed angry about after that was that if you felt like you needed to see what was happening with Logan, you should have talked to me about it first. I'm never gonna say no to something if you need it, or if it's something that'll make you happy. I don't think I'm capable of that kind of no."

"I wasn't thinking. I never think things through enough." She took a deep breath and it felt like her body wasn't even capable of sitting upright. She could feel the defense she'd built up to protect herself from the Kaplans start to crumble, and she was afraid of it. She wasn't sure there was much of a person beneath all of her sarcasm and anger.

"I still love you. I always will." Anna looked over at him, even though he wasn't looking at her. "If we ever get back to Earth and Mercury is waiting for you, then I'm happy for you. You deserve the best and every bit of happiness together. I don't even know what kind of person I am anymore, not after . . ." Anna shook her head. "I used my anger and sarcasm to hold me up. Beneath that, I don't know if there's any part of me left. Nothing good, anyway."

"Of everyone I've ever met, the only person I can think of with more anger and possibly more sarcasm is my sister. Was my sister." He admitted, since he wasn't sure if Khadi was still alive or not. "Whatever you were with the Kaplans, whatever they did to you, you never have to be that or feel that ever again. We've got this. They're either dead or gone, and if they're gone, we'll make sure they catch up with the dead part."

"God, I hope so." He didn't really say anything about what he wanted with Mercury if she was still alive, so she was going to take his friendship as it was. "Are you sure you want to stay down here with me until they figure something out?"

"The crazy shit that finally got us in here was my idea, and this is one of the only buildings that's still standing. I don't think there's a whole lot of work I'm missing out there, and even if I am, they can handle things without me this time around." He looked down at her and reached up to run a hand over her opposite shoulder, though he didn't let the touch linger for long. She hadn't been specific about what exactly was activated by touch, but he didn't want to make anything worse for her. "I love you. And I just spent half a year thinking you were dead. I'm not going anywhere."

Anna leaned into him even more once he touched her, and she hoped that Charles would figure something out. She hated feeling the need to push away from Orion, and she fought it, but it was exhausting to do so. "Thank you. For believing that I might still be alive."

"I'm always going to believe in you." He turned toward her and couldn't help but lean into her to kiss the top of her head. He had been living out in the forest for months, not to mention the hunting he'd been doing for the past week, so he was sure he didn't exactly smell like the sterile, obsessively-clean environment around them, but she wasn't pulling away, so he certainly wasn't going to either. "No matter the odds, no matter how many people call me a fucking idiot for it, you're the most believe-in-able person I know. I'm honestly a little disappointed you didn't blow this whole place up on your own, but I'm sure it wasn't for lack of trying."

"I managed to put a couple of bullets in Stephen, but that was about it." She was disappointed in herself too, but he was right, it wasn't as though she hadn't tried.

"You shot Kaplan? Nice. Please tell me you got at least one of them through his nuts." He smiled down at her and leaned back against the wall, just to be close to her without causing the look of pain he could see building up on her face.

"I fucking wish. That dick is the most disgusting piece of flesh. No matter what he says about it." Anna knew she was one of Stephen's favorites because he wanted to break her but also because he wanted to use her body repeatedly. She hated that he had ruined the fun of sex by raping her repeatedly, but the drug was incredibly consuming. "At least I'm not like some of the women here. He utterly destroyed some of them."

"We questioned some of the Deltas on our way in and they all refused to even give us their names. They just went by their numbers. There was one Alpha left on the way too, and he just . . ." he shook his head. "I'm never gonna ask you about what happened here. I don't want to know, and I'm pretty sure you'd rather not talk about it. All I care about is that what happened to them isn't gonna happen to you." Even if he wasn't touching her, she could see the look in his dark eyes as he looked down at her. He had missed her for months, and she was alive. He couldn't take his eyes off her.

Anna reached up and ran her hand gently against the side of his face, and her heart broke at the real feeling of touching him. God, if this was all a fucking dream, then she didn't ever want to wake up. "I never thought I would see your eyes again. I missed them so much."

"They missed you too." He smiled under her touch, closing his eyes briefly to savor it as a few more tears fell from the eyes she had missed. "We're gonna be alright. We're gonna figure this out, get you off the stuff they put you on, and then . . . well, then we're gonna figure everything else out. We don't exactly have a get-back-to-Earth plan just yet."

She nodded as she thought about it, and she attempted to stay as close to him as she could. "If we never get back to Earth, that's okay. I could be happy here with you." Anna didn't know if Logan, Mercury, their families or children were alive, but it almost seemed too much to ask. Too much to hope. She was free. Orion was alive, and he was with her. She was happy for that, and anything else would make her happier, but living on Eleusis with Orion would make her happy too. It wouldn't be torture. It wouldn't be the edge of death. It would be a life with someone she loved.

"I think I'd be alright with that." He took her hand, even though he knew it was hard for her. He just wanted her to know that he meant what he was saying. It was a different world. A world that was starting to get better. At last.

8

Pain. Had he ever lived his life without it? Had he ever, for a moment, known what it was like to live without some kind of pain or another? It didn't feel like it. It felt, and had felt for days, as if he had been in pain since the day he was born. The sun didn't rise without pain. It didn't set without pain.

Logan thought when they moved him to a zero-gravity cell, there would be less pain. He had been wrong. His entire body felt wrong in zero gravity, and his legs . . . god, his legs . . . what he wouldn't give for a hacksaw just to cut them both off and be done with it. He had never once considered suicide in his life, but every time he looked at the ropes binding him to the wall, he thought about putting them to a very different use.

When they took him out of the zero-g cell, he didn't even open his eyes to see where they were taking him. He didn't know if they were taking him to yet another surgery or if they were taking him out to show him off around Prime. It wouldn't have been the first time. He couldn't care anymore. All he could feel was the pain.

He was fairly sure he had suffered some kind of psychotic break days before, but every time someone came to ask him questions, he knew enough to keep his mouth shut. It wasn't as though there was anything else they could do to him that they hadn't already done. Pain was pain. Once he had met it and counted it a close acquaintance, they couldn't give him any more than he already had.

"Where are we going now?" He asked with his eyes still closed, trying to keep his breathing even, against every instinct he had. If he was conscious, his body was screaming at him to breathe heavily. The pain required it. He had to be better than the pain. Even if he really wasn't.

"You're going to see another doctor." The voice said as he was pushed through hallways, and not slowly. The entire journey was jarring and sharp, just to make him feel as much pain as possible.

"But don't worry, I'm sure you'll appreciate this one too."

"Great. You know, I never really fully appreciated doctors' appointments when I was a kid. If I had known I had this to look forward to, I would've enjoyed them even less." He sighed, since he didn't want to see another doctor. Of all the things he didn't want to do in the world, seeing another doctor took high priority. "Have you had your checkup recently? You sound a little sick. I think your humanity might be infected."

"I've been checked. All good." He was rammed into a wall just before they made a halting stop in front of thick, glass doors. "This doctor is supposed to help you with your physical therapy. You need to get to walking soon."

"Do I?" He tried to make his tone as light as possible. If he could be a pain in the ass, it would be slight compensation for what they had put him through. "Why would I need to walk when I've got slaves like you to carry me anywhere I need to go?"

"Funny." Once they got clearance to get through the glass doors, there wasn't much of a trip before he was pushed into another room, and the nurse moved around loudly before she came back to his side with a needle. "You'll like this stuff. Until it wears off, because then you'll just want more. We're finally going to give you some pain medication." And without any warning she stabbed the syringe in his neck and inserted the blue liquid, which stung at first. "It'll kick in by the time the doctor gets here."

He grunted a little at how much it stung moving through his veins, but he could tell that she hadn't been lying about it being a painkiller. At least it partly was, anyway. He opened his eyes just a crack to see who he was talking to, but just shook his head once he'd gotten a look. "Somebody really ought to tell you idiots that you're too young to be on the wrong side of history." He groaned as the effects spread, and opened his eyes again to see his captor heading for the door of yet another nondescript room. "I know you're probably expecting a 'thank you' for the meds, but you'll have to settle for just a little less hate behind the usual Fuck You."

"I know you get around, but no thank you!" The nameless woman yelled back before she was gone completely, leaving him alone and in silence for a long time before the click of a door sounded again and someone walked in. The person didn't walk far into the room before they stopped, remaining closer to the door rather than getting closer to him.

"They told me I was seeing another doctor." He said without

opening his eyes. It felt too good to stay still and see nothing for a while. If he saw people, he would dream about them. He would add them to the catalog of people he hated. He didn't want to do that. "So which kind of doctor are you? The kind who's going to cut me open or the kind who's going to parade my surgeries in front of a bunch of med students? Those are the only kinds I've seen while I've been here."

He could hear the doctor slowly cross the room to get closer to him, but still no one touched him. "I don't really specialize in male healthcare, unless they're in the womb." A familiar voice replied softly, and he could hear the tremble in it.

He was already halfway to jerking himself upright by the time she got the comment out, but a hissing wince stopped him in his tracks before he could do more than push himself up on an elbow to look at her. Once he saw her, though, he pushed himself to sit up the rest of the way, no matter how much it still hurt to do so. "Mercury." He breathed her name like it was something holy, and stared at her eyes like they might disappear if he blinked. "Is it . . ." he hesitated, but still didn't take his eyes off her, "they sent an actress before, days ago, I think. But I knew the difference. Are you . . . Are you really . . ."

"An actress?" She said in both confusion and horror, since she still couldn't believe the measures the Consortium would take to mistreat people. She moved the rest of the way to him and reached out to take one of his hands in both of hers. "I'm really here. I don't know why, and I can only assume it's meant to make things worse for you. But I'm really here."

He held her hands a little too tightly, still looking up at her from the gurney they had wheeled him in on, but she could see the moment he chose to give up and believe it was really her. He dropped his head and lifted her hands so that he could kiss the back of her knuckles, resting his face against it afterward. "They're going to do whatever they want to do to me. Nothing I can say one way or another is going to change their plans."

Mercury was crying almost as soon as she saw him, but she had been able to hold it back until that moment. It was terrible to see him in his condition, and any anger that she had once harboured against him was long gone by now. He had suffered the weight of the world, and she wasn't going to make him suffer any more. "They keep making me listen." She said softly as she stepped in a little bit closer to him, but she knew they had given him pain medication, so she hoped it was helping. "I never know if you're still alive. But I did want you to know that we're okay. I'm alive. The children are alive. All of them. Gwen has been helping me take care of them, she stays with me most of the time."

He let out a breath that was halfway between a sob and a sigh of relief, shaking a little as he held tightly to her hand. "Kiss them for me." He said quietly, taking a shuddering breath as he folded her hands in both of his. He eventually recovered enough to look her over before he met her eyes. "Are you and the twins alright?"

"We're okay. They're bigger than they should be. Or I am. One or the other." Mercury stepped in the rest of the way so she could hug him. It started out gentle but then she was holding tightly to him even with a belly between them. "We're going to get out. Kam says she's working on a plan."

He sighed all over again once he was holding her. The strength she had gotten accustomed to from him had faded in the time since she'd seen him last, and he still didn't move his lower-body at all in holding her close. "Trust Kam to be working on a plan. I'm glad to hear she's alright too." He ran his hands over her back and dug his fingertips into her muscles to savor the feeling of her there with him. "I can't tell you much about us on the ground. I expect that's a part of what they want to get out of putting us in the same room. But we survived the attack in the mountains and we've been working ever since."

Mercury wrapped her arms around Logan's neck and she leaned her head down into his shoulder as she continued to cry softly. "And those on Eleusis?"

He shook his head against her neck. "Both Twists were destroyed in our attack. We've been able to intercept some memos out of their communications, but there's nothing that talks about anyone we sent. We just don't know. Communications between planets weren't sustainable for long without the Twist."

She nodded and held tighter to him. "They told me everyone was dead." Mercury said softly and she turned her head so that she could kiss the side of his head. "I'm so glad you're alive. Our sons deserve to have you in their lives. Lynnette too. We'll get out of here and find a safe place for all of us."

The kiss surprised him, but he had no idea what she had been through, aside from being forced to listen to him screaming. Maybe they had even made her watch his surgeries. He would never have wished that on her. Nothing even approaching it.

When he leaned back to look up at her, it was a very different man looking back up at her. His hair and beard had been shaved 'for medical reasons' as a part of his initial surgeries, and the stubble that had grown back in its place only served to make him look more harsh than he ever had before. There were scars on his scalp and along his jawline she had never seen before, and the storm in his eyes had turned to steel. The man who looked out from behind them, though, who looked straight into her eyes, was hers.

"I'm so sorry, Mercury." He said without letting go of her. "I don't know if it even means anything after everything that's happened, and I don't know how you . . ." He shook his head to rid himself of the thoughts that had momentarily plagued him. "I used to think, when all this started, that the worst mistake I'd ever made was joining the Initiative in the first place. But that wasn't true. The biggest mistake I've ever made was hurting you. I've been reliving it every day since, and there's nothing I want more in the world than to go back and undo it. There's nothing I wouldn't give to make that right."

"Don't relive that every day, I don't want to cause you any pain, Logan." Mercury moved so that she could run her fingers over his face, over the stubble and over the scars. "I'm not angry with you anymore." Mercury pressed her forehead to his and kept her hands on his cheeks. "I still love you, I never stopped loving you. This isn't your fault, and you've more than paid the price for whatever you think you've done. When I was angry with you it was because you were my life, and then my whole life was turned upside down because of what happened between you and Anna. I wanted to hate you so much, but I didn't, and I don't."

She kissed his lips lightly before she leaned back and looked into his eyes. "And they lied when they told you that I abandoned you and the cause. I agreed to go back to the Consortium because they threatened to kill the children. Or get rid of them. Either way, I'll do as they say if it keeps you and the children safe. But I'm always on your side."

"Everything the Consortium does is one kind of lie or another. I would never have believed anything they told me about you. I know you better than that." His hands moved to her sides, holding onto the jumpsuit she wore as he stared back up at her with tears running silently from both eyes. He couldn't even speak as he held her, savoring a timeless moment that he knew would eventually break. But he was going to live in it for as long as he could. "I told you once that I would tear the world down for you." He gripped her sides tighter, the man he had once been, the strength he'd once had, still in him somewhere, even if it had been buried by pain. "I mean to make good on that promise soon."

Mercury wiped at his tears with her thumbs and she nodded. "I believe you, Logan." She ran her hands over his head and she hugged herself to him tightly. "Whatever they do, just don't give up, okay? Don't give up, and I won't give up."

He rested his head against her chest and held her as tightly as he felt was safe given how pregnant she was. "You know I won't." He ran his hands over her sides, and turned his face just enough to kiss her collarbone, his tears still leaving cool trails along her skin as he sighed.

"They're going to come and take you away. That's the only reason they would let us see each other, is so that we'd have to live with the knowledge that they have us both. So the fear of what they'll do to either of us is real. But I'm not afraid. I'm going to keep fighting." He pulled away just enough to look up in her eyes again. "The rallying cry I left on Earth, the one that's making the rounds of the world, is 'who wants to live forever?' I didn't completely think it through at first, but I think I'd answer that I would. On certain terms. So long as you were a part of that life."

"I will be." She ran her hands along his face again and looked around, but no one was coming in for him just yet. "I can give you a massage to help with your back. They said that we would have some time."

"I'm sure your back is bothering you more than mine right now." He glanced down at her once, then moved to scoot himself backward on the gurney. It was a fairly standard hospital bed that had been wheeled into the room, with pristine white sheets and locked wheels at each corner. "Just stay with me, if we have a while. The last time you were this pregnant, I remember you being tired most of the time."

She wasn't actually sure if they would have a while or not, but she was going to pretend like she believed them. Mercury got up onto the gurney and faced away from him so that her back was facing him. "You do that a lot, you know." She replied with a small smile that he could hear instead of see. "I'll offer something and you counter-offer. It's okay to receive, you know." She glanced back at him so he could see her small smile. "And yes, when I was this pregnant before, I was tired. That version of me did not know true exhaustion, though. Imagine four children under the age of two and having only the capability of waddling everywhere. Sometimes they think it's a game if I can't reach them. Especially Declan and James. They are the worst troublemakers together. Leo and Lynnette are much better behaved, I have to say. Leo tends to watch everything, and Lynnette only follows when she's sure something good will come of it."

"I suppose she's her father's daughter that way." He laid back down, and pulled her along with him so they could relax, if only for a few minutes. It felt too good to have his arms around her to think about possible futures. He wouldn't allow the fact that they had only been given the moment's reprieve so things could be made worse later. All that mattered was Mercury, and having that moment together.

"I missed their birthdays. All of them." Leo and Lynnette had been born in early August, and their own twin boys had been born in November. They had all hit a year old without him. Or Orion or Anna, for that matter.

He took a deep breath and pushed away the sadness of his tone, since he wouldn't spend the little time he had with Mercury dwelling on sadness or missed opportunities. Dwelling on missed opportunities was a certain method of missing even more. "Twin boys are always going to be trouble. I have some experience in that area. I'd be a little disappointed if James and Declan weren't constantly in some kind of mischief."

Mercury shook her head. "Well, then you can chase them around when you see them next. I've had to fish toys out of the toilet too many times." She leaned back into Logan's embrace and closed her eyes. She didn't want to think about him on a gurney or the two of them stuck on Prime. She wanted to think about a better life out there somewhere, a better life back on Earth. There were so many things she wanted to tell him.

"Oh, and when they're teenagers? I'm not dealing with overly hormonal boys fighting over the same pretty girl. That's your fight, Mister." Mercury didn't remember ever having a conversation quite like the one she was having with Logan, in fact, she rarely remembered a time when she was the least bit bossy around him, but she had changed a bit since he left her for Anna. She was less needy.

The moment of pause that response got from him was enough

for her to know he was duly surprised at the change, but he gave a brief laugh at it, and leaned in to kiss her cheek in response. "Alright, I'll fight that battle. So long as you fight the same battle a couple years later when these two start fighting for thee same reason." He fanned his fingers out over her side as if to help her hold the babies inside her. "How far along are you, anyway? I know you said they were bigger than they should be at this point, I just don't know what this point is."

Mercury looked down at his hands and appreciated the simplicity of the action and the moment, since she had felt so utterly alone in the parenting department that even a moment of shared concern was refreshing. She put her hands on top of his and then traced her fingers along his skin. "About thirty-two weeks. But they're each already a little over 2.3 kilograms. Normally a single baby at thirty-two weeks is just under 1.7. I shouldn't be surprised, considering Leo is definitely larger than his sister and Orion is . . ." She stumbled a little, since she didn't know what tense to use with Orion, but she tried not to dwell on it. "Orion is a large man. As you know. Still. These girls are growing faster than I anticipated."

"So you're likely to go early, then." He didn't sound particularly worried, since she'd had an enviable time of her first round at childbirth, but the situation was vastly different that time around. Nothing about it was within their control, while everything with the boys had been completely on their own terms. "2.3 kilos, for crying out loud. I don't think I weighed that much when Liam and I were born, let alone eight weeks shy."

"I know. They'll be alright if they come early, but I don't know what to expect. If they will, or if . . . I just don't want them to get so big that they cause trouble for themselves in here." Mercury glanced at her belly and leaned back into Logan again. "I don't want to do it alone either."

"If I have anything to say about it, you won't." He promised quietly, with another kiss to her hair as she leaned back against him. "I'm glad you've had some of the others around you, at least. I've had . . . well, we've all had a lot of time to worry over what's happening everywhere else. I imagined a lot of things. I'm just glad you've had the others around you and the kids."

"It's my fault that we were discovered." Mercury shook her head slowly. "My parents were looking for me and they found me, which means the Consortium was watching their every move."

Logan knew her parents were looking for them, but that was the whole reason why he and the rest of the council hadn't reached out to make contact, because her parents were too high-profile. "I can't fault parents for going in search of any kind of news about their daughter. It doesn't make it your fault that we were found, any of us. The fight was a matter of time, it just didn't go the way I had hoped." He held her a little tighter as he remembered hearing she had been taken and the Twist was no longer working. "The fight that's coming . . . is going to be a very different situation."

Mercury looked around after he said that, but still no one came in to separate them. "Are you scared?" She asked honestly as she turned a little so she could face him a little more. "I don't know what I can do from here. I don't . . . with the children and these babies on the way, I don't know what to do."

"Just be safe." He reached up to caress her face, drawing his fingertips down along her neck to help convince himself that she was really there. "Just defend yourselves, stay safe, stay together as much as you can. Everything else . . ." He actually smiled and leaned in to kiss her lightly. "I wish I could tell you. I really do."

She felt her heart jump as soon as he leaned in to kiss her, and she was too stunned at first to really do anything, even though she had already kissed him once. Everything was so complicated, it always was. Kissing Logan was simple. Kissing Logan was kissing a man she still loved, even if the other man she loved was still alive somewhere. Kissing Logan was feeling alive and feeling hope for something other than being a Consortium rat for the rest of her life.

Mercury leaned back in after he pulled back and she kissed him in return, giving him a little more behind the kiss than she had the first time. What if she never saw him again after they took him away? If she never saw him again, she wanted to remember kissing him, she wanted to remember he was a brave man who had endured so much for her and for their children. She wanted to remember that they loved each other.

He couldn't hold her as tightly as he wanted. He couldn't hold her as long as he wanted, because he knew they would come to separate them quickly. If they weren't talking, there was no chance for them to pick up any useful information by eavesdropping. He didn't want to stop. He didn't want to go back to a world where Mercury wasn't there with him. "I love you." He said desperately between kisses, because it would never be said enough. "No matter what they do, it won't change that. You're better than they are. You deserve a better world. Our children deserve a better world. I want to see it with them. With you."

"I love you too." She whispered against his lips, and almost as soon as she said the words, she could hear doors opening to allow people into the room to separate them.

Mercury kept her eyes on his. "I want so many things, and I want it with you too, Logan. Please, don't let them take you away from me again. Please." She begged before she kissed him again, but then she felt a forceful hand on her shoulder. Mercury sounded pained when the kiss broke, and she turned to glare at whoever stopped it. "You said we would have plenty of time to talk!"

"Which clearly neither of ye wanted, since yer done talkin', ain't ye?" The guard pulled her away to her feet and glared as she stumbled to regain her balance.

He took a syringe from his pocket as another pair of guards dragged Mercury away, but Logan hit him from behind before he could administer the drug. Logan could barely stand on his own feet, but he dragged the man to the floor to hammer his smug face with white-knuckled fists. The man had clearly been expecting nothing of the kind, and was getting the beating of his life.

"Logan!" Mercury cried out, since she didn't want them to hurt him any more than they already had. "Just don't hurt him anymore, please! Please!"

Eventually one of the guards who started to restrain her stepped up and took a wand from a pocket of his vest to electrocute Logan. The shocks left him and his assailant both twitching on the floor, but the guard pulled his comrade away to recover in safety while Logan continued to struggle and pant on the ground.

"You're all dead." Logan growled as he glared up at them. "The second you laid a hand on her, you picked the wrong side."

The guards displayed the same condescending confidence Mercury had seen from the Alperts, already feeling sorry for Logan and all other rebels for a battle they assumed was already won. They ushered Mercury out of the room, and the last she saw of Logan was a needle getting shoved into his neck to put him to sleep. Mercury was a wreck all over again as they shoved her back into her unit, and she couldn't help but continue to cry even after she heard someone come in. Was there ever going to be a time when she wasn't crying over Logan Bickford?

$* * * * *$

An hour later, a message came through showing Mercury the footage of Logan when he woke up. They tried to convince him it had just been a dream, that she was really dead and he would really never see her again. He didn't believe them, but they kept trying to convince him anyway, and eventually he just stopped responding. Obviously his pain medication was beginning to wear off, but he wouldn't even give them the satisfaction of showing that he was in pain. He turned over on the gurney and faced away from them, toward the side she had been lying on. They could try and convince him of all kinds of things, but they couldn't convince him out of believing in her.

Mercury didn't hear anything from anyone else for the rest of the day, but eventually a call came through to her unit. She had a few calls come through as medical consults, but this was from a number she didn't recognize. She and Gwen had gotten the kids to bed about a half hour before, so it seemed unlikely that she would be getting a consultation at this hour.

When she accepted the call, the room that came into focus was a familiar one to her. The numeral VI, highly stylized, was visible in the background, off to one side of the large desk behind which she had often played as a child. Her parents were both present, sitting there as if it was one of her weekly calls home from medical school all over again. The only differences were the growing quantity of white hairs along her father's sideburns and the look of deep concern on both their faces. Their confidence in her had never wavered in medical school or as she began her career, and the lines in their faces made them seem almost strangers.

"Mercury." Her father breathed with a sigh of relief he couldn't quite hide. "They weren't lying, they actually let us through."

Mercury was stunned to see her parents and she just stared at the screen for a solid minute. "Mom? Da?" She asked as she foolishly reached out to touch the screen as though she would get to see them. "I didn't even know if you were still alive . . ."

"We didn't know if you were either." Her father said as he reached right back as if to meet her fingertips. "They didn't tell us anything after we were separated, and then . . ." He sighed and rubbed at his forehead without taking his eyes off the screen. "Are you alright?"

"I . . . I just saw Logan. They . . . they've been . . ." Mercury shook her head, since she didn't want the Consortium to cut her off for talking about it. "I'm so scared."

"You don't have to be scared, sweetheart." Marcus said a little frantically. "You're going to be alright. Just . . . The Alperts told us that you agreed to try and work on their behalf with some of the other rebels. I think that's great, sweetheart. You just . . ." There was meaning in his eyes that she could see because she knew her father well enough. Did the rest of the Consortium know too? Did the Alperts? Her father wasn't a man who was easily intimidated and he was rarely afraid. He looked afraid, but she could see he wasn't. He knew something he wasn't saying. Even if he was trying to say it anyway. "You just need to hold on, alright? Things are going to be alright."

"Hold on? I've been trying, Da." Mercury's voice cracked, and she hated how weak it made her sound, but she couldn't help herself. "It just keeps getting worse. I don't know who is alive, who is dead, and if I'm going to die soon or not. I don't want to die. I don't want Logan to die."

"Things are going to change for us soon." Marcus said with the same kind of duality behind his eyes. He took a breath before he continued. "Even before the attack in the mountains knocked out both operating Twists, we were working on construction of a new one, but the refinement process for the materials required takes a long time. Still, we expect that Twist to be completed in a few months, at the last estimate I heard. You know what's going to happen when that's active." He sighed, still looking conflicted.

"That's why they want you and as many of the other captives as possible to assimilate yourselves into the Consortium way of life. Up here or back on Earth, either way. Once we have another working Twist, things are going to change. We're holding on for that, and we're not going to move before that and take risks we don't have to. Once we can be everywhere at once, we'll offer the rebels the chance to surrender and everyone can go back to living their lives. We just have to make it a few more months."

Mercury nodded, though clearly she hoped it was sooner than a few months. "Of course. It's not that much time, I understand." She still looked pained as she thought about it, but she just stared at her parents. "I'm doing what I can to help everyone else here. It's not easy." She made it sound like she was trying to convince people into the Consortium, but she wouldn't do that. Ever. "The Alperts said I could go back to the way things were. And the children would be safe."

"We're looking forward to seeing our grandchildren again." More true emotion showed through in his face, followed by a deep breath to steel himself against the conversation they needed to have again. "I know what you mean about it being difficult sometimes." He sounded like he was just making conversation, but he gave Mercury a brief look and a pause as if he wanted her to hear more than he was saying.

"Back on New Year's, there was some trouble on Station Twelve. We had to send some military units to intercede, nothing to be done, of course. The incident shook up quite a few of the other Captains, especially those of the greater Stations. I've been spending a lot of time with them and their staff, and my own staff, trying to explain things to them, help them see reason. It's difficult with things as tense as they are and the rebels down on the ground making all their alliances with some of the larger political Unions. But it's important work."

"I didn't know that there were problems elsewhere." Mercury said honestly as she wondered what in the world that her father had been going through. He was alive, though. That was what mattered to her. "Is it too much to hope that eventually we'll all live in peace?"

"No." Her father said without any hint of duplicity in his eyes or face, even though he didn't mean what the others from the Consortium would assume he meant. "No, I don't think that's too much to hope for at all. I want to see you and our grandchildren grow and live long, happy lives. I believe that's possible, and if we continue the work we're doing, we'll get there." He managed to give her a smile, but there were still tears on his face. "They, um, they said they'll allow us to send you some things, as long as they're vetted for going into the holding area, of course. Your mother has some blankets we'd like to send for the children. Is there anything else you need? Anything we can get for you?"

Mercury didn't know why, but hearing they had blankets for the children made her even more emotional, and fresh tears slid down her cheeks. "Pictures? Can I have photographs?"

"Of course." Her father said with a smile. "We, um, we've got loads we can send you, of course." He looked down at something else in his terminal for a moment as he took a breath. "It, um, it looks like if we get them off soon, they should all get to you by the fourteenth or so." He looked back up at her after he said so, and there was that reservation in his eyes again, filled with things he wanted to say but didn't. "I wish we could be there to see you and the children. They've said we'll be allowed to visit soon, but they haven't said when that is, exactly. But as soon as we can, we'll be there."

She nodded and looked between them as her mother finally chimed in, but she knew why her mother usually stayed quiet. Every time her mother tried to say something, her voice broke with the tears she was trying to hide for Mercury's sake. Her parents were being threatened and controlled by the Consortium as much as she was. Her mother told her to take good care of the babies and to give them lots of love, and Mercury cried even more. "I love you both so much. I hope I can see you soon."

"You will. It'll be alright." Her father continued crying along with her and her mother. He was someone she almost didn't recognize from her childhood, and she could see in both of them that every way she had been tortured with Logan, they had been tortured with news of her, or a lack thereof. "Peace is possible. Once this rebellion is finished, we can begin working to rebuild the life we had before, all of us. We're all working toward that. Just don't lose hope."

Once the rebellion was 'finished.' Not 'crushed,' not 'defeated,' but just 'finished.'

"We'll see you soon, Mercury. We're proud of you, and we love you."

"I love you too." She reached out to touch the screen again but they were gone in an instant, and she dropped her head into her hands and cried harder. This was not the life she had envisioned for herself that day when she signed up for the Initiative. This was not what she dreamed about and hoped for. This was a nightmare, and she desperately needed it to end.

9

"Sure. No big deal." Liam said under his breath as they made their way down the corridor. He was less certain, with every step, that they had, in fact, put together a good plan. Even if most of it had been his idea, he wasn't sure, at the moment of execution, if he would actually classify it as 'good.' Maybe 'passable' would have been a better descriptor. "Just act natural when my DNA identifies me as the single most wanted man in the universe right now. No problem. I'll get right on that."

He was walking behind and slightly to the right of Fatma Salem, the long-sitting Captain of Station Three. Khadijah had more than delivered on her promises to make the connections that needed to be made, but convincing the hard-headed captain to do her part in what Liam admitted was an absolutely insane plan had been fairly difficult. It didn't surprise him that the older widowed Captain had taken a fancy and a half to Khadijah upon meeting her in person. The two of them were stubborn enough to put up a blockade that no force in the universe was likely to move. Yet there he was trying. Because of course he was.

The dye job on his hair and beard had been extensive, and according to Fatma's people, would last for several months and confuse the hell out of anyone who tried to swipe a casual DNA sample from him. Both hair and beard had been buzzed within an inch of its life and dyed a fiercely dark blue, a rather popular color on Station Three, known for its eccentricities in body modification throughout the known world. He had been even less enthusiastic about the small spike through his lower lip, but he had to admit it placed him immediately into a certain category of person. Namely, the kind other people were better off not staring at too long unless they wanted a fight.

He walked along behind Fatma on their way to the luxury liner that was waiting for the captain and the rest of her entourage. It was scheduled to pick up all of the Captains of the various stations under the Consortium's control and take them to Prime for their annual trade summit. The flight to pick up all of the main leaders of Orbital humanity was as much a part of the summit as the actual meeting hosted on Prime, and was not an affair that any of the Captains was permitted to miss. Behind Liam and Khadijah, dozens of security officers and trade officials, all hand-picked and fiercely loyal to Fatma, accompanied them down the hallway, with a few of Liam and Khadijah's own people sprinkled in.

"Besides," he continued as he glanced around for the thousandth time, "I'm a bodyguard. Aren't I supposed to look a little jumpy? I feel like that would be natural for someone in my position. Fake position."

Khadi glanced over at Liam and shook her head. "No, you're supposed to look like you could kick someone's ass, not like you're going to pee your pants if someone jumps out at you." Khadi was also disguised, but her disguise was meant to draw attention away from her face and from everyone else around her as well. She had put in some contacts and had used a lot of makeup to make herself look like she was not a guard, but entertainment for someone as well-known and loved as the Captain herself. The jumpsuit from the shuttle was long gone in favor of a deep purple dress that was a match for her altered eyes, cut deeply in the front and short enough for her to feel the guards watching her from behind while they waited for a hopeful chance the dress would move just enough to get a peek. "Don't you know how to, you know, strut? Look confident?"

"You know, strutting isn't really something I had a whole lot of use for before . . . well . . . now." He did his best to walk casually, but spending a few weeks on board a space station had not been quite enough experience to give him the easy predatory grace he saw in most of Fatma's bodyguards. "I've always been more the type where it's all fun and games until somebody pisses me off."

"They took your girl. Doesn't that piss you off enough?" They had enjoyed each other's company a few times while they had waited on Three for the day they could finally meet with the Captain and get everything moving, but they had kept it casual. Or, at least, she had.

When he looked over at her, she could see the anger behind his own contact-covered eyes. Aside from the time they had spent together horizontally (and vertically, and a number of other angles), they had gotten to know each other fairly well on a personal level, and she'd had the chance to see just a little bit of the temper he had otherwise only told her about. He kept it under control most of the time beneath a genuinely fun-loving demeanor, but there were other times when she had caught him sitting on the edge of his bed and staring out into the darkness of space for long minutes at a time. He had a wallet he carried with him containing physical pictures of each of his wives and his children, and he had a single picture of him and Gwen that had been taken just a few days before the attack on the Bickford estate.

As he glared over at her, she could see his hand go to his pocket where he was carrying those pictures, but it didn't linger there long. "I'm plenty pissed off." He eventually said as he turned his eyes forward again. "I'm just saving myself for the people who deserve it. Which is nobody here."

"You never know around here. Just pay close attention." She felt bad for prodding him, but he was there for one big reason, and that reason was his fiancee. Sure, he wanted to help the greater good, but he mostly wanted to get Gwen back.

Khadi turned her attention back to the Captain for a while and they made it onto the ship without any problems, which was a slight relief. The Captain said she wouldn't discuss matters until they had arrived on Prime, so Khadi moved to sit down next to Liam. "Sorry." She said in a low voice. "I say things I shouldn't."

"You say whatever you want." They were seated relatively close to the Captain for their maneuvering seats, but the ship itself was larger than many of the smaller Stations, and the accommodations were sumptuous, to say the least. He shifted uncomfortably in the seat, since it was a kind of luxury he hadn't been accustomed to in space.

"I'm not gonna spend every second of my life pissed off." He eventually said as he came back down from snapping at her. "That's always been my brother's way of doing things, and it's gotten him . . . well, it's gotten him places I don't really want to go myself. I'm here to get her back, but the only way I'm gonna get close enough to do that is by laughing my way into it. The only reasons the Captain even allowed us to come along is because 1) she doesn't want to piss off the rest of us, 2) you're easily the hottest fucking thing I've ever seen outside of Earth's gravity, and 3) she thinks I'm mildly funny. I'm just . . ." He shook his head and sighed, already letting go of his anger for the time being. "I'm not cut out to be a rebel. I'm in this because the people I love already are. The fight doesn't come as easy to me as it does to some."

"Clearly I'm not a fighter." She motioned down toward her dress. It was uncomfortable to say the least, but she was more accustomed to uncomfortable clothing than she was to wearing comfortable clothing. The corset underneath was definitely pushing her breasts into a new dimension. "I don't want to be either. But I didn't want to do nothing. You didn't even believe I had the pull or maybe even the brains to get us here in the first place."

"I float corrected on both counts." He admitted, looking her over in the dress at her gestured invitation. Not that he needed one. The dress was its own kind of invitation. The docking clamps of the ship began the process of disengaging, and he did his best to keep from clutching the arms of his seat as the ship began to maneuver away from the station. "I'm just not sure why she's still stalling. We unfolded everything to her, and she knows we don't have a lot of time. If this is gonna work, we *need* Three. There's no way this works without them."

"She's stalling because she wants something. And she never does anything alone. She wants someone else to go in on it too." Khadi glanced over at the older woman across the ship from them who was handed a drink before she headed into her office onboard the ship. "What do you think, do I flirt with her?"

"I don't know. If that by itself would've done the job, I think we'd be in business by now. You were hitting her pretty hard back in her office." He said it without judgment, but there was still a slight edge of something in his tone. She had been paying attention almost exclusively to Fatma during that particular meeting, but she hadn't missed the fact that Liam had been having his own kind of thoughts throughout the proceedings. They had been together enough times for her to tell that he was making more out of the relationship than she was. "If you think it'll help soften her up for when some of the other Captains get on board, though, be my guest."

"She's been widowed for a while. Lots of people think the reason she's been tougher the last few years is because she's been lonely after her wife passed away." Khadi looked at Liam, since he looked like he had bitten down on something sour. "Cut it out. We're not dating. Don't be so jealous."

He did his best to put the look away, with moderate success. "We may not be dating, but I can still be reluctant when it comes to trading favors for influence. Not something I've ever been comfortable with. Especially with people I like."

"We're doing this to save the world and orbit. I'm sorry if you think my methods make me sleezy." She frowned at him, since she didn't like being judged when she was just trying to help. She sank a little lower in her chair, clearly changing her mind about what she should do.

"That's not what I'm saying. I'm . . ." He sighed, clearly already defeated in the conversation. "My brother's done a lot of shit I didn't like in the name of this war. I've been up and down on him about it, but that doesn't mean he wasn't right to do it. I just . . . I'm a simple person. I'm a farmer. I tend to live my life thinking I can live it on simple terms. Nothing up here is simple." He gripped the arms of his chair a little as the ship jolted, but so did everyone else around them, so he didn't really look out of place doing it. "I'm not judging you for anything and I'm not sitting here thinking you owe me something you don't. This isn't a world I belong to."

"That's because the 'world' is down there. This is Orbit." She responded not coldly, but matter-of-factly. "I'm just trying to help." She emphasized again. "She has everything to lose, in her mind. The Consortium doesn't want to fuck with Three. And she's alone on top of it all. I'm just trying to encourage her to help. You say you're not judging me, but then you look disappointed when I suggest showing off my tits."

He gave her another one of the looks that she'd gotten from him the entire time they'd been on Three. The kind of look that was never accompanied with anything vocal, and might never be. His usual jovial self took over in the next moment, though, and he smiled as he leaned his head back in the seat. "I'm a fan of those tits. And if you were trying to convince me of something with them, whatever it was, I'm pretty sure I'd say yes. Go get her. She's got a lot to lose, but she's got a lot to gain too."

Khadi looked at him for a moment and she wondered what it would be like to be loved by Liam. She'd never been with anyone that was in a polygamous marriage. She didn't have any claim on Liam, even if she wondered what it would be like. Khadi leaned over the seat and into Liam so that she could kiss him. She kissed him long and hard before she pulled away. "Stop looking at me like that."

He gave her a confused look after the kiss broke. "You kiss me like that and then you tell me to stop looking at you like this. On a scale of one to mixed-signals, you're a twelve, baby."

"I like you." Khadi said afterward. "But the way you look at me is unsettling. No one has looked at me like that." She touched the side of his face and sighed. "So stop." Khadi didn't have any emotion behind it, but she was pulling away slowly. She did have a Captain to convince.

Fatma had a private office/cabin for the trip, as all the station Captains would, though it was nothing compared to her quarters on Three. The compartment had barely enough room for a long zero-g bed that could convert into a chair for meetings and a few other chairs along the sides of the room. There were cabinets aplenty for storing possessions for the trip, but at the moment, Fatma was alone, apparently sitting back to review reports on her personal device. She looked up when Khadi appeared, and didn't seem in the least bit surprised.

"I hadn't expected you until we at least docked with Six, but I don't mind people arriving early. Late would have been irritating." Fatma was an older woman, but she had aged gracefully while losing none of the iron in her soul that had propelled her to authority on Three at a young age. She had been the youngest person ever to attain the Captaincy of a station, and she had ruled it without a mentionable challenge for nearly thirty years. It made her senior among all the sitting Captains in orbit, even though most of them hated her.

Her hair was a flawless silver, falling in perfect braids down over her left shoulder. The right side of her head had been shaved and the hair follicles cauterized away when she was a young woman, and the tattoos she wore there were in a glyph pattern that only those who attained her personal favor were permitted to wear on her station. The pattern continued down in an uninterrupted wave along her neck and down across her heart, where it spiraled between her breasts and disappeared beneath the shirt she was wearing.

Fatma's face showed the hardness of age, but none of its wear and tear, as smooth and strong as it had ever been. Her olive skin showed no signs of softness or the laxity that often came with age, and her perfectly black eyes were as sharp and piercing as a hawk's. Her shirt and trousers were those of an officer on leave, not a monarch, but she wore rings on each and every finger, of varying styles and metals. She had always been more of a legend than a lady, and she seemed to prefer it that way. "Please, close the door behind you. We want to make sure people get the impression you'd clearly like them to get."

Khadi felt as though she should hesitate at a comment like that, but instead she went along with it as though the comment didn't matter and she closed the door. "I thought you liked me."

The look on the woman's face was deeply amused without being cruel. "Oh, I do. If I didn't, I would've left you and your friend behind and just said no." She nodded to a seat near hers so that Khadi could have something to hold onto as the ship jostled and accelerated toward its next destination. "I've followed your career, you know. You caused quite a stir several years ago when you actually turned down the Playboy shoot. Isabella was heartbroken." She smiled and put aside the file she had reviewed, stowing it in a compartment beside the chair.

Khadi sat down as directed and made sure she was sitting up straight and had her full attention on the Captain. Not that her attention could possibly be anywhere else, not in a situation like this. "You followed my career? Really? I just . . . wow." There were plenty of models out there, she wondered what made her more attention-grabbing than the rest. "I declined Playboy because it is more centered on the male-gaze. I did other photoshoots that were more tasteful. The lucky ones get to find out the truth behind the photos for themselves. That's always what I've told myself, anyway."

"Lucky is a good word to apply to those who do, I'm sure." She had no need or reason to hide her appreciation of the effort Khadi put into attracting her attention, and she looked her over appreciatively before meeting her eyes again. "Anyone who wants to keep some mystery in this world certainly has to do so on purpose. The Consortium is in the business of finding and solving mysteries, not tolerating them."

Fatma opened a drawer set into the wall of the room and flicked a stylized clear sphere in Khadi's direction. There was a nozzle to one side to drink from, and she could tell by the way the light refracted through it that it was a module of Shine. It was usually a lower-class drink, but the woman seemed to have maintained her taste for it. "I followed your brother's career as well, until he left for the Initiative. Not much mystery to that one."

"He seemed fairly simple. I don't think he actually was. Is."

She caught the sphere and then took a drink from the Shine within it before she said anything else. "What attracted your attention, if I may ask? You're a busy, powerful woman."

"You turning down the Playboy shoot was actually what alerted us to you first." She took a drink of her own and shut the cabinet to relax against the straps of the lounge chair/bed. From Khadi's perspective, they were still speaking more or less face to face, but still, the sight of the powerful woman on a bed was a provocative one in any context. Especially given the last person she'd seen wrapped up in the straps on a zero-g mattress. "Very few say no to something like that when it's offered. Isabella did, back in our own time, but in her case, it was because her wife objected." She gave Khadi a smile over another sip of Shine.

Khadi followed the Captain's example and took another drink, but she was smiling back. "She was beautiful and flawless her entire life. I was told she was one of the nicest people to exist, which is unheard of for models. I mean, we're catty and dramatic. I know I'm a bitch at least half the time."

"She was kind." It was clearly still difficult for Fatma to talk about her wife, but she concealed the difficulty well. "But she had a sharp mind for what was necessary. She had a gift for seeing the way things would play out. Anyone who chose to play chess with her was making a huge mistake. She could always see ten moves ahead of anyone. I threatened to make her a commander more than once." She glanced at the door and then back at Khadi. "She told me to go to war with Prime ten years ago. Clearly I didn't listen."

"Why not?" She leaned a little closer, since she was all about learning as much as she could, and if the Captain was going to tell her, then she wanted to know.

"Because it wasn't worth the lives." She said without hesitation. There was no regret in her eyes or her voice as the same stern tone saturated her words that Khadi and Liam heard during their first meetings with the woman. "The regulations and restrictions imposed by Prime have always been a weight on my people, and on the rest of Orbit, for that matter. But going to war would have cost lives, not just ours but theirs. Innocent people die in wars. The guilty speak at the funerals for a photo opportunity. When we were ordered in to assist with the Kenyan crisis, I didn't hesitate. Those were actions that needed to be taken and a government that was abusing its people every day. It was necessary. It cost lives, but they were lives duly spent. War with Prime . . . is a different matter."

"Not this time." Khadi emphasized as gently as she could, but she realized maybe gentleness was the wrong approach. "The Consortium is going after the small stations for now, but when they turn against Three, it's not going to be the way you think. They won't come after us with guns, they'll turn people from within, turn us against each other and say that internal government needs to be re-established. They'll overthrow you and get what they want before you can even stop it. You know how the people on Three are. Ambitious. Active. Overzealous sometimes. We wouldn't be on Three if we weren't looking for a wild, busy, or infamous life."

"I know my own people." She shot back, but without any anger in the statement. She sighed afterward, and made a few gestures on a pad nearby to open a graphic that Khadi had been looking at for most of her life. It was the usual method of representing all the major Stations of orbit, with Prime and the other eight major stations taking up the majority of the space, and smaller stations aligned according to the faction to which they belonged. There were a lot of moving pieces and subgroups to the way orbital government worked, but Three was a clear anomaly even under a simple graphic.

It had no subsidiary stations aligned with it, and it gave no direct intervention access to any other subgroup. It was beholden only to Prime. "The one guarantee I need from you and your friend is the one guarantee you can't give me. You can't guarantee things won't be worse if we succeed. I've seen what happens when a power vacuum is introduced on even a small scale. You yourself should remember just a few years ago when the Saleo photography firm scandaled its way out of business. Hundreds of photographers and videographers out of jobs and dozens of them stepping up to try and start their own companies on the ashes of Saleo. When the dust settled, there were twenty people dead and five different companies that are still fighting tooth and claw today over every contract. What you're asking me to do is to create the same exact situation, only on a global scale."

"I'm asking you to step up and make a stand, yes." Khadi looked up into the Captain's eyes. "And I can't promise you anything. Except that I can say it will get worse if we do nothing. I can't say it will get better if we do something, but I know it will get worse if we don't." She sighed heavily as she looked the older woman over.

"The Consortium as it is . . . they're a force of destruction. They say they work for the betterment of humankind, but over and over again they look like a mad scientist. We need a new government. A smarter government. You've been Captain for thirty years. Don't tell me you don't know that there are too many crazies in the Consortium. I've dealt with some of those on the Board at the big shows. They take and take and take. We shouldn't have to front their bill anymore."

"I've never said I liked them. Or wanted to defend them. The trouble they get into, the difficulties they make for themselves, is and has always been their own problem. I've made that clear on more occasions than you have clearance to know about." She took another swallow of her Shine, then left it on a latch at the arm of her chair that was there for the purpose.

"I know more about how much destruction they're capable of than they want me to. Which is part of why I've managed to coerce them into leaving Three alone for so long. If your rebellion hadn't come along and blown up Nine when it did, I imagine Three would have been their next target, just to consolidate their rule and get me out of their way. I can sit here and agree with you until we circle the sun again, but the kind of action you're asking . . ."

"I have no interest in putting together the broken pieces of the world myself. If I did, I might have listened to Isabella years ago and done this myself. Nothing I've seen from the rebels gives me much hope that they're going to be a better replacement than the Consortium we already have. The only one I've seen or heard of who I could respect is either your brother or your friend's brother, the cripple. But he went and put himself in Consortium custody and there's no guarantee your brother is alive. The rebellion feels to me like it's on its last legs and it's limping to me to give it some kind of new life again. And nothing about that makes tactical sense."

"You are a stubborn woman, aren't you?" Khadi said with a short laugh in an attempt to relieve the tension, since she wasn't good at staying serious for too terribly long. "You need to relax a little." She replied with a smirk and she took several gulps of her Shine. "Logan wouldn't have given himself up if it wasn't a part of a plan. And Earth . . . well, they're just looking for a crack in the Consortium's armor. Eventually they're going to find it. The

Consortium is going to go down in one way or another. The real question is if you want to be with them or against them when it happens."

"There's never only two sides in a war." She said it quietly, more as a lament than an attempt at an argument. "And there is no crack. At least not one that can be exploited for very long. The Consortium has enough Earth-based countermeasures to take out any fleet that launches before it can leave orbit. If Earth could handle the Consortium, you wouldn't be here talking to me. They would have launched and we'd have had our war by now. If I stand with the Consortium, or if I stand aside and stay out of it, their rebellion fails. That's why you're here."

"Except it seems like nothing I say will change your mind, so I don't know why you agreed to see me." Khadi said with an edge of defeat in her voice. "Even my tits aren't working, and usually they're an amazing distraction to powerful people."

"They're very effective." Fatma said as she unhooked the restraints that were keeping her settled. The ship had been stable for some time, which meant they were allowing inertia to do its work for the time being, and they were as truly weightless as it was possible to be in orbit. She floated closer to Khadi and stabilized herself with one hand on either arm of her chair, her dark eyes burrowing into Khadi's soul the closer she got.

"I want to give you what you want. You and the rebels. The Edge has always been a place for fighters. We're nothing if we don't have a war to fight, whether it's personal or professional or patriotic. If you were in my place, what would you tell my generals to convince them that this is the right war to fight?"

"I don't know. None of them are going to want to fight for Earth-born. And half of them don't care about the other stations. So unless it's personal, I don't know. Maybe Eleusis? Everyone wants to go there, but I'm beginning to believe no one is going to go there except for the elite Consortium people."

"If they had it their way." Fatma agreed. "They offered me a position as head of security with the Initiative. When I turned them down, they took one of my security officers. Victoria. I never have quite forgiven them for that." She considered, still floating nearby just to enjoy the sight of Khadi from closer quarters. "Eleusis might be enough. If I chose to fight for the rebels, can you or your boyfriend make that kind of promise? That our people and I would be permitted to oversee security for the colonizing forces they keep saying they'll send?"

Khadi was caught off-guard by the boyfriend comment, and she felt a desperate need to address that first. "First of all, he's not my boyfriend. He's got two wives and a fiancee already. Secondly, I'm sure he and his brother would agree it is only right for you and whoever you deem worthy to oversee security. Without you, the rest of us may never see Eleusis at all. With you, many more of us probably will."

She was surprised at how vehemently she denied being Liam's girlfriend, and it showed in the look she gave Khadi when she was finished. "I'm familiar with your boyfriend's marital status. I also naturally had you spied on while you were staying on Three." She let that sink in for an amused moment and gave a smile, which was almost as terrifying as her naturally fierce expression. "But I'm glad you think they would agree with our natural involvement. That is a step in the right direction with regard to establishing some kind of order in the wake of all this, at least as far as I'm concerned."

"Any people who want to go to Eleusis from Earth are going to have to undergo training and serious detox. They won't be fit for security detail for some time, that's obvious. But our people already know how to fly shuttles and we aren't all in the middle of dying from CV." She said as though it was obvious. If Earthlings wanted to go to Eleusis, it was going to take more time for them to be ready for it than everyone else. "And even if you spied on us, that doesn't say anything. We slept together. That does not mean that I am in a relationship with anyone."

"You didn't just sleep together. You stayed over. In my experience, that implies something more than just sex. But what do I know?" She shrugged and looked Khadi up and down again, some of her silver hair falling forward over her shoulder in the movement and moving toward Khadijah's own as if reaching out to draw her in. "It's been a while since I indulged myself with a connection that lacked attachment. I was never very good at it even in the beginning."

"Really?" Khadi moved closer to the Captain, though she felt immediately overwhelmed that it was obvious the Captain actually was interested in her. Khadi found herself often attracted to both women and men, even though she gravitated toward men. Really she gravitated toward anyone who she felt comfortable around. "Aren't you lonely? I imagine a woman like you could have anyone you wanted."

"You're one to talk." Her eyes trailed down over Khadijah's exposed chest, and she drifted up a little to change the angle Khadijah had to keep in order to keep eye contact. Tall a woman as Khadi was, it wasn't often someone forced her to tilt her head back for any reason. Especially one who was hovering over her to check her out. "You're more of a knockout than I ever was, but you've never been married." Her hand moved slowly in a caress down Khadijah's cheek and along her ample cleavage, clearly taking the liberties that Khadi was offering without pushing for more. "It's not always about having anyone you want. It's about having *the* one you want."

Her mouth suddenly felt too dry to respond quickly, and Khadi hesitated in her response but she licked her lips in an attempt to get them to work. Her pulse was racing, mostly because one of the most powerful women in the world was paying her attention. Very close attention. "Marriage never felt right, even though I do want to be married eventually. I just don't know if the right person for me exists. I'm what you would call a handful. Also I'm rude. Among other things."

"You're also not afraid to argue with a bitch who has a few dozen trained killers on board who would throw you out an airlock at a word without even asking questions." Fatma gave her an almost sweet smile as she said so, her caress moving even lower as she watched Khadi squirm under the attention. "And you believe in a cause you've got no reason to think you have any business getting involved in. You don't strike me as a politician, since you'd have had contingencies and counteroffers when you came in here. You're not military like your brothers, or you'd have tried to push me along the angle of glory and duty. You came in here with nothing but what you believe. I respect that."

Khadi decided to be brave even though the Captain had probably just threatened her life, and she reached out to run her fingers along Fatma's face in a gentle caress that was warm and friendly. Clearly she was open to letting the Captain touch her however she wanted. "You're right. I'm here because I believe in this. And maybe it doesn't matter because I'm one little person, but this is going to change everything."

"With or without us, I see." Fatma breathed quietly, close against Khadi's lips. "You are *not* one little person, Khadijah." She met Khadi's eyes and moved in the rest of the way to take her lips hostage. The touch was gentle, but commanding, as if Fatma was drawing something more out of her she was already willing to give, savoring it as her hands moved over the younger woman to lift her out of the seat and press their bodies together mid-air.

Khadi was so stunned at first that she almost forgot what to do, since she really wasn't expecting the Captain to kiss her and she wasn't expecting to think the Captain was a good kisser. She almost had to pinch herself, but she was quick to jump into it as soon as she convinced herself it was real. Khadi was an excellent kisser, and she definitely wasn't going to hold back from Fatma. Hell, if the woman needed to make out, it wasn't going to hurt to help her out.

It was one thing to be a good kisser, or good at other things, but it was something completely different to have decades of experience behind just how good a person was. Fatma wasn't just an excellent kisser, she was hypnotic, assertive, and the way she moved anticipated and accentuated every shiver that came out of Khadijah. It wasn't uncommon for the lovers Khadijah had taken to be intimidated by her, but Fatma had no such problem. She was forceful, she was demanding, but she was generous with her own touches in return.

Khadi was gasping by the time the kisses broke momentarily, but her hands were clinging to Fatma's clothing. She wasn't ready to end it yet. "Holy shit. You can kiss."

"Decades of practice, I should damn well hope so." She didn't move like a woman with any restrictions, and she certainly didn't kiss like one. "So can you. I can tell you're a lot like me. You like to be on top."

"Most of the time. Sometimes I'm up for anything." Khadi went back to kissing Fatma with force, and she was certain it wasn't just the Shine talking.

By the time either of them had any intention of coming up for air again, it was because the ship jolted slightly with a course correction, and they hit the side of the bed, putting them into a brief spin until they hit the floor, still tangled up in each other. Fatma actually laughed, a deep, rich sound that seemed almost unnatural coming from so severe a woman, but clearly her mood had been lightened by the experience. "I could keep you captive in here the rest of the trip."

Khadi laughed and rubbed at the spot where they had hit the bed before she gave the Captain another short kiss. She'd been lost in the experience with the Captain, and it was both insane and awesome. Hands, lips, limbs had been everywhere. "Am I that good?"

"You are *very* good. Give it a few more years and you'll be unstoppable." She kissed Khadi one more time herself and held her face between her hands as the younger woman's lips tasted all the way down her chest. "But as greedy as I am, I'm not going to hold you quite that long. I have business to attend to. Especially if I'm going to be fighting in your war."

"My war? It's my war now?" She asked as she turned her attention up to Fatma's eyes, which were unwavering no matter what her age. "Does this mean you're going to help us?"

She still held back, though she didn't take her hands off Khadi as she returned the look. "If you can extract a promise from your rebel . . . 'council,' I believe you call it, that I and the others under my command will be permitted to lead the security forces on Eleusis, then yes, I will help you. I will not," she followed quickly, "turn over sovereignty of my Station or executive authority within it, and I will require that all units presently beneath me in the chain of command remain so, but I will accept a place as one of the senior commanders of the impending government, and a seat on its governing council, such as I presently hold." She kissed Khadi again almost sweetly. "Those are my terms. If your council can accept them, then you can rely on my support."

"They will agree. I'm sure of it." She responded with a few more kisses, since she was definitely all good and riled up. "They would be stupid not to give you whatever you wanted."

"We agree on that." Fatma said with a grin and a kiss that felt final. "Go give my terms to your people. We should be nearly to our next stop, and I'll have meetings with the leadership coming aboard." Her hand slid over Khadi's dress (askew as it was) to leave a few lingering sparks in her veins as she pulled away. "And if at the end of this, you've decided that being a polygamist's wife isn't the life for you, come and find me. I'd be happy to set your modeling gossip pages humming with rumors of exactly what I've been allowing you to do to me behind closed doors."

Khadi laughed again and smiled at the older woman. "Thank you. For listening to me when you certainly didn't have to. And for . . . well, lots of fun." She watched the woman for a moment longer before she worked on straightening herself up. "I don't know what I want. But I'm glad to know you're up for it."

"Maybe under leadership other than the rest of the Consortium, I'll find myself a little more free with what I'm up for. I am approaching retirement, after all. I have no intention of allowing my golden years to be boring." She gave Khadi another playful smile, then picked up the sphere of Shine she had offered to Khadi earlier and floated it in the beautiful young woman's direction to take away with her. "Be quick about an answer regarding my terms. If there's anything to be done, I mean to do it before we reach Prime."

Khadi grabbed the sphere and cheekily grabbed another before she used her long legs to push herself back out of the Captain's personal quarters. How long had she been in there, anyway?

She rushed over to Liam with a smile on her face. "She agreed. As long as we agree that she and the rest of Three are in charge of security on Eleusis." She held out a sphere of Shine for him. "I told her we would be insane not to agree."

Liam looked cautiously optimistic about the answer, but eventually shrugged and took a sip of the Shine, which he apparently liked quite a lot. "That . . . is a very unique burn at the back of my throat. Wow. You're right, they would be insane not to agree to that. They're not gonna be happy about it, but that's the nature of politics, I'm gathering."

He knew Khadi well enough to know when she was energized from having a good time, and he hadn't been the only one in the cabin wondering just how entertained the Captain had been by the entertainment she'd brought along. Now that she had come back out, there were even more whispers going around, but he kept himself from listening to them.

"Good job getting that out of her." He said with a noncommittal nod as he took out his communicator. It had a mode that was only to be used for urgent-level communications, but he imagined the council members would consider their success an urgent matter. He switched it to that mode and sent the message quickly, then shut it off to wait for a reply.

"Thanks." Her cheeks burned a little, since he wasn't looking at her. "She said she wanted an answer before we get to Prime." Khadi took another gulp from her sphere and licked her lips afterward. "How, um, how long was I gone?"

He gave her a sarcastic look and made a show of looking at his communicator. "Almost an hour. We should be docking with Six here in about twenty minutes, by the last position report I saw."

"Okay." She was quite energized, mostly because she wanted to talk about what happened, but Liam wouldn't want to hear. "I didn't intend to be gone that long. Sorry."

"You don't have to apologize for anything. You got it done. Something tells me I wouldn't have had quite the same effect." He gave a short laugh, but it was a little forced, under the circumstances. "I've just been out here talking to some of the guys about tattoos. You people have your own fucking language with these things on the Edge, seems like."

"Most artists have to be approved by station leaders. It's hard to find training and equipment, so it makes them a bit rare." Khadi looked at the sphere in her hand and she decided to chug the rest before she said anything else. "She told me to find her again if I didn't want to be a polygamist's wife."

He had been sipping at his own, and he actually choked a little at that, but he reached out to catch the drops of shine before they got too far, and held them in his palm as he coughed and looked back over at her. "Observant little head of state, isn't she? What, did she have a camera in our room and enjoy the footage?"

"She said she did." Khadi glanced back at the Captain's quarters. "She told me that sleeping with someone is one thing, but staying is another. She also kept calling you my boyfriend, which is entirely inaccurate. Never once have you or I spoken about any kind of relationship status."

"No, you've been pretty keen to avoid that topic of conversation." He finally managed to get the rest of his drink down with a grateful sigh, and closed up the sphere to set it spinning in front of him. He was clearly not accustomed to being in zero gravity, since the novelty of it still delighted him on a basic level. "Well, if you do decide that being a polygamist's wife isn't something that interests you, it's good you know you've got one incredibly powerful connection that's also open to being pursued."

"I didn't know the polygamist wanted a fourth wife." She said quickly, though she tried not to sound defensive. "I thought we were just having fun."

"The polygamist is right here, and doesn't typically talk about himself in the third person." Liam answered with as sarcastic a smile as he could muster. "I told you at the beginning of this that I never rule anything out. I came on this trip to find Gwen and bring her home. Just as much as I want to get her home, I want to get home to Rachel and Bree. I want my family together, safe, and happy. That's my main . . . reason for existing."

He might have been set up by Logan in the first place in a relationship that hadn't been his idea, but he had come around to be grateful to his brother for doing it, and it was something he had embraced and run with for himself.

"Alongside that and apart from it, I like you. You already know that. Yeah, we've been having fun up here, but I . . . don't even do that lightly. I like you, I like being with you, and I even like fighting with you. Because you're usually right, and it's usually because you know a shit-ton about things I've got no fucking clue about. I'm aware of how good it is to fight with somebody because you can learn something from them while also enjoying being with them."

He shrugged, since she seemed more confused and appalled by the conversation than actually interested. "I'm saying it's something I would think about. Complicated as it would be. I like you enough to say that it would be well worth thinking about."

Khadi opened her mouth and closed it a few times and just stared at Liam. "What? Really?" She was too stunned to really have a detailed response, so she didn't even try. They barely knew each other, really. Other than arguing back on Earth since they'd been forced to work together. Their chemistry was unreal, if the last few weeks constantly together was any indication. "You are crazy. We fight just as often as we fuck."

"And if we can keep that ratio going permanently, I see a *whole* lot of fucking in our future. Not to mention some killer make-up sex. Not something I have much experience with, I admit. My relationships with the others go pretty smoothly, as a general rule. With you I'm getting this fortune-telling vision of plates and glasses flying at my head in the same room and on the same night as I fuck you on the kitchen counter until you've made up for trying to kill me with a mixing bowl."

"Why would I have to make up for trying to kill you? If I'm throwing a mixing bowl at your head, you probably deserve it." She stared at him with his blue hair and different-colored eyes and shook her head. "You are insane. Seriously insane. We aren't compatible. Outside of our genitalia." They did fight a lot, but not like she fought with her ex. Liam would goad and tease, not nitpick and criticize. He was so very different from anyone she'd been with in Orbit.

"Alright. Keep telling yourself that." He relaxed back in his chair with a last glance over at her, checking his communicator for a response even though communication delays would mean at least a few more minutes before the fastest of responses would get through. "But I'm hearing a lot about how crazy I am without hearing anything that sounds like a 'no' out of you."

"Shut up. I didn't say yes either. You're just trying to get me to agree with some fucking mind-ninja trick." She was glaring at him like usual, playful or not. "Aren't you? You're trying to trick me into marrying you so you can fuck me on your kitchen counter with dangerous shards of glass on the floor. You need your head examined."

"Again, lots of comments on my sanity, no actual refusals." He gave her a playful glare of his own, and his communicator finally chimed with the agreement of Jason and the rest of the council. Liam began unfastening his restraints with a glance at the Captain's cabin, where she had received no other visitors since Khadi's . . . whatever it had been. "If you'll excuse me and my head, in need of examination or not, I'm gonna go close this deal real quick. You let me know if you come up with other ways *not* to say no when I get back."

"I didn't say yes!!!" She tossed her sphere after him and realized too late that she was already throwing glass at him. He really did ninja her brain. "You're infuriating!"

The glass hit him in the back of the arm and bounced off, nearly hitting another person's head before a more-cognizant guard managed to snatch the sphere out of the air with a glare that was anything but playful.

"Sorry, man, I'll get that tossed away." Liam extended a hand for the sphere and took it from the guard with a thumb back in Khadi's direction. "Head's a little off on that one, if you know what I mean. Damn shame, too."

"Shut your damn mouth!" She yelled after his comment, since she didn't want him spouting off that she was crazy. She was not crazy. He was crazy. And stupid. Even if he was hot. And she did like him. He was still stupid.

* * * * *

The retinue from Six came on board before its Captain, and the differences between the personnel from Three and those from

Six were apparent even beyond the uniforms both were wearing. Those from Three bore the fractal insignia of their units, while those from Six, while some were also dressed as security officers, were mostly trade officers and corporate executives in the latest style of formal fashion. Their appearances were well-kept and civil, as was expected of those who oversaw the primary manufacturing and energy management systems of the greater orbital Stations.

Marcus and Claire were some of the last to board, both of them dressed to impress and clearly aware the trip to Prime was every bit as important as the summit itself. That year, the trip was actually the more important of the two pieces, in Marcus' mind.

On the way to their private cabin, Marcus saw the person he'd been told to expect, and he had an unexpectedly severe jolt run through him at the sight. The last time they had seen Khadijah had been at their daughter's wedding, since Mercury had married the woman's brother, after all. The woman was difficult to forget, even with the contacts he assumed she was wearing to hide her brilliant eyes. He pulled himself to a stop near her, even though the rest of their entourage had left. "Excuse me, you wouldn't happen to know which direction the private cabins are in, would you? They've remodeled this liner since last year's summit and I appear to have gotten turned 'round."

Khadi's eyes widened but otherwise her own feelings were well-hidden. She knew the Finnegans would be boarding, but seeing them again definitely reminded her of Mercury. It made her insides ache for Orion all over again, since she missed her brother so much, but none of it was betrayed by her facial expression. "Certainly." She said politely. "Let me take you there so you don't get lost."

"Ah, that's very kind, thank you." Marcus accepted graciously. There wasn't much opportunity for conversation in the narrow corridors leading through the ship, but when they reached the office that had been set aside for them, Marcus nodded to their officers, who had gotten settled into the correct section without any help from Khadi. He turned to face her and reached out to take her hand warmly afterward. "Thank you very much. I'm sure we'd have been quite lost." He pressed her hand between both of his, and she could feel a small slip of paper pass into her grip. Apparently sleight of hand was a part of the Irish Captain's skill-set.

Khadi closed her hand around the paper and gave the man a

smile and a nod. "Let me know if you need anything else. I'd be glad to help. We still have a bit of a ride yet."

"Don't I know it." A tiny bit of honesty crept into his tone as he met her eyes. He knew something, that much was obvious. Even though it had been rumored that he and his wife were the reason why so many people from the Bickford estate had been kidnapped, he knew something.

She and Liam had been sent into orbit with Marcus and Claire being an unknown quantity, along with so many of the other Captains. There was just so little interaction between Earth and Orbit it was difficult to know where any particular member of the Consortium's own leadership stood on the conflict personally.

When she turned away and had a chance to look at the note he had slipped her in private, it was as brief as it was filled with meaning. *6, 7, 8 ready. 2, 3 may be a problem. 4, 5 need convincing. Confident will be ready if 2 or 3 leads.*

Khadi looked at the note and read it a few times before she turned back and knocked on the Finnegan's door that just closed moments before. When it opened and she was face to face with Mercury's father again, she smiled at him. "I forgot to mention to you that Three is providing complimentary beverages, new brews, if you're interested. Would you and your wife like anything to drink?"

"Are they?" He said with appropriate delight, looking over at Claire to verify with her as he held her hand. She'd come back in on a tense conversation between the two of them, but they clearly weren't exactly soldiers. It was natural that they would be tense given everything that was going on. "Yes, I think that sounds quite welcome at this point. Please give our best to Fatma."

Khadi nodded again with a continued smile. "I'll bring something back to you straight away." She met Marcus' eyes once more and turned away to go take his note to Liam, if the bastard was done being an ass. Even if he wasn't, the information was too important not to tell him.

Shit was about to get real.

10

Stephen felt like they had been hiking for days, but he knew it was only because the days were longer on Eleusis, and it had only actually been a little more than a single day since the morning of the attack. Henry had barely spoken to either of them beyond agreeing they needed to stay together for a greater chance of survival, and he'd led the way in a particular direction the entire time without saying where he was going.

They managed, in their wild dash for safety, to pick up a few guns and a few bags of rations that were placed in the emergency exit tunnels as a precaution against just such a circumstance, but Stephen knew better than to think they would last forever. Mostly they were tired, but Henry had assured them he had a destination and at least the beginnings of a plan. They trusted him that far, if not much further.

"I always meant to come farther inland." Stephen said quietly enough that only Maria could hear him. Henry was a few dozen meters ahead of them, moving with his usual grace across the landscape as if he had been born for Eleusis rather than the world that designed him and his brothers. "I was told the hills only get more severe the further in, but this is something else."

Maria glanced back a few times as though she expected something would show up to help them, but all they saw was Eleusis wilderness all around them. "I never wanted to come out here until we had a house out here." She admitted honestly, since there was no reason not to be honest. "A beautiful mansion nestled away, not . . . like this."

Stephen had been an indefatigably optimistic person ever since he'd woken up from his coma in Maria's care, and even after the attack and the crushing defeat they had suffered, it was hard for him to let go of that attitude completely. "That would have been ideal, you're right." He nodded up ahead at Henry.

"So long as we can manage to make some kind of home for

ourselves out here, though, the planet is a big damn place. And when the Alperts do manage to get the next Twist built, they'll come along and get us anyway, whether we're back at the compound or out here. There's nowhere in the universe they wouldn't be able to find us eventually." It wasn't the first time they had talked about the eventuality of getting picked up, and he imagined it wouldn't be the last. "But even if that never happened, I can think of worse places to spend the rest of our lives."

"I'm surprised some of our toys haven't come running out here after us. Most of them are likely to die without us in the next couple of days, and the rest won't last much longer than a week at most." Maria sighed heavily in disappointment. "It was going so well."

"It was." He agreed, squeezing her hand as they made their way up a particularly steep hill after Henry. They stuck to the lower portions on the way, but he seemed interested in climbing that one for some reason. Stephen didn't ask questions. "But all the data has been saved, everything is backed up, we can still continue once we've regrouped."

"You're right." She squeezed his hand in return, though she was utterly exhausted otherwise. Before the rebel attack she had already been extremely tired, and now she was fighting to avoid collapsing to the ground. "Henry! Are we going to stop before we collapse?"

"You want to stay exposed out here on the hillside for anybody with a set of binoculars to see you?!" Henry shouted back, his patience wearing thin. "Be my fucking guest!" He turned a corner along the hillside as he said so, and stepped into a sudden dense cluster of trees that was nestled into a cut that looked like it had just sheared right off the side of the hill into a rockslide below.

As they got closer, they could see, in rather grisly detail, the hide and sprawling limbs of a Behemoth draped through the branches of the dense trees like a tent, but with the way Henry was making noise and moving with confidence, it was clear the beast was dead. Still, the fetid stink of it was prevalent.

"Watch your head in here. If you cut it on my traps, you'll do the rebels' jobs for them." His voice came up from a hole in the hillside inside the fragmented rockfall beneath the Behemoth corpse, and they could hear his footsteps moving down a set of stone steps he had set into the ground. Artificial light winked up at them from far below to illuminate the stairway down.

"Did you kill that thing?" Maria said with a pinched expression, since the smell was absolutely abhorrent. "You really have lived out here like a native."

"There are no natives." He said harshly as he led them further in. There was a place where the hall splintered into three different tunnels, and instead of taking any of them, he bent over and moved a stone on the floor out of the way to reveal a ladder leading down. "If you want to live, don't go down any of those." He said with a glare, before heading down the ladder himself.

"Some extreme lengths for privacy on a planet without a native population." Stephen went last, pulling the stone back into place over them as he descended the ladder.

"I'm not fond of visitors. Even friendly ones." Henry grumbled as he got to the bottom of the shaft, which was naturally-occuring, it seemed, since it pinched and widened in various places until it came out on a much deeper and much larger shaft that was completely dark beyond the ladder's end.

The home, if it could be called such, was a pocket in the wall of the larger cavern where their voices echoed and there was a faint sound of distant water, though no signs of it on the floor of the living space. There was a single cot with blankets and, off to one side, a rack of hanging animal corpses with cuts of meat drying on them. The artificial lights of the place were tiny globes strung in every corner of the necessary space, making the whole place feel like a ghostly kind of residence after the dim light of Eleusis' sun.

"There's food and water down here to last however long we need to. I've got reserves tucked away in the rest of the cave, just no reason to waste power lighting it. The hill above us works as a signal post for the satellite in orbit. We should be able to establish a communication lock here soon, once the system resets."

"I'm glad that we have a way to establish a connection at least." Maria's tone continued its work to convince herself of their chances. "Once they get the Twist working again, then we can get out of here and they can blow the compound to bits. Not that the rebels don't have their own problems by now with all of the people getting sick or dying without us there."

"Makes me wish I was there to see it. Just a little." Stephen said with a smile, finally looking over at Henry, who was busy making himself comfortable and checking on the various bits and pieces of his home to make sure everything was as he had left it, especially the food and the water catch-systems. "Thank you, Henry. For leading us here."

"My deal with the Consortium has never changed." Henry said without looking back at the two of them. "I work for you and lend you my skills whenever you want them, I get to do it from here, on Eleusis. They get the Twist working again to take you two home, that's fine by me, but this is my planet. I'm not leaving. Best thing you can do to return the favor I'm doing keeping you alive is to forget how to find this place and leave me the fuck alone once you're gone."

"Whatever you say, Henry." Maria said with her hands up, since she wasn't about to try to drag away the man that was keeping them alive. If he wanted to stay on Eleusis, then he could. They didn't care what he did with himself after they were gone. "Eleusis is your planet. No one is going to try to take you away from here. Least of all, us. We just want to wait it out until we get a ride out of here."

"Fine." He grumbled, still clearly uncomfortable with having anyone else in his home. He flicked a switch and a thousand other small globes of light came on, illuminating the rest of the spacious cavern. There were too many small pieces to it to be taken in all at once, but Henry didn't stop to give them a guided tour before he started away.

"I've got things to check in on here, if we're going to be here for a while. If you need to take a shit, do it over there and put the cover back when you're done, it'll go downstream. And if you're gonna fuck . . . well, you'll have to find your own place for that. I'll bring back some of the pelts I've collected, that'll have to do as a mattress for you."

"I'm too tired for any of that right now." Maria looked over to Henry and then to Stephen. "And if you two want to fight over me for that, you'll have to do it later. I could definitely do with some kind of mattress though. We should have some kind of comfort in this cave, after all."

It was almost an hour before Stephen managed to get the connection working with Henry's equipment, and Henry only came back to the lived-in portion of the cave long enough to drop off a pile of pelts for them to sleep on. The satellite launched into orbit in the early days of the Eleusis Initiative had been put in place primarily to map the planet and provide a Twist-powered communications array with Earth, relaying data only rather than a larger physical transport connection. The band was set to permit audio only, but Stephen was still glad to hear Vance and Gehrig's voices on the other side.

"The compound's been overrun." Stephen said quickly, since they were never certain how long the backup communication was going to last. "Montgomery, Maria, and myself were the only survivors that we know of. The rebels overran the place using the indigenous fauna. We escaped through the tunnels. Be advised; if you re-establish the Twist, the compound will be held and fortified by rebels upon your arrival. We counted 157 at our last thermal imaging."

Victoria almost never sounded happy, but she sounded particularly irritated when she replied. "Are you three completely incompetent out there?" She growled, since they had their own share of problems they were dealing with at the moment, especially with Bickford in custody. "We didn't want to have to take over the planet all over again. It should not have been this difficult to maintain control."

"Lest you forget, we lost almost our entire military contingent in the very first wave of their attack. Which was a complement *you* decided was sufficient to defend the compound. You anticipated less than half the numbers that initially attacked us." Stephen wasn't about to let things be squarely their fault. Everyone had made mistakes. "There's almost nothing left of that compound as it is. Everything relevant has been uploaded and sent back to orbit for later analysis and future projects. When you get the Twist working again, you might as well send in a warhead and just carpet the place. We can begin again at one of the other sites."

"Then you better not be close unless you intend to die with them." Victoria replied sharply, since she was tired of cleaning up after the Kaplans. "Both of you were given a second chance with this assignment. If you know what's good for you, you'll figure out a way to get rid of more rebels in the meantime. We'll contact you to give you some kind of warning when the Twist is working again. Are there any other disappointments you have to report at this time?"

"We lost the compound and everyone there is going to die when you get around to it. I believe that's plenty for the time being. Has the timeline for the new Twist been altered at all, or are we still expecting June?" Stephen had never had much patience with people judging him for things that were outside of his control. Getting invaded by the wildlife certainly qualified.

"The new timeline has not been altered. As it is, even if it were, we've no need to inform you of it until you need to prepare for it to be activated." Victoria was still extremely angry, clearly. "Logan Bickford is now in our custody. Our current efforts are focused on whatever the rebels are stirring up on Earth. We'll get back to you when we can."

"Fair enough. We'll wait to hear from you. We'll check in . . . closer to June, just to make sure everything is still on schedule. And we will work on the rebels in the meantime." He wasn't sure what else to say, since they didn't have much else to offer, so he ended the connection and tossed the communicator back on the desk where it came from. It felt good to lie back on the furs just because of the exhaustion persisting in his limbs, but at the same time, they were underground on a strange planet with only Henry for company. "It's going to be a long four months."

Maria laid down next to him and curled into his side and closed her eyes. She never knew what to say to Vance or Gehrig, since she was a scientist and they were military-minded. "Four months is nothing if we can get rid of those pests in the end. At least we got out together."

"That's all I care about." He agreed, putting an arm around her to pull her into a tired kiss. "We should get out of these clothes. They're going to have to last a long time. Unless the frontiersman here has extras tucked away somewhere." The cave was a comfortable coolness after the long hike from the compound, and Stephen didn't hesitate to shed his clothes and help Maria out of hers. They'd been naked and worse in front of anyone that mattered.

* * * * *

"It's getting so much worse." Anna said between gritted teeth.

She kept her eyes tightly shut and kept herself away from touching anyone as she sat in her cell. At first it was easier to fight the effects of the serum on her body, but after a few days without Maria and Stephen around, it was wearing on her. She was taking deep, measured breaths, and she could feel her baby kicking around in response to her distress, but she couldn't shake the need that was eating away at her.

She was sweating so profusely her hair was wet around her

face and she was rocking back and forth slightly to attempt to distract herself. Orion hadn't left her since he arrived, but now even having him in her cell was becoming too much. No one was allowed to touch her except Maria, Stephen, and Henry. Or, at least, not without their permission. At first it had been worth fighting those rules. Now it was painful to even think about fighting it just to sit close to Orion. "I don't know how much longer they expect us to do this. I can't do this."

"They found a solution." He repeated to her for the dozenth time in the past half hour. Charles and Jeeta had been working on the cure around the clock ever since the compound had been fully secured, but the rest of the news he received by way of his communicator hadn't been heartening. He hadn't told Anna about any of it.

She didn't need to know that every single person from the Delta batch was dead except for one, who seemed to be responding to the new treatment. They had been the most severe, so Charles had focused on that batch first, as futile as that had eventually been.

Dozens of people dead, with a dozen more from the Echo batch already dead as well. Several had volunteered to drink their daily dose connecting them to Maria and Stephen, but without the two of them around to give orders, to be pleased, they were suffering just as badly as Anna.

"They're finishing up the batch now, they said. It should be just a few more minutes." Even as he said it, he knew he was doing the same thing he'd done with frustrating passengers back when he'd been nothing more than a pilot. "Just a little farther" was the second oldest lie in history, as far as he was concerned. Right behind husbands telling their wives their dresses did not, in fact, make their butts look bigger.

Anna was nodding as though she was trying to indicate that she could keep pushing, that she could go longer, but she was really losing her mind. "You can't stay in here with me. Please." She begged as she looked across at him with tears falling down her cheeks. "Maybe if you get out of my cell, it will be a little better. I'm so sorry."

"You should have told me." He knew he couldn't touch her, as difficult as it was to keep himself from doing so, but he got up at that suggestion immediately and stepped out into the hallway. If he was already that far away, he knew he might as well step across the hall to give her even more space. He couldn't imagine he smelled very good either, given that most of the rebels had paraded through the extensive shower facilities on hand and he had refused to leave Anna's side since they took over the place. "Better?"

"A little." She leaned back against the wall and tried to take deeper, more even breaths. His distance did help with the order that no one was supposed to touch her other than the Kaplans and Henry, but it still didn't assuage the need that was literally destroying her brain.

"I knew there was a reason why I stayed mostly away from recreational drugs." She said between heavy breaths. "This is fucking terrible." Anna took another deep breath before she finally opened her eyes again after leaning her head back against the wall. "Okay, if I have a heart attack or a stroke or something, you have to get Jeeta down here to get Olivia out, okay? She's little but maybe she could survive."

"You're both surviving." He said insistently, wishing he could get closer to reassure her more directly. "I'm not losing you again. Not now." They spent most of the preceding few days catching up on everything she could stand to talk about that had transpired over the past five months, and everything he could tell her about life in the camp. Her brother Cory came back and forth to see her for himself, but Cory had changed in the months they had been trapped on Eleusis. He'd lost an eye, for one thing, getting into a fight with a tree-dwelling predator in the forest, but he'd had time to heal from the injury until he could joke about it. He had avoided Anna for the most part because he didn't want to make her condition worse.

"There's something I haven't told you about yet. But I've been meaning to." Orion slid down to the floor, conserving energy as well as he could until Anna's cure arrived to save her life.

"You've been keeping secrets? Man, that's really not the best way to rebuild a marriage. Clearly I didn't take my own advice before." Anna moved so she could lay out on her bed, since her back was killing her among other things. "Spit it out, then."

"I went to our mountain." He admitted as he sat against the bars of Charles' cell. "A couple months ago when we had those really crazy storms that came for a few days and went again, we decided it wasn't the time to try an offensive, and Cory had just taken down a Behemoth by himself while it was sleeping. Crazy bastard. So we were all eating pretty well, just trying to stay out of range of here.

"I went out with Zoe and a few of her people to get a feel for some of the inland terrain, see if there were any surprises. We climbed our mountain, I went and took some rocks and laid out the foundation plan for our house. Got it all mapped out and claimed. I never did any surveying work, obviously, so I just figure, fuck it, if we get out of this, all of us, and we get the chance to colonize this place, I'm just gonna say that whole damn mountain is ours. Top to bottom. Make it easy on the real estate parceling."

Anna didn't even know what to say to that, since Orion hadn't even known she was alive a couple of months ago. She also was stunned he was thinking about their mountain and their house, and not some prime real estate for himself and Mercury. "I don't deserve you." Anna confessed softly, her voice cracking a few times as she spoke.

"What, because I put some rocks on a hill and decided it was mine? Any asshole can do that." He never understood what it was she didn't think she deserved, and he imagined he never would. "I'm not sure I've ever gone looking for something in life because I thought I deserved it. Even if I had, I'm pretty sure any sense I ever had of what I did or didn't deserve got shot to shit back on Nine. It's not about what anybody deserves, it's about what we can get and what we can make of what we got. But if it was about what people deserve, you'd still deserve better than me."

"I cheated on you. And you're still willing to give me a second chance, even though Mercury is a much better person than I am." Anna moved all over the bed in her physical distress, but talking was giving her some distraction at least. "I don't want you to be with Mercury because she's better than me, I want you to be with me. But I also have a likelihood of dying here in the next day or so, so there's that."

Orion was quiet for a while after that, his thoughts spiraling in the same way they had a thousand times in the months they'd been separated. "At some point along the way in the mountains, I decided to believe that the Match program never actually put you and me together. I think the whole cross-matching between the four of us was just a way for the Kaplans to take a situation, poke it with a fucking stick, and see what happened. See what it would take to push two legitimately, if not perfectly, happy couples, and get them to trade sides. I believe that, and have ever since the mountains. I've got no idea if that's true or not, and I wouldn't believe either of those motherfuckers if they told me one way or the other. But it doesn't matter.

"Mercury and I chose the system, when we got started. We loved each other, and we make each other happy. I don't think either of us ever questioned that. She's carrying my daughters, if she's still alive and she hasn't exploded yet. But we chose each other because we work. That's not a bad thing, and I thought, at the time, that it was the best thing to do with my life. If everything had gone according to plan, maybe it would have been. But that's not the world we live in. The world we live in is the one we choose to make. And in a world like that, I'd rather have you next to me every step of the way."

"You're making me cry even more. I can't tell what's sweat and what's tears anymore." She tried to tease, but she was shaking again from the withdrawal. "I don't even know when I realized it, except that I don't think I needed to realize anything, really. As terrible as that sounds now. I fell in love with you in a situation that was fucked up. But I fell in love with you because you're you. There's no way if I was put with Stephen Fucking Kaplan that I would ever fall in love with him. No one made me love you. I just do. I want to live on our mountain and promise you every day that I'm never going to hurt you again. If I survive."

"Don't promise me that every day. That would get repetitive. Unless you're promising it in body language, in which case, promise all you like. That kind of repetitive, I can get behind." He didn't know what would make her situation worse, but he did his best to keep her spirits up as best he could.

His communicator went off, and she heard him move on the floor to read it. "They're coming." He said excitedly, but she could see his face fall a little bit out of the corner of her eye. "They said they've got it figured out, and that it's worked on some of the others, but that you're probably not gonna like it. Whatever the fuck that means."

"Great. Piss off the dying pregnant woman even more." She grumbled as she attempted to sit up again, though it wasn't easy. "It better fucking work, because I'm literally dying here."

It was only a few minutes before Charles and Jeeta arrived, with a tall glass of liquid that made her immediately thirsty by how much her entire body had been craving the effect it normally had on her. Jeeta held it just outside her cell as Charles hobbled over, leaning on a cane, his tone direct and precise as always.

"You've got two choices. You can either die of withdrawal right now, or shortly, at least, or you can allow someone else to take over the Kaplans' special place in your brain's chemistry. If what I'm seeing chemically is correct, we should be able to taper you off over the course of about a month to where your chemical reliance on that person fades to a safe level for you to cold turkey the rest of it out of you, but in the meantime, your brain chemistry has grown dependent on external forces for validation and direction at a chemical level."

He placed the glass on a ledge where she could take meals, still meeting her eyes. "This will be much like the initial dose you took, opening up receptors for binding protocols. Your general has ordered that Orion take rein for you and a dozen or so others to rehabilitate them as well. Carl himself is taking most of them, and Aiko is taking those who show the least current need for rehabilitation. Bottoms up."

"Wait, what?" Anna glanced at Charles for a moment but her attention was immediately drawn back to the glass and she could feel herself almost gravitating to it, even though she desperately did not want to. "Orion is going to be my . . . master?"

"Chemically speaking, yes, that is an accurate summary." Charles looked over at Orion with a neutral shrug of one shoulder, then back at Anna, waiting for her to take the glass. Taking it herself was a part of the process of the brain's assimilation of the drugs.

"Wait, I'm not . . ." Orion was saying as he forced himself up to his feet.

"Going to help her survive? That's rather uncharitable of you." Charles said with an offhand glare at Orion before looking back expectantly at Anna.

"Better him than anyone else." Anna agreed and waddled, slowly, across her cell and took the glass without any more hesitation. "I'm sorry in advance." Anna looked down into the glass and then tipped it back for her first gulp. "I'm mostly sorry because I'm a fucking horny bitch even when I'm off this stuff. And not pregnant. But my body is in control. I can't stop it from being psychotic. We're animals."

Charles' eyebrows rose a little at that confession from her, but he'd heard just as bad or worse from Anna over the course of their captivity. She had lost the capacity to surprise him long ago, if she ever truly had it in the first place. "And on that note, I think we'd best be elsewhere. We'll see to it that the doors are closed tightly on our way out."

"You're leaving?" Orion was confused by that kind of assistance, since there was no guarantee what they'd just given her would work with reference to him instead of the Kaplans. "How fast does it usually take effect?"

"It doesn't take long." Anna headed back toward her bed. "I'm assuming a little bit longer than usual considering your 'information' is new to my system. Who knows. But I'm getting naked, because that's one less thing I'll have to worry about." She paused and sighed. "You have to tell me to."

"You weren't allowed to get naked before unless somebody gave you permission?" That seemed like a strange thing to exercise dominion about, but strange was the least of the adjectives he could have used with regard to the Kaplans.

"No, I just didn't like to get naked for them, so I was usually forced." She kept her hand close to the zipper of her jumpsuit, but it didn't move closer. "Come on, please? This thing is starting to feel itchy."

Orion felt strange giving orders, but he stepped up to the door of her cell as a test, looking down at her with a hand on the bars as he cleared his throat awkwardly. "Take off your clothes." He ordered in what he thought was a fairly firm voice, but he was a long way out of the mentality of giving orders when he was there with her.

He could see her shoulders visibly relax and her whole body seemed to follow after he gave her an order, she even groaned after he said so, and she started taking off her jumpsuit. "Oh, that's better. Thank you."

It was strange for him to see her actually enjoy being told what to do, since that wasn't who Anna was at all, but if it helped her, he was certainly going to keep going with it. "Any orders that Stephen, Maria, or Henry previously gave you, you're ordered to forget them completely. They no longer apply to you or anyone else. I want you to ignore any restrictions they ever placed on you."

She nodded and he could see a visible shiver run through her body as he gave her another command. When she had the jumpsuit off, she was naked underneath, since undergarments were entirely unnecessary for the Kaplans. Anna focused her gaze on Orion. "Can we go take a shower?" She was looking him over like she wanted to devour every order, but he would have to talk first. She didn't jump until she was told. The drug slithered its way through her too easily. "I feel so gross. Especially after all that sweating."

"You and me both. Lead the way to the closest one. Or whichever one you'd prefer." He kept his distance, just in case she either wasn't open to being touched yet or it was still potentially painful.

Anna quietly walked out of her cell (and internally rejoiced she could actually leave it) as she led him down the hall to the open showering area for the prisoners. The only time Anna ever saw it was alone, or with . . . someone she didn't want to be with. It was pristine and white and open with showerheads all around. Even naked and pregnant, though, she didn't look like she was less confident standing in front of Orion than she ever had been. The inside of her mind, though, was a different matter. She was struggling with every errant thought in her mind, but she desperately wanted to feel like she could be strong.

She went to turn on several spigots before she turned and looked at Orion again. "Would you like me to undress you?"

He had seen the shiver of relief from her before when he gave her a command, and as much as it went against his own inclinations to be bossy at all with his lovers, especially Anna, he stepped into the communal shower and nodded down at her. "I *would* like that. Do it."

"I feel like I should be apologizing for something." Anna said when she was close enough to touch him, but then she did her best to undress him, even though he had to bend over a few times. He was still incredibly tall, and she was still short. At least that hadn't changed.

She tossed his shirt over toward one of the active spigots so that it would get rinsed. Anna stared at his chest as soon as it was exposed and she started to cry all over again. She never thought she would be this close to him ever again. "Can I touch you?"

"You don't need my permission to touch me or anyone else." He reached up cautiously to brush his fingertips along her cheek. The Anna he'd known would have done what she wanted when she wanted it and made no apologies to anyone. He hoped she was still somewhere underneath what the Kaplans had done to her, but he hadn't been around her long enough to know for sure. "Touch me all you want, however you want. I plan to do the same to you."

She actually whimpered as soon as he touched her, since it felt like she had been literally starving for a master's touch, and she couldn't help but turn her face into his fingertips. Anna felt as though if he took his fingers off of her skin she might actually die, so she hoped he wouldn't stop touching her. "I'm glad they never caught you." She spoke softly as she stood there in front of him. "They didn't break me completely, but if they had you, they would have."

His caress didn't stop at her cheek, but his other hand did take hers to move it to the waist of his pants, reminding her to get him stripped in the hopes that it would thrill the pharmaceutical part of her brain. "Even when I found out they had you, I never once worried they had broken you." His fingertips tucked themselves along her neck until his thumb could tilt her head back to look up at him. "One of the first things I remember you telling me is that you're anything but fragile. I've never since had reason to think you were."

As soon as he reminded her he had given her the command to undress him completely, she was quick to act, since her body absolutely demanded it. She tossed the rest of his clothes with the others under the water and felt freer to touch him again. Anna backed up toward some warm water and enjoyed the spray.

She instinctively reached her hand to a soap dispenser in the wall without needing to look for it, then brought her soapy hands back to his skin. It would take time to wash off days of sitting with her when he probably had better things to do. Her hands were still trembling a little, but she was doing her best to try and let her relief work its way through her body. "Tell me what else you want."

"Right this second, I've got just about everything I want." He tilted her head back beneath the water and started working his fingers through her hair once his own hands were reasonably clean. She wasn't in as desperate need of a shower as he was after living in the wild and bathing on the shore, but he wanted her to feel that she wasn't going to be a slave anymore. That someone was going to take care of her for a change.

"I want . . ." he searched for something, then actually smiled a little as she continued to work the soap into his skin. "I want you to think back to the mountains, those first few months after we got out of Nine. Finding that one maintenance shaft just to see how far we could echo before people started yelling at us."

Anna gave him a small smile as he ran his fingers through her hair and she thought about their life in the mountains when they were back on Earth. Sometimes her memories were so vivid and other times it seemed like they were a past version of her, a different story and a different woman. She could remember herself as an impetuous and ambitious woman, always trying to get things done and make a difference. Now she just wanted to find a quiet place to exist, to make a home and house and be left alone. She didn't want to make a difference. She just wanted to live. "I remember." She replied softly. "It feels like a long time ago. It feels like a different Anna."

"It does feel like a long time ago." He continued working through her hair and rubbing some of the tension of the past few days out of her shoulders while she soaped the rest of his body. "I thought being stuck in the mountains would make me antsy. I thought it would make me feel like I was bottled up all the time, that I would need to move, fly, things like that. And I did miss it, but not as much as I thought I would. I thought being stuck here on Eleusis was gonna be the same way. That I would end up hating this place and wanting to be anywhere but here."

He shook his head, and his long-fingered hands moved to cup her face gently, his thumbs brushing a kiss of their own over her lips. "All I want is to make a home with you and the kids. Somewhere. Doesn't matter where. I'll fight this war until it's over, if there's war left to fight, but I just want a life."

"That's what I want too." She kissed his fingers back as soon as his thumbs ran over her skin, since she had ached and dreamed for the chance to kiss him again. Anna gripped onto his arms with her slippery hands as her lips begged for more than just his fingers. "I did so many stupid things. I thought I was doing something for the greater good, but I don't care about that anymore. I just want to live. With you."

"We can do that." He said confidently, as he ran his hands down over her breasts and her sides as the water covered her and set her skin steaming. "If you want to take an order from me, take that one. Live with me, here or back on Earth, wherever we go." He leaned down within an inch of her lips, pressing his forehead against hers. "And don't apologize. For anything. That's an order. Whatever happened back on Earth, I stopped being mad about a long time ago, and nothing that's happened here has been any fault of yours."

Anna still felt regretful and apologetic for hurting Orion the way she had, but for as long as she was under the control of the drug, she wouldn't be able to voice it with a command like that. And living with him wouldn't be a pain or a struggle, it was what she wanted. "Does that mean we can get married again? That I can be Mrs. Al-Jabbar again?"

"Well, technically, you are still wearing your ring." He looked down at her soap-covered hand and the tattoo that surrounded her ring finger. He reached down to interlace his fingers with hers, taking some of the soap from his body so it was easier to run his hands over hers. "You can be anybody you want to be. Including Mrs. Al-Jabbar."

She gripped his hand tightly as soon as he interlaced their fingers and she stepped in closer to him. "I want to kiss you. But I'm a little afraid this isn't real and this is a nightmare where you won't kiss me back."

He reached up with one hand to wipe the water from his face, and was finally starting to feel clean after what felt like a lifetime of dirt and sweat. "I'm done with nightmares." He leaned down and kissed her almost frantically, having barely held himself back from doing so until he was sure that touching her wouldn't be painful. Once he did, and it was clear that pain wasn't what she was experiencing through the touch, his hands moved to cup her full breasts and he stepped in close enough that she could feel the rest of him against her like a memory from another life. His hands massaged up over her shoulders in the kiss but then moved to her lower back, holding her pressed gently against him with her baby slightly in the way.

Anna was noisy as soon as he was kissing her and touching her in every which way, and she kissed him back just as frantically with her hands sliding all over his body. Only part of her actions were fueled by the drug, and really only the intensity of her actions was affected. Everything else was desire and love for the man in front of her, the man that she'd nearly lost and somehow managed to get back. She knew how lucky she was that Orion was alive and he was there with her and he wanted to be with her. Anna wasn't going to waste that kind of luck. She pressed her body into him as much as she could even with a baby bump between them, since she wanted to feel him against her. "I missed this so much. I missed you so much."

"You're not gonna miss me ever again. You're going

nowhere." He said almost threateningly as his hands moved down to grip her backside, though it had him bent over her until he had her completely folded against him. There was a narrow bench that ran around the entire shower area, and Orion quickly moved the shower spigots they had commandeered so the warm water would continue flowing over them, then sat down to pull Anna into his lap. Once she was sitting on top of him, it was easier for him to hold her, to kiss her, to do anything and everything he wanted with her.

Anna kissed all over his face between kisses against his lips, and her arms were locked behind his neck as she sat on his lap. She was still squirming on top of his lap with every one of his touches, since it made her more needy every time he kissed her or touched her. "I need . . . more instruction." She nipped at his bottom lip. "I need more of you."

"What kind of instruction?" He asked almost teasingly, but he could feel just how hungry she was for him, and he was no less anxious for her. "Oh, you mean the instruction where I tell you to fuck me until you see stars. That instruction."

He shifted himself beneath her and spun her on his lap so that her ass was against him and her baby bump was no longer a hindrance. Then he laid her head back over one of his shoulders so he could kiss her while his hands roamed over her. It was one of his favorite positions with Anna even when she wasn't pregnant, and it felt like coming home to have her so open and exposed in his arms again. "Do that. I want to see you as satisfied as you've ever been in your life."

Anna certainly didn't hesitate to move so she could slide herself down on top of him, but she took her time, because she wanted to cherish the feeling of him. For the first time in what felt like a lifetime, Anna wasn't in distress and she wasn't in pain. Anna wasn't being raped, she was being worshipped. She wasn't being tortured, Orion was taking care of her. He was touching her with love and affection, and it was the best kind of balm on her scarred soul. She was so happy she was with Orion and she wasn't withering away that she almost couldn't even control her body or the pleasure she felt from everything. "I love you." She said several times as she started to move, her body accommodating his incredible cock in every way it could. Anna felt like she couldn't tell him enough.

"I love you too, Anna." He moaned against her ear, his arms

locking themselves around her as she settled against him, both of them breathing together, rocking against each other in ways that had long since grown familiar. The room filled with steam around them, and the sterile scent of the soap overpowered everything else in the air. But the only thing that mattered to Orion was the taste of Anna's skin beneath his lips, the feel of her rocking herself on top of him to take him completely. He wanted to banish the memory, the reality, of everything she had endured in that place; he wanted to stand on their mountaintop and watch the entire compound fall away into the ocean, but for the moment, he settled for holding her, being in that place alongside her.

It didn't take much for Anna to orgasm the first couple of times, between having Orion with her and a drug that made her absurdly horny and obedient, but she was pushed into a perfect pleasurable oblivion each time, moaning his name. Especially because he was so attentive to her needs, Orion wreaked havoc on Anna's mind and body, and she hoped it was healing her in some way or another. After a third orgasm, she was starting to feel as though it was becoming unfair. "Are you holding yourself back on purpose, Giant? Don't you dare."

He smiled broader than he could remember doing ever since they'd been stranded on Eleusis, at the fact she was back to calling him names. "I wouldn't . . . dream . . . of holding back with you, Shortie." His hands moved down to her hips as she slammed herself into him, and she could feel his teeth graze the back of her shoulder as he gasped for air. When she wanted something from him, she almost always got it, and he had been without her for too long to have any desire to hold back any longer.

When he cried out her name against her ear, his hands shuddered in their grip, moving in spasms over her sides and thighs as she rode him straight through his own climax. She was the only woman he'd ever been with who had always known more about how to please a man than even Orion knew about how he liked to be pleased, and it appeared she had never stopped being amazing.

He held her against him afterward, kissing her frantically everywhere he could reach as he panted for breath. "You . . ." he laid her head back so he could kiss her lips, "are still a dangerous fucking woman."

Anna didn't know why she was crying, but she was crying as she kissed him afterward, and she didn't even care about the tears.

She just cared about Orion and finally sharing her body with someone she *wanted* to share it with. Feeling loved again, feeling love at all. "Dangerous, maybe." She said between her tears. "And definitely only yours."

They stayed there beneath the hot water until it began to turn cool. Even when they shut it off, they stayed there in the shower clinging to each other and relishing the silence. The tiled room was so still their breaths echoed off the walls, and Orion felt as though the last five months were slowly draining out of them both, running down the drain like the refuse that it had been.

They had both gotten clean under the shower while it had been hot, and for the first time, Orion felt like he could walk through a free world and take a free breath. "Come on, baby. Let's find you some decent clothes, not that fucking costume they had you dressed up in. And I'll see if Zoe and her crew managed to find me at least some pants that might fit."

Anna looked down at herself and then up at Orion again. "Then can we sleep? I want to sleep in your arms."

"Yes. Then we can absolutely sleep." He promised with another kiss as he helped her stand up. "We'll get some sleep and tomorrow's going to be a different world."

11

"Hey! Delta! Echo!" Carl shouted across the room at the one remaining Delta and some Echoes who were still alive after a few days without their fix. Everyone had been medicated more or less successfully, though very few of them were happy about the arrangements. "Up on your feet! Now!"

The Delta and some Echoes had a bad habit of kneeling down and trying to do things for everyone else around them, sometimes the other slaves, sometimes the rest of the rebels who had invaded. Some of the rebels were more willing than others to accept what they were attempting to do, and Carl was attempting to maintain some kind of order. "Get over here and follow me around if you absolutely *have* to have somebody to do things for." He wasn't going to tolerate somebody bowing and scraping to somebody else.

He took them around a corner to the lab where Aiko had set up her own personal command post, mostly seeing to the wounded who had garnered some kind of injury in the attack (there had been blessedly few of those, thanks to Orion's planning and the work of the engineers) as well as organizing food storage and inventory to make sure they could feed and sustain everyone inside the compound walls. There was more than enough work to go around, and Carl was going to see that everyone was put to work.

"If I tell you three, as your highest-priority order, that you're to do everything Aiko tells you to do; that you're not to harm or obey anyone else, and that you're to otherwise do whatever the fuck you want so long as you stay within the compound, will that keep you from bugging the shit out of everybody else here?"

The Numbers looked at each other and tried to figure out how they were going to obey Carl's command, but then they all looked at him and nodded. "We can do that." One said, even though she didn't sound confident.

"Good." He said more harshly than they probably deserved. "If you start feeling the need to get bossed around again, come find me, don't just go renting yourself out to whoever's around. Got it?"

Aiko looked over at Carl and shook her head. "I'm beginning to wonder if they're ever going to snap out of it."

"They've only had a few of days. If they don't snap out of it, we'll . . . just have some housekeepers until somebody figures out a better option for them. Right now I'm just worried about keeping them from giving out blowjobs to every single cock they walk past."

He walked up behind her and looked down at the makeshift bassinet she'd made out of a laundry basket and some blankets behind her. David seemed less peaceful indoors than he had out in the Eleusis wilderness, but Carl couldn't fault the boy for that. The outdoors was all he'd ever known. He put his hands on Aiko's shoulders to massage them as he looked, not over her shoulders, but straight over her head, at what she was working on. "How's everything looking in here?"

"They've locked down some of their information remotely, but I think we can make contact with someone. I'm trying to make contact with Jason. He's the only one who can crack all of this with his connection. Charles could, I'm sure, but I don't trust him like I trust Jason."

"They all look the same to me." He said with a brief laugh at his own joke. He'd been in a much better mood since they actually took the compound, though the former slaves still irked him. "I want him working on the slave problem right now, until we know we've got a plan that'll actually work to bring everybody down out of their brain-chains. He seems like he's done some pretty good work on that so far. We'll see what else we can do with him if he manages to keep pace. The guy is a Montgomery, and judging by where he falls in the alphabet, he's just about as old as Xander. The guy's secrets are keeping secrets from each other, if he's anything like the rest of him."

Aiko turned around after David looked settled, and she tilted her head back so that she could look up at her husband. "Did you get something to eat? You've been running yourself ragged."

"I grabbed a couple of the ration bars. I also set a couple teams to raid the supply warehouse looking for anything that either approximates barbeque sauce already or can be made into a decent one. We've got enough smoked meat going around right now to last all of us for weeks, but I really, really hope they manage to put together a decent sauce." They had a different set of concerns following their victory than they had before, but that certainly didn't mean they had less to worry about. "Everybody should be able to get some decent sleep tonight, for a change. I've got most people settled in quarters, there are teams sleeping right now who'll be on security for the night, and we'll all feel a whole lot better if we get a solid eight for once."

"There are beds." She said with a smile. "Beds in rooms where people aren't right next to our house all of the time. Units with a few rooms apiece so David can have his own room and we don't have to worry about your snoring waking him up."

"Hey, you snore too. Just . . . I'm guessing not as loud as I do." He conceded with a shrug. "I claimed a unit that looks like it was servants' quarters next to Douche and Douchette upstairs. I took one sniff of that room and immediately assigned a team to start cleaning it out and burning everything inside. I've seen my share of fucked-up places before, but that . . . anyway, we've got some breathing room in ours. And I already checked. The bedrooms are pretty well soundproof."

"I could use a decent shower." Aiko said with a smile up at her bulky husband. "It's a whole new line of thinking when you feel like you might lose fingers and toes in the Eleusis cold to having a nice place like this. Even if the Consortium built it."

"I don't give a shit who built it so long as they've vacated the premises. Which, after three days of going over this place with the finest-toothed-comb I can find, I'm pretty sure they have. There's one tunnel we're still watching to see if anybody tries to sneak back in, but everything else we've either caved in or chained up. Pretty soon we'll get to work on the walls and be fine and snug for the winter."

He leaned down to kiss her, but his smile fell a little the moment after. "Three bodies we haven't found in the mess, though. The three I was hoping most to find, of course. I could hope the Behemoths took their heads off and we'll never know which body parts belonged to them, but I'm not really known for that kind of wishful thinking. My money's on them still being out there someplace."

"Then the Eleusis wilderness will take care of them." Aiko said reached a hand up to run it across his cheek. "It's the three of them against Eleusis and us. They won't last long." She pulled him down into another kiss and she tugged on his beard a little. "Are you keeping this?"

"I was thinking about it." Razors weren't something they had access to out in the wild, so having the option of shaving it off had him hesitating. "First few weeks it itched like a motherfucker, as always, but now I don't mind it so much. You have a preference either way? I take requests. You didn't seem to mind it much when we were stranded out here the first time around."

"It's pretty soft, so not really, but I don't know. I just like looking at you." She smiled brighter and pulled him down into another kiss. It was easier to be a little more romantic when they weren't worrying about dying *every* second.

Carl was anything but subtle or reserved, especially with Aiko, so as she kissed him, he lifted her up with his huge hands on her waist and placed her on a shelf nearby in the room so he could kiss her easily. It wasn't the first time he'd tossed her around as he saw fit, and he knew it wouldn't be the last. "I'll keep it a while, then. Find a razor somewhere around here and get rid of this mess on top of my head, that's happening as soon as possible, but I'll keep the beard. David seems to like trying to yank it out of my face anyway. Wouldn't want to deprive the kid of the satisfaction."

Aiko laughed softly again and looked into Carl's warm eyes as he held her up on a shelf. It shouldn't amaze her that he could toss her around so easily since she was small and he definitely was not, but it was still quite an experience whenever he actually did it. She ran her hands over the hair on the top of his head even though he said he was going to get rid of it. "What do you think is going to happen now? The Consortium can't send anyone after us, it would take a generation for them to get here. Even if they did, we would have time to prepare."

"I doubt the Consortium was planning to rely on just a few Twists for everything they wanted to do. The fact that they didn't send any reinforcements here while we were gone tells me they really don't have any others to use, but I'm sure they'll still be working on a new one. They built it once, they'll find a way to do it again. We'll just have to be ready here when they do." He shrugged, since without knowing more about what was happening across the galaxy, there wasn't much they could do to prepare. "We'll have this place squared away, get the walls back up, get some . . ."

"Excuse me, Commander?" A voice came from the doorway, where two figures stood. Charles found a cane of sorts to lean on as he walked around, but Jeeta still remained close enough to catch him if it gave out, which it had several times. The strange-looking man was carrying a communicator in his free hand, and was holding it out to Carl with a quiet smile. "Phone call for you. Long distance."

"Long distance? The fuck does that mean?" Carl made sure Aiko wasn't going to fall down off the shelf where he'd placed her, then stepped away to take the communicator from the man, at which point the voice from the communicator spoke up.

He means it's Jason, Commander. Jason's voice came through the communicator, sending Carl's eyebrows to the ceiling as he looked back at Charles.

The albino shrugged as if it were nothing worth commenting on. "I may or may not have overheard the thing you were most desperate for was contact with Earth. The communications array in the compound has functions on a kind of small-scale Twist, I just had to patch in and override a few dozen systems." He looked back at Carl's disbelieving face with another small shrug. "I might also be the smartest person you've ever met. I'll go back to work on the slaves now. Just thought you might want this, now that everyone is stabilizing."

We're not finished with our conversation, Charles. Jason's voice said almost threateningly before Charles could turn away.

"We are for now, little brother." Charles didn't look at the communicator as he said it, and wouldn't have looked at Jason if he were present. "We'll talk again later. There's work to do." He left it at that and started to head out of the room, leaning heavily on his cane and a little less on Jeeta beside him.

Aiko found a way to jump down without seriously injuring herself and she ran the short distance to get to Carl and the communicator. She and Jason weren't . . . friends, really, but they were something. They had a history. "Jason?" Aiko asked even though she'd already heard him talk. "You're really there?" They lost contact a long time ago, or it felt that way.

In fairness, Jason answered with a short laugh, *I have a little more right to be surprised about you surviving than you do to be shocked about me still breathing. I'm still rather de-centered from all of this, while you, by Charles' report, are standing at ground zero.* He laughed again, and she actually heard him sigh on the other end of the connection. For most of the time she'd known him, he'd been cold and calculating, but maybe having a family of his own for a few years had changed that about him. *It's good to hear from you, Aiko. I'm glad you're well.*

"You don't need to worry about us. Well, certainly not Carl and I. We're experts about Eleusis as far as anyone can be an expert." She let out a deep sigh. "Can you update us about what happened on Earth? What's happening now?"

Yes. I can give you a full rundown on just about everybody's whereabouts. Even if not all the news is good.

Charles let his brother's voice fade as he walked down the hall with Jeeta, his thoughts churning in ways he hadn't experienced in a very, very long time. The world . . . everything he had been told while he was in captivity was being wiped away bit by bit by the facts even his cursory investigations had uncovered since being freed from his cell.

So much about what the Consortium had tried to sell him was bullshit . . . Anna hadn't been a plant after all . . . at least not as far as he could tell. Things were still . . . no, he had to hang onto some things, he had to trust some kind of facts. He really was free. Still trapped on Eleusis, but really free. He wasn't being stopped from doing what he wanted to do, from contacting Earth. No one could fake the answers to the test questions he had given Jason. No one else knew those things. Unless the Consortium had recaptured Jason and was using a vocal synth . . .

No. He had to hang onto some things. He had to let himself believe that facts could be facts. Otherwise he would never leave the prison they had constructed for him. He couldn't believe that everything was a lie, that everything was a prison . . .

"I need a minute." He whispered to Jeeta, squeezing her shoulder once before he moved to a chair in the hallway to sit down. People were moving purposefully back and forth every few minutes, carrying something or guiding a group of others to some destination they hadn't known how to find, but Charles ignored them. He had to ignore them for the time being. They didn't matter. Only Jeeta mattered. Only reality. If there even was such a thing for him anymore. He settled into the chair and leaned forward to rest his forehead on the head of the cane, taking slow, deep breaths with his eyes closed.

Jeeta gave him some space for a few minutes, but eventually she knelt down on the floor next to his chair so he would know she was right there with him. "What can I do?"

He shook his head at first, since his first impulse was always to refuse help when it was offered. People who were offering help were usually looking out for weaknesses they could later exploit for their own benefit. That was the nature of people. That was the history of his life. He wouldn't let it be his future. Afterward, though, he put a hand down on top of hers as she rested it on his knee.

"It's just been a long time since I was anything approaching free. I've gotten good at being a prisoner, where your enemies are the people on the other side of the bars. I don't know how to do this anymore." He squeezed her hand and forced his eyes open. He had to take in data. He had to observe the world in order to form conclusions about it. Closed eyes did not eliminate the need for further data.

"There's a . . . project of mine, which I'm betting the Consortium kept here on Eleusis to keep it close to me. Just in case. Once I got access to the compound systems, I identified a couple places they might have hidden it. High security that they don't want anyone noticing. I'll need your help to get to it."

"Of course." The soft-spoken woman said as she squeezed his knee gently. She had been "hired" a long time ago to take care of him and to give him a friend so that the Consortium could use her against him. They succeeded in using her, but only because she really did care about him, and she hoped he really did care about her too. "You know that I'll do whatever I can to help you."

He nodded and pushed himself back up to his feet to continue down a different hallway. He remembered the layouts of the compound buildings from a brief look at their systems, so navigation wasn't a problem, even if he had to manage it without raising his head too much on account of the brilliant lights. His eyes still couldn't quite handle real sunlight, even on Eleusis.

"This is the first time you've been free in a long time too." He said as they started on a long stretch of corridor that looked as daunting to him as a marathon, but they had things to do. "You've been locked up an appreciably terrible percentage of your life either looking after me or being tortured by people trying to torture me. What do you do now?"

"I stay here with you, as long as you want me to." Jecta held onto his hand while he hobbled along with his cane. "I love you, you know. You've never believed me before, at least you say that you didn't believe me. But no one is forcing me to do anything, least of all forcing me to tell you that I love you."

He squeezed her hand as she said so, since it wasn't the first time she'd told him. "I told you when we met that love isn't something I understand." He knew enough about himself to know that there were certain elements of the human experience to which he was either not privy or to which he had never been fully exposed. If he had ever loved anyone, it would have been Henry, back when they were very young, living on their own as brothers on Earth, but that particular nerve ending had been cauterized decades before. "I know I care about you more than any other living person. That you were the first person I thought of as soon as I stepped out of my cell."

Jeeta nodded and she leaned in to kiss the side of his head and then his cheek before she just continued walking alongside him. "Maybe when we have a home of our own, you'll learn how. If you want to."

That got a small smile from him, since there were a thousand manipulative answers that could have been given to what he'd said. He had considered the possibility of most of them, but as usual, Jeeta hadn't come back with any of them. "Where would you want that to be, do you think?" His accent for Punjabi hadn't gone away over the years of his captivity, though he knew he didn't have to speak it, since she spoke his own native English just as well as he did. He hoped she understood that he continued to do it as a way of being closer to her, instead of taking it as one of his usual pretentious habits. "Someplace here on Eleusis, or would you rather go back to Earth somewhere?"

"I like Eleusis well enough." She replied without hesitation in her own language, since she wasn't at all offended by his use of it. "But Eleusis needs adventurers and discoverers. Earth needs problem-solvers. I fall much more into what Earth needs than the other way around. What about you?"

"I don't think I'm up for too many adventures." He felt old, which was what had been bothering him for a very long time. He had been young for so long, and he knew he still should be. There was no reason for him to be otherwise except what he had been through. He had no idea if he could get back to what he should have been or not. That was what he was angry about, beneath everything else. "But I could be useful on Earth, if there's an Earth worth defending or helping at the end of all this."

They reached his destination, which had been disregarded by

the rebels as nothing more than a supply closet. They had raided the shelves and carted off everything that looked like it was worth anything, and Charles couldn't fault them for missing the less obvious storage near the back.

He ran his hand along the back wall of the storage closet until he came to a seam he was looking for. A portion of the wall spun at a touch, and his handprint was accepted on the panel there, since he had programmed it into compound security a few hours earlier. At that acceptance, the wall above the shelf slid aside to reveal a case roughly the size of Charles' arm, heavily locked and heavily reinforced.

All he could do was shake his head at the extra security they included. "It's almost cute how they seemed to think they could keep this under lock and key forever." He slumped to the floor once he pulled the case out, and heaved a grateful sigh once he could rest a little. Some manipulation of the lock unclasped it, and he pushed back the lid once he looked around to make sure they were more or less alone in the hallway.

What was inside appeared, at first glance, to be a kind of armor for a single arm. The panels were smooth and simple, and appeared to contour so that it would cover one arm and part of a person's shoulder. It was a plain and efficient grey, with a panel at the fingertips for controls that had long since gone dark. "I'm glad they were never stupid enough to destroy this thing. It's not the best thing I've ever done or made in my life, but it's damn close."

Jeeta sat down gracefully next to him on the floor and looked over the item that he had in his hands. "What is it?"

"It was my solution to the problem they gave me." He slid it onto his arm, but she could see from the way it had been originally designed and the emaciated remains of his arm within it, just how much less of him there was than there once had been. He made a few gestures on the control and growled at a red haze that came over the panel. "They didn't destroy it, but they did manage to lock it out from my safeguards. I'll have to spend some time working backward around them." He took it off and put it back in the case, then leaned back against a wall just to look over at her.

"It's what will get us home. It let me stay ahead of the Consortium for about ten years. They wanted the Twist tech from me, but what I ended up giving them was the dumbest version of it I could come up with that would still work. This . . ." he tapped the case with his cane, "this is the way it should have been if I had been developing it for someone worth giving it to."

Jeeta's eyes widened as he explained what it was, and she stared at his arm again. "This could change a lot of things very quickly. But I don't need to tell you that."

Charles looked tired, but even a short walk could do that to him without any difficulty. He patted the case once and closed his eyes as he caught his breath.

"It breaks all the rules." He said with a sigh. "For almost ten years, I hopped around the world like a god. Didn't share it with anyone, didn't tell anyone else, didn't do anything honestly worthwhile with it. When I eventually got bored enough, I told Henry. We visited Eleusis together, the two of us. I didn't know he worked for the Consortium. I didn't . . ."

He choked off that train of thought and forced himself to open his eyes instead of wallowing in everything he'd done wrong. "I need to repair it. If I can get it working, I'll offer it to the rebels, but I don't want to give them false hope of getting home."

"Okay. We'll keep it to ourselves until you're ready to share it, if you want to. It's yours, after all. You invented it. You get to decide what to do with it." She placed a hand gently on his shoulder and she took a deep breath before she moved to get up. "Let me go get you some water, then I'll help you back to your new room."

He put a hand on her shoulder to stop her from getting up, and instead raised his head, with some difficulty, to look up at her. He didn't say anything for a long while, which wasn't uncommon from Charles. His thoughts moved so quickly that he sometimes got taken along for a ride by them, and forgot to come back immediately. Eventually he reached out to pull her in close, settling her on his lap to wrap his arms around her. His legs had seen the greatest damage from the Consortium's torture, but his arms had been more or less untouched, and it was the only thing about him since she'd known him that showed any strength at all.

He hugged her against him as he took a slow breath of the scent of her. It wasn't the first time he'd shown her actual affection, but every other time they had been pulled apart by the Consortium or some new form of torture had been implemented to separate them. Part of him was still waiting for just such a thing to happen, but he held onto her anyway. "I'd prefer it if it were *our* new room."

Jeeta was always quick to show him affection whenever he

would allow it, and as soon as he was hugging her against him, she had her arms around him, hugging him back. She was surprised, however, that he wanted to share a room with her. He was a particular man, she knew that, and she wasn't bothered by it. It was why they had picked her for him, because of all the people they could trap into being his companion, they picked someone who was perfect for Charles. They were serious about wanting to break him in every way that they could. "Are you sure? It won't bother you if I'm there?"

"I'll be a great deal more bothered by myself if you aren't." He knew it wasn't the most romantic answer he could have given, but if he had given her a romantic answer, it would have been because he had calculated it to be such, and he didn't want to be that with Jeeta. "I've been living mostly without you since I met you. I have no interest in distance. From you."

"I have no interest in distance either." She agreed and gave him another hug as long as he would allow the physical affection to go on. Jeeta put a hand up to his cheek gently and smiled at him as she pulled back slightly to meet his eyes. "Maybe someday you'll be interested in intimacy too. We'll start with sharing a room and see what you would like after that. I'll never expect more than you are willing to give, or more than you want to give. I promise."

"The only reason I don't want more at the moment is because I'm fairly certain, even given your recent history of prolonged comatose periods and the potential for loss of muscle tone from such an inert state, that you would snap me in half." The barest twitch at the corners of his mouth indicated a joke from him, but he very rarely actually smiled, at least that she had seen. "I do, however, intend to dedicate myself thoroughly to any physical therapy my attending physician prescribes. In that and in so many other things, I place myself entirely in your capable hands."

"Snap you in half?" She asked with a laugh. "Way to make a woman feel larger than she would ever like to feel." Jeeta kissed his cheek and continued smiling at him. "We'll work on your physical therapy so you can walk again. Not for my benefit."

"I would never call you large." He said as his eyes flicked downward. "Not you as a whole, at least. I reserve the right to comment with that adjective on specific body parts." He reached up with one hand to caress her cheek, his fingertips feeling gently over her skin as if it was the first time he'd ever touched anyone. He made no move to get up or leave their spot, but as he caressed her jawline and the side of her neck, his eyes looked up to meet hers. "Do you think we can trust them? Mister Tanaka and the rest of his people?"

Jeeta didn't answer right away because she was thinking it through, and thinking about the little exposure she had with the rebels so far. Eventually she nodded and met his eyes again. "Yes, I think we can trust them. But I also think we need more time to see what they are really like. I don't want anyone else using you again for their benefit without giving you what you're due in return."

He agreed with that wholeheartedly, and glanced down at the case next to them once, as if to make sure it hadn't been spirited away while his attention was even slightly diverted. "Whatever happens, this stays with us. At least until I can build a better version. I've had years in solitary confinement to refine my ideas for it, and I'm certain I can do it better with the right resources. But it stays with us, even if I help them fight their war. I won't be put in a box again and I won't have you taken from me again. Under any circumstances."

Jeeta agreed and hugged him again, since she hadn't moved off of his lap. "I am worried about something else, though. I'm worried that if we run into someone from the Consortium again in all of this, or if the Kaplans and Henry come back somehow, that you'll be convinced that I'm not here for you. I don't think there's anyone else in the universe that matters to me anymore, and if I lose you, I lose everyone. I don't want you to be convinced I'm not absolutely on your side."

Anyone else might have gotten defensive at that kind of statement, but Charles actually appreciated her honesty, since he tried to be honest about his own doubts and fears with her as well. He had never told her as much, but he knew already that if Jeeta really was the Consortium's final and best weapon against him, they would absolutely succeed in what they wanted. If Jeeta turned against him, then the last string holding him to any semblance of caring about the world would snap. He would tell them whatever they wanted to know, because if Jeeta was a plant, then there was nothing in the world worth holding secrets to protect.

"Once I get this working again, I'm going to go looking for them first." He said quietly, watching her eyes and subtly leaving his fingers along her neck as he spoke. Her pulse was steady, and he wasn't even sure if his fingers would pick up an alteration or not as they had once been able to do. But they remained anyway.

"When I find them, I'm going to take one of Carl's guns and I'm going to go for them myself. When that happens, I want you with me." His voice fell almost to a whisper before he took a breath and leaned his head back against the wall. "When I find them, if you really are working for them, or for the Consortium at all, the only thing I've ever wanted to ask is that you shoot me in the head once you have what you want. This kind of mobile technology will undo anything it's set against right now, you said it yourself. If you're not this, if this still isn't real . . ." there had been too much damage to his eyes during the torture for his tear ducts to function as a normal person's should have, but he didn't cover up the slight catch in his voice fast enough for her to miss it, "then shoot me, take it, and do whatever the fuck you want with it. I'll even key it to your bio scans before I go so you can use it yourself."

"This *is* real." She assured him, since she didn't want him thinking for one moment that it wasn't, even though she knew it was a real concern for him. "I've never been 'working' for the Consortium. They pulled me from my life and said they were going to kill my family if I didn't do what they told me to do. I had no idea what they would tell me to do, but of course I agreed. I can only assume they've killed my family by now. There's nothing I can do either way for them, but my feelings for you are real."

Jeeta moved a hand so that she could run her thumb over his lips. "My feelings have been real for a long time. They were never fake to begin with. I know why they picked me *now*, because you never would have opened yourself up to someone if it wasn't real and genuine. But I didn't ever tell them anything or give them anything they didn't observe from us interacting. They wanted me to, which is why I think my family is probably dead. They probably killed them before they even brought me here, but there's nothing I can do about that. I just need to know how I can prove to you that this is real. I'm real. My feelings are real."

"Then I'm at another one of the Consortium's self-defeating crossroads." He closed his eyes briefly under the feel of the caress, but opened them sharply as he reminded himself not to permit too much time without watching the world. "If you are a Consortium agent, then I'm lost, but I permitted you to suffer for something you deserved in attempting to torture me with your own pain. If you aren't, then I've permitted someone who loves me to be repeatedly abused and her family to be killed for the sake of keeping secrets and paying the price for crimes I committed against the Consortium myself."

"You didn't permit anything. They did what they did because they could. Even if you gave them everything they wanted at every turn, they still would do what they wanted. If they tried to promise you anything, they never would have kept their promises. You aren't responsible for anything." She pulled her hand away from his cheek slowly, since she didn't know if he even wanted to be touched by her. Especially if he still felt there was a possibility she was a really good actress and liar. "Don't program anything about your invention to respond to me. I don't want your invention. I want you."

He didn't answer her about the invention, but he would still program it to respond to her. He needed to know, and if she took it and used it without his knowledge, then he would know. "I want you too, Pranjeeta." He rarely used her full name, but he had told her candidly long before that he thought it was beautiful. "I want the you I think I know. The you I want to believe cares about me. I want to know what's real." He admitted, not for the first time. "I've spent most of my life functioning under the basic assumption that trust of any kind is a fallible construction, and that people simply choose to set their personal bar lower or higher in terms of the lies they will permit themselves to believe. I never wanted to change that. Not until you."

He closed his eyes as his hands moved down to her waist, then leaned his head forward against her collarbone, taking in the warmth of her and the closeness of her. He had once held interpersonal relationships to be something so cheap, so . . . anti-intellectual. Things merely tangible couldn't possibly have lasting value. Now he would have given anything to be able to lock himself in that simple moment for the rest of his life. "I want to know what it's like to exist past that wall. To believe something a part of me is always going to know can't be conclusively proven, but continue to believe it anyway."

Jeeta ran her fingers along the back of his neck and along his head gently and carefully, her fingers tracing senseless lines along his bare head. "I hope there's some way I can prove to you the immeasurable way that I feel about you. I worry that it will take dying for you to prove it, but I have little else to live for if you don't want me around." She traced her fingers down the back of his neck again. "Come, will you let me help you to your . . . our room?" She didn't know if he still wanted her to stay with him or not. "I don't want you spiraling into doubt over this. I just wanted you to know that I'm worried about what you think of me here. I'm worried you'll cut me out and cut me off and go on without me."

He shook his head without moving away from her. "I won't. I will promise you that." He moved away enough to look her in the eye again. "Life or death, doubts or certainty, I'm with you." He looked up in her eyes for a long time, then leaned in to actually give her a kiss, his lips taking hers as unexpectedly as they also happened to be expert at something she'd had no reason to think he had any skill in whatsoever. The kisses they had shared previously had been rushed, fearful affairs, always broken up by Consortium agents when they had barely kindled into life between the two of them. The hallway around them, however, was silent, and there were no Consortium agents rushing to dictate how they were going to live their lives. It was only her, and Charles claiming her lips as his own while his arms wrapped tightly around her back.

Her pulse jumped slightly but simply out of shock, since she wasn't expecting him to kiss her. Once he started kissing her, though, it was like his hugs, she would take it and run with it without hesitation. Knowing Charles, she might never get the opportunity again.

12

A month felt like an eternity. Every day felt longer and longer as Mercury knew Logan was somewhere but she couldn't get to him. Mercury tried not to let it show as she went about her life; attempting to do her research, taking care of her children, and going along with Kameron's newly-hatched plan to get them out. It seemed like an impossible plan, but she knew if Kameron could actually get all of the tools needed, Kameron would always be unstoppable.

Mercury also had the small problem of contractions when she knew she wasn't prepared for her babies to be born. They would come on for an hour or so at a time, but then go away, and she hoped it was because she had the will to stop it from happening. The logical, scientific part of her brain violently disagreed with that hypothesis, but she had to convince herself she had some kind of power over it.

She didn't want her babies born in captivity. She didn't want them born so they could be taken away from her and poked and prodded like a science experiment. The only way to keep them safe was to keep them in. Even if it was nearly impossible.

The strangest thing about her half-captive/half-free life was that the smallest noise was always a potential sign of something changing. Since giving her greater freedom to move about Prime upon request, there had been days when her requests, even the simplest ones, had been flatly denied without any stated reason, but there had been other days when she was encouraged to take her children out wherever she saw fit.

The only person who had put up a convincing enough performance of being subservient to the Consortium's demands had been Melissa, and so she was allowed out to accompany Mercury on some of her walks. She and Kameron had staged a number of loud and sometimes violent arguments for the benefit of the Consortium's monitoring, and they appeared to be working.

It wore on the two of them, since the arguments were sometimes genuine, but that was what it took to sell the fighting. Melissa's freedom and the possibility to gather resources was another part of the plan, but it was far from an easy one.

"You got a message." Melissa said from her side of the bench. She was sitting close to Mercury's stroller, and she picked up the communicator as she continued to bounce William on her knee. Kassie was always left back in captivity when she left, but she was glad to get William out occasionally, at least. "They, um, they're letting you know that they've added a new physician to Logan's case." Melissa handed the communicator over to Mercury absently. "They said he's on his way down here to consult with you about something. Do you want me to stay?"

"If you would." She held a hand to the side of her incredibly-massive stomach. Orion's twin girls might just snap her in half, which was not an easy task. Mercury had Declan and James in the double-stroller, and Leo and Lynnette stayed back with Gwen. "It's easier to deal with them when I'm not alone."

"You're not. Even when you are." Melissa gave an attempt at a smile and looked down at Mercury's wrists, putting out a hand to turn her arm a little. "These are healing up nicely. I swear, you bounce back from everything faster than anyone I've ever known. Are they still itching at all?"

Mercury shook her head as she looked at the tattoos Melissa had drawn onto her skin. They were beautiful and perfect, and she was grateful and amazed by the woman's talent. The pain wasn't terrible, and she was right, they were healing quickly. She never would have thought much about it before, but now she knew it was due to genetic alterations, it felt different to her. "The ointment you told me to use has helped. I find myself staring at them sometimes. It helps me feel closer to both of them."

"Well, you can't get much closer than your own skin." Melissa gave William a kiss afterward and moved a little closer to Mercury, so she would feel someone else was there with her. William was a paranoid little boy, to say the least, and unlike Declan and James, he showed almost no interest whatsoever in exploring the small plaza where she and Mercury had decided to take the boys for the afternoon. He stayed close to Melissa, as one of the few people he knew, and eyed all the glass and steel surrounding them with the utmost suspicion. The only known trueborn son of Eleusis, he never quite acclimated to being in a closed space.

"That looks like your doctor." Melissa nodded down a hallway past Mercury as a man in a long white coat approached.

Time was a strange thing. The brain was an even stranger thing. So it only stood to reason that memories, where the two met, would sometimes be the strangest thing of all. There was nothing particularly outstanding or noticeable about the man as he walked toward her, aside from the fact that he looked her in the eye and never once looked away once he saw her.

She recognized the pained look in his eyes before she recognized the rest of him, simply because there was that little to remark upon where he was concerned. Roughly her height, brown hair, brown eyes, a pleasant enough face, and a regulation haircut. The pain in his eyes was the only thing that managed to reach into her memories and connect him with the world before she'd entered the Initiative.

"Mercury." He breathed with a conflicted sigh once he was close enough. "It's . . . amazingly good to see you. Even under the circumstances."

It felt for a moment as though Mercury was stepping back into a different life, since the last person she expected to see was Dr. Greg Voss. The last she'd seen of him was a painfully awkward goodbye. Before everything. Before the Initiative. "Greg. Dr. Voss." She corrected, since she didn't know if he considered them to be on friendly terms or not. He said it was good to see her, but she felt guilty for the way she left things. "It's . . . I hardly know what to say. I feel as though it has been a lifetime since I've seen you last."

"It has been." Greg agreed and approached slowly so she would know he wasn't there to do her any kind of harm. His face and posture were a whirlwind of different emotions, but he kept his hands at his sides as he got close enough to see the boys inside their stroller. Only when he saw them did he finally smile. "Your boys are beautiful. I . . . was told you had twin boys and that you're carrying twin girls. The redhead takes after his mother."

Mercury smiled as well as she looked over at her boys. They were in a stroller that had the seats facing each other, and while they looked content with their toys, she was sure they would be throwing the toys at each other in no time. "They are beautiful. And yet so much trouble." She said with a laugh before she motioned toward Melissa next to her. "I'm sorry, I didn't introduce my friend. Melissa, this is Dr. Greg Voss, we worked together on Station Seven before I entered the Initiative."

She was mostly watching Greg, since she didn't know how to describe him, other than that they had been friends. Their history was a little bit more than that, but she didn't know if that was appropriate to talk about. He had strongly opposed the Matching program because he insisted that they had a solid friendship between them that could blossom into something more. She hadn't been convinced, clearly. "Dr. Voss, this is my dear friend Melissa."

"Pleasure to meet you, I'm sure." He said with a polite nod. Otherwise, though, he stayed a few steps back from the stroller to give Mercury and her friend some space, and actually put his hands into his pockets to keep himself from fidgeting. "And I'm . . . still Greg, Dr. Finnegan. If that's alright." He said it with a tentative smile, obviously not sure exactly how to approach things between them since it had been so long since they'd seen each other.

"Of course. Greg." She replied just as politely. "And I'm still Mercury." Mercury laughed softly as she looked down at herself. "Or I will be eventually. I'm Mercury plus two at the moment."

That got a small smile out of him, but it was a shadow of the usually-confident Greg she had previously known. He pulled a chair from a nearby table closer to the bench where they sat in the middle of the plaza, then pulled out a tablet with her file pulled up in mid-air for his review. "They told me you've had some intermittent contractions. How far preterm did you end up delivering the boys?"

Mercury's smile faded quickly, since she hadn't reported to anyone about the contractions. She didn't want to report them, since she didn't want to be admitted. The babies weren't due yet even if her insides were running out of room. "I thought the message said a doctor was coming to talk to me about Logan?"

Greg's smile fell as hers did, but for slightly more complicated reasons. "I . . . wasn't aware of what they told you. I just know what they told me." He seemed reluctant to continue, but sighed and forced himself through, as she had seen him do countless times when talking about a diagnosis that wasn't favorable to a patient.

"What they told *me* was that I've been assigned to attend you through the birth of your girls. While I'm doing that, I'm supposed to refrain from mentioning the dozens of veiled threats they issued regarding Logan and their intentions toward him once they begin whatever mockery of a trial they intend to hold for him. I'm also *not* supposed to tell you about how they intimated that I should convince you to take me back instead, since they're certain they'll convict and execute Logan. In dragging me here from Seven and assigning me to you, they're hoping that a friendly face will draw you away from him and more completely back into your old life here in orbit. But those are all the things I'm *not* supposed to tell you about." He said bluntly, since he obviously didn't mean to go along with any such commands.

"What I *am* supposed to do, though, is check in on your status, given your recent contractions, and work with you to put together a plan for exactly how we're going to get these two girls into the world safely."

Mercury took time to digest everything he said and she nodded slowly. "You're not even going to *try* and seduce me?" She was trying to tease him and make the situation lighter which she never would have done before when he knew her. "I'm at a low point. One husband died, the other on death row, and I'm so pregnant these babies might just fall out of me. Especially because I'm sure I'm dilated to at least a three and I haven't told anyone about it yet."

That got a look of obvious concern from him, but he blinked a few times at her attempt to tease him, even in such a situation. "Well, if you're dilated to a three, I don't think any attempt I'd make at seducing you would be much help for your situation." He gave her a hint of a smile, but there was still pain in his eyes and the possibility of a tear at the edge of one of them. His feelings for her had always been much deeper than hers for him, and it seemed the intervening time hadn't changed that.

"You've always been such a support to me and a true friend." She said gently, and she pushed herself up off the bench again (with much effort) so she could get closer to him. Mercury glanced back at Melissa, but she knew Melissa would understand what she was about to do. Melissa was acting a part herself, after all, convincing the Consortium. "Thank you for being so honest with me." Mercury moved so she could whisper into his ear. "We can do whatever we need to do in order to convince the Consortium my mind has changed. I don't want you to be punished or tortured along with the rest of us."

He put his arms around her once she was close enough, but he didn't make anything more of it than just a hug, though it did give him the chance to whisper back into her hair. "Ever since things went south on Nine, I've been working for your parents trying to find a way to contact you. I don't care what they do to me, so long as you're safe. I'm here to take care of you, but I won't have to for very long."

He hugged her tighter, taking a deep breath while she was close to him before he pulled away to look her in the eye, speaking a little louder. "You're my only case here, and I'm at your disposal, so I'm not going anywhere until we've got healthy babies and a healthy mother. Separately, not all tangled as you are right now." He lowered his hands to run them over her stomach, feeling expertly for anything she might have missed.

It was strange to have his hands on her, since she remembered the time they were intimate, and it was very different than this or anything she ever experienced with Logan or Orion. Greg was a good man. And she knew he had deep feelings for her, but she had never shared those feelings. She hated the idea that maybe she led him on, but she never actually did so knowingly. Her babies kicked and squirmed even while he touched her belly, since they were active little girls. "I've had back labor for about two days now, and it's getting worse. But I'm not ready for them to come. I can't protect them as easily if they're not inside. The boys went full term, but they . . . well, they weren't as big as the girls are."

"I see." He said in the neutral way they didn't actually train doctors to get perfectly right, but which all doctors seemed to have about them regardless of shared training. "If you're that far along, then we really should get you to a delivery bed. Do you have someone who can watch the boys?"

"That's me." Melissa piped up with one of her characteristically brilliant smiles. "Well, me and some others back in, you know, prison. We pass everybody around, and we can pass these two around for a while until their sisters get here." She gave Mercury an encouraging smile and got up with William on one hip, his little arms around her neck as he held onto her. "We'll just have a sleepover for a little while. It'll be fun."

"No, no, no. It's not happening right now." Mercury shook her head as she looked down at herself briefly before she glanced back at Melissa and then at Greg. "I've got more time. A week, two . . . maybe." Lies. All lies. She knew he was right and it was likely she would have her babies in less than forty-eight hours, depending on how quickly things progressed, but she didn't want to think about it. Someone she loved was supposed to be there. Not a bunch of Consortium doctors in an Orbit hospital where they would likely take her babies away to experiment on them. "Orion was supposed to be with me. Logan. They were supposed to let me see him again. They'll take my daughters away if they're born here."

Greg moved his hands to her arms, keeping eye contact with her as much as she would let him. "I'm not rushing you anywhere, or trying to hurry this along in any way. If you want to go see Logan, I've been authorized to take you there." He said each word slowly, almost methodically, to make sure she could process them through her panic. "We're gonna take this as slow as you want, and make sure everything goes as smooth as it can. For now, I'm recommending that it's best for you not to stress about the boys while we're waiting on the girls. Let's get them headed in the right direction and then I can take you to go see Logan for a little while. Does that sound okay?"

Mercury glanced at the stroller and moved away from Greg's touch so she could get closer to her boys. Declan reached his arms up so she would pick him up, but James didn't seem to care. Mercury ran her fingers through Declan's hair and picked him up so she could kiss him and hold him. She looked over at Melissa afterward. "Are you sure this is alright? You know how my boys are."

"There's still more of us than there are of the kids." She said with her same bright smile, swaying to amuse William, who still looked scared of the world, but mostly just hung onto his aunt like a contented little baby animal. "We'll be fine. You know us. We've got to do some reordering anyway to make some room for the girls' bassinets." She looked over at Greg in mild alarm as he moved closer to her, but she stood still as he stepped in with a hand on her shoulder. Mercury could see her face as Greg leaned in to whisper through her shining blonde hair into her ear, and saw her eyebrows steadily march upward on her forehead as he spoke. Mercury had no way of distinguishing between panic and excitement in the woman's expression, since that was just who Melissa was. "Are you . . . ?!?"

"I'm sure." Greg said calmly, patting Melissa's arm afterward.

"Okay. I, um, okay." Melissa was flustered by whatever he'd said to her, but she hugged William a little tighter and cleared her throat. "Okay. Okay. That's . . . okay. Sure. I will. Right. Sure. It'll be okay, Mercury." She finally got her attention back on the one of the three of them who was most deserving of comfort at the moment. Melissa managed to put her smile back onto her face in the process, though it had been rattled by the moment. "It'll be okay. We'll take care of the boys, I promise. You don't need to worry about them."

Mercury looked even more concerned, since she had no idea what Greg said to Melissa and it was causing her to panic all over again. She looked between them but kept her emotions mostly bottled up so a camera couldn't see her true feelings. "If you're sure." She asked again, since she wasn't feeling very confident, but she also knew she couldn't watch her toddling boys while she was in labor.

Melissa nodded a little more confidently, having gotten control of herself, and she stayed by the stroller while Mercury gave her boys a hug and a kiss each goodbye. She set William to stand on one part of the stroller while she pushed it, which seemed to amuse the little boy to no end as Melissa headed off through the plaza. A few guards followed quietly at a distance, as always, but they didn't interfere with Melissa at all while Mercury could still see her.

Greg watched them go along with Mercury, then took a few steps in another direction, his hands back in his pockets. "It's this way. Would you prefer I got you a chair? You might be more comfortable."

"No, no chair. I'd rather waddle, if that's okay." She let out a short laugh afterward and she looked over at Greg. "Should I be worried? I don't know what you told her . . ."

"No, you shouldn't be worried." He reassured her, then turned and offered his arm, if she wouldn't take a wheelchair. Anything that kept the Consortium's resources focused on their little torments would help. "I haven't seen anything on any of the scans of the girls that makes me nervous about their delivery, and if you managed with the boys more or less on your own, I'm sure you'll be fine with the girls. They're measuring long as of the last scans, but their heads aren't oversized."

"Thank goodness." She looked down at her belly again. "We didn't have medication down on Earth, not that we could use for birth. It happened fast with the boys, but it was painful. I remember Logan talking me through it the entire time. I remember his voice more than anything else about the entire thing until I heard baby cries." She sighed heavily as she stared at her still-moving stomach, since the girls had even less room than the boys had. "At least they already have names. Fiona and Farrah. I just feel guilty that they have to come into life like this."

"They're beautiful names." He smiled down at her belly as they walked, slowly, passing people who moved to keep their distance to go about their business. No one wanted to be associated with a known rebel, and more than a few conversations around Mercury always centered on questions of why the Consortium was permitting her to walk free after what she'd been involved in.

"They'll come into the world surrounded by people who care about them. Who care about their mother." He didn't look at her as he said so, but he still kept his pace slow and even beside her. "These past years . . . especially since what happened on Nine, I've been moving around a lot. I even got a research grant for six months and went down to Earth. I mostly worked with the Mediterraneans, but I had some time and leave to go traveling. I went to see Spain, France, England. Even went to Ireland, thinking you might have gone back there in hiding after what happened and I'd just . . . come across you somehow." He shrugged.

"I thought Earth was going to be this terrible, barren, blasted wasteland. But it isn't. It's beautiful and it's open and it's warm. The people down there are open and beautiful and warm." He glanced down at her stomach with a weak smile. "Your daughters might be born on this station, but this isn't where they're going to live. I'll do whatever I can to make sure of that."

Mercury rested her head on Greg's shoulder for a moment so he would know how much she appreciated that he cared about her and it was touching to her that he was looking out for her. She held a little tighter to his arm after she lifted up her head from his shoulder. "I wish I'd had a chance to see those places too. To do research like you did." She looked over at him and smiled. "Going to Ireland would be great. I don't know what I would do, or if it would feel like home in some ways."

She shrugged and let out another long sigh. "There wasn't much I wanted from life, you know? I wanted to do my research and deliver babies and have a family of my own. I thought that being a part of the Initiative meant I would get to do that on Eleusis. That's all. I don't know how my life turned into this when I never had any intentions or inclinations to become part of a rebellion."

"I . . . never pegged you as the rebellious sort, that's for certain." He gave her a more genuine smile, moving with her toward one of the many thousands of lifts that wove their way through the station from one level to the next. There were almost two million people housed on Prime, and the place was far from simple to navigate.

"Some days I wish I had gone, to be a part of it. Other days I'm glad I didn't. Mostly I . . . I don't know. I wanted simple things too. Bring some lives into the world, maybe save some lives in the process, seemed like a pretty good living. As for my research . . ." he laughed, but it didn't have any humor in it. "That got confiscated just a few weeks after you left for Nine. I pieced most of it together on my own before I left for Earth, but it was still . . . the second time I pieced things together, I knew what kind of a huge pile of shit I had stepped into, and I buried a drive with the information on it down on Earth. Just in case. When I got back, that's when I reached out to your parents. I never wanted to be a rebel, but I won't be party to something that's . . ." he shook his head, since that statement didn't need to be finished. "Loving certain people puts us all in places we wouldn't otherwise have chosen for ourselves, I think. And that's not always a bad thing."

Mercury watched his face as he spoke, feeling another spike of guilt when he mentioned loving someone. It was true for her, but she was feeling as though he was talking about himself more than anyone else. "The people here are still good. I hate that the Consortium is trying to pit us all against each other, Earth versus Orbit, eventually versus Eleusis. The Consortium is corrupt, but most of the people aren't. I worked with good, caring doctors. I had genuinely kind and understanding patients. Pure, sweet babies. But the Consortium has turned this into a war that didn't need to be. Earthlings want to be liberated from the poison that the Consortium created, and that's it. This is just . . . too much. Too many lies by so few people."

"So few people who maintain a hell of a lot of power." He said quietly. There were too many surveillance systems all over the station for him to even be afraid of them, so he was speaking openly and inviting the consequences, whatever they were. They wanted him around to take care of Mercury for the time being. After that, if there *was* an after, they could do whatever they wanted to him.

"Your rebels are changing that. From the rumors I've heard circulating about what's going on down on Earth . . . they have the leadership scared. And with good reason." There was a hesitancy in his voice that Mercury remembered from times she'd heard him lie, but he also glanced up looking for cameras. Was he lying because he thought they were being watched, or did he *want* to be caught with that particular lie? There were too many possibilities to know.

Mercury didn't push more of the conversation, since she didn't want someone to show up and yank Greg away from her when she needed him. At least when he was with her, she knew he was okay. If he disappeared, they might kill him. "Why are they letting me see Logan? Do you think they'll let him be with me during the delivery?"

"I'm not sure if they'll let him leave confinement. But the clinic where I'll order you a bed isn't far from his holding. So under guard, he might be permitted. I'll see what I can do. It's at .6 Gs, though, so it will be a little closer to an aquatic birth than a standard-G procedure." He squeezed her hand on his arm as the lift moved them through the station sideways, blitzing past entire arms and the vast plazas for which Prime was so well-known in orbit.

"I don't know what they've said about him here. Logan, I mean. But he's not bad or crazy. He's not cruel. He's strong and kind. But he's a leader. He's not a psychopath. He's a good man."

"I stopped trusting anything in the news reports a long time ago." He gave her a sympathetic smile. "The fact that you love him and you're as devoted to him as you are is enough reason for me to trust him. Besides, there's research suggesting that all good leaders have to have some psychopathic tendencies. It's part of the job. I don't hold it against him."

"I know the research." She let out another short laugh. "You know, he used to ask me all these questions to see what I knew about things? And he would just sit there as though he was utterly fascinated, when I knew he had to be bored. Who wouldn't be bored? But I loved it. I loved talking about research that didn't matter to him, but it mattered to me. I miss it. I miss being a doctor so much." She'd been given research. Consults. But it was nothing like the life she had before, on Seven.

"You're still a doctor." He reassured her as the lift began to slow toward its destination. "You've just had a slightly different patient base the past couple years than you used to. You've been working on birthing a new world in addition to babies. That requires one hell of an obstetrician."

Mercury gave Greg a genuine smile after a comment like that. "You are sweet." She replied gently as she gave him a kiss on the cheek. "I'll try to remember that when I'm in active labor. I tend not to be as fun to be around."

"No one is fun in active labor. Nobody." He answered with a sheepish grin, though she could see that he'd turned slightly red after the kiss. "But unlike the last time, we do have medication here, and I verified with them that I would be permitted to utilize the full standard array for you. Stories about Logan have . . . circulated . . . among doctors in the past month. There's no way I was letting that happen to you."

"Are you sure what you're going to use is . . . the right medication?" Mercury hadn't allowed anything that came from a syringe to enter her body after what happened with the Kaplans. "They . . . have access to some incredibly scary drugs."

"I'll be testing it first. I brought three nurses and an anesthetist from Seven that I've worked with before. Farouk, you might remember him. He's a good man. I trust them. They'll be the only ones in the room."

He moved with her once the lift stopped, into a part of the Station that was a great deal less open and inviting than the portion they had come from. The corridors were narrower, and she could tell by what she passed that she was in a sector fully devoted to being a detention block for the Consortium. The eyes that looked back at her through some of the doors were empty and angry, and the lights were dim enough to let the men and women behind the doors appear less than human. The doors were incredibly thick, reinforced with brackets on every side to make them airtight and seal them away from the hallway.

"Quick warning." Greg said as they made their way down the hall in roughly half-gravity, bouncing just a little with every step. "I've never had much of a criminal background myself, but I've got a cousin who landed in here a few years ago. Stupid kid." He cleared his throat before continuing. "They're called Suicide Cells. Every one of them has a button and a hatch inside for the prisoner to space themselves if they decide to do that rather than face trial. They get out of it with some assisted suicide legal loophole from centuries ago that they've kept on the books this whole time. So just . . . when you see him, be careful that there's no touching buttons."

"I don't want to touch anything except him. I haven't seen him except for just one time . . ." Mercury shook her head. "Other than the horrific videos they keep streaming into my room."

He just nodded. "I wish I could tell you those were fake. But I've seen a few of them." They were authentic, which meant that for most of a month, Logan had been having episodes of excruciating pain. Usually in the middle of the supposed sleeping hours, when he couldn't get the rest he needed.

Strangely, and conversely, the videos had also shown her an image of a Logan that was getting . . . better. He was in horrific pain most of the time, that much was clear, but when she'd seen him the first time, she had seen the kind of distressed state he had permitted himself to get into. He had been strong before, but the way he'd held her that day had shown a kind of prolonged weakness.

The man in the videos she was sent, though, was never wearing anything besides prison-issued shorts, and he was a person she didn't even recognize. His hair and beard were growing back, slowly, and she had seen an appreciable difference in his musculature between videos.

She wondered why they were permitting him to get more physically fit until Diego had pointed out that the current version of Logan looked dangerous. Exactly the way the Consortium would want an accused criminal to look if he was about to stand trial for terrorism.

"I can't lose him too." Mercury said in a voice just above a whisper. "I don't know what to do, but I can't lose him."

"Don't worry about that right now." He patted her arm and took a turn down the corridor, since he clearly knew where he was going. The cells were empty for a long while as they walked, but eventually they reached the end of the row, where there was a clear glass wall between Mercury and Logan.

He hadn't seen them approach, and from the way the glass appeared a little hazy, it seemed it was coated on his side not to allow him to see out. Inside the cell, though, Mercury could see the door Greg warned her about, with a large warning sign next to the exposed button for escape.

Logan himself was nowhere near the death button. Instead, he was on the ceiling doing a bizarre kind of pull-up that involved him leveraging his entire body until it looked like he was doing a pushup on the ceiling, after which he fell to the floor beneath him and did several normal pushups. After those, he jumped to the ceiling again and pulled himself up into another rotation, working furiously for several repetitions until he fell to the floor and stayed there, panting and covered in sweat despite the cold temperatures in the wing. It was cold enough to get a small shiver out of Greg beside her, even though they were both fully clothed, while Logan was still in only his prisoner shorts.

As she watched him get back to his feet, he walked over to a wall and grabbed onto a pair of bars set into it, before pressing a button in the center. The console lit up, and Mercury could see him mouth the word 'water' before he closed his eyes and a torrent drenched him, spraying him with enough force to almost break his hold on the bars in the wall. As it slackened, he took a few gulps of what he'd managed to catch, and cupped his hands under the last bits of the torrent to drink what remained. It was clearly the only way they hydrated their prisoners.

The rest of the water drained out through the grates of the floor, and he wasn't given anything as useful as a cup to drink from. Even so, once he had gotten a sip, he went back to his exercises, still dripping in the chilled air, his eyes focused on only what was in front of his face to the exclusion of all else.

Mercury winced as she watched, since she couldn't believe what they put Logan through, but she should have been used to it by now. The Consortium knew no limits to their cruelty and torture. "How do I talk to him? When can I go in?"

"I'm waiting on the cell access from central monitoring." He looked at the panel beside Logan's cell, and he could see his own request for access pending, it just hadn't been answered yet. Monitoring wanted them to wait, it seemed. "They're taking their time. They'll let us in once they think you've gotten the message they want you to get. Seems to be their way." He said almost dejectedly. He hadn't brought Mercury down there so that she could be tortured or witness Logan being tortured. Even as he sighed, though, apparently someone listening decided their game wasn't fun anymore, since the panel glowed green, and the seals on the door clicked open.

Logan immediately dropped from the ceiling onto his feet and seemed to bounce from the floor back up onto the cot he'd been given for a bed, falling into a crouch as he watched for who was coming in to see him. Whatever else the Consortium's torture had accomplished, it had certainly succeeded in making him wary.

Mercury hoped he wouldn't just outright attack her, but she wasn't going to hesitate to go in. There wasn't time to hesitate, especially if she didn't want to have her babies in a prison cell. "Logan?" She said just loud enough as she waddled her way in, since there was no way she could run anymore. Even with less gravity.

She could see his body lose its tension as she approached him, but he was hesitant about stepping down off his cot. "Mercury." He sounded more confident than the last time she'd spoken to him, but there was something wrong with his voice. It had been damaged, possibly beyond repair, by what he'd been through, but the man had never looked stronger.

"Are you okay?" It was a silly question to ask, she knew as soon as the words came out of her mouth. "I'm sorry. Of course you're not okay. I . . . I don't know what to say. I'm sorry." She repeated as she watched him carefully.

"I'm . . . alright." The look on his face was more . . . wild . . . than she had seen, but it was as Greg had said, it was exactly the way the Consortium wanted him to look. She could see dark circles of exhaustion under Logan's eyes from what was certainly a chronic lack of decent sleep, and there were open wounds on his exposed legs that were still left over from the surgery he'd been put through, never having healed properly. Even so, he was standing on his feet, and though she could tell he was in pain, there was no outward cause for it. It was just a part of his life, and he seemed to have accepted it.

"They keep telling me you're dead." He approached her slowly. He knew what he looked like, and he didn't want her to be afraid of him, or think she had any reason to be. "They keep telling me different ways you died. One day they'll tell me they re-established contact with Eleusis and they brought everyone home. Then they tell me about torturing and killing them. Then they tell me they rescued them again. Then they come at me until I tell them I believe what they're saying. Then they start again the next day." He shook his head, still resolute, but clearly shaken by the experience.

"Induced psychosis." Greg said quietly from behind her, speaking to Mercury and not to Logan, though he was close enough for Logan to hear. "There was a . . . study done on a cult that practiced it last year in Argentina. Methods of . . . intentionally fragmenting a person's perception of reality until they would be diagnosed by an unknowing physician with true psychosis."

"Sounds about right." Logan glared at the man, though it was clearly unintentional. It was just the way he looked at people who weren't Mercury anymore.

"Just don't believe anything they say. Don't let them do that to you." She said gently as she closed the distance between herself and Logan. If he was going to hurt her, then he would. Mercury refused to be afraid of Logan, she refused to let the Consortium damage her relationship with him. They had been through enough. She reached out to touch him when she was close enough, and she ran her hands up and down his arm until she took his hand and pressed it against her cheek.

"I'm alive. They're not going to kill me, they want me to work for them. The babies are coming, though. I'm going into labor." She admitted, even though she didn't want to. "Greg is my friend from before, on Seven." She looked back at Greg briefly but then looked up into Logan's eyes again. "He's going to help me, but I want you there too."

Logan looked back at Greg a little less suspiciously, but he knew the name from what she'd told him during their time together. "Greg, huh?" He looked the man up and down as he reached up to hold Mercury's hand against his face. It was good to feel something warm for a change. That was the worst part of all of it, the lingering, non-lethal chill of the world that seeped into his bones. "I thought you'd be taller."

"I thought you'd be scarier." Greg shrugged, not rising to the fight or the lethal jealousy in Logan's eyes. "I'm here to help, and she really needs to get to a bed. Sooner would be better than later."

"Alright, lead the way, then." Logan said a little hesitantly, looking around like a scared animal at several holes in his cell through which Mercury safely assumed they had sent various torture implements to break the man. "If they want to stop me from going with you, they'll figure out a way. But I'm sure as fuck not staying here by choice." He squeezed Mercury's hand and looked back at her as if his soul was hanging onto hers to stay afloat through the look. He wasn't broken, she had seen broken minds before, but there was something unhinged about him. Sanity and belief in what he was looking at were a survival mechanism for him, and rationality was something he had to white-knuckle just to stay in the moment with her.

Mercury held onto his gaze in the moment without saying or doing anything before she put her other hand up on his face and pulled him into a soft kiss. "I'm here. This is all real. I promise you. Don't let them take you away from me, okay?"

He knew she said she was going into labor, but if she was able to stop for a moment, then he was going to stop with her and savor it. He had spent too long in solitary confinement, too long in pain, not to take every single moment and make the most of it. "I'm not as far gone as they think. Or maybe I'm further gone than *I* think. I don't know which. It doesn't matter." He shook his head and kissed her back, his beard still dripping with the water they had sprayed him with. Steam rippled off his body from his own heat in the cold room, but he didn't seem to notice. "Nothing is taking me from you. Never again."

She didn't care about the water on his face or his body. All Mercury cared about was taking the moment she had been given and holding onto Logan while she could. She hugged herself to his bare chest, even with her giant belly between them, and she held herself against him with her arms around his back.

She could feel the pain of another contraction coming on, but the only obvious thing about it was that she tensed. Mercury didn't make a sound, she didn't wince, her breathing changed a little and she tensed. It was how she had avoided telling anyone about anything, just by hiding it. But he could feel it, even if she was doing her best to hide it. "I'm holding you to that, Logan. Don't leave me."

She could feel the shaking in his arms as he put them around her, but he didn't let go, and didn't move away. He had to take a few shaky breaths before he could take one full one, but eventually when she tensed again, he moved to pick her up as if she were nothing more than a small child, cradling her against his chest. He headed out of the cell with a glare at the doors, as if he expected them to slam shut on him as he was walking through, then nodded to Greg as he started half-jogging, half-hopping down the corridor in the lower gravity. "Lead the way, Doctor. She's not having these babies in a fucking Suicide Cell."

Mercury turned her face into his chest as soon as he was cradling her in his arms, and she closed her eyes as he carried her. She was paying more attention to Logan than to anything associated with her labor, since having Logan there, being held by him, that was a priority in her brain. Even though her body might disagree. "I'm worried they're going to take the babies away." She admitted in a whisper against his skin. "I've been having contractions for a few days now, but I didn't tell anyone. Labor can go on for so long, I just . . . I want to keep them inside where they're safe."

"They'll be safe." He promised, but he knew it was empty. He had no way of keeping it, no way of being sure about anything in the world outside of his own mind. "They're your daughters. They are who they are. Nothing can take that away from them. Or from you." It was clearly some kind of mantra that he'd repeated to himself over the weeks he'd been in captivity, but the words had force behind them. They had to pause at the end of the cell block for Greg to get them clearance back through into the free portion of the station, and Logan looked down at Mercury as he held her a little tighter through another contraction. "You're going to be alright. We're together, and we're going to stay that way." There were a dozen guards on the other side of the door, all armed, to escort the three of them, but no one made any move to try and separate them as they followed Greg toward the clinic.

"You're carrying me and you're walking. Are you in pain?" She was so wrapped up in herself and seeing him again that she hadn't even really paused to think about all the progress he'd made. However, she knew it had to be progress that was made in the most painful ways possible. The Consortium would have made sure of that. "I can walk, I don't want to make things worse for you."

"If you're walking, I'm not holding you." He said without answering the rest of her question. His legs especially had been in near-constant pain ever since the Consortium had done surgery on him. The nerves had to be regenerated from scratch and they kept giving him medication to speed up the process as much as possible to make sure he would be ready in time for his trial. They kept telling him it would begin the next day, then that it had been delayed, then that it would begin in a year, then a week, never the same, never an answer that could be relied on. He held Mercury tighter as he pushed away the circling thoughts put in his head during his time in a cell. He wouldn't let them take away from his time with Mercury. He wouldn't. "I prefer holding you to any other alternative."

She curled into him instead of attempting to reason with him, mostly because she selfishly wanted him to keep holding her instead of walking. Every moment felt stolen, and she would steal as many as she possibly could. Mercury rested her head against Logan's shoulder, since she was glad to be in his arms again. Even for a short time. "I love you so much, Logan."

It was hard to tell in the dimly-lit hallway whether the droplets falling from Logan's eyes were tears or if he was still drenched from before. His face was hard and his eyes were crazed in their focus, but he stopped when they reached the clinic. Greg had to go in first with a few of the guards to show them where he intended to house Mercury. Logan took the chance to lift her up closer to him in a kiss, then rested his face against hers. "They can do whatever they want to me, try to make me believe whatever they want, but I won't doubt that. I love you too, Mercury. We're going to get through this. All of this. These girls are going to grow up in the kind of world a child deserves, not the cage you or I had around us from the beginning."

Tears slid down her own cheeks after that, and Mercury kissed him again before she just held his face in her hands. "We can go back to Earth." She whispered against his lips. "The CV . . . it's not a disease. It's poison. As long as we can put an end to that, babies can grow up and have full and long lives again."

Some of the wildness left Logan's eyes at that, and the confusion that replaced it made him look a little more like the man she knew. "The whole planet? You can . . . it can be removed from the whole planet?"

She nodded slowly, her forehead rubbing against his as she did so. "It will take a long time for the effects of the poison to fade and to get rid of the poison in the first place, but the Consortium, back then, did this. There *has* to be an antidote. They murdered billions of people and turned Earth into what it is on purpose. They blamed it on some explosion, but that's not true. The Alperts told me themselves. Probably because they plan on killing me, but it's the truth. They're continually poisoning Earth every single day by allowing it to go on."

Logan knew the same history the rest of the world did, and he knew the same story about the explosion at Banang Co. Everyone who lived on Earth in the past few hundred years knew it. He took in the information without questioning. His hands tightened painfully on her as he thought through what she'd told him, and she heard him let out a groan of pain that went beyond anything the Consortium's torturers had managed to get from him.

"Their days are numbered." He promised with a malice in his voice that Mercury had never heard before. She had seen what he did to Stephen Kaplan, and she had watched him thrash under torture in the videos, but even after what she had seen, Logan never seemed like a dangerous person. Not before. The man who held her, however, was something different.

They were allowed into the clinic under guard, and Logan laid Mercury down on the bed indicated by Greg, where a team of nurses stood by. Their guards lined the hallway outside, two of them just inside the door to keep an eye on proceedings. No one made any move to keep Logan at a distance, but one of them did go to a monitor at the side of the room while the nurses hooked Mercury up to an IV.

"Dr. Finnegan." Dominic Alpert's voice came from the screen where the guard stood watch. He and his wife sat at the table in their unit where Mercury had been invited for dinner, sipping at glasses of wine. "We're so glad to hear your daughters are about to join us. We understand this is a difficult time for you, but we wanted to express our congratulations in advance. You have the best of all possible care around you, and we're certain that things will go well."

Mercury didn't respond as she bit her lip through another, stronger contraction but she stared at the screen. "If you really want to congratulate me, you'll promise me that they won't be taken from my care. I know better than to ask for mercy on Logan's behalf, but he's their father now, you know. Orion is dead."

"I'm sorry, Doctor. I'm not able to promise you that at this time." Dominic's voice was as placid and polite as ever, as if they were having a conversation about toothpicks instead of a person's children. "It's not suitable for a child of any age to be in the care of a known terrorist, after all. Your children will be . . ."

"Dominic." Logan cut the man off and turned toward the screen, putting himself between the Alperts and Mercury, as if their line of sight would make a difference. "Be careful what you promise or threaten. You shouldn't say things you can't follow through on."

Dominic actually appeared taken aback, for the first time that Mercury had witnessed. Clearly he thought their torture of Logan had been more successful than it actually was. "I think you'll find there are very few promises I am not able to follow through on, Mr. Bickford. Especially given your current status as criminals. Both of you."

"Crime is a point of view, in some cases." Logan watched Dominic smile, and smiled right back. "And if you're thinking you can use that line in the trial to nail my coffin shut, you just keep on thinking that, if it makes you feel all warm and fuzzy inside." Dominic took another sip of his wine, apparently content to let Logan say whatever he wanted and hang himself, so Logan looked at Sara instead. "What about you, Madam Vice-Tyrant? You were much more talkative during our last conversation, I figured you'd want to make yourself heard here too. This is the second-to-last conversation I'm gonna have with the two of you."

Sara smiled just as her husband did. "You're in the way of my view, Mr. Bickford. You see, you're right about what those children deserve. A good life. A happy life. Once they're cleared in a couple of days of any health issues, we were thinking of adopting them ourselves. So if you don't mind, I'd like to watch my daughters come into the world."

Logan didn't move, and didn't take his hand away from Mercury's behind him. Instead, he stared down the Alperts for a moment and lifted his head as if he was listening to something far away. "We can fight over whose daughters they are later. But I'm curious, I've sort of lost track of time with all the fun I've been having down here in the Suicide Cells. What's the date, Mrs. Alpert? I want to make sure I remember my daughters' birthdays in the coming years, after all."

Sara raised an eyebrow as she looked at Logan through the screen. "February the thirteenth, Mr. Bickford. At this rate, those girls will be a beautiful Valentine's present for us." She couldn't see Mercury through Logan, but she spoke louder anyway. "You can enjoy them for a couple of days, Dr. Finnegan."

"February the thirteenth." Logan's lips drew back in a smile that Mercury couldn't see, but she could feel it through his hand, the way his entire body seemed to relax under the news. He leaned his head back a little without looking away from the screen. "What time is it, Greg?"

"It's almost midnight." Greg said without sounding confused or surprised at the question. Time of day didn't really matter on the stations, which was why Mercury and Melissa had been strolling around so late in the day with the children. There was no visible sunrise or sunset in many of the large areas of each station in orbit.

The look Mercury had seen earlier was back in Greg's eyes, as if Greg knew something no one else in the room knew, except Logan. "It's 11:57 exactly. PM."

Logan's smile got even broader, and on the screen, Dominic's smile dropped just a little more. Logan squeezed Mercury's hand and looked away from the screen long enough to glare at the guards before he looked back at the Alperts. "Dominic, Sara, I have to say, it's been a pleasure being tortured by you. But in twenty-four hours, you and I will have our final conversation. It will be seen by the entire world, all of humanity that we can reach. It will begin with both of you down on your knees, and it will end when I kill you both with my own hands."

"That's quite a plan you've conjured, Mr. Bickford." Sara heard Mercury let out a soft groan behind Logan. "You better see to it that our daughters enter the universe safely."

"Oh, I was around the last time she delivered twins. She's stronger than you give her credit for. I'm not worried." He continued smiling, and he looked away long enough to look at Mercury and let her know he was still there with her. The confidence in his eyes was something new and unexplained, but it was there, as completely as it had ever been. "It's going to be okay." He promised.

"We know about the invasion you're massing in the Mediterranean, Mr. Bickford." Dominic cut in just to break off the moment and deny Mercury the chance to respond. "We know about the second fleet you've massed off the coast of Taiwan where your rebels didn't think we would find it because of the interference there. They've been gathering for the last week. We dispatched our own fleets three hours ago to both locations. They will be annihilated before your daughters are born." Logan had his back to the screen, but nothing Dominic said wiped the smile off Logan's face. In fact, it only seemed to get brighter. "We'll make sure the event is covered as well as possible with the onboard cameras of our craft so that you can review it later. It's important to document these things."

"Yes, it is." Logan agreed without turning around, reaching up a hand to caress Mercury's face once the contraction passed, reaffirming to her he was there, and nothing was going to happen.

"Greg?"

"Thirty four seconds." Greg answered without explaining, and when Mercury got a glimpse of the Alperts past Logan as he turned around, they were finally no longer smiling. Instead, they were both looking down at their communicators, which were going off in a panic.

"Watch the ground, Nic. Sara. You have no idea what's going on down there, you have no idea how much of humanity you have pissed off, and most importantly, you don't know your own people." Logan growled, since his voice was so broken, but his voice was firm.

"Watch it all. I want your eyes wide open when you see the world fall out from under you." Mercury could see on the screen as the Alperts got up quickly from their table, but the lights in their unit went out a second before the camera cut off to snow. The lights in the clinic around them began to flicker as well, switching over to emergency systems as they began to fail.

"Logan?" Mercury asked nervously, since he seemed to know what was going on, but to her the whole station was in trouble and she was in labor. "What's going on?" She looked over at Greg too, since there were more people she cared about on the station than just the two fighting to get out of her. "Are we in danger? James, Declan, they're still . . ."

"They'll be alright." Logan promised, though he had no way of knowing for sure.

Greg stepped in to assist, all of his nurses working in the near-dark to make sure all the machines were working off emergency power only. Out in the hallway the guards shouted back and forth to each other in confusion. They tried to establish what their orders were, since their communicators weren't working. "Your friend took them back to the cells, and they'll be alright in there. They're all together, and your friends will keep them safe. All of them."

"He'll have most of the locks sealed tight by now." Logan assured her, glancing back at the door to the room. It wasn't a large delivery room, and had been a little crowded with the nurses and the guards, but the guards inside the room had gone into the hallway to deal with the confusion. Logan looked at one of Greg's people who was checking on supplies in a cabinet near the door. "Nurse?" He nodded meaningfully at the door. "Would you mind?"

The man took the hint, but didn't make a big show of moving toward the door until he reached it and slammed it shut all in one motion. The door locks clicked audibly in the silent room, and though they could hear the shouting of the guards outside, none of them managed to get it open. All doors in all parts of the Station were designed to act as fail safes in the event of a breach to the vacuum of space in any location. When a few guns went off outside, all that followed was ricochet and more screaming from the guards as someone was hit with their own fire. Logan couldn't have cared less.

"They're out there and we're in here." He looked over at the window as they turned and the bright Earth beneath them lit up the dark room, but it passed quickly with the station's rotation. "We're alright. You just focus on the girls. We're going to be okay."

"Okay." Mercury looked up into Logan's eyes and she gripped even tighter to his hand. "You helped me through last time. I could not have done it without you. I'm glad you're here with me." She tried to take a deep breath afterward. "I wish Orion was here too."

"Maybe he will be, on the other side of this." He settled in on the bed with her, exactly the same way he had when their sons had been born, and kissed her forehead, completely ignoring the rest of the world. Mercury could still hear the soldiers in the hall shouting, but Logan ignored all of it, his eyes on her and her alone. "You can do this. Just breathe."

13

Mercury lost all sense of time once her body kicked into active labor, which was only a few hours after Logan had carried her into the room. During the hour or so of active labor, the pain was so intense she felt as though she wouldn't survive it, but somehow she managed to get her daughters out of her body. She had an IV, but they hadn't had the chance to get any pain medication before the lockdown happened, so she birthed her daughters entirely unmedicated.

She was exhausted as she laid back on the bed, Fiona at one breast while they cleaned up Farrah, the second and slightly smaller girl. They both had a lot of dark hair on their heads and similar cries, though not exactly the same. They were beautiful even though they were bigger than both their brothers had been when they were born. Both girls had a beautiful shade of skin that was darker than Mercury's, but she also knew it would probably get a bit darker still when they had all the melanin they would eventually have. It took time for their little bodies to develop, after all.

"How did I survive that?" Mercury sighed as she pushed a sweat-drenched pile of hair back out of her face. "I think these girls were trying to kill me."

"They weren't trying to kill you. They were just comfortable where they were and cranky about being somewhere else." Logan assured her as he patted Fiona's back lightly. "You did great. I'm amazed you were up and walking around as long as you were to come down and get to me. You should've been in bed yesterday."

"I didn't want to give birth. I was afraid of what they were going to do." Mercury looked down at Fiona and ran her fingers across the back of Fiona's head along her fine and soft hair. "What's happening out there? Are we still safe here?"

"We'll be safe until someone comes to get us." He assured her as he looked over at Greg, who had taken up a position near the window, along with the rest of the nurses. They all seem to have been well informed. Logan wondered who had recruited them. Whoever it was, he was grateful. It was just after seven in the morning, and he would have been standing near the window with them if Fiona and Farrah hadn't just entered the world. "We should have about another hour or so until things start getting really interesting."

"They're launching another squadron." Greg reported from the window. "That makes four that I've seen. All headed for the ground."

"Good." Logan said with a nod. "When I fill out the Alperts' report card, I'll remember to note they follow directions well."

Eventually a nurse brought Farrah over and smiled as she held out the wrapped baby to Logan instead of Mercury. Farrah wasn't crying, so she thought it was safe to hand off the baby without Mercury having to feed her first. Mercury watched as Logan took Farrah and she felt herself relax even more as Logan held the baby. "I'm glad to see you haven't forgotten how to handle a newborn."

He gave her a quick, smiling glare, sitting beside her in black hospital scrubs because it was the only clothing the room held that would fit him. "It hasn't been *that* long since James and Declan were this size. It feels like it sometimes, but it hasn't, really." Farrah didn't seem interested in opening her eyes, but Logan ran his fingertips over her forehead to let her know the world wasn't going to hurt her. "They're beautiful, Mercury. Even if they were trying to kill you, try not to hold it against them."

"They are beautiful." She looked at Farrah in his arms and then into Logan's eyes. "I worry that they're too beautiful. It's only going to give us trouble." She hoped he really was okay with helping her raise someone else's children, because she wanted to have a family with him, and they had a big one already. "Though James, Declan, Lynnette, and Leo will be enough trouble as it is. Maybe we will be experts quicker than I think."

"I don't think we'll have much choice, honestly." He smiled down at the little girl as she stretched herself out and then crumpled back into a tight bundle again. Clearly she wasn't used to having so much room to move around. "But children are all trouble, no matter whose they are or how beautiful." He leaned over carefully to kiss Mercury with both girls held gently between them. "Her mother is the most beautiful woman I've ever seen in my life, and she turned out alright. I'm not worried."

Mercury smiled at Logan and reached out with her free hand to run her hand along his cheek. "You know, you should keep the scrubs." She teased, even though it felt so strange to be able to tease anyone, let alone Logan, since she believed he was dead or dying for so long. "Maybe you can be the doctor this time."

"You think so?" He looked down at himself with a grin. Her comment had gotten a few laughs from the nurses as well, who were mostly pretending they could all ignore each other while they were only a few feet apart. Logan ignored them completely in favor of paying attention to Mercury. "Maybe I will. But you'll always be better at it than I am."

Mercury smiled even brighter, because she hadn't seen his grin in so long. "I missed that smile. I'm glad to see it didn't go away forever."

"You have that effect on my world." He leaned in for another kiss but Farrah began fussing in the middle of it, squealing as she reached out blindly for something she was too tiny to even define. "I think this one wants you back. Is Fiona finished?"

Fiona had fallen asleep at her breast so she slowly moved the sweet sleeping newborn to her belly and reached out for Farrah. It took some assistance for the little one to latch onto her breast correctly, but Mercury was a professional at getting her babies fed. It felt as though it wasn't that long ago that James and Declan had weaned because they needed to be on a bottle during the times when someone else was caring for them. "I think Fiona looks a little drunk. Can you re-wrap her for me?"

"I'll try. I was never much good at that." He moved Fiona slowly to a blanket that one of the nurses held out for him, and quickly swaddled her into a tight bundle in the crook of his arm. He still remembered how, and it felt strangely like the best thing that could have happened within the confines of his own brain. So much of the world had been lies, so many deceptions, so much pain and uncertainty, that remembering how to do a simple thing from a simpler time was so therapeutic he almost wanted to cry. He held the little girl close as he went back to sit beside Mercury, and he looked up at Greg again. "Anything yet?"

"Not yet." He said cryptically. "I've seen a few flashes that I thought looked possible, but nothing definite yet. We're not at a great angle."

"Angles aren't going to matter much pretty soon." Logan bounced Fiona against him gently. "Make sure everything's secured. We need to be ready."

"Probably a good idea." Greg nodded to the nurses, and they all began moving around the room and putting equipment away if it wasn't essential, locking cabinets and pulling out straps to tie other things in place all over the room, including a single belt for Mercury herself that would allow her to hold herself to the bed.

"Are you going to explain anything to me?" Mercury draped a blanket over Farrah and tugged her gown back into place over her other breast. "I'm no longer in labor. I think I can handle the truth."

"The truth?" Logan laughed and glanced up at the window before looking back at her. "The truth, my love, is that I am even crazier than you thought I was, and I'm about to prove it."

* * * * *

"People, if you do not want your dicks on my cutting board, you had better start getting me some fucking answers!" Vance's voice boomed out through the control chamber, one rank after another of systems operations monitors working furiously at everything they could think to try. They had been in the room all night, and the scent of human sweat filled the hall, not the least of which was Vance's own.

It had been hours and hours of false starts and false victories, and everyone in the room had learned not to speak up unless they thought they had made actual progress. Vance's glares were second only to Gehrig's beside him as the two of them and their lieutenants circled the room watching every monitor to make sure everyone was working as hard as they could.

"I've got internal motion sensors back online, sir!" One of the technicians cried triumphantly, typing furiously in mid-air to try and push his discovery and get actual results.

"Fucking finally!" Vance floated over to the man and collided with the terminal behind him with a grunt. He brushed himself off quickly and watched over the man's shoulder as he worked, gliding through the Station systems that monitored all of Prime. "Where are they?"

The man's sweat beaded up on his forehead and began to drip into his eyes before he reached up with a sleeve to wipe it away. The microgravity at the center of the station was essential to some of the cooling systems for the operational computers, but it didn't make things easier for the technicians who had to work on them. Droplets of sweat and a not-insignificant collection of vomit floated through the air from all the nervous technicians. "Where are who, sir?"

"The rebels, you fucking cunt! If the whole damn Station went dark, you don't think that just happened by chance, do you?" He smacked the man on the back of the head, but to his credit, the man kept working anyway. "Check current sensor logs against data from right before the lights went out at midnight. Account for all discrepancies and start scanning for biometrics that aren't supposed to be here."

The man worked feverishly for several minutes as Vance stewed, allocating parts of the task to some of his comrades nearby as the rest of the technicians all worked on their assigned systems to try and push past whatever hellish system virus the rebels had dropped on them. Above their heads, the horizon of the world spun steadily around the glass dome that separated them from the vacuum of space, each pane decorated with geometric patterns that broke the sky into beautiful pieces that no one in the room had looked at in hours.

Vance wanted to leave with the taskforce that had been sent to Earth to deal with the gathering fleets of rebels as the Earth's nations finally showed their colors, but no, he had been required there on Prime. Watching a bunch of technicians fail at doing their jobs.

"There's . . . no one, Sir." The technician said hesitantly, since he didn't want to disagree with the Director. "All scans show the correct number of people, including the five children who were born station-wide during the blackout. Their scans are already in the system and they're the only ones who weren't accounted for prior to things going dark."

"Then why the hell are things still dark?" Vance didn't bother arguing with that kind of result, since he could see the data for himself on the screen, but all it did was confuse him. "If they weren't going to attack while our systems were out, then why take them out? Just to show that they can?"

"No, to distract us. And keep us vulnerable." Victoria said some distance behind Vance and she glanced from screen to screen, even though none of the screens had the answers she wanted. "We have to mobilize everyone we have for an attack here. And you and I need to get to Bickford and Finnegan, because whoever shows up here is going to be looking to liberate them."

"They're across the entire damn station." Vance shot back, glaring at the doors. "Even if our people were cutting toward them, it would take hours to get to them." The large doors at one end of the chamber had long since been cut open by technicians scrambling to get to the central hub just after midnight.

Vance thought the attack came from inside the station, by someone infiltrating the control hall and taking over the systems. But when they arrived, there had been no one but a frantic night crew proclaiming that they didn't understand what had happened. Vance assigned crews to pry open and otherwise cut their way through the locked passages of the station as quickly as possible, to re-establish mobility, but they simply didn't have the equipment to do the job.

"We're completely blind to anything going on here or on the ground. We need to know what's coming at us before we can do anything meaningful about it." It was the same argument they had most of the night, but there was no other way to move forward. They had long since given the order for people to be mobilized, armed, and placed at every conceivable location as their teams managed to cut through the station doors and re-establish some kind of chain of communication, but it was slow-going.

"Well, we better figure something out. Because there is no doubt in my mind that Bickford had a hand in this." Victoria said as she tried to get information off of her communicator, but it was touch and go.

"Ma'am, this is . . . they're actively cutting this off, Ma'am." Another technician said with worry cracking his voice. "I managed to get around the programming block to reboot the external sensors, and they're still . . . working, we're just being blocked from seeing the data. The particle nets are still working, debris monitoring is still working normally, I saw that before it got cut off again, but the data is being intentionally mishandled before it can get to our processors."

"Why do we care about this? If we can't see it, we can't see it?" Vance butted in, too angry to stay quiet.

"Because if they can keep us from seeing it, they could keep it from working if they wanted to, and the station would have fallen apart in the past seven hours by damage from debris. It means whoever's doing it, they don't want to kill the station completely."

"We need to see who is coming." Victoria said impatiently,

just as her communicator chimed. When she checked it, she noticed a video connection from none other than the Captain of Three. "Fatma is contacting me. Somehow."

When the call connected, it was spotty and scattered at best, but Fatma sounded frazzled. The woman never sounded frazzled. "What . . . hell . . . on down there? You're the on . . . person I can reach. We're out of . . . no li . . . guida . . . nothing! I thought you had the . . . bels under con . . . on the ground!"

"We're working on it!!" Victoria yelled back when she replied, though she knew the yelling didn't help at all. It wasn't as though yelling fixed anything about the situation. "We can't find the damn rebels anywhere. Maybe if we start threatening the ones we have, we can squeeze some information out of them."

"You've had them for months!" Fatma yelled back, and Gehrig could almost hear the woman laughing behind the scream. "What the *fuck* have you been doing this whole time if not threatening them and trying to squeeze information?"

"We have been. Just apparently not enough." Victoria growled as she stared down at her communicator. "Are you laughing at me, *Captain*?" She asked in a tone that was definitely threatening. "What the fuck is wrong with you? This is Prime. If they invade us here, they'll come after you next."

The communicator continued to crackle in and out of active reception, but the only sound that could be heard answering Victoria for a long time was Fatma's high, rich laugh, joined by many more as background noise. The laughter came with no explanations, and eventually cut off abruptly. In the silence, the control chamber seemed to get brighter, somehow, but as Vance and Gehrig looked around, there had been no change in the lights throughout or in the monitors in front of the terrified technicians.

A scream sounded from across the room, and everyone jerked in their restraints at the possibility that the rebels had finally landed in some kind of force. Guns were drawn and people instinctively dove behind secure panels, but the screaming didn't stop. When everyone recovered enough to see what the screaming was about, all they saw was a group of technicians off to one side who were screaming and scrambling away toward the door as fast as they could, looking . . . up.

Dozens of faces turned toward the glass ceiling in unison, and more screams erupted all around the room.

The darkness of space beyond the window was filled with

light.

Not the lights of ships or of space debris being broken up by their lasers, but brilliant, powerful lights from dozens of other Stations, all coming straight for Prime.

The horizon had, at some point, stopped spinning around the edges of the glass, which meant that Prime itself had stopped spinning. Microgravity ruled on Prime, and all the incoming Stations seemed to slowly align with the mother station of Orbit. Three was closest, its bright, clear docks visible as they began to align with Prime. No Stations were built to exist while chained together, but they had all been built by the same engineers with the same docking mechanisms and many of the same design features. As Three turned to bring itself into line with Prime, everyone in the control room could see that they didn't intend for the contact to be a collision, but a docking, on an epic scale.

To add insult to injury, external sensor systems came on around the room, showing a hologram of exactly what was happening outside. Dozens of stations, of all types and sizes, were moving to dock with Prime. Three and Two were docking on the immediate ends of the station, while Four through Eight were attaching themselves in turn to Two and Three. Stations higher in number and much smaller in size were moving to dock with Prime all along its length, like locusts landing on a field to devour it whole.

"That's . . ." Vance couldn't even react beyond the screaming and the choreographed chaos looming nearby, the slow dance of the stations all converging on Prime at once. "That . . . can't happen. That's . . . it's not . . ." Such a thing had never, to his knowledge, even been attempted in orbit. No two of the greater stations had ever *docked* with each other, let alone all of them at once. His mind reeled at the logistics alone that would be involved. "That can't . . ." he repeated numbly, since the implications of Fatma's laughter were painfully clear the closer the other Stations came.

You should have known this day would come. Jason's voice spoke through every terminal and every speaker in the room, his words hanging in the air in holographic print that faded slowly when he was finished speaking. *You should have known better than to make enemies out of your own people, especially when you have nowhere left to run.*

"Don't let them board!" Victoria screamed over Jason's voice, since she wasn't about to just stand aside and let the other stations do whatever they thought they could to Prime. Prime was the biggest and greatest station of all . . . it wasn't going to fall prey to the others. "Lock down everything! Mobilize the guards to all the entries!"

"With what systems?!" Vance shouted right back, since they had struggled for the last seven hours to get anything working at all, and they still had nothing to work with, including their own internal communications. He was oddly calmer now that he knew what the hell was happening, but his calm wasn't a sign of being optimistic about their chances. "You! You're in charge here unless we come back. Priority is communications. Anything you can get. You six, with me."

He shoved himself toward the exit to the room, and growled in frustration as he and Victoria and those he had barked at pushed themselves along the corridor toward the few open hatches they had managed to cut through. "The only dock we can get to is this one, which means the only threat we're gonna be able to deal with is Three. Until we can get communications back, we're just gonna have to hope that the rest of the station is awake and watching their damn windows."

"I'll kill Fatma myself if I get the chance." Victoria growled, since she couldn't believe her former captain would do this to Prime, to one of their own. "How the fuck did this happen and no one knew? Someone should have known!"

Vance thought about it quietly for a long time as they moved through the corridors. When they arrived at the docks, their own people gave orders for defense while Three positioned itself against them for possible points of entry. Eventually, he just shook his head. "Bickford. That bastard." Vance growled as he checked his gun and glanced over at Victoria. "I haven't gotten any internal monitoring reports from the other stations for a month and a half, ever since he was taken into custody. I didn't even notice because we were too busy watching the Scandinavians and the Mediterranean, monitoring rebel ship movements, communications . . . He was right. We've been watching the ground."

"Well, I'm going to watch his brains splatter against the wall if I can get to him before his friends do." Gehrig replied sharply as they attempted to prepare for whatever Three had in store for them. Victoria wasn't going down without a fight, even though it looked like everyone else around them wasn't interested in dying for the cause. "Shoot at anyone stupid enough to defy my orders! We told them no entry, and if they break through, I want them dead!"

Vance waited beside her in the silence that followed, his eyes fixed on the large cargo dock where Three intended to place its boarding bridge. They could hear the mechanisms on the station's exterior making the connection and pressurizing the loading bridge. It was just a matter of time before the process was complete.

"Three has thousands." He said quietly, so that only Victoria could hear. "Even if every single fighter here on Prime is awake with a gun in their hand, I don't know if it would be enough. Not with half our fleet deployed to Earth and no word when they'll be back." He didn't look over at her as they waited. He didn't have to. "You and I both know how this is going to end, Victoria."

"Then it won't be without consequences for them." She replied without looking at Vance either. "If I'm not going to die on Eleusis, then I'm going to die right here. But damned if I don't take down as many fuckers as I can while I can do it. They deserve to die for turning against their own."

Vance didn't say anything as the machinery in the distance continued, the stillness of it all settling on everyone present. He was a leader, but he had never been the military power Victoria was. He thought he would grow old and die on Eleusis during the colonization. But in a matter of hours, that became an impossibility. He only had two options, death or surrender. He doubted Three would even permit him to surrender. Besides, if his options were a violent death or the rest of his life in the kind of box where they had put Bickford, he would choose violence. "Goodbye, Victoria." He said quietly as the cargo doors began to pull open across the docks from them.

"Goodbye, Hugo. It's been a pleasure." Victoria replied, and she looked over at him briefly to give him a nod. However, as soon as the cargo doors had any kind of space between them, her focus and her gun turned to the gap and she opened fire without any warning. Whoever was coming through first was the dumbass that was going to pay. The doors continued opening as she kept shooting, but at least she was backed up by her own once she opened fire.

14

"I'll . . . I'll do as you say, Mis . . . Mrs. Tanaka." The former slave had been ordered not to go groveling on his knees to anyone or call Aiko by 'mistress' any longer, but chemically-programmed habits died hard. He, like so many others, had come begging for their daily dose of the obedience serum, since many of them were suffering the effects of withdrawal after the step-down program Aiko had devised to rid them of the burden of their addiction. "I . . . thank you." The man was easily in his fifties if not his sixties, judging by his appearance, but he was weeping like a child as he expressed his gratitude for the saving that he hadn't even asked for in the first place. "You are . . . we didn't know . . . if . . ."

"It's okay." She said as gently as she could, though it was sometimes hard to be so gentle all the time. Their minds were fragile, and the last thing Aiko wanted to do was raise her voice to people who cowered so easily. "I'm glad we were finally able to make something work. The Kaplans left a lot of their information behind, and so . . . well, I'm just glad you and the others seem to be doing so well."

"We . . ." he had a difficult time meeting her eyes, though it was so hard to avoid since she was so much shorter than he was and she insisted on looking them in the eye when she spoke to them, "some of us, me and some of the other Echoes, we were wondering if we could work for you, Mrs. Tanaka. They took us because we were people who wouldn't be missed back in Orbit, and we've been away so long . . . we'd like to go to work for you here. The winter is coming, we know, but this building has ways to support growing food. We can still work to plant and grow some food here."

Aiko looked into the man's eyes for a moment without saying anything and she looked away and around the room. "We were talking about staying here in the compound because it's better equipped. If you stay here close to us, I worry about your progress." She and Carl assumed that eventually a Twist would be re-established and the prisoners could rebuild their lives elsewhere. "They're trying to find a way back to the stations. You don't want to go back?"

The man looked slightly terrified of that possibility, but she already knew that was part of their conditioning. He shook his head, trying his best to look resolute. The effects of their medication had worn off considerably since they had started tapering off, but it would be much longer before the psychological effects faded completely.

"Most of us aren't interested in going back if we don't have to. I know it's partly because we were told never to leave the compound, but going outside the walls to build farms . . . it's still scary for most of us, but less than going back to Earth would be. As we get better, some of us might feel differently, Mistress. Miss." He immediately flushed apologetically red, but carried on anyway. "But for now we'd like to be useful. It's still a new planet. There's a world of things that need to be done."

"Alright." Aiko tried to give the man a reassuring smile. "Certainly, you can stay and help. I need some help too, some assistants to help me in my lab. We can have rotations so everyone can help in different areas. I think that will help. And we're going to do some rebuilding and remodeling in here so that this looks less like a compound and more like a big . . . living space. Apartment building. Something. Something less clinical and military."

The man nodded enthusiastically, since what she said was even slightly indicative of her wishes, and therefore quickly found a home in his brain as a goal he could work toward. "I know a few of us used to be technicians back in Orbit, and I know at least one of us was a structural engineer. We can get started on plans. We've got enough rubble to work with around here to last us until rapture."

He was one of the Echoes who was most able to speak for himself, which was why his fellows had asked him to be the one to speak for them as well. "A couple of us worked in 'ponics too, I'll make sure they know they're assigned to your lab. I'm sure they'll be glad to help with whatever they can." The man began to drop to his knees out of habit, but stopped himself before doing more than just dipping toward the ground, and cleared his throat. "I . . . I'll go see that things get moving, then. No autumn days to waste. Thank you, Mrs. Tanaka."

"No, thank *you*, for wanting to stay here with us. Michael." They had given names to people who couldn't remember their own, and Aiko was determined to use names instead of numbers. She didn't want them to be Echo-12345 forever. She wanted them to be people again. Eventually. "Don't hesitate to come talk to me again if you need to."

"I will." He backed away toward the door and kept his eyes on the floor as he turned to leave. Some habits were going to take a very long time to break, especially since the people didn't even seem to notice they still had them most of the time.

"Well, I'd say that's progress." Carl made sure to keep himself mostly out of sight with David in his arms while the man visited with Aiko. She had a way of putting people at ease and setting their minds toward their future. He, on the other hand, was good at giving orders. Not the best person to assist with the rehabilitation of recent slaves. "And I can't say I blame them for wanting to stay here. Not that sad about the prospect myself, so long as there's some way we can get William back."

"Jason told us Will is alive. As long as he's alive, there's a way to get him back." She said with determination, since she wanted her son back so much it was a physical pain in her chest. "I miss him so much."

Carl got up and moved closer, since he felt the same way. "He'll be two next month." Even knowing they would probably get to talk to their son on his birthday was a comfort, but painful at the same time. They had to figure out a way to get home, but Jason assured them that there were other things going on at the moment that required the full attention of the rebels. The Twist would have to wait. "I'm sure Kam will throw him a party or something. Heaven knows he's got lots of company among the other kids his age."

"I'm sure he's grown so much . . . and I missed it. I just want him back." She moved closer to Carl and looked at David in his arms before she looked up Carl again. "Knowing us, I'll get knocked up again before we can even get him back."

"The only reason you haven't gotten knocked up already is because we were fighting a war. Now we're building apartments and planting winter crops. Peacetime is babytime." He smiled down at her and put his huge hand along her cheek to caress her neck. "We'll get him back. And once we know we're not gonna get shot at or drugged in the night, you and me are gonna go prospecting to find us a hilltop for me to build us a palace on. Orion already claimed his, but the one next door looks pretty good too, at least to me."

"A palace, huh?" She smiled brighter as she put her small hand on top of Carl's large one. "I like the sound of that. A palace on Eleusis." She turned her face so she could kiss the inside of his hand. "Do you think Orion and Anna are going to be okay? I didn't tell them about Logan and Mercury, since they didn't really need to know about them being the Consortium's prisoners. Not while Anna is . . . recovering."

"He tells me she's getting better. It's just . . . slower. For reasons I'd rather not think about where my best friend is concerned." Orion had mentioned a few of the things slowing down Anna's weaning off the drug, mostly centering on the fact that she was enjoying being addicted to her man. "Plus, she's still more worried than most that the Kaplans are still around somewhere. They kept her on a pretty short leash while she was here, so I'd say her paranoia about it is pretty well founded."

"They probably *are* around here somewhere, unfortunately." Aiko said with a shake of the head. "I think her paranoia is proof of that. There's probably some attachment because it is their blood that activated it inside of her. If they're still alive, she has reason to be paranoid. We do too. She needs to be watched, I don't want them sneaking in and commanding her to go on some kind of killing rampage. She's not just a farmgirl. She's an assassin."

"If their drug works, she should be bound to Orion now, not them." Carl didn't sound completely certain even as he said it, and he wasn't sure he would want to see it put to the test, but he was saved from thinking any further along those lines by a knock on the door of Aiko's lab, and a pair of faces he hadn't seen for several days. "Jeeta, come in. I meant to send somebody looking for you two earlier today, I was starting to wonder if the two of you decided to go prospecting."

"We just wanted some privacy." She said by way of simple explanation, but really it was Charles who wanted time to work. Jeeta was simply his assistant. They stayed in the same room and slept in the same bed, but they remained platonic roommates, more or less. She helped him with his physical therapy and his work. That was the life they'd had together for the days since they were freed. "But now we wanted to come and speak with the both of you."

"Sounds ominous." Carl said with a smile that he hoped would be returned. He sighed when it wasn't. "Well, come on in and speak your peace, then." He sat back on a chair with David in one arm and Aiko on one knee. He raised an eyebrow when they both came in, Charles shuffling behind carrying a steel case in his free hand. "You brought me a present? You shouldn't have."

"The present is not for you, Commander. Not directly." He placed the case on a table at the side of the room and unlocked the latches on either end, but didn't open it. Instead, he stood by it as if reluctant to have it out of reach. "I know I'm a stranger to you, and you've got at least one good reason named Henry to distrust my family. But I need to ask you some questions before I talk about what I came to discuss."

"Ask all of us or just Carl?" Aiko glanced over at David once and then back at Charles. "And it's not just Henry. Jason has done his fair share of dragging your genes through the mud. Xander too."

"Jason and Xander have sacrificed more than someone as young as you are can comprehend." Charles said with a lethal but subdued glare in her direction. "Anyone who has given as much as they have to the world inevitably makes some mistakes and miscalculations in the course of doing so." He looked back at Carl, heaving a quiet sigh and trying not to be as confrontational.

"But to answer your question, I need to ask all of you. There are pieces of information I require, and assurances I require as well. I will understand if you are unable to give these assurances, but any refusal to give them will result in the withdrawal of my support. I am sorry to be so blunt about it, but I cannot . . . I will not compromise on my terms once I give them. I know this is confusing, but you will understand why."

Charles opened the case beside him, and turned it toward Carl and Aiko, letting them see the device inside, curved and armored as it waited for his arm. Or Jeeta's. He had programmed it to work for her without her knowledge or permission. It was something he had to do.

"Fifteen years ago, Henry and I were captured by the Consortium. We were living in Morocco at the time. We had just split from Xander. He had some business in the Amazon. They took us to Prime, torture, confinement, use your imagination and then make it worse." He shrugged, not wanting to dwell on that time. It was nothing compared to what happened afterward.

"They came to me a few months after they took me, gave me the news about Eleusis, the contest they had put out to find a faster way to get here. The fastest was too slow for them, so they solicited my ideas on the subject." He glanced down at the device in the case. "They gave me the resources to conduct the research I told them was necessary. The other contestants were thinking in terms of existing technology. Instead, I invented the Twist."

"You inven . . ." Carl had no reason to disbelieve the man in front of him, and did nothing to try and keep his jaw from dropping to the floor. "You . . . oh, you better make sure you're standing behind bulletproof glass when we tell Orion. He came in second place in that contest. Behind you, I guess."

"His course was very nearly perfect, I'm glad to know it was his. I look forward to congratulating him on it. From behind a bulletproof barrier." Charles nodded, but continued on anyway. "I invented the Twist in its correct form, with no containing framework, designed to create instantaneous site-to-site connection. I used the technology they helped me create to escape and destroyed all evidence they retained of its design. I remained in hiding for ten years, after breaking out Henry as well.

"At the end of those ten years, the Consortium offered Henry a deal if he captured me on their behalf. He did so."

Charles glanced at the device again, lovingly. "This is keyed to me and to Jeeta. It will kill anyone else who attempts to use it. The Consortium forced me to give up the Twist technology by means I will not describe, but the version I gave them was the version you and they have utilized thus far, limited in scope, difficult to construct, difficult to power. The technology needed to be limited, hobbled, or the Consortium would have wiped out the world by now." He could see understanding in their eyes, so he went on.

"What I need to know, the assurance I require, is that if I agree to utilize this technology, *my* technology, on your behalf, on behalf of your rebellion, that you will at no time attempt to take this technology from me by force or attempt to copy it. I will oversee its use, I reserve the right to deny requests for transport for any reason, disclosed or undisclosed, and in exchange, when your rebellion succeeds, I will live in a place of my choosing and will be provided compensation and support as I will stipulate. Those demands will be modest at the time I make them."

Carl took in the entire speech with his jaw still hanging open, but eventually forced his mouth to close. "That's a hell of a lot of addendums. And a hell of a lot of power to keep for yourself. Agreeing to that would make you the single most powerful person in the universe. No contest."

"My ambition has never been power." Charles answered quietly. "Power is easy. My ambition has always been to be left the fuck alone. It turns out to be vastly the more difficult of the two."

"So you don't want anyone to be able to travel between planets once you go into hiding? If you're the only one who can use it, then you are begging to have the whole world come after you all over again. I mean, you could leave now if you want to, right? Go wherever you want? Why stay here with us if you can make your dreams come true already?"

"I have spent quite enough time alone with my own dreams." He said without explaining any further, but Carl saw the man's fingers twitch to hold Jeeta's hand tighter. "More to the point, I have as much or more to hold against the Consortium than any other living creature. If I can help you restore what they've destroyed or improve what they have tried to corrupt, I'll consider it honest revenge."

"Making the world . . . two worlds . . . better places as an act of vengeance?" Carl asked doubtfully. "Not the best motive I've ever heard."

"I might be willing to negotiate the exclusivity of my control over the Twist, in time." Charles admitted, rather than continuing his discussion of vengeance. "Trust is not a thing I take lightly. Nor will I ever. And it will take a great deal of convincing for me to believe that adequate safeguards can be placed on the technology to keep it from causing undue harm. Technology such as this is to nuclear weapons as nuclear weapons themselves are to children burning ants with a magnifying glass."

"We would be incredibly grateful for your help, Charles. Our son William is still out there, and along with everything else, we want to get him back. But we're not going to try to force anything from you or with you. That's not how we work." Aiko looked over at Carl and back at Charles and Jeeta. "What did you think we were going to do when you brought this here? Attack you? Have you arrested and thrown back into a cell? We aren't interested in any of that."

"No, I didn't think you were." He answered with a sigh that

was still relieved, no matter what he'd said. "As I said, trust isn't something that comes easily to me." He glanced over at Jeeta, then down at the device in the case, his fingers trailing over it like a beloved pet. "I have one other request, and then, given those assurances for the time being, I will place myself at your disposal."

Carl's mind was racing with the preparations that would need to be made to get back to Earth as quickly as possible, especially given Jason's reticence to answer any detailed questions over their previous, tenuous connection. "You've put a lot of requirements on this already, you're really gonna add one more?"

"This one will please you." Charles assured them, as he worked the device out of the case and onto his arm. It sat there comfortably, and he was always surprised at how light it was, for all the power it contained. "I'd like you to assign a few of your soldiers to go with me to kill Henry and the Kaplans. I've located them a few dozen kilometers northeast of here, in a fortification my brother built underground."

Carl's face was back to disbelief, but he certainly wasn't going to pass up that kind of opportunity. "The satellite scans can't get through Eleusis bedrock to scan underground."

"They can if you alter what they're scanning for and the bands they're scanning, in a very localized area." Charles explained, doing his best to keep from sounding like he was explaining something to a petulant toddler.

"How did you even know to look there, if it has to be so localized?" Carl shot back suspiciously.

"Because I helped him build it." Charles answered without further explanation. "Do you agree to my terms?"

Aiko couldn't imagine why they would possibly refuse. "Of course. We can't have them wandering around Eleusis alive. Especially considering all the damage they did. You, um, you should probably go talk to Orion and Anna, though. I think they'll want to go with you. And if you want soldiers, they're better than most."

"I'll go too." Carl said as he handed David back over to Aiko, who still hadn't left his lap through the entire conversation. He looked over at her as he got up with a sigh. "I'll need to witness to the council back on Earth that they're dead, along with all the other witnessing and answering I'm gonna have to do."

Aiko didn't know what to say to that, since she didn't expect that Carl would volunteer. She felt a little nauseous when he did.

"Who . . . who is going to stay here with us?" Aiko and Carl had hardly been separated since even before the first time they were trapped on Eleusis, and she felt too attached to him to want him to go. Especially if the Twist suddenly didn't work again and she was trapped on Eleusis or elsewhere without him.

"We won't be gone long." Carl assured her with a brief kiss. "Can the gate, door, whatever you want to call it, be left open for long with that thing?"

"It's actually much easier to sustain than to open, so there is greater efficiency in leaving it open rather than closing and reconstructing, unless you require it to be open for a period of longer than a day, for local planetary travel." Charles said as if it was the most matter-of-fact thing anyone had ever said.

Carl just shook his head. "If I live to be a hundred, I'm never gonna get used to you fucking Montgomeries." He turned back to Aiko, one large hand on David's back. "We'll be there and back before anybody even knows we're gone."

"That's not true. I'll know you're gone." Aiko said sadly, though she did want William back, and if he could go and get William, it would be worth it. "But if you have to go . . ." She didn't like using a guilt trip, but still, she wanted Carl to be well aware she didn't like him leaving. She selfishly wanted him there with her.

"You know I do." He kissed her again as Charles and Jeeta headed out of the room. He didn't see the harm in letting them get a head start, as slow as Charles was. "I'll be alright. You know better than anybody how not easy I am to kill. Besides, I ain't come this far to be done in by a couple little shits like Stephen and Maria."

Aiko didn't let him move very far away before she yanked his shirt back so she could kiss him several more times. "This is our planet, you know. Yours, mine, Will's, and David's. I'm not staying here without you. And don't come back all torn up either."

"Can't promise that. Henry can be a nasty son of a bitch. But he's Charlie's problem." His huge hands moved over her as they were left alone in the room, starting something he intended to finish later. "Have I ever mentioned how sexy it is when you get bossy? I might have to go find another planet for us to claim just to watch you get that sexy steely side going."

Aiko just smirked. "Really? You, the big, bulky warrior man, you like to be bossed around by a tiny, nerdy woman?" She giggled but his hands were getting her riled up in other ways. "I mean it, though. You better come back to me. You're my world."

"And you're mine." He said and meant it. "Eleusis might be our world, but you're all I need of mine. I'll always come back to you." He kissed her one more time to make sure she could feel the promise in her bones, then turned to go. If he spent too much time saying goodbye, he'd be around another week.

Orion was stunned into silence at the proposition set in front of them. The fact that neither he nor Anna were presently dressed wasn't helping him manage his shock either. Anna had decided to wake him up in the most delicious of ways, and he had to admit that his brain still hadn't quite recovered.

"Okay, let me get this straight." He looked over at Jeeta, since at least when she talked he didn't feel like he was three years old listening to a lecture on astrophysics, and Carl was quiet. "He invented the Twist, there's a portable version, and you want us to go with you to kill the Kaplans and his brother Hunter Henry. Am I missing anything?"

"No, that's the simplified version." Jeeta looked at Orion, mostly because his nakedness wasn't nearly as offensive to look at. Anna's lack of decency was something, but she almost couldn't blame the woman. "We'd like to go sooner than later, though." She said politely, though she didn't really want to be polite about it.

"Do I get to call dibs?" Anna looked over at Charles. "I mean, you already called dibs on Henry a long time ago, which is fine, though I would gladly kill him too. But Stephen Kaplan, I want to kill that motherfucker myself. And shoot both him and Henry in the fucking balls."

Orion actually smiled at the fact that Anna was able to even speak that kind of threat against her former masters, since it was one more sign of how she was coming out of her previous control. Every day she seemed to be farther and farther from who she had been when he found her, and he couldn't be happier about it. "No argument from me. You want a jumpsuit or do you want that short skirt so they can get a look at what they're never going to touch again?"

"I want you to tell me what to wear." She replied with a smile as she ran her hand over his skin, simply not caring about anyone else around, even though she was still quite naked. Even with Carl nearby, Anna was done with caring about what other people thought, and she had lost enough time with Orion. She wouldn't ever pass up a chance to touch him ever again, and she would never be touched by another person again. Her body was hers first, then Orion's. Anyone else could rot in hell. Her method of attempting to heal was reclaiming every part of herself and not allowing anyone else's abuse to claim her. Every touch she allowed and asked for erased a little more horror from her mind and body.

He halfway rolled his eyes at the request, but then nodded toward her wardrobe. "Jeans and a t-shirt, then. I don't want them seeing any more of you than they've already gotten, and if you're gonna be shooting somebody in the nuts, probably best to wear something you don't care about getting bloody. I like you in that skirt."

"Fine." Even pregnant she was still pretty spry and flexible, and it showed in her speed as she hopped up. Anna hurried to comply with his order and anyway, she wanted the Kaplans dead. She really, really, *really* wanted them dead.

Orion went and got dressed in the only pair of shorts he'd found that actually fit him well, and didn't bother with a shirt, as usual. He'd gotten accustomed to living without one out in the wild, and didn't see the reason to change. He pulled on a pair of good boots, though, for which he had become immensely grateful. "You expect them to know we're coming? Henry would know about you designing the Twist and everything, right?"

"I don't know if he'll be expecting us or not. But sensors are showing that he's stationary at the moment and has been for the past hour. So he's either asleep or waiting on an ambush. I don't particularly care which. You can injure him, and by all means disarm him, but I want to talk to him before he dies." The look on Charles' face was ice cold, but his fingers twitched a little as if he was already holding a gun.

"If you want to talk to him, we're going to have to restrain him somehow." Anna finished getting dressed. Her jeans didn't button all the way, but no one had maternity clothes in the compound. "He's a fucking psycho who never listens to anything. Unless . . ." She glanced backward as if she was looking for something and she looked over at Charles again. "Don't you have some of the serum still?"

Charles raised an eyebrow, since he already followed her train of thought. "All those months in a cell across from you, and I can't recall ever seeing you with a sufficiently malicious streak to use something like that on another person. But it won't work. The serum doesn't work on me, and won't work on him. Just as I suspect it wouldn't work on you." He flicked a look over at Orion. "We 'designed' types are deficient in some of the areas the drug is designed to control."

"You 'designed' types still have weaknesses. Hit him with an immunosuppressant or something beforehand. I don't know. I would sure like to give that bastard some orders myself." Anna persisted, since she had imagined so many ways of exacting revenge on Henry.

"I'm going to kill him, not capture him." Charles said flatly. "Henry has betrayed everyone in my family, and killed at least two of us himself. He's of no use as a prisoner, and he would only escape, no matter how well-designed his prison. If I had my own way . . ." a dark kind of malice moved through Charles' hazel eyes as he looked back at Anna, and she saw Orion take half a step back from the man under the kind of vicious cruelty the cripple was clearly capable of imagining, "I'd have him dying for centuries. But in the interests of time and efficiency, I will settle for him merely dying."

"I'm not saying he wouldn't die. It would just be nice to make him dance a little beforehand. But we'll do it your way, magic-portal-man. Let's go, then. No need for all the excess jabber." Anna was in a stage of emotional 'healing', which meant being even more brash and unthinking than the previous version of herself, at least toward everyone else except Orion. She didn't want to be depressed over what had happened to her, not when she had Orion back. So the next best thing was to pretend like it didn't have an impact on her. It did, but she didn't want to show it. Repression would work, for now.

When they were all dressed and armed with several guns each (just in case), Charles walked over to the door of Orion and Anna's chambers and locked it, then turned out the lights, to leave them in almost complete darkness aside from the small stand-lamp next to their bed. "Behind me, please." Charles asked, and waited for the other four to comply before he tapped on one of the keypads in the device on his arm.

He had most of the sequence pre-programmed. It was only a few taps before a laser grid formed itself in the air beside their bed, just as a precaution and a targeting measure, and a hole in space formed at the center of the grid. The hole expanded outward as if pulled by invisible hands, stretching into a wide oval shape that even Orion could pass through comfortably.

The reason for the light being turned off quickly became obvious, as the dark cave spread open in front of the group. Carl went through the opening first, stepping cautiously onto dry rock without making a sound, and moving aside so Orion and Anna could follow. They could tell that they were in a broad, empty space, with the smell of dead animals nearby, the salt of curing meat hanging in the still air. All five of them were through quickly, and the hole closed behind Charles with the same complete lack of ceremony as it had opened, no light, no heat, no show of destructive force to mark its passing.

Across the cave, in the only patch of light visible aside from the acute phosphorescence of the lichen all around the edge of the nearby pool, the five of them could see their targets. Henry was lying back on a cot, apparently asleep or pretending to be, while across the living space, Stephen and Maria were on a bed of animal skins. He had her on her knees with a fistful of her hair in one fist, the violence of their lovemaking (if it could be called that) audible and echoing through the entire cavern.

Anna's confidence buckled as soon as she saw them, and she gripped onto Orion's arm with a force that was painful. She couldn't move, not because she wanted to watch them, but because she didn't want them to know she was there. She didn't want them to force her to join or do anything else they had forced her to do. The arm that held a gun in her hand was already trembling, though it wasn't necessarily from fear of them, it was a fear she wouldn't be able to do it.

"You're not there anymore." Orion whispered down into her hair, his hand resting calmly on her shoulder. "You're not *theirs* anymore." It wasn't quite an order, but he hoped the reminder would help, even if he wasn't sure it would.

Anna's breathing was still irregular as she stood there, but she moved her arm just enough so she could pull him closer. "Tell me that I'm yours. Only yours. Please."

"You are your own." He answered from beside her, one of his long arms stretching across her torso to hold her against him as she watched the pair across the broad pool. "You're your own woman first, foremost, and always. Then, only after that, are you mine. But me being a greedy son of a bitch, I will take every bit of you that you give me."

Anna nodded since she was reassured she was her own person and she belonged to Orion more than anything else. She hoped it was a truth her brain might trick her into believing. She kept a gun solidly in her hand but turned her attention to Charles and Jeeta, since they were ahead of everyone else, and she wasn't going to open fire until he was ready.

Jeeta looked back at their companions and looked over at Charles again as she helped him stand. "Do you want them to handle getting him into custody?"

He smiled down at her, though she wasn't that much shorter than he was, and she was a great deal stronger, at the moment. "Thank you for the vote of confidence." Was he actually teasing her? Being so close to revenge had put him in a clearly better mood. He turned to look over his shoulder at the waiting soldiers, then leaned against the rock so they could all draw close enough to listen to him. "General, there is an outcropping of rock just below their sleeping quarters, roughly four meters from my brother's bed." Charles was interrupted momentarily by Maria screaming, but he was merely silent a moment before continuing in the darkness. "He will be armed, most likely with a knife hidden in his cot. You are the best matched in this group to subdue him."

"Sounds like fun." Carl actually grinned and started moving. It was good to be taking orders from someone for a change instead of giving them. Leadership was fun, but it was also its own kind of burden.

"Captain, Anna . . ." he looked over at Stephen and Maria, who were now facing away from them after the progress the five of them had made around the pool. "I believe you said something about shooting him in the balls. Is your aim that good from this angle?" The rutting pair were only a dozen meters away, after all.

"Right now? I don't know how good my aim is." Anna stared at Stephen and Maria some more, since she was still having a hard time. She was stronger than this, wasn't she? She shot Stephen before and nothing had stopped her, but she also hadn't been looking at him when it happened. "I'll settle for the ass first. He'll get too distracted if his dick is falling off. I want him to know who is killing him."

Anna watched Carl's progress until he was close enough to react whenever Henry reacted to the noise, and then she didn't think. She just aimed for Stephen's disgusting ass and fired. After she hit him in the ass, she aimed for his side so she could at least put him down, and she shot at Maria's side as well. She didn't want them crawling after weapons.

The cave was a flurry of screaming and wild motion for a minute and a half, only after which anyone knew what the hell had happened. As soon as Anna had gotten off her first shot, Henry had started awake and brought a knife up in time to catch Carl mid-tackle.

The two men wrestled on the ground next to his cot, but Carl was far too large for the fight to be anything close to fair. Before long, Carl had Henry's arms twisted behind his back until he dislocated both the man's shoulders, and pressed him forward onto his knees. Carl had a knife wound in one arm that he had turned into Henry's attack, but it was like he didn't even notice the blood pouring down his arm. He would handle it later.

Across the cavern, Stephen and Maria fell to one side as they were hit, and Orion was there beside her to shoot them both a few more times in the legs to prevent them from escaping. Neither of them were armed or had thought to keep a weapon close by during their playtime, and they laid against the stone of the cave groaning in pain as they looked up in panic. Stephen reached out blindly with one hand to try to find Maria's, and latched onto her wrist as soon as he found it. Both of them were in too much pain to say anything at first, but the hatred in Stephen's eyes as he looked up at Anna was tangible.

"Hello, Kaplans." As soon as Anna was able to get over to them, she gripped the gun tighter in her hand. She wondered if they would try to give her a command. She wondered even more if she would want to respond to it. "Here we are again. Only this time I'm not going to let you get away alive."

"Don't shoot." Stephen said between gasps of pain, devolving into grunts as he got angry. "You're shooting the wrong people. Your rebels are the enemy, not us."

Anna felt her grip loosen slightly, but she took a deep breath afterward and forcibly tightened her grip. "Who would you want me to shoot? Carl? Orion?" She turned slightly toward Orion, but her hand with the gun didn't move. "They didn't rape me repeatedly. Torture me. Attempt to destroy me. You did."

"It was the best you've ever had. Or ever will." Stephen looked her up and down again, confused both at the fact that she was still alive and that she wasn't moving the gun. "Shoot the fucking giant! Now!"

She hesitated and she knew he could see it, but she shot Stephen in the shoulder instead. While he was screaming, she decided to speak again. "You said shoot." Anna stared at him, clearly ready to shoot him again. "I'm not going to shoot my husband. I'm going to kill you and your fucking disgusting piece of trash wife and I'll finally be free of you."

"You're never going to be free. Not as long as you live." Stephen threatened through gritted teeth. He already thought he was going to die once. He wasn't going to stop fighting until someone forced him to stop. "You're always going to remember. Every single time. You'll remember every single time, even when you think you've forgotten, and you'll never have . . ."

"Memories fade." She moved the gun lower and shot him right in the crotch, just like she wanted to. "But your small dick was always going to be the first thing to go." When Maria tried to throw herself at Anna for shooting Stephen again, Anna didn't even save any special torture for Maria.

"What a waste of a brain." She said before she shot Maria twice in the head and looked back at Stephen who was still in pain from his dick. She thought about giving him a chance to say anything else, but then she shook her head and shot him in the throat.

There was no more fight in either of them once she was finished raining lead on them both. Stephen gagged a few times as Maria's body fell across his own, but his sightless eyes soon glazed over, staring up at the roof of the cavern as the blood continued to pour from his throat. It was a gruesome scene, with part of Maria's skull fractured off along Stephen's ribs, but both of them lay still as the echoes of the gunshots died with them.

Orion moved slowly to put a gentle hand on Anna's shoulder, one finger at a time, to let her know that he was there with her. "Two nightmares down." He eventually said into the stillness. "Two fewer for the world to worry about."

Anna felt sick, not because the Kaplans were dead, but because the adrenaline from murdering them was too much. The murder was two more tick marks on her murdering tab. She really was a terrible piece of shit. "I didn't think I could do it."

"Most things are that way. Until you do." He squeezed her shoulder and turned her to face him, leaving the corpses behind. "And that's the last time you're gonna have to use one of these for a while, I'm hoping." He put a hand on hers still holding the gun numbly, and pushed it down slowly so she could move out of the posture she'd taken to kill someone.

Anna let the gun clatter to the ground and she stepped into Orion and buried her face into him. "Do you promise? Can I be a normal mom with a house and kids and you and nothing else to worry about? I don't want to be this person anymore."

"You can do that." He promised, holding her tightly against his chest as he looked over at where Charles was advancing slowly on his brother. Henry wasn't making any sound as Carl held him in a kneeling position, making it impossible for the man to escape. More importantly, there didn't seem to be any other threats present in the cavern. The three of them seemed like they really were the very last of the Consortium's presence on Eleusis.

"Hello, Henry." Charles said as he got closer, leaning against a wall for support once he was close enough to speak one on one. He was holding his arm where the Twist rested, since it was heavy enough to fatigue him after wearing it for only a few minutes. It didn't matter if he showed weakness in front of his brother anymore. Henry was going to die, and they both knew it.

"Hello, Charles." Henry said through clenched teeth. They might have been designed to be superior, but he wasn't immune to pain. "Do you have a rack already set aside for me?"

Charles shook his head, almost sadly. "I considered waiting until I had one, but I am no longer that patient. I've considered a lot of things for this moment, none of which seem sufficient." He looked up at Henry with icy apathy in his eyes. "In time, I'll forgive myself for allowing you to die quickly."

Henry nodded, appearing content with that kind of answer. "There's a question you've wanted to ask me for a long time." He fought through the pain to speak calmly. "You've always been too proud to ask me, too full of yourself to actually speak the question out loud, but you've always wanted to know. You've always wanted to know because you've never been capable of understanding. It might be the only thing you can't understand." His eyes were just as cold as Charles'.

"The answer to the question you've never been able to answer, is that we should never have been made. We should never have existed, and therefore, it's right that we don't. One by one, I made sure we would be erased. George, Frank, Isaac, they were easy. Accidents. Brandon was harder. They got Jason entirely on their own, without my help. Devon was an honest accident, I had nothing to do with him. I don't know anything about Edward. He was like Xander, always just a little too fast for me. But you . . . you I almost didn't take. You, of all of them, you I liked. Because you understood. You always understood. You hate everything because we're wrong. You hate the world because you know you don't belong to it, and it doesn't belong to you."

Charles shook his head, looking down at the ground between them. "I never hated the world, Henry. The world depresses me. Because I understand it too well. And I understand how much a part of it we are." He looked up again, with difficulty.

"You took our family away, Henry. All of us . . . together . . . imagine what we could have accomplished. Instead, you picked us apart, made us afraid to stay close to each other, all the while you were the reason why." He opened a panel on his device and glanced up at Carl. "You can release him, General. He knows what this is."

Carl put Henry face-down on the ground and then pushed off him, stepping up and away to get closer to Orion and Anna while he watched the confrontation between the brothers.

Henry got back up to his feet, with some difficulty, since he couldn't use his arms very well with both shoulders dislocated. As Charles had said, he didn't make any move to get closer, just stood and clenched his teeth in pain as he watched Charles. "May I ask where you're sending me?"

"There was a beach house where we lived for a year in Morocco." Charles said as he worked on his device. "It's probably the most peaceful place I ever lived. Delivered groceries, landlord who didn't ask questions, clean water. We stayed there so long because you were waiting for me to lose my edge, which I did." He gave one final tap, and a laser grid appeared on the cave floor behind Henry, so bright it hurt everyone's eyes to look at it at first. When everyone in the cave adjusted, they could see a beach hundreds of feet below, with waves rolling up on it gently. The salt smell of the ocean filled the cave, the cry of gulls audible from far below. "It was the last place I trusted you. I buried you there in my mind a long time ago."

"All this work and you still didn't get what you wanted." Jeeta stayed as close to Charles as she could while the confrontation continued. "Because if he wants me for his family, I will be it for him. And you didn't destroy them all. You failed."

Henry looked back at Jeeta, then gave Charles one more glare before he turned back to look down on the beach far below. "The world will kill the rest of you soon enough, if the Consortium doesn't do it first." He sighed and shook his head in resignation as he watched the waves pour in over the sand. "I hated that fucking house."

Charles shook his head and raised his gun. "Dying the way you lived, Henry. Even your last words are half-ass." He let a shot ring through the back of Henry's head, spraying forward through his eyes as he fell forward through the Twist. Once he was out of sight, Charles stepped up and took aim at Henry's falling body, then fired over and over again to completely empty the clip before he hit the ground, sending sprays of blood flailing through the air to paint the sand around the corpse upon impact.

Jeeta let him stand by himself for a moment to stare but then she rushed to his side so he wouldn't fall. She latched onto his arm, but she never once tried to touch anything other than his arm. "Are you alright?"

He took his time, but eventually nodded, unable to take his eyes away from the small speck of his brother on the sand far below. "I'm glad our family ghost is dead." He took a step back when he could force himself to do so, and tapped a command on the Twist to close the portal, leaning on Jeeta as the world slowly returned to darkness inside the cave.

Once it seemed like Charles was settled against a wall to recover from Henry's death, Carl stepped a little closer. "Hey doc, you mind? The wife sees me come home with this, she's gonna be pissed. I'd like it to be mostly gone or at least covered by the time we get there." He drew closer to Jeeta after grabbing some spare rags from Henry's collection, still looking worriedly over at Orion and Anna.

Orion led her away from the two bodies, but they were still at a distance from the other three while he held her, letting the world settle in a little more with every passing moment. "He can get us back to the kids." Orion said with a hand along the side of her face. "Leo might be taller than you by now."

"If he's . . . okay." Anna wasn't completely convinced that her children were alive, even though she desperately wanted them to be. "Charles never said he was going to share anything, did he? He just wanted revenge."

"I was selfish enough to want revenge first." Charles answered from the other side of the cavern. In absolute stillness, all sound traveled fast. "But I have as much reason as the rest of you to hate the Consortium. My device and I are at your service, at least until your war is won, then we can discuss the best use for it in whatever world follows." He looked over at Anna and Orion, then back at Carl, as Jeeta finished a simple bandage for the cut in his upper shoulder. "General?"

"Back to the compound first." Carl said unsurprisingly, looking around at the dismal space where he would never want to be stuck. "Then we gather up everybody who's still gunning for a fight and anxious to get back to the other side of the galaxy." Charles obliged them with an open Twist, and Carl headed through first, as he had last time.

When the others were through and the Twist was closed, Carl unlocked the door and sent a quick message a few floors away to Aiko, letting her know he'd be back shortly, sufficiently unharmed.

"Orion, you and Anna start spreading the word and organizing units and armaments. We don't need any guns here on Eleusis any longer, so you might as well make sure everybody's armed to the teeth for the trip home. Charles, you contact Jason and Xander, tell them we're coming and that they'd better be ready for Christmas in February with that Twist of yours. We'll have all our people suited up and ready out on the grounds in two hours. If they're still fighting the war, it's time we got back to help."

15

Khadi didn't know what she was expecting when Three actually docked with Prime, but she didn't expect to hear gunfire over the radio connection as she sat in a room with Fatma. Liam insisted on being part of the front line once they docked, and she winced as the gunfire continued to get louder. "They didn't even try to talk. Or reason. They just . . ."

"Victoria knows better." Fatma was looking at a holographic representation of the docks, showing vitals on all her soldiers as well as scans of the enemy locations from Prime's internal sensors. "They know if we've come this far, talking wouldn't do them any good. I had hoped for a surrender, but she's too much like me. She'll never give that order." She touched one of the holograms to open a frequency to the commander in question. "Pull Harrison's squad back. Twenty seven at their thirty and six." She didn't wait to hear a response, she just closed the connection to watch as her orders were obeyed.

"There's nothing we can do until they're dead? Until we can get through?" She felt sick to her stomach watching and listening, especially knowing that Liam was in there.

Their last conversation had been an awkward one. It had been a strange confession of feelings and also her reminding him (though he didn't need to be reminded, he told her) that he was here fighting for his fiancee. Then neither of them made any attempt to talk about what they might want further than the time they had spent together. Even though they confessed they had feelings for each other. Khadi didn't know how to be a girlfriend or a wife of a man who already had three others. And she still wasn't convinced he would even like having her around for more than a good time. They really did fight a lot. It wasn't cruel or hateful fighting, but Khadi didn't think it was a good idea.

He told her he thought her opinion was wrong. They fought some more. Had more mind-blowing sex. Then he was gone.

"How long do we have to wait?"

"Until they've got the docks and some of the surrounding corridors cleared. The sweep pattern we've laid out will take us through the industrial sector first, and it should be a pretty easy sweep, but we've got a long way to go between here and the cell blocks where they're keeping your friends. Then we move on to handle the central offices."

Fatma sounded lighthearted about the entire enterprise, even though gunfire was still ringing through the radio and some of her people were turning red as they were wounded or killed. That was the nature of war, and it was what Fatma had been trained for her entire life. "We should be able to move in ourselves in just a few minutes. They have fewer in the dock than I was expecting."

Khadi hadn't looked at the screen for some time, since she couldn't force herself to do it. "Can I ask you . . . I mean . . . is he okay? He's not dead, right?"

Fatma gave her a kind smile, and shook her head afterward. "You models. Open books, the lot of you."

She made a few gestures on the screen, and one of her soldiers, all of whom were in an electric kind of blue to go along with the primary colors of Three's insignia, lit up green instead. Another flick of Fatma's fingers sent the man's vitals to a corner of the screen where Khadi could keep an eye on him. His vitals were good across the board, and the small diagram of him showed no injuries except a small patch of red along one side of his torso. A tap showed that he had bruised a rib at some point, most likely because he simply wasn't used to fighting in zero gravity.

"He's doing well for a non-soldier, actually. He's smart enough not to get in the way of everyone else who actually knows what they're doing, which is more than I can say for some of my own. And he has better aim. He's already got two and a half notches." Fatma sounded genuinely impressed, but she wasn't concentrating on Liam completely. Her eyes were flicking over the entire battle, and highlighting different areas where she was sending recommendations to her commanders inside the dock to advise them on movements.

"I'm not an open book." She defended first, but she watched Liam's vitals for a moment before she forced herself to look away. "I just don't want him to die, okay? He's on a romance mission to get his girl back."

"I know. He's a bona fide hero." Her eyes twinkled with

amusement, both at Liam and the fight in front of her. The woman was *enjoying* herself. "Heroes don't have much of a shelf life, in my experience. But I'm still enough of a romantic myself to hope I'm wrong about that, for your sake."

She gave a few more orders regarding a rogue group of resistance fighters that slid behind her people, and looked worried until her people cleared out the pocket and continued on their way. "If you want something to distract yourself, take that other terminal and start looking for the Alperts and the remaining Board members. I want to know where they are and I want to make sure they stay isolated until we can get to them. I'll let you know if your knight takes a hit."

"He's not . . ." She glared at the woman and growled as she moved over to the terminal to start helping. "He's not my knight. I just like the guy, okay? It's not a thing."

"Open book and full of fiction." Fatma laughed again and went back to giving orders. "I-squad, start your sweep of the fourth-quadrant corridors, I want you pushing through to clear a path for some of our friends from Five on their way. Play nice. O-squad, you're right up the middle. Clear and secure along your way, you'll be reinforced by Four in ten minutes. Once you get to the E-ring, hold for further orders."

She was having the time of her life watching what happened inside, but as she watched, Khadi saw her face grow a little more somber. There was no trace of real pain or regret as she looked at a single enemy blip that faded first to red and then winked out completely to show a darkened framework of lines drifting through the dock under its own inertia.

"Victoria." She shook her head with a sigh, and watched the small frame of lines drift until it hit a wall and was caught against a support beam. "Goodbye, old friend." She flicked the screen to clear the frame so it wouldn't distract her from everything else, and blinked once to restore herself to the fight.

"Anubis, there's a few hiders under the passenger port at your 90 and 46. Clear them out and it looks like our work is done in the dock. Spread out when you're done and wait for the rest of the party. Good work so far, people, keep it up."

Khadi wondered how the Captain could both mourn a friend and be pleased with death at the same time, but she wasn't about to question what was going on. She worked on the terminal in front of her and glanced up a few times to check on Liam. He was definitely working his way through, but it would still be a while before he could make it to the prisoners. She hoped he found the person he was looking for.

The only thing that managed to distract her completely was a ding from the screen in front of her instead. "I found them, Captain. The Alperts."

Fatma's smile was both beautiful and lethal as she glanced over to get a look at the location. "Good work, Gorgeous." She praised with a wink before she swiped through her display to identify the cleanest route between the dock and the bunker surrounding the Alperts. They were at home in their unit, the last place Fatma had expected to find them. They had guts, she had to give them that.

"White." She snapped once she identified the route. "Can you get me a path between here and there?"

Except for the last few bulkheads, yes. Jason answered slowly, as if he couldn't spare thought for all the words at once. The man was working steadily since the blackout to infiltrate every system he could, and Fatma was slightly concerned about the reach the man had attained. Not that she would ever admit it. *They've got those sealed off in ways I'm not even sure about. You might need to cut your way through once you get there. I've got station 19 docked right over them to physically cut off any escape pod they might have stashed, but they don't have any boarding capabilities. You'll have to get at them from the inside.*

"And you're positive they don't have a Twist in there they can use to get out?" Fatma asked doubtfully. She had agreed to work with the rebels, but that didn't mean she trusted them.

My blood is type O positive. That's the only type of positive I've ever been in my life. Get your people there and cut through and you can let me know. If they've got one, I would think they'd have used it by now, but you're the military genius here. I'm just the genius.

"Just open the corridor as my people make progress, kid. And keep the cheeky remarks to yourself." Fatma snipped back.

I'm older than you are, young lady.

Fatma glared at the holograph without saying anything, since the comment had actually managed to surprise her. Who the hell was this guy?

She closed the connection with a grunt. She really hated dealing with the snot-faced rebels, but they had proven effective. She wasn't going to ask questions beyond that. Not yet. There would be a time for that later.

"You coming?" Fatma moved away from the holograph,

taking a small projector and shoving it in one pocket while the guards and commanders all around her began final checks on their weapons. She checked the pair of guns under her arms and the two knives at her waist as she waited for Khadi.

"Me?" Khadi said in surprise, since she wasn't a warrior or a fighter, but she supposed she could handle herself with a gun. Orion had made sure of that. "You want me to go with you?"

"Hey, you're the one that came back up here to convince us to go to war. You didn't want to sit out what you started, did you?" Some of her people around her laughed at the taunt, and it only made Fatma smile wider. They were all insane, grinning and laughing at a time when bullets were flying. "Don't worry. I like your ass, I'll make sure somebody's watching it."

"It's a great ass." Khadi agreed as she glanced backward at her backside. "I worked hard for it. But seriously, you're getting off on this, aren't you?" Khadi grabbed the gun that was handed to her and she followed after the Captain. "I mean, your ass is pretty nice too."

"You have a great show, you celebrate." Fatma shrugged as they moved down the corridor of her own station in perfect unison with the rest of her fighters, every one of them trained on how to fight and fly in zero gravity as smoothly as a moon in orbit. "I fight a good war, I celebrate. This is my profession. Everybody gets off on what they're good at."

"Apparently." Khadi replied as she followed perhaps a little too closely behind Fatma. "My profession is that I look pretty and I do it with a bendy body and a snippy attitude. So I'm gonna follow behind you and let you look the part with the gun."

"Smart girl." Fatma drew one of her guns as they floated through the access bridge and into Prime. They looked around at the rest of her people posed at various entrances in case the native defenders managed to cut their way through to try and retake it. The front lines had done their work and the other teams, including Liam's, were already off on their own individual tasks. Fatma had her own job to do.

* * * * *

Liam grumbled as he drifted down the hallways of Prime. Not only was he getting more cranky the longer he stayed in zero gravity, but Prime felt like it was roughly the size of the entire midwest.

"How . . . many . . . of you . . . fuckers . . . *are there*?!?" He let off a few more rounds, most of them finding a home in someone who shot at him. Most of the soldiers Fatma sent with him were purely on the offensive, which meant Liam was lagging behind them. He was comfortable with that. He preferred to stay behind columns and on the *not*-getting-shot-at side of all bulkheads until their enemies were mostly cleared. The training they received on Three probably included lessons on noble suicide, he decided.

At the moment, though, he found himself ahead of the rest of his squad, for reasons he couldn't explain until he saw a huge wall of people with guns, all of which were pointed at him.

And this is why I hate zero gravity. He thought as he panicked, already spinning end-over-end as he fell/floated toward the enemy. The squeal of terror he let out wasn't dignified, but it was apparently confusing enough, and when they didn't fire immediately, he had an idea. "Soldiers from Three! They're invading the station!" He screamed, flailing and pointing ineffectively back toward the soldiers he knew were hiding and regrouping behind him. His earpiece must have fallen out somewhere along the way.

What do you know? That actually worked! He thought again to himself as he floated past the block of guards. They closed behind him and kept their eyes on the hall he'd floated out of, a few of them shouting orders at each other to stay sharp. He finally stopped against a column and spun around it before he braced himself and took some cover. They were gonna be really mad when he shot them all in the back.

He managed to injure more than a dozen of them before the rest of his squad got worried about him not answering his earpiece and came to rescue him. They took out the rest in a single wave, then descended on him with disapproving glares.

"Tarja, I don't even want to hear it. Everything was *exactly* according to plan." He glared at the leader of the squad, a severe blonde who had violently protested at having to 'babysit' him. "Anyway, why are we down . . ." Liam flinched as he got pelted in the face with an earpiece that one of the other soldiers had flicked at him. "Ow!" He grabbed it out of the air before it floated away, and shoved it back in his ear. "Harsh! I'm on your side!"

Take better care of it this time. Fatma's voice sounded in his ear. *Down the hall marked 10881B. Third corridor on the left, there are another dozen guards.*

"Wait, I thought you said the cell block was still half a mile away?" Liam moved in the direction ordered, floating after the rest of the soldiers from Three like an awkward sea turtle following a perfectly-flowing school of fish.

It is. We thought your brother and the doctor would be with the other prisoners, but they're down here. With two babies. Don't get them shot.

"Two babies? Mercury wasn't due until . . . oh, fuck it. Like anything happens on a schedule anymore." Liam followed after the squad with a sigh and checked his gun to reload it on the way.

Mercury had fallen asleep, amazingly enough, but when she heard the nurses tell Logan someone was coming she sat up slowly and looked around in a panic for her babies, though they were in little isolettes next to her bed. "Logan? What's going on? Who is coming?"

"Well," Logan squeezed her hand to let her know he wasn't far away, "whoever it is, the guards outside are shooting at them, so I'm pretty sure I like them." The shooting outside the hall continued for a long time, and Logan eventually moved off the bed closer to the windows to watch as bodies slowly drifted into a weightless pile at the end of the hallway.

When the shooting finally died down, Logan could see a few more soldiers come down the hall, and the sight of them made the nurses and Greg move away from the door.

Logan didn't have a gun or any other kind of weapon, but the doors had been sealed ever since the power had gone out in the rest of the station. They were supposed to stay locked up wherever they were until . . .

The lock clicked open without anyone getting anywhere near it, and the door opened to admit a man with shocking blue hair and piercings in his face. Other than that, there was something familiar about the man that Logan couldn't quite place.

"What the hell, Mercury?" The man in blue hair said, and his voice shocked Logan out of his confusion, but not quickly enough to speak. "Fatma said Logan was gonna be . . . AH!" Liam screamed and recoiled. "You . . . What the hell?"

"You're one to talk! You look like you got face-fucked by a smurf!"

"And what are you doing, auditioning for a prison movie?"

"You pierced your . . . that's just wrong, man. That's not . . ."

"Hey, this is the *only* thing I got pierced. It's part of the disguise."

"Yeah, well this was part of something else."

That silenced Liam temporarily. "Your legs?"

"Working. Long story."

"Can't wait. Wanna get back to the war?"

"Do we have a choice?"

"No, not really." Liam pushed off the door and took Logan in a tight embrace. "Honestly, I'm just glad you're still alive. Earth has been losing its shit with the radio silence they put out about that fucking gauntlet you threw down."

"Yeah, well, they weren't quiet up here." Logan let go of Liam and turned back toward Mercury, pulling himself closer to her bed and the newborns. "Can you move, or would you rather stay here until things are cleared? The next stop," he glanced over at Liam, "unless plans have changed," he looked back at Mercury when Liam shook his head, "is the cells, to make sure the kids are alright."

"Don't leave us behind." Mercury slowly moved from the bed. She was all kinds of sore, but she wasn't about to get left behind again. The nurses rushed around to pack her bag with medical supplies for her and the babies, but everyone was going with her. Mercury looked over at Greg, since she wouldn't be able to shield both babies adequately. "Will you take one?" Greg was a doctor like she was. Neither of them were trained to be fighters and warriors. They were healers.

"Of course." He moved quickly to unstrap the isolette so he could instead wrap the baby against his torso where he could most easily protect her. He ended up taking Fiona, cradling her against his scrubs but hanging back to let the fighters go out first.

Logan didn't get far ahead of Mercury, but he did stop long enough to grab a few of the guns from the deceased Prime soldiers. "You have much trouble convincing Fatma and the others?"

Liam shook his head and gulped. "I had, um, help."

"Help? What kind of help?" Logan didn't like the sound of that.

"Long story, brother. Not the time." He turned to look back at Mercury. "Your parents are here too. They had most of the Stations wrapped around their little finger before we even popped the idea to them."

"They were trying to tell me to hang on when I talked to them last. I could tell they had a plan, I just didn't know what it was." Mercury held Farrah firmly against her chest after wrapping a sheet against her body like a toga against the scrubs she'd eventually changed into. Farrah was cocooned against her body and she held a bag of supplies against her shoulder. "Hopefully we can find a way out close to the prisoner block. There are too many children there. Gwen was living with me, helping me with the children."

"So she's okay?" Liam asked immediately, spinning around in midair, obviously forgetting that he was in zero gravity. He bumped into a column as a result, and groaned in pain, but righted himself quickly enough that it was obviously not the first time it had happened.

Mercury nodded. "She's okay. She misses you all the time. She kept saying she wished she had kept a picture of you, but she always said that whenever she came out of her room, so I suspect it wasn't a desire based entirely on sentimentality."

That made Liam grin. "I'm gonna have to talk to her about that. And make sure she's got pictures to take with her from now on."

"What, in case we have to launch a revolution and save her from being imprisoned again?" Logan smacked his brother in the back of his head on the way down the corridor. "Just make sure you get your face back to normal before you start taking pictures."

"Let's hurry." Mercury encouraged, since she didn't want to stay any longer than she had to. "Where are we going to run to? Who is willing to protect us?"

Logan hung back a little to take Mercury's hand, and shook his head. "No more running." He squeezed her hand, but pulled up short as they came out on a broad plaza that had turned into a war zone.

There were dozens of fighters spread out all over the area, but many, many more fighting for the other stations than there were fighting for Prime. Logan and Mercury could see Tatyana and Xander behind a bench taking fire at a group advancing on them, but they didn't seem concerned. Bullets were flying everywhere, but the fighters from Three did an excellent job of keeping attention off Mercury and the others with her.

"Your parents didn't just collaborate with the other stations to rescue you. They collaborated with all the other stations to end this damn war. They're not here to save us, they're here to end the

Consortium."

The firefight in front of them was bloody, and fast-paced, but the soldiers from the other stations moved too quickly for the Prime fighters to answer, and the plaza was clear in a matter of moments. The fighters had ample time to gather up their wounded before they formed up in front of the next sealed compartment door and moved on, punching toward the cell block one relentless corridor after another.

"End the Consortium? Is that even possible?" Mercury didn't stop moving, though. Stopping meant death in this place. "We still have to have somewhere to go . . ."

"Home." Logan said thoughtfully, as they moved down the halls behind the tide of the war. The inhabitants of Prime were beginning to understand they had lost, and they started to lay down their weapons rather than risk becoming part of the trail of bodies. Logan was glad they were starting to understand sooner than later. "That's the only place that matters. Home. We'll make that wherever you want. So long as it's with you, it's home."

Mercury held his hand tighter and she felt her eyes filling up with tears again. "Home. If we can't get to Eleusis, I want to go back to Earth. That's home to me right now."

"Then that's where we'll go." He promised with a kiss when they stopped. They paused at one corner while the soldiers ahead of them took their time clearing out one particular corridor. More and more, they forced people back behind doors and locked them so that they couldn't be opened again without an override, rather than killing everyone they encountered. No one had any interest in wasting lives if it could be avoided.

They've got the cell block on a completely stand-alone system. Jason's voice said into Liam's ear, when they were finally close. *I can't access it, and I don't imagine you want to take the time to look around for the right kind of access port. I've cut off the Prime-side programs that access it, but I can't override them myself. The people inside should be safe.*

"Should?!?" Liam shouted down the hallway, turning more than a few heads at the sudden noise, all of whom quickly got back to their own business. "What the fuck do you mean, *should?!?*"

I mean should. You'll have to find a way to break in yourself. I suggest an approach utilizing something big and heavy. You should be good at brute force.

"Well yes, now that you mention it, that *is* a talent of mine." Liam growled.

The prisoners inside had been informed of dangerous intruders, and most had moved to the furthest units, but Kam and a few others prepared for whatever was trying to break in. She had managed to create a few weapons, though they weren't nearly as good as the Consortium's. Kam moved closer to the entrance anyway.

The hall outside their cell block had been dark ever since midnight, and they didn't have any windows to the station exterior to tell them anything about what was going on. Three of them had taken up positions ahead of the others with Kam's weapons, Diego and Jela on either side of her as they watched the door.

"What do you think?" They'd heard gunshots and banging outside the cell block doors for several minutes, but nothing had made it through yet.

Jela was more nervous than the other two, but he had the least experience fighting. "Some other prisoners broke out? Trying to cause chaos? That's why they locked us in with radio silence?"

"Doubt it. We're rebel prisoners. They have us in lockdown because they don't want anyone to get to us." Kam had created her own pulse gun, and she sent out a warning pulse that would have given an uncomfortable shock to anyone close to the door. "We don't want any trouble!" She yelled, even though she didn't know if anyone could hear her.

"Ow! Damnit, Kam!" Liam's voice had always been easy to tell apart from Logan's, and the scream of pain was genuine. "Ease up on the firearms and back the fuck away from the door. It might go boom."

"You could have said something before now, dumbass!" Kam and Diego backed away and motioned for everyone else to stay far away. "You're clear!!"

The next thing that came through the door was a large bank of chairs that had been bolted to the wall in the corridor. They lost a lot of their momentum coming through the doorway and got tangled in the debris, but some of the glass and twisted metal still sprayed the prisoners. Liam and a few other soldiers pulled the seats back through, and Liam floated in once it was clear.

He shook himself free of some lingering shards, and grabbed hold of a door frame just inside to look around at the prisoners, panning quickly over everyone present. A few had started cheering, but those mostly died down at the sight of Liam. "Yeah, I'm blue. Let's get past that. Gwen?!?" He wasn't going to apologize to anybody for having priorities when it came to who he wanted to find. "Gwen, are you here?!?"

When there wasn't an immediate response, Kam got closer again. "She was up most of the night once Mercury went into labor, watching over the kids. She's probably still asleep, she buries herself . . . what the fuck am I telling you for, you already know that! There's Mercury's unit. Mel has the kids." She pointed to a door that was pretty far back.

"Okay, all I needed was for you to point. Thank you." He rushed past the group toward the room indicated, using a few of the still-shocked prisoners as leverage to get him there.

When he burst through the door, Mel was already on her feet with a knife in her hand and all four children gathered into a safer corner of the room. She let out a deeply relieved sigh once she recognized him, and put the knife away out of reach of the children. "Liam! You scared the hell out of me!"

"Good to see you too, Mel. Where is she?" Liam was having a hard time staying calm after everything he had been through, and he was too close for pleasantries.

Melissa grinned. "That one."

"Great. Start packing up the kids. We're getting out of here. Logan and Mercury are right behind me." He didn't stick around to get an answer from her. He moved to the room she indicated and opened the door almost reverently.

Despite all the crazy that was going on outside the room, Gwen was in her underclothes and sleeping with her whole body exposed except her head buried under several pillows to drown out the noise. She hated sleeping in the jumpsuits, so she went for semi-comfort in her ugly Consortium-issued underwear. He could barely hear her muffled groan. "Just fifteen more minutes, Mel? Please? I'm so tired."

The room was exceptionally dark, since the only light coming in was from the flashlights Melissa had in the main room. Liam floated in through the door and kept his distance from the bed, though he wanted to do anything but. He didn't want to be the victim of violence from her immediately upon waking up, which her tone made likely. He took a deep breath and looked her over as he sighed. Gods, but he had missed her.

"I'm here for a proposal that's long overdue." He had rehearsed the line more than a few times in the months since she had been taken, and he wasn't going to apologize to anybody for how cheesy he knew he sounded. "I hope you'll forgive me for being so late in getting around to it."

There was nothing but silence and no movement for a moment as Gwen laid there and tried to figure out if she had actually heard something or if she dreamed something. Slowly but surely the pile of pillows lifted up so she could peek out from underneath them. "Is someone in here?"

Liam cleared his throat. Apparently that hadn't gone as smoothly as he imagined. "Um, yeah." He probably should've spoken up, given the pillows. "It's Liam. Here with a rescue. And a ring. Which apparently the pillows got in the way of you hearing just now, but I promise, it was romantic as fuck."

"Liam?!" She yelled once she heard him clearly and she jumped up like a crazy person, flinging pillows in every direction before she launched herself at him in the dark. His voice was proof enough for her, even if she couldn't see very well. And if it was someone playing a trick on her, well, they were getting a show with her mostly-naked sleeping habits.

Liam was ready for her assault, though she seemed to have missed the memo about the station no longer having gravity to keep anything in position. Her leap from the bed slammed them into a wall, but he didn't care. He gripped her tightly against him and kissed her furiously, though he felt a little guilty when he felt the spike in his lower lip poke her in the middle of the kiss.

"Ow." She said after kissing him a few times, since the pain wasn't going to stop her at first. Though the difference was definitely giving her pause. "What the hell is in your lip? It hurts. Also how the fuck did you get here?"

"I had to blend in with some of the psychos on Three. My head is also blue. Don't freak out." He sighed against her neck as his hands roamed her back, groaning at the feel of her safe and whole in his arms. "Long story short, we convinced all the other Stations to flip on Prime and gang up on the Consortium brass. All the other Stations docked with this one. I have never seen so many pilots shitting themselves simultaneously in my life. Broke in, bang bang, still lots of shooting going on out there, but I'm not here for out there. I'm here for you. *Fuck* I've missed you."

Gwen didn't know why she was crying after a description like that, but she was definitely sobbing as she held onto him. "I've missed you too. I'm so sorry I couldn't get into the bunker. I was trying to help Mercury and then . . . it just went to hell. It's been a fucking nightmare here. They take our blood all the time like we're lab rats. Especially the kids." She clung to him as though holding onto him was keeping her alive, since she had put on a front of being calm for so long. "I thought I would never see you again, never go home and see Rachel or Bree again. Never get mar . . . wait, did you say you just proposed?"

"Aaaaaand now we're back on the same page." He kissed her again, then worked his way down her body as they floated together in the darkness. His lips savored the taste of her skin, the warmth of her neck, the cool skin of her breasts that had been without a blanket. Eventually he had slid down her body to run his hands over the back of her thighs, looking up at her as he pretended to kneel in mid-air.

He reached into his pocket and pulled out a wallet that he had carried around for months. He fumbled inside the wallet to get through the layers of securing ties he had placed on it to make sure it went nowhere, but eventually worked the ring loose and held it up to catch the light from the flashlight in the other room. "I said it was long overdue, but I hope you'll forgive me for being late."

"Oh my god. This is happening. This is fucking happening. In a space prison." Gwen looked at the ring in the darkness and held out her hand, since she didn't care if it was nothing but string at this point. "We don't have to have a ceremony or anything, right? Bree said she wouldn't throw a fit as long as we have a private shindig at home."

"As far as I'm concerned, you're mine already." He slipped the ring onto her finger and kissed the back of her hand on his way back up to her lips. "Not like there's gonna be much of a government left to tell us what we can and can't do after all this. I say you're mine, and we can have all the shindigs you want, big or small, as soon as we get home."

Gwen went back to kissing his lips several more times, since she couldn't believe any of it was real after believing for so long that it would never happen. "I love you so much. Thank you for saving me. And loving me. And giving me so much." She was still crying, but she didn't apologize for that. "And I really hope we don't get shot leaving this place because I haven't had sex in a *very* long time."

That made Liam grin as he wrapped her legs around his waist and groaned under the next kisses they shared. "Believe me, we're gonna fix that as soon as humanly possible. The second I'm reasonably sure nobody's gonna shoot at us, or we can find someplace decently bulletproof, you and I are gonna start making up for lost time."

"Thank god. Cuz I didn't even have a picture of your incredibly sexy face." She bit down playfully on his bottom lip and tugged it between her teeth for just a moment. "Masturbation sucks compared to your incredible cock."

"And don't you fucking forget it." He groaned at the way she latched onto him, and every kiss was a reassurance he wished they had enough time to get reacquainted properly right then and there. "Right now, you need to get some clothes on and we need to move. And I promise you, that is the one and only time, for the rest of our having and holding, that I am ever gonna tell you to put clothes *on*."

"I'm gonna hold you to that. Especially cuz I hate the clothes they gave us." She let go slowly, even though she didn't want to. "Are Mercury and Logan okay? They . . . they made us watch some fucked up shit, Liam." Gwen said as she grabbed her clothes as quickly as she could. "They operated on Logan a bunch of times and they never gave him any medication. They kept him awake. It was worse than anything any cinema or imagination can make up. It was . . . they made us listen too. Sometimes in the middle of the night they would wake us up with it."

Liam couldn't even imagine being forced to listen to something like that, let alone actually being . . . "I . . . didn't know any of that."

He looked back out into the main room, where Logan and Mercury caught up and Logan was hugging all of his children. There were six of them. Somehow, sleeping with two women, Logan had wound up with six kids to his name, while Liam had been through three wives, a fiancee and a fuckbuddy, and was working on his fourth. That didn't seem right to Liam, but he wasn't going to question it in the middle of a rescue.

"He's alright now, I think. He's walking again, which is more than he was doing back on Earth." He caught her in another kiss on their way out the door, sighing with his forehead against hers. "I am . . . not good enough at talking to express how happy I am that you're alright. I love you, and we are never getting involved in another revolution to take down a tyrannical government again. My hand to god."

Gwen couldn't help but giggle and she nodded in agreement

with her forehead still against his. "I thought I was going to die here. You're literally my savior right now, and I love you even more for it. You left Earth behind to save me. I love you so much. I'm so happy to be your third Mrs. Bickford."

He hugged her tightly, finding himself unable to do anything else. "You're worth it. Even though I have to say, I am *not* a fan of zero gravity. My body is not built for this shit." He kissed her again and moved with her through the door just as Logan held the door of the unit open for everyone to leave. It hadn't taken prisoners very long to get moving, after all.

"Can you get everyone back to Three?" Logan asked Liam as the last few prisoners gathered around them, including Kam and Melissa with Will and Kassie clutched against them.

"Yeah, probably. With the help of the crazy squad out there." He nodded to the guards from Three who were watching the doors, then waved a little apologetically, since they heard him. "Why? What are you gonna do?"

"I've got to be here to finish this." Logan said with an apologetic look over at Mercury. He wanted them to go home, but going home and having a safe place to call their own meant erasing the people who wanted them dead, once and for all. "I got a report from Fatma that they've been cut off at the Executive wing. They can't get in even from the inside. I've gotta go up there and figure out a way through to the Alperts and the remains of the board, or else this will never be over."

Mercury frowned and held Farrah tighter against her chest, but she gave Logan a nod, since she knew he was right. They needed to change the world to be together, it seemed, but she couldn't deny that to have a quiet life meant eliminating the Alperts. "All right. But this is the last time. I hope, anyway." She took a deep breath and sighed it out slowly. "Hopefully we will be safe on Three."

"We will." Liam promised, which got a few surprised looks from those who hadn't been around him for the past few months. "Fatma is actually pretty cool. Once you get past the whole super-killer side of her, anyway. We'll be alright there." He looked up at the doors and braced himself against a column to get ready to move. "Logan, be safe hunting executives. Don't do anything stupid."

"I think it's a little late in the day for that kind of advice, don't you?" Logan said with a ghost of a smile. He was still holding tightly to Mercury, since the last thing he wanted was to be parted from her.

"Logan," Melissa asked, since Will was being a pain and Kam was distracted trying to calm him under all the confusion, "have you . . . has there been any word from Eleusis?"

Logan looked up at Liam, since he didn't have anything to report on the subject. Liam just shook his head. "Nothing that we've heard, I'm sorry. Not since the Twists were destroyed. But Jason was never able to pick anything up from Consortium chatter either. So we don't know anything for sure either way."

Melissa wasn't very happy about that answer, but she shook her head and gave Kassie another kiss instead of worrying the subject any further. "Just . . . hoping. We'll keep doing that, I guess."

"It's what has kept us going this long." Gwen said as she gave them a smile when she finally got a chance to look down at her glittering ring. "Sometimes hope becomes reality. It's fucking awesome."

Logan smiled genuinely at the fact Liam had found Gwen intact, and watched them go before he turned back to Mercury, holding her as tightly against him as Farrah's presence would permit. "I meant what I said about going home. This will be over soon, and I'll do my best to stay away from getting shot. My plan right now is to die of all the grey hairs these kids are going to give me as I watch them grow up."

Mercury nodded again, though she wished she wasn't agreeing to let him go. "I don't want you to go." She admitted, since she hated all of the times in the past when she had stayed quiet and she wished she had spoken up. "I just got you back. You have to promise me that you and I are going to go home together. I don't want to hear anything else."

She had seen a lot of parts and pieces of Logan through his stormy grey eyes, and foreign emotions still circulated in them as they fixed on hers. Still, the abiding part of him she had always seen was how he felt about her, the love he had for her acting as a calm center of the constant storm in his thoughts and soul.

"I came up here, gave myself up to them to act as a distraction and a sideshow while the rest of the council made today happen, to get you back. I knew it was a risk, I knew they might try everything in the book to break me or just drop me into nothing. But I came up anyway, and if it got me here with you, I would do it all again. I promise you we are going home together."

"I believe you." She confessed gently before she kissed him again, and again, and again. "We both have made it through hell and back. Several times. We deserve to be together on a farm, living our lives exactly the way we want to. I won't settle for anything less than a full life with you, Logan."

"Nor should you." He agreed, hugging her again as he wound his fingers through the hair at the base of her neck, holding her tightly. The hells they had passed through were alive and well in both their memories, and in the way they gripped each other as if to hold off the eventual separation, however temporary they both intended it to be. "I love you, Mercury. The moment our business is finished here on Prime, I'll find you and we will get back to Earth."

"I love you so much, Logan." She whispered, but no less sincerely. "I will wait for you and the life we can have together. We have an entire family between us. You mean so much to me." Mercury held him as tightly as she could without hurting or disturbing Farrah. "Be safe. I can fix a lot of things. But not everything."

"I'll make sure that fixing anything is the last thing you'll be doing for me when we get home." He gave her a subdued smile as he pulled away reluctantly. He spent so much time on the edge of sanity, wondering if he would ever be able to be anything like his old self if he did manage to get free, but all he had to do was hold onto Mercury. She was a fixed point in his soul, and no amount of tampering from other sources could change that.

"Stick with Liam. I'll try to make short work out of keeping my promise to the Alperts." He floated through the wreckage of the doors and down a corridor with an escort of a dozen fighters from Three. Every one of them was dangerous and focused, while others helped move the prisoners through the corridors back toward Three and the safety it promised.

16

"This is . . . we're really going to get there?" Anna held onto Orion's hand, since even though they had managed to walk through the Twist once, she was afraid it wouldn't work to get them into Orbit. The last place she wanted to be was on some crazy station. "I'm still not convinced this is all even real, to be honest. I'm fairly certain I have severe brain damage."

"Any idea what's going to convince you, if amazing sex with me doesn't do the trick?" Orion asked, more casually than he felt. They were hanging back to let Charles finish his calculations for Twist placement, since it was by no means a simple endeavor to land on a space station that was in orbit half the galaxy away. Most of the other fighters would be going through ahead of them, since Orion and Anna didn't actually intend to do any of the fighting themselves. "I've never had my brain fucked around with the way you have, but at least to me, it seems like reality in general is just a matter of deciding this is what you see and going with it."

"Maybe I *imagined* the amazing sex. If so, my brain is fucking awesome and I take back the discouraging tone I used when talking about brain damage." Anna held Orion's hand tighter and tighter, though she doubted she could actually do any damage to him. He was insanely strong. She'd felt his muscles herself many, many times. "I just want this to be over."

"I keep thinking it will be." He said as the Twist opened up ahead. The things Charles could do with it had been . . . well, Orion hadn't tried too hard to wrap his brain around it.

The day before, when Carl complained about the fact that they didn't have adequate weapons to take back to Earth with them, or any real clothing, Charles had broken them into a private armory in southern Egypt and then a department store in Manhattan. The entire compound had been resupplied in a matter of hours, all the while everyone watched Charles with a growing sense of both respect and dread.

The amount of power at the man's fingertips was tailor-made to boggle any mind that tried to comprehend it.

"I mean, I'm used to thinking it's all about to be over, just not in a good way. Now it actually seems like, with what they told us about all the Stations, it seems like it might be actually over in a good way soon. That's . . . I mean, I didn't exactly think our life was gonna be all doom and gloom or anything, but I could've lived with just having you all to myself with us and our kids out in the middle of nowhere someplace. Yeah, it would be life in hiding, but it'd be life on our terms. I never imagined a life where we wouldn't even have to hide." Orion continued, vocalizing what they all honestly believed.

"Me either. Not after everything that happened in the Initiative." Anna agreed as they all started through the Twist. "Let's just get all the kids back." She glanced down at her baby bump and gave Orion as much of a smile as she could. "I've got one here, so we're good there."

"Yeah, hold that one in for just a bit longer. I don't want you popping before your time." He poked her stomach once as they started walking, but as soon as they were through, it was clear they had walked into an active war zone. The switch from Eleusis gravity to zero gravity made Orion feel like he was about to throw up because of how sudden it was, but he adjusted as quickly as he could and hauled himself along the wall where so many others already latched on.

He recognized the part of Prime where they'd landed, and he looked around warily while re-checking the gun at his side. "This is the Executive Wing." The corridor was narrow, but it was also clearly intended as a service area. Just beyond them, past the mass of the other rebel fighters who'd come from Eleusis, Anna could see a broad plaza filled with crystalline sculptures and brilliant manipulations of light.

Some of the sculptures were reduced to flying shards of glass by the first wave of Zoe and her psychopaths, who insisted on being given the first shot against the Consortium brass. Orion didn't want to be anywhere near all the fighting between Zoe's people, Carl, and the private security forces of the Board and the Alperts. He knew for damn sure that Anna didn't want to be close to it either.

"This way, come on." He motioned the other direction down the corridor, past the still-open Twist. "Zoe and the others will draw the private security back toward them. Let's see if we can't get these access ports open and let the rest of the army do its job." The Twist didn't care about locked doors or blockaded private wings of space stations, but it would be a lot easier to get a door open than for Charles to reconfigure the math to get a Twist open somewhere on the other side of the door where it wouldn't kill someone in the process.

There were numerous times in her life when Anna found herself tinkering with something she shouldn't. She even remembered times when she'd helped Logan on his farm with his gigantic farming machines, since she was so little and she could wiggle in and out of places he couldn't. When it came to the station, though, Anna pried off screens and dug into the wiring in an attempt to make something open even though it shouldn't. "I hope they don't mind that we're ruining all their pretty shit."

"You know, I think they'll live." Orion said as he stayed behind Anna, letting her work on the access panel she'd found without interruption. He let off a few gunshots seemingly out of nowhere, but he steadied himself against her ass after the recoil as she saw a few of the private security people drifting in pain at a distance down the corridor. "You know, or they'll die. Doesn't make that much difference to me at this point, really." He let off a few more shots as more personnel realized that someone was going for the access doors. Apparently they didn't appreciate that.

Anna found it a little remarkable that the sound of bullets flying really didn't even break her concentration, though she didn't know if she should attribute her comfort to her life being that fucked up or because Orion was there protecting her. It was probably Orion. Probably.

Eventually (after getting shocked a couple times) Anna rewired the doors to bypass any computer commands (especially after disconnecting the computer interface) and she looked over as she finally got them to open. "Open sesame. There we go."

The rebels on the other side were just as surprised about the doors opening as the security inside with Anna and Orion, but the firefight that ensued was nothing short of cataclysmic.

Orion huddled with Anna against the wall, just hoping and praying to avoid bullets ricocheting through the corridor. Most of the bullets fired found bodies, though, and Orion could see wave after wave of the security forces nearby mowed down by the fighters coming through. He smiled at the uniforms that flowed over the walls and slid through the air in packed formations, blazing symbols of their units on every single shoulder in wild colors.

"They brought Three!" He felt a surge of pride in his home such as he had very rarely felt before, and shouted before Anna saw his head rock back and some drops of blood go flying where his head had previously been.

His body went limp as it recovered from the shock of the hit, drifting for an agonizing moment through the air before his hand clutched at hers again. "Ow!" He screamed as his body twisted away from hers, still under the momentum of the gunshot, though he was trying hard to correct it.

"Orion!" She pushed herself after him immediately, since she didn't know what happened or where he had been hit, but she was imagining all sorts of terrible things. Even though he'd screamed, she was terrified of a deadly head wound. "Orion?" She asked fearfully when she grabbed onto his arm. "Please don't be dying. Please."

He finally stopped spinning, but he still tried to stay between Anna and the rest of the fight, even if his eyes were squinted in pain as he held her against the wall. "Not dying. I don't think." He had a hand up to where he'd been grazed, but blood was still coming off the wound. "Might have a skull fracture, though. Fuck, that hurts! Never had one of those before." He winced again, but then looked down in panic as something tugged at his leg.

Cory came up from beneath the two of them, and steadied himself with a foot hooked into the mess Anna made in the wall panel. "Here, I've got it." It was difficult to get used to seeing Cory wearing an eyepatch, especially one as rough and home-made as the one he'd made for himself on Eleusis. The look in her little brother's face that would have allowed her to keep calling him her little brother was long gone, and had been replaced with a seriousness that made him much more closely resemble Ben than his former self.

He was all business as he tore off a piece of the rag he held and balled it up on top of Orion's wound, then wrapped another bandage around Orion's head tightly to hold it in place. "I thought the point was for us to shoot the other guys, not get shot ourselves."

"Yeah, I must've forgot for a minute. I'll try not to let it happen again." Orion groaned as Cory worked, but Cory's eyes narrowed as he glanced up. "Your three o'clock, low."

Orion jerked his head to see what Cory was talking about, then lifted his gun and fired on the three who came around an inside corner to reinforce those getting massacred in the access corridor. "Thanks."

"Hey, the one eye I've still got works just fine." Cory finished with the bandage and looked around again before looking down at Anna. "You get some too, or just the easy target here?"

"I'm okay. He's twice my size and he decided to be my human shield, so I'm okay." She was forever grateful that Cory was okay, and somehow he was always saving her ass. Even though she should have been the older sister that was saving his. "Don't you end up getting shot either. I'm not losing either one of you to these Consortium fuckers. They've taken enough already."

"I think for once, we're the ones doing the taking here." Cory gave her an optimistic smile, but the look in his one good eye was still murderous. The world had changed, and everyone in it had changed to suit. "I'm gonna go head off anybody else coming around the corner and play lookout. The not getting shot thing applies to you too. We already thought they killed you twice."

"We're going home soon." She promised her younger brother, since she knew that he went to Eleusis with her to support her in bringing down the Consortium, but he'd not only lost an eye for it. He had a baby waiting for him back on Earth, and she knew he was desperate to get back to his baby and Larissa. "Once this is finally over."

Cory nodded, but didn't seem like he actually believed her. He was excited, but things had changed so much in the preceding years, he had given up on ever really knowing up from down. Orion shook his head as her brother moved away, taking up a position the way Orion himself had taught him. Cory checked the corner in a different place than the one he shot from, and moved, for all the world, like the soldier he claimed not to be.

Orion found the two of them a safer place to hide as the shooting continued in the access corridor, but soon the gunshots died down, and a few lone shots signalled the end of the battle for the entry. Men and women from Three poured into the Executive Wing by smooth dozens. Orion was glad none of them fired on him or Anna in the process of sweeping through. They'd all chosen brightly-colored clothing to distinguish them from the steel greys of the Consortium's fighters, but Orion had never been certain it would be enough to keep their own allies from shooting at them.

"If I . . ." Orion blinked a few times and tried to steady himself against the wall of the mechanical corridor they had hidden in, "if I, like, pass out here sometime soon, don't take it personally. It's not like I'm gonna die of a bullet graze. I just . . . I'm not sure I can . . " he shook his head to try and wake himself up, but he had lost a fair amount of blood from the free-flowing head wound before Cory had bandaged it, and he felt like he was going to pass out at any moment.

"I'm going to find a medical bay or something." Anna held firmly to Orion, but when she looked up and peeked out, she felt her stomach drop as though she had seen a ghost. "Wh . . ." She had darted back in but then she looked out again, and sure enough, surrounded by Station Three fighters . . . "Logan?" She called out, since she wasn't getting shot at so she figured she was among friends. Ish.

Most of the army floated past her, intent on their work deeper inside the Executive Wing, and no one responded to her calling for Logan. She had to grab Orion to keep his now-unconscious form from floating into a wall and making his head wound worse.

When she had him secured against the wall, a man in black scrubs came down the hall looking like the station was his own personal victim and he just happened to be in the middle of a killing spree. The man had a jagged scar down one side of his face, and wasn't even carrying a weapon, but the people around him followed his orders to make sure no corner was left unturned.

The man sent a few to investigate the blind mechanical hallway down which Orion and Anna had decided to hide, but he did a double-take as he looked up at the two of them. He watched them with a shocked expression, and kicked off of someone else nearby before the look on his face finally connected with Anna's memory of what his face looked like before they were separated.

"Anna!" His voice was a broken, gravelly shadow of what it had been before, but clearly they had both turned into different people since the last time they'd seen each other.

Anna pushed herself toward him immediately and connected with him before he could even really do anything, since she was amazed he was alive. She wrapped her arms around his neck and just hugged him. "Oh my God, I can't . . . you're alive?!"

"Me? You're the one everybody thought was a ghost!" He

hugged her tightly, ignoring the fact that there were still soldiers moving past them in the hallway and the sound of gunshots still rattled the corridor from hundreds of meters away. "You're all . . . how . . . oh god, is Orion . . ." he saw the man's floating and bandaged form once he looked over Anna's shoulder in the embrace.

"Do you think that I would be hugging you with his dead body back there and not in fucking hysterics?" She gave him a scolding look before she looked back at Orion. "Cory bandaged him up. A fucking bullet grazed his head. I didn't see a hole, so I think he was telling the truth about being likely to live. But I don't know where to take him. I'm not a fucking doctor. Do they have like . . . medical healing tubes or something I can stick him in and it'll magically make him better? I think I saw like fifty SciFi movies where they had shit like that in space. I'm not sure he'd actually fit in a normal-sized tube, though . . ."

"No tubes that I know of. We've got medical staff standing by all the way from here to Seven, they're docked the far side of Three. Medical transport!" He barked away from her, in a tone that was instantly obeyed. Two soldiers who had been administering first aid to superficial wounds came bounding off the walls toward them. One of them extended a stretcher from a case they were hauling, immediately going to Orion as Logan indicated to get him stabilized. The stretcher was, predictably, much too short for the giant, but his legs weren't injured, so they bound them in place and padded his head for transport. With quick, efficient motions, they entered diagnostic measurements and patient information for quick processing.

"Mercury and their twins are back on Three, along with Leo and Lynnette." He added quickly, since he knew Anna would want to know her children were alright. He didn't have the time to ask about the fact that she was obviously pregnant, but he knew that conversation would be had eventually. If she was already showing as much as she was, it was likely that he was the father. "That's where most of us who were in the mountains together are gathering, if you want to join them. I'm here to deal with the Alperts and end this thing once and for all."

"They're okay?" Anna felt like bursting into tears just hearing her children's names, but she watched them take Orion and she knew she should be by his side. Anna wasn't conflicted about her emotions, but she was conflicted about where she was needed the most. "I thought they were dead. I thought all of you . . ." Anna just took a deep breath as her voice shook.

"Charles got us here with a Twist. And the Kaplans are dead. I killed them myself. There's no mistaking bullets to the head and another to the throat." Anna cleared her own throat after that. "They had me as their personal . . . prisoner for a while. A long while. Do you . . ." She watched Orion get further and further away, but there was nothing she could do for his injury. "Do you want me to go with you to face the Alperts? I mean, we kind of started this together, right? Running into that burning house together after it was crushed by a falling space station . . . we were the face of the rebellion before we even knew it."

He nodded, but remembering back that far, crisp and clear as the images were, it seemed like lifetimes had passed. "Who is Charles? Nevermind, don't answer that. We'll talk it through later. If you're up to it, let's get to it. The rest of Prime is either locked down by now or it's been swept clear of any military resistance. It should be just the Board now." He hugged her again with a deep sigh, shaking his head against her hair. "I'm glad to hear about the Kaplans. The people here on Prime had me captive for about a month, up until this morning. Sounds like it's my turn to settle the score. I'll tell you about some of the other shit we've found out on the way there."

She didn't let go of him right away and she took his hand for a moment afterward and squeezed it tightly. Anna smiled up at him, even though he looked nothing like the Logan she had known her entire life. "This little girl may just have to have 'Victoria' for a middle name after today. Though Olivia Victoria seems a bit much."

He held onto her hand as they coasted through the hallway, and he held onto her with a death grip of his own as he looked her up and down to take in the sight of her pregnant again. "It might be a bit much, but I think it's warranted. Where did Olivia come from?"

Oh yeah. That conversation. Anna's cheeks flushed slightly, since she didn't really realize until then she was going to have to confess she'd been seeing Oliver at the same time she'd been with Logan. "Her father." She said without looking up at Logan at first.

"I . . . was seeing Oliver too." Anna said in a small voice. "Our relationship was never really defined, I . . . I didn't know what you wanted or what I wanted and then shit literally blew up and . . . they caught both Oliver and me and they tortured him. They confirmed that the baby was his. And then they made me shoot him and bury him with my own two hands." She could have told Logan that Oliver led the Consortium to their location in the mountains, but it didn't matter now and she didn't even want to tarnish his memory by saying it. She knew why he did what he did. She also knew he regretted it. There was no reason to tell Logan everything.

Logan's expression fell, but more at the fact that he was dead than at the fact that Anna cheated on him. She was right, they had managed to place each other in a terrible place, and he certainly wasn't going to hold something like that against her. "I'm sorry he's dead, and that they put you through doing it yourself, especially. Neither of you deserved that."

He squeezed her hand, and stopped them at a corner, cushioning the change in momentum with his own body before he pushed off again. "There was a night where I made my own mistake back then too, just so it's . . . clear and there's no more damn secrets. Big difference is, instead of there being a kid involved, I'm pretty sure my mistake is gonna marry my twin brother as soon as we get back to Earth. So, you know . . . there's that."

"Talk about keeping it in the family, Bickford." She said teasingly, feeling a little more like herself as she held onto Logan's hand. He was still her friend. Amazingly, somehow, they were still fucking friends, after the nightmare they had lived through and still hadn't quite gotten out of. Anna laughed a little and shook her head. "At least you didn't ask her to compare, right? I mean, that would be just wrong."

"In my defense," not that he had much of one, "she'd never fucked Liam when I slept with her. Or I didn't know she had, anyway. I only figured out he was the twin she's actually and genuinely into after the fact. Still." He shrugged, since there was no talking his way out of it.

"You always do get the really pretty ones." She shook her head again and squeezed his hand in reassurance. "I'm totally including myself on that one. If I don't believe I'm as beautiful as the rest of them, it will hurt my ego. Pregnant women don't need a wounded ego."

"You absolutely belong in that category." He swung them

around a final corner, and drew up short at an elaborate corridor with a set of highly ornate doors at one end. There were dead guards on either side of the doors, and blood slowly binding to the perfectly-stylized white crystals of the doors.

"We've no' gone in yet, Sir." A soldier nearby said gruffly, looking up from a tablet that he turned to show Logan and Anna. "Scannin' shows the servants and other staff bailed a few minutes ago, but we've no' seen the fuckers themselves. Servant passages are cut off and they should 'ave nowhere te go."

Logan glanced at the insignia on the man's shoulder and nodded with a hand on his arm. "Thank you, Sergeant. How is the rest of the station?"

"All's quietin' down, Sir. We've got twenty-three Board members under arrest and a few hundred other prisoners, willing surrenders or otherwise."

"That's good news." He looked up at the doors and sighed. "Shadow me and have someone keep a camera running. The world is gonna need to see this." He squeezed Anna's hand and moved to the door, floating with one hand on the handle for a long while without doing anything. Eventually, he took a deep breath and actually knocked politely.

Anna almost burst out laughing when Logan knocked on the door, but of course no one actually came to answer. The Alperts had to know that they were going to die. There was no way that anyone would dare keep them alive after all of this. "Well, aren't you polite." Anna held in a snicker. Then she decided to knock herself. "Come out, come out, wherever you are! The people you tried too many times to get rid of are here for dinner!"

Anna's jab got a laugh from all the guards around them, including the ones who had been holding cameras even before Logan gave the order for them to do so. Logan tried the latch of the door, and was surprised to find it already open. He imagined he had Jason to thank for that.

The chambers of the Alperts were pristine and perfect, with a few small inconsistencies that Logan attributed to the inevitable stress that came with certain death. Most of the furniture was such that it would magnetize itself to the floor if a lack of gravity was detected, like most bulky items in orbit, but there were a few floating piles of shattered crystal moving like broken schools of fish through the room. "Well, if I knew what was coming, I'd probably start throwing things too." Logan commented as they moved through the otherwise-empty chambers.

A few guards went ahead of them to clear the route of any surprises, but the guards stopped when they reached the end of the hall. One held up two fingers and pointed into what turned out to be a sumptuous dining room. The guards weren't shooting and didn't seem particularly concerned, so Logan assumed the Alperts didn't appear to be armed.

He had only seen them twice, once at his first interrogation and then again just before Mercury delivered her daughters, but they were easy to recognize, as public as they were. They were seated in two chairs at the far end of a long, elegant table, glass pods of wine set in front of them in small racks intended for zero-gravity use. Neither, unsurprisingly, seemed happy to see him.

"I did promise the two of you a final conversation." Logan moved into the room, letting himself drift along the row of chairs that sat facing the pair until he reached the middle of the table. He drew himself to a stop so he could look down at them, doing his best to keep his knuckles from turning white as he gripped the chair.

Anna didn't say anything until she was beside him, but she could see Sara open her mouth to speak and Anna shook her head. "I know, I know. You thought I was either dead or a Kaplan lab rat, right? Well, they're dead now. I killed them myself. And the serum you encouraged them to create, you know the one. The one where you control people's minds and bodies with shit that looks like water? Yeah, fuck that. Your fucking servers are getting wiped clean of that nightmare. Nice fucking try."

Dominic looked back at the two of them, attempting to maintain his composure even in the face of his own annihilation, but the mask he wore was thin. "Let me guess. Charles."

"Who?" Anna looked at him like he was an idiot. He was going to try to identify Charles when he knew he was being filmed? No way. She wasn't going to out Charles when she knew she wouldn't be standing there if Charles hadn't fixed a Twist for them. Charles wanted to disappear. She wasn't going to even blast his name on anything. "I don't know who you're talking about. The rebels took over the compound on Eleusis. It doesn't belong to the Consortium anymore. It belongs to the rest of humanity."

There was a play of emotions in Dominic's eyes Anna could see clearly, even though she'd never spoken to the man before. At first, he seemed intrigued by the fact she wouldn't out Charles, but then the inevitability of his own situation seemed to creep back in on him. Nothing could be interesting if he wasn't going to be given the chance to investigate it. "This . . . action . . . this revolution you believe you've won, will do nothing but set humanity back three hundred years. To a time when the nations could do nothing but squabble amongst themselves for tiny drops of power. Small ideas from small minds."

"Three hundred years is right about where I would set the clock back, if I had that kind of power." Logan continued glaring, but he wouldn't stoop to their level. He wouldn't place himself in any way on par with them. "The two of you, along with every other member of your governing board of directors, are under accusation under the authority of Unified Earth, of which I am the highest executive authority. You have previously confessed to those crimes of which you are accused. The actions of Unified Earth here today have been carried out with the intent of bringing you to answer the accusations against you, and to face judgment for your guilt."

He gestured to the wall, and was glad when Jason obliged him by taking over the projection equipment in their dining room. Scenes of their conversations with Mercury, board meetings Jason found about the true nature of CV, and a dozen other conversations about their intent to subjugate certain percentages of humanity to form a perfectly obedient world on Eleusis. All played around the room to let the Alperts know the evidence against them, and it was irrefutable.

"The two of you, along with many others, have conspired for years, for generations, to commit an ongoing genocide against the people of Earth. You are guilty of thousands of other crimes, but as they say where I'm from, there's no point beating a dead horse."

Sara looked over at her husband and then looked back at Logan and Anna again and shook her head. "You don't know what you're doing. You don't know what you're stopping by doing this. Earth was already tearing itself to pieces hundreds of years ago, before we were even alive! Eleusis needed something different. Something better. Humanity that wanted peace. Not war and power. And science is nothing without experiment and progress. We were working toward the betterment of humanity, not the detriment!"

"You know, I used to wonder if you people could hear yourselves." Logan said as he shook his head. "Except, the problem is, I know you can. You know what you sound like, you just don't care." He reached behind him, and glanced away to catch the gun that one of the soldiers obligingly floated toward him. He set the gun in one of the wine racks on his side of the table so it was in easy reach, then looked back at the Alperts.

"What humanity wants, what the vast majority of humanity wants, is to be left the fuck alone. What your slice of the human race wants is to mess with everything you can touch because you think you know better. I've seen what you call science. The world has seen it. Hell, the world's been breathing in what you call science every day for the past three centuries, and dying slow deaths at fifty on account of it. You're not scientists. You're raping, genocidal tyrants who hold up a fucking bunson burner every time somebody criticizes your program. You tell them to back off while you go looking for the truth you want to hear. No more." Logan picked up the gun and backed away from the table, motioning to the guards by the door to come in and restrain the prisoners.

Dominic did his best not to struggle while he was being manhandled, but when one of the guards shoved him down like he was nothing, like he was some kind of trash, he thrashed in the man's grip and fought back for a single moment, before something bit into his shoulder and made him cry out in pain. He instantly stopped thrashing, and couldn't feel his left side at all.

Eventually, he and Sara were forced up onto the table, still in restraints, on their knees with their ankles bound together and locked against the gold and crystal flatware.

"I hope you're proud of the world you're making, Mr. Bickford." Dominic said as he glared up at the man floating in the air over them, holding at his side the gun that would end Dominic's life. "The kind where anyone with a big enough gun can do whatever he wants. That's not just the pre-Crisis world, that's barbaric."

"Then call us barbarians." Anna said at Logan's side while she glared at the Alperts. "We are the barbarians who ran into a burning house to save the lives of innocents that *you* killed with your jettisoned space station. We are the barbarians who joined the Initiative to do something *good*, to go to Eleusis and build something great, while you decided that our good intentions were only good enough to turn into a fucked-up science fair project. *We* are the Barbarians having babies when we're barely old enough to take care of them just so we have some kind of life before your virus steals the rest of our years. I'd rather be a fucking barbarian than someone like you."

Logan reached out and squeezed her hand after that speech, since he couldn't have said it better himself, and he wasn't going to try. "If either of you believe in any higher power, now's your chance to make your peace with it."

Dominic shook his head, not in denial but in condescension and disbelief. "The only thing that's ever mattered is preserving the outward and upward trajectory of the human race, and here you are putting it back on a collision course with its own self-destruction. If there is a god, or gods, all they'd be doing is laughing at us." He wouldn't completely lower his head, but he did look over at Sara once with defeat in his eyes before he closed them and gritted his teeth to wait for the inevitable.

Sara looked between Logan and Anna and shook her head as well, but then she looked over at Dominic, though he wasn't looking at her any longer. "I love you, Dom. It's been great while we have had it."

He opened his eyes again to look over at his wife, and she could see him straining with one bound hand to try and hold hers, though neither of them were in a position where that was possible. He didn't speak again, but he held her eyes as Logan moved through the air to brace himself on a chair behind them.

"I'm glad to hear you enjoyed genocide so much. Really warms the heart." He cocked the gun and held it to the back of Sara's head. Years before, he might have had more difficulty even contemplating the idea of committing any kind of violence against a woman, strictly because she was a woman. After hearing her choice of last words, though, Logan felt no shame whatsoever as he pressed the barrel to the back of her head.

"For crimes against humanity, you are both found guilty and sentenced to die. Do so in the knowledge that the rest of us are here to dedicate the remainder of our lives to cleaning up the mess you and your kind have made of our universe." He didn't hesitate once he had finished the sentence, only making sure that both Alperts had heard and understood him before his gun went off twice with quick and lethal precision.

He waited only a moment as what was left of the Alperts drifted toward the other side of the room, then kicked both corpses so that they floated ignominiously down the table. He turned back to Anna and took her hand as he put his gun away, headed back toward the soldiers.

"Let's get this sector closed off and finish securing the rest of Prime. We've got a lot of work to do, but none of it is here. Get moving."

"Orion?" Mercury asked softly as she stood next to Orion's unconscious body, though she knew he should be waking up by now. She'd stitched him up herself, and she'd applied a numbing gel so that it would eliminate some of the pain from his head. He was fortunate to avoid a fracture, but he had lost a lot of blood. "Can you hear me?"

"Mmm." Orion groaned as the world came into focus, though even after he blinked several times, nothing about his surroundings was any clearer. The accent speaking to him sounded familiar, though, and through his hazy mind, he blinked a few more times to try and bring her into focus. "You . . . sound a lot like this woman I used to know. She was a doctor too. But she wasn't as blurry as you are. You're very, very blurry. Are you aware of how blurry you are? You should have a doctor look at that."

"A woman you used to know, huh? Did that bullet wound knock me out of your head?" Mercury looked the wound over again, but she had to open up his eye and shine a light in it, which probably wasn't pleasant. "You're having a normal pupillary response, so your vision should clear. It's probably the medication that's causing it."

He was barely conscious when she started asking him questions, but after she shined a small and angry sun directly into his eye, he jerked awake, and looked her over as he continued to blink the lights off his retinas. "Mercury?!?" He shook himself and reached out to grab onto her tightly out of nowhere, pulling her down with him against the gurney he hadn't realized he was still strapped to. "You're here! Wait, why are you here? You're not big on putting bullets *into* people."

"I didn't put a bullet into you, silly, I mended you." She kissed his cheek and hugged him as tightly as she thought was wise while he hauled her onto him. He really must have forgotten that she was still supposed to be pregnant. "I've been here on Prime for a while. They kept a lot of us locked up here, all the children too."

He let go of her at the mention of the children, and seemed to remember that she was supposed to be carrying some, since he looked her up and down. "Did they . . . the kids . . . we just got word that there was a fight going on and we needed to touch down in the Executive wing, but they didn't give us specifics about . . . where are . . ."

"They're here with us." She looked back at the isolette where Farrah and Fiona were sleeping side by side, since she wouldn't allow them to even be a room away from her. They had to be with her. Orion hadn't required surgery anyway, and so she didn't feel guilty about demanding she keep her newborn daughters close. The boys were too much trouble to have around a wounded person, though, so they were with the other children.

Mercury kissed Orion's cheek again and started to cry, but then she moved to grab the isolette and float it closer. She picked up Farrah who let out a little squeak and showed off their beautiful daughter to him. "They decided the best time to be born was in the middle of a crisis."

"Oh, no, I'm sure that's not how it was." He pushed himself to sit up, hooking his feet on the gurney to stay in one place as he reached out to take Farrah and hold her for the first time. "They've got too much of their dad in them, from the look. They heard there was a fight happening out here and didn't want to get left out of it." He looked down at the little girl and ran a thumb across her tiny cheek when she tried to stretch and couldn't get out of her swaddling blanket. "And which half of Fifi are you, exactly?"

"Fifi?" Mercury replied with a laugh and gingerly sat down on the edge of the bed next to him. "This is Farrah. The one that was running a little behind her sister over there. Though you wouldn't really know it, they both pretty much weigh the same. Farrah is only an ounce smaller. For now."

"Yeah, well, she probably already pooped that out, didn't she? Yup. She probably did. Now you're even." He pulled the little girl up into a kiss and let her hang in mid-air for a minute so he could look her over. The girl didn't seem to mind, since she'd been in a more or less weightless environment for the majority of her existence so far. "Are you alright?" He looked over at Mercury just past the swaddling cloth of the little girl between them. "I mean, there weren't any complications with the birth or anything?"

"I think the only complication was pushing out seven and a

quarter kilograms of baby. Each one is a solid three and a half kilograms. I nearly passed out during Farrah from the exertion. You make some big babies, Orion Al-Jabbar."

That made him laugh, and he set Farrah spinning for a minute just because he could, before he took hold of her again. "Yeah, I'm trying to feel guilty about that and I can't. They're pretty adorable for being less than a day old." He got up and went over to Fiona, setting Farrah back in place next to her sister so they would know they weren't alone. With one hand teasing at the black hair on Fiona's head as she tried to sleep, he looked back at Mercury. "I'm guessing Logan and Anna are alright, since the first thing you told me when I woke up wasn't that they're dead?"

Mercury nodded, though she still looked concerned for Orion, since she kept looking up at the bandaging on his head to make sure it wasn't bleeding through. "Logan went to end things with the Alperts, and I was told that Anna volunteered to go with him since you were being brought back to a medical bay. She made sure you were taken care of before she went, but from what I've been told, it's been taken care of by now. They should be returning here soon."

Mercury scooted closer to Orion and ran her hand along his cheek. "It's so good to see you. They told me so many times you were dead." He could see his name inked into her wrist as she touched him, but she didn't pause to explain her tattoos. She just wanted to be there and stare at him while tears streamed down her cheeks.

Now that he was a little more awake, his touch was gentler as he pulled her into a hug, mindful of the fact that she'd just given birth and had two new babies to keep an eye on. "We knew there had been an attack on the mountains, but we didn't know anything beyond that. They tried to feed us a lot of bullshit too, but we just . . . a lot happened on Eleusis. But there was a Montgomery brother there that fixed a Twist and brought us back here. I didn't know . . . we had all started settling in, once we overran the compound, planning on what we'd do if we had to spend the rest of our lives out there without ever setting foot in our own solar system again."

"Seems like exactly what the Consortium loves to do. Force people into making decisions based on very limited resources." Mercury hugged Orion as long as she could, since the nearness of him was so comforting. "I'm so happy you're alive. And more or less alright, as long as you tell me you aren't in a lot of pain."

"I'm not. It's just my head. I can tell you gave me some pretty good drugs." He reached up gingerly to touch the bandages, but otherwise left it alone. "If they've dealt with the Alperts, and the rest of the board . . . that means it's over. It. . . it actually worked."

He wasn't having any easier a time thinking about it than he had when he was talking with Anna before, but with Mercury, he knew she would understand just how rocked his world was by the possibility. It required imagining a world without the Consortium, the single reigning constant of humanity for the past three centuries.

"It actually worked." She repeated before she looked up into the dark eyes that she still loved fiercely, and probably always would. She loved the man behind them even more. "I don't know what that means, or even what is next. I don't know if someone worse steps in, or if chaos takes over. I do know it means there's no one left who cares about how I live my life. That's something, right?"

"That's a fucking lot, if you ask me." He said without letting go of her, shaking his head in disbelief. "But if Logan was the one to pull the trigger on the Alperts, he didn't do it because he was mad. He did it to send a message. That's how your . . . how he works." Talking about Logan brought up a lot of complicated baggage between the two of them, just because he wasn't sure where things stood. He knew that he loved Mercury, and always would. But things with Anna felt . . .

He cut off that train of thought. He'd just woken up with a head wound. It was not a good time for dealing with the tangles he'd gotten himself into.

"He sent a message alright. He also declared himself the leader of the Unified Earth. I'm not sure what that means, and he wasn't exactly elected, so I don't know what kind of consequences that will have. Hopefully people will be happy and supportive as a whole. I really liked living on Earth." Mercury moved a hand gingerly to check on his bandages again and she met his eyes once more. "I think that's where we all go from here. Us rebels, I mean. Back to Earth to figure things out. Your family is still there. A lot of families are still there waiting. My parents will go with us. We have time to sort things out."

He was relieved to hear about his family, since he'd spent just as much time worrying about them as he had about Mercury and the children ever since he'd been trapped on Eleusis.

"Unified Earth, huh?" There had never been a particular name for the rebellion they joined, though various factions had gone under different aliases at different times. Orion had never been much of a fan of any of them. "I like it. Certainly sends a message. That is, of course, if Earth is in the mood to be unified." He knew that was a complicated question, so he shook his head and leaned in to kiss Mercury's cheek as he held her. "I can deal with some time on Earth. So long as nobody's shooting at me for a while and there's a hot shower. It's amazing how much I missed showers. It went: Family, Fast Food, Showers. In that order."

"I think we're finally going to be able to breathe the air freely and not worry as much about being hunted down. At least I hope that's the case." Mercury cherished the kiss on her cheek, but she leaned in and kissed his lips again. She had no idea where any of them stood on anything, really, especially knowing that Logan and Anna had faced the Alperts together. Mercury knew how she felt and what she wanted, but she knew nothing was simple between any of them. The last she had seen of Orion, they had been happy together and looking forward to the birth of their daughters. She loved him deeply, and always would. "Thank you for coming back to us."

"Like I was just gonna stay on Eleusis for the hell of it." He returned the kiss, his long-fingered hands cradling her face as he savored the touch. Mercury had been his partner through so many things, understood him so completely, so easily. Mercury felt like home. "Thank you. For our beautiful daughters. And for being here when I got back."

She pressed her forehead against his before she kissed him again without saying anything, and she smiled afterward. "Now we get to see how they grow up. They may look like you, but I'm going to laugh if they end up developing an accent like mine."

"I'm not sure what a cross between an Irish and an Arabic accent sounds like." He grinned as he thought about it, since he wasn't sure he had ever run into anyone with quite that mix of heritage before. "Whatever they sound like, you're likely to have something with these two you've never had with anyone else. Women you actually have to look up at." He knew they were likely to take after him in terms of height, especially since Mercury herself wasn't a small woman. "But don't worry, they won't be taller than you until they're at least twelve."

"I'm glad I've got a solid decade of authority, at least." She laughed and kissed him a few more times. "I don't think Leo is going to like it if they're taller than he is."

"He'll live with it if they are. Boy's got almost two years of a head start on them, they'll probably catch up when they hit puberty before he does, but my money's still on him in the long run. Him and . . ." he cut himself off, since he knew nothing was certain between the four of them, and he could see the same kind of acknowledgement in her eyes as he continued. "Well, any kid with giant genes is gonna be competition. I know we've got a ton of kids running around already, but Earth and Eleusis are both big, empty worlds. Plenty of space for tiny humans to grow and roam."

"We're all one big family now, regardless. We've got too many half-siblings to not be a family no matter what happens." Mercury shook her head and sighed as she tried to relax next to Orion. "I don't know what's going to happen anymore, to be honest. Everything just seems . . . surreal."

"That's what happens when somebody changes the rules." He ran his fingers through her hair, closing his eyes against her just to hold onto her, then opening them again to watch the babies in their isolette because he didn't want to miss a moment. "But surreal is better than real and broken. I'll take a life without being hunted. Hell, I'll take a life where I don't imagine I'm gonna have to point a gun at somebody else and pull the trigger ever again. Where I can go back to being some kind of pilot and you can keep on bringing screaming babies into the world. I never thought that was too much to ask and now maybe it's finally not."

"Did you want to have so many screaming babies, though?" She teased as she looked up at him while he ran his fingers through her hair. It was loose instead of braided. An unconscious habit from being around Logan. "Right now we have six children between us all under the age of two. And we'll probably lose Gwen, since Liam proposed to her."

Orion shrugged, but he was smiling anyway. "Kids are chaos. Adding more chaos doesn't make it worse, it just means the chaos reaches a little farther. Coming out of a place where we were only allowed to have so many kids, it's kinda nice not to have somebody telling me what we can and can't have. And Gwen and Liam? Really? Did not know that was happening."

"It's happening, definitely. He and your sister seem friendly too. I didn't think your sister wanted to be friends with anyone." She teased before she kissed his cheek again. "I told her to stop by here after I could get you to wake up, so she'll have been alerted by now. She should be here to see you soon. Apparently she and Liam made a special trip to Three to convince the Captain to join the resistance. They changed the war, if you ask me."

"Khadi?" Orion asked in sudden and clear confusion. "Friends? With Liam?" He raised his eyebrows and glanced at the door. "Oh, she and I are gonna have to have some conversations about that."

"Conversations, huh?" Khadi said from the doorway as though just mentioning her name caused her to appear. In reality she had been lurking outside to make sure she wasn't going to intrude on a heavy makeout session or something. It seemed tame enough to make an entrance, so she did. "What kind of *conversations* do you think you're going to have with me, big brother?"

Orion glared, still holding onto Mercury with one arm. "The kind you're gonna listen to. But they're also the kind that can wait. Right now, I'm just glad you didn't get yourself killed while I was stuck on Eleusis." He moved to pull Khadi into a hug when she was close, since he had been just as worried about the family he'd been born into as the family he had started for himself. "I'm also gonna need to hear about how the hell you convinced the Captain to join up with the rebellion. I know she's an angry bitch, but I didn't figure she'd take orders from anybody."

While Khadi didn't look any sort of guilty at the mention of Liam, she definitely looked guilty when he asked about the Captain. She was silent for a moment as she hugged her brother a little bit longer. "There may have been some heavy making-out involved. She did offer marriage, though, if I was interested. You wouldn't know it, but she can *kiss*."

"Ugh!" Orion exclaimed as he let his sister go violently enough to send them both moving backward toward the walls of the small bunk. His face looked like he had just swallowed something incredibly sour, and he shook violently as he tried to expel that image from his mind. "Sure, she's just what, two times your age? That's . . . ugh . . . nope. Can't do it. Nope. Nope, I'm suddenly much more okay with you getting friendly with Bickford the 2nd than I was a minute ago. Blech."

"Okay, wait, who said anything about me getting friendly with Liam?" Khadi thought she'd kept it quiet pretty well, except . . .

well, before. Maybe not as quiet as she thought. "Liam just got engaged. And *excuse me*, but my lips and my tits may have changed this war so don't get all judgmental now."

"No no no, I'm done talking about the captain. I'll worry about bleaching my brain later. The only time you get defensive is when you're guilty." He glared across the room as only an older brother could, slowly floating closer both to her and to Mercury as he made his case. "And yeah, he might have just gotten engaged, but the way that guy does things, that doesn't mean much." He watched her face as he spoke, and he knew his sister well enough to know he was on the right track. "Holy shit! You . . . oh wow. Okay, feeling a little sick about that again. It'll pass. Might just be the head trauma. You're gonna have to tell me all about exactly how that happened sometime. Because I . . . phew. Do Mom and Dad know?"

"You are assuming a whole lot of things right now, Orion!" She was getting louder and she didn't want to get louder. She didn't . . . it wasn't serious. She and Liam had enjoyed each other's company, he rescued his damsel, now they were both moving on. "Mom and Dad don't know anything because there is Nothing. To. Know." She crossed her arms and glared at her brother. "Here I come here to see my wounded brother back from the dead and you're going to lecture me on who I . . . on random people that don't matter?"

He gave her a sarcastic look, glancing down at the way she folded her arms as further proof of how defensive she was about the accusation. "If I didn't give you shit, you'd immediately assume the Consortium had scooped out my brain and replaced it with somebody else's. I'm your brother. It's my duty in this life to give you a hard time about each and every choice you make. Especially about who you . . ." he drew himself up short with a mocking look, "supposedly don't have any particular feelings for."

"I mean, really, do you see me with someone who has three other wives? I couldn't even handle my ex, and that was just me. I'm terrible at relationships." She needed to shut up. "Not that I was even *thinking* about something like that. I'm just saying. It sounds ridiculous. Also, he is incredibly full of himself and just as annoying as you are." Khadi was nothing if not confrontational and argumentative. "I'm glad you're not dead. Don't die. But I thought you'd be nicer than this, especially with a head wound."

"Head wounds usually make people cranky, not nicer." He

dropped the subject without conceding he was wrong, since he didn't think he was. Instead he just floated over to her and pulled her into another hug, letting go of the argument for the time being. There would always be another one whenever Khadi was involved. "I'm glad you're not dead too. And good work with the captain. I'm never gonna be able to say that with a straight face, but if you had a hand, or a pair of tits, in convincing her to fight for our side, then I'll say it was a job well done."

"Thank you." She said with definite pride in her tone. "Just don't tell mom and dad about that." Khadi continued hugging her brother, since she really was happy that he was alive and mostly well. "They lost enough, I'm glad they didn't lose you too. They shouldn't have to pin their hopes and dreams on me, that's just sad."

"You're a model. Hopes and dreams are kinda what you stand for." He said with a shrug, then turned back to take Fiona from Mercury, since he wanted to see the other children. "Come on, I want to see the kids and then send a message down to Mom and Dad letting them know we're all more or less intact. If we can even do that yet. I saw all the terminals blacked out during the fighting."

Mercury let Khadi take Farrah since Khadi was just as excited to see the babies as she was to see Orion, and Mercury found it strange that her arms were free for the first time basically since the girls were born the day before. She hooked her arm with Orion's free arm, since she wanted to stay close to him. "It will be a while before they restore full functionality around here, a lot of systems were damaged. But if there's still a working Twist, who knows, maybe we can talk to them within a few hours."

"Here's hoping." Orion floated out into the chaotic web of halls that was one of the main residential corridors of Station Three. He knew vaguely where he was, since he'd grown up partly on the station, but it felt almost nothing like home with the lack of gravity. He doubted ship systems could be expected to continue working without rotational gravity for more than a day or two, but he tore his mind away from the technical aspects of everything in favor of the children.

He moved so that a giggling, floating Leo could catch him around the neck, and hugged the little boy tightly as Lynnette hit him in the chest. He was careful with Fiona as the little ones crawled all over him, hanging on tightly so they wouldn't drift away. "Has *nobody* given you two a haircut while I was gone? Good grief, it's like a cloud!" He teased Leo as he kissed the boy's head, where his hair was sticking out wildly in the lack of gravity to hold it down. As always, the boy was the more rambunctious of the two, but Orion felt himself start to cry as he held them both tight enough to make them squeal.

Both the children were saying Dada and making all sorts of noise that was nice to hear, since it was further proof that they were alright and well, even though the Consortium had undergone a lot of monitoring on the children. Mercury had assumed when they were imprisoned that it was only a matter of time before children started disappearing for good, but thankfully they had never actually gotten to that point. "We told them every day that you would have all sorts of stories about Eleusis. So you'll have bedtime duty for a long time until you run out of stories."

"Oh, I've got plenty of those." He agreed, not taking his eyes off the kids as they hung onto him and examined the new baby in his other arm who was rubbing at her face. "Not sure most of them are appropriate for little ones, but I'll try and edit them to make them just a bit more kid . . . friend . . . ly . . ."

He slowed down as he looked up, since the doors at the end of the corridor had opened while he spoke. Anna and Logan floated in with a contingent of guards that assigned themselves to Logan. Charles was nearby as well, with Zoe and her squad in a permanent ring around him to watch his back. Orion was grateful for that, but the moment was an incredibly strange one, to say the least.

Logan looked up at Mercury and Orion where they hung in the air with some of their shared children, then looked around until he found Gwen nearby, who had been watching the boys with Liam. He moved to them first, to take James and Declan in a tight hug, though James somehow slept through all the excitement. He wrapped James tightly against his side, then lifted Declan to give him a kiss and a tight hug as he and Anna floated up toward Orion and Mercury. "Glad to see the head wound wasn't too bad, Captain."

"Glad to see captivity didn't kill you, Bickford." Orion said without any anger or acid in his voice. "What are we calling you now? President? Prime Minister? Emperor, maybe? Just saying. You can kind of pick and choose, here."

"I believe Prime Minister is what we plan to go with." Logan said with a subdued smile. "Trying to keep things as parliamentary and diplomatic as possible as we work to set up a new government and all the representation that goes with it."

"That works. But you could've gone with Emperor. Just saying. Missed opportunity." Orion returned the subdued smile, since he knew better than to think that he and Logan would ever be friends. Still, he didn't dislike the man. He couldn't, after everything they'd been through and everything they had been part of.

Anna smiled brighter when she saw Orion, even though she knew it was possible he wouldn't want that house back on Eleusis now that he had Mercury with him again. She darted away from Logan so she could scoop up her babies from Orion and squeeze the life out of them as they giggled and hugged her back. Anna never knew she could feel so happy to see someone again, so thrilled to know that her babies were alive and well and . . . smiling. Untarnished by the Consortium.

Both Leo and Lynnette patted her belly but she kept kissing their faces all over. "I'm never leaving you two again. Never, ever." She held them both on her hips and looked back at the crazy family that was hers, and her eyes zeroed in on Cory specifically. "Hey, Charles!" She said as she looked away from her brother for just a moment. "I know this is a big fucking deal, but do you think maybe you could let some of us go back to Earth the 'special' way?"

Charles glanced up when he was called, and made sure both Jeeta and Zoe's crew were with him when he pushed off to go reach the complicated family. "I'm very sorry, Anna, but I've been informed by the general that I take my orders from the Prime Minister as of now." He threw a sarcastic look at Logan. Clearly authority wasn't something he was fond of in his life.

"You take requests from any of these three as if they came from me." Logan glanced around quickly. "There was a space set aside on the estate for the Twist when we moved between there and the mountains. Cory, can you help him with the coordinates?"

It took a few minutes for them to find the precise location and put through a test slit in the air to make sure the space in front of the manor house was clear of interference. Once that had been established, Charles cleared people away from a section of the station wall that opened of its own accord onto the facade of the Bickford Estate. Cold air whipped through the station at the Twist's opening, since it was February in the midwest, but it was only a few dozen meters to the house.

"Cory, run ahead and let everyone know we're coming." Logan gave the order quickly, but with a smile, as Cory launched himself through and landed in a roll on the ground on the other side, already running for the house.

The transition wasn't an easy one for anyone, awkward as the switch from zero gravity to gravity was, but they all managed it eventually. Logan didn't go any farther at first than the dead winter grass just past the Twist, staring up at the manor house as if it was something from another life.

"Home sweet home." He looked around at Anna and at Mercury, both still beside him, with Orion behind them, the rest of the former prisoners streaming around them to get to the house and get back to their loved ones as quickly as possible.

Anna watched her brother as she held her children and stared at the Bickford estate, since it was home, but still everything felt . . . so different. "Your sister has a baby in there. Can you believe that? It's my brother's kid. So weird."

"Yeah, if you want weird, I've got a story about Khadi to tell you sometime soon." Orion said from behind them, shaking his head at the tangle he didn't want to even contemplate at the moment. He had never lived at the estate himself, only having visited for a few days when they were gathering midwesterners to join the rebellion. Still, the place looked like what he imagined a home should look like, should feel like, with life running through it and a welcoming front door.

Logan still stared, but he looked back at Anna with a smile before he started walking. "Part of me thought I would never come back here."

"I was pretty certain I was going to die on Eleusis." Anna looked back at Orion for a moment before she just stared at the Bickford estate. "I'm kind of hoping I can live in a house there someday instead."

Orion smiled, but Logan wasn't looking to see it. Instead, Logan took a few steps toward the house, staying close to Mercury in the process. "Let's get these kids inside and someplace warm with some beds set up for the night." He looked off to the side where Charles was looking up at the sun, holding Jeeta's hand beside him as people continued coming through the Twist.

"Charles, when you're finished, please get with your brothers and retrieve them as well. There's also a contingent of people in

Colombia which I need you to retrieve. Jason can put you in touch with Renata, and Renata will know who to bring with her. I'd like to have a meeting with some of those present in three hours. That should be enough time for you to get everyone together."

Charles didn't look happy about the mention of his brothers, but he nodded anyway, since he had meant what he said about working for the rebels. At least until he could figure out a safe way to put the technology in someone else's hands so that he himself could get away for a while. "Yes, Your Excellency." There was plenty of mocking in the address, but he would do as he was asked regardless.

"Good. That's three hours of peace, at least." Logan grumbled quietly, but loudly enough for Mercury to hear, at least. Mercury squeezed his arm to reassure him and Anna shook her head.

"I'm not calling you that." Anna said as she hoisted her heavy son on her side so that he wouldn't slide to the ground. "Nope. Not doing it. Not even a little bit."

That made both Logan and Orion laugh, which led to a moment of slightly tense silence, but all four of them ignored it as they headed for the house. All four of them knew what happened, what changed, but none of them could say for certain exactly what would happen next. Instead of thinking about it, they had children to care for and people to see whom they had spent months missing.

Decisions would come later.

18

Jason leaned back in his chair in the center of the living room with his hands over his face, as he rubbed out the tension of the last few days. The targeting for the various stations had easily been the most complicated thing he had ever attempted in his life, but they all docked and were all intact. That was all he had asked for.

The reports that flowed in after the fact were almost more than he could handle, but he ignored most of them. Everyone wanted him to do something all at once, and nobody was going to be happy about being ignored. Jason couldn't bring himself to care. It was the middle of the afternoon there on the coast, and Bekah was, mercifully, in her room taking a nap.

"Baby." He said quietly, without opening his eyes. The house was almost always quiet, and Jason was grateful. He needed the peace and quiet, and the peace and quiet meant that nobody was shooting at him or the people he loved. He had to admit, he was a little surprised their location had remained a secret for so long. Every day he went to bed thinking one of the many alarms he had placed around the house would wake him up, and every morning he woke up with nothing changed. He didn't know how to live in a world of peace. He needed to learn. "Baby, there's something in here you need to see."

"Hm?" Jessie replied as she opened her eyes, since she had dozed on and off while Bekah slept, though she was trying to read a book. Sleep was just much more enticing. "See what, Jase?" She opened her eyes and rubbed at them as she slowly got up.

"Crews are doing sweeps of Prime." He turned in his chair to look over at her as she approached from the couch. They both had been awake for much longer than they should have the day before. Jessie had run some of the coordination between the other Station captains and she watched some of the surveillance feeds that needed close monitoring while he was doing other things. It had been a rough few days for everyone.

"This is the list of the reported deceased from one of the crews." He scrolled down through the list once she got closer, and reached the name Carmina Hammond. A wire-frame diagram of the human body came up beside her name, showing with clinical detachment the dozen or so wounds from which she had died. A blow to the head had finally killed her, but she'd taken multiple stab wounds all over her body, had both her legs broken and had severe lacerations on her knuckles. She clearly hadn't gone down without a fight, but she had gone down.

Jessie stared at the screen for a long time without saying anything before she looked over at Jason and then glanced down at her hands. "I'm glad she's gone, then." She said simply before she took a deep breath and breathed it out slowly. "I still have nightmares sometimes she'll find us and do it again. Or take Bekah."

"No more of those." He reached out and took one of her hands before he pulled her down to sit with him. A single gesture dismissed all of his systems, though they were ready for him to return to work just as quickly. He tried to make a point of dismissing everything else about the world when he was with Jessie or Bekah. The single-mindedness of fighting a war was something that came naturally to him, but he worked against it to spend time with his family. "No more of a lot of things, with the Consortium erased."

"So . . . what do we do now?" She sat with him, but was always uncomfortable sitting on his lap, since she felt like she was too heavy. "Do we stay here? Go back? I worry about Bekah sometimes, since she's not around other children."

"Well, there are a hundred and thirteen children at that estate right now within six months of her age. She certainly wouldn't lack for friends." Jason held tightly to her, always wanting her to know that he wanted her close. "With Charles . . . resurfaced . . . we can go wherever you want. But I think going back to the Bickford estate would be a good start. We can figure out what it is we want to do from there."

He pulled her down into a kiss, venturing a hesitant smile. "I would say you could try and turn some of Bickford's farm into a vineyard, but I don't think that part of the midwest is particularly suited to it. Besides, I like ours here."

"Vineyards still thrive there, just not quite as well, and certainly not in the winter." Jessie kissed him back after he kissed her, and she held onto him for a while. "How do you feel about everything now? I mean . . . there's still a lot to do, but . . . no one is going to be hunting us down anymore, right?"

"I'm sure there will still be some lingering problems from the Consortium fleet, but the Mediterranean and the South Africans mostly handled them a few days ago. Three launched their own people to finish what they can find." He shrugged and kissed her again. "There's always going to be aftershocks following something like this, but whatever it is, it can be managed. The moment we got the Stations on our side, we went from being the hunted to the ones doing the hunting."

He still couldn't quite believe everything, especially since his own small family was so far removed from it. On the coast where they lived, nothing whatsoever happened, just like the majority of the universe. But he was grateful for the pieces far away that changed.

"If I know Bickford, my brothers and I are going to be even busier now than we were before all this happened. The difference is that now the things we'll work on hopefully won't be life and death every second of every day. Whatever he has me doing, I won't let it come before you and Bekah."

"Are we holding you back?" She knew they had to be holding him back somewhat. He was a genius, after all, and even though she wasn't stupid, she certainly wasn't at his level. Maybe their daughter would be someday. Or any other children that they might have.

"On the contrary," his smile lost its hesitancy, and he leaned back in the chair to press her fully against him, "I think you and Bekah are the only people in my life that have consistently pulled me forward." He kissed her neck as he held her close, and sighed against her hair. "When I met you, I had plans, I had schemes, I had all kinds of ideas about what I wanted to make the future into, and exactly how much I wanted to make the Consortium suffer for what it had done to me, to the planet. But I didn't have dreams. Computers don't dream, even human ones, which is all I was created to be. Everything I have that's ever made me more than that is from you."

"You're the first person who made me believe I was worth something." Jessie replied as she kissed Jason several times. "I still don't really understand why you picked one of the bitchiest women to be matched with, you cheated the system for a strange matchup." She kissed him harder. "But I love you. Even if you are crazy and too smart for your own good."

"I am all of those things." He admitted freely, since he had called himself worse. He knew she still had a difficult time with him much of the time, and that, while getting away had allowed them to live in peace, living so separately from the rest of humanity had taken its toll on her. "I'm also the luckiest son of a bitch that ever came out of a test tube. Cheating the system is the least of what I would've done to get to you. And that was when I barely knew you. If I had to help break the Consortium all over again just to have you, now that I know you, I'd do it twice just to make sure."

He shifted beneath her to get comfortable, considering the effect her kisses were having on him, and gave her a mischievous smile the next time he met her eyes. "But if you think *I'm* too smart for my own good, wait till you meet Charles. He makes me look like an idiot kindergartener, and he's got the problems to match."

"Hm." Jessie said in a way that definitely made it sound like she wasn't exactly thrilled to hear that, but she kept kissing him. He knew how to make her feel desired. "You would do all of that for me? Really?"

"I'd do more than that. But I'd do that for a start." He kissed her roughly, his fingertips pulling at the edges of her dress to run his hands over her thighs. "When I told you I meant to make a life with you, I meant it. And now we can." It was still incredibly strange to consider, and he knew it would take even his exceptional brain some time to wrap around it. "I mean to make it a good one."

It was still strange sometimes that they could be so open with each other since they were in the middle of nowhere. Even Bekah was still too small to even understand most things, but they were rarely intimate if Bekah was awake. Jessie, however, still had definite body-image issues when it came to being in the open. As he ran his hands over her smooth thighs, she squirmed a little on his lap as she tugged at her clothes gently. "No one wants to see that in broad daylight."

"Good. Then all that time introducing myself and insisting I'm no one finally makes sense." He kissed her hard all over again, not pushing her to do anything she was uncomfortable with, but letting her know he definitely wanted her, light or no light.

Jessie kissed him even harder and squirmed a little bit more.

"Maybe if you close your eyes."

Whatever request he got from her, rare as they were, he had always done his best to comply immediately, and closing his eyes was no exception. He still gave her a loving but sarcastic look as he complied, his hands doing the seeing for him as he rested his head back against the chair.

"No one left, of your brothers," She asked cautiously as she kissed him and eventually tugged off his shirt. "They aren't going to try to kill us, are they?"

"My brothers? No. I don't think so." Jason still had his own insecurities about being seen in broad daylight, but she had seen all there was to see if his scars and the mess the Consortium had made of his body. If she was still interested in seeing it again, he wasn't going to stop her. "Xander might have wanted to a long time ago, but he's had more than enough chances to do it before now if he wanted to. All Charles ever wanted was to be left alone. I don't think he's ever killed anyone in his life. Not that I've been around for most of it."

"Just as long as no one wants to kill *us* anymore." She kissed along his neck and ran her hands over his body as though the scars were just a part of him. She truly didn't even see them anymore. All she saw was a man who loved her despite all of her flaws and she loved him back. So much.

She might have insisted that he keep his eyes closed, but he knew his wife's body well enough to navigate just fine without his sight. He pulled her dress up along her thighs until he could pull it over her head and throw it aside, relishing the bare feel of her beneath.

Out on the coast, living to themselves, they had done away with a number of things that were usually considered either necessary or advisable for public life. Undergarments had been one of the first things to go, and Jason hadn't missed them a single moment since. He spent most of his time in loose shorts and a simple shirt, and one of the first items on his list when they had arrived on the coast had been to arrange a shipment of beautiful and comfortable dresses for Jessie. There were hundreds of them, of which she had only kept and really used a small percentage, but he kept them coming anyway, and most of them ended up on their floor.

Even with his eyes closed, when he leaned into her, his lips and his tongue found the most sensitive parts of her breasts to worship, and he did so without restraint. Parenthood taught them both many things, but among the most important lessons they learned was there was never any guarantee how long Bekah would sleep. They needed to take advantage of every moment for either decent rest or indecent play.

Jessie was always amazed at how well he knew her body and how good he was at teasing her whenever he was given the opportunity. She groaned as he paid her very close attention, all the while she squirmed some more on his lap. "Is this . . . our celebration for victory?"

"One of them, maybe." His hands joined in on the celebration eagerly, since once he got going with her, he was as single-minded in pleasing her as he was in every other aspect of his life. "You're too good to celebrate just once."

Jessie kissed him hungrily with every touch, and every kiss they shared made her need him even more. His hands were just as dangerous as the rest of him. It was amazing to think that they were free from being hunted, that they were rebels who had actually won, and her tormentor was dead. "Do you think there will be a cure that will save me?" Jessie was the only one in danger anymore from CV. Bekah was the product of Jason, so she was probably immune. "I really don't want to die in ten years."

"You know I'm not gonna let that happen." He knew she had asked him to close his eyes, but he opened them to look up into hers as he said so. "With everything we know now, with some of my bugs working to break through every secured server the Consortium has ever kept anywhere on the planet, pretty soon I'm going to know everything they've ever known, about anything. I imagine I'm gonna spend the rest of my life combing through all of it, but there are treatments already to counteract the Crisis toxin if we leave Earth. I'm betting Bickford is going to make it one of his first priorities to assign a science team to figure out how to scrub it from the planet. If it is possible."

He kissed her again to bring them both back to the moment, and his kisses were hungry as they moved back down over her neck to her collarbone. "If I have anything to say about it, you and I are going to live forever. There's never going to be a time when I'm ready to let go of you."

"You can keep your eyes open." Jessie said softly before she pulled him back into a kiss instead of letting his lips wander. Both of their sets of hands seemed to be in competition to tease the other person the most. "Live forever, huh? Promise you won't get bored?"

"I can't promise I won't get bored. I can, however, promise that I'll never get bored with *you*." He was just as eager in the competition as she was, since he loved it when he pushed her past the point of no return and into realms where she took exactly what she wanted. He groaned under her own torments and redoubled his efforts, his long fingers taking every advantage to distract her from her own insecurities with the thousand ways he wanted her.

While Jessie did miss being around other people (even though most people would say that she wasn't the friendliest person in the world) she did like the freedom of exhausting her husband and being exhausted anywhere they wanted. Jessie and Jason went at each other until they were panting on the floor, though she hardly remembered getting to the floor. She was nearly asleep again when she heard chiming from somewhere in the direction where they had started, by his screens. "Is someone contacting you?"

"Probably." He said sleepily, and he didn't even bother opening his eyes. He just barely caught his breath and was content to fall asleep with Jessie leaning against his side on the carpet when the communicator started chiming. "But I'm pretty sure I don't care right now. I'm not sure I can even walk, let alone carry on a decent conversation."

Jessie grinned. "Good. I like to exhaust you." She teased as she turned into him and ran her hand along his body again. "You know, if we are going back, maybe Mercury can explain to us why we haven't gotten pregnant again."

"I don't think she can tell us it's been from lack of trying." They certainly hadn't been doing anything to prevent it, but in spite of a few late cycles, there had been no sign of Bekah getting a younger sibling. "I think she's old enough now to learn that she'll have to fight for things occasionally, though." Their daughter seemed exceptionally bright for a toddler, already speaking more than either of them was comfortable with. Jason grinned at the possibility of her having to deal with a younger sibling. "She can be bossy with a little brother or sister for a change instead of trying to order the two of us around all the time. That'll be a nice change of pace."

He kissed Jessie roughly at the thought of another child. They'd had multiple conversations about the possibility of more children, and Jason still wanted as many as they could have. He opened his mouth to speak, but his communicator went off again, and he growled as he laid his head back on the carpet. "I hate it when they're persistent."

Jessie pouted. "Don't we deserve some peace and quiet? Not that we were being particularly peaceful or quiet just now, but still."

"I prefer you anything but quiet." He teased with a well-placed kiss along her breast as he moved to answer the communicator. If he didn't, they wouldn't be left alone. There was no information to go along with the call, which made Jason immediately suspicious, but he answered it anyway. "Yes?"

You and your wife might want to put some clothes on. Bickford wants a meeting with everyone in two hours. Charles' voice spoke through the communicator, eerily close to Jason's but more harsh and with a very different accent.

Jason looked back at Jessie with a frown, but he didn't look concerned. "Bickford's always been kind of a demanding cunt, but that doesn't mean he always gets what he wants. Is he demanding us there just for a meeting or are we being summoned permanently by His Excellency?"

Just for the meeting right now. But I've already given orders that a suite in the Bickford mansion be cleared out for you. For all three of us, actually.

"Are you trying to tell me you're going to live within three kilometers of another living thing? By choice? Because then I'd agree that you really must have brain damage."

I do. And I'm still smarter than you. Let that sink in while you're packing up your things. You can move later if you want, but at least get dressed. Every time I've tried to target you for the last two hours to pick you up, your biometrics have been indistinguishable from your wife's.

"Yes, well, I'm a big fan of being indistinguishable. You should try it sometime."

Shockingly brilliant observation, Little Brother. I've never once considered sex as an enjoyable activity. You truly are a wonder. Contact me when ready for transport. Don't be late.

"That was a little awkward." Jessie said softly as soon as she figured the conversation was over. "I didn't know anyone would be monitoring our biometrics."

"He wanted us to know he could." He said with a grumpier expression than the one he'd had on his face just a few minutes before. "That and as far as I know, human intimacy is still kind of a foreign language to him. Imagine me when you first met me and then make it worse."

"You didn't have any problems shoving me against a wall and letting me know what you wanted." Jessie said with a raised eyebrow, since she remembered their first kiss vividly. "I have no complaints."

"I still don't have any problem doing that." He grinned down at her, enjoying the sight of her stretched out on the floor and satisfied. He knelt over her and took his time kissing her thoroughly, savoring the last of their interlude together. "I'll make sure the rest of the house is locked up and begin packing up our things if you can see to Bekah's necessities. We don't have a great deal to take along, and I have no intention of letting go of this house, so things might as well remain as they are, as far as I'm concerned."

Jessie got up slowly but she nodded as she briefly looked around. "Back to the Bickford Estate. At least we will be around other people. And possibly free childcare."

"Oh if it's not already on the menu, you can believe I'll be hounding Bickford to put it there." It had been one of the best things about being in the mountains, and he hoped they could see a return to it soon.

He kissed her one more time before they began putting their clothes on, groaning at the warmth of her he always cherished. "I love you." He said out of nowhere. "I don't tell you that as often as I should. But I do. Every day and every night."

Jessie smiled brightly while she went to grab her tossed dress. "I love hearing you say it. And I love you too." Jessie grinned at him as he put his clothes on. "I'll show you again later so you know for sure."

"If I ever turn that down, put me in a body bag and drop me in the ocean." He grinned as he tugged his shorts on.

* * * * *

It was chaos at the house as soon as Cory stepped inside, but the message about the rest of the rebels being freed and returned from Eleusis had passed through the house like wildfire. He had passed both Rachel and Bree as they ran toward the entrance of the house to find Liam, but however many people he asked, he couldn't seem to find anyone who knew where Larissa was.

It took almost ten minutes for him to finally get a reliable direction for his wife, and he shot down the hallway at a sprint. He'd been away for too long, and if he could shave seconds off the remaining time, he was damn well going to do it.

He eventually got to the indicated door and gingerly opened the door. He hoped that there was a baby on the other side he didn't want to disturb by coming home. The lights were out inside the room, so he crept inside as quietly as possible, looking around by the half-light coming in through the heavy-curtained windows. There was a fan running across the room even though it was fairly chilly inside the house, but he couldn't see much.

"Rissa?" He whispered quietly, waiting for his eye to adjust to the near-darkness.

There was silence for a moment longer until he heard someone clear their throat. "Cor . . . Cory?" A sleepy voice replied as a tiny lamp turned on and there was Larissa in a rocking chair with a baby at her breast.

The light was enough for Larissa to see him by, but the man she saw bore only a slight resemblance to the one she had married. At his first opportunity, he had gotten rid of the soldier jumpsuit he'd worn for months on Eleusis in favor of a simple white t-shirt and a decent pair of jeans. He might have looked like a farmer, but he'd been a bigger man when he left. Beneath the shirt, Larissa could see nothing but lean muscles from months of hard work. His hair was cut short, his beard had grown in around the many scars on his face, and the patch over one eye proved itself not to be just a trick of the shadows as he got closer.

His smile was still Cory's, though, and as he stepped up toward the rocking chair, he slowly went down on both knees to look up at her. He put a hand on the arm of her chair, but extended his other hand to touch her leg as if it had to cross a vast distance to reach her. He sighed audibly at the touch, and half-closed his one remaining eye briefly to savor the reality under his fingertips. "Hey you." He whispered, not wanting to disturb the sleeping baby she held.

"Hey you." She replied in a broken whisper as tears immediately ran down her cheeks. The baby at her breast was asleep anyway, so she pulled the baby away gently and pulled her shirt back into place. "My god . . . I didn't know . . . I'm so glad . . ." she didn't even know what to say, since she had gone back and forth so many times, was he dead, was he alive? "This is Annabelle." She finally said as she held out the sleepy baby. "She looks just like you. No mistakin' she's yours."

He tore his eyes away from Larissa long enough to look over the baby as she lowered the girl gently into her lap at his eye level. He reached out a cautious finger that shook constantly on account of a nerve injury he'd taken in his arm, and caressed a tiny wisp of the girl's brown hair. "She's beautiful, Rissa." His one good eye still produced tears, the one beneath the patch had lost the ability to do so, leaving that side of his face dry as he looked back up at her. "I hope she's been an easy baby so far. I never in my life meant to leave you to do this on your own."

"I know. It happened, you did what you thought was best." Larissa slowly got up from the rocker and put Annabelle down before she turned around and launched herself at Cory. "You're alive!" She whisper-yelled as she wrapped her arms around him and clung to him. It looked like she had gained some weight while he was gone, but it had gone entirely to her chest, hips, and backside. Her face looked more or less the same. "You're really here, right? This isn't a dream?"

He was stronger than he had been the last time she saw him, and he picked her up easily when she wrapped her arms around his neck. He shook his head against her hair in answer to her question, swinging her around once with a quiet laugh. "No, no dreaming. It's me, in the flesh." He looked around for any other doors in the room, and found one near the rocker. He turned off the lamp and moved quietly through the door into what appeared to be Larissa's chosen bedroom, then shut the door as quietly as he had opened it. He had every intention of seeing his daughter, but he wanted to see his wife first. As soon as the door was closed, he had his arms around Larissa again and had her up against the wall beside the door to kiss the life out of her, with half a year of missed opportunities behind the touch. "God, I missed you so much."

"Wow, Cor . . ." She was clearly impressed by his strength, not that he wasn't strong in the past, but Larissa was also never a tiny girl. Both her brothers were substantial men, and she was a woman with curves. Especially now. Larissa kissed him hungrily, but clearly she had questions too. "You're so . . . and your eye . . . what happened?" She ran her fingers just below the fabric of the eyepatch. Clearly she didn't care that he had lost an eye, she just cared that he was alive. Larissa didn't even give him a chance to respond before she went back to kissing him and pulled his shirt off. She groaned softly when she saw the muscles underneath. "Oh . . . wow. You've . . . changed a bit."

"Six months in the middle of Eleusis-Nowhere and anybody would get like this, I'm pretty sure." He was less playful than he had been, but his smile still had a hint of his usual exuberance to it. "We got stranded outside the compound and picked them off for a few months, till Orion was a crazy enough bastard to figure out how to flush them out. I lost my eye the first day, a bunch of shrapnel from an explosion." He didn't sound upset about it, and he wasn't, since he had long since processed the loss while he had bigger things to worry about. He told the entire story between kisses and his own attempts to rip her own shirt off, sighing against her skin as he kissed her, each sigh a testament to how much he had missed her.

"I can't believe . . . you went through so much." Larissa said between her own kisses. She ended up almost completely undressed by the time he finished explaining. "I'll make you a new patch. One that's more comfortable." She added before she yanked him back to the bed, which had been entirely hers until that moment. "After Logan and Liam went away, things got hard around here. A lot of people thought we were going to be targeted. A month ago, Taylor Lind tried to convince me to marry him." She added it in quickly so that it wouldn't seem like a big deal. "He kept sayin' I needed a man and Annabelle needed a father and you were dead and I needed to recognize it." Larissa shrugged, though he could see a little bit of guilt in her eyes. "I never said anything out loud, but I worried you really were dead. Not that I would have married Taylor, but I still worried. Nothing happened." She assured him quickly so that he wouldn't worry.

From the dangerous look in the eye he had left, Larissa could tell he was going to have some words with the man. "Fuck Taylor Lind." He said with a possessive kiss. They fell together onto the bed once their clothes had been violently cast aside. Her hands got a thorough opportunity to explore the chiseled workmanship Eleusis had wrought on her husband, as well as some of the scars he wore that hadn't been there before. "I made you a promise before I left that I would come back. I fought like hell on Eleusis to make sure I kept it, and I'd rather not fight at all, but if I ever have to, I will, to make sure I get back to you and Annabelle."

"You don't have to fight anymore. And I would never have married Taylor Lind." She wrapped her arms around him and hauled herself close to his definitely-chiseled body. His improved body made her even more self-conscious about hers, though, since she knew she had gained some weight. "Though one look at you and every other woman around here is going to tell you that you should let Taylor have what he wants so you can have someone else."

"Fuck them too, then." He kissed her roughly, though he'd never been at all rough before he'd left for Eleusis. He'd never been particularly soft or unattractive, but he'd still been very much a young man. The months on Eleusis had sanded off whatever remained of that identity. "You have never been more beautiful to me than you are right this second, right here. And that's not just the six months of celibacy talking."

"It's not? Are you sure?" Larissa slid her hands all over his amazing body and kissed him just as roughly in return. She knew he had never been so rough before, but she didn't mind. All she cared about was that Cory was back and he was alive and that he still wanted her. "Six months is a long time."

"Fucking right it is." He laughed breathlessly again as his hands moved over her hips, riding up to caress her breasts gently, since he was sure they were still sensitive if she was nursing. "I missed *you*, not just this. And if you don't believe me, I've got pages and pages of really, *really* bad poetry I brought back for you from the other side of the galaxy to prove it." His lips moved down over her chest as he said so, taking in the taste of her as if she was a pleasant dream he couldn't wait to have again.

Larissa gasped in pleasure as he kissed down her chest. Months felt like lifetimes when she truly wondered if he was dead. "I missed you too. Every minute of every day, I wanted you here with me. I didn't write anything, but I would love all of your poetry." She replied before she moved so that she could be on top of him. She didn't want him to have to work at anything, and she desperately wanted him to be happy. "I love you, Cory Prince. I love you so much."

The trails of their tears were still wet on both their cheeks as she wrapped him up in her, and he wrapped his arms around her tightly once she had him. Their gasps echoed against each other between their kisses, but the language they spoke was the same. Home was there between them, and they would never let it go again.

* * * * *

Melissa grinned at the chaos inside the house. It clearly made Kassie nervous, since she kept looking all over the room. Melissa shushed her gently and giggled at the maelstrom of happy tears that swept through the house and spilled into every hallway.

"It's okay, baby, everybody's just saying hi. They missed each other." She and Kam were informed that Aiko and Carl were part of the force that slammed the coffin shut on the Consortium, but things had been so crazy on Prime and Three that they hadn't seen them before coming back to the Bickford Estate. Charles was still bringing people in that Logan had required, though, so she and Kam and the two children stayed by the windows to watch.

"Look, Kassie, he's opening another window. Maybe this one is for your Auntie Aiko." She looked over at William in Kameron's arms, and though he looked just as confused as his cousin, Melissa didn't imagine understanding in the boy's eyes when she mentioned his mother's name. Will might have been the quietest baby boy Melissa had ever seen in her life, but he was incredibly perceptive.

Kam was just as quiet as Will as they watched, and while Kassie squealed when the portal opened again (Kam was amazed how much like Melissa their daughter was, even though Kassie came out of Kam's body) and Kam actually held her breath when she saw Carl and Aiko come through. Will was already reaching out for his parents even though they were on the other side of a window, so Kam moved quickly as soon as the portal closed and they were through. "I told you they would come back for you, Buddy."

Carl and Aiko were both a little disoriented to see the Bickford Estate, since neither of them had been there before for any real length of time, and the place was a little overwhelming in terms of sheer size. Carl had David in a secure bundle held against one shoulder, but he saw Kam coming out with William almost immediately after they stepped out of the Twist.

"There's that ugly mug. Just like his dad, poor kid." He grinned at the little boy reaching out, and just to see Kameron and Melissa alive and well. "Thought for sure your big mouth would've gotten you killed by now, Fitch!" He called across the distance, bouncing David against his shoulder to keep him entertained.

"I guess I'm just a lucky bitch!" She yelled back, and Melissa jabbed her side for cursing in front of the kids. Kam smirked and set William down so he could go running after his parents. He stumbled a few times, but he was a pretty solid walker/runner. Mostly a runner.

Since David was secure in Carl's arms, Aiko took off running and scooped up Will as soon as she could. Once he was in her arms she showered him with kisses and squeezed him so tightly she hoped she wasn't hurting him. "Mommy missed you so much! You're so big!"

"So big!" Will said as he threw his arms up while she held him, grinning like a fool at his mother as she showered him with kisses.

"See, I told you he talks." Melissa jabbed Kam again with a grin, bouncing Kassie as the reunion continued in front of them. She was glad it would be just her and Kam and Kassie again, but she had enjoyed having William around.

"He talks to you, I guess. Never could get him to talk to me." Kam smiled as she watched Carl show David to his big brother who didn't look at all impressed by the baby. "Just wait until Kassie gets one of those to have around. She'll make that face too."

"Maybe we can get around to that." Melissa said as she flipped some of her hair behind her shoulder, both because it was annoying her and because she knew Kam liked it when she did. She gave her wife a flirtatious smile before turning her attention back to Kassie. "It *is* my turn, after all."

"Hell yeah it's your turn. I don't want to do that again for a while." Kam stepped in and pulled her wife into a heated kiss, with Kass on the opposite hip. "Except we're going to ask Mercury to do it the way that we don't need to get a man involved. I don't want anyone touching you just so we can get another baby."

"We'll still have to pick who it is." Melissa draped an arm around Kam's neck and tossed her hair back again, this time very much just for Kam's benefit. "But I don't want anybody else touching me either. I might enjoy cock a little more than you do, but I'm a whole lot more interested in *you*." She kissed Kam hungrily, enjoying the fact that their family felt like it was back to the way it was supposed to be and they were in a place they actually wanted to stay. "We can go see Mercury in a couple months. I want some time with you to celebrate being free before I start feeling gross and weepy all the time and puking my guts out every morning."

"You don't know it will happen to you. Knowing you, you'll be one of those pregnant women who feel great all of the time and I'll hate you a little for it." Kam smiled and she kissed Melissa a few more times. "Celebrate being free. God, I can't even really believe it. What the hell am I supposed to do if I'm not running around with a gun?"

"Oh you're still gonna be running around with a gun." Carl interjected nearby with a laugh. "I'm sorry, did you forget you work for me? I did not fire you. You are still very much employed. You and your gun both."

Kam looked over at Carl and smiled. "Thank god. Or whoever I need to thank for that." She widened her grin and looked at Melissa with a shrug, since she knew Mel wasn't exactly thrilled to hear her job would still include weaponry. "You have your gun and I have mine. Yours just leaves prettier results."

"I don't know. You were getting pretty artistic with your gun back on Prime." Melissa didn't like Kameron being in danger, and she didn't like it when people shot at her, but she had kept tight hold on both the kids during some of the fighting when Kameron had been hard at work. She had never actually seen Kameron in the middle of a fight before, and she had freely confessed at the time that her militaristic wife was dead sexy when she was kicking ass. "Not that I'm hoping you have to shoot people all the time. I'm a freak, just not that kind of freak."

"You're the best kind of freak." Kam said with a smirk before she looked back at Carl and Aiko. "I really fucking hope . . ." She winced at Mel's jab over her cursing. "I really hope that Bickford brings back that childcare thing again. I could use a break like that."

"Shit, I'm just glad we're all back on the same planet." Carl laughed with an arm around Aiko, but he was glaring at Melissa. "Go ahead, jab me. See what happens."

Kam saw Melissa raise a challenging eyebrow and she just grabbed her wife's face and distracted her by kissing her again. "Don't poke that bear. He bites." She kissed Mel again and nodded toward the house. "Come on, let's get back inside. If that fu . . . if that portal opens again, I don't want to be near it."

Carl traded children with Aiko once they started toward the house, and he bounced his older son up in the air with one hand the way he had six months before. A grin split Carl's face when it made the boy laugh the same way it had before, since he knew how quiet William was under normal circumstances. He dropped the boy back into his arms on the way into the house, his head barely clearing the top of the doorframe, as usual.

"You know Bickford isn't gonna give us much of a vacation." He said to Aiko once they passed the chaos of the dozens of reunions happening simultaneously across the mansion. "He hasn't demoted me, that I know of, and he's actually got the rest of the world paying attention to him now. He's gonna put us both to work until we're buried in paperwork up to our eyelids."

"That's okay. I imagine most everyone around here is going to be buried in work. Especially Mercury and the rest of the doctors after a day like today. In nine months she's going to be rushing from one reunion baby to another." Aiko laughed softly before she kissed David's forehead. "We won't be here forever. Just until things settle enough that we can go back to Eleusis. You owe me a palace."

"I do. It's true. Need to get one of those Montgomery supercomputers to help me out with the blueprints. One of them has to have an architectural background in his back pocket, right? They do every-fucking-thing else." He smiled at William as the little boy wrapped his little arms around his neck. He put a huge hand on the boy's back to reassure him that they were going to be staying together, and closed his eyes as they waited for a hallway to open so they could get farther from the chaos.

Aiko didn't say anything else as they wandered until they found someone who could direct them to an empty suite of rooms. Once it was just the four of them in a quiet suite, Aiko sighed and sat down on the edge of a bed. She looked over at Carl with Will and she gave them both a smile. She wished with all of her heart that Kazuo could have been there celebrating with them, and she missed him every day, but she was grateful for what she had.

"Thank you, Carl." She said suddenly as he played with Will. "Thank you for giving me a chance after I had lied to you, for loving me, for taking care of our family. I never imagined any of this when my parents sent Kazuo and me up to the Initiative."

"Believe me, neither did I." He smiled back at her and kicked off his boots, since he was going to be comfortable as quickly as possible if they had a break to relax. "Before I put my name in for the Initiative, I was a guard on Three working for Station Security. And now for some reason people listen to me when I give orders." He shrugged and moved closer to her on the bed to sit down, shaking the whole frame as well as her and David as he did so.

"I imagined I was gonna get stuck with some woman who was pretty unhappy about being stuck with me, and that I was going to take orders the rest of my life until something across the galaxy managed to kill me. None of this was even close to being on my radar." He let William loose on the bed to jump and bounce on the pillows, which he did with a huge grin on his face, but no open laughter. Strange kid. "Especially not you." He kissed her in a moment where William seemed unlikely to harm himself, with one of his huge hands on her waist.

Aiko kissed him back several times before she spoke, though she still held David close to her the whole time. "I'm your fantasy girl, right?" She smiled brighter after that, since she knew the answer already.

"Even more now than you were when I met you." He agreed, tracing a thumb along the contours of her smile. "Now I actually know you. And I know enough to be a little bit scared of you. Which I have to say, is always a turn-on." He kissed her deeply and reached out casually afterward to keep William from jumping off the bed to his detriment. "I'm not sure we ever talked about you having a fantasy of your own, but I hope I manage to meet it."

"You're the fantasy of a lot of women, big guy. Just look at these muscles." She ran her fingers along his outstretched arm while Will continued jumping even with his father keeping him safe. "You love me for me. What else could I possibly want?"

Carl usually had an ego the size of a small country, but he had never felt that way when he was with Aiko, mostly because they had completely different skill-sets. He never considered himself particularly inept until he'd met her, but even with her, she never made him feel as inferior to her as he knew he was. He was grateful for that, and for a great deal more. "I'm gonna build you that palace." He promised with a deep kiss. "And as soon as these two boys are old enough to watch their younger siblings, I'm gonna make sure one whole wing of the place is designated clothing-optional. I want peace, I want quiet, and I want you naked. Not in that order. That's the kind of life I'm gonna make for us. No matter what Bickford decides to throw at us in his whole New World Order."

Even after all the time they had been together, Aiko's cheeks still flushed whenever he talked to her like that, and he knew good and well how much she liked it. She was a bookish girl with a god for a husband. "That sounds amazing."

His grin agreed with her, and he kissed her and both their children, just glad to be home. "I'll go get us some food for the room and find somebody to watch the kids for the meeting in a couple hours. Your parents should be along pretty soon, once Charles gets the connection to Colombia settled. Anything else you want me to go foraging for?"

"Something cooked. And delicious. They've got a grill in this place, right? Tell Logan to light up a grill." Aiko thought of the very idea of Carl doing that and she shook her head. "I'll stay here with the boys and wait for you to bring something back. Whatever it is."

"I won't be long." He kissed her again as he stood to get his boots on. He looked around the room, taking it in like every other place they had run off to in their short life together. He hoped there wouldn't be too many more to add to the list. Staying in one place and making a life for themselves would be a welcome change after all the chaos, even if the chaos was absolutely worth it.

19

Gwen sat at the table with Rachel and showed off her ring while she held Chrissy in her lap. Chrissy was happy to see Gwen again, which was incredibly sweet to see, though Bree just about lost her mind when Liam came through the door.

One, he was alive and she was so proud, but two, his hair was *blue*. Rachel clearly wasn't a fan of the blue hair or the lip spike, but Bree just didn't know what to think of it. What she *did* know was that she wasn't pregnant anymore and her husband was home. That was all that fucking mattered in the end. She reached out to run her hand over his face again as he drank some coffee. "I still don't know what to think. Rachel says we should shave it all off."

"You know, this *is* still my face. I do get some say in the matter." Liam teased, but he kissed her fingertips every time she touched his face, relishing the fact that he was home and surrounded by his favorite people in the world. "Besides, the stuff they gave me is gonna fade over the next couple months. So shaving it off just means I'd have blue stubble for a while instead of an actual beard or hair. Would you rather have me bald?"

"Yes!" Rachel said from across the room, since she thought he looked absolutely ridiculous. "What is wrong with a bald man, exactly?" She held onto Bree's new baby, since she really liked the newborn stage. Newborns weren't nearly as much of a handful as the crawling, toddling, walking monsters the others had become.

"I think the blue hair will kind of grow on you." Gwen said without getting up, but she was bouncing Chrissy in her lap. "It's the lip spike that really should go. That thing hurts."

"Ugh, okay, okay, fine, I've been overruled." Liam cried out in defeat. "You know, I only need one of you to be on my side in something to maintain a tie, and you can't even give me that." He sighed in resignation and leaned his head back. He had to reach up around Bree to get both hands to his mouth, but he pinched the clasp of the spike free from his lip. He pulled the spike itself free with a wince and held it up as evidence of his sacrifice. "There, concession made, by overruled majority."

Gwen and Rachel cheered while Bree moved in closer to kiss him and make it all better. "Don't pout. You still look like a badass to me, Mr. Bickford." Bree laughed while the other girls continued to cheer. "You still have your blue hair, right?"

"Only until the supplies I just ordered get here." A voice said from the doorway to the room, where Logan stepped inside with a smile. He was happy to see his brother back with his entire family, whole again in ways he hadn't been in months of plotting and politicking. "I ordered a kit from the same vendor that Fatma used to turn you blue, that will turn you brown again. Whether you use it or not, I leave up to you and your, um, democracy." He glanced around the room, since he could tell it wasn't a very popular look among his wives at the moment.

Rachel jutted out her arm immediately in Logan's direction as soon as he appeared. "See? Logan looks real good with his hair like that. What is so wrong with that?"

"Thank you, Rachel." Logan said with a smile as Liam's mouth just gaped open in mock offense.

"Okay, fine, you know what? I'll go shave it all off tonight. Then you can all be married to a fffffreaking cue-ball." He really was trying to watch his language around his verbal children. Even though Anders and Beckett were playing with cars along one side of the room, he didn't really want to take any chances on them learning bad habits from him too early. "Would that make you happy?"

"Yes!" Rachel agreed.

"I don't know . . ." Gwen hesitated, she was getting used to the blue and it didn't look *that* bad.

"I don't know either. Are you blue *everywhere?* Cuz I'm sure as hell not fu . . . sleeping with a smurf." Bree added, even though she knew Rachel wanted them to back her up.

"That, I trimmed down already, thank you very much. I did have time for a shower and some maintenance before I came back here so as to be presentable." He knew it didn't really answer the question, but he just smiled at the round of laughter the comment got from everyone present. He looked up at Logan while they laughed, glad that his brother could stop for a change and appreciate some laughter in the world.

"Something you needed, Logan? I heard your edict about a

meeting earlier. I'll try to be there, but I'm not making any promises." He glanced around the room again with meanings that no one needed interpreted.

Logan rolled his eyes. "I won't pull you away on business. I do actually love you that much, and I would prefer your wives not harbor murderous intentions toward me." He did glance at all three of them in quick succession, though, settling on Gwen briefly before he looked back at Liam. "I'd like to talk to all of you about how things can proceed from here, if that's alright. To make sure we're all on the same page. It's a big house, and it's also a heck of a lot more busy than it has been in a long time, if ever, but it's still ours. I want to make sure it runs the way we want it to."

"I've already had people ask me if I'm going to run the childcare facility." Gwen looked up at Logan but held Chrissy close as if Chrissy was her own baby. "It seems like people are looking for some privacy."

"I can't imagine why." Logan teased, pointedly not looking at the other two women in the room who hadn't had the chance yet to spend any time with their husband since his return. "If you would take up that responsibility again, I would be very grateful. Not tonight or in the next day or two, even, but whenever you're able to get back in touch with your former caretakers to re-establish operations." He glanced away at Rachel and Bree afterward, not wanting to leave the two of them out. "I'd ask the two of you as well to oversee the rest of the practical affairs for the house overall. It's my intention that the three of us, myself, Liam, and Larissa, each house our families here, but there are quite a few others I plan to invite to live here as well."

"So what are you gonna do, commute from here to Prime every day by Twist? Just because?" Liam wouldn't put it past his brother to do it just to make a statement.

"No, I intend this estate to be the center of operations for my government." Logan dropped into the silence that followed, broken only by the sounds of Anders and Beckett playing along the side of the room. "I've already tasked Ben and Cory with reaching out to several construction companies to see who is willing to barter construction work and materials for Twist access time in order to begin work on an office complex in the western fields. They never grew as well as the rest of the fields did anyway."

"You're gonna . . . here? Right in our backyard?" Liam was

incredulous, but he knew in the next moment that he shouldn't have been surprised. "Gotta send a message that things have changed, I guess."

"Exactly." Logan agreed, looking around at his three sisters-in-law again for their own opinions and insights.

"No reason to start anywhere else when you have the land and manpower here." Rachel replied as she bounced just enough to keep Dax asleep in her arms. Dakota, Bree's second son, was a dream baby. So sweet and easy. "I'd like to help too, maybe with the books? Eventually?"

"I'll need all the help I can get, and I'd be grateful." Logan said earnestly, since he knew how gifted Rachel was. "I imagine for the next several days and weeks, most of the nations of the world are going to be too busy trying to piss me off for me or my administration to accomplish anything useful, but we can talk more about whatever positions you're interested in as things develop. I'd rather not make anyone else in my family more of a target than you already are until things quiet down somewhat."

Rachel nodded and when it got silent, Bree shook her head. "Don't look at me. I'm not volunteering for anything. Someone has to be sure to be here with the kids or clean or make meals and shit. Hell, Liam may need another wife just to help me if the two of you are going to skip out on me."

Liam choked on his coffee when Bree said that, but did his best to play it off as a legitimate accident. Logan looked just as confused as everyone else in the room, for which Liam was grateful. He didn't need to be outed in front of the wives whose good graces he was trying to keep.

"Yeah, well, when we all started this thing, you did say four was the lucky number." He teased over in Bree's direction, then shook his head. "Right now I'm much more concerned about just staying here, living a little while in peace, and enjoying these babies. Y'all can go and take government posts and official positions later on as soon as you get sick of me again." He kissed Bree, since she was the closest at the moment, but he got up from the table to get a refill on his coffee. It also gave him a chance to pass Rachel and give her a kiss as well, even if she scrunched up her face at the blue of his hair.

All three of his wives stared at him after his choking coffee incident, but of course Bree was the first to speak up. "We're not going to get sick of you. I just lived a nun's life for six hellacious months. When I was huge. And so horny. No. Not gonna get sick of you."

"She even wanted to spoon with me. I locked my door just to make sure she didn't sneak in." Rachel said with a look over at Liam. "I'm surprised her vagina lasted this long without you."

"And that's my exit." Logan said from the doorway, chuckling to himself at his brother's predicament. "Gwen, you'll let me know when you've got childcare up and running? We shouldn't have quite as many people hanging around here a week from now, but there will still be a need for it at all hours."

Gwen nodded and looked into Logan's eyes for a moment before she got up from the table with Chrissy in her arms. She walked over to Logan and gave him a brief hug. "Thank you for everything you did." She lowered her voice to a whisper. "He knows everything so I hope it won't be awkward."

"Oh, don't worry, it's awkward." Logan returned the brief hug, still laughing. "But I think that'll fade with time. I hope so, anyway." He glanced past her into the room with a broad smile, more easy and free than any she'd ever seen from the man during their time in the mountains. Liam was the brother who smiled, not Logan. Apparently victory agreed with him. "I'm glad you're happy, Gwen. Truly. And I'm glad you're safe, after everything that's happened."

"Me too." She wore a grin of her own as she looked at the ring on her hand and looked back at Liam. "The blue hair isn't too bad, all told. He's alive. That's all I really care about." She squeezed Logan's arm and then smiled up at him too. "What about you? Are you going to be happy now? Smiling has got to be much better than scowling all the time."

"Right now I'll stick with smiling. The scowl will be back soon, though, if I know some of the world leaders I'll be dealing with." The look of solid resignation came over his face again briefly, as she'd seen it so many times, but he wasn't going to focus on that at the moment. "Oh, and I'm just going to assume that you three are going to handle planning the wedding? I took care of the last one, and I told him in no uncertain terms that he was on his own for any others he added in the future."

"We got it handled." Bree said as she clung to Liam's side, since she definitely did not want to stop touching him. "She says she doesn't want a big shebang, but if nothing else, there's going to be a shit-ton of booze. I'm not pregnant. That means I need to get drunk."

"Perfect logical argument if I ever heard one." Logan grinned from the doorway and began his retreat. "I'll see you whenever your wives choose to take mercy on your soul, Liam. Thanks again, you three." He gave them all a quick smile and turned from the room. Dinner was cooking and just about ready, but Logan didn't want to be around when they started chopping up his brother into their own preferred pieces.

"I doubt we'll be the only ones about to get married after all this." Liam looked across the table at Gwen with a smile, since he had always loved watching her with his children. It was a large part of what had drawn him to her in the first place, really. "I know Diego was talking even before all this that if we ever saw peace again, he wanted to do a big ceremony for all four of his, because they never really got the chance to do it right in the first place. Plus, who knows, maybe Logan and his whole crazy mess will finally get itself sorted out." His tone didn't make it sound as if he thought that outcome was very likely.

"Who do you think it will be?" Gwen asked as she went to sit by the table again, since Chrissy wanted to bounce on her legs again and she was all too happy to oblige.

All of the women looked at each other and of course Bree was the one who had the loudest comment. "Mercury is the knockout. If he's smart, he'll pick her. They were good together. He and Anna have a history, but that's just it. History."

Rachel looked mildly concerned by that comment. "I don't know, Liam and I have been together a while, that doesn't mean it's worse because we have a history. Right, babe?"

"Oh no, I'm a *big* fan of history." He agreed with a wink in Rachel's direction. He had known and been with Rachel the longest, ever since Margo's departure from the family. He was glad of all the time they'd had together to learn about each other and draw closer, even if they didn't tend to make a spectacle out of it the way Bree enjoyed. "I really don't know what's gonna happen, though. Not enough to lay any kind of stakes on it, anyway. I doubt Logan himself knows right now either."

"Well, they better figure it out and stick to it." Bree replied with a shake of her head. "We don't need any more drama in this family. We've had enough for several lifetimes." She leaned in and kissed Liam's neck and tugged on his shirt. "We've got time before dinner, right? Can I steal you away?"

They were a very long way from being on any kind of schedule as they had been previously, and Liam knew better than to think they would be back on one reliably any time soon. He was strangely comfortable with that.

He returned the tug to her own shirt and glanced at one of the doors nearby in agreement. "Go on, I'll be right behind you." He sent her off in the direction of what had previously been her room, where he knew he'd be able to find her quickly in the chaos that was their house. He finished his coffee and got up, trailing a hand across Gwen's shoulders idly on his way to Rachel.

With Bree on her way out of the room and Gwen temporarily focused on their three eldest children, the room seemed private enough for him to take a moment with Rachel and Dax. He kissed the back of the little boy's head first, gingerly, so as not to wake him up, then took a lingering kiss from Rachel. "Hopefully you haven't got plans after dinner." His hands settled along her waist, keeping her as close against him as the little boy asleep at her shoulder would allow. Rachel was commonly the busiest of his wives, so he did his best to be considerate, even back on their scheduled days, of her own time and plans.

Rachel smiled up at him and pulled him back into another kiss. "I do. You." She replied softly as she looked into his eyes, all the while her chest filled with all kinds of emotions that really only Liam saw the full extent of. "She's not any more needy than I am for you, I hope you know. She's just louder than I am."

"Yeah, well, we'll see if you can still say that when I'm through with you tonight." He teased quietly, taking her in a kiss more scandalous than the two of them would usually indulge in with another of the wives so close by. He had been gone for half a year. It was a time for exceptions to rules. "I missed you too. I can't tell you the number of times the last six months I wished you were around; then was just immediately grateful that you were safe, even if you would've probably been better suited to do half the shit I've been doing than I was."

"I'm not better suited for any of that stuff. I wanted to be here with the children, and with Bree. God, can you imagine if I had left Bree in charge around here?" Rachel looked mildly horrified as she shook her head. "I'm not sure there would have been an estate to come home to." Rachel kissed him a few more times and caressed his cheek with her free hand. "I love you. I'm so happy you're home and that you brought Gwen back safely."

He laughed at the thought of Bree in charge by herself, and didn't contemplate the possibility very long. Bree was an exceptional mother and an amazing wife, always the first to support him or get in the face of anyone who gave him shit, but she was not the most organized or personally responsible woman he'd ever met. "I love you too, Rachel. It is . . . amazingly good to be home." He kissed her a few more times, and left a promissory kiss along her neck as he pulled away. "I'll see you at dinner. And for dessert."

Rachel smirked and gave Liam a nod, but after he started to walk away, Gwen jumped up from the table and rushed after him before he disappeared. "I love you too." Gwen added before she kissed Liam on the cheek. She held up Chrissy who gave Liam a kiss as well. "See you at dinner, you stud."

If he was being honest, he did feel a little like an animal that had been put out to stud, but he wasn't going to act like he was mad about it. Things with Gwen were still new, all things considered, and he was truly impressed with just how easily she fell into rhythm with the rest of his family. "I love you too, Mrs. Bickford." He had teased her the day before about getting used to it, and he meant to make sure she had ample opportunity.

Gwen actually giggled, but she hoisted Chrissy back onto her hip and then backed away to see to the boys. "Tell her to be nice. Rachel hasn't had a turn yet."

"Great. First I'm a stud, now I'm a carousel. Y'all need to make up your minds." He grinned back at her as she rejoined the boys, but she could see him take a deep breath to steel himself before he set off to follow Bree. He had some inkling of what he was walking into, but with Bree, it was always best to be mentally prepared for anything.

* * * * *

Jason felt immense trepidation as the Twist opened on the Bickford Estate. The mansion nearby had always sounded larger than life whenever people described it to him, and it more than lived up to its reputation, especially with the life nearly bursting out of its seams. Charles hadn't responded to the transportation request with anything but a set of coordinates and a time to be ready, so Jason knew better than to go looking around for him when they arrived.

Instead, he saw Xander and Tatyana near the house, apparently waiting for them. Jason took a few cautious steps closer, with Jessie's hand in his, looking back and forth between the two of them as he considered what to say. He settled on something long before they were actually close enough to talk. "Here's a relevant question, then." He gave Tatyana a pointed look. "Are we all still friends even when we aren't fighting a war?"

Tatyana's cold stare made February in the midwest feel warm by comparison, especially when it flicked to Jessie briefly. "No one would have called us 'friends' in the first place, White."

"What would you call us, then? Co-terrorists? Not as good as a tag when we're no longer going to be doing much terrorizing." He knew neither of them wanted to think about the fact that the war was effectively over, but it wasn't a fact of the world that he was going to let them ignore for very long. "I would like us to be friends. If that's possible." He glanced over at Xander. "I don't exactly see either of you being traditional enough to make me call you my sister-in-law," he cringed a little as he said it, since history was a long and twisted memory for all of them, "so I would like to be able to say we're friends."

Tatyana just glared back, her face as unreadable as ever. Without answering the question, she reached out to squeeze Xander's arm and then stepped away, looking at Jessie. "Your rooms are this way. The Bickfords carved out a Montgomery wing."

Jason gave Jessie a reassuring smile as she was led away. He didn't trust many people in the world, but he trusted Tatyana. He knew a day might still come when she would find a reason to kill him herself, but she wasn't Carmina, going after those dear to her enemies just to cause them pain. He hoped they were on better terms than that. With Tatyana it was always difficult to tell.

"She's mostly been angry at you for skipping out to the west coast just when things got serious around here." Xander filled in once the ladies were gone. "Frankly, a lot of people here were. Me included."

"Well, every single one of those angry people can go fuck themselves." Jason shrugged and dropped the bag he carried to the mostly-frozen ground so he could put his hands in his pockets. If Xander wanted some kind of confrontation, then he would get one. "Everybody does selfish things once in a while. The only difference is, some of us do it because we actually choose to protect our family. Not abandon them to people who want to torture them in the name of science."

Alexander's face, *his* face, as it should have been, turned to a stormcloud in a heartbeat. "We've all had reasons to do as we've . . ."

"I was six." Jason said, somehow without the abundance of anger that he had stowed behind the sentiment for his entire life. "And because you couldn't be bothered to so much as look back as you ran, maybe give your little brother some cover fire, it was another sixty years of torture and experimentation before I was even able to so much as hit puberty, let alone escape."

He consciously relaxed the clenched fists in his pockets as he spoke. "If I died, even so much as a month ago, I would have died blaming you, at least in part, for everything." He allowed himself a final moment to seethe, then let out a slow breath. "But with the Consortium behind us, if I've spent the rest of my life permitting ends to justify means, then it would be hypocritical of me to do anything but conclude that the end of the Consortium, and our survival, has justified whatever means you and I resorted to in order to reach this point. You did what you did, and so did I. You are who you are, and so am I."

Xander considered the speech a while in silence, but eventually gave the tiniest shadow of a nod. "I can live with those terms. Whatever else you've been, you've always been my brother, Jason. I never stopped looking for opportunities to get you out."

"It doesn't matter." He wasn't going to let Xander feel better about having done his best when he failed. The best any of them could do anymore was move on and do their best to forget anything and everything that happened. "What does matter," Jason's eyes flicked to one side, to a small pocket of air nearby that looked just slightly out of place, "is whether our one known surviving brother is going to stop snooping on other people's conversations and condescend to join us in the flesh."

The spot of air hung for a moment, but then expanded quickly into a person-sized Twist, allowing Charles to step through with Jeeta at his side. She didn't stay long, but she did give Charles a quick glare as they stepped through, as if to say she had warned him against trying to snoop on his brothers.

"It's very nice to meet you both." She said to Jason and Xander, smiling at them quickly before she turned and took the Twist apparatus off Charles' shoulder and formed it along her own. Jason caught a brief flash of surprise from Charles, for some reason, but understanding and a mild glare quickly followed. All Jeeta did was glare right back, and gently shoved their frail brother toward the two of them as she turned to walk away. "We'll have plenty of time to get to know each other later, I'm sure. I'll leave the three of you to do your own catching up."

Charles lingered next to the two of them for a long time as Jason and Xander looked him over. He had done his own spying on both of them sufficient to satisfy his usual suspicions about people, but he still wasn't completely certain either or both of them wouldn't try to kill him. Especially after the speech Jason had just delivered about being left for dead.

"I suppose you also blame me for the whole left-for-death-and-experimentation vendetta, yes?" It was easier to look at Jason. He had less history with Jason, all of it before the man had turned six years old so many lifetimes ago.

Jason shook his head, but didn't so much as blink to look away from the challenge. "I'm not usually hurt by things I expect. You were always a self-absorbed prick, Charles. You leaving me to the Consortium wasn't a surprise. I imagine you calculated at the time that my capture increased your odds of getting away free."

"It did." Charles admitted without apology. "But when I re-ran my estimations after we reached safety, I believed we could have doubled back for you without risking our own safety to an unacceptable degree. That being said, Henry's actions afterward made that course of action impossible only seconds after I had completed that calculation." Charles' voice was every bit as cold as Jason remembered it, but there was so much more behind it than there had been before. Xander had been only a boy of sixteen, Charles only two years younger, the last time the three of them had been in the same place. Another lifetime indeed.

"I checked in on you, during your time with Hyacinth." Charles admitted. "I started to suspect Henry of murdering others of us by then, so I made no move to make contact, lest he find you through me. But I was happy to see you free of them on your own terms."

"I wonder what that looks like." Xander's glare was more cautious than angry. "You being actually happy about . . . I don't know. Anything."

Charles gave the kind of infinitesimal shrug that Xander could remember being infuriated by even as a child. Some things never changed. "Perhaps we'll find out in days to come." Charles didn't sound completely confident that he would ever know what it meant to really be happy, but that was a question between him, Jeeta, and his own twisted mind to answer.

"The others are dead." Charles continued, as if it was the most logical route for the conversation to take. "Henry claimed he found and killed all those who remained of us except the two of you. The only reason he never killed me, I believe, is because he enjoyed the pace at which the Consortium was doing so themselves. Henry never had that kind of patience."

He looked back and forth between Xander and Jason, stepping just a little closer so that the ring of their conversation tightened into something approaching an intimate circle. In the dry light of a midwestern February, Charles' skin was like sickly snow, his scalp and face completely devoid of hair, his cheeks sunken by protracted malnourishment that would take more than a few weeks to heal. Beside him, Jason's scars peeked out through the neckline of his shirt, teasing at the horrors beneath and the limitations with which he had been left by those who hunted them. Beside him, Xander stood as a mirror of painful perfection, his full beard softening his scowl.

All six hazel eyes exchanged ghosts as they darted back and forth. The years that Jason had known under experimentation and constant attempts at escape. The creative horrors that Charles had endured and the emptiness of the few freedoms he had enjoyed. The agony of Xander's revolutionary life, watching friend after friend die for a cause they would never see realized. They had crawled through different hells, but had emerged, forged by the same fire.

"My terms for handing over the mobile Twist were simple." Charles continued. "I required Carl's assistance in killing Henry, which he happily provided. In exchange, I was assured that I would retain ultimate and complete control over the usage of the Twist technology. It was a rash and stupid choice on his part, but it was his agreement. Bickford has chosen to honor it, with the understanding that I remain in the employ of Unified Earth, answerable to him and those he designates." He rolled his eyes at the term, since the divisions on Earth and in Orbit were so vast and multifaceted that nomenclature alone could never hope to solve them. But that was someone else's problem.

"I have autonomy in which passages I permit and which I

don't, under that sovereignty, and I don't trust anyone but Jeeta with power like this. Including the two of you." He always had a talent for making insults sound like statements of fact, since a statement of his opinion was not an insult, it was just relating a specific detail. "Even if I wanted to stop you from using the Twist, though, I couldn't. The mechanism is coded to certain portions of my genetic sequence and, consequently, to yours as well." He paused, looking at the two of them. "I don't trust you. Yet. But everything I have seen so far tells me that the correct course of action would be to give you the opportunity to earn that trust. And maybe the opportunity for you to learn to trust me again as well. Once I can complete two more mobile arrays, I'd like to ask the two of you to join me in fulfilling this function for the new government."

Jason stared back at him, trying to think three steps ahead when they both knew Charles had always been smarter. Charles couldn't fault the man for trying, though. It was what he would have done under the circumstances.

Xander, on the other hand, stared only briefly and then hung his head with a humorless laugh. "You know, when that thing blew up in the mountains, I was . . . I'm gonna say maybe five percent relieved. Not because it stranded everybody on the other side of the universe but because it meant I wouldn't have to fuck with that thing anymore. I should've known better than to think I could get off that easy."

"Yes, you probably should have." Jason agreed, without looking away from Charles. "If we agree to help, we'll be doing so under our own autonomy, beneath the UE sovereignty. I won't answer to you. Even if I do eventually decide to trust you."

"In design and execution matters, you will still defer to me." Charles had to walk a line. He couldn't let them or anyone else walk over him, but he had to give. That was what Jeeta had told him constantly. He had to give some things up in order to gain more. It was a method he had stayed away from his entire life, but he could reflect on the evidence of what that pattern had achieved and say honestly that he was finally open to alternatives. "There are still improvements I expect to make with regard to capacity and a number of other traits, but for everything related to design, you will consult me. You know I do not exaggerate when I say that a failure to do so could, and in all likelihood will, be catastrophic."

"In that case, you will defer to me when it comes to restrictions and favoritism when it comes to who gains access to it." Xander challenged, not even looking at Jason. "Let's face it, neither of you are exactly known for your people skills. It's gonna be a long list of people chomping at the bit to get access to the Twist for whatever reason. I'll do a better job gatekeeping that than either of you."

"And neither of you have the necessary expertise to judge the prioritization of its scientific applications." Jason interjected calmly, since they could all see how the balance was already shifting and settling between the three of them. "I will coordinate those efforts. Which means no one gets to start using it to go looking for new planets to settle on without consulting me first. Believe me, I've already started getting demands and offers."

Their eyes shifted back and forth between each other as they all contemplated the balance, but no one needed to firmly agree to know they had struck a kind of shaky and temporary equilibrium. It might never be easy, but all three of them knew that the other two were the closest thing they were ever likely to have to a friend in the world, aside from their own lovers.

"What's out there?" Xander eventually asked, looking pointedly at Charles. "Don't even pretend you didn't look."

Charles looked down at the ground, taking a shaky breath that shivered out of him rather than sighed. "The center is what would be expected." He eventually admitted. "The act of twisting space becomes distorted if the center is crossed too closely, I haven't had time to do more accurate measurements. I'm sure you'll do plenty of those." He nodded at Jason without meeting the man's eyes. "As for the edge, the closest one to us . . ." he shook his head. "What's out there made no sense, even to me. And though it pains me to admit it, I don't believe that answer is as important as coming to a better understanding of what's right here first."

It didn't take Jason long to nod his agreement. "Amen."

The three of them stood quietly against the wind, as if they were waiting for some force of nature to come along and separate them again, but none came.

None would come.

"No more running off." Xander eventually broke the silence. "For any of us. We're all that's left. We do this, we do it together."

Jason didn't have to contemplate that, since he and Jessie had made the decision to stay at the Bickford estate already, and he had no intention of ever abandoning his brothers the way they had once abandoned him. "No more running."

Agreement was more difficult for Charles, since he hadn't intended to offer up such a promise upon first meeting his brothers again. He was still tempted, at every moment, to take his technology and run with Jeeta to the other side of the world where they would never be found. That was why she had taken it with her, he knew, and she had been right to do so. They needed to rely on each other, the three of them. They were family, or at least they would try to be.

"No more running."

* * * * *

Like so much of the Bickford Estate, the dining hall was designed as if the original owners intended to feast the entire district all at once. Liam couldn't remember it ever used in a formal or celebratory meal, even during the ceremonies when he and Logan had their weddings. Until the house had been filled with rebels hiding out from the Consortium, the large hall had been an easy repository for furniture that wasn't wanted in other parts of the house, and a wide-open space in which he and Logan had played as children without the fear of breaking anything. One of their baseballs had come close once to hitting one of the beautiful high windows near the ceiling, but it had merely dented an impossibly-high light fixture instead. Liam could still remember how terrified and relieved they had both been at the time, but looking up at the dent in the ornate wall-lantern just made him smile.

The hall couldn't hold everyone who had descended on the estate, but someone (Rachel, he guessed) directed people to set up every table that could be found in the house all in one place so that the celebration of the Consortium's defeat could continue unabated, shared over food as every other good thing in the history of humanity had been. Down the center of the dining hall ran what seemed to be a single long table with a dozen differently-colored tablecloths uniting it.

The extreme end of it had been reserved for Liam and his family, but most of those already sitting at the central table were those who had played a leadership role in the events of the past few days. The entire Tanaka family was along one side, including

Aiko's parents and their three grandchildren, the Montgomery brothers had accepted seats close together, all of them and their significant others talking across the table as Jessie and Jeeta passed Bekah back and forth between them.

As Liam moved to take his own seat (Why did the end of the table have to be so far away? Walking was not his strong suit at the moment) he could see that his brother and Orion and Mercury and Anna had conspicuously avoided taking seats for themselves anywhere in the room. Logan held a plate in his hand as he moved from table to table, talking with everyone present. Mercury was with her parents at the side of the room, corralling her children and eating in between the bites that she could get her sons to take. Anna was with her own siblings, with Leo and Lynnette making the rounds of the entire Prince clan while she held onto Annabelle. Orion was nowhere to be found at the moment, but his parents and sister-in-law were at a small table to one side of the room, along with Orion's nephew.

The other Al-Jabbar that Liam looked for was also absent, but any thought of her quickly fled from his mind as he eased himself down into the chair at the head of the table with a sigh.

"Food." He said to no one in particular, rubbing his face once as he leaned forward gingerly on the table. "Food . . . is necessary."

Bree snickered from where she sat by the table, though she already had a plate in front of her and a baby at her breast, since she had a blanket covering one side of her body and one hand to eat with. Rachel and Gwen had the other monsters under control while she fed the newest monster herself. "You know you loved it." Bree replied with a satisfied grin, since she felt amazing and relaxed. She would need another round of Liam soon enough, though. "Better build your strength, Liam Bickford. A few hours does not make up for six months of abstinence."

When he groaned, Rachel showed up with a heaping pile of food since the toddlers were all strapped into high chairs and were relatively safe as they made a mess. Chrissy sat with Margo and Jela at another table. Liam told all of the girls that he had spoken with Margo and she was healthy and safe. They were all glad to see the proof, even if they didn't have much to say to her or her new husband. Especially because Margo was pregnant, which had happened much quicker than when she was with Liam. She was in a relationship that made her happy, though, and none of the other women would speak against that.

Rachel kissed the side of Liam's head as she handed him a fork and a spoon and put a cold beer down by his plate. "Round one."

He groaned again at the sight of the food, and leaned his head back to look up at Rachel gratefully. "You are my hero." He took Rachel's hand and kissed her knuckles gratefully before he started eating. He got a few bites in and then reached out to pull Anders closer against his corner of the table. He wasn't going to just let his wives do all the work when it came to their children. The little boy was almost two, and was fierce on the subject of mac and cheese. "Any more surprises pop up while I was in captivity?" He asked Rachel and Gwen, moving quickly to avoid getting kicked by Bree nearby.

"No more surprises." Rachel replied before Bree could say anything in reply to Liam's comment, and then she moved to give Beckett some more fruit before he got angry over his empty tray. "You better hush and eat your food before you get yourself into trouble." Gwen giggled and Bree gave Liam a look that said he better listen to wife #1 or he would regret it.

Bree and Gwen turned back to their meals before they noticed someone headed their way. Bree looked up to see a beautiful, tall, obvious-model walking directly toward them. "Hey, Liam, isn't that the girl that we talked about before? The model?"

Liam choked on the potato in his mouth as Bree mentioned a 'model', and he looked up to cough as he watched Khadi approach. Apparently she and her brother had been talking outside the dining hall, since Orion was on his way to sit with his parents and his sister-in-law with Leo now riding on his shoulders. Liam only briefly noticed that detail, however, as he watched Khadi get closer. "I, um, I don't know what you're talking about."

"You don't know what I'm talking about? Don't you listen when I talk? She took those crazy pictures . . . I know I showed you." Bree adjusted Dax under the blanket so that she could move him to her other breast. "Damn, who would have known she's related to Orion? I never would have guessed. I mean, I see it *now*, but damn . . ."

Gwen studied Liam's face a little between bites as Khadi and Orion got closer and it looked like they were going to walk past. She wasn't sure if Liam was going to say anything, but then he turned his attention back to his food.

"Liam?" Khadi said as she paused, even though she could feel Orion's glare on the back of her neck for a moment before he moved on to find a seat next to their parents. When Liam looked up, she just smirked. He looked so guilty it was hilarious. But also it was awkward. Wasn't it awkward? The last they'd spoken wasn't really speaking as much as angry making out and then all hell broke loose and she hadn't seen him since. He'd found his fiancee. "Just thought I'd stop and formally meet your family. I think I've spoken to some of you briefly."

He gulped, cleared his throat, and looked back and forth between Bree and Khadi. "Oh, *that* model. Right. I remember now." He cleared his throat a few more times and looked around the table. There was a reason he never played poker.

"This, um, everybody, this is Khadijah. We worked together on the whole rescue-plan thing. She was a lot of help in getting some of the stations to see things our way these past few weeks. Also, the blue hair was her idea, so if you're still not sold on it, you can partly blame her." Anything to get the spotlight off himself. "Khadi, this is Rachel, Bree, and Gwen. Also my boys Anders and Beckett. Dax is under the blanket there and Chrissy is over there with her mother." He gestured vaguely across the dining room toward Jela and Margo, where they were laughing at something Chrissy had done.

"Three boys and one girl, huh? The Y is strong with this one." She tried to joke, but she was just as awkward as he was. This was a bad idea. Clearly if he wanted to see her or even talk to her, he would have called out, but now he just looked guilty. He told her before that it didn't have to be a dirty little secret, but clearly that was a lie. "Well, nice to meet you. Liam is good on his feet. He pretty much organized the whole thing up there, getting the stations to work together and all that shit. I just convinced someone to have a meeting." She looked over the three women and let out a slow breath. "I'll see ya around."

"Wait, hey, you're a model, you can't just walk away like that." Bree reached out to grab Khadi's arm before she got too far. "I mean, it might be fun to *watch*, but don't just leave. I don't know how Liam could forget the pictures I showed him. You're so pretty! I mean, seriously. It's unnatural." The other women nodded since they were a little intimidated by her, which said a lot, since Liam knew how to pick his women.

"Well, to be honest, your husband, great as he is on the job, he's kind of an ass." Khadi said with a smug look. It felt like she was going to get in the last word, and she really liked getting in the last word. Since surely, guilty as he looked, he wouldn't shoot back a snarky response. "He basically told me it was unlikely I could even arrange a meeting, since my fame was no good. I mean, I *am* famous."

"Yeah, you are." Liam did, in fact, shoot back, looking up (way, *way* up) at the woman with the guilt quickly turning to pure snark on his face as he began to forget his present context a little. "And what motivates famous people more than anything else? Calling them out on what they are or aren't hot enough to get done. Sure as hell worked on you. Got you to actually get to work instead of whinging about how you weren't sure if she'd see us or you weren't sure if she would go for the plan or not. One little challenge to your Wow Factor and you were off and running to prove something." He sat back in his chair with one arm resting on the back of it, the spitting image of confidence. "Mission accomplished."

Khadi's glare only deepened as he sat back and looked like he won. "Seriously. I could just smack that grin off your face, Liam." She growled at him, and she clearly was not paying attention. "Are you trying to say I'm not hot enough? Because I am. Clearly. She went for it, and *she* even proposed."

"You are hot enough." Bree assured her while the other two remained quiet. "You're right, he's definitely a dumbass sometimes. I mean, clearly he's dumb enough to sleep with another woman and not even *warn* his wives that he bagged a model."

"I am not . . ." He sounded like he had something in mind to finish that sentence with, but it ended up just trailing off into ineffectual nothingness. "I'm . . . Okay, so I'm pretty stupid, but I'm not . . ." again, there was no recovering from the hole he'd gotten called out into, so he just stopped trying. "I . . . am not getting out of this with dignity. Anybody got a sword handy I can fall on? Anybody?"

Gwen laughed at that, as well as some of the people nearby who heard Liam get called out and Rachel shook her head before she stood up and held out her hand. "Nice to *officially* meet you, Khadi. Apparently Liam can't handle keeping his pants on. But we love him too much to get mad at him and his penis."

After that kind of response, Bree burst out laughing. Rachel was rarely *that* open, and it was hilarious. "Even Rachel!" Bree cackled even though she still had a baby at her breast, but Dax didn't seem to mind. "Okay, so I have to know, is he still as swoony for a first-timer as he was with us? Because Gwen has been around a while, her opinion is already skewed."

"Hey!" Gwen said as she gave Anders some more mac and cheese. "I'm not that much of a Liam-veteran! We're not even married yet! I just barely got this ring!" More people were paying attention and trying not to be obvious about it, but the women did not stop for Liam's benefit.

When Khadi floundered and couldn't come up with an answer, Bree decided to question her further. "I guess my real question is, did he woo you or did he just sleep with you? Cuz apparently he can't do one without the other if you look at his track record." She pointed to the other two women.

"I . . . uh . . . I mean, I never thought about this kind of arrangement before . . ." Khadi fumbled and tried to be honest without being a liar at the same time.

"Before you met Liam?" Bree pressed further.

"He didn't, like . . . he didn't propose or anything, but . . ."

"He better not have proposed to you before he proposed to me!" Gwen added as she thought about flinging the mac and cheese at Liam. "That's not even fair. I was in prison!"

"Dear God, Liam." Rachel scolded as she sat there next to him with her food still mostly untouched. "If you can't keep it in your pants can you at least stop making women fall in love with you? Seriously. We're not going past four. I refuse. No more than four. So turn off the 'fall-in-love with-me' crap. We can't let you out of our sight for anything."

"There's no 'fall-in-love-with-me' crap! There isn't!" Liam protested wildly, since he really hadn't been doing anything on purpose, as usual. He hadn't even liked Khadi until he had actually gotten to know her a little better.

He looked back and forth between all three of the women he was married or almost married to, attempting to defend himself from all sides at once. "There was no proposing, there was no arranging, and there was definitely no swooning. This one does not swoon. Swooning is not happening. I . . . I am gonna get another beer. Anybody want anything?" He held up his bottle, which still had a good amount in the bottom, then he seemed to realize he was still holding a partly-filled bottle. Liam chugged the rest before he held it up again and waited for requests like nothing had happened.

"You are not getting up." Rachel said in a tone that meant business, and Gwen hopped up instead.

"I'll get you another beer, Liam." Gwen looked both entertained and a little sympathetic toward Liam, but there was a twinge of jealousy too. Not because Liam may have thought about adding a fourth wife, but because she barely got him back and barely had a proposal. She didn't want to lose that 'newness' just yet.

"Why don't you sit down, Khadi?" Bree motioned to Gwen's open seat. "We'll make room for one more."

Liam knew his family was attracting stares, but his family always did that, it seemed. He had long since gotten past that part of it. He hadn't wanted to make a spectacle out of his own family drama, and had intended to talk through things with all of them later on, at least after all of their reunions.

As Khadi moved to take a seat, Liam leaned back in his chair and grabbed an empty one for Gwen right at the corner beside him for when she returned. The fact that Khadi sat down at all said a lot, and the look he gave her held volumes about the crap he was going to give her later for proving him right, but there in public was not the time or the place for it. "Thought you were planning on sticking around for a while on Three with Fatma?" Okay, maybe it was a *little* the time and place for it. "Change your mind?"

"Maybe I did." She replied softly, but her tone was still sharp. She didn't like him being right about anything, but clearly he liked to rub it in when he was. If they were going to have a relationship, it would be the craziest thing she ever did, but she was thinking it would be worth it. "You pretended you didn't know me." She hadn't looked at him after she sat down, but now she was. "It seems more like you changed *your* mind."

"I was giving you an out. Except that apparently if I bicker with somebody, it means I've slept with them, so that didn't work real well." He gave Bree a mildly accusatory glare, since she had been the one to call him out. Not that she'd been wrong.

"It wasn't the bickering." Bree finally pulled her now milk-drunk son off of her breast and covered herself back up before she wrapped him up in the blanket. "It was how you knew exactly what to say and do to poke and prod in all the right places. No one knows how to do that with a stranger."

Khadi looked at Bree and Liam and she sighed. "What if I

don't want an out? Do you still want me out?"

Liam shook his head and managed to smile at least a little, though he knew he was far from hearing the end of it from his other wives. "No, I don't." He knew that was a statement that fundamentally changed things for all of them, but he went on quickly. "Things are sort of chaos all around right now, and I know you're gonna be going back and forth to Three to help get things settled. If Logan hasn't tapped you to help out with that stuff yet for him, he will pretty soon. So I know you're gonna be back and forth." She was an Orbital, after all, which was one thing that made her fundamentally different from anyone else in his family, and from anyone else he'd ever been involved with in any way.

"We don't have anybody pointing a gun at our faces anymore, so we can take it as it goes." They had gotten to know each other pretty well during their time in orbit, but Khadi hadn't had a chance to get to know the rest of his family the way Gwen had before they'd gotten involved. If Khadi was going to be involved with him, she wasn't going to be involved just with him, but with the rest of those already attached to him.

"You should stay." Liam looked down at Anders beside him. The little boy had run himself ragged through the course of the day, and even with mac and cheese still in front of him, he was starting to nod off. "Here, help me with this guy real quick. I don't want him falling asleep face-first in his dinner."

When they managed to get the tray off the highchair and set the food aside, Anders started to fall forward as he nodded off, but Liam couldn't quite get to the buckles on the chair to get him out. When Khadi helped and managed to unclip the boy, his sleepy arms pushed Liam's away in favor of the softer, smoother skin that he recognized by nothing but touch. Anders reached out for Khadi with his little eyes still closed and a quiet whimpering cry beginning in his tiny chest, at least until she picked him up. Once she did, he laid his head down and was immediately still, heaving a tiny sigh as he started to relax into sleep on her shoulder.

Khadi looked over at Bree, and Bree just shrugged, since she already had a sleeping baby in her arms. Rachel was taking care of Beckett and Gwen was slowly making her way back with Liam's beer, but a lot of people were stopping her on the way.

"He looks pretty comfortable with you." Bree nodded toward Anders. "And we could use some more help, if you tell Logan where to stick it and stay with us."

Liam didn't contradict Bree's offer as he looked back over at Khadi with a nod. He knew the whole relationship was something new for her, and he was trying to make sure he wasn't pushing her into something faster than she wanted to be pushed. But he was quickly learning that with Khadi, pushing was the best way to make something happen. There just wasn't much guarantee of what would result from the pushing in the first place. "It's a big house. And I guarantee we've got everything down here that you had up there. Except Shine. That, we don't have. That, I am gonna miss."

"Yeah, sure." Khadi said softly so she wouldn't wake up the little boy on her shoulder. "I'll think about it. If you can find me a room that's my own but not in the way. And . . . we'll see if it can work."

"Alright." He agreed, smiling at the way she looked with Anders sleeping on her. She was back to dressing like the model she was, her clothes fancier and more elegant than just about anyone else's in the room, but standing out was one of the things she did best.

When Gwen got back to the table at last, Liam took the beer from her gratefully and put one hand across her lap to hold her close against him once she sat down. It was more than a little surreal, being surrounded by all four of them at the same time, but he knew he needed to start getting used to it at some point. "Thank you. *So* much." He took a long drink of the beer and sighed, not entirely sure what to say with Khadi now at the table. He just knew he wanted Gwen to be close so that they could hold onto what was between them, that he was looking forward to their wedding, and the celebration of a new beginning that it would be for them. "Everybody making jokes about how fast you'd sink to the bottom if you got tossed in the ocean?" He glanced down at the ring everyone had stopped her to see on her way back to him.

"A few. Mostly they're just happy for me, and probably because if I'm happy, their kids get better care." Gwen teased as she kissed Liam, even though he was still in the middle of a circus. "You're a lucky son of a gun. You have some gorgeous wives, you know."

"Oh, don't I know it." He agreed very quickly, looking around at Bree and Rachel to make sure they knew he included them in that thought. Bree at least was smiling a little bit, though Rachel still seemed both exasperated and yet amused about what was happening. "I am well aware that I am the single luckiest sonofabitch ever born. And yes, I am aware that for the foreseeable future, I am also going to be the most romantic and attentive sonofabitch ever born as well." He had never been particularly put in the doghouse by any of his wives, with the exception of Margo, but she was no longer with their family. Even so, he had never had it as a goal just to avoid the doghouse. He wanted to be living in the penthouse at all times. "I mean, that's an everyday thing for me under normal circumstances, but still, sometimes you have to punch it up a little more than others." Like when he had 'bagged' a model without warning his other wives first.

Rachel eventually leaned in closer and kissed Liam on the cheek before she whispered into his ear. "You've reached your limit, Liam Bickford. Do you hear me? I am not joking. I don't want to share you past three other women."

"I absolutely hear you." He said again, returning the kiss to her cheek before he met her eyes so she would know he was serious. "Believe me, I have no desire to be any more shared either."

"Good." Rachel sat back and slid Beckett out of his seat so she could hold him in her lap. She seemed calmer once she had Liam's word, and even a little more relaxed.

Gwen kissed his other cheek but remained in his lap, since she much preferred his lap to the other chair he'd put out for her. She was sure that no one really liked to share Liam except for maybe Bree, and even Bree had definitely kept Liam all to herself only hours ago. If they all wanted to make it work, it would work.

Bree patted the back of the baby on her shoulder and she just continued smiling over at Khadi. "So, tell me. Do *you* mind sharing? Cuz I had the hardest time getting some fun things going until Gwen showed up."

"Told you." Liam said to Khadi with a hint of a smile hitting the edges of his lips. It was hard not to smile with Gwen on his lap and Bree talking about 'fun things' happening. He looked back over at Bree with an easier smile. "I told her you wouldn't last five minutes without bringing it up, but I'm impressed. You made it almost fifteen."

Bree tossed her red hair with a grin. "You scrambled my brain a bit earlier. I'm still trying to get it back in working order." She raised an eyebrow at Khadi and smiled a little brighter. "You did say a woman proposed to you. Makes me wonder what you did to get that kind of offer."

"You don't have to answer that." Liam shot back at Khadi, though he was smiling, since he'd given Khadi grief about it himself. "This is Earth. You have the right not to incriminate yourself."

Khadi laughed softly. "I'll keep that secret for now. Maybe I'll share later. I think I've caused enough trouble for one day."

With things appearing temporarily defused, Liam took a few bites of his potatoes, since he didn't plan on making it all the way through the meal. He'd had a chance to get a shower after spending time with Bree, but he had more than worked up an appetite in the process, and he had no intention of taking any kind of break any time soon. Rachel hadn't been joking earlier when she said she was just as needy as Bree, just quieter. If anything, Rachel could be the most exhausting of his wives when she really wanted to be, and if the glares she was giving him were any indication, she really, really wanted to be.

It was going to be a long, but incredible week.

20

Every time Logan believed he was out of the craziest period of his life, the world turned up the voltage.

A month after the invasion of Prime, however, life finally, at long, *long* last, appeared to be settling down.

Relatively speaking.

"Let me say again how grateful I am for your help in the negotiations with the Americans, Prime Minister." It was a little strange for Logan to need help negotiating against those who should have been most eager to join up with the cause of Unified Earth. He lived right in the center of the North American continent after all, but there had been more than a few close calls between the UE district (which he and all his neighbors had declared to extend fifty kilometers from his estate in every direction, including the Prince farm and many others) and the North American Union to which the Midwest District had previously belonged.

Carl had deftly fended off the few violent threats that were extended to them by agents of the previous government keen on acquiring the Twist technology for themselves. Eventually the other governments of the world had helped put sufficient pressure on the NAU to leave the UE compound alone and give it the independence it required.

Logan knew he hadn't left the world much choice, and the world was slowly catching up with the same realization. Nothing could fight the Twist, and Charles had proven he was ruthless in the ways he could find to apply it, for good or ill.

"Without your diplomatic offerings, I'm afraid the conversation would have taken a great deal more wrong turns than it did, and I'm thankful that you were willing to lend it. If there is a way in which I can show that gratitude, Prime Minister, please don't hesitate to let me know." The woman had never given him permission to call her Gretchen, and so he hadn't, even after the victory on Prime and her formal recognition of his authority.

"Hm. Well, I felt it was owed and I felt as though it was necessary, of course. I don't make decisions lightly. Prime Minister." He was a leader in his own right, of course. She certainly wasn't the only Prime Minister in existence. "Are you calling me simply to thank me, or is there more involved here, Mr. Bickford?"

"Logan, please." He said with a smile, since it wasn't the first time he asked her to call him by his first name. "No, this call was just to thank you. I believe the parliament is coming together nicely since the NAU came on board, and I expect it will be full soon. I'm glad that we can be friends now that we're on the other side of all this, and I look forward to working with you in the years to come. Seems like enough of a reason to warrant a phone call to me."

"Interesting." She said in her same annoyingly calm voice. "Well, I appreciate the call. I know as well as you do that every minute of every day is a busy one. And you have small children."

"I think it'd be more accurate to say they have me, but that's children in general." He gave a genuine laugh, unafraid of what she might think of him for such a flippant emotion. "I'll let you go, then, Prime Minister. I'll notify you when the suite for your ambassador is ready."

"Thank you. Our ambassador is eager to make her way to you, as are most, I think. You've changed the world, Mr. Bickford. Everyone is keen to know where you are interested in seeing it go from here." The prime minister could be heard typing in the background as soon as he mentioned leaving her to her work. She almost never stopped working. "Until we speak again, Mr. Bickford."

"*Tot de volgende keer*, Prime Minister." He said with a smile he hoped she could hear, then closed the call. She was the last phone call he needed to make that morning, so he slid the communicator away from him on his desk. As far as he was concerned, he couldn't get the thing far enough away. He knew the feeling wasn't likely to go away any time soon.

The house began to feel empty again after most of the rebels returned to their own native lands, but it didn't approach the feeling of emptiness it had held for most of his childhood. Cory and Larissa had made it their personal project to transform the place back from a refugee camp overrun by people into a home again, and even in the space of just over a month, they'd done an exceptional job.

Logan himself had taken over an entirely new suite of rooms than the ones in which he'd grown up. The rooms prior held too many memories of his life before the Initiative, and besides, there had been no good place to house the children near him in those rooms. His new suite had a bedroom, a living room, a full suite of four guest bedrooms, and a door to lock it away from the rest of the house. Just beyond it was his office, accessible from his new bedroom, and beyond that, the rest of the damned universe, which always seemed to be waiting for him as soon as he opened the door.

"Good morning, Renata." His smile wasn't going anywhere anytime soon after the conversation with the Nordic Prime Minister, even if his plans for the rest of the day were mildly terrifying, at least in some respects. "Please let Charles know I'm requesting his presence in the gate room at his convenience, no hurry." He pulled on the coat that hung on its designated hook next to the door, shrugging it over his shoulders and relishing the feeling. The coat Larissa made him had been with him through everything but his torture on Prime, and life just felt right when he wore it. Besides, it was going to be chilly on Eleusis. "What do you think, Renata? Care to stroll across the galaxy for the afternoon? Have a look at construction?"

"Just a stroll, huh, Sir?" Renata chuckled and shook her head. "I still have a lot to do this morning, my boss keeps me pretty busy. I'm not sure he'll let me off for a 'stroll'."

"Well, I won't tell him if you won't." Logan said from the door with a last smile. "You're my chief of staff now. That gives you plenty of room to make people concerned requiring quality inspection results, asking pointed staffing questions and generally making people nervous. Come on, you know that sounds like fun."

"Yes, doing inspections sounds like great fun." She teased as she shook her head again. "Mercury was hoping to go, you know. She told me she wanted to check on the birthing facility. She didn't say anything to you because you told her it was going to be called the Finnegan wing. I don't know that she cares for that."

He sighed. That had probably been a step too far, but he wasn't sure he was willing to take it back after the ground on the wing had already been broken. "In my defense, she *did* design it." He shook his head and went for the door. "I'll talk to her and make sure she comes along. Try not to think less of me if I decide to cave on the subject of the name."

Renata watched him carefully since she, like everyone else, was curious who their fearless leader would end up being with. Or maybe he wanted to live the single life for the rest of his life. No one could tell for sure. "Or Anna. Anna has been working with designs for the residential areas. Maybe she could go with you?" He didn't have a tell. He was so hard to read.

"I should probably bring Orion too. Carl and Aiko are already there, so that would cover all projects under construction. Administrative, Medical, Residential, Research, and the air strip." He gave her a smile as he saw her eyes narrow at him slightly. "Please let those on this side of the galaxy know that I'll be waiting for them in the gate room."

"Not even a little crack? I mean, come on!" Renata sighed as she started contacting the parties he requested. "Everyone wants to know, you know."

"Is there a pool going?" He asked from the doorway. "I know of several from the press, but I mean here, among the local staff."

"If there is, I'm not in it." Renata looked up from her ever-present tablet. "I just want to know. You all just . . . went your separate ways. Except you haven't. You've seen both women on dinner dates a few times. Gone on walks with both. It's ridiculous how fair all of you have been. I don't even know what to think."

"Excessive fairness. Hm. I've been accused of a lot of things in my life, but never that. I don't think." He wanted to ask Renata what her thoughts were, but he valued their friendship and wanted her to remain in the dark a bit longer. "I'll say this, I promise you'll be the first person I notify beyond my own family if a decision is made. Does that help at all?"

"No. Not really." She replied honestly before she tapped on her tablet a few more times. "I've notified all the parties you've requested to meet you at the gate. Sir." She said with a slightly annoyed expression, even though she knew she had absolutely no right to prod him about his personal life. "Eventually I'll need to know numbers for my wedding, you know. If you're going to bring a plus-one or not."

"I will keep you informed." He said with a final laugh before he headed down the hallway. He respected the woman greatly, but sometimes nettling her was just too much fun to pass up.

He passed the room where Anna was staying on his way, and

came down the hall just as she was closing it behind her, apparently having received his message.

"Nice day for a trip across the vastness of space, don't you think?" He had his hands in the pockets of his coat as he walked, looking more like his old self than she had seen him in a long time. His hair was growing out again, as was his beard, and he'd gained back some meat on his bones instead of being so unhealthily wiry as he had been forced to become on Prime. The grey in his eyes was lighter than she had seen since they first went to join the Initiative, the storm having passed with the battles they won together.

"It is for me. The gravity there isn't as heavy as it is here. Or it doesn't feel that way." She laughed as she looked down at her still-growing belly. It wouldn't be much longer before she would have a newborn of her own, while Mercury's twins were already a month old. "And it's nice and chilly there right now. Just what this pregnant woman needs."

"Getting to that part of it, huh?" He hadn't had the chance to be with Mercury during the latest stage of her most recent pregnancy, but he'd been with her through the first, and as smooth as everything had gone for her with the boys, she had still been fairly miserable for roughly the last month. "You could go up and see one of the stations for a while if you wanted, you know. I'm sure Doc Weber would be glad to have you as her houseguest on Seven for a while, plus I thought I saw something about Sierra being pregnant right now too. Plenty of commiseration and no gravity to make you feel miserable."

Anna shook her head without even looking up at Logan. "No, no space stations for me. Nothing about being in space brings good feelings to me, not now. I'd rather be miserable on a planet, either Earth or Eleusis."

"That's fair." They passed a sitting room that looked out toward the fields where construction projects were well under way on the administrative center for the Unified Earth government. It was something new, and he was looking forward to seeing how it would shape things for decades to come. Maybe even centuries.

"One of the reasons why I always have them come to me. Plus it's kind of fun watching them struggle if they're accustomed to lower gravity." He knew that wasn't the most charitable way to feel, but not all the station captains were excited about the new regime, even the ones who had fought alongside him in the takeover.

"Well, people should get used to things everywhere, right? Earth, Space, Eleusis . . . we're all supposed to be one big, happy family eventually." She smirked and looked over at him finally. "Good thing we're pros at all of it."

"Speak for yourself. I'm still one short on that list." She had given him grief about it once upon a time, but that had been a very different life. A very different set of circumstances. "Today is the first trip I'll have made to Eleusis. Even if I was ten steps away from it about a hundred times back in the mountains."

"Well, I'm glad you decided to join in on the fun." Anna replied with a smile before she glanced down at her communicator when it beeped. "Why is Renata asking me if I'm your plus-one to her wedding? I didn't know she was getting married!"

Logan rolled not just his eyes, but his entire head, even though he was smiling. "She's moved on from dropping strong hints to giving me outright grief at the continuation of this . . . situation. Apparently it's the water cooler gossip of the entire government that the four of us still aren't married. And yes, she and Pete are getting married in . . . I want to say June. She put it on my calendar already, I've forgotten. Nice guy. Pretty terrified of me. You know, just the way I like them."

Now it was Anna's turn to roll her eyes. "Well, I'm not terrified of you, Logan Bickford." She reminded him before she went back to smiling at him. "Everyone wants to know your business because you're the Prime Minister now. If you don't pick a First Lady, then you're going to get a shit-ton of offers." She teased as she reached out to grab his hand and squeeze it gently. "I think we've all done this the right way. Taking things slow between the four of us. Figuring shit out without genitals touching. That's the hard part."

"That has absolutely been the hard part." He agreed, but he was also in agreement with what she said overall. It hadn't been something that the four of them exactly sat down and had a meeting about, but while everyone had been expecting them to pair off and ride off into separate sunsets, they had all taken a step back into their own families and their own renewed lives in the new world, so that they could see that world clearly enough to think about what mattered.

The kids flowed between all four of them in an almost comic circle of shared custody, but Logan certainly hadn't minded. He loved them all, even the ones that didn't belong to him by blood, because he loved their mothers. "I do think we've been doing it the right way, but I don't think any of us have any intentions of doing it for much longer." He said as they got closer to the gate room. He didn't mean for it to come off as ominous as it did, but it was an important decision. One that would shape all of their lives, since they all silently agreed in every glance that the choice would be the last of its kind.

"Yeah, I think it's nearly time to make some kind of decision. I'm not made for abstinence." She teased as she squeezed his hand before she looked up at Logan with a grin. "Can I get a kiss at least?" Anna smiled and raised her eyebrow after she requested the kiss.

They all might have been celibate for a month, but that didn't mean they had been cold. Logan put an arm around her waist to pull her into a warm kiss. It was always good to see Anna, and it was even better to be close to her.

Anna smiled after the kiss and looked into Logan's eyes. It was good to feel . . . almost normal again. Logan was her longest and closest friend. She never wanted to lose that. "You're pretty amazing, Logan Bickford. I'm lucky to have you in my life, no matter what happens."

"You're your own kind of amazing, Anna Jeanine Prince." He kissed her one more time for good measure, grinning the whole time. "This time the middle name isn't because you're *in* trouble, it's because you *are* trouble. Not that that's new information for you at this point."

She just shook her head, even though she was still smiling. "Don't go around using that middle name too much. I don't want the kids to pick it up and the next thing I know, I'm hearing Anna Jeanine all the time." She laughed softly before she looked down at her belly. "But you're right. I am trouble. Never gonna change." She kissed the back of his hand and then kept walking with him hand in hand. "Mercury and Orion coming too?"

"If they're awake. I know Orion had a late flight last night before he Twisted in, but hopefully they'll be along. I want his opinion on the air strip and I need him to check out some of the drone work that Jason recovered last week." Talking about Orion's work made it easier to answer the question, though he knew he wasn't answering it fully. "I've also been informed that Mercury is less than happy with me for naming the birthing center wing after her, so I want to make sure she has the chance to yell at me as soon as possible."

"Mercury? Yell? Is she capable of that? I can't imagine her raising her voice for anything." Anna paused. "Okay, sure, maybe some things but I don't want to know those details. Regardless, I can't imagine her yelling at *you*. Why did you name the wing after her if she didn't want you to? That seems like a bonehead thing to do."

Logan rolled his eyes again. "It's a pretty commonly-known fact that I took my current position by conquest. Not because I'm smart or qualified in any way. Bonehead is one of my many middle names."

When Mercury got the call to meet in the gate room, she was in the middle of a meeting with Jason and Jessie regarding the fact that they hadn't been able to conceive any more children. She had just given them the results of their testing, and Jason looked over at Jessie with accepting resignation. "Well, I have to say, that figures. I should have known they were shooting me full of something during the Initiative." It turned out that Jason's body didn't naturally do most of the things a body was supposed to do. "So how does it come, then, shots? Pills?"

"Oral medication in the form of pills would be less invasive, though I'm not certain they would be equally effective. I can use the same dosage of liquid that the Initiative used, though the side effects might be more apparent. It would probably be my suggestion, though, to go with a liquid. You might experience increased hormonal reactions, though. Possibly increased aggressiveness, libido . . ."

"Increased libido is . . . difficult for me to conceptualize at this point." Jason said with a grin, though he doubted Jessie would thank him for being so frank about their sex life. They were talking to a doctor, after all.

Jessie shook her head but she didn't make any further comment about the libido issue. "Will it harm him to have to take the medication? It's not worth it if he's going to be harmed."

"There's no lasting side effects that I've seen if it's used for less than six months. After that, if you still have difficulties, we'll discuss another route. I don't think you'll have to wait long with the proper dosage."

"Liquid dosage and increased libido . . . you're right, I doubt we'll make it quite to six months." Jason smiled again and squeezed Jessie's hand. "Thank you, Doctor. As always." He stood and shook Mercury's hand, thinking back to the first time they had met and the trust they showed in each other during their days in the Initiative. It had been a long road since then, for all of them.

"Of course, Mr. White." She said with a kind smile as she glanced over at her communicator and she shook her head before she went to escort Jason and Jessie out. "Looks like I'm being asked to go to Eleusis. This should be interesting."

"There was a time when that would have been a highly unusual request." Jason said with a laugh. "As it is, I'll just say have a pleasant trip and plan to be home by dinner. I hear Carl brought back a couple of blue-backed herbivores that Aiko and the others haven't quite decided on a species name for yet, but is supposed to be delicious." Jason smiled until they got out into the waiting room of Mercury's temporary clinic, where they could see Orion in a chair that was clearly too small for him, waiting with a pained expression on his face.

Mercury was immediately concerned when she saw the pained expression. "Orion? Is everything okay?"

"Do you . . ." he asked slowly ". . . have anything . . . to cure . . . a very . . . very acute hangover?" He asked slowly, eventually opening his eyes to look up at her. "I asked Barry if he brought some Banana Juice down from orbit, but he said he used up the last of his supply during all the celebrations a month ago and hasn't restocked."

"Come in here." She shook her head, still smiling a little. She did not enjoy seeing Orion in pain, but she did enjoy seeing him in general. Once he was in her clinic and she said goodbye to the Whites, she closed the door and went to her personal pharmacy. It was locked in three different ways to prevent anyone breaking into it, but eventually she found what she was looking for. "This is something Aiko modified. It should be fast-acting, according to her. What were you celebrating now?"

"Not celebrating." He took the shot of green liquid and cringed at the taste, but he hadn't specified he needed medicine that tasted good. That was an impossibility he'd long since given up on. "Well, kind of celebrating. Khadi needed to talk through her complicated love life after I got back from my red-eye, and that girl drinks more than I do. I think if somebody gave me a choice between being a giant and having a high alcohol tolerance, I'd have taken the alcohol."

"No one said you had to drink with her." Mercury said with a laugh but she laughed softly so she wouldn't cause him any more pain. She went and got a cold drink from a small refrigerator. "Drink this too. You need to re-hydrate. This is fortified with electrolytes and vitamins."

"Thank goodness for people with functioning brains." He downed the glass quickly and headed toward the hallway with her. "I hear we've been summoned by His Majesty." He said through still-squinting eyes. "Was that a hangover-induced hallucination, or was that real?"

"No, that was real." She watched him just to make sure he was okay. "He wants to go to Eleusis. I don't know why today of all days. He's never been. I haven't either."

Orion walked beside her in silence for a minute as they headed down the hallway. His eyes opened a little more with every step they took, and by the time they were two wings away from where they had started, he was looking a little more like his usual self.

"I'm glad you're going now, instead of before." He smiled and put an arm around her shoulders beside him to hug her against his side playfully as they walked. "If you'd gone before, you'd have been required to have a gun in your hands. Even if I know for a fact you can kick some ass when necessary, that doesn't mean I'd ever want to see you need to. Peacetime is a much better time for a visit."

"I'm no good with a gun." She shook her head and sighed. "Logan wants to name the birthing center the Finnegan Wing. That's too much, right? It sounds terrible."

"I think it sounds great." Orion knew that probably wasn't the answer she wanted to hear, but it was the one he had to give anyway. "It's the first hospital on Eleusis. You're lucky he didn't try to name the whole thing after you and call it good."

"Did you talk to him about this? Did you two decide this was a good idea together?" Mercury's smile turned into a small glare. "I know I'm a good doctor, but a lot of people are good doctors. I don't need that kind of recognition. I didn't do anything special. Most of the revolution I spent delivering babies and being saved over and over again."

"I think the whole 'delivering babies' thing is why he decided to name the place where people deliver babies after you, actually." He shrugged, smiling at her instead of returning the glare. "The getting rescued thing . . . they don't usually name things after people for that, but that's not something to hold against a person either."

"I don't know, the both of you nearly died too many times just to rescue me. I think it's something to hold against someone." She shrugged as well, but she reached out to loop her arm through his, since she wanted to be close to him and keep him from falling over at the same time. He looked like he was getting better with each step, but she wanted to make sure he was alright. "Do you want to stay over and help with the girls tonight? I still haven't been able to convince them to take a bottle during the night."

"Sure, I can do that." He squeezed her arm against his side and chuckled at the thought of the girls. "They just prefer you to something artificial. Can't say I blame them for that."

Mercury laughed as well and jabbed his side gently with one of her fingers. "They take a bottle just fine when they have to go to the care center. It's only when they know I'm around, the little princesses." She laughed again. "But it's hard to keep up sometimes. It's easier when I have help, especially if the boys are there too. Though they're getting a little better at sleeping through the night."

"Now they are. Can't say I'll miss all the wakeups once they fully sleep through." He sighed afterward, though, since he probably would miss it. A little. He'd had a lot of long nights with the boys when he and Mercury were together, but that felt like another lifetime. "The princesses have only been around a month. Give 'em a little more time before they're willing to close their eyes on the world for very long. Or on you."

"Makes me feel a little bit like a milk machine or something." She said with a small laugh. "Anyway, they're fine for now, or so I'm assuming. I haven't heard anything otherwise. But I still don't want to go to Eleusis and see 'Finnegan Wing' on the construction site."

"I don't think they've gotten to the signage yet. I'd be impressed if they had." He opened a set of double doors for her to get out into a main artery of the house, opulent and spacious as everything else in the mansion.

"No matter what we do," he said a little more thoughtfully, "no matter what we say or do about it now, I've seen . . . a lot of things this past month about us. Khadi keeps herself on top of everything that's running around in the media, but all of us are already turning into legends. And every time the Montgomeries manage to completely remove their pictures from the web, they just get more famous. The birthing center on Eleusis is the least of the things that are going to end up being named after us, I'm afraid. Not much we can do about that. People know too much about all of us."

"I wanted to be known as the doctor who cures CV. Not that I wanted to be famous, but that I wanted to make an impact on humanity in that way. This is just . . . being a victim and a speculated love interest for the two infamous men of the rebellion. I wanted to be remembered and known for something good." She sighed and looked down at her feet. "There's plenty of other research to dedicate my time toward, research about you and our children. But I spent so much of my life studying CV. It's just something I need to get past."

CV still wasn't cured, and no one really had an answer as to how, but they did know the answer to the mystery behind CV's origin. If the Alperts had known of an antidote, apparently it had died with them. And CV had adapted and mutated enough as a present toxin to eradicate it without more information.

He knew the revelation of CV's true nature had haunted Mercury ever since the victory over the Consortium, but he'd never pushed her to talk about it. "I felt a little bit of that when I found out about the Twist, back on Nine." He admitted, walking slower. "It was like I had been irrelevant for half my life and I just hadn't read the memo. I wanted to be the guy who flew the ship that got us to a new world." He shrugged, since he'd had a long time to get past his own failed expectations. He knew it was still very new for Mercury.

"I don't think it's something you need to get past. The only reason you're not going to be remembered as the doctor who cured CV is because there was no actual infection. You will, however, be remembered as the doctor who figures out how to cure the planet of it. The way I hear it, there's a shitload of atmospheric scientists and biologists who've been trying to work out how to leech the chemical out of the world's ecosystems and so far they've got shit to show for it."

"I don't know if I'll even be able to accomplish that, but I'll try." Mercury held his arm a little bit tighter before she looked up at him again. "How are you feeling? It seems as though Aiko's 'hangover cure' is helping."

He glared at her a little for the abrupt change of topic, but if she didn't want to discuss it any further, then he wasn't going to push it. "I'm good. I'm a little lightheaded, actually, so I think it's working a little *too* well, but I imagine that's because she formulated it to work on Carl, not on people half his weight. That man should be able to drink if anybody can, but he's probably the biggest lightweight I've ever seen." He grinned down at her. "I'm fine, though. A little lightheaded I can handle compared to some of the shit I've had to deal with."

They were getting close to the ornate lobby Logan had designated as the gate room, where Charles or one of his brothers typically worked with the Twist dispensations. It was heavily guarded by several people Orion and Kameron had designated as trustworthy, but Orion knew that in case of any kind of foul play, the person holding the Twist would be the most dangerous person in existence no matter what guards they had around them.

Mercury slowed down as they got closer. "I don't think I'm ready to go to Eleusis." She said abruptly, but she usually wasn't one who showed her fears so easily. Around Orion, though, she was clearly a little more open. "I . . . what if something bad happens? I can't leave my children again. I can't lose them."

"We don't live in that world anymore." He stopped with her so that he could look her in the eye and hold both her hands. "I've been back and forth to Eleusis a dozen times in the last month, just looking over the site and visiting Carl and Aiko. Charles . . . I mean, I thought I was done meeting people so smart they scare me after you and I got married. Holy shit was I wrong about that. There's nothing to be scared of. We're gonna go there, look over things, and be back in time for dinner. I know how crazy it sounds, but that's the world we live in now. The world is full of crazy. No place more than this house, I think."

Mercury nodded, even though she was still dealing with severe emotional baggage. Apparently being hunted and kept prisoner was enough to crack a person, and she was still trying to figure out what to do with herself afterward. "Are you sure, though? Are you really sure that we don't live in that world anymore?" Mercury wasn't sure, even though an entire month had passed in peace.

"I'm as sure about that as I am about anything else." He didn't try to move them any closer to the gate room, lingering in the hallway for a while just to be around Mercury alone a bit longer. "I think Logan would like to believe the Consortium was over the second he pulled the trigger. I think most of the world would like to believe that, me included. But no one's that stupid, including Logan himself. I know there's been some problems with the remnants of the fleet they dispatched and some clear problems in the Central African territories, but it's different than it was. The ideas and the people aren't just gone overnight because they lost, but I still believe it's fundamentally a different world now. I'm not saying we don't still need to lock our doors, but I don't think there's any need for nightmares. There's too much to be excited about, too much new going on to be afraid."

"I never used to be afraid of the unknown." Mercury admitted as she turned herself toward Orion and stepped into him for comfort. When he pulled her in easily, she buried her face into his shoulder and turned her face to kiss along the side of his neck. "I don't want to be now. Easier said than done."

"Saying is always easier than doing, seems like." He said in a light tone, holding her tightly. He returned the kiss to her cheek, long fingers reaching up to comb through her hair as he held her. "It's gonna be a long while before we all really stop looking over our shoulders. But what's important, at least to me, is that I don't believe that's the kind of world our kids are gonna grow up in. Not the way we did, and not the way the others did down here either. It's gonna be a better world for them than it's been for us, and we made that happen."

Mercury nodded slowly and just let him hold onto her before she tilted her head back just enough to look into his eyes. She moved closer to kiss his lips gently, but there was still quite a bit of emotion behind the kiss. "Thank you for being strong for all of us."

"If all this has taught me one thing, it's that I'm not as strong as I thought I was." He thought back to all the times on Eleusis that he'd kept going out of sheer desperation and nothing else, and shook his head as he kissed her again. "The times when I was, it's been because I had good reasons. You being one of them."

Her expression of concern softened as soon as he mentioned that she was a good reason for him, and she kissed him a few more times. "Do you think we've been doing the right thing to make a decision between the four of us? Taking our time? Going back and forth between pairings? It seems like a logical way to do things, but I don't know if 'logical' means 'best'."

"I think it's the first time in all of this that any of us have really had the chance to think through things because we *want* to, instead of needing to on some level." He smiled, thinking back, and his arms looped around her waist as he slouched against the wall to be at her level, as always. "Not that I needed any kind of force when I first met you. But we both submitted ourselves to the Match program because the Initiative deadline was coming up. Nothing wrong with that, but it had its own ticking clock behind it. That's one period of my life where I've got no regrets. Not many of those around. But I think it's good that we've been giving ourselves some room to take a breath. I'm not sure if there's just one way I could say is the 'best' when it comes to something like this, but I think we've done what we all need. That's good enough for me."

"I suppose you're right." She agreed before she smiled and kissed him again with one of her hands running across his cheek. "There's no best with this. A decision has to be made eventually." Looking into Orion's dark eyes gave her confidence and usually a smile, so she eventually stood up a little straighter and tried to look as though she felt confident. "Alright. We should go, I suppose."

Orion nodded and stood back up to his own full height, looking down at her as he left a caress on her cheek. "I love you." He said as the preamble to a gentle kiss. "We're going to be alright, all of us and all of the kids. You'll see."

"I sure hope so." She slid her hand into his before they started walking again, even though it was a short distance away.

When they got into the gate room, though, Charles was the only one present, tinkering at his ever-present workbench where he was constructing who knew what. The Twist he used lay nearby, one large wall of the sizable room standing blank and slightly scarred from the inevitable heat that was produced at the Twist's initial opening.

"His Majesty is late to his own party. As usual." Charles said without even looking up. Doubtless he had seen them coming on one of the several security monitors at the side of the room. Anna and Logan were pictured on one of them, talking in a hallway the same as Orion and Mercury just had been. "Good thing you two brought coats. It's fairly chilly on Eleusis today. Tonight. It's about half an hour from sunset where you're going."

"I really don't think he enjoys being called 'His Majesty'." Mercury said with a slight frown as she looked at Charles, but she tugged on her coat and buttoned it up over her scrubs. "Are they close? Part of pretending to be brave means not standing around and waiting."

"I know a little about that, oddly enough." Charles still didn't look at her when he spoke, just as he rarely condescended to look at anyone, but he did slip on the Twist with another glance at his monitors. "Yes, they're close. And the other side has already been notified." He keyed in a few things and inspected a final, dizzying display in the air in front of him, then flicked his fingers toward the blank wall.

It glowed red with a latticework of warning light that did no harm, then the air split in the spiraling gate that no one in their right mind ever really got accustomed to. It warped the world and screamed it was just wrong to every sense, but it quickly stabilized, and appeared to be nothing more than a frameless gateway between the room they were in and a grassy spot just outside the walls of the compound. "You two can get a head start or you can wait. I get paid either way." He went back to work tinkering, completely ignoring both them and the wonder of his own creation in favor of whatever problem he was presently working to solve.

Mercury looked back as though she would see Logan walk into the room, but when she didn't see him, she looked up at Orion again and held his hand tighter. "Alright, well, you'll have to lead the way."

Orion held her hand, but he was still looking at the monitor as well before he stepped through, taking in a deep breath of Eleusis air. The differences between Eleusis and Earth were usually subtle, but that difference in the air, he could have taken a breath with his eyes closed and his ears stopped and still knew where he was.

They took a few steps to get clear of the Twist, but Orion looked over at her with a smile as if they had just completed a voyage of a hundred years. "Welcome to paradise, Mercury. It's had some trouble recently, but I still think it deserves the title."

Mercury was greeted with a chill that she hadn't really expected, but Eleusis really was breathtakingly beautiful. She looked around at the vibrant colors, even in the fading sunlight, and she could see the construction off in the distance as well as hear the sounds of people working amongst all the other sounds of Eleusis.

She wondered what it would look like in the spring if it was so colorful even when things were dying off, but she knew that eventually she would actually see the spring for herself as well.

Eventually, when the infrastructure was built for the hospital and some residential areas, Mercury thought it would be good to live on Eleusis, at least for half the year. That way she could go back and forth between Earth and Eleusis, since she still wanted to do work on Earth too, especially to eradicate the CV toxin. "It really is beautiful."

"Told you so." He nudged her playfully as she took it all in, watching the wonder in her eyes with a smile. It was good to see the razor edge of wondrous curiosity find its way back into her expression, however tenuous or foregrounded with fear it was for the moment. He was about to say something else, but they heard a door open behind them on Earth, and he glanced backward at the Twist as Anna and Logan came through, obviously a little surprised to see the two of them already on the far side of it.

Logan stood there for a moment looking through at Mercury and Orion, heaving a slow sigh at the incredible distance between them that they could overcome with a single step. "Thank you, Charles."

"Of course, Your Majesty." Charles still didn't look up from his other work, but gave them a dismissive wave to forestall any further attempts at conversation.

Logan glanced down at the first step of Eleusis turf with obvious trepidation, but he eventually looked down at Anna. "Shall we take a walk, then?"

"What do you want to see first?" Anna said as she kept holding onto Logan's hand, but she smiled at Orion. "Newbies." She said loudly enough for him to hear, since both Logan and Mercury still looked awed.

Logan took his first steps onto Eleusis soil and sighed unconsciously, as if he'd been afraid it would burn him upon arrival. "I . . . I think everything would be a start. I'd like to see everything." He smiled at Anna, and at Mercury when he said it. He even had a pleasant, if distant, nod for Orion as the man towered above all of them.

"As much as I'd like to see everything, though, I should probably have a walk through the compound and have a look at construction. Besides, I'm told I'm scheduled to get yelled at this morning. Evening." He glanced at the sky and shifted his frame of reference as if the entire day had gone by already, then looked over at Mercury with a warm smile.

They remained paired off but started walking together toward the compound, even if it was slightly awkward. "I'm not going to yell at you." Mercury finally said to break the silence. "I don't know why Renata told you, but regardless, I don't think the wing should be named after me. I'm not a hero."

"I think that depends on who you ask." Logan said quietly in his own defense, but he was still smiling. "Besides, things don't usually get named after heroes. They get named after people who are important to their founding. And you are. Most of the people who've been given First Right either had you deliver their babies or they're going to live longer lives because you were the one who thought to get CV immunization supplies before we hightailed it off Nine."

Logan had allowed very little talk of colonizing Eleusis so far, since he wanted to take the time to consult with the various governments of Earth and Orbit and push them for real unification before he allocated colonization resources or permitted Twists to the planet. So far it was working, but one concession he made was with those who had survived the Initiative and fought directly in the rebellion against the Consortium. Those had First Right of occupation, and he had drawn all the engineers and workers for the compound's reconstruction from that group.

Most of those they passed as they strolled into the compound raised a hand in greeting, and Logan smiled at all the faces he recognized, even if they kept their distance. "They'd end up naming something after you. If not the birthing wing, I've heard talk of naming one of the northern-hemisphere archipelagoes after you. The soil in the pictures is this ridiculously bright red and so are some of the plants and flowers, just to blend in. They might do it anyway, even with the hospital." He doubted she would find it amusing, but the fact made him smile regardless.

Mercury shook her head. "You can stop those things from happening, you know. You just don't want to." She continued glaring at him for a moment longer before she went back to looking around. "Well, I can't stop it from happening, but I can say that I would prefer not to work in a place named after me. I don't need that kind of pressure. I'm already feeling enough stress just being here."

Logan gave her a sympathetic look, but didn't say anything else for the time being. One of the construction supervisors came up to him and handed off a report that he vaguely remembered asking for the day before.

"I think I'm gonna go check out the airstrip." Orion said as he began to pull away. "Maybe take a look in the hangar and see what Charlie and the others decided to pull out of the Moroccan station last week." He glanced between all three of them, but eventually, his eyes settled on Anna. "Feel like taking a look?"

Mercury pulled her arm from Orion's so he didn't feel responsible for keeping her sane and calm, since she knew she had to handle her own emotional issues. She gave him a small smile when Anna agreed to go with him, and she gravitated toward Logan even though he was looking over a report.

Anna squeezed Logan's hand and moved away so she could go with Orion to check out the airstrip. They were the two that knew how to fly a shuttle, after all, Orion being much more skilled at it than she was. "Do you think we can test something out? It's not completely dark yet."

"You read my mind. You should be careful how you do that." He smiled at her as they rounded a corner, the hangar and the air strip beyond coming in sight. There wasn't much to the place as of yet, and the air strip was far from the most complicated thing under construction. It was going to be a little over a kilometer in length by the time they were finished with it, but at the moment it was nothing more than a bare and sand-packed strip of bare earth. There were no crews working on it in the fading light, but there were a few men and women working in the hangar who greeted Orion and Anna both when they came in sight.

"Hey, Rosetti, did they get the pods last week like they were saying they were going to?" Orion asked as he took the man's hand briefly.

"Yeah, yeah, we got six of 'em." Rosetti answered with a smile that knew something, though he refrained from saying exactly what. "Got one already prepped that just came back off a shot out to one o' the islands. Tanaka wanted some samples brought back, usual drill, nothing messy. She's all set for ya if ya want it."

"Sounds good, haul it out." Orion grinned at the sight of the mostly-glass pods on their storage racks. They were one of the first things he'd learned how to fly and one of the first things he'd taught Anna to fly as well, and it felt a little more like home whenever he had one around. "You still remember how to throw one of these things around, right?"

Anna was doing a happy dance from being told that they had

a pod ready, since she really wanted to get in one and explore Eleusis from the sky. She looked ridiculous with her pregnant belly and shaking her booty, but she was grinning like a fool anyway. "Of course! Though I'm not sure if I can fit behind the controls. I guess if *you* can, then I can, right?"

Her happy dance made him laugh, but he shrugged as the pod rolled out for them. "I think you'll fit just fine. These are a different internal variant than the one you learned on, but all the controls are the same." The pods she learned with came with three planks inside that passed as seats, all of them facing out from the center. The one in front of them was designed for only two people, and both faced the same way, one strapped in behind the other. Orion slid in first, securing himself in the rear seat, which had just barely more room to accommodate his height. He adjusted the netting for the primary seat so that it was back against him, to make room for her pregnancy. It would be a tight fit, but it didn't look like he minded. "Alright. What's the Earth phrase? Just like riding a bike?"

"I don't think you can use that phrase if you don't know how to ride a bike." Anna climbed into the primary seat, though she had all sorts of butterflies in her belly in both nervousness and excitement. They pretty much felt the same, but they were enough to get Olivia kicking in her belly. "Even Olivia is ready for this."

"Attagirl." He patted the side of Anna's belly as she wiggled into place, then closed and sealed the hatch to allow the pod's systems to come online. "Alright, if you don't remember something, ask, but otherwise, I wanna see how much you remember. Atmospheric flying is gonna be a little different than vector manipulation out in the vacuum. But these things are pretty fucking hard to actually crash, so just have fun with it and try not to kill us all on purpose."

"God, if I wanted to die, it would have been easy to do that already, thank you very much." She shot back at Orion but she was smiling when she looked back at him. "This is awesome." She powered up the pod, shivering a little at the familiar sensation. "Let's get moving."

She heard him gulp violently as she shot them straight up in the air under the pod's power, but once they had some altitude and she had them tipped to look down at the ground, Orion felt himself calm quickly. He always felt calmer once he was mid-flight.

The altitude she gained for them, floating ever higher and higher over the compound, made it feel as though the two of them were putting everything they had both endured on that ground behind them, looking down on it from a place where it could no longer touch them.

"Looks like a big damn mess from up here." The whole compound was ripped to shreds, and most of the barrier wall was still in pieces, but there was at least the beginning of a restoration. The two pieces of the compound that hadn't been part of the initial design were the air strip and a long pier that jutted out from the compound into the sea. Both made the compound look as though it was there to reach out into Eleusis rather than try to wall off humanity in its own tight little bubble. "A beautiful mess, but still, a big damn mess."

"Give it five or ten years. It'll look better eventually." She looked over the same construction and compound, then pointed them toward the water. "Let's go see if anything tries to jump out and eat us when we fly over."

"What was that you *just* said about not dying?" He asked with a laugh, then slid his hands up to her waist. One of them slid past to point on her instruments to a spot that afterward blinked at his indication. "We can get eaten by massive Eleusis sharks some other day. And yes, Aiko says those are a thing, so I'd rather not right now, if it's alright with you. There's something I want to show you farther inland."

"Oh fine. Ruin all the thrill." She gave an exaggerated sigh before she turned the pod to head in the direction of the spot that Orion indicated. She took one hand and caressed the top of his hand as he rested it on her waist. "I missed you."

"I missed you too." He wove his fingers with hers as she flew casually, and the seats were so tightly stacked against each other that she could easily feel him move behind her to get more comfortable as his hands rested on her waist. "Why do you think I picked the claustrophobic pods? That's how much I missed you."

Anna laughed. "This was the only one that was ready to fly. Don't even try to make it sound like you did it." She tried to get as relaxed as she could but it wasn't easy. "So where are you taking us, Captain?"

"Hey, it's Commander now, thank you very much. I got an insignia and a fancy piece of paper and everything." His hands never left her once he'd touched her, but he clearly wasn't answering the question. "You'll see. You'll also want to take this pass a little higher than the others. The drafts through here get crazy coming off the sea for some reason."

"Yes, Sir." She replied with a smirk, since she did miss following his orders for the last month of abstinence. "Commander. I'm sorry for my error."

"Damn right. I earned that promotion." He grinned and guided her through the tall hills of the coastal region, watching the horizon splayed out like a spiked carpet beneath them in every direction. It seemed to smooth out much farther inland, but Orion was content to stick to the hills near the compound for the time being.

Eventually she came around a bend in the hills between two of them at a low-gliding sweep just barely off the tree-tops, but that put them face to face with what appeared to be the tallest hill in the range, covered in the tall scrub-grass that seemed to cover the rest of the plains outside of the thick forests that preferred the lower slopes. A few resilient trees dotted the slope itself, but it stood with a few rocky outcroppings against the wind and the rest of the world.

"Up near the summit." He pointed a commanding finger as she flew. "There's a broad dip of a ledge about thirty meters from the top on the far side. Mostly out of the wind, good place for a pod landing. Let's see if you can still park."

"Of course I can." She said confidently, even if she felt shaky at best about it. Anna followed his directions about finding a good landing spot, and once she spotted it, she was furiously looking over the controls and all the information with quick eyes to make sure she made the landing as smooth as possible. The wind whipped them around a bit, but eventually she was able to lower the pod more or less where he said it should go. "Hey, I got pretty damn close."

"Yeah you did." He laughed behind her, looking over her shoulder to check the landing was secure and the pod had powered itself down to conserve power for the return trip. They were excellent in space where they could conserve power, but inside an atmosphere, they were a little more limited. Even so, they had plenty to get back where they came from.

He opened the hatch and let Anna out first, then slid out after her, holding her hand the entire time. The wind wasn't as fierce right against the side of the hill, and in a few steps, they came around the side of it into a kind of fold in the landscape where the wind was barely noticeable as anything more than a rushing noise in the distance.

"Don't get me wrong, I'm glad we've got the Twist and it's gonna do some amazing things for the human race, but nothing beats flying. That's just my opinion." He took her hand as they walked, both because they were so high up on the hillside and because he just wanted to be close to her.

Anna immediately entwined her fingers with his, even though hers were small and his were twice the length of her own, it seemed like. They looked strange together, she knew that, but she adored him anyway. "Nothing beats flying." She agreed, even though she wanted to say that being with him sure as hell beat flying in her eyes. "Well, maybe *something* does. But it's hard to beat."

Orion's answering grin didn't have to ask her to clarify what she meant, since clearly he agreed. "So I really tried," he stumbled a little along one bend of the hillside, but they weren't in any immediate danger of falling to their deaths, so he regained his balance fairly easily, "I really tried to figure out how to get this thing up here without using Twist magic, but eventually I caved. Xander thought it was hilarious that I waited so long to ask. Just didn't feel right to have anything up here that wasn't made by hand, but some things you just want to get done." They came around the shoulder of the hill to face toward the sea where they had flown over, and Anna could see something shining along the curve of the hill. The closer they got, the stranger it looked, and the wider Orion's grin became.

The hill, she could see, had been cut away as if by some precise deity who had no fear of heights. The place that had been cut away was a steep slope where the hill seemed to curve back in on itself, and instead of bare rock, the bulge had been replaced by a smooth glass wall looking out and down on the valley below. The turf of the hill flowed up over the roof of it, making it invisible from above, and the glass reflected none of the light of the sun across the sea in the west.

He was leading her toward a door set into the side of the glass as it curved into the hill. On the other side of the glass, a small but comfortable two-person unit looked out on Eleusis. It had almost nothing by way of amenities aside from a shower tucked away in one corner, but there were curtains that could be drawn over the wall of windows and a comfortable bed facing the sunset.

She could see all the seams and fittings around the room where the different modular pieces of it had been carried in and set carefully in place, disturbing Eleusis as little as possible in order to make a comfortable shelter away from the winds outside. They still howled past the windows, but it was a quiet, rushing song against the glass, as if there was something about Eleusis itself that could only be heard up on that hilltop.

"Oh wow, Orion." She looked the entire structure over and hesitated to open the door. "This is a beautiful getaway. Good thing you know how to fly to get yourself up here." She looked around as soon as they stepped inside, since she was just amazed and a little afraid. The glass made it seem like one wrong move and they were going to tumble off and plunge to their death. "It's so peaceful."

"I thought we could use some of that, after everything else." He stepped inside after her (he had to duck, since clearly modular places were not built with giants in mind) and gave her plenty of time to look around the limited space. Rather than being scared of the fall, he was leaning on the glass when she finished her inspection, watching her with a smile. "It's not what I envision as an end result. Eventually, when I get a chance to build the rest of the house up on top of the hill, I'm thinking I'll attach it to this spot with a stairway or an elevator or something. Maybe put a secret passage in a library or something that leads down here for a getaway. But it's a place to stay the nights while the house is in progress."

Anna was so distracted by everything that she just wandered until she sat down on the very edge of the bed, since she didn't want to disturb the precision of the covers. "Wait, what did you say?" She eventually said when her brain caught up with him. "You thought *we* could use some peace? Like, you-and-me 'we' or like, 'we' as in rebels in general, or just people in general?"

"I mean we." He said ambiguously, then took a few slow strides toward where she sat on the edge of the bed. Rather than moving to sit beside her, he bent down when he got close and leaned on her knees as he looked her in the eye. He parted them gently and knelt between them, his hands taking her in as he moved himself in close, sliding up her thighs to her hips as he looked up in her eyes.

"I mean us. As in you and me and the kids. I mean a life, as in peaceful nights yelling at the kids for throwing popcorn at the screen and helping them with their math homework. I mean long days working our asses off and long nights when the only things that go bump are you and me and the occasional kid out of bed past lights out. I mean we." He pulled her down into a brief kiss, still looking up into her eyes afterward. "I mean all that, if all that is still something you want to have with me."

Anna was so stunned that she didn't even know how to respond except to nod at first until the tears came, and then the curse words. "No shit? Really? You want all of that with *me*?" She just kept nodding and crying. "I still want all of that with you, more, as much as I can get! I . . ." Anna had been so certain she wasn't a part of his picture that she was having a hard time. "Fuck. I thought you . . . I want you, Orion. Only you."

His hands moved up over her sides as he kissed her after that answer, taking in a deep breath as if to inhale the moment and hold it forever. There were tears in his own eyes too, but he wasn't afraid to let them fall. They both knew how long a road it had been for them to reach that moment, and he couldn't stop touching her.

"I love you, Anna." He eventually said, once his hands had worked their way up her body to cradle her face. "I'm going to spend an Eleusis lifetime loving you. No matter what happens, no matter what else is in store for us, it's gonna be my mission in life to continue blowing your fucking mind at all times. That's the kind of life we're gonna have up here. I'm yours, and that's for life."

Anna kissed him several more times with their tears pressed together in each kiss, but she didn't care. She was still blown away by the fact that Orion wanted to spend the rest of his life with her and not with Mercury. "I love you too, Orion." She eventually said between kisses, even though she also wanted to apologize yet again for ever messing it up in the first place.

She did remember, however, that he had ordered her never to apologize for it again. While the drug wasn't in her system anymore, somehow his orders still held some weight in her mind. "I promise you I'll never take anything for granted. I'll do my best to never hurt you. You're the best thing that has ever happened to me, Orion."

"I'm not done happening to you. Not by a long shot." He kissed her again as he got back to his feet, then slid onto the bed so that he had a leg on either side of her from behind, and they could look together out at the sunset, washing the skies in the blue light of Eleusis' star and the violent purples and deep reds that resulted in the clouds. He wrapped his long arms around her to enclose her completely, leaning down to kiss her neck as he took her hand.

"I would've brought a ring, but it looks like you've still got the old one." He caressed over the ink on her finger with a quiet chuckle against her hair. "I'll get you another one anyway if you want one."

Anna laughed softly as he looked over her finger and she was entirely enveloped by the giant man she could now say was her husband again, even without any ceremony or anything else. "Well, if you're offering, I mean, you're a Commander now. What's that pay?"

"Right now? Jack shit. Room and board plus favors from people whose asses I've been professionally saving for a while, I guess. Still got a few of the Echoes hanging around wanting to be my butler or something, but that's not happening. I'll have to take it up with Carl and figure out what he's gonna start paying me." He pulled her hand up to his lips so he could kiss her tattoo, then his lips moved to her neck. "Maybe I'll ask one of the Montgomeries to use scanners and find some diamonds here on Eleusis. Sounds like the kind of thing Xander would go for. If it's bling you want, I'll make sure it's bling you fucking get."

Anna laughed again and she turned around in Orion's embrace so that she could go back to kissing him. "Does this mean that I can strip you naked now?" She kissed him harder, since she definitely did not want to stop. "That's why we're here, right? To make this place ours?"

He laid back on the bed under her kisses, certainly not resisting that kind of impulse. "Oh, this place is already ours. All I'm up here to make mine is you." He started removing her clothes just as she tugged at his, kissing her the entire time. The fact that she'd said yes, that she had still wanted a life with him after a month back on Earth in her old life . . . was more than he had honestly hoped for. He thought that life with Logan would call her back, but he wasn't going to stop to question the decision she had made, or the decision that he had made. He wanted Anna, and wanted a life with Anna, more than anything he'd ever wanted in his existence.

The world around them was dark, but Anna couldn't care less. All she cared about was Orion, and now that she knew he wanted her too, there was no doubt in her mind that they were perfect for each other. Logan had once been the perfect match, for a past version of her. But the present, the version that mattered, wanted Orion and no one else. There was no wondering, no doubt. She just knew.

The sunlight died as the last of it fell on the heap of clothes they left on the floor, but Orion watched something more beautiful move against him on the bed. The bronze of his skin and the pale flush of Anna's slid against each other like an extension of the evening, and he ran his hands over every delicious inch of her as if to reclaim her for his own.

She was free of the drugs that had enslaved her, free from any kind of control. They were both free of the fear Eleusis had been to them for the majority of the time they'd been there, and the world was theirs for the retaking. When he was inside her, it was like he could feel the heartbeat of the reclaimed planet celebrating alongside them, feel the reclaimed life they had taken for themselves opening up in possibilities ahead of them.

"Good god . . ." he moaned against her ear, his hands shaking as they gripped her against him. He was careful about her pregnancy in the way he touched her, but he had never treated her as if she was breakable, and that was no exception. He wanted her, he wanted her without limits, and that was exactly the way he took her.

"So good." Anna replied with a whimper and a moan of her own, since she was utterly lost in him. It had never felt so right as it did in that moment. There was no guilt. There was nothing that made her wonder if she was with the right person or not. It was fucking bliss. "I love you." She managed to say before she unraveled and cried out in pleasure, since he was relentless and amazing and her entire body was consumed with pleasure.

After a month without her, his climax wasn't far behind her own, and he abandoned himself to it completely, clinging to her as tightly as if she was the other half of himself. It was how he felt, trapped ecstatically inside that moment, that he was complete, and would never again be otherwise. Every movement she made against him was a celebration of that connection, the wholeness that had come back to the world with her pressed against him.

"You . . ." he breathed into the glorious, panting silence, "are perfect." He kissed her as the room went completely dark, the stars just barely out, one of them the sun under which they had both been born. "Spectacularly . . . fucking . . . perfect."

"We're perfect." She replied in her own gasping breaths. "We're perfect together." No matter how many mistakes had been made along the way, somehow the two of them had managed to figure out a way back to each other. The Consortium had done a great many evil things, but in the end, she was grateful for Orion in her life. Even if it hadn't started the way that either of them had hoped, he was her universe.

* * * * *

The review of the construction in the compound didn't take very long, and really hadn't been necessary at all, from what Mercury could see going on around them. Everyone was in the process of going back to their own residential units for the day or calling in an authorized Twist to get them back to Earth, but Logan continued on his way through the compound. The hospital had not, in fact, gotten to the point of adding the sign that would declare the birthing wing hers, and even the foundations for that wing hadn't been laid yet. It was going to take some time before people would be living with any regularity on the planet, with the exception of the few adventurers who decided they were simply never leaving again.

"No, I didn't, there's some committee somewhere that I'm supposed to meet with about that. Renata would know." Logan shook off the question, since he quickly accepted just how buried he was with things to do. He patted the arm of the man who'd been questioning him and sent him on his way toward the Twist with a smile. Then he continued walking, even though he and Mercury had traversed the entire campus and reached the edge of the long beach.

For the first time in the walk, they were alone. Just as many people flocked to Mercury as had sought Logan, since most of them had some kind of connection with her, directly or indirectly. Logan looked over at her with a sigh, before glancing back gratefully at the fact that no one followed them out onto the sand. "Talk to most of these people and it's like we didn't just fight a war a month ago. One of these days I'm going to have to ask one of them how they manage that."

"To their credit, the world, both worlds and the space between, they're all different places." Mercury had her hair in a bun on the top of her head from her appointments to keep it out of the way, but now that they were enjoying the breeze and the sand, she let her hair loose to blow in the chilly Eleusis air. She looked out at the water and looked down at the sand, picking up a piece of Eleusis sea glass, as green as the color of her eyes. It was flat and smooth and beautiful even in the chilly weather. "This place almost seems like it's in my imagination somewhere. It's so untouched."

The moment she took her hair down, Mercury could see all the strain of the world and thoughts of anything behind them vanish from Logan's eyes. "Part of me would rather leave it that way." He walked slowly beside her, reaching out to roll the sea-glass through his own fingers before he handed it back to her, preferring her eyes to the facsimile of her beauty in the glass. "Just to know that there's someplace like this in the universe. Peaceful, beautiful, thriving without us."

The only part of the beach where the presence of humanity intervened was a pier that jutted out into the sea a hundred meters away. The waves broke against it in the evening breeze, spraying white foam against the dark pylons. "I don't know if I'll ever live here, but if I did, I'd like it to be someplace like this, out on the coast. Maybe that's the midwest in me always looking for an ocean and only ever finding a puddle."

"I like the idea of homes in both places." She watched the water spray against the pier before she bent over again to pick up a shell. Her time on Earth had been the same as his, in the mountains or in the plains, never near so much water at once. "That way I could come here and work if I had patients that needed me, and I could continue to study CV on Earth. I'm still trying to figure out where I'm needed, if I'm even needed at all. CV might be impossible to eradicate on Earth, and any good doctor can deliver a baby."

"You're always going to be needed." They were meandering down the beach in the vague direction of the pier, but they were far off the beaten swath the construction vehicles left, the tracks already starting to fill in with the foliage as if Eleusis simply would not tolerate the alteration. "And you're more than just a good doctor. You're a genius in your field and out. You could take whatever position you wanted in the world, work on whatever research you wanted, and always be home in time to read the kids a medical journal or two to put them to sleep."

"I hope I'm as good as you seem to think." She held out the shell for him to see, since it was a beautiful mix of iridescent blue and purple. "What about you? Do you want to live here or back on Earth? I know you're a big deal on Earth. I'm just curious what you would prefer."

"I'm not a big deal anywhere." He contradicted gently, examining the shell closely. "I'm just the guy who managed to pull the trigger. I know better by now than to think that makes me anything special." He rubbed some of the salt from the shell to polish it between his fingers as they walked.

"I'd like to go back and forth too, but I'll probably be spending most of my time on Earth. There's too much there to be handled. It's going to be James and Declan's generation that actually gets to live completely on Eleusis, not ours. Maybe I'll set up a retirement home here somewhere. I could live with that." He gave her a cautious smile and flipped the shell like a coin in his hand, watching it catch the sunset in perfect ripples of color.

"Most of the time I'm still trying to wrap my head around the fact that we . . . can. Do both. Live both places. Walk from one end of the universe to the other. Pretty soon the Montgomeries are going to expand their search and start finding other planets like Eleusis. Then there will be even more homes for humanity, more branches . . . it's too big for me to hold onto. Which makes sense, I suppose."

"They can worry about the rest of the universe. That's too much for one person to worry about." She gave him a warm smile before she ran a hand through her wavy hair so that she could brush it over the side and expose one side of her neck. It whipped into her face, so she tried to toss some of it aside. It had gotten exceptionally long in her captivity.

Logan watched her in fascination that he did nothing to hide. The few wisps she couldn't seem to draw away whenever she pulled her hair aside were teasing along her cheek when he reached up to brush them back with the rest. The caress continued down the exposed side of her neck and then moved down her back over the coat. "We'll have to come back here in the Eleusis spring, you and me." His arm remained along her lower back as they walked, and he hoped she would stay close to him. "I don't see many vacations in either of our immediate futures, but I love seeing you free like this. Whether it's home or here."

Mercury stilled for a moment when he ran his fingers along her skin and kept his hand at her lower back. She knew he meant to keep walking, but she couldn't just play off what he said. "Do you think it's a good idea, you and me?" She hated feeling like she had to ask, but she did. When he rescued her on Prime, he thought Anna was dead. Now if he wanted to live on Earth and Anna was there, she was worried about his relationship with Anna. He said on Prime that hurting her was a big mistake, but she still wanted to know what he thought. She didn't want to put herself at risk for more pain, especially because she wasn't sure how she could have even prevented it the first time. She wasn't sure she could prevent anything like that at all.

He wasn't surprised at her hesitation, since the end of the war had changed things for all of them. They both thought they had lost the others, but he meant everything he told her back on Prime. He stopped in front of her, reaching up to brush her cheek again and hoping she wouldn't pull away.

"I've thought . . . probably a thousand times about what I could say to you today." He took in a deep breath, as nervous as she had ever seen him. He was well-practiced at appearing calm even if he wasn't, but she was even better-practiced at reading him regardless. "And I still have no clue. Nothing I can think of seems like enough. I thought about trying my hand at poetry and that went . . . terribly. I thought about singing and that was even worse. I used to write you letters after the fight in the mountains. Every few days when the world turned into too much, I would go back to my closet and write you one and then tuck it away because I had no idea if you would ever be able to read them. I don't know what happened to them, maybe they got destroyed when the Colombia base was deserted, I have no idea. I've tried thousands of ways to think of how to tell you what I want from our life together, and all of it comes up laughably short."

Mercury's expression softened when he said he wrote her letters, and there was something about that confession that made her really want to read them. "You wrote me letters? But weren't you with Anna?"

"Not . . . before the battle. Not really." He shook his head, since it was far from his proudest moment. "Anna and I have always known how to be best friends, and I think she'll always be that. She's someone I trust to always be on my side. But when we first got married, we were both . . . up against a wall of one kind or another. We've both loved each other since we knew how, and it was just this . . . explosion of things that had been bottled up. I think when things happened back in the midwest, we went back to that, for a while, but we just . . . never really stayed on the same page. We've talked about it a little since Prime. We got in each other's way, and that's not the way I want to spend the rest of my life."

It was hard to talk about Anna because things ended so strangely and so abruptly, with the two of them being separated for six months, but he wasn't blind. He could see the way she looked at Orion, and he was glad for it, to the core of his soul. "We're going to be involved with Orion and with Anna for the rest of our lives. There's no way to change that, and I can't even say that bothers me after everything that's happened. They're both good people and they're both good parents."

"But no, when I was down in Bogota trying like hell to pull the rebellion into some kind of focus, it wasn't Anna I wanted next to me, it was you. When I imagine watching James and Declan chasing their first crush around the schoolyard in elementary school, you're the one I want yelling at me for rolling my eyes. When things get hard on Earth, and they will," there had already been signs of exactly how things were going to progress politically, as some powers resisted the unification he had put forward and others embraced it, "you're the one I want to talk things through with at night. Not because I want to put you through any of that kind of stress or those hard times, because I don't. But you're the one person I know who . . . gets it. Who understands."

He was on a roll with no sign of stopping, hours of thinking about what to say all pouring out in a flood that he couldn't stop once it started. "I also can't wait to be a spectator in your life. Hopefully with a front row seat. I know the revelations about CV have undermined a lot of what you wanted to do with your research, but I know you better than to think you're going to let that slow you down for long. I mean it when I say you're an amazing doctor, and whatever it is you choose to apply yourself to for research from here on, you're going to be amazing. I want to be there for that. I want to be next to you to watch you being an amazing mother to James and Declan. To Fiona and Farrah. I want to be part of your life, because it is going to be amazing. I want to be whatever kind of husband you need me to be, so that you can be the amazing person you are."

"I don't know how things would be with us." Mercury's once-analytical tone was more fearful, more cautious, but she still held onto her core of weighing the positives and negatives of every situation. "We're both different, after everything that's happened. I still . . . I want things to be the way that they were, but not entirely. I don't like knowing I was too naive, but I also know that my preferences weren't from naïveté. I just . . . I know we're both different, and I want that to be okay. I don't want to worry about jobs or anything else driving us apart. Because if we're together again, I don't want to worry about losing you again."

"The only thing you're ever likely to lose me to is a board meeting or a screaming toddler from time to time. And I have the authority to do something about the board meeting now." He decided as soon as he chose to really take the position of Prime Minister that he would never attend a meeting he didn't have to, mostly for the sake of his own sanity. "And I have no intention of ever letting things get the way they were in the mountains. We were both working our asses off and the boys were infants. We didn't have time to be us, together or apart. I'm not gonna live like that again. I won't do it. Here pretty soon, I'm gonna start appointing representatives like a crazy person and start delegating like it's my job."

He put out a tentative hand against her waist at the bottom edge of her coat to pull her in gently by a belt loop. "I was naive too, in the beginning. But my preferences weren't just from playing games either. We both might be different, but so long as I've got the authority to make it happen, things are going to run the way I want them to run." The hard look in his eyes made any threat of consequences for disobedience unnecessary. Mercury knew how Logan could be when things didn't go the way he required them, and with all the power he'd been given, he had more than enough leverage to enforce his will on the majority of the world. "Most of all, I want you. On whatever terms, whatever it takes, whatever I need to be or do."

Mercury looked into Logan's grey eyes for a moment and she was silent for a little while before she spoke again. "Do you still want a big family? Can we have a real wedding? With a white dress and everything?"

The questions made him smile, and his other hand joined the first to hold her against him on the sand. "We can have the wedding to end all weddings. And my answer on family has never changed. However many you want to have is how many we'll have. If you keep on coming up with twins, that house back on Earth is gonna get really full, really fast, and so be it."

Mercury didn't hesitate or fight it when he pulled her in close and she gave him a small smile as she looked up at him. "I want to change my last name for good, too. So if you're going to name it the Finnegan Wing, it won't matter so much if I'm a Bickford."

"No, I guess it won't." He had no problem agreeing to that, and his hands moved up under her coat to hold her tighter. "And I can rescind the name of the wing if you really don't want it there. But any chance I get to commemorate you or honor you, I'm gonna take it."

"It's alright." She eventually conceded, since she didn't think it was that bad. "My parents only have one child. It can commemorate them too." Mercury reached up and ran her fingers along his cheek and smiled up at him. "Can I kiss you now?"

It felt like a shadow of their previous life tentatively coming to life. Just the fact that she asked permission sent a tingle down his spine. "Now and any time you want. Preferably every single day for the rest of our lives."

Mercury smiled brighter and immediately leaned in for a kiss that started gentle at first, but the longer the kiss lingered, the more heated it became. "It's been a long time . . ." she said between kisses. "Before the attack . . ."

"For me too." He sighed through the kisses, holding to her tightly. "Where do you want to go?" He began undoing the buttons on her coat. It was chilly but not truly cold, and the world felt much warmer after those kisses. "The whole universe, anywhere you want, but preferably somewhere with a bed."

"Anywhere in the world?" She asked as she continued kissing him while his hands opened her coat. "Ireland. A nice, beautiful hotel in Ireland."

He nodded with a grin at her answer, and pulled out his communicator once her coat was open. One of his hands remained inside it to hold her close while the other held it to his ear. "Hey, Charles. Good of you to pick up. Quick favor. I need you to find the nicest hotel in Ireland and put a Twist between my location and that room. Then get Renata to book it for us. Yes, I'm aware that this is a frivolous use of world-changing technology. But that entertains you, so you're gonna do it anyway."

Logan couldn't stop grinning, especially since it only took Charles a few more seconds to open a Twist a few paces away from the two of them that opened on a beautiful room decorated in dark wood and intricately-carved furniture. It was roughly the same time of day in Ireland as it had been on Eleusis, and through the open Twist and the windows of the hotel suite, they could see their own sun setting just as they could see the Eleusis sun setting over the sea opposite the opening.

"Thank you, Charles." He took a last look at the beach and stepped through the opening without letting go of Mercury's hand.

Mercury held tightly to Logan's hand, and when the Twist disappeared, she gasped softly as she looked around. They were in a perfect room, beautiful and luxurious. "It's so beautiful." She shrugged off her coat and carefully put it over the back of the nearest chair.

"Lock the door." He said in a quiet command, shrugging off his own to throw it on top of hers before he stopped her for a kiss on her way to the door.

Mercury was unable to hide the shiver that ran down her spine after she kissed him and she rushed to lock the door, but then she was quickly back to Logan with her hands exploring him easily. "It's locked."

"Good." His tone and his touch approved, his eyes stuck on her rather than taking in the opulent room around them. He had warned the staff in the child care center they might have to watch all their children for longer than just a few hours if the day went the way he had imagined it might. The way he hoped.

His hand slid up over her shirt to her neck, holding her in a kiss that was heated but controlled. For the time being. "Go test the bed for us. See if it's good enough." They had discussed so many things in such depth over the time they had been together, there was almost no end to the things they knew about each other. They knew how firm the other liked the bed, which side they preferred to sleep on, what kind of sheets they liked or didn't. There was a universe of shared knowledge between them that had been set on a shelf for almost a year, but was still anything but forgotten.

Mercury went to the end of the bed and took off her shoes before she crawled up onto the fancy bed. She felt out of place in her scrubs, but she hadn't known she would end up engaged to Logan before she came back from Eleusis. She would have dressed better. "It's quite firm." She replied as she laid back and sprawled out on the bed. "Not as soft as I'm used to, but you will like it."

"You're in it. I already like it." He approached the bed slowly to enjoy the sight of her, his mind turning back to the night the two of them had decided to go along with the Initiative's requirements. There was no Initiative now. There was no Consortium. There was no one to require anything of them at all, and everyone who had tried was forgotten. He kicked off his shoes on the way, "And you'll be staying on me, not the bed."

Mercury went back to smiling again and she scooted back on the bed playfully as he approached, clearly on the prowl. "On you, huh? In my scrubs? Do you need a checkup, Mr. Bickford?"

"The scrubs won't be staying in the bed." He leaned down on the high bed and balled up his hands in the comforter, then started pulling it toward him with her still on it. He pulled faster once he had her going, until she slid right up against him on the edge of the bed and the rest of the comforter fell away at his feet.

Mercury was still grinning and giggling as he pulled her right up to him. "That's a very nice comforter, Mr. Bickford." She started kissing him again once she was close enough, though. "Does that mean you want me to take them off?"

"It means I plan to leave them in pieces." His touch was gentle for the time being, but she knew from previous experience just how strong he was, and how lethal he could be with the hands that roamed over her as soon as she was close enough. He cupped her face in the last gentle kiss he gave her, then leaned her back on the bed before his hands ripped straight down the front of her scrubs so his lips could kiss down her chest.

She gasped softly as he kissed across her skin, still as pale and freckled as ever, since most of her freckles had gone into hiding under her shirt, apparently. "Am I going to have to walk out of here naked?" She was wearing a simple bra underneath, nothing fancy as her scrub top slipped off her shoulders and away from her body.

"Yes." He answered simply, but a threat nonetheless. "You're going to walk out of here naked and directly into my bedroom." His hands took their time pushing aside her shirt, and left it around her waist so that it was holding her wrists lightly in place.

His lips took their time on the full curves of her breasts before his hands joined them. "And the same rules are going to apply in that bedroom as always did before." He worked his way back up to her lips and moved to join her on the bed, his body harder and stronger than she'd ever felt him before. "Which means we're both wearing too many clothes."

"Hm. You're right." She wiggled a little beneath him, since it had been so incredibly long. So long since she'd had sex, even longer since she'd been with Logan. Just as it was with the boys, her full breasts seemed even fuller after having her babies. Mercury tugged at Logan's shirt, though, since she wanted him bare just as much as he wanted her bare.

The sunset hit him as he pulled his shirt off over his head, throwing it aside like it had angered him. He stepped back from her enough to shove his jeans to the floor and kick them aside, standing in the gold and orange glow of day's end to look down at her. He had been the strongest man she'd ever met the first time they'd been together, but the years between had made every part of him hard and unyielding. That included the part of him she wanted most at that moment. Every part of him except the smile on his face.

His hands took a firm grip at the sides of her pants and pulled them off along with her panties all in one motion, discarding them on the floor without taking his eyes off her. He leaned over the bed and kissed up from her waist as one hand unhooked her bra and pulled it away, freeing her breasts as well as her arms, so that the two of them were left bare on the bed.

He hovered over her like a storm about to break, every part of him reminding every part of her of exactly what her body knew he could do to her. It had been almost a year since they had last been together, but there were things he made impossible for her to forget. A single light caress was all it took for him to lay her arms back behind her head, resting on the spray of scarlet hair like a halo of fire on the dark sheets.

"Tell me you're mine." He commanded quietly, a single fingertip tracing the length of her arm all the way to her neck and across her lips before it began a long, torturous journey down over her chest.

Mercury was breathing slowly but deeply as her body was on display for him. Nothing had changed, really, except the tattoos on her wrists. Her body bounced back exceptionally quickly after childbirth, and her curves were as voluptuous as ever. She took another deep breath as tears pricked at her eyes when he made his command. "I'm yours, Logan. I could not and would not want to belong to anyone else."

His answering kiss reminded her exactly what it had felt like, in the world they had shared before, to have her senses commanded by him. Every touch erased the stress and trouble from her body, every kiss rebuilt the world they had shared between them. They were nations away from anyone who even knew where they were, half a world away from any task that was waiting for them in the life beyond each other's arms. All that mattered, all her body was allowed to feel, was the brush of his beard against her neck, his rough hands as they owned her body piece by piece. His lips on hers were the conquest her sighs had been waiting for, and when he pressed himself into her, his moan was an echo of her own.

She groaned almost as soon as he slid into her, and while her arms were above her head, she desperately wanted to touch him. Mercury looked up at him hovering over her, and every movement made her gasp, slow and measured as they were at first.

"Logan . . ." Mercury moaned his name between breaths, since she couldn't believe that being with him again was real. The tears that prickled before were silently sliding down her cheeks, since she was so happy to have him back. He was alive, he loved her, and he was hers. No sharing. Just hers.

Their world ended at the edges of the bed, as far as Logan was concerned, and the two of them moved in unison as they rediscovered every piece of each other. He rolled to his back and took her hands, entwining his fingers with hers as she rocked atop him. There was no difference between the glow of the sunset and the fiery curtain of her hair. There was no barrier between them, no conflict, no hesitation, and no restraint. Logan's neck arched in a moan beneath her, gasping out of need.

"Yes," he growled in satisfaction, "Yes, Mercury. Just like . . ." he couldn't even finish the demand, though his body was demanding enough to speak for itself. What he demanded, she gave, and what she needed, he was all too happy to provide.

Mercury loved hearing the pleasure she could provide, and when he said her name between his moans, it only motivated her more. She moved quicker and harder, desperate to mend everything that had been broken before with every new memory in the making. "I love you." She said several times, since she wanted him to know that between every pounding heartbeat, she loved him. Adored him. Cherished him. More than anything else, she wanted a happy life with Logan.

He had never before held himself back with Mercury, and wasn't about to start at the beginning of a new life. He had no defense against her, and wanted none. His hands gripped at her frantically as she rocked freely against him. She knew his body well enough to feel exactly when she had him at his breaking point, and his mouth opened in an uncontrolled cry as he slammed himself into her. He wanted . . . he wanted . . . he wanted . . .

"Aren't you . . . going to tell me?" She asked in a tone just as needy as his. Mercury held herself back for a command, a command to let herself go, a command to push him to the point of no return, she would take them all. "I need . . . to hear . . ."

Another loud moan rolled from his chest at her request, but he looked up as she writhed, shaking with the effort of holding back. He pushed himself up beneath her with a gasping threat in his eyes, until his chest was pressed against hers and her legs were wrapped around his waist. His arms encircled her as they rocked against each other, both of them open to the other in every way two people could open themselves to another person. She knew him well enough to know why he wanted the closeness. He wanted to watch her come apart at the seams, and the heat inside them both meant to see it happen.

His pace quickened as he regained some of the control, pressing her tightly against him. When he managed to speak, his voice was a ruined, ragged whisper, but her body knew the command anyway. "Come for me, Wife."

That, along with a few more precise movements, and Mercury tilted her head back and completely unravelled in his arms. Her whole body tensed in the moment of bliss, but she didn't stop moving even as she repeatedly cried out his name. There was nothing like this, nothing like this moment between herself and Logan. She was glad she was still able to have it, and to have him. They fit so perfectly in so many ways, it was soul-bending.

He was strong enough to have left bruises when he joined her in his own climax, but she was far from fragile. His arms clutched her to him desperately, the sensation stretching out through his entire body as it reverberated against her own. All the tension, all the strength in him fled completely in that moment. It left the world a silent place, containing only their satisfied gasps and the cry of birds outside the window calling out to the sun before it was gone for the night.

He kissed her skin ponderously as his entire body echoed with their lovemaking. Eventually he looked her in the eye, reaching up to smooth sweat-dampened strands of fire away from her face. "I love you so much, Mercury." He said when he could finally speak, still cradling her against him as they caught their breath.

Mercury never thought of herself as an emotional person, and really, she often thought of herself as not emotional enough. In that moment, though, she was crying all over again and clinging to Logan as he looked her in the eyes. She wasn't sobbing, she just couldn't stop the tears from running down her face. "I didn't know anything could feel like this, the way I love you. After . . . after I lost you . . ." She couldn't really describe the anger and the pain in the same way she struggled to describe the enormity of the way she felt right now. "I didn't know . . . if I could feel this again."

He kissed her tenderly and wiped away some of her tears, but afterward, he just held her against him, nuzzling her cheek with his own. For Logan, the world had felt like a damned place ever since the attack on the mountains. The prison of the mountain, the prison of the chair to which he'd been confined, the actual prison on Prime in which he had been . . . he put those thoughts aside. Even their memory had no place in Mercury's presence.

He knew it would take some time for them to settle into the world they had made for themselves again, but as they held onto each other, they got a piece of it back. "The only thing that's ever going to take me from you again is old age. And I plan to do everything I can to put that off as long as humanly possible."

He kissed her shoulder, wondering with a split second thought about some of the things he knew about the Montgomeries and their longevity, and how much it applied to Mercury, or to Carl, or to their own children. He banished such thoughts, since they did no good to dwell on. He didn't want to imagine putting her through the ordeal of watching him grow old while nothing changed for her until much, much later. "This right here is the world you and I are going to come back to every night for the rest of our lives. Whatever we need to do, wherever we have to be, there's never again going to be a reason for us to spend a single night apart. And I don't intend to."

Mercury kept her arms wrapped around him so that the

closeness of their bodies kept her warm as they pressed together. "Every night. I'm holding you to that." Mercury found his lips again and kissed him several more times before she said anything else. "I would give everything up for you, I hope you know that. I love being a doctor, but I love you even more. I will travel the universe with you, if you need me to."

He shook his head after that kiss, and laid back on the bed to relax with her on top of him, as promised. "I'm never going to ask you to give up what's important to you. We still might go travel the universe, though, if that becomes an option." He smiled and brushed her hair away so he could see her as his hands massaged over her back. "I want you to be happy, more than I want anything else in the world. That means I want to do everything I can to get you to your goals. Every single one of them."

She continued raining kisses on him as her tears tapered off. "I'm really happy that you don't mind having a wedding. I know my parents would want to see it, since things . . . well, things were different the last time. They weren't accessible. And I want to wear a beautiful dress. Just for you. I got a tattoo for you. The dress will be less painful."

"Clearly you haven't worn very many wedding dresses." He laughed at the things he'd heard from his own mother as a child about the pains she'd taken with her wedding dress. He had found the stories annoying at the time, but he hung onto them like every other memory of his parents. He wondered, briefly, what they would think about what he'd become. What Liam had become. He didn't have to wonder if they would have liked Mercury. They would have loved her as much as he did. "When I say the wedding to end all weddings, I mean it. It's going to be the kind of thing they put in history books with a date kids are going to be irritated they have to learn for a test. It's what I wanted to give you in the first place. And now . . . well, now I'm good for it."

He savored the kiss that followed, as the light from the sunset faded from the room and left them in the darkness of their private world. The stars would be out to watch their lovemaking soon, but Logan made no room to close the curtains, since it would mean moving away from Mercury. "Do you remember . . . there was one night back in the mountains, I think the boys were maybe six months old, it just barely started to get cold again. You came in, I was already asleep, you did that thing and I couldn't walk for about an hour?"

Mercury laughed softly against his chest as she ran her fingertips over his skin. "I remember. It had been a hard day for me, but when I came home and saw you, all I could think about was how pleasing you would make me so happy." She slid her hand lower, since they were no longer joined, but she imagined it wouldn't be too long before they were again. "I was always trying to find ways to surprise you. I do not want to admit how many video clips I watched in order to learn some of the things I did. But I remember. It requires being incredibly limber."

"You've certainly never lacked in that department. Or in any other." He growled under the kiss as she touched him, every night they spent together flying through his mind at once. They had always been a release for each other, they had always set it as a goal to create a place for each other where they could let go of everything else. A simpler place, a warmer world. The memories of staying in their unit in the mountains, taking care of their sons when they were small, something as simple as the two of them leaning back on the couch with a child each, everything brought a smile to his face.

In the beginning of their relationship, things had been a game between them, just an act they could put on to avoid penalties. He remembered the first moment he embraced it, and his mind reeled, pleasantly for once, at how great the distance was between that moment and the present. He had been acting like her lover then. He planned to be her husband now, and always.

"Do that again."

EPILOGUE

"Mel!" Kameron yelled from her own dressing room, since she and Melissa were not supposed to see each other, but damned if she was going out like this. "What did you do with the dress I picked out? This is not that dress!!"

"Oh yes it is, baby!" Mel yelled back from her room. Kam could hear a whole chorus of giggling from Melissa's room, but then, the entire area where they were located was mostly made up of giggling. "I just made a couple *tiny* changes here and there."

"Tiny?!?" Kameron looked at herself in the mirror. The slits in the sides of her dress nearly showed off the fact that she wasn't wearing any underwear, and the previously conservative neckline was now plunging. Not to mention her comfortable three-quarter sleeves were now straps. "The whole central region is going to see my bare ass and my nipples hanging out! I'm going to wear jeans and a t-shirt, this is fucking ridiculous."

"No! Come on, nobody's gonna see your ass except me!" Melissa whined and pleaded from several rooms away, eliciting all-out laughter from everyone else in the area getting ready, some of whom were having their own shouting conversations. It was going to be a very, very busy day. "You're gonna look so hot! Not that you don't in t-shirt and jeans, but this is our wedding! Just this once!"

Kam growled as she looked at herself in the mirror for a moment longer. She had wanted to wear a dress, but she had wanted to wear the dress *she* chose. This monstrosity was entirely so that she was Mel's arm candy, which was not terrible, but she was going to catch all sorts of hell for it. She could just hear people asking her where she could hide her gun.

Instead of yelling at Mel anymore, she decided to leave the conversation hanging and stormed across the hall where the men were getting ready. She barely knocked before she pushed her way inside. "Guys, tell me this is ridiculous. I cannot go out there in this."

"You can absolutely go out there in that." Orion said from the middle of the mass of men, many of whom had panicked upon seeing a woman walking through the doors, until they noticed that it was Kam. His comment got a chorus of agreement from the tuxedos and other sets of formal attire around the room, but he separated himself from the group to inspect the dress more closely. "*That* is a hot wedding dress. You are hot. By definition, the two of you go well together. Scientifically. Own that shit."

"Did she tell you to say that?" Kameron said as she looked down at herself again and just shook her head. "She *had* to have it altered? Sneaky sneak. She's gonna owe me so much . . . well, she's gonna have to work real hard to make me forget about this thing."

"Yeah, I don't need to hear about the kind of work you make your blonde bombshell do behind the scenes. Or behind the curtains, as the case may be." He tugged at the skirt of the dress with a grin. "If it makes you feel any better, hers is worse. And I don't mean just a little bit worse. I mean a *lot* worse. I mean, better, for those of us who can appreciate incredible tits from a respectable distance," there was a chorus of Amens from the rest of the grooms grooming themselves to get married, which made Orion grin, "but worse than this. As in a lot worse. You're not gonna be self-conscious walking next to her. You're gonna be too busy turning into a fucking slip 'n slide."

Kam smirked at first but then she turned her smirk into a glare that she threw back at Orion. "Goddamn you, Al-Jabbar. Did you really have to say that? The last thing I want is for any of you thinking about me as a fucking 'slip n' slide'." She was really curious what Melissa's dress looked like after that comment, though, and it was enough to distract her from being furious about her modifications. "I can't believe I got kicked out over it either. I'm staying in here with you guys."

Orion looked around at the ocean of testosterone in the room and shrugged. "Feel free, you're certainly welcome. But we're a little short on makeup. We'll be glad to just sit around and ogle you until it's time to go." He grinned at her and followed her look around the rest of the room.

The room had previously been a large gallery for entertaining within the Bickford estate, but had been converted for the day with a few dozen mirrors and stands, just as most of the neighboring wing had been turned into a series of dressing and makeup rooms for all the day's brides. There were five weddings in total to be solemnized that day, and there had been four grooms in the dressing room before Kam arrived. They were dressed in a variety of styles and to varying degrees of formality, but all of them were constantly checking and rechecking themselves in the mirrors.

One of those getting ready was Carl, who looked down at her with a black *hakama* wrapped around his broad shoulders. Any other man might have looked subdued and stoic in the wedding costume. Carl looked even more dangerous than usual. "Wear the dress, make the girl happy. When she was doing my ink last month, she couldn't shut up about it. She's been dreaming about being super-bridezilla with somebody since the first time she got sweaty looking at her high school teacher's tits. Her words, not mine."

"I do make her happy, thank you very much, you ass." She growled at the man who was probably three times her size and could easily hide a katana in his getup. Kam looked far more feminine in that moment than usual. Her hair was curled and she was even wearing light shades of makeup. She also had a stud in her nose, thanks to Mel's new fascination of learning how to pierce people along with tattoos. They both had gone through the "oh god oh god oh god" together and Kam yelled at Mel repeatedly not to close her eyes since she was the piercer. "Though she seems to think if I want to make her real happy my wedding present will be either a stud in my tongue or rings in my nipples. Fuck no am I letting her do that shit. She needs to pierce more people first."

"So that other people can suffer from her mistakes until she gets it right. I understand. That's you being charitable." Carl was relentless, but Orion stepped in to give her a side-hug, since he didn't want to mess up what she'd done with herself. The straps looked like they might break off in a rough wind. "If you're gonna puke, I'd go get it over with. Wheels up in thirty."

"Puke? I'm not going to puke. That was when I was knocked up. It's her turn next." She looked Orion over. "Maybe we should get you to donate. Or that hulk over there." She replied with a glare back at Carl. "Mind donating some of your baby juice to a couple of gorgeous ladies? We already have one half-Asian baby, we can shake things up with your spawn too."

Carl just shook his head. "You're gonna have to take that one up with Aiko. She's got first claim on anything coming out of me that can even remotely be called 'juice.' But only ask if you want a boy. Doc Red did the testing and apparently that's all I make."

"Dear god. A boy like you? That might destroy her lady bits. Never mind." Kam said with a shake of the head. "Poor Aiko. You better make sure Mercury can find a way around that. She wants a girl."

"We've talked about it. If the testing is wrong and we manage to pop one out in the next few tries, fine with me. Otherwise we're gonna have to pick one up off the street." Carl checked himself over obsessively in the outfit, but the look on his face said he actually liked it more than he thought he would.

"So kidnapping. That's your child-care plan. Very nice." Orion shook his head and straightened his uniform, though he could still see Kam in his mirror. The uniform was very different from anything he'd worn as a part of the Consortium, much simpler and less ornamented, but his rank was clearly blazoned on his sleeve and he had several decorations along one shoulder to show the honors he'd been handed (by Carl) for service during the war with the Consortium. Carl had decided to keep the fractal insignias of the various military divisions, and so his other shoulder was a blaze of color that matched the tattoo he had on his skin beneath it.

"Also," he said to Kam in the mirror, "you don't want mine unless you want your kid taking meds the rest of their life. That's what Leo and the girls are gonna have to do, and what I'm gonna be doing from here on out. Unless I want to grow through the ceiling and die of heart failure at forty."

"Pass on that. But at least there is a solution." She said with a shrug before she tugged at her dress a little more. "Do you guys feel nervous? I feel nervous. But she's already my wife. I even upgraded her ring. I just feel fucking nervous."

"I was nervous until I actually got into this outfit." Carl smoothed the folds of the robe against his chest. His broad grin spoiled the stoic look, but he didn't seem to care. "Somebody get this man something sharp besides himself!" He cackled at his own joke and cracked his neck, clearly more than a little excited.

The other two men in the room had intentionally dressed differently, but there was nothing they could do about the fact that they looked similar. Liam had never been a formal person, even for his first wedding, and he clearly wasn't about to start. He wore a white shirt and black slacks with a patterned red vest and tie. The cufflinks in his sleeves were a Bickford family heirloom, and added just a touch of something resembling class to his appearance. Otherwise, his hair was as shaggy and wayward as it had been for most of his life, setting an unruly counterpoint to his polished clothes.

"You want nervous?" He asked over his shoulder, still fighting with the cufflinks to get them in place. "Try getting married to one while the two you're already married to are bridesmaids, and while a *fourth* one . . ."

"Nobody cares, Liam." Logan cut his brother off with a cold chuckle, grabbing his suitcoat off the back of a chair beside him. His black suit had infinitesimal red pinstripes running through it that were invisible unless someone was close enough. His coat was long in a current fashion popular in orbit, cut deeply over his chest and long enough to brush the back of his knees. His shirt had no collar, only polished red jasper stones in place of buttons marching down from his throat. He kept his hair and his beard trimmed close, and he cut an imposing figure, even standing beside Carl. "You picked your hot mess, you're the one that's got to deal with it. Plus, don't even act like you don't love it. Nobody's buying the stress."

"I do." Liam agreed, though when he repeated it, it sounded like he might be practicing. "I do, I really do."

On the other side of the hall, there was a little more activity going on between the group of brides minus Kameron, and their bridesmaids and even a few flower girls. Each of the brides had bridesmaids in different colored dresses, but all of the brides were wearing white, even if their dresses were vastly different. Bree and Rachel helped Gwen while Khadi was nearby, only she was helping Chrissy with her tiny little dress.

"You look so beautiful." Rachel said with a smile as she helped straighten out Gwen's dress, and Bree put on her veil so that it was pinned at the back of Gwen's head into the bun she had on the top of her head. Gwen had a few ringlets here and there around her face, and she had stunning diamonds dangling from her ears, which were a present from Khadi. The present from Rachel and Bree was that Gwen was going to have Liam all to herself for a solid week. It was a hell of a present.

"You could have worn my dress." Bree said as she thought back to the stunning and utterly scandalous thing that still hung in her closet. "I killed in that thing."

"Yeah, well, that thing is basically a sheet of strategically placed pasties." Gwen shook her head. "This one is much more me." The skirt had high slits that exposed her legs, and there were spots of lace fabric around her waist and capped sleeves that gave a fun 'peekaboo' kind of feel. It was both classy and relaxed at the same time, and she felt her dress suited her perfectly. "Anyway, I don't have the boobs for it. I mean, look at Mel." Gwen nodded toward Mel who was absolutely stunning in her gown, especially with her plunging neckline. "Some of us got it and some of us don't." None of them, however, had it quite like Mercury, who truly looked like the belle of the ball.

Mercury's long hair was down and naturally fell in dark red waves over her back and shoulders, but her dress was absolutely stunning. It was embellished with crystals all through the corset-type torso and even along the skirt, which went down to her feet. The dress was haltered behind her long flow of hair, and everything about her seemed to sparkle. She looked like some kind of royalty, but she didn't have anything to say about it, really. She just hoped that Logan would like it. After Gwen mentioned Melissa, she looked over at the tattoo artist and smiled. "You really do look quite stunning, Melissa. Kameron will love it."

"Thank you." Melissa did an obligatory twirl to send the bottom edge of her dress flying (which was also an excuse to show off her heels, which she kept raving about wanting to wear every day, everywhere she went). It looked at any moment as though her dress was simply going to open up and throw her naked into the world, but that seemed to be the way she liked it. The skirt was full and flowing with a slit over one leg that came right up along the inside of her thigh, and the thin trail of fabric on her torso barely covered her breasts and opened all the way to her waist. She might have been wearing white, but her tattoos covered her more than her dress did, and were much more colorful. Her blonde hair was in perfect curls, and her smile outshone the rest of the dress. She was having the time of her life just getting ready.

"You look gorgeous too!" She ogled Gwen openly when she was finished with her twirl, since she put a slightly different spin on being around for the other brides to get ready. "When Bree told me about how the two of you met, believe me, a wedding dress is not the first thing I pictured you in." She winked and raked her eyes over Gwen's dress, giggling the whole time.

Gwen laughed but her cheeks turned red as she looked over

at Bree. "You have a big mouth." She sort of scolded, but Bree was not easily embarrassed or put down.

"What?" Bree did some ogling of her own, but mostly right back at Mel. "It's not a secret. So what if we like to share?"

Everyone started laughing but eventually turned back to their own mirrors. Anna helped Aiko as much as she could, though she had no idea how traditional Japanese wedding attire was supposed to look. Aiko had on a beautifully embellished white kimono, and between Anna and Aiko's mother, they were trying to tie it up just right. In so doing, though, Aiko was the most modest of them all, but she wasn't flashy enough to want to show off her tiny figure anyway. She kept to herself, but she was smiling the whole time.

Anna, who finished getting ready before the rest of them, was in the shortest and possibly simplest dress of all the women. Her dress was cut at mid-thigh while most everyone else's was much longer, but she was about comfort as well as beauty. There were sewn flowers and crystals here and there on the iridescent fabric and the top of the dress went over one shoulder while leaving the other one bare. Her hair was down except for a few strands that were pinned back, and she was wearing flip-flops because the girls had insisted that she shouldn't go barefoot on a farm. Being raised on one, she didn't see the issue, but she obliged anyway.

"It's almost go-time, ladies. Let's bring down the fluffing and the hairspray a bit. We don't need to destroy the atmosphere any more, it has enough problems."

Very few men were permitted in the brides' hallway, but there had been a few needful exceptions. Marcus and Claire, dressed in the finest orbital fashions of the day, stayed near their daughter as Mercury put the finishing touches on her appearance, but her work was mostly done. Aiko's parents were both nearby as well, her father more of an emotional mess than most in the days since the battle. He had never been the same since Aiko and Kazuo had left for the Initiative, but he was smiling and happy to see his daughter so happy on her wedding day.

No one came for Gwen, but she was surrounded by Liam's family. More than a few who she worked for back in the mountains sent wedding gifts of various kinds in gratitude for everything she had done for them and their children. No one came to stand with Melissa either, but she seemed not to notice or care, flitting from one of the rooms to another to admire everyone in anticipation.

Ben and Susan were the last to arrive, Ben in the best suit he had for the occasion, though it paled in comparison to the rest of the grooms and groomsmen. He had stood with Liam during his first wedding, but he was going to be there for Anna instead, in a very different capacity.

He didn't say much as he took his big sister's hand and twirled her around, but he eventually smiled. "Dad would've approved. He was always about keeping it simple. It's a good way to stay happy."

"Dad was smart." She stepped out of the twirl and into a hug, even though Ben was rarely the huggy type. "Thanks for being here for me. Walking me down the aisle. This is the last time I'm going down an aisle, I promise."

"I believe you." Her family had been skeptical of Orion at first, even back in the mountains, but they had warmed to the giant eventually. Even Ben had to admit the guy was funny, and he made Anna happy. That was all that mattered. "Right now I'm just working on not pissing myself in terror at what's gonna happen in the future. I mean, not this, I don't care about you, you're fine, but I'm eventually gonna have to do this for Emily, for Ginny, for Madeline, for any other gorgeous little girls this one manages to manufacture," he nodded over at Susan with a quiet smile, "it's just . . . yeah. Little terrifying."

"Well, at least you're practicing with me. I'm easy. I just might dance down the aisle to give you the utmost embarrassment so nothing can get worse from there." Anna teased as she finally let go of her brother. "If you would rather I embarrass Cory, that's up to you."

"No, I would not." He wasn't going to do anything that would take Cory away from Larissa, even long enough to walk Anna down the aisle. The two of them had been almost sickeningly inseparable ever since the battle on Prime, and Ben wasn't going to compromise that sentiment between them.

Ben looked up as Anna's bridesmaids gathered, since there was a multitude of women who very much wanted to be part of the ceremony, and an equal number of men for Orion. One in particular caught his eye and raised an eyebrow, since the woman showed up to stand as a bridesmaid in a soldier's uniform. "It's like Kam all over again." He looked the woman over. "Except . . . more scary."

"Don't tell Kam that." Anna looked back at Zoe and laughed

softly. "Zoe found herself a man too. Except I don't know if he's with her because he's scared not to be, or if she's just that good to him."

"Hey." Zoe said as she tugged at her uniform. "He's a doctor. He doesn't need to be scared of me." She glanced over at Mercury and then at Anna again. "I don't know what keeps him coming back, I'm just glad that he does."

Behind their conversations, like a force of nature without an off-switch, had been a kind of low buzzing, a constant hum to the world that simply wouldn't quit. It was the middle of June, and it should have been hot outside, but Ben felt cool breezes keeping the entire estate pleasant under the cloud-dotted sky on his way in.

Outside the house, on the massive field beside the house at the foot of the former observation tower, crews spent the last few weeks setting up thousands upon thousands of seats. Representatives from all over the world were in attendance, both for the five-way wedding and for the opening of the Unified Earth complex that had taken place the day before after months of construction. The hum was a thrum of idle conversation that strummed through the ground like a small and constant quake, as the world waited to celebrate its leaders and those it had come to call its heroes.

"Ready to go do this?" Ben asked with an arm extended, Anna's bridesmaids falling in behind her. "Again?"

"Oh, I'm ready." Anna said with a grin as she looked back at all the brides lining up as well. "Talk about a big fucking wedding, though. At least I'm not pregnant anymore. Olivia can hang out with Susan and Emily, right? I told the care center to bring all the kids up."

"They'll all be here. Don't worry about them. This is all about you. You ten." He rolled his eyes, since he'd found the idea of the multiple weddings entertaining from the beginning, but he had to admit, the exterior was incredibly impressive.

Xander showed up right on schedule, looking over all the brides with Tatyana beside him. Neither of them wore rings, and they certainly hadn't invited thousands of people to gawk at them just because they felt like spending their lives together, but he still smiled at how extraordinarily happy everyone looked.

The apparatus on his arm was slightly more streamlined than the one Charles had brought back with him from Eleusis, but it was every bit as effective. "Alright, brides. Your boys and your chosen lady had their spotlight on the way up. If you're gonna run for it, now's the time." He looked around the hallway briefly and almost sighed. "No takers. I figured with five of you crazy people there would be at least one runner. I'm disappointed."

He tapped a few times on the device on his arm, and five doorways opened all over the hall, with a slight haze over them that was an improvement Xander had added to prevent people on the other side of the Twist from seeing through to their side. He pointed to each one in turn to line up the girls in their particular places, then stepped back to watch along with everyone else.

The wedding venue itself had been set up in a gentle bowl in the fields, with a five-sided platform raised in the center. At each apex was a small, decorated stage for each couple, and five aisles radiated from the center like beams of starlight.

At the end of each aisle, there was a small white platform that was marked explicitly off-limits to the crowd, on which each of the girls' bridesmaids began appearing. Some parts of the crowd immediately started applauding at the sight, while a general hush came over the rest as people rushed to take their seats and cameras everywhere began to flash. The world was so clear it was difficult to believe anyone in attendance had ever seen anything but sunny skies in their lives.

Mercury seemed more nervous as the time got closer for her to walk out, but she held onto her father's arm with a vise grip, since he was the only person supporting her at the moment. "There are a lot of people out there." She said softly, since she wasn't great with a *lot* of people. Doctors were one-on-one people, usually. This was a crowd and a half.

Marcus smiled and patted his daughter's arm. "I only see one. And he's the only one you need to concern yourself with right now."

At the end of the aisle, past the applauding crowd and the small procession of her bridesmaids, Logan stood on the part of the platform set aside for the two of them. There was a gentle ramp up to where he stood, but there was no one standing beside him, unlike the rest of the grooms already present. He was waiting for her alone, and his eyes were fixed on the haze of the Twist, knowing she was beyond it, waiting for her.

The rest of the world didn't exist for him either. Only Mercury.

Mercury's stomach was twisted in nervous knots, but she took a deep breath and took a step alongside her father. Before they knew it, they were through the haze and she was still walking at a slow pace toward Logan. She knew that a thousand different thoughts were going through her mind at once, but she felt happy, even if she was extremely nervous. Logan looked so handsome that she drank in the sight of him as she walked, letting the rest of the world fall away, as if just a loving look from him had commanded it to do so.

The sun seemed to follow Mercury down the grassy aisle, every part of her blazing with light beneath the afternoon sky. The eyes of the world and of the crowd surrounding them spun around the entire circle, people standing and moving and craning their necks to get a look at everyone.

The bouquet of brilliantly-colored flowers Melissa held covered more of her than her dress, but she strutted down the aisle in confident steps, grinning every time someone in the crowd called out at her and actually giggling every time someone whistled. Her eyes were stuck on Kameron at the far end. She looked incredible, and Kam could see a familiar hungry expression in Melissa's eyes that made her strut turn just a little bit predatory as she got closer. The dress, about which she'd had mixed emotions, was not long for the world, once Melissa had half a chance to get her hands on it.

Kameron didn't look away from Melissa even once. They had started out as something that was really a bit of genius on Kazuo's part, but had never been intended to be anything permanent. However it started, though, nothing felt more right than watching Melissa walk down the aisle toward her in a beautiful wedding dress.

Aiko was even more debilitatingly nervous than Mercury, but she had the most exotic bouquet of flowers to hide behind. Hide she did, mostly, except when she caught Carl's eyes. She walked down with her father toward the monstrous man that was her husband in word already. Aiko's flowers were all genetically altered by herself, mixed Eleusis and Earth, and they were a stunning display of color that she was proud of. It was easier to think that people were looking at her tie-dye flowers than at her.

Carl felt mostly disbelief every time he saw Aiko, morning, noon, and night. He had been told, during their first period of abandonment on Eleusis, about Jason rigging the Match system to place them together. However mixed his feelings about the man were, he was unabashedly and purely grateful for the means by which Aiko had come into his life. Their relationship began as something artificial, but no machine had made them what they had become. He still couldn't believe she loved him, even after having two children with her. He only knew that there was nothing in the universe he wouldn't do for her, nothing he wouldn't give to have just one more day beside her.

Liam's grin threatened to break his face in pieces as he watched the aisle in front of him, and before Gwen came through, he had to kneel down and scoop up Chrissy, who had toddled up to the platform without dropping a single one of the flowers in her basket. The audience around him was incredibly amused by the girl's performance, and he couldn't help agreeing. He kissed her gently and told her she did an amazing job, then handed her down off the platform and back to Khadi, who snuck down to the front row to help encourage the little girl forward while Bree and Rachel made their entrance.

As soon as he saw Gwen step through in white, though, all other sensations in the world ceased to matter, and he pushed himself back up to his feet with his hands clasped in front of him. She looked incredible, and he felt his heart explode all over again at how amazing it was to have her joining the family he had only begun to create.

Gwen was nervous, but she was smiling, especially having Bree and Rachel behind her, since they supported her and brought her into the family just as much as Liam did. She gave Liam a small wave down low and then grinned behind her flowers. She mouthed an "I love you" and kept grinning like the young, crazy-in-love girl that she was. She had run away from home to be a rebel, she had served the rebel cause by taking care of babies, and now she was marrying the love of her life in the most unconventional way possible. She wanted for nothing.

Orion glanced to either side when the rest of the brides appeared to uproarious applause, but he turned his eyes back to his own aisle as he fidgeted at his side. He wasn't sure why he was nervous, but as soon as Anna's bridesmaids came out, he felt himself settle down. By the time Anna stepped through, all Orion could do was smile. He could see her almost dancing her way down the aisle toward him, and he couldn't resist the urge to laugh just once at how free she looked. The sound was swallowed up by the crowd all around them, but he could still see the echo of it in

Anna's own smile. They had been to the other side of the galaxy and back, they had faced down governments, scientists, and all-purpose assholes, and they were still together. The bounce in her step put a warmth in his heart that would never leave.

Anna kept bouncing and smiling even though she knew Ben probably wanted to shake his head at her side, but she eventually blew Orion a kiss. Then, before she even got to halfway, she paused, kissed her brother on the cheek, and pulled her arm away so she could run the rest of the way to Orion.

That move and her exuberance had the entire crowd around her applauding and cheering, since everyone loved to see an enthusiastic bride. Orion laughed as she sprinted up toward him, petals falling off the agitated flowers in her bouquet as she went, and snatched up by the nearby crowd as remembrances of the day.

He picked her up as soon as she reached him and swung her around once completely before setting her back on her feet. "Trust you to make a wedding into the hundred meter dash." He said with a laugh as he held her steady, the crowd cheering all around them.

Anna was laughing as he picked her up and held her, and she kissed him even before she was given permission to do so. She didn't care about permission. Anna leaned in and kissed his cheek before she whispered into his ear. "Don't lift me up too high. I'm not wearing any underwear. I'll give people a show, but not that much of a show. That's just for you, big guy."

"Oh I knew there was no underwear going on as soon as I saw this pajama shirt you're calling a dress." He couldn't stop smiling, especially at her last comment. He leaned down again to whisper in her own ear. "You'd better keep the show to a minimum. I'm not wearing any either and these pants are *not* built for that. Believe me."

Anna giggled and looked toward the officiant with a grin. "This is going to be short, right? I do, I do?" She looked up at Orion as he slowly let her slide down his body back to her feet. "I get a sparkly ring, though, right?"

The man laughed along with everyone else in the audience at Anna's antics, but he was more stoic than most. Orion's former commanding officer was a man with generous amounts of grey at his temples, but the rest of his hair was a faded purple, as if it had been his natural color and was greying with time. He had more piercings in his ears than Anna, but otherwise he radiated authority, and couldn't have been happier to see his former Captain getting married.

"We'll try to keep it as short as possible." He said quietly, glancing around to see the progress of the other brides in reaching their spouses. Anna had short-circuited the symmetry of the program, to no one's surprise, and most of the others were still walking up to the platform. It was decided that the couples would speak their own vows privately, for the public to see by other means later, but that all of them would be declared wedded at once when those were completed. For the time being, Anna and Orion were left to themselves to watch the others approach nearby.

Logan watched Mercury walk toward him with his heart about to beat out of his chest. He knew he needed to appear calm, but it was a long way off from what he felt. The months since they returned from the Irish hotel had been some of the busiest and happiest of his life, and he had no expectation that it would change any time soon. The roaring of the crowd didn't detract his attention from Mercury to see what Anna was up to. All he could see was the brilliance of the woman with whom he intended to spend the rest of his life.

"Hello." Mercury replied softly but with a bright smile as she finally made her way up to Logan. She hugged her father and kissed his cheek before he told Logan all about how he better take care of his daughter, which only made Mercury smile even more. When they were more or less alone, she reached out for one of Logan's hands. "You look so handsome."

"Trust me, no one is looking at me. I don't have the words to even begin." He held her hand in both of his, still reeling from the sight of her. Everything in his life before that moment had been a shadow compared to her, and he knew everything besides her would always pale for the rest of it. "Is everything as you wanted it?" He asked quietly, knowing that people were watching them closely for every movement, knowing that people would analyze and over-analyze everything he said. He couldn't have cared less. All that mattered was Mercury.

Mercury gave him a small nod and she continued smiling. "There's a lot of people." She replied just as softly before she looked away for just a moment at the large crowd. She took a deep breath before she looked back at Logan's unwavering grey eyes. "All I can really think about, though, is you. Everything is for you."

He nodded slowly, still not quite able to speak, then lifted her hand in his to kiss the back of her knuckles. "My whole life, I've never been much of a religious person. Then you walked down that aisle and I started believing in goddesses. One goddess, at least. And that's more than enough for me."

Mercury's cheeks flushed as she thought about perhaps the goddess he was talking about, the name that he had given her. "Venus?" She stepped a little bit closer to him, since holding his hand hardly felt like enough. Not when the only thing she could feel was a magnetic pull toward the man she loved so much. "Your Venus?"

"That's the one." He agreed, giving a low sigh of pleasure that only she could hear, just at her proximity. That was all it took with her, just being around her, and the world was a different place.

Mercury squeezed his hand and took a deep contented breath of her own. "Thank you for doing this for me. After everything, it's so good to have this. Something real to hold onto. Memories to look back on."

"We get to make them first." He said with a slightly less stoic smile, then turned toward the officiator. He had asked Mercury's father to be the one officiating for them, as a Station Captain, and at a nod from Logan, the man stepped back toward the center of the platform with the other four officiators, and began to address the audience.

Logan found that he couldn't even listen to the comments Marcus made regarding their reason for being there that day (as if it wasn't incredibly obvious to everyone present). All he could see or understand was Mercury there ahead of him.

Once Marcus was finished with his brief remarks, the words of the couples were relayed around the entire gathering, the vows echoing in every ear, snippets of all of them for all to hear, in a chaos of devotion that everyone gathered could see.

Orion cleared his throat a little more dramatically than necessary before he began to speak, holding both Anna's hands in his as he fumbled through his own brain to make sure he still remembered his vows, or near enough. "Anna." He stalled, just to clear his throat again. "A lot of things have changed since the day we met, but a lot of things haven't. I still like flying things, you're still short, and the Earth still typically spins around the sun. We didn't change those things. But we have changed each other, and

I think for the better. There are a lot of things in the world that still might need to change. But one thing won't. I love you. Now and forever, or as long as you can stand me, whichever comes first. My money is on forever." He smiled, his thumbs caressing the backs of her hands as he held them. "There was one night, back in . . ."

". . . the mountains," Liam grinned at the memory, though he was going to have to be sparse on details, "when I remember you and me talking about what you wanted out of life, eventually. Marriage, kids, someday. All hypothetical. All based on the possibility of you finding the right guy." Liam gave her a wink as he squeezed her hands. "I knew the second you told me that. I knew I wanted to be that guy, and I wanted to be able to give you the life you weren't sure you were ever going to have. I knew I wanted you to have that life and I wanted you to have it with me." He glanced briefly aside at Bree and Rachel, and even flicked a look over at Khadi before he settled his eyes on Gwen in all her glory in front of him. "I love you, Gwen, and I want to be that guy for you for the rest of your life. I want to chase the kids with you, I want to watch the stars turn beside you, I want to wake up one day when I'm . . ."

". . . seventy-five and all . . . wrinkly and gross . . ." No one in the audience could imagine Melissa looking wrinkly and gross at that moment, and she was still smiling as she said it, since she had a point she was trying to make, "I'm going to be right behind you from this day to that one. I'm gonna love you until you can't stand me anymore, I'm gonna ink and decorate every inch of that gorgeous body of yours that you'll let me decorate, and I'm gonna . . ." she was getting on a roll, holding herself in closer to Kam as her vows got more fervent and then backing off, just a little bit, as she remembered they were still in public. "I want all of it. All the kids we're gonna have, all the beauty we're gonna bring into the world, and god, the fights! God, I can't wait for the fights! I am so excited about the fights. You have no idea. I want to fight. That's how much I love you. I want to fight with you until the neighbors are calling to report a murder, I want to fight with you until the walls shake, and then I want to . . ."

". . . find out how in the world I managed to keep you." Carl's voice was always steady, but it had shaken more than once in the course of his vows, and not because he was delivering them in Japanese. "One of these days, I might understand it. Until then, the plan is to just be grateful for it. There's no war I wouldn't fight for you and there's no peace I wouldn't make the most of right beside you. I love you to the other side of the universe and back, and from now until the end of whatever the fuck time is. Ever since I met you back on Nine, I've been . . ."

". . . yours." Logan said simply. There were only so many declarations to which he considered the world entitled, but he wasn't going to leave any doubt in anyone's mind as to his devotion to his wife. "Everything I am, everything I ever will be, is yours. Not because I promise it, even though I do. Not because a law makes it that way, but because it's the truth. All I am is yours, heart, mind, and soul. I love you, Mercury, with everything that I have."

Orion squeezed Anna's hands in his, shifting the way he stood and avoiding looking straight down, since he was so tall he could see right down his soon-to-be-wife's dress. Maybe she had done it on purpose. "This I vow," he said in the only formula they had all agreed on, "that I am yours, in sickness and health, for better or for worse, probably mostly for the worse, where I'm concerned . . . for richer, for less rich . . ."

"This I vow," Melissa finally said, when the rest of her tumbling vows had run their course, "that you're never getting rid of me, that you're always going to know how much I love you, that I'll be the best mother I can be to all of our children. And that things will never, ever be boring. I vow that you will always . . ."

". . . be able to count on me," Carl stumbled a little more in Japanese, but just because his brain was so scrambled otherwise, "for anything, at any time. That I will smile and nod when you talk about science as if I have a clue what you're talking about. That I will support you in every goal you set for yourself, in every way that I can. That I will not rush into gunfire anymore unless absolutely necessary. That you will never forget . . ."

". . . how important you are to me, and how grateful I am for every day with you." Liam was like his brother in many ways, but the single tear running down his cheek was a clear and obvious difference between them. It wasn't alone on his cheek for long. "I vow that you'll never be taken for granted, that I will always make you laugh. Well, I'll always *try* to make you laugh. Can't promise I'll actually *succeed*, but I'll always try. I vow that I'll be whatever you need me to be, that I'll always do my best to make a safe and laughing home for our family. I vow that I will never . . ."

". . . be without you, if there's anything I can do about it." Logan and Mercury both knew just how much he could do about it. They had never been apart for more than a few hours since the hotel in Ireland, and he didn't intend to be away from her for any longer for the rest of his life. "I vow that in everything I do in this life, you are the other half of me. That I will stand beside you in your dreams and make them real. That I am yours so long as I live."

After such incredible vows, all of the women felt daunted to go next, but Anna was the first to start them off. She had given herself a running start from the very beginning, after all. "Orion, it has never been hard to love you, even when it was hard to stay alive. I should have known from the beginning that it would be impossible not to fall in love with you, because even that first night we spent together playing video games . . . I knew you were amazing. Your heart is as giant as the rest of you," she said with a grin, "and I am so . . ."

" . . . lucky to have met you." Kameron said as she looked at Mel with an intensity that consumed her entire body. "I had resigned to living a mediocre life, even though Kazuo was not a mediocre man." Kameron looked toward Aiko's family since Aiko was on the next platform over, but then she looked back at Melissa. "You are the best thing that has ever happened to me in my entire fucked up life. You brighten my world. You push me. You love . . ."

" . . . me exactly the way that I am." Mercury said as she continued to get lost in Logan's perfect stormy eyes. "You never expected me to be something I'm not, you never gave up on me, and you believe in me. You conquered the world to find me, you conquered everything in your way." Mercury held even tighter to his hands, since her hands were starting to shake. "I'm better because I met you. I'm better still because you love me, and I love you. I'm stronger . . ."

". . . because you make me strong." Aiko said in unfaltering Japanese, but it was her native language, after all. "I didn't even know you in those first days we spent together, but I wanted to be important to you. I wanted you to feel as though you mattered to someone and that you were worth caring about. I didn't know I would fall in love with you, but I'm glad that I did. You know so much about me, you trust me. I trust you with my life because I know that you know what you're doing, even if you get injured quite a bit." She said with a small laugh. "Even if we have all boys . . ."

" . . . I am so happy that you love me enough to let me be a part of this beautiful family that you have created." Gwen said as she looked from Liam to Rachel and Bree, and then back at Liam again. "I didn't think I would ever care to settle down anywhere, even if it was something that I wanted. I was afraid of it. I was afraid of falling in love. I fucked things up on purpose, but you didn't let me keep it that way for long. You pushed, you came after me, you showed me how important I was to you and your family. I fell in love with you because falling in love with you is as easy as breathing. You make me feel as special as every other person around you, and you're incredible at everything you do. I've never felt love like this before."

As soon as the women were done telling their little stories about the crazy men and women that they loved, they started with their vows as well, some of them sounding more nervous than the others, but all beaming at the people standing across from them and holding their hands.

"Melissa, I vow, with my heart, soul, and everything else that is a part of me, that I will never stop loving you. I love you more every day. I worried for so often and so long that you would one day look at me and think that you made a stupid fucking choice, because you are everything. You're so incredibly kind and funny and so fucking beautiful . . . and you're the best mother to Kassie. My heart, soul, being is entirely yours and will belong to no one else. Never . . ."

" . . . will I ever go without you, never will I want to be without you by my side." Aiko squeezed Carl's hand as hard as she could, which was rather pathetic considering his immense strength. "I can't sleep without you near me, I can't think without knowing you're okay, and one day, we'll make it back to Eleusis and live . .
.

" . . . as long as we possibly can, as people in love, but also as a family." Gwen started to cry. "Damn it, I told myself I wasn't going to cry, but then I saw you cry, and that just messed me up." She dabbed at her eyes with her knuckle and continued smiling at Liam. "We're all going to be by your side, we're all going to be behind you in whatever challenges come, but I can't speak for them entirely." She replied with a laugh. "I can speak for me. I'm yours, Liam, whatever people might say about it, or about us, they don't know us. They don't know anything about how we feel, how we love . . ."

" . . . they don't know what we truly mean to each other, but no one needs to know everything." Mercury took a few steps closer to Logan, since she hated distance between them. "What you need to always remember is that nothing in this world, in any world, matters more to me than you. I had once dedicated my life to medicine, but now I dedicate my life to us. Things will never be perfect, they're never meant to be, but I am comfortable with trial and error." Mercury chewed on her bottom lip as her cheeks flushed, but she was still grinning. "I'm yours . . ."

" . . . always yours, Orion." Anna looked up at her giant, towering over her. "I don't care what comes. I want to live on that mountain on Eleusis. I want to have a bunch of children that tower over me by the time they turn five. I want to hear your laugh every day and to tease each other until we can't anymore. You saved me, Orion. You saved me in so many ways, you saved my life, you saved my heart and soul, you saved me from myself. You are my everything. I will always love you."

The skies above the massive gathering were dotted and speckled with clouds, and the sun shone down its radiance on all the couples as their vows were spoken. In the kisses that followed the officiators' proclamations, the applause and the cheering from the crowd set the rolling midwest plain singing with emotion and exuberance, but as the kisses began to break, the sky began to break along with them.

Fireworks shot up from all five corners of the assembly, raining brilliance against the sky's blue radiance. As the fireworks blasted the annunciation of the solemnities, though, the sky was torn apart in all five corners, then five more, and more, and more, in spinning, widening gaps in reality that twisted their way into life only to multiply against themselves.

The crowd hushed into whispers of awe as the Twist gates opened in a dizzying variety above their heads, darkening the midwest landscape and dazzling it at the same time with the display of worlds beyond their own. Planets turned beneath foreign suns through some of the gates, while others opened to show the blazing passage of an icy comet. Nebulae in every visible color decorated the edges of the assembly, opening and closing so quickly the eye could barely focus on one before another took its place, shining fantastic beams of power and purity down on the attendees.

The gates moved from astral images to atmospheric and planetary perspectives, shifting to open in thousands of places all at once on Eleusis itself, easily recognizable to those who had been there. The verdant landscapes opened like a lush mirror in the sky beneath a different sun, winking down at the newlyweds with an approving smile. The Eleusis oceans rolled with possibilities unknown, hundreds of landscapes passing in a blink. Some might have been from Eleusis, some might have been from Earth. Some might have been from yet other worlds untouched by human eyes until that moment. None could say.

Above the central platform itself, as the multitude of Twists diminished and gathered themselves away into the brilliance of the midwest sky, gates opened to show five different binary star systems, one above each newly married pair. Each Twist showed the stars spinning at impossible speeds around each other, so close that flares reached out from one to the other within the dance, all pulsing with life and power unimaginable.

The audience finally recovered enough from the show to cheer and applaud as the final Twists disappeared, but they were shocked into further oohs and aahs by the sudden appearance of hundreds of Twists to blot out the sky, each showing a different star. The immense possibilities hung over the assembly as the couples began to descend the platform beneath them, each holding hands and watching both the strange skies on display and each other.

Logan glanced at the displays, but his eyes were on Mercury as they stepped down to join the crowd that came to wish them well. Crews were already moving quickly to dismantle the stage and convert the entire area into a reception venue, where the thousands in attendance could eat and drink and dance and celebrate with them for the evening. None of the newly married couples would stay long, but it was expected, and Logan wanted the entire world present to force them into socializing with each other. It was something he meant them to get accustomed to in the years to come.

"You outshine them all." He said against his wife's ear as he pulled her in close, cherishing the last moment of solitude beneath the alien stars before they would be confronted by endless well-wishers.

"I shine for you, Logan." Mercury said as she kissed him again, both of her hands on his cheeks as she savored the moment of truly being husband and wife in front of the entire universe. "No one planned for this, but sometimes it's the things we don't plan for that turn out the best." Mercury kissed him once more before she just stepped back to admire him.

Anna hadn't stopped kissing Orion even though people were clamoring for their attention to wish them well, but Anna just wanted to run away with her husband. She and Logan had run away, once upon a time, in a different life, as different people. Anna wasn't thinking about Logan, or Mercury, or anyone other than her giant husband. "Did I mention I'm not wearing panties?" She said against his lips before she kissed him again.

"You did." He laughed and glanced down at the parts of her he knew were bare beneath the dress. "Did I mention I can't fucking wait to get you somewhere alone so we can take full advantage of that fact?" He had to lean far over to kiss her, but as they walked off the platform, he left her on a higher step and hopped off to put himself at the right level for kissing her, his hands still on her waist. "We need to do that as soon as possible, or I won't be responsible for what happens to this uniform."

She giggled as she walked with him, still completely oblivious to everything else going on around them. Anna had eyes only for Orion, that was perfectly clear.

"That dress." Kam said into Melissa's ear as soon as their kisses broke, but she went back to mauling Mel as soon as she could after she said it. "I just want to rip it off. Right now."

"It won't take much." Melissa said with a teasing giggle, tossing her hair playfully off to one side. "I bought two, just because I wanted to see how hard it would be. Just a few little tugs and a couple well-placed rips and I'm all yours. I checked." She glanced down at the thin strip of actual covering immediately over her waist below the plunging torso and the high slit along her thigh, then grinned back up at her wife. With that suggestion, the dress did actually look as though someone had been in the process of ripping it from neck to waist and floor to crotch when the dress stopped barely short of accomplishing that goal. "You'll have it in shreds in seconds, and I can't wait."

She kissed Kam fiercely, pressing herself into her wife with a moan she did nothing to hide. "I'm gonna take my time shredding yours. God, you look delicious."

Kam tugged on a few strands of Melissa's hair before she

leaned in and kissed slowly down Melissa's neck. "We don't have anyone waiting for us. Not really. I say we ditch this party, swipe some wine, and then let me taste how delicious *you* are." She slid a hand down Melissa's side to tease along her hip. "I have no fucking patience when you're teasing me like this."

"Why do you think I picked this dress?" Melissa pulled away and bolted in the direction that looked like it had the lowest density of people. Most were either moving to set up for the evening's festivities or heading in a different direction to congratulate the other newlyweds. A few photographers did remain to snap pictures of both of them as they ran for it, but neither of them could stop laughing.

Carl bent down and scooped Aiko up in his arms, partly because he could and partly because he intended to keep her above and protected from the mass of people around them. There were a number of people snapping pictures of him and his tiny bride, but Carl was still watching Aiko, not the rest of the crowd.

"I know we've been Mr. and Mrs. ever since the Initiative, but I'm glad we got to have it in front of your parents this time." Aiko's mother, recently appointed as a director over one of the many institutes that Aiko herself would help to coordinate, had been the one to officiate their wedding, for which Carl felt particularly honored. "Sorry if I fucked up the language too badly. I've been back around English-speaking people too long. It's high time you and I went and got ourselves stranded again, I think."

"You were great." Aiko said with a grin as she kissed along his face and neck while he held her above the crowd. "But I'd be happy to get stranded with you." Aiko pressed her face into his cheek. "I love you so much."

"I love you too." He said in Japanese once again, since he did know that one phrase particularly well. "We'll go get stranded again soon. William and David are gonna need another little brother in the next year or two, and fucked if I'm gonna let that kid be born on Earth. Nope. This is no longer our planet." He glanced down and then back up at the thousands of stars seeming to burn close overhead. "For tonight, though, we are gonna dance and then Charles is gonna put us back on our mountaintop. I stocked that son of a bitch yesterday with everything we're gonna need for weeks. Hope you got plenty of sleep last night."

"Sleep? Who needs sleep?" Aiko giggled as she kissed Carl several more times. He really was her warrior in shining armor.

Gwen rushed up to Liam and giggled when he twirled her first before he brought her in close. "We get a whole week!"

"Oh, they finally told you, did they?" Liam laughed as he kissed her again, his hands sliding over her wedding dress to fully appreciate the outfit. She was both incredibly sexy and perfectly cute at the same time, and he just wanted to twirl her over and over to watch her face light up in the motion. "They can be pretty generous when they want to be. They're probably hoping I manage to knock you up." It had been some time since Gwen had been on her black market birth control, but Liam wasn't worried about their lack of conception so far. They had all the time they wanted, and plenty of kids to keep them busy besides.

"Well, that's just a strange thing to wish on a newlywed." Gwen continued twirling and kissing Liam. "You are so handsome. I'm so fucking lucky."

"Have a look in a mirror. I'm the lucky one here." He picked her up to twirl her in the middle of a kiss before slowly setting her back down on her feet. "I love you. I hope you're ready for an exhaustingly happy life."

The crowds went on for hours, and aside from Melissa and Kam, the rest of the happy couples found themselves surrounded and tossed from group to group, always with new well-wishings and new stories people had long waited to tell them.

As the sun dipped low and the celestial display above them turned even brighter by contrast, two men sought out Carl and Aiko, initially giving her a fright before they made it clear their intentions were peaceful. They were nearly Carl's size and looked similar enough to be eerie, and explained that they had been seeking out the rest of those involved in their experiment for years. Carl had brothers he had never known, but who were very interested in getting to know him. The family Aiko had shown him how to have would grow, even beyond what he had imagined.

Those who approached Mercury were less obvious in identifying themselves, but a number of women took her in hugs too warm to be warranted from strangers, looking back at her with features in a thousand different combinations that were every bit as flawless as her own. The leavings of the Consortium, the remnant of their many and varied experiments on the human race, had all flocked around the sister they had recognized in her during the war. People stood up to fight because of her. People had changed minds and expanded ambitions because of her. People had been brave because they had seen her own bravery.

Every congratulations on her happiness came with offers of assistance, requests to be of service, stories of gratitude at what had been done. Those from Earth thanked her for allowing the truth about their own world to come through, as she was credited with eliciting from the Alperts the truth about CV. Some of them told her that they were involved in laboratories trying to solve the problem, a worldwide network of minds and hearts dedicated to healing, all inspired by her resilience and tenacity. They all shared the same dream she did, of raising their children in a world that would let them live their lives in peace.

There weren't as many unexpected visitors who talked with Anna and Orion, but most of those that did were either grateful for their resistance and rebellion, or they wanted to know what it was like on Eleusis. Anna always talked about Eleusis with great positivity, but she also warned that it would take a lot of time, construction, and peace between leaders to really encourage population growth on Eleusis. People seemed to understand, even if it wasn't the answer they were probably seeking after.

In a moment of peace, Anna darted to a dessert table and came back with cake that hadn't been smashed in her face. She could still smell the frosting up her nose from earlier when Orion had been relentless. "I will share my cake with you if you don't shove any more up my nostrils."

"I . . . might agree to that. Temporarily." He was hungry, after all, though Zoe had been a considerate enough bridesmaid to make sure he and Anna both got something to eat, if only a few bites at a time. He allowed Anna to feed him a piece and gave an appropriate groan, since it really was that good. "We should get married more often. That's fucking delicious."

"How many times do you want to marry me, exactly?" She teased as she took a bite for herself and then moved from standing next to him to sitting in his lap. It was nice to be left alone for a little bit. "It is fucking delicious cake. Everything has been incredible. Best party ever. Ten stars."

"There's a lot more than ten up there." He looked upward with her, smoothing out her hair so she could lay her head on his shoulder to look up at the incredible display above them. "Maybe Leo and Lynnette will go check that one out someday." He pointed up past her at a red giant at a huge distance from the Twist, which was looking at it through the hazy atmosphere of a planet where it appeared to be raining. "That one over there looks more like Olivia. All, you know, quiet and beautiful." The baby had been one of the easiest Orion had ever seen, for which they were all grateful, and the planet he pointed to had a long, motionless valley of twilight stone that faced up to a white dwarf star, seeming to look down on the valley with almost no filter between it and the landscape.

"You're such a romantic." Anna said with a grin before she turned her head slightly to kiss along Orion's neck before she looked back up at the sky again. "I adore you, Mr. Al-Jabbar."

"And you are everything." Orion wrapped one arm around her waist to hold onto her while the other rested on her knee, his fingertips constantly reminding her of coming attractions. He kissed her exposed neck when she looked back at the stars, closing his eyes briefly just to enjoy the moment, the edge of all possible futures. "I love you too, Mrs. Al-Jabbar."

"Come on." She patted his knee after a few more moments of silence. "I want to grab some more food and then sneak out of here. What do you say?" She raised her eyebrows suggestively and smirked.

Mercury, who had danced with her father and seemingly a thousand other people before she made it back to Logan, was all too happy to step away from the festivities for a soothing glass of wine. She wasn't known for being a drinker, but she figured it wouldn't hurt. "You said that you had new rooms made up for us?" Previously it had been 'Logan's' room that they were staying in, but they both agreed that something new and decidedly both of theirs from the beginning was probably a good idea.

He nodded as he sipped at his own glass, a mischievous smile slipping through afterward. "I did say that. Would you like to see them?"

Mercury nodded, since she was feeling overwhelmed with all of the attention and people anyway. Their children were being cared for by her parents and Logan's sister for the next week. "Yes, please. This is all just too much for me now, I'd rather have just you for company."

"That can be arranged." He took her hand to bring her back a little into the private world they shared, and handed off his wine glass to Renata, who he'd been talking to before Mercury came back to him. He gave her new husband a brief glare just to make sure the man knew he had reason to be afraid, but smiled at

Renata. "Please make my apologies to anyone I didn't get to speak to. We're out of here." He was already taking out his communicator and dialing Charles, glancing at one of the entry frames the brides had used earlier in the afternoon nearby. "Charles, the new rooms, please. Thank you very much."

Mercury was always so surprised by how prompt the Montgomeries were. She found some of them to be better company than others, but they didn't seem to get under her skin like they did with so many others. "Thank you, Charles!" Mercury replied a little loudly, only because she wanted to be heard and the communicator wasn't near her face. She finished her wine before she was willing to give away the glass. Maybe the tingling feeling she was experiencing was connected to the volume of her voice. She wasn't sure.

Logan laughed at the volume of her shout, but led her away and twirled her one more time as they approached the platform. The frame for the Twist turned red-latticed first and then opened on what appeared to be just another patch of grass, but Logan was still smiling. He turned once, with Mercury, to wave at the crowd applauding their getaway, and paused briefly to smile genuinely at the sight of one couple dancing in the distance. None of the Montgomeries had wanted to actually participate in the massive wedding themselves, but it still warmed his heart to see Jason and Jessie swaying together on the converted dance floor, completely oblivious to the rest of the world.

He stepped through with Mercury and sighed gratefully when the Twist closed behind them. A quick look around told her that they hadn't actually gone very far, but the Twist kept anyone from trying to follow them, which was all either of them wanted. The closest corner of the Bickford estate was only a hundred meters away, and they could see the edge of the international complex a kilometer beyond that. The thousand Twists hanging in the air identified the party grounds where things would certainly rage well into the night, but they were well out of sight of any of the actual revelers themselves. It had been easy to miss one more spot of construction in the middle of everything, but the place in front of them was more than just another government office.

The house was mostly glass and steel, but she couldn't see inside from where they were standing. It was three stories, with balconies and porches jutting out in random intervals and a high, open entry. Flowers were planted all across the front of the home.

As he led her inside, it was obvious that none of the pieces inside had ever been used or lived-in. The house itself was almost entirely empty, with very little furniture or decoration to be seen. Everywhere was open space and potential, awaiting their own touch and their own lives to fill it.

"There's six bedrooms, aside from ours." He glanced up at the second floor, which was mostly open on the greatroom at the front of the house and had a number of doors leading off the extended landing. "So, you know, we have room." He grinned at himself, since he was rather proud of the design, and he hoped she liked it as well.

Mercury smiled and then took off her heels (which she hadn't needed in the first place) so she could leave them by the door. As soon as she took any further steps, her large dress swished beneath her. It had been bustled in the back so that her train wasn't a mile long behind her, but the dress was still quite a presence. "It's beautiful, Logan." She twirled slowly in the middle of the floor to look around the house before she looked back at Logan. Everything about her was perfectly done up, even the paint on her toenails. "We'll see how many rooms we'll actually need."

"So what, you're thinking this won't be enough?" He teased as he spun her around barefoot on the thick-carpeted floor. "I figured some of them could share, at least when they're young." He spun her around and kissed the back of her neck, as he tugged at the complex laces on the back of the dress.

She enjoyed the fact that he could pick her up and swing her around as though she was some petite woman, which she was not, but she enjoyed feeling that way anyway. "You have big dreams for a big family, Mr. Bickford. We already have two babies and two toddlers roaming around."

"If I wasn't prone to having big dreams, Mrs. Bickford, I would have nothing at all." He couldn't stop touching her or kissing her whenever he got the chance, standing with her in the middle of the expansive entryway with their entire house and their entire future ahead of them. He worked at her dress until it was loose enough for her to get out of it if she wished to do so, then spun her back around for another breathless kiss. He had missed her while they were separated by crowds of strangers. "As it is, I have everything. So I'll hang onto my big dreams for a while."

"Everything? I hope not *everything*, since I hope you still want for something." She kissed him a few times before she let the dress fall away, only to reveal some very fancy underclothes that were just as white and pristine as her dress had been.

"It's possible to have everything you want and still want more of it." His eyes moved over her hungrily before he examined the attire with his hands as well, drawing her into a warm kiss. "It's possible to have a goddess who is my entire heart's desire, and still be greedy for chances to fall down and worship."

Mercury gasped every time his hands trailed over a sensitive part of her and his fingers tugged at the sexy lingerie she wore entirely for him. "I love the way you look at me." Mercury stepped in closer so that she could go back to kissing him while his hands wandered. "I love the way you touch me. But I mostly love that you're entirely mine and I'm entirely yours." She had a beautiful sparkling emerald and diamond ring to show for it, too, but she didn't care about the ring like she cared about the man.

Sneaking away from the party was harder than Orion had expected, but subtlety had never been his strong point. Being a giant made subtlety almost impossible, even in a crowd. Eventually, though, he and Anna managed to slip away separately to meet at a spot behind the food tents, and Orion called in a Twist so they could make their getaway.

"I have never in my life been so happy to see an empty house." They stepped out in front of the Prince house, worlds away from the raging party at the Bickford estate. Everyone else from her family had been in attendance at the wedding, of course, and her siblings were going to be Liam's houseguests on the estate grounds for the next week to leave Orion and Anna completely alone. As soon as the Twist closed behind them, he leaned down and kissed her deeply in the middle of the open grasses, then picked her up and threw her over his shoulder to stride toward the house.

Anna squealed as soon as he tossed her over his shoulder and at first her hands flew back to cover her exposed ass, but since they were alone, she just let it go. "Do I look like a giant sack of flour, you giant?!"

"You're actually pretty tiny as sacks of flour go." He reached up to smack her exposed ass on their way to the house, and dropped her to carry her in both arms through the threshold, since he had to duck to get through. "So no, you do not look like a giant sack of flour. You look like a tiny and incredibly gorgeous woman, and bear almost no resemblance to a sack of flour whatsoever."

He didn't stop once they were inside except to close and lock the door behind him, heading farther in toward the stairs leading straight up through the middle of the house.

Anna wiggled as he held her even though she knew he might potentially drop her. She had faith that he wouldn't. "I even went all smooth for you down there. I spent a lot of time freshening up for my groom."

"That's my country girl." He laughed as he smacked her exposed backside while carrying her. "All comfort and casual on the outside, all kink and crazy underneath." He finally got to kick the attic door closed behind him and ascended the last of the steps to get to their oddly-made living area. Rather than putting her down on her feet, he swung her so she could land on her knees on the side of their bed, where it was easier to kiss her and for his hands to wander as they had wanted to for hours.

Anna's dress was so easy to be rid of that she just yanked upward, pulled it over her head and tossed it aside between kisses. True to her word, she was bare below the waist and had only a strapless bra on for support. She went after Orion's clothes as soon as she was almost bare, since his would take longer. "In this very room I received my invitation to the Initiative. That changed everything. The decision to go."

"I was up there, getting the same news." He mused as she stripped him, grinning as she attacked his uniform. He let out a grateful moan when she yanked away his pants, since it really had been incredibly uncomfortable to be contained all afternoon with her looking as gorgeous as she did. There had been some times during the dancing when he had needed to immediately excuse himself to go sit down or end up in every tabloid on Earth. A single twist of his fingers against her back and he tossed aside her bra, looming over her with his uniform shirt open and his pants discarded at his feet. "If I'd've known I was on my way to this moment, I'd've been in a bigger hurry."

Anna grinned up at Orion as she ran her hands along his skin. He was so gorgeous she hardly knew what to do with herself. "We were very different people then." She replied as she looked up into his dark eyes, and she wrapped a hand around him to haul him down into a kiss. "We were always supposed to be together, to end up like this. There was just a hell of a road to travel to get here. More like across the universe and back."

"I don't mind." He kissed her heatedly, and moved to lie

beside her on the bed just to get comfortable. They were going to be there for a long while, if he had anything to say about it. His hands moved over her constantly to take in her gorgeous curves, and he moved her right on top of him, her hair playing tricks with the fading sunlight coming in through the window across the attic.

"What matters more is the universe still in front of us. And none of that scares me. Nothing scares me when I think about you being there with me or being sprawled out in a bed somewhere for me to come back to." He held her against him to kiss her neck, her chest, everywhere he could reach in celebration of their solitude and the future ahead of them. "Nothing is too much for you. If you can handle me and all my crazy, you can handle anything."

"I think the opposite is true. It's not about me handling you, it's about you handling me." Anna hovered over him as soon as she was on top of him, and when she moved her hands to grip his shoulders, she smiled at the new glittering ring she wore. A brilliantly multicolored stone from Eleusis. "Earth, Eleusis, Orbit, they're still pretty fucked up." She said with a laugh before she leaned down and kissed Orion. "But at least we're alive, in love, and together through it all. That's all I ever wanted. A good life."

"A good life." He agreed with a smile. He liked watching her admire the ring, since he hadn't wanted her to have the tattoo by itself. He had a tattoo of her name to match, but he also wore a wedding ring of his own to show he was hers. His fingers raked her back and gripped her tightly as she teased him, groaning already in anticipation of everything ahead of them. "I think a good life should start with a solid week of incredible sex. What do you think?"

"Mmmm." Anna agreed without words at first while she kissed him a few more times and teased him just a little bit more. "Hell yes."

The End

For Now

ABOUT THE AUTHOR

D. Brumbley is a husband/wife duo from Kansas City who spend most of their time in each other's heads. In suburbia the duo lives in a simple house with a dog and two feisty kiddos. One half of the duo loves football, baseball, libraries, and romance. The other half of the duo likes D&D, Fantasy novels, Marvel Comics, and cheesecake. A country girl and an east coast boy met online, became best friends, fell in love, and somewhere along the way decided that telling stories together would be fun.

Best. Decision. Ever.